KU-535-191

SUSPECTS

David Thomson was educated at Dulwich College and the London School of Film Technique. After seven years at Penguin Books, he became director of film studies at Dartmouth College, New Hampshire between 1977 and 1981. He is the author of a dozen books including the acclaimed *A Biographical Dictionary of Film*, biographies of Warren Beatty and David O. Selznick, and three other novels, *A Bowl of Eggs*, *Hungry as Hunters* and *Silver Light*.

Thomson is a regular contributor to *Film Comment*, *New Republic* and the *Independent on Sunday*. He was on the selection committee of the New York Film Festival and he wrote the screenplay for *The Making of a Legend: Gone With the Wind*. He now lives in San Francisco.

Also by David Thomson

A Bowl of Eggs
Hungry as Hunters
Silver Light

Movie Man
Wild Excursions: The Life and Fiction of Laurence Sterne
A Biographical Dictionary of Film
America in the Dark: Hollywood and the Gift of Unreality
Scott's Men
Over-exposures: The Crisis in American Filmmaking
Warren Beatty and Desert Eyes
Showman: The Life of David O. Selznick

For
Tom Luddy

Wright Morris, *Reflection in Oval Mirror, Home Place, Nebraska,* 1947

SUSPECTS

David Thomson

Minerva

A Minerva Paperback
SUSPECTS

First published in Great Britain 1985
by Martin Secker & Warburg Ltd
This Minerva edition published 1995
by Mandarin Paperbacks
an imprint of Reed International Books Ltd
Michelin House, 81 Fulham Road, London SW3 6RB
and Auckland, Melbourne, Singapore and Toronto

Copyright © 1985 by David Thomson

A CIP catalogue record for this title
is available from the British Library
ISBN 0 7493 9678 4

Printed and bound in Great Britain
by Cox & Wyman Ltd, Reading, Berkshire

This book is sold subject to the condition
that it shall not, by way of trade or otherwise,
be lent, resold, hired out, or otherwise circulated
without the publisher's prior consent in any form
of binding or cover other than that in which
it is published and without a similar condition
including this condition being imposed
on the subsequent purchaser.

Is this a novel,
or a non-fiction book about movies?

My answer must be both. It is film criticism and movie history, but it is a fiction in which the material (the life) is the world created in a genre of movies. This is not just a way of warning readers of the rules of the game. It is a reminder that fiction has no hold unless we believe in it, and that movies use the exact poignant imprint of so many glances and faces to make a dream. So try to read without having to slap me, and ask how much your own "real" experience treasures imaginary beings and absurd possibilities.

David Thomson
November 1984

Jake Gittes

Noah Cross

Ilsa Lund

John Clay

Axel Freed

Eileen Wade

David Staebler

Judy Rogers

Kit Carruthers

Waldo Lydecker

Laura Hunt

Helen Ferguson

Dickson Steele

Laurel Gray

Roy Earle

Marie Garson

Henry Oliver Peterson

Gwen Chelm

Alma McCain

David John Locke

Maureen Cutter

Al

Joe Gillis

Max von Mayerling

Guy Haines

Pete Lunn

Kitty Collins

Amy Jolly

Norma Desmond

Julian Kay

Walter Neff

Phyllis Diedrichson

Wilson Keyes

Debby Marsh

Harry Lime

Kay Corleone

Skip McCoy

Cora Papadakis

Frank Chambers

Jimmy Doyle

Francine Evans

John Converse

Jack Torrance

SUSPECTS

Vivian Sternwood

L. B. Jeffries

Lars Thorwald

Alicia Huberman

Alexander Sebastian

Walker

Chris Rose

Ma Jarrett

Cody Jarrett

Brigid O'Shaughnessy

Casper Gutman

Victor Laszlo

Richard Blaine

Elsa Bannister

Adeline Loggins

Jay Landesman Gatsby

Norman Bates

Bruno Anthony

Dolly Schiller

Bernstein

Susan Alexander Kane

Raymond

Mary Kane

Sally Bailey

Gilda Farrell

Hank Quinlan

Ramon Miguel Vargas

Jeff Bailey

Bree Daniels

John Klute

Mary Ann Simpson

John Ferguson

Judy Barton

Smith Ohlrig

Howard

Evelyn Cross Mulwray

Harry Moseby

Paula Iverson

Travis Bickle

Frederick Manion

Mark McPherson

George Bailey

"Each man's life touches so many other lives."
—Clarence the angel, in *It's a Wonderful Life*

"Round up the usual suspects."
—Captain Louis Renault, in *Casablanca*

At this time, in the evening, with fifteen hundred miles of moist heat sighing against the house, I let my unsteady heart beat in its paper prison. . . .

JAKE GITTES

Jack Nicholson in Chinatown, 1974,
directed by Roman Polanski

In November 1901, at the Tulip Tree, a whorehouse on Stockton Street in San Francisco, where she worked, the nineteen-year-old Opal Chong gave birth to Jacob. She was a Eurasian who named her child after Jacob Schwartz, an agreeable policeman whose patrol included that stretch of Stockton. The infant was allowed to live on the premises, and Opal (a star of the house—she was alluded to occasionally, with awe, in the social column of the *San Francisco Chronicle*, written by Herbert Kane) was permitted a second room of her own by the proprietress, Adeline "Lady" Ray. The other girls spoiled Jacob whenever they could, but Opal went from carefree to strict. She was not as imaginative a whore after his birth.

Jacob was acquiring Chinese and pocket money from errands for the house laundry when the Tulip Tree was leveled in the San Francisco earthquake of 1906. Opal perished in that disaster, but only after she and her son had been trapped seven hours in the debris. Later in life, Jake told the story that his mother protected him from the full weight of a collapsed beam, and instructed him in the pleasuring of a woman before she expired. He never made this story plausible, but listeners took it as a sign of his romantic inclination.

The boy's education and welfare were assumed as duties by Mrs. Ray and the policeman Schwartz. They put him in an orphanage in Sacramento and had his name changed to Gittes, apparently after a lawyer who had been disbarred a few years earlier. "Jake" Gittes had few visitors in his years in Sacramento, and he left the orphanage in 1918 with a reputation as a dark schemer, a promising middleweight and the chronic teller of tall stories.

1

Moving to Los Angeles, and fighting as "Chink" Gittes, he had a three-year ring career that included a bloody but honorable draw with Harry Greb. He gave up the game when he was obliged to "lose" two fights in a row for gambling coups. It was in one of those thrown contests that he suffered a broken nose, leaving him with a somewhat nasal intonation and recurrent respiratory problems, so that he was sometimes known as "Snort."

Jake retired from the ring in 1922 and was then a worker with —soon to be manager of—a swimming-pool construction company that employed mostly Chinese labor. It appears likely that Gittes was personally responsible for some fanciful novelty designs—for instance, the Cobra Pool at Rudolph Valentino's Falcon Lair home. Apparently thriving, the company was driven into liquidation when one of its pools was shown to have a defective chlorination system, as a result of which a Silverlake child had died of cholera. Jake always believed that the "accident" was linked to his refusal to take out insurance with the local police.

Thus, in 1925, having learned fatalism, Jake Gittes joined the Los Angeles Police Department. He was promoted and in 1928 he was assigned to Chinatown as a detective. A distinguished career might have been his but for the Iris Ling case. Another Eurasian, and the owner of a small, prestigious brothel, she and Gittes became lovers. But Ling was under pressure from a Tong gang, and Jake rashly promised police protection—it was LAPD practice to stay aloof from native disputes in Chinatown. Iris was found, wandering and incoherent, in the Santa Monica mountains, blinded and abused. No arrests were ever made, and Jake resigned from the force in helpless disgust.

He next set up the J. J. Gittes Detective Agency, specializing in divorce work. He was experiencing a modest if rather flashy prosperity when, in 1937, he was drawn into the affairs of Evelyn and Hollis Mulwray. This led Jake to investigate the part played by Noah Cross, Evelyn's father, in the manipulation of water in southern California. In love with Evelyn—by then a widow—Jake was there in Chinatown when police shot and killed her after she had wounded her father in an obscure family altercation. In the investigation, Judge Robert Evans said Jake had acted with "disastrous good intentions . . . and culpable naiveté, especially when you recall the clever pug he was."

For a year he did not leave his Los Feliz apartment—a victim of hepatitis and melancholy. He drifted thereafter, but found work farther north in 1942 at an internment camp for the Japanese. He married Aioshi Ichikawa, an internee, and there were allegations after the war that Jake had run a ring of prostitutes in the camp for munitions workers in the area.

By then, however, he was in Japan. In 1946, he and Aioshi went to Tokyo, where Jake returned to the swimming-pool trade with a partner, Alex Dawson. A daughter was born in 1949—Iris—and Jake became rich enough to travel in the East. Rumors spread from Macao to Manila that he was an operative of the CIA, and it is known that in 1960 he was in Saigon supervising the installation of an exotic indoor pool for Madame Nhu.

In 1972, Aioshi (still resident in Tokyo) said she had not seen Jake for four years; she was then in personal charge of the swimming-pool/golf-course design company. Iris, a photographers' model in Hong Kong, said she had met her father in Saigon in 1971, and reported that he was in poor health, suffering from jaundice, but working for a gaming club known as the Red Sash.

Dead or alive, present whereabouts unknown. There can be a lurking poetry in reference-book style: official statements with a hint of suspiciousness, as if one were hard of hearing between the lines. I will never let Jake die.

> *All those movies, hundreds a year for fifty years, with only seven or so story structures in all of them. I can see through the window the street lamp on the corner saying Bedford Falls is safe and civilized. And there is the light in my window that anyone passing by might call tranquil home life, or anxiety's tireless friction.*
> *I write by night.*

NOAH CROSS

John Huston in Chinatown, *1974,*
directed by Roman Polanski

What follows can be no more than notes waiting for the publication of Gore Vidal's biography of Cross, so often announced and postponed, yet still promised as *Noah's Flood: The Wealth of America*.

Noah Cross was born in 1870 in a prodigious rainstorm that prompted his name. He was the son of Julian Cross (1828–99), a leading Virginian and tobacco farmer, and Minna Russell (1851–91), granddaughter of Lord John Russell, British Prime Minister from 1846 to 1852. That couple met in London in the early 1860s (when the lady was only a child) during a secret mission undertaken by Cross on behalf of the Confederacy. Married in 1868, Minna went with her husband to live in Charlottesville. Her life there was made wretched and abbreviated by an asthma played upon by the rich, humid air, by her husband and by the fatal onset of lung cancer, which she ascribed to "living, willy-nilly, in America's fuming humidor." Her son was her single consolation, and local lore had it that he would sleep in her bed on thundery nights, up to the age of twelve.

Noah studied history at the University of Virginia and graduated in 1892. A noted horseman, he entered the cavalry and, as a colonel, he took part in the 1898 skirmishing in Cuba, where he was wounded in the right thigh. In the aftermath of these hostilities, Cross purchased land in Cuba very cheaply—"for what I had in my pocket"—and this became the basis of the Cross Fruit Company.

With both parents dead, Cross inherited lands in Virginia and Derbyshire, England, as well as the family tobacco interests. Leaving these under wise management, he went west and spent a year riding in the Sierras. In 1901 he built a house for himself near Los Angeles, and in 1902 he married Hester Doheny, the daughter of the oil magnate Edward Doheny. Their daughter, Evelyn, was born in 1905, but Hester died of influenza in 1919. In four generations, no Cross woman lived past forty.

The first decade of this century was a period of vast business expansion for Cross. By the time of America's entry into the First World War, *The Wall Street Journal* estimated, he was growing 8 percent of the cigarettes smoked in the U.S., canning 12 percent of its fruit, and "effectively licensing" the water flushed away by Los Angeles. This last accomplishment was the result of a collaboration between Cross and William Mulholland of the Los Angeles Department of Water and Power that took possession of water from the Owens River Valley for use by the city. Officially an urban policy, it only proceeded after Cross had purchased key acreages, the value of which kept rising in direct proportion to the population of Los Angeles. This enterprise provoked angry controversy (Upton Sinclair called Cross "The Great Rapist"), but Cross repudiated every charge by quoting Mulholland's first estimate of the water in the Owens Valley: "There it is—take it."

What *The Wall Street Journal* of 1917 could not know was that Cross was also a silent partner in the Hughes Tool Company. In 1909, he had gone to the aid of Howard Robard Hughes and Walter Sharp when they needed capital. Cross remained a shareholder in that company until it came under the control of Howard Hughes, Jr., a man Cross could not endure and about whom he said, "In the old days a tycoon was a man who, tastefully I daresay, threatened *other* people. This gray-suit cowboy is perpetually alarmed about his *own* health. No good will come of it."

Also in Los Angeles, it was Noah Cross who had prevailed upon a young "photoplay artist," Cecil B. De Mille, to make his film *The Squaw Man*, in the village of Hollywood. Thus Cross deserves much credit for bringing motion pictures to Los Angeles: he had, in 1910, helped arrange the co-opting of Hollywood into the city of Los Angeles in return for its water supply. Cross and De Mille became fast friends, and it was through that contact, in 1921, that Cross joined the board of Paramount. He is alleged to have told its chairman, Adolph Zukor, on that day, "My life—make that," little guessing that soon after his death the same company would treat parts of his career in *Chinatown*. It was De Mille, also, who introduced Cross to the actress Norma Desmond—their affair resulted in his setting her up in a mansion on Sunset Boulevard which she retained in the fierce suit that followed his boredom with her. Some felt his admission of it drove her mad. (Actresses sit on a narrow ledge, and they are preserved by our response, our loving them.)

When Edward Doheny was implicated in the Teapot Dome scandal (1922–24) it was his son-in-law, Noah Cross, who went out of his way to pay off witnesses and journalists. For those services, Cross gained entry into the oil industry, links that would prove instrumental in the eventual sale of Paramount to Gulf & Western, at which point Cross is reputed to have told his colleague Zukor, "What you have never had to find out, my dear Adolph, is that under compelling conditions a board may do anything."

It was in 1921 that Cross's daughter, the sixteen-year-old Evelyn, married Hollis Mulwray, the diligent head of the Department of Water and Power, when she became pregnant with her father's child. This child was named Katherine. In his nineties, Cross would talk privately about the matter: "Evelyn should not have been so much

5

cremated, without autopsy

around that summer," he said. "My wife had died and . . . it was a provocation." By then, however, Cross's longevity had transcended morality: it is the survivors who present history, and for Noah Cross life was always larger than its crimes.

The Depression brought scarcely a pause in Cross's progress. By 1935, he was reckoned to have a personal fortune worth over $500 million. It was in 1937 that his son-in-law, Hollis (salaried at $32,500 a year), began to threaten Cross. As the matter grew uglier and more confused, a private investigator, J. J. Gittes, was involved—both professionally and romantically. Hated by Evelyn, attacked by Hollis and hounded by Gittes, Cross found fresh impetus in his old zest to survive. Evelyn was killed by the police after wounding her father. Katherine went to live with her grandfather. But Katherine Mulwray killed herself when she was eighteen: she was found drowned in the Hollywood Reservoir. Cross had her cremated, without autopsy. He could get things done.

In his last decades, Cross retreated—to Galway, in Ireland, where he bred, rode and talked to horses; and, until 1959, to Cuba. No waning in his faculties was observed, apart from a little arthritis from his several old wounds. His empire swelled still, always under his scrutiny. He dabbled with a volume of memoirs, *Deep Waters Run Still*, never finished. We must wait for Mr. Vidal to find confirmation of whether or not he was a patron of, and advisor to, Gregory Arkadin, Eva Perón or Warren Beatty.

He died, early on the morning of June 18, 1972, in Ireland, of a massive heart attack, while on the phone to Washington, D.C.

> *I will never quite escape the sway of Noah Cross or the urge to imitate him. It would amaze anyone who knows me, but I could have been like him, could still put on a Stetson and drawl away. He was as grand and convincing as an actor. But I am real and splintered. I have hundreds—well, seven or so—to please.*

ILSA LUND

Ingrid Bergman in Casablanca, *1942,*
directed by Michael Curtiz

Although only a hundred miles from Stockholm, Askersund, the country estate where Ilsa Lund was born in 1918, was an idyllic enclave made claustrophobic by the dire feud that prevailed between her parents. The girl could do nothing except hope to outlast its withering effect. We know how valiant her spirit was because, until the moment of her unexpected death, she never backed away from the sincere hope that lives could be improved. But in her last photographs, we see the grave marks of disappointment.

Her father was a count whose small fortune was wiped out by the Kreuger speculations exposed in 1932. Her mother was a determined feminist at war with her husband and horrified to discover her own pregnancy. The country people had a notion that Ilsa was "simple," but that was only the servants' gossipy view of a child who never took sides and was invariably frustrated in her attempts to love two people who hated the sight of each other. The mother died when Ilsa was only eleven, of an illness that seems to have been just the breaking out of unmanageable rage. The girl was left alone with a morose father whose one need for his wife had been as an enemy.

So it was that Ilsa became infatuated with one of the young men servants in the household. They had a clumsy, furtive affair and he told her they would elope. But when the moment came, his nerve failed; Ilsa faced humiliation and misery if she stayed. On her own, and with very little money, she made her way to Germany in the summer of 1937.

In that terrible country, she was like a refugee from another century. But in Munich, and then later in Berlin, she was employed at a school for languages, first in a menial capacity, and then, when her German was more secure, as a teacher of Swedish. It was a bare existence in which her peace of mind was further eroded by the daily persecution of Jews. She intervened once or twice in street brawls and was once detained by the police. It was this incident that made her German pupils persuade her to leave Berlin. The language school had premises in Paris, and she went there late in 1938.

In Paris, she met an American expatriate, Richard Blaine. Not only

7

were they lovers in that time of phony war; Blaine also served as the mentor she had never had. A former labor organizer in America, who also claimed to have fought in the Spanish Civil War, he introduced her to the works of Marx, Trotsky, Victor Serge and John Reed. Their relationship was stormy: he was a heavy drinker and she challenged his brutally despairing attitudes too much for his comfort.

Blaine quit Paris on the eve of the German occupation, but Ilsa remained behind. As a national of a neutral country, she was able to live in Paris teaching languages to German officers. Late in 1940, she was approached by "Octave," a leader in the Resistance, who wanted to exploit her contacts in the enemy high command. She undertook several assignments for Octave—a hungry, lazy, rootless man—and had "Elena" as her code name.

Early in 1941, she was sent through Lyon to the vicinity of the Swiss border to rendezvous with Victor Laszlo, a Hungarian partisan who had escaped from a concentration camp. Together they traveled by way of Biarritz and Lisbon to Casablanca. Unbeknown to Ilsa, Blaine was then established in that city as a café proprietor.

It was widely assumed that Ilsa and Laszlo were married, but that was only a cover which inhibited Ilsa's reawakened feelings for Blaine. In truth, she never warmed to Laszlo and had early misgivings about his genuineness. But thanks to Blaine's assistance, she and Laszlo were able to obtain the scarce letters of credit that permitted departure from Casablanca. And so they made their circuitous way to America.

In New York by the fall of 1941, they were hailed as heroes of the struggle against fascism. But security agencies were not satisfied that Laszlo had indeed been in a concentration camp. Some wondered if he was a Nazi plant; others felt that he was a quixotic opportunist bizarrely touched by good fortune. In the words of the official report, ". . . it was so contrived an escape from German authority that it seems to have required the personal attention of Germany's ace, Major Heinrich Strasser." Later on, it was impossible to measure the balance of truth and masquerade in either Laszlo's boisterous identification with Communism in the years after 1942, or his tearful coming clean to the House Un-American Activities Committee in 1949. In all of this, Ilsa was an unhappy bystander, estranged from Laszlo but under suspicion by association. It was an undoubted relief for her when Laszlo died, of emphysema, in 1952—he had kept up a vulgar society trick of smoking two cigarettes at the same time.

Ilsa's American period was as unsettled as the rest of her life. She again taught languages, being proficient by now in five. She did some work subtitling the early films of Ingmar Bergman, and she was for a while the intimate of writer Delmore Schwartz. He refers to her in his collection *Vaudeville for a Princess*:

> And we shall never be as once we were,
> This life will never be what once it was!
> There is no prospect for tomorrow's thrills,
> Now and Tuesday, I must remember Ilsa.

More recently, research by Gail Levin has suggested that Ilsa may be the tall blonde woman, naked but for a blue sleeveless wrap and red high-heeled shoes, standing in the doorway in the Edward Hopper painting of 1949 *High Noon*. There are other mysteriously austere sexual icons in Hopper's later work that might be Ilsa Lund.

It was in 1955, against the concerned urgings of the FBI (still uncertain of her ideological allegiances), that Dag Hammarskjöld, Secretary General of the U.N., hired her as a personal assistant. True to their very close working relationship, she died with him in 1961 when his plane crashed in West Africa on its way to Kinshasa.

JOHN CLAY

Sterling Hayden in The Killing, *1956,*
directed by Stanley Kubrick

On a windless night, a little after nine p.m., how long would it take the engines on a DC-7, warming up, to disperse the contents of a large suitcase full of notes to the value of two million dollars?

John Clay, Johnny, was born in Oakland, California, in 1920. His father was a railroad conductor and his mother looked after the seven children. Twice a week the father was home with dry accounts of how the train had made its way between Seattle and Los Angeles. There were men who rode the freights then, going up and down the coast looking for work. Mr. Clay tipped them off, awake or not, whenever he found them, in the way he took a toothpick and coaxed shreds of meat from between his teeth after a meal. "Don't you ever let 'em ride?" asked Johnny. "No, sir," said his father, "against the rules."

"You miss some, I bet," reasoned his son. "If I see 'em, I don't miss 'em."

A suitcase forty-six inches long, twenty-eight high and a full fourteen inches deep—18,032 cubic inches. All those numbers, and all the notes with numbers on them. These were the notes taken in at Bay Meadows racetrack that day, small bills, crumpled, torn, some put back together again with Scotch tape in a last hope of a killing.

Johnny Clay was too big for school by the time he was fourteen. So he went away from home and down to the San Joaquin Valley. There were supposed not to be jobs, but Johnny knew where to go and he spent his teens following work between Modesto and Bakersfield. He picked almonds, artichokes and so on, all the way to zucchini. He was picking things he'd never eaten. By the time he was eighteen he was as hard and straight as a pole, and he smelled of onions. No washing could get rid of it. He used to think he was growing in that Valley himself, that strange reformed desert where canals and aqueducts patrol the earth and will not let it die. He counted the vegetables as he picked them, the boxes where he and the other pickers stacked them, the trucks that went out every night, and then all the other operations like the one he was on. It gave him a feeling for the millions in America.

No one ever knew for sure—the beauty of this robbery was that no one ever knew just how much—but about 4,000 fifties, 20,000 twenties, 80,000 tens, 100,000 fives and 60,000 ones. Over a quarter of a million bills, and an estimated total of two million dollars.

Johnny rode the trains in those days, and he still knew which ones his father was on. All the Clays had the timetable by heart. So sometimes he would slip aboard at dusk on a long uphill, and he'd be back home just a few minutes ahead of his father—with dust in his hair still—and he'd look up when his father came in and he'd say, "Still throwing 'em off the freights?"

He boxed a little, he was so impressive physically, but Johnny didn't know how to put another man away, and they said he didn't punch his weight. He looked good in the ring, but no one believed he was going anywhere. In 1941 he went into the navy. He served all the war as a seaman. Torpedoed once, and then again, his ship was sunk at Leyte Gulf. He was in the water once, and a small boat the other time, thirty-one hours and eleven days, seeing sharks all around the first time, and counting out the food and the days the second time. If he had been a prince or a president's son there would have been a book about him.

This case had been purchased at a pawnshop. It was strong, and it had metal corner pieces. But one of the fasteners didn't work; it flapped like a broken wing. And Johnny had no time to get a strap to put around the case. A strap would have made it all right. Johnny thought afterward that he could have used the belt on his pants.

When he came back from the war he was two hundred pounds and only twenty-five, so he fought some more. He wasn't as gentle a man either; anyone could see that the war had hardened him. They called him "Seaman" Clay on the bills, but it wasn't quite right, and though Johnny kept winning he never looked confident. People would always bet against him, no matter that he was the stronger man. Then one hot August night in Stockton in 1948, Ezzard Charles nearly killed him. People relaxed and said they'd always known it was going to happen.

So Johnny got out of boxing. He knew some gangsters, from Tahoe, and he fell in with them. They used him as muscle in the casinos. Johnny heard of jobs they were on, and he asked to be let in, but the others kidded him that he was punchy. So he watched these jobs and worked it out why most of them failed. And then in 1950 he went after one of the casinos in Reno. All on his own, with a plan. He studied the place and saw how at five a.m. on the third Sunday of the month there was a way to take everything. It was over a million, they said. The job worked, and Johnny was free for two months because no one could believe it was just one man. But they caught him, in Eureka, with all the money, except what he'd spent on meals and gas. He could have lived four hundred years on it at the rate he was going.

The case was on the top of two layers of luggage at the outside corner, so when the little motorized cart taking it to the plane swerved, the case fell off and a bump on the concrete broke it open.

They sent Johnny to Alcatraz in 1951. He was mild and patient about it, and he never ate all the heavy foods they gave the cons there. He ate moderately and worked in the yard while the others were up on the top bleachers looking across the Bay at the city, asking themselves how all the people could go about their business every day with the prison only a mile and a half away in the sunshine, and men festering there. But a prisoner is likely to be more philosophical than a free man.

Johnny was in a cell with Kola Kwarian, and Kola taught him chess. It nearly broke Johnny's brain to see how many moves you could figure. But there were just sixty-four squares and just thirty-two pieces to play with. So he worked it all out and got to be a fair player,

11

though he could never beat Kola. One day the Russian told him a story about how an emperor once had held a city to ransom. He'd said he'd take a sack of grain on the first square of the chessboard, two on the next, four on the next, and so on, geometric progression. At first, the people thought that would be easy. But Kola laughed and he told Johnny there would never be that much grain in all the history of the world. Johnny nodded quietly, for he had always known the world must end.

The cart swerved because of a dog. Today, there'd be no chance of a dog getting out there. But in 1956 airports were less formal.

In Alcatraz, Johnny planned the Bay Meadows robbery, and when he got out he went straight ahead with it. It only needed five of them. Marv Unger put up the seed money. George Peatty, the cashier, opened the door to let Johnny in behind the scenes. Mike O'Reilly, the barman, had brought the gun in earlier in the day, and left it in his locker so Johnny could use it for the holdup. Randy Kennan, the cop, would put the bag of money in his car and drive out; who was going to stop a police car? There were two others for smaller things: Nikki Agoglia to shoot Red Lightning on the far turn so everyone was diverted, and Kola to start a fight in the bar to get all the cops' attention.

Two million dollars, and it worked. Except that Johnny could see notes spilling no matter how careful the cashiers were. And then later, out in Daly City, when he transferred the money from the duffel bag to the suitcase, there was some left on the ground. So maybe it was only $1.9 million in the case, going to the plane, warming up to fly to Boston, with Johnny and his girl Fay at the gate. Then the dog and the swerve. When the case opened it still took eleven seconds for all that money to be whirled away by the aircraft engines, and they were only thirty feet from the case. The money had been thrown in like dirty laundry. There were people at the airport for years afterward looking, and you still hear of notes being found. But officially they recovered $632,127.

They sent Johnny back to Alcatraz and he died there in 1960.

> *Is the order of these entries significant? I do
> them as they come into my head, but my head
> keeps running back to system. So design and
> randomness bump together, skirmishing, like
> lovers.*

AXEL FREED

James Caan in The Gambler, *1974,*
directed by Karel Reisz

"We will see that the boy is brought up nicely," A. R. Lowenthal encouraged his daughter, Naomi, in 1943. She was holding her baby, a foot long, with yards of fine white robes reaching to the floor. The child was born swarthy, with piercing brown eyes and a sensual mouth. No one could remember seeing a baby who paid such attention so early. "He has the stare of a victorious general," said Lowenthal. "Or a painter?" suggested Naomi. Her husband, Lowenthal's son-in-law, a frail man named Rudolf, stood by like a stranger in the three-stage family rapture. He noticed his own weakness in his new son's face, but he was too reticent to say the word *gambler* out loud. Anyway, he died a year later, of a perforated stomach ulcer, with so many things unsaid.

A. R. Lowenthal, Armyan Lowenthal—he added the *R* much later for rhythm—had come to America from Lithuania in 1911, when he was fifteen, with "nothing except wit and balls and will." He had won a reputation as a king of style, and a killer in business. By the middle 1920s he owned a chain of furniture stores in the New York area which he still supervised and for which he remembered every smallest detail. He was an awesome figure for any family, a giant of achievement and appetite, nearly a monster of success. No flaws showed in his castle.

His own wife had dimmed in his light. Their daughter Naomi had elected very early to please him. In bringing forth a son, she had met the wish always uppermost in his mind. A.R. looked on Axel—a name he had urged—as if he were a golden bowl smuggled across a continent for his delight alone. The old man loved to hold his grandson, humming long passages from Mahler and swaying the tiny bundle in time with the sweep of his own romantic longings. Secure, old, and weak in the heart, A.R. dreamed of further glories. Axel's chestnut eyes watched him with intense curiosity, certain somehow, no matter how immature, that he would have a contest of wills with this gray-haired dear. He conceived the urge not to please his grandfather, even if it destroyed him, Axel, in the process.

A dedicated mother and a rich grandfather made a brilliant child.

13

He was eloquent at five. He could sketch quickly, dance with grace, play the piano by ear, tell stories to his elders, captivate strangers, play games with a skill ahead of his years. He was like a perfect child. But he had a momentous temper that could turn him into a dervish of violence in an instant. It was beyond his control, a passionate anger always directed at playmates or people on the street, but so dramatic it served to put a dark cloud around him in the eyes of others. It was self-destruction, not yet aware of its true target.

He went to Harvard in 1961, becoming best friends with the sons of Latin American dictators and Brahmin families. He wooed the daughter of a branch of the English nobility and married her. He was, for the short duration of the marriage, mentioned in Burke's Peerage. But he moved with equal ease among mobsters, bookmakers and loan sharks. As his father had known, Axel could have been a lord, a poet, a banker or a killer, but gambling became his abiding interest. He would be locked in writing a textual analysis of Donne and Marvell, only to reach out for the phone and put a thousand dollars on Boston College to beat the spread against DePaul. He read every newspaper he could find, but only the sports sections. He loved the games, not for their beauty or the prowess they required but because of the odds and the likelihood that hovered above them, like bees near flowers on a hot day.

This went on for several years, the scale rising. He could be breathtakingly rich one day, and then a week later forced to borrow twenty dollars from Naomi. Sometimes he was a center of cheerful groups; sometimes he hid from his creditors. Not that either state pleased him. The indecision was his greatest gratification, the risk. There was no winning so great, no luck so magical, that he would not bet until it crashed down.

Nineteen seventy-four was the last chance, the last crisis. After that there was no going back. One night at a private casino in Manhattan, he lost $44,000. It was the largest debt he had ever had. Axel got up from the table exhilarated by the magnificent danger, smiling with love and a killer's kiss at the casino management, discussing how he would pay them back. "Soon, Axel, soon," they said. "Sure," he answered, "soon." They were so businesslike; he was such an amateur. His amusement always hurt them and made them feel shabby. They could guarantee an extra slash of the razor when the time came.

Then he went to see Billie, his current girl. She was a model, lithe, thin, blonde, Californian, the most unsuitable sexual prize he could find for a scholar and a Jew. She was butter next to his anchovy. He went to the college classroom and talked about Dostoyevski: he was a part-time professor, a natural at existentialism, a firebrand for *The Idiot*, *The Gambler* and Karamazovian bargains with destiny. He went to his mother for $10,000, a stay against execution. He went to a birthday party for A.R. on the beach. He explained his whole predicament to Naomi. So as not to spoil her father's day, she gave Axel a check for $44,000 along with the advice, "Come to terms with why you're doing this."

He scooped up Billie, and took her to Las Vegas. "I'm hot as a pistol," he assured her, and there in a Nevada casino, at blackjack, with 18 showing, he did not so much ask as tell the croupier, "Give me the 3," with a force so great that the woman was not surprised when she flipped it over for him. He won $90,000, the most he had ever won. But he lost half of it again when Brown beat Harvard at basketball, and another $50,000 went away when, in the last second, Seattle turned it on the Lakers 111–110. He bet all he had left on another game, and won. It was desperate and ecstatic. "If all my bets were safe," he said, "there wouldn't be any juice."

He went back to New York, and the Mob sent men out to catch him, hold him by the ears and bring him in. "You owe us," they said. "Sure," said Axel. "But I'm broke. Stake me again." They said, no more. He would have to do something for them. There was a black kid in his class, Carl Spencer, on the basketball team, the star forward. Get him to fix the spread against Syracuse. "How?" said Axel. Impress him, they said, the kid respects you, genius. And as he was going on this drab mission, one of the mobsters called out, "Hey, Axel, one day you'll be killing someone for us."

He grinned, lustrous with exaltation. The game was fixed. Spencer was ashamed. The debt was canceled. Axel had a clean slate. So he went up to Harlem into a black club, demanding the best whore in the place. He insulted the pimp. "What do I have to do, nigger?" And the whore cut his face with a knife. With the bliss of nearing disaster, Axel looked at his wound in the mirror.

EILEEN WADE

Nina Van Pallandt in The Long Goodbye, *1973,*
directed by Robert Altman

Frederick Gould was an eminent King's Counsel. He specialized in litigation and society divorces, and he acted in England for Mrs. Wallis Simpson in the divorce that freed her to marry King Edward VIII. Eileen, born in London in 1938, was his second child. The family stayed in town, living in the Boltons throughout the Blitz, though Eileen and her brother John, with their mother, were evacuated to Devon for parts of 1941–42.

Eileen grew up a tall, attractive blonde girl, a pupil at St. Paul's School for Girls. She sang at school, and took the part of Ado Annie in a production of *Oklahoma!* Her father wanted her to go on to Cambridge, but an unfortunate misunderstanding over her entrance exams sent her instead to a finishing school in Switzerland. While there, she added several foreign languages to her education and perfected the straightfaced lie, a ploy that some had noted in her at an early age. It was while in Switzerland, in 1957, that she became the mistress of the American business tycoon J. J. Cord. The affair lasted only one summer, but through Cord's graces she was able to go back and forth between Europe and America for the next few years, an assured resident alien.

She did this and that: she managed an antiques store on Wilshire Boulevard in Los Angeles, she had a stud farm in Galway, and she was a literary agent in Paris. But in 1962, in London, she set up the first of a small chain of health-food shops—Nuts—that were known during the sixties as a trendsetter. Eileen herself traveled in the Mediterranean and North Africa, obtaining the best possible supply of grains, nuts and pulses, raisins, dates and other dried fruits. In 1966, she wrote her *Health Food Cookbook*, which was a big success when published by Penguin.

In London, in the mid-sixties, Eileen Gould was a frequent figure in the gossip columns: she was alleged to be a close friend of Albert Finney, Andrew Oldham and Tony Godwin, then the editorial director of Penguin Books. She also spent several summers on the island of Ibiza, and it was rumored that she had acted as a middleman in the sale to major galleries of paintings done by Elmyr de

Hory—who had a studio on the island—but "signed" by Dufy, Matisse or Utrillo.

Late in 1967, the British Customs and Excise confiscated a consignment of dried apricots sent from Morocco to London for Nuts. The barrels were found to contain several pounds of high-grade hashish. Eileen Gould protested that she had no knowledge of this secret ingredient; and the police could find no clinching evidence that she had been involved in the illegal importation of drugs. However, the affairs of Nuts came under close scrutiny, and in 1968 Eileen sold the company for £1.1 million to the Trust House Forte group.

With the proceeds, she traveled—to the Mediterranean and to America—and farther afield, to Africa and the South Seas. It was in Tahiti, in 1970, that she met Roger Wade, the novelist. Wade (1918–73)—real name Billy Joe Smith—had been a soldier captured at Bataan and a prisoner of the Japanese. A wanderer and a sailor, after the war he had lived in Sausalito, and started to write—*A Man Cannot Stand Confinement* (1949), *Vienna and Johnny and Old Nick* (1957) and *Undertow* (1964). These were all best-sellers, and they allowed Wade—his adopted name as a writer—to buy a series of sailboats. However, by the time he met Eileen, Wade was an alcoholic, more inclined to talk about his next novel than get on with it.

They were married in 1970, on board his schooner, the *Aquavit*, in Pailolo Channel, off the island of Maui. The couple sailed back to California and took a house in the Malibu Colony. Wade struggled to write a new book and Eileen opened a health-food store in Santa Barbara. It was not a happy marriage for very long, and Eileen started an affair with Terry Lennox, a Malibu neighbor and a former baseball player.

It was in 1973 that Lennox's wife, Sylvia, was found beaten to death and Terry Lennox disappeared. In fact, he had been driven to Mexico by an old friend, Philip Marlowe. Eileen stayed behind and hired Marlowe to look for her husband when he disappeared on one of his drunken binges. This was only a way of making gambler and gangster Marty Augustine, as well as the police, believe that Terry had killed himself in Mexico from remorse. Eileen flirted with Marlowe, and one night at Malibu, as they were becoming intimate, the drunken Roger Wade walked out of the house and into the Pacific, where he drowned.

Not long after that, Eileen sold the Malibu house and went away. Marlowe played a hunch. He went to Mexico, to the small town where Terry Lennox had been certified dead and buried. He talked to the local authorities, and guessed that they had been bribed. So he waited and explored, and he talked to kids in the sunny squares and to old men in the sleepy bars. He met a drunk named Firmin who told him he had seen a blonde woman, nearly six feet tall, with hair the color of sunrise. Tequila sunrise, thought Marlowe, but he checked it out.

Marlowe found the villa where Lennox and Eileen were living, and he went there one day when Eileen was at the market. Marlowe had liked Wade; they had sat on the beach one afternoon seeing how much they could drink. Lennox laughed when Marlowe told him the story. Nobody cares, he said. Nobody cares but me, said Marlowe. You're a born loser, sighed Lennox. So Marlowe shot him, and when Eileen got back she had food for two with her lover floating on top of the pool.

There has been no word of Eileen Wade since then, nothing to pin her down. She had money, but she was the kind of woman people notice. There are no charges against her anywhere. Marlowe never put in a report. Maybe Eileen went farther south. There was a story in 1980 about a white woman running a resort hotel in Sulaco. And that's where Frederick Gould retired in 1974, the law set aside.

DAVID STAEBLER

Jack Nicholson in The King of Marvin Gardens, *1972, directed by Bob Rafelson*

Four times in ten years, different doctors have suggested he try reducing the dose. David Staebler doesn't welcome the thought, but he has always been obedient and self-pitying enough to suffer under the system. It's important that he treat this warning about scaling down the drug as if it came from the IRS, or some other arrangement of initials stamped into the spine of the state, an authority not to be denied or questioned. David has always expected to be taken and exploited; his tender sadness is waiting for it, and his flat, ironic voice was trained not to give any sign of the pain. You'd never know about the pain, if you didn't notice the unalleviated morbid song in that famous voice. "This has been 'Etcetera,' I am your host, David Staebler . . ."—a calm accountant, describing disasters in the early morning hours, making them up, sometimes slipping in true horror, but no longer sure which pills kick and which are clever placebos.

David and Jason Staebler were born in Philadelphia, in 1936 and 1938—"in that order," Jason added for years. He was so much more convinced than David, so much more worldly, that everyone took him for the older. Yet Jason wanted to be spoiled; he wanted to cling onto the chance of being the "kid" brother. David looked at him with the gloomy awe of an innocent who has met a wizard. While they were still boys, a kind of deferential slowness overtook David so that Jason was always beating him—to the punch, the dinner table, or the dream. It was Jason who lived on the spur of moments, deciding what they were going to do; while David, with eyes like a dark pond in shadow, waited to be ruffled by the wind. David had only two advantages. He remembered everything and then gradually, over the years, he retold it all as stories. He built Jason into a legend on the radio, and it did for the poor guy, long before that set of bullets ripped him apart in Atlantic City.

Their parents were both killed in 1938, on Sunday, October 30, when their car was in a collision just outside Grovers Mill, New Jersey. They were on their way back from New York to Philadelphia, two happy young people, not long delivered of their second child, returning from what they called "another honeymoon" in the city. They had everything to look forward to; they were listening to the car radio, spellbound in the dark, a fragile cabin buzzing along the road, touching, their hands held on the ledge of their two thighs . . . when a panic-stricken truck came out onto the highway. Their hands were still locked, and the radio was still playing . . . or so it went, according to David's bewitched account of how radio came to be his metier.

The boys were brought up by their grandfather, a movie projectionist in Philadelphia. He was a dour, conscientious man, ruined by the death of his daughter, their mother, who gave the boys a steady-paced routine for life, stable to a point of emphasis, that had not the least effect on them. Both Staeblers grew up crazy. They were intelligent and they could pass, but they were out of their minds and into that night in which young married lovers met their death. Jason was supposed to be the wild and reckless one; after all, he got himself killed for a reason no one could ever quite put into words. But it was David, and it is David, who has already told five different stories about how his parents died. All on "*Etcetera*," all heart-rending and as arresting as a vision in moving headlights. Not one person in Philadelphia has ever called up to say, "But a year ago, you said that . . . " David Staebler's fleeing from the truth holds sway in the night airwaves of that city. People may raise their eyebrows, but they let the storyteller go on. It lets David suppose that no one's listening—one more nail to put in the coffin of himself, his arms reaching up and tapping it into his wooden top.

David went to Temple: he studied literature and ran the campus radio station. By his senior year, he had seven separate voices and characters on the air, he was always on the radio, those eyes so planed away of their own shining, always craving the red light, "On Air." Jason left school at sixteen, and by the time he was twenty he was running a chain of grocery stores in the Poconos. There are still those in the area who say that Jason Staebler was a merchandising genius, that he could have been an emperor in supermarkets. But he got bored easily, he was always changing his plans, always talking about Hawaii, or Alaska, or South America. He may never have read a book, but he couldn't abide hard facts. He wanted the melting life of fiction, and he lived out scenarios in the way David let them creep into the night air, like fog.

Anyway, by the late 1960s, the brothers were apart. They didn't "know" where the other one was—except that David still lived at home with his grandfather, and always worked for the same radio station in Philadelphia. So Jason knew, just as David could count on it that his brother was somewhere close but unexpected. They went years without a word or a call, always expecting to bump into each other. Jason had made a promise that they would both be big, kings of Marvin Gardens, by the time they were forty.

David was thirty-six when the call came. He was on the air, telling a story about how he and Jason had once watched their grandfather choke to death on a fishbone. "My brother and I became accomplices forever. 'Don't ever say a word about this,' said my brother." David was drawling the story into the microphone, and the city and the grandfather were absorbing it in the same mood of stoic wondering. Then the call came from Jason: come to Atlantic City, right away.

David went, always available for disaster, always punctual and giving of himself. Anxious to please, horrified by the possibility of not being liked. It was his need for company, his fear of being alone, that made for so much trouble. Yet he was a retiring fellow, drifting into the bathroom in the middle of the night to practice a soliloquy, a gaunt loner sufficient to inspire a young woman's fervent insistence that he should have the john and all the time he needed—"I know you're an artist." So she peed out of the window, and David didn't ever get to screw the fabulously pretty Jessica, the stepdaughter of Sally, to whom Jason, in Atlantic City, seemed precariously married. Though the gloomy David was sure his brother was fucking Jessica too. He only had to look at Sally's burnt-out eyes, and see how she hacked off her hair on the wintry beach, letting the copper hanks burn in a fire that was the best reason for being out there on so cold a morning.

Jason had this plan for a casino and a hotel in Hawaii—he had Hawaiian shirts already packed. David was to direct entertainments there: seances, charades and wakes, presumably. They were going to make their fortune. It was 96 percent finalized. But it was all bullshit. Jessica had looked to David once amid the buzz of Jason's plans, and said, "I wish you didn't really think I was part of all this." "Well, aren't you?" David had asked. And Jessica nodded and grinned, "Of course I am. We all are."

And just to stop him talking, just to halt the inane momentum of packing and the gravitational absurdity of "going to Hawaii," Sally shot Jason. She sobbed in Jessica's arms afterward—it never had much to do with betrayal. Jason's pitching had to be stopped.

But David went on. He took the body back to Philadelphia, he organized the funeral, and so on. And he went back on the radio, not a whit more or less fatalistic than he had been before. But friends told him he was depressed, and so he made depression his new brother. He went on drugs that slowed and blurred him, but he got used to them and he can still spin those infinitely sad myths into the night, like a kid lying on his bed tossing curve balls at the ceiling so that they bend round the light bulb, never hitting it, always missing explosion.

JUDY ROGERS

Natalie Wood in Rebel Without a Cause, *1955,*
directed by Nicholas Ray

They lived in a four-bedroom house in Altadena, after Ed Hopper came out of the army. He got a job as a salesman for an ice-cream company, and in the years between 1946 and 1955 he won salesman-of-the-year three times. Judy, the elder child, was born in 1937, a pretty girl whose looks had turned angry and suspicious by the time she entered high school in 1951. No longer did she go to her dancing lessons; on weekends, she never went riding; and she had given up

21

her suitable circle of friends. In high school, she went with the rougher boys. She was interested in cars, movies and being out late. The happy Hopper home was filled with recrimination. Ed Hopper took to slapping his daughter's face when roused. There was a perpetual flush of disgust on Judy's cheeks mixed in with those ignominious pimples. With a bottomless supply of ice cream, she had always been beset by baby fat and acne, and she loathed her own weakness.

By the time of her senior year, Judy was going with a bunch of hard-faced kids—Buzz, Goon, Crunch, Moose and so on—who looked too old for high school. That's when Jim Stark came to the school: his family had arrived from back east somewhere. He was a weird kid, shy but bold. He made friends with Plato, the fruit; but he gave Judy a glance that let her know he was straight. And he got into a chicken-run with Buzz his first week at school after the two of them started a fight outside the planetarium.

Judy was Buzz's girl, not that she'd gone all the way with him yet. But others kept off. Still, just before the race began and she was giving both the guys some dust, she didn't know which one she wanted to win. Then Buzz sailed over the cliff, like a car in a movie, and before he hit the rocks and the water she thought that she didn't really know him. Jim looked after her then, and the two of them took Plato into L.A. to an empty mansion off Sunset Boulevard. That's where the other kids came after them, and Plato got out this gun and shot Crunch. Then he took off and got into the planetarium. The cops came and Jim went in to try and get the gun off Plato. He borrowed the gun for a while and took out the clip, so it was empty when he gave it back. But Plato got scared when the cops put the lights on and he ran out waving the gun, so they blasted him. It was the worst thing Judy ever saw. She hated the cops more than she felt for Jim.

But Plato's death brought them closer together. She saw later that it was a pressure from which they were too vulnerable to escape. So when they graduated, they married. Both eighteen. A marriage with four worried smiles from the parents.

Jim enrolled at UCLA. They lived in a tiny apartment on Gayley Drive, and Judy worked as a waitress in Westwood while Jim drove a cab four nights a week. They didn't see too much of each other, but a son, Caleb, was born in 1958. They were hard-pressed then. Judy couldn't work as much. The costs of child-care were high. And in his junior year Jim was put on academic probation. They fought whenever they were in together. It was plain to Judy that their teenage romance had been a brief passion encumbered by marriage. Jim had a circle of friends he never talked about. He was secretive. If Judy heard any of their names he became angry.

In 1959, she moved out. They both called it a trial separation, because they were too hurt to face the truth. Judy moved to Anaheim, where her father had got her the manageress job at a fast-food outlet. Within three months, Jim had stopped calling. She lived with Caleb in an apartment, helped out by some money from her parents and some from Jim's father. She vowed she'd never marry again. But in 1962 she met a doctor, Herbert Rogers. He was forty-four, divorced, with two teenage daughters who lived with him most of the time. He wooed Judy, and he talked to her about psychology in a way that impressed her.

He offered her his house in Menlo Park, a large family and no need to work. He seemed like a good man, kind but disciplinary with Caleb. So in 1963, she married him and moved north. Three years later she walked out, sick of his greedy daughters, worn out by his tiredness and the terror with which he viewed the failure of a second marriage. Moreover, he was very conservative, critical of young people and mocking of the antiwar movement.

The rebellion in Judy was rekindled. She took Caleb and moved into a Haight-Ashbury commune. Once there, she became active in the antiwar movement. One day in April 1966, she got a call from a voice she knew:

"Hey," it said. "Anniversary."

"Jim?"

"Good guess."

"What anniversary?"

"Day Plato got it."

She had forgotten. Jim wouldn't tell her where he was, or how he had found her. Judy mentioned it to a woman in the house, and she wasn't surprised at all, so Judy worked it out that Jim was known to the group. As time went by, she reckoned that it was a kind of anarchists' cell, and Jim was something of a leader. He came by one day in the summer with an Oriental woman who didn't speak English. He talked to Judy and they took Caleb to Golden Gate Park. He asked her what she thought about the war. After that, Judy got trusted with more important jobs.

On October 11, 1968, she was killed, driving over the Bay Bridge when a homemade bomb she was carrying exploded.

KIT CARRUTHERS

Martin Sheen in Badlands, *1973,
directed by Terrence Malick*

It was only as I came to write this piece, and thought to study the map of all the small places Carruthers passed, that I had a surprise. There on the Rand-McNally Road Atlas, page 77 in my edition, about fifteen miles in from the western edge of South Dakota and on a line with the Montana-Wyoming border, there is a small red square and "Geographical Center of the U.S." It's in there near Antelope Butte and Haystack Buttes, just to the west of a line you could draw between Rapid City and the Slim Buttes battle site. Carruthers must have gone right by it, but I doubt if he stopped to notice or think about it.

If you consider the map of the whole country, then I don't see how it can be called the "Geographical Center." For a start, it's a whole lot closer to Canada than to Mexico, and maybe only half as far from the Pacific as it is to the Atlantic. I always heard it said that Kansas City was the middle of America, or the nearest large place, and that Bedford Falls, Nebraska, was the heart of the country, the mathematical midpoint. So it came as a shock to see this red square in South Dakota. It makes me wonder whether there may be others all vying for the honor. Not that it's much once you've said it. It reminds me of a book I read about the race to the South Pole between Captain Scott and Amundsen. When they got there, both of them, they couldn't be sure they were there. No red markers—just white as far as they could see. So they marched around for miles just to be sure that they'd stood on the damned pole itself. As for the center of America, you might have to do the same, unless you have a sure feeling where it is.

This Carruthers was an old-time desperado, some said; I thought he was a new breed of disgrace. I knew the country was in trouble when it celebrated him so. These are the facts:

Kit Carruthers, b. Birdeye, Arkansas, 1933, never knew his father; his mother did laundry and went in to Memphis at night

1938–47: some schooling, yet he could barely read

1947–50: went with a traveling preacher, named Powell, who worked the roads between Fort Smith and Nashville. Carruthers was his assistant and his advertising manager, and he often played the part of a country boy who had been struck blind, so that Powell could cure him. He was also abused sexually by Powell, until one day Carruthers beat him to a standstill and quit

1950–54: on the road, Carruthers would say he was a wounded veteran of the Korean War. He tried to join the Army, the Texas Rangers and the state police of both Oklahoma and Kansas, but he was rejected for lack of education and psychological instability

1954: ninety-day sentence in Amarillo, Texas, for shoplifting

1955: occasional disc-jockey and raconteur on Arkansas radio station, but he was fired for persistent use of obscenities on the air. He said he just couldn't eliminate them

1955–56: worked for a chain of supermarkets as manager for stunts and promotions

1956–57: arrested for brawling in Wichita, Kansas; assigned to State Mental Hospital for observation, and released

1957: drifted north; time in McCook, Nebraska, as railroad maintenance man

1957–58: into South Dakota; barman in Rapid City, fired for haranguing customers; to Fort Dupree, worked as member of a garbage crew.

On June 8, 1958, Carruthers went into the offices of the local newspaper and demanded to be interviewed. A reporter sat with him, to humor him, and the young man said that as "a decent, enterprising American who liked to listen to the other man's point of view, I have got nowhere." He added that he was about ready to do something. A week later, he supposed that the paper was not going to run his story. On June 17, he met Holly Sargis, and June 29 he shot and killed her father, set fire to the Sargis house, and he and Holly drove away, toward the buttes. She was an impressionable girl, and all agreed he was a rousing talker.

They led the life of hideaways that summer, living in the forests and then beating out across open country into Montana. The thing that tickled him was stopping off in small towns to take a look at how he was doing in the newspapers. In that summer he shot Sargis, and two, three, four, some hunters that stumbled on their tree house, then five, an old friend of his, six, seven, the two kids who happened by—he shut them in a shelter and fired into it—and then a policeman who came after them, that's eight.

He was stopped finally on a back road in Rosebud County, not far from the Little Bighorn battleground. He was taken back to Rapid City in South Dakota to be tried. He gave interviews and pleaded guilty, and when the judge asked if he had anything to say, he talked for twenty minutes, saying that Holly Sargis hadn't been old enough to know what was happening, and how he'd started to get respect after he killed some people. Then he said he hoped he'd get the juice, and he did, in the state prison, January 23, 1959. In his last interview, he asked to be known as "The Dakota Kid" after he had died, and if he didn't rise again. But he had donated his body to science, and they cut him in pieces.

WALDO LYDECKER

Clifton Webb in Laura, *1944,*
directed by Otto Preminger

In 1935, at the peak of his fame, and just before the scandal that ensured this would be his only honorary degree, Waldo Lydecker was dressed in an academic gown at Pembroke College and asked to speak to the senior class. He surprised the occasion by offering not some barbed remarks on how young ladies should behave, but a heartfelt tribute to the example set by Charles Dickens. Among his few intimates, it was remembered that he sometimes quoted from the English novelist, did own a set of first editions, and may have inspired a passion for Dickens in the young Welsh actor Emlyn Williams.

The journals of Waldo Lydecker cannot yet be published: too many mentioned and mocked there are still alive. But I have had an opportunity to examine them (my thanks to the Steffensen Collection at Wesleyan University) and I believe that this will be the first public revelation that "Waldo Lydecker" was born Walter Little, in 1893, in Portsmouth, the English south-coast port, where Dickens had been born, eighty-one years earlier.

He was the son of Elsie, a boardinghouse keeper in the Fratton district, and of a sailor, Arthur Little, who was lost at sea in what we must now call the first Battle of the Falkland Islands (in 1914). Young Walter, an only child, grew up with few advantages and poor schooling, earning coppers collecting glasses in Portsmouth public houses and being an errand boy for sailors on shore leave. Fond of horses and always slight, he was an apprentice jockey in the years 1908–11, familiar at the various stables and racecourses in southern England. However, a controversy over his rough riding at the

Goodwood meeting of 1911 put an end to his career, and it was noted that, thereafter, he went into employment with bookmakers.

At around the same time, he fell in with traveling theatrical companies, working as an actor and a writer of romantic lyrics. This seems to have been a happy time, in and out of scrapes, as Walter roamed that lovely, gentle part of England, playing Malvolio at Haslemere one evening, and taking bets at Plumpton races the following afternoon. There is some evidence that Walter appeared a few times on Fred Karno's houseboat at Tagg's Island, on the Thames, and the possibility that he had shared the homemade limelight there with the young Chaplin. More intriguing still, although no text survives, it is clear that Walter adapted a stage version of *Nicholas Nickleby* that played in Brighton, Bournemouth and Portsmouth in 1914—"the last summer of enchantment" Waldo once called it in his New York column.

He was conscripted into the British army in 1916, shortly after the death in Rye, Sussex, of Henry James. Walter had been employed in the James household, to read to the dying novelist, a task that may have accounted for the rather stilted grace of his speech. Whatever, he went from reading *Dombey and Son* to James to khaki and drill in a few weeks, and he might have died in the Flanders mud but for an emotional involvement with a lieutenant (Walter was only a private) from one of the nation's most distinguished families (the de Winters). No action was taken by the authorities, and no evidence preserved. However, in 1917, Walter Little was discharged, without comment, and sent back to England. The country had changed, and Walter was not the same blithe young man. He had influenza in 1919, and was never strong again. There were incidents with the police and a squalid business with a canon at Chichester Cathedral.

Escape came in the form of work as a steward on the Cunard line, and so Walter Little arrived in New York in 1920. The city and the prospect of a fresh start there thrilled him, and a year later he quit his ship at the docks and hailed a cab.

The next few years are vague: the journal ceases, as if its author were busy transforming himself. It is certain that Walter Little went to Los Angeles, to the new picture business. While there, he became Wallace Lydell, an extra and a stringer for gossip columns. But in 1928 he surfaced as Waldo Lydecker, running a salon in Santa Monica that never let its own notoriety detract from the verve with which it pronounced on the stupidity or iniquity of others in that city. Waldo started a column for a Hearst paper, rose quickly to syndication, and

27

appeared to relish the fear and loathing of many film stars. Without stooping to sensation, let me just say that he was by then a promiscuous homosexual who ran the dangerous gauntlet of reporting on liaisons and human mishaps observed among his own circle of associates. Attacked once or twice, he adopted a walking stick and did nothing to discourage rumors that it sheathed a weapon.

It was in 1931 that Waldo moved to New York to make the nation as a whole his target. In an interview given at that time, he indulged the legend that he was Hungarian and of noble birth. This was the foundation of his reputation as a model of Manhattan manners, correcting speech and table arrangements, advising on dress and deportment, but always, somehow, remaining a law unto himself. It was the Lydecker secret that while he intimidated others with etiquette, he behaved like a libertine of insult, deploring, criticizing and making himself a fountain of sarcastic rebuke, all in the name of politeness.

In addition to his column, he had a regular radio program on CBS, a potpourri, in which he wearied of current affairs, recommended restaurants and designers, and read from Dowson, Swinburne and Tennyson. There were books—*How to be Insulting but Forgiven* (1934) and *The Caustic Christmas Book* (1937)—overly mannered, to be sure, but amusing still and forever spiked by the nervy line drawings of Norman Clyde, Waldo's close friend in those years.

Lydeckerism was characteristic of the smartest American cities of the 1930s—glamorous, heartless and addicted to fads and cults. In fact, Waldo had a healthy streak of ordinariness: he enjoyed Laurel and Hardy; at home he fed on rice pudding and blancmange; and even when he posed in his marble bath, at the typewriter, for Cecil Beaton, he took care to wear shorts in the water, of what looks like a very garish plaid. He lived on Park Avenue in two apartments knocked into one and furnished with ostentatious "taste": "It's lavish, but I call it home." He was fond of bogus antiques that deceived guests, and he was a sleeping partner in the company of "Lejon Fils, Paris" (to be found in Hoboken), specializing in Louis XV reproductions.

By this stage he was too prominent to escape the public censure that followed his arrest in Central Park for soliciting a sailor. He was fined $5,000, and he "retired" from his column for over a year. He came back eventually, for Kane papers, but never with the same space or brio. His nerve had been shaken; there was a new edge of jittery malice in his talk and writing.

No longer feared, sometimes laughed at, he was lunching at the

Algonquin one day in 1942 when Laura Hunt, fresh in advertising, approached him to endorse a pen for which her agency, Bullitt's, had the account. That he accepted impressed Miss Hunt as a testament to her winningness. Waldo's diary says simply that he appreciated how a young actor in the restaurant noticed him only when the "glaringly luscious" Laura appeared.

The entire patronage of Laura Hunt was for ulterior motives: she was bait in a time when he feared his own looks were fading, not much helped by a new mustache. He made her, "if it counts for anything to make this city notice a selfish sexpot from Nebraska who will give as much head as it takes to get ahead." He would say anything for a laugh. Behind her creamy back he ridiculed her—especially to Tavorian Jacoby, the painter he coaxed into doing what he regarded as a swooningly vulgar portrait of Laura. In time, Miss Hunt discovered his real scorn and did anything she could to oppose him. "My dear," he said to her one night, "if you only had real intelligence I would have to kill you."

Laura threatened to expose him, and he urged her to do her worst. He felt his life was a bore, marginally alleviated by a teenage protégé named Falco. Perhaps Waldo meant to murder Laura that sweltering weekend in August 1944; perhaps he knew that Diane Redfern, a model, was staying in Laura's apartment and put both barrels of buckshot in her face as a warning. Whatever the answer, self-destructiveness had set in, and his fate was fixed when—in the course of the investigation—Waldo made an erudite pass at the detective in charge, Mark McPherson, and then explained its raw meaning. Forty-eight hours later Waldo was dead, shot by McPherson's assistant in Laura's apartment, as he lunged theatrically at the heart-shaped face he had made famous.

> *I cannot write that without flinching—my arm jumps out—to protect her, or is it because I have imagined myself aiming at her? In the years since, I have sometimes cursed Laura and supposed her desire accounted for my action. We imagine others with so much more zeal than we ever see ourselves. We are like close-ups in a movie, staring into the dark so that we do not have to face the camera or the discipline of being seen.*

> *Am I jealous of Waldo, because he discovered*
> *Laura when I wanted to be her* auteur? *We*
> *watch in a crowd, sure the picture is ours alone.*

LAURA HUNT

Gene Tierney in Laura, *1944,*
directed by Otto Preminger

"Only prettiness," I say out loud in the quiet house, flipping through the packet of photographs in Laura's file. The prints fall like rubber leaves, preserved but unnatural. I put them in order long ago to trace her life. There is always the same body—from when she had a career as a model—a promontory of bare shoulder and the taut slopes of her breasts, arising from this or that cast-satin evening gown, or the season's most tastefully risqué swimsuit. There are painted clouds behind her, ghosts of sky. But what was risqué in the 1940s only makes her smile naive now; unless you were young then and grew up with her.

Her body has a hundred heads on it, all turning to be seen, to catch some fleeting lens or lover, to monopolize a nightclub flashbulb. In every picture, the face wants to gobble up its watchers. But look at twenty pictures and you notice it is those "pretty" eyes that are at bay, and her face that is being eaten. The mouth is open, and the teeth are polished tablets. Her tongue, in the dark slit of her lips, is as blatant as 1942 or 1943 allowed, and sometimes there is a saucer of saliva in her mouth, ice to skate on in December.

I would as soon do without these photographs; there will be no illustrations. The sharp corners and the clammy sheen of these prints feel dangerous. They make anyone they "take" the viewer's slave, an unfree being, a woman "taken in photography." The movement in movies is redemption for the death in photography.

To look at Laura's glossiness here I could despise her. Put the stills away and I can recall the trembling white woman who took me to her cool body at the Pierre and let an afternoon swell with unspoken healing. It must have been a very sudden, chaste love we made; there was nothing expert about it. I have kept her pictures, but I seldom look at them. I do not want to make a shrine of her or what we shared. If we did share. Two people can come away from such an afternoon in love, or in love with love, but strangers in their sense of the words. And if I ever felt, leaving the Pierre, that knowledge or wisdom had come down on me like grace to save me—even now I say "healing," pouring the word into the wound—I had to learn that the brief touching had ensured all the rest of the damage. The afternoon had prepared me for the night.

Laura Hunt was born in Omaha, Nebraska, in 1920, the younger of two daughters, the Hunt girls teenage Omaha called them in the 1930s, when it seemed possible that their parents, two tall worriers, might have in one characterless home the best actress and the prettiest girl in America. Their father was in insurance and their mother was the maker of some forty-five thousand wholesome and lacklustre meals in a scheme of regularity which never quite blanked out the speck of a visiting madness. Once a year, when the prairie wind stirred her nerves, their mother went domestically crazy, taking apart clothes she had made or snapping the handles off every cup in the house. Then she was sensible again, and her life resumed its level, grounded stretch. Every few years, their father bought sets of new crockery at a sale.

The other sister, Mary Frances, was three years older than Laura. She was not unappealing, not unappealing, but she deferred to her younger, more accessible sister; she was somber in her expressions and outlook, except when on the stage. There, and only there, Mary Frances Hunt came to life. People who had seen her acting sometimes passed her by backstage, no matter that they were on their way to give her flowers and to tell her she had a remarkable future. But I married her.

"Muffy," said Laura one day, "if you looked like me you would be Margaret Sullavan, but if I acted like you I would only be . . . Hedy Lamarr. As it is . . . " I know, I heard it, and winced at the smart, three-quarter accuracy. The true dilemma was much stranger. On stage, Mary Frances was beautiful, but she had not one spark of Laura's lust for getting ahead and pretending. Laura could worm her way in anywhere, she was slippery and convincing. But Mary Frances waited to be asked, and stood back from crowded elevators. It was called timidity by most people, but there was an iron door of suppressed vanity there, a fearful pride too great to speak. She was a great actress, but too shy or too ashamed to talk about it.

Laura was a poor actress, fussy and overdone: in one gesture on stage she became blurred. So she drifted, from regret, into being a liar and a user. There was no plan or malice to it; it was the sign of how much her prettiness troubled her. But so close in age, they grew up together, Laura with beaux and secrets, Mary Frances with Electra, Hedda Gabler, Perdita in *The Winter's Tale* and an implacably closed-off inner self. Which I once thought I could free. For, in 1938, rather than risk New York and the theater, Mary Frances Hunt had a breakdown: it was called marriage, to put the theater out of bounds. She is alive today, alive tonight, upstairs like a threat, but she has never got over it. Laura found herself alone, all the more determined to leave Nebraska and impress the world, but guilty because she was a mere pretender, untouched by acting's genius.

She started east in 1939, and in Iowa she entered a beauty contest under the name of Mitzi Glass. It was a hysterical adventure to disprove her own reputation. But, mortified, she won and had to smile for the slow photographers of Des Moines. One of her prizes was a ticket to Hollywood—"Good God!" raged Mary Frances—but Laura went steadily east, out of love with herself, yet wooed twice on the train. In retaliation, she surrendered to a traveling salesman who called her "doll" and roughed her up when he was satisfied. "My lovers are always disappointed," she said years later at the Pierre Hotel. "They expect me to be Cleopatra, but I am as plain as Nebraska!" Did she think I was let down?

For two years in New York she was a photographers' model, kept by several men, indulged, idealized and then dropped so often that she became brittle if not breakable. She might have been more in the city, but she was too hostile to herself to try hard, and too attractive to want for much. She lifted herself out of this dismal hole in 1942 for nothing but money. Laura went into advertising, so that she could sometimes send a check back to Nebraska. The challenge reminded her of her old ability to get whatever she wanted.

And so, in 1942, she broke in on Waldo Lydecker's solitary lunch at the Algonquin and asked his austere celebrity to endorse a fountain pen for an advertisement.

"Does it work?" he asked her, signing the menu.

"Does it matter?" she replied, dipping a breadstick in his hollandaise and sucking it clean.

They neither of them appreciated it, but Waldo and Laura were two "personalities" yearning to escape their base selves. He schooled her, and did not think of touching her. She learned about fame, imposing herself, and how the means of mass communication told the dreamy public what to think. "I am always addressing the vast unknown," said Waldo, "just as you in your photos are looking out at those you will never meet. We are both of us without private character." She met influential people, and she found that she enjoyed advertising just because she saw through it: it was a way of bringing prettiness to any cause or commodity, spreading the joke. It was a language not spoiled by aging or lack of substance. Laura Hunt was one of the first in America to guess that people bought magazines for the legendary prospect conspired in by all the advertisements. It was a new culture, movies in your lap.

Murder altered Laura's outlook. It brought a defeatist respect for violence that lasted all her life. It introduced her to Mark McPherson; and it helped her see that someone else, Waldo, might think less of her than her own estimate. She had been with men who disparaged their manliness: Waldo and Shelby Carpenter, the whimsical Kentucky cad who had not outgrown the wish to please everyone. McPherson reminded Laura of Mary Frances: he was haunted, he blamed those who flinched from his darkness, and there was that same hunched intelligence that expected rejection. McPherson made love to Laura as if she were his prisoner, a suspect he could grill for his pleasure. She liked that. She felt aroused when he put her in a small, stale interrogation room, turned the light on her and began to whip at her with questions from the shadows. "I'd reached a point where I needed official surroundings," he said. And there, on the small scuffed table where confessions were signed, Laura arranged her voluptuousness and dragged his ungiving force into her. "Slut," he whispered when she came, and her eyes leapt in appreciation.

They were married in 1945: one daughter, Paula, was born in 1946; and then a year later Mark beat Laura so badly that no careful surgery could hide disfigurement. She never charged him, but the city threw him off the force. There was a divorce, and he went away with nothing much except that portrait of her—the thing he had fallen in love with and which no one else liked—and her last present to him. (Or last but one—there was that other cruel gift.) Mark McPherson went away, as if unfit for the world. Laura was sure he would not be back—as if she had disposed of him. He went away, but I never forgot him. It may sound foolish or conceited, but I trusted I would find him.

Laura was finished as a model. But she had a daughter to support, and she guessed that television advertising was the coming rage. She made Bullitt's, her agency, the leader in that field for fifteen years. She produced commercials, bringing the product together with visualizers, directors and actors, and foreseeing that commercials could be as beautiful and suggestive as small movies.

She married Shelby Carpenter in the 1950s, but it was a marriage that barely disturbed the lives of the two people. A few years later they divorced, though remaining at the same level of frosted amiability. She moved to Los Angeles, consumed by work and Paula's education. She sent the girl to Smith, and she saw in 1969 that Paula got a job at the ICM agency in Los Angeles. From that start, Paula Hunt became a powerful young packager in the entertainment industry. I saw her at the funeral, and we talked a little. It was not comfortable because I could not forget the rumors, after Laura's suicide, that Paula had outmaneuvered her mother in an agency deal in 1971, taking a batch of clients Laura had regarded as hers.

But when we buried Laura, Paula turned to everyone there, let her brown eyes swell with love and told us, ''The modern awareness of personality would not be as it is without the career of my mother. She gave meaning to the old American dream that a nobody could be someone, and she did it with flair, with style, and with love.'' The little speech appeared next day in the trades, like a handout. There is a frenzy from Nebraska, it is the mania of being in the middle, without seabreezes, of being unknown, and I have sometimes felt it in silk sheets on a hotel bed or in PR prose, a tremor in the smoothness.

I am not cut out for this—God help me.

> *I have always called her and thought of her as*
> *''Mary Frances.'' Yet I never use anyone else's*
> *middle name. It sounds a declaratory but con-*
> *flicting name, or is that only because I know*
> *her? I wonder how different it would be if she*
> *were only one or the other?*

HELEN FERGUSON

Barbara Stanwyck in No Man of Her Own, *1950,*
directed by Mitchell Leisen

There are two Americas. I know you have heard this before; there are countless two Americas: north and south, Atlantic and Pacific, straight and crazy, National League and American League, the rising and the falling, blue cheese or creamy Italian. Let me suggest one more—I know it, because I have crossed over a few times.

There is the America of the Interstates. This is a land like an airline map, of major cities held in place by straight lines, a grid of business, population and the certainty of being in the mainstream. Then there are the old back roads and places where no one would go except to live quietly in a small town with a main street and one of everything a town requires—a school, a church, a bank, a cemetery, a hotel verandah for the old-timers and a scarlet woman about whom they can make up stories. Take any state in the Union. Look at its map and find the green lines of the Interstates; then look away at the "empty" holes the green lines contain. Imagine the life there, with so many content to be unknown, and others who hope to get away and be recognized. This is the America torn between refuge and prison.

Helen Ann Ferguson was born in one of the holes, at Bridgeport, California, in 1921. It's sixty-five hundred feet up, in the Sierras, between Yosemite and the Nevada border. There are sparser holes. Bridgeport has skiing, extravagant scenery; it's not far from Mono Lake, on a road to Bishop in the south and Carson City to the north. But it's not on a main route; the Sierras are closed in winter, and Bridgeport is left to itself. The passable highway, 80, goes from Reno to San Francisco; and beyond Reno 80 is Salt Lake City, Cheyenne, Omaha and Chicago. Bridgeport, California, and Caulfield, Illinois, must be about the same distance from the rush and throb of 80.

Ann Ferguson, as she liked to be known, was the daughter of Bridgeport's dentist, an only child who became a capable housekeeper when her mother died in 1936. Ann made her father proud: she brushed her teeth, she studied and she led an active, uneventful life. She did well in school, but never disputed her father's opinion that it was foolish to send a girl to college. She took a short course that qualified her as a dental nurse, to help her father. She enjoyed cross-country skiing, and in the summer she was part of the swimming-and-tennis gang. She had boyfriends, and her father was mild to all of them, hoping that would avert seriousness.

Ann was twenty-five when, suddenly, an upper front tooth went rotten. Her father pulled it and made the replacement. He took every care to make it fit, but he never saw that her full confidence in him had gone. Then Ann got involved with Jeff Bailey, who had taken over the filling station in Bridgeport. He was a mysterious figure, from far away, a man who paid his bills and never sought acceptance. In retaliation, the town called him a loner; but he was most alone in his own mind, and that was a little eased by the friendship of Ann and Dickie, a deaf-mute boy who helped at the station.

Bailey—it is an old name—had been a detective, mixed up in New York gambling. There had been a woman and a killing, and Bailey had ended up feeling used. He had removed himself as far as he could, to a hole in the country; but then he had decided to make his living at the roadside so he could see who passed by. One day in 1947 someone recognized him, someone lost, on a back road, stumbling on a find. The old associations closed in, unsettled business, with debts to be paid and old attractions awakened with a glance or a forgotten perfume. Ann did whatever she could—no matter that her father and the town warned her about Bailey—but Jeff was found dead in a crashed car, along with the other woman from out of the past.

Ann left Bridgeport. She went to San Francisco and met a man, Stephen Morley, whom she had encountered in the last frantic days of the Bailey episode. Morley had been an operative for a lawyer named Eels; he was a gambler, too, a ladies' man, adept at the smaller forms of fraud and extortion. He seduced Helen Ferguson (she had made a small change in her name to get Bridgeport out of her system), and he made her pregnant. When she went to tell him, she discovered that he had left for New York. There was a note telling her not to be upset.

She waited awhile, and then she followed him east. He was living in a cheap apartment on the Lower East Side with a blonde, Carol Mather. When Helen showed up, he laughed at her and said how did she know he was the father of the child? Helen believed he would relent. He did see her from time to time, when Carol was working; he slept with her again, and though she despised him Helen could not appreciate that she did not need him. One day she called on him, knocked on the door to the apartment, and felt the horror of subterfuge and indifference when at last an envelope was slipped underneath the silent door. It contained some money and a rail ticket back to San Francisco. It all smelled of a gardenia scent she knew as Carol's.

On the train, she met a friendly couple, the Harknesses, Patrice and Hugh, not long married. They started talking for a simple reason: Helen and Patrice were both pregnant, and due at about the same time. Hugh Harkness had been in Europe on government work, and he had met Patrice there. She was an orphan: her only family was his, and she was on her way to meet them for the first time. They would get off at Chicago, and thence to Caulfield, Illinois (between Moline and Normal), where the Harknesses lived.

But the train crashed in Ohio—the Maumee disaster of July 3, 1948. Helen and Patrice had been in the ladies' room at the moment of impact; they were laughing and talking, and Patrice had asked Helen to hold her wedding ring while she scrubbed her hands (the smell of oysters from dinner). Helen slipped it on for safety, and was thinking of life's ironies when the crash occurred. In the hospital, she was known as Patrice Harkness. The real Patrice had been killed, as well as Hugh. But the shock had started Helen's baby, who had come into the world—delivered amid mud, flashlights and the groans of distress —as the son of Mrs. Harkness, the woman wearing the ring.

She hated the dishonesty, but she was on a slope of providential force; and she had envied the couple on the train their future as rich as her warmest memory of small towns. Helen Ferguson went to Caulfield as Patrice Harkness, delivering a grandson and a hope for the future to Donald and Grace Harkness, who had lived there all their lives, consistent, quiet and attentive, like readers. As she met them, Helen felt fake, stepping into a myth. Her son was christened Hugh, and the dead Hugh's brother, Bill, came home for the event. Helen liked him, but she knew he looked at her in a quizzical way; he noticed her false tooth.

Helen slipped into happiness. The Christmas holiday was the best she had known, even if the fear of betraying herself never went away. She guessed that Bill was falling in love with her; she thought of her own son as Hugh Harkness. When she looked at him in a grandmother's arms, her thoughts were no longer framed by the deception. And then Stephen Morley appeared, a blackmailer now.

He had read of the crash, and gone to identify the body. He had looked at Patrice Harkness in the morgue and smiled. Yes, he said, poor Helen Ferguson, and the unborn child, too. But he had heard the story of two pregnant women in the ladies' room and seen where the other one, Harkness, had her address. It's the Irish in me, he chuckled, as he reconstructed the chance plot.

He came to Caulfield and learned that Helen would be rich when Donald and Grace Harkness died. So he extorted money from Helen, and he compelled her to marry him: they drove to Iowa to do it. Helen wanted him dead. Grace, who learned enough of the story, planned to get a gun and shoot him; her own heart was bad, and she might as well do something bold and useful before she died. And then, one morning, in the rooming house in Caulfield, Morley was found shot.

a woman you search for

The two women were ready to own up, for they both suspected Bill
had done it. But the police smelled gardenia. Carol Mather had shot
her lover after learning he had married someone else, and put on extra
perfume to be more herself.

The shock killed Grace; Donald died fifteen months later. Caulfield
was agog when the story came out, and in 1951 Bill and Helen,
married now, moved away with their son, Hugh, determined to give
him a happy home in one of the quiet, secret places in America. Let
them go, there are perils enough in those quiet holes.

DICKSON STEELE

Humphrey Bogart in In a Lonely Place, *1949,
directed by Nicholas Ray*

"The king sits in Dunfermline town, drinking the blood red wine."
That line is set in my mind, like a stain in wood. I must have learned it
in school, in Bedford Falls, on a winter day when the heating system
clanked and grumbled and I wanted to be out skating, with Violet
winking across the classroom, so sure she knew what I was thinking.
The line has come back to me over the years, whenever I hear the word
blood. Sometimes I get a little more of the poem; it goes on for pages, I
think, about a sea captain sent on a mission by the king, Sir Patrick
something or other. I think I recall that he has to find a woman—at
sea? or on land? I don't know. I can hear the class reciting a line about
the king's daughter and Noroway. What does it mean? Lines you
can't get out of your head, and the notion of a woman you search for
but never quite find?

I never knew that Dunfermline could bring it all back, too; it's rarer
than blood, I suppose, and so it might be more piercing. But I didn't
know that Dix Steele's people had come from there, a town in
Scotland. Two brothers, Andrew and Fergus, left there as young men
in 1907, to come to America. They settled in Trenton, New Jersey.
They had a hardware store and they started a mechanical repair shop;
they were sure that the automobile was going to be big, but trouble.
They worked every hour they could find, and they bought themselves
a good old house on Spruce Street. Then one day, in 1912, Andrew
was called to look at a bus that had broken down. It carried a traveling

38

theatrical company, on its way to Philadelphia, and there was a dancer in the group, a Spanish woman, Adele Santana. As Fergus tells it, she took one look at Andrew and decided to have him. He had barely talked to a woman in his life, and here was this one, just as bright and noisy as a parrot. I asked Fergus why she snapped up his brother, and he answered, "Oh, there had been a wishing in Andy all along. She knew it. She touched it." He may have meant that literally; somehow this tango dancer put her hot skin against his, and he was done for.

They were married, and there was the boy, John Dickson Steele, born in 1914. Adele left them all when the child was two. She took off for the West, saying she had to be dancing again. Andrew died three years later, technically of the influenza that was so grim in Jersey. But he was a broken man before that. So Fergus became the boy's guardian as well as uncle. He brought him up without a mention of Adele and Dix, I suppose, studied Fergus's milky skin and sawdust hair and wondered about his own carbon looks. But there are things we can never tell our young, matters of shame and pride that we long for them to find out, but that are past our telling.

Dickson Steele grew up clever and strange. He had no close friends, but he was always in demand. He could mend anything, or take it apart and explain how it worked. By 1930 or so, he was learning to fly, and he spent a lot of his time at the airfield in Trenton working on planes. Fergus wanted him to go to Princeton, and he was rich enough then to pay. But Dickson put it off several times, and he didn't go to the university until 1934, when he was twenty.

At the end of his freshman year he dropped out. He had done well enough, with distinction in engineering and literature. But he was bored, or displeased, and he took off for Manhattan. He knocked around there in 1935 and 1936, and somehow the hawk on *Time*'s cover, Jed Harris, took a shine to him. Harris was about the best known stage director in the city—he did *The Front Page* and *The Green Bay Tree*—and possibly the wickedest man in America. If you can go by reputation. You can't, but there's no harm in warning people. Harris had a genius for cruelty: it excited as much admiration as horror. He was like a fictitious villain, but alive and breathing and doing it to someone you knew. It was power that really attracted him. As a director, he let a story out slowly on stage so that you felt *his* control. It dripped on you.

It was Dickson Steele who drove Harris across America in the fitful spring of 1938, when Harris was preparing *Our Town* and wanted to say he'd studied small places. That's when they came to Nebraska, and Harris had his infernal night of talk with Mary Frances. I don't call that Steele's fault, or even proof of evil in Harris. It was understandable, what he said. She *was* an actress, still desperate to do it and just as desperate not to. They moved on, with Harris surer how to put on the play, and wreckage behind him.

Harris, I believe, told Dickson to get back to Princeton, and wrote a letter for him to the university saying he was not to be overlooked just because he was odd. So in the fall of 1939, he was a twenty-five-year-old sophomore, who got a name for cutting up professors in cross-talk. He had learned from Harris and given up all thought of hiding his difficult nature. But he was out again in 1940, and off to McGuire Field where he enlisted. They loved him. He had his license already, he knew engines and he was a natural killer.

Dickson Steele rose to colonel in the air force. He was in combat in Europe, flying fighters in the Mediterranean, and thereafter he was stationed in Britain, a leader of the big bombing raids sent against Germany in 1944 and 1945. He was a fine officer, hard but inspiring, adored by his men. The war excited him; it gave liberty to all his hostile feelings. Pilots were encouraged to paint signs on their planes to show how many "kills" they had.

He came back with a novel, *Brucie and the Spider*, published in 1946. Such an unnerving tale, about an American flier in Scotland during the war who meets a girl, Katriona Bruce, falls in love with her, begins to think she is a witch, and hears she has been murdered after he has gone away to win the war. The pilot remembers then all the little things that made him think there was another man, another darker lover, in her life. It was a short book full of rock and cold, harshness and tenderness. The novel was a critical success, and it did well enough to get Dixon Steele—he had made that his working name—out to Hollywood.

He did scripts, but none of them was produced. He drank on the money and he grew quarrelsome. There were stories of fights with producers, and once he took a plane out at Santa Monica and buzzed a studio executive's house at Malibu.

It was in 1949, while he was struggling to do another novel and sell a script, that Dix got involved in the Mildred Atkinson case. She was a hatcheck girl at a restaurant. He saw her reading the very novel that he had been hired to turn into a script. Rather than read the book—a fat bore of a thing—he took her back to his place at the Virginibus Arms on Camden. Later that night she was found strangled. Laurel Gray, who also lived at the Arms, said she had seen Atkinson leave, alone, but then Laurel fell in love with Dix. Brub Nicolai, one of the detectives on the case, had flown with Dix. He hated having to investigate his old commander; but he could never forget the completeness of Dix's nature as a killer. In the end, they decided that Atkinson's fiancé had killed her. But Dix's nerves snapped along the way, and he even threatened to strangle Laurel once when he thought she doubted him.

She left him. Dix wrote another novel, *The Evening of the Day* (1952), about a man who is suspected of a string of rapes and killings. There were people who couldn't finish the book, it was so disturbing and true. But it was a hit, and the movie was a triumph for Montgomery Clift. Dix worked less; he remained friends with Nicolai; and he knew Laura Hunt when she was in Los Angeles.

I corresponded with Nicolai, but there was not much he wanted to say. Was the LAPD ever satisfied about the Atkinson case? There were other, similar murders in the fifties and once or twice Dix came under suspicion. "He would laugh at me," Nicolai wrote. "And he'd taunt me: 'Just because I write mystery stories, you think I'm fit to be a killer.'"

His last novel was *Beneath Suspicion* (1964), about a police chief who plays a game with the world. He kills his mistress, knowing that he will be called upon to investigate the crime. When the trail goes cold, the man commits other murders to rekindle interest. The book was a sensation: the more so because Dix had given up company by then, living in Topanga Canyon, seldom seen in public. He died up there in 1970, wealthy, a man of letters, a distinguished soldier. But there were some sure he was a killer.

There was a new book, three-quarters done at his death. Laura was his agent then, and she told me it tells everything—even without an ending. I don't know. An ending is important; it can say the writer has been pretending, or not. The book was locked away in her safe, and, as I said, she is dead.

> *I don't know where that safe is. It might be untouched in the office still, or waiting on some L.A. dump, battered and rotting, about to fall apart, so the pages can scatter with the ash and the seagulls. Or be found by a red-hot publisher?*

LAUREL GRAY

Gloria Grahame in In a Lonely Place, *1949,
directed by Nicholas Ray*

I wonder why incest is such an American fascination? Is it because of our superstition about coincidence bringing the proper strangers together in the new desert land so that their magical coupling wipes away the loss and separation of leaving Europe? But if we believe in Mr. and Miss Right, then we must suppose an author who made them but deliberately flung them in opposite directions. It takes something like storying to crisscross the emptiness. We have formed a taste for lucky encounter, for intersection and unrecognized coincidence, for the story turning round to examine the storyteller's face. And because we aspire so much to love, we think of this instinct as incest. Yet the chance of coincidence makes us suspicious, too, nervous that the narrator is sleeping with the story, that nice girl who seems to be ours in the daytime. Don't we know when we see the lovely lady on the screen that the very camera has had her?

If she had been less famous or less rich when she died, in 1970, Laurel Gray might have been in an asylum. But that is how we are, here; we buy or talk our way to freedom, and our craziness lays claim to all the visible world. Laurel Gray had rights on the invisible, as well. She was a celebrated seer, who had virtually no contact with other people. Her house in Laurel Canyon was arranged so that she could live as fully in the spirit realm as possible. Perhaps she died from lack of substance, forgetting to breathe in her desire to feel out the future.

Who could have imagined that ending when she was born, in Grosse Pointe, Michigan, in 1926? She was a granddaughter of the man who had funded Henry Ford's first company in 1903. It was said as she grew up that if Grandfather had been more resolute, why, all those cars would be Grays. But he had only invested his money (and it was only a little of his money), watched it grow and then let Ford buy him out in 1917. Laurel was born in a crowd of Grays sure of their place in the century, nearly neutralized by comfort and unaware of the foolishness in being so rich but remaining in Detroit.

Old Gray is the only man I ever heard of who really lost it all in 1929. For all those stories of suicides on Wall Street and families ruined, Gray is the one case that checks out. He lost an eight-figure sum: Laurel was three then. Of course, there was six-figure money left, the loose change, as well as a house, cars and a skeleton crew of servants. Laurel grew up plump, pretty and spoiled; she wore silk underclothes as a child, and there were Maine lobsters brought in twice a week. But the mood of the family was crushed. She lived in the shadow of a greater past, in a family that began to see how Detroit society now looked down on them.

Laurel didn't much care. She took it as it came, tutors, private schools in the East, and the wartime summers at home and at Charlevoix. She moved with military men and older people; she used to sing at supper parties at the Chicago Club; there were stories of an abortion in 1944. In 1945, she went to Hollywood, on the say-so of a producer she had met.

She was in a few pictures: you can see her in *The Harvey Girls*, in the chorus on "The Atchison, Topeka and the Santa Fe" number. For a year, 1946–47, she was married to Henry St. Andrews, a real-estate dealer from Santa Barbara. He had a ten-year-old son from another marriage, Lindsay, and the 20-year-old stepmother was always moved by the beautiful, timid child. They were better company than ever Laurel and St. Andrews managed to be. Even after the divorce, she would call the boy and take him to museums and movies. Lindsay was never robust, and he had an analyst who said Laurel was good for him. As for Laurel, she moved into an apartment at the Virginibus Arms, she had a good settlement from St. Andrews so long as she never remarried, and she tried out for movies sometimes. She had a masseuse come to the place three times a week, a woman who had been a theosophist and met Krishnamurti at Ojai. She went by the professional name "Miss Adele." She talked to Laurel about the handsome young Indian who was supposed to be the reincarnation of Madame Blavatsky, and about his teachings as she worked the oil into Laurel's bare back to the beat of samba music on the radio.

Laurel always sensed something about Dickson Steele; but she was sensing things about most people. Lindsay St. Andrews was off at St. Paul's and, time after time, they used to write to each other on the same days. There wasn't a plan about it. Maybe they had a rhythm. But Laurel suspected it was something deeper. And she thought Steele was dangerous, all through their affair. That was what attracted her—the aura of violence, and the mystery too, the feeling that there was a story there waiting to be read. She guessed he was a murderer, and she told Brub Nicolai what she felt.

43

Nothing was ever proved. Laurel went in fear for several years, yet it was not just fear. When she heard footsteps following her, or when the phone rang at night and then stopped without a word when she answered, she thought this was it, coming true. She was thrilled. She called Lindsay one night—he was at Yale then—and she had picked on a moment of great crisis for him. Laurel drifted into spiritualism as a business, carried along by this knack. She never advertised, but word got out that she was good. Once or twice, Nicolai consulted her on police matters; he never made it official, he never said where the hunch came from, but he got a reputation for instinct.

It was in 1959 that Laurel and Lindsay married. They were only ten years apart, with no blood ties. But what were blood ties compared to the way they thought of things at the same time? It made news, and there was gossip; some people talked about incest. Laurel replied that while they might have been stepson and stepmother in this world, it was likely they had been brother and sister in another. But she didn't sleep with him, and she took lovers to disperse what she called "those distracting impulses"—this said with a comical shiver. Lindsay sold fine art in Beverly Hills, and they had an intricate double act, bringing paintings and spiritual solace to several homes.

They moved into Laurel Canyon, and there were people in the sixties who spoke of "Laurel," meaning her *and* the place, with hints of magic or danger there. Then Lindsay walked out, calling her a sick, grotesque woman who didn't wash enough and sat in trances in front of daytime television. He was killed in a car crash in 1966, a year after the divorce. Laurel was reported to have murmured, "A Ford, of course," closing the door on reporters. But it had been a Mercedes, on Highland.

To be a spiritualist, I suppose, you must be very selective. When you're wrong, you forget it. When you're right, it verifies the system. Gamblers work the same way. So most people decided Laurel was a charlatan, and a handful believed in her. But she stayed up in the house, with servants to look after her. People saw her by private consultation, except for Joan Didion, who wrote a piece on her for the *Saturday Evening Post*. It was a good article, funny, dry and touching, as if Didion knew this was a deluded woman yet an actress with her own odd poetry. The article contained some of Laurel's predictions—most of them wrong and forgotten now. But everyone remembers the one about an appointed outrage coming, killers and wolves slipping down out of the hills, "retribution . . . somewhere like Beverly Glen or Cielo Drive," Laurel had opined. That was published nine weeks before Manson. A year later, Laurel died, of cancer. She hadn't seen a doctor in fourteen years. She was forty-four, and I suppose in that long a time most of us will experience one astonishing coincidence or premonition. Or did the Manson gang read the *Saturday Evening Post* and believe in destiny?

ROY EARLE

Humphrey Bogart in High Sierra, *1941,*
directed by Raoul Walsh

All these people going west, have they got names to be blessed? It's like being way off from a line of trees, toward sunset, watching people walking through them, all going in the same direction. While the sun beats on your eyes, you study the people, and then you start to feel that the trees are moving too, just ebbing out toward the west, like stick people staggering into the fire.

It's all one motion, I think, the way so many people came west from Europe, and then west again across the country. And these were not nomads. They were the members of families who had lived in one tight place for centuries. And then in the space of a couple of hundred years, they cut off their own heritage, because they were persecuted, because they were poor and always would be, or because they were angry and difficult, and they headed west. But where do they go when they have got as far as they can go, and when they see the kingfisher color of the sea? Can they ever stop?

The great-grandfather of Roy Earle was a cider farmer in the Calvados region, in Normandy, France. The name then was Oeul. He was a Huguenot, and he came to Boston in 1836, though he'd never once in his life seen Paris. There must have been some commotion or upset, something that urged him to get away; no one knows what it was now. You can see the birds go south in August, but don't ask them if they know why they're doing it.

Roy Earle was born in Rush Creek Valley, Indiana, in 1902, in lush farming country, with a creek and a hole where the catfish basked on afternoons. His father grew corn and vegetables, and kept pigs and chickens. In the Great War, as Roy was growing up, his father got enough money selling corn to buy the farm. But he remembered how hard it had been, for him and *his* father, and he expected Roy to work after school without asking for anything. Roy loved the farm and the country, but there was a knot of anger in him.

When he was seventeen, he went to Indianapolis and worked in a factory making parts for cars. But he never got on with the boss, and one day he attacked him and beat him up. The boss pressed charges and in 1920 Roy got a six-month sentence in the city jail.

So, after that, he went back to the farm, no matter that his father treated him like an outcast. That passed away a while, but Roy had a friend in the next town whose brother had been a bank robber. They all hung out together in 1921 and 1922, and Roy got talked into joining them. There were small towns in the south of the state, and the young men held up a couple of stores and a bank without ever alarming or hurting anyone. But no one they robbed was ever going to take them on. Then, in 1924, with some help from Chicago, they went after a bank in Lafayette, and the three of them were caught. Roy got three years in the state penitentiary.

When he came out in 1927, he moved on to Chicago and he was a part of the Mob there, whether he knew it or not. In 1931, he held up the biggest bank in South Bend, and a lady was killed in the shooting. There was a manhunt, and they got Roy and he was sentenced to life in Mossmoor in 1932. He was thirty, and "life" then meant another thirty years before anyone would remember he was there.

But something happened. Some of the old Chicago people put in a word for him. They must have put some money in too, because they got Roy out of jail in 1940 on a pardon. There was noise about it in the papers, but the authorities said that Earle was a sick man. He'd been ill at Mossmoor and he looked thin and gray when he got out.

Of course, the money that had sprung him didn't forget. The Chicago organization told Roy to make his way to California; he could pay his dues there. They gave him a car and in the spring of 1940 Roy drove out by way of Des Moines and Denver to Los Angeles.

He had never seen mountains, or known air as clear. Some days, he reckoned anyone could make a fresh start there. He met a girl, Velma Goodhue, who had a bad leg. Roy thought that maybe if he could raise the money for her to have an operation, she might think of marrying him. So that's how he got drawn in on the Palm Springs Hotel job, along with Red Hattery and Babe Kozak, and Louis Mendoza, a clerk at the hotel. There was a woman with them too, Marie Garson, a dance-hall girl.

They did the hotel, and got away with $500,000 worth of jewels and cash—or so the hotel claimed. Velma had the operation, but once she could dance with anyone who asked, she saw Roy as a sad-looking, middle-aged guy. Roy had trouble fencing the stuff. He knew he was being double-crossed by the Mob, and he killed a man named Kranmer, who tried to take the jewels from him.

So Earle was on the run, with Marie Garson, who was in love with him. He went into the Sierras, around Mount Whitney, and the manhunt closed in on him—"Mad-Dog Earle," as they called him by then. He clawed his way up into the rocks, but it was cold at night, and he had nowhere to go. A sharpshooter got him on the second day, from half a mile away. The press said what a wretched end it was, but Roy really loved the mountains and the views and the streaks of iron and copper color in the rock as the sun went down.

MARIE GARSON

Ida Lupino in High Sierra, *1941,*
directed by Raoul Walsh

Before the two bridges were built in the 1930s, the Golden Gate and the Bay, San Francisco was an island city that relied on ferries to Oakland and Sausalito. The city was made so that the Ferry Building could be seen all the way down Market Street. That point was the eye and ear of the city, and Marie Garson was born a shout away, at Mission and Beale. Her father was a seaman on the ferry, and her mother had been a housemaid in one of the big mansions on Russian Hill. Marie was born in 1919, and the ferry boat hooted its way home through the fog on that November night.

The father was a big, boastful man, a tyrant in the house, and a boyo in the bars. But in the 1930s, as the new bridges felt their way across the water, spelling the end of the ferries, he drank more. He became morose and brutal, and he beat Marie and her mother. In 1936, Marie packed a bag and hitched a ride on a truck going south. Two days later, she was in Los Angeles.

She met a young writer, John Fante, and lived with him on Bunker Hill. It was her first gasp of happiness. She worked as a waitress and read his stories and they made each other feel good. Sometimes they took a bus down to the beach in the evening and swam in the darkness.

He told her great stories, and she loved to keep warm in his arms. But he grew gloomy over his poverty and one day another man flirted with her when she served him. His name was Kozak, and Marie could not get his tough face out of her head.

She moved in with him, and he put her to work at a dance hall: she was an available partner for anyone with a dime. Marie hated it, but she was in awe of Kozak and she slept with some of his cronies if he suggested it. They were small-time crooks too, and it was when they got involved in the Palm Springs Hotel job in 1940 that she met Roy Earle. She liked his rueful eyes, and the scorn he had for Kozak: one glance of his taught her what to see. Marie could tell that Earle was soft on someone else, but she stuck with Roy, hoping that if she stayed loyal and patient he would come round. They had only a summer together, but Roy loved her and trusted her, and she thought of him as a father.

When Roy was shot, in the Sierras, Marie took his dog, Pard. She realized later that the ring he had given her—from the spoils of the hotel robbery—was enough to get her a small place in Culver City. She had a job on the assembly line with the Hughes Company, and that was how she met several fliers. There was even a weekend when Hughes himself noticed her, flew her down to Mexico and had dinner with her. He didn't speak to her again, but he never treated her badly and he had her made a supervisor.

After the war, Marie heard about a "club" being run near Muroc Air Force Base by a woman known as "Poncho" Barnes. She had been a flier herself and had taken over a desert property for the rest and relaxation of the men at Muroc, many of them test pilots. Poncho put in a pool, there were horses, and a bar with a row of bungalows next to the main building, where private parties could be held. Poncho was hiring young women, and she naturally favored anyone with aeronautical connections.

So Marie moved up there to the Mojave Desert, and she started to have a good time. Poncho was the law on her property: the air force let her be, and the pilots had nowhere else to go in the vicinity. Marie took Pard with her, and somehow out in the desert she began to collect stray dogs. Poncho called them "the hounds" and some nights a group would go out hunting rattlesnakes with flashlights. Marie fell in love with one of the pilots, a kid named Bobby Kaufman. They had been married four months when he crashed, out in the desert, in 1948. Killed.

Marie stayed on at the club until 1954, when it closed down. She moved into the nearby town of Lancaster; she liked the desert, and she had plenty of friends on the base—the name of which was changed to Edwards in 1948, after another pilot who was killed. Marie opened a kennel in Lancaster, a way of making a business out of her dogs. And she settled to the life there. She died in her house in the summer of 1969. She lived alone, with only the dogs, and her body was not found for a week. The dogs had begun to eat her, but I don't think the worse of them for that.

> Yet in a movie, dogs are pals or killers, never
> unknown. In movies, this garden path and that
> picture on the wall are all poised with meaning.
> Everything in the frame seems chosen, asking
> us to work out why it is there. Is there nothing
> spontaneous?

HENRY OLIVER PETERSON

Robert Morley in Beat the Devil, *1954,
directed by John Huston*

"I was, I fancy, thirty years or so ahead of my time," H.O. told Michael Parkinson on British television in a merry interview of 1973, the year before his death. "Until the age of about fifty, you see, my life was as spotty as your handkerchief—no offense, I trust. But after that I became quite respectable, and I am pleased to feel today that a modest amount of affection and gratitude flows towards me from people I have never met and who—should that be whom?—I daresay would be thoroughly dismayed if they did meet me. This little talk of ours will probably blow my cover for good. Still, I have enjoyed myself, and that's the thing, isn't it?"

He had been born in 1908 in an upstairs room of the Leg of Mutton and Cauliflowers, a public house in Leatherhead, Surrey, run by his parents. He grew up there, amid the smell of beer, a fat little boy too much accustomed to finishing others' meals. He was, apparently, a natural, fluent liar from an early age. "My father thought I was a scoundrel, but my mother was fond of me and I took gross advantage of everyone. That sounds horrible, doesn't it?'' he said to Parkinson. "But such candor seems to be expected of one nowadays. Shady characters are so much more popular now.''

The boy was sent to Whitgift School and expelled in 1925 for cheating. His father had an interest in a garage on the A24, and as a young man, H. O. Peterson built up a secondhand car business on its premises. "I never knew the first thing about motors, but neither did the customers. I could sell with style and, in those days, you know, most people thought it was such a serious thing to have a car that they became very solemn in the selling. I treated a car like a new hat, and people liked it.''

The business flourished, but in 1932 Peterson was given a six-month sentence in Brixton for petty fraud: "Checks or something, I can't remember. It could have been any one of a dozen naughti-nesses.'' He was a cheerful prisoner who spent the time learning contract bridge—"Best thing that ever happened to me.'' The day of his release, he saw a vacant property at the top of Brixton Hill—"I saw that the hill was a very hard pull for cars, and I twigged''—he bought it and opened H. O. Motors. Success again: "Streatham was getting very posh then, and I had a special thing—colored cars, pretty ones. They'd all been black or gray before. There were gangsters then in the flats by Streatham Hill, and I did very well.''

But in 1937, the Inland Revenue called for an audit, and eventually the business was wiped out by fines and confiscations. "Seemed a shame at the time, but I really should have gone to jug for it. I had to sweeten a few pots to stay out.''

In 1938, he took a steamer to Rio de Janeiro, having recently been hired by Sebastian, the coffee merchant. "South America then was heaven. I stayed there all the war years, happy as a sandboy.'' He dabbled in coffee and beef, in minerals—"all manner of minerals'' —and he resided in Santiago, Chile, where he once more went into the business of cars. He also made friends with St. John O'Hara. The couple were All-Chile Bridge Champions in 1942 and 1944: "We'd have had forty-three too, but O'Hara was on cocaine the entire time. He opened three spades once on a hand you could have played *misère ouverte*. Dear fellow, though.''

After the war, it was bridge that brought Peterson back to Europe. He and O'Hara were defeated only in the semifinals at the Lisbon Competition of 1948, on a hand that is regarded as a classic. Their opponents were Gutman and Cairo:

O'Hara

♠A6
♥Q10
♦Q965
♣Q10532

Cairo   Gutman

♠1097   ♠KJ85432
♥J97653   W   E   ♥K2
♦J84   S   ♦1073
♣A   ♣K

Peterson

♠Q
♥A84
♦AK2
♣J98764

The bidding went to 6♣, with Peterson playing the contract. (On the very first round, West had ventured 2♥—unjustifiable, but a shot in the dark that would prove effective.) West led the 10♠ and Declarer won with the ace. He then led a low club from dummy and was not surprised to see the ace and the king collapse on it together. At this point, West led a small heart. Peterson recalled the earlier bid and decided that West had the king. He therefore played the queen from dummy. That disclosed the king with East, won in hand with the ace. But now there was a heart loser—whereas, if he had played the ten from dummy the queen was still a winner. One down. "That's what makes the game a joy," said Peterson, as Gutman and Cairo advanced to the finals.

His reputation in competition bridge brought forth an invitation from the *Daily Telegraph* to be their bridge correspondent. Peterson accepted, and he became known for his astute analyses derived from fictitious and sometimes fanciful hands that were being played amid some Agatha Christie-like intrigue—"It was all done in the space of a column, taxing sometimes, but such fun." This approach was regarded as showy and frivolous by many cognoscenti, who noted that Peterson's own prowess at the tables had suffered accordingly. "Bridge is a very strict regimen if you mean to succeed. Too grim for me, I fear."

Nevertheless, Peterson and O'Hara still played in Europe, and it was shortly after the Trieste tourney of 1953 that they found themselves in Ravello, near Naples. Peterson claimed later that the

British East Africa Uranium Company had been meant as a jest and that the death of Paul Vanmeer had had nothing to do with him. "There was this major, you see, Ross he called himself. And he simply had to be killing people. I think it was brain damage." The ugly voyage of the *Nianga*, the ordeal in north Africa—"too sadly true," sighed H.O.—and their eventual arrest by the Italian authorities were fit for a romance. The charges were eventually dismissed, but Peterson was left at a low ebb, especially when the final, piteous disintegration of O'Hara—long anticipated—occurred in Ravello prison. "He was a sweet little fellow, but unless he had drugs and a few women before lunch there was nothing you could do with him."

Peterson wandered unhappily for a few years, dismissed by the *Telegraph* and shunned by old friends. Then, one summer, he was laid up in the Dordogne with gout and, in the space of six weeks, all from memory or imagination, he wrote *Some Pleasant Hotels on the Continent*—casual but shrewd, and an unexpected hit when published by Constable in 1958. Another publisher approached H.O. to do a more thorough work, and so in 1962 there appeared the first edition of *Peterson's Guide to Touring in Europe*. So far the book has had eighteen revised editions, it has survived H.O.'s death, and it continues to be researched and compiled from offices in Fetter Lane. Reliable, courteous and opinionated, "A book for ladies, gentlemen and their vehicles on the loose with a low budget and higher hopes"—to quote from H.O.'s first foreword.

GWEN CHELM

Jennifer Jones in Beat the Devil, *1954,
directed by John Huston*

There is a statue of Gwen Chelm on the northern plains of Zimbabwe, striding toward the west. It is larger than lifesize. Her hand is arced above her eyes so that she can look toward the sunset. Sometimes the tall wiry grass waves around the plinth, but the statue is itself windswept or agitated by her own romantic ardor. The stone folds of her skirt are blown back, and the fine intricacy of her hair stands out from her head like the depiction of electricity in a comic book. She would have loved the statue, and although the woman is forty or so—Gwen Chelm's age when she died—it is a statue of a girl ablaze with eagerness and hope.

Gwen Perkins was born in Budleigh Salterton, in Devon, in 1928, the daughter of a clergyman. It was a quiet, industrious upbringing, with Gwen a faithful follower of the Allied war effort: there were maps in her bedroom, with flags to show the progress of every campaign. In 1944, her last year in school, she put on a pageant that traced the events of D-Day, as if it were a miracle play. She herself played a Joan of Arc of the Resistance who heard the voices of saints and turned the tide of battle in Normandy by crossing enemy lines.

It was in 1946 that Gwen went to London, to work in a team of young women who composed verses for greetings cards. She was known for her notices of bereavement. But the limits of the job became oppressive and in 1949 she joined the magazine *Picturegoer*, writing the synopses of films and reviewing them. It was in this capacity that she met Harry Chelm, a buyer for W. H. Smith's. He was the son of a newsagent in Earl's Court. The couple became engaged in 1950, and married in 1951, the year of the Festival of Britain.

Harry Chelm was a decent, straightforward man, stupid and reliable. But he did all he could to keep up with his young wife's romantic inclination, and he felt excited by the rapture with which she told and lived out entirely false stories about themselves. He supposed this process was dangerous, but he never denied the stories in public, and blushed if they seemed to require a nobler Harry than he could be.

It was in 1953 that the Chelms set out for Africa. Harry had an uncle in Kenya who was too old to run his small farm, and he had written to England asking if the young couple would care to take it over. It was in Italy that the Chelms encountered Billy Dannreuther, H. O. Peterson *et al*. Gwen insisted on an affair with Billy, and she furnished every evidence of illicit carnal relations despite her own determination to remain virtuous. It was only later, in Africa, that she regretted her abstinence. Harry loyally believed that she had been unfaithful, and that she was passionate and impetuous.

In fact, Gwen never shook off her sensible approach to all matters. Her vivid fantasy life deceived others, but it did not convince her. The days in Africa were long, hard and tedious, but Gwen worked on the farm and took care of the accounts. Harry became more caught up in politics—this was the process that led to him being knighted in 1967 and being called "the obliging Chelm" by Jomo Kenyatta.

The farm spread; it became prosperous. Managers were hired, and

Gwen Chelm was freer to travel. She went to visit a cousin in Rhodesia in 1961 and became fired with that country's political dilemma. Secretly, she worked as a friend to the freedom fighters, a fund raiser and the author of several of their pamphlets. This work led first to her affair with Winston Ntali (assassinated in 1969) and then to her own death in 1971 on a guerrilla raid in the rolling grasslands where her statue now stands with this inscription: "Gwen Chelm, a great believer and a citizen of Zimbabwe." There is a small plaque in the church at Budleigh Salterton and, sadly, there is the six-hundred-page life, *My Wife*, by Sir Harry Chelm, which nearly smothers her gentle turbulence in detail.

> *I read about a young woman photographer. She had a face like a hook. The more she pictured others the more her pale face begged, "Know me. Remember me." She killed herself. Someone in the book said there are two kinds of people—voyeurs or exhibitionists. Suppose we can be both at the same time? Show-people and watchers.*

ALMA McCAIN

Tuesday Weld in I Walk the Line, *1970, directed by John Frankenheimer*

You may come upon a young woman sometimes in the Tennessee hills who has a sly beauty, one you recognize a second or so after you've looked. She's outside a store, wearing sneakers in the mud, and you wonder, Is that something rare or just a flat, dull sensuality, with the look of a battered fifteen-year-old who has never washed properly? Then she notices you looking. A slow smile creeps up in her face and you see green eyes and lips that look swollen. There's a real beauty, you think, a flower in the backwoods. But while you're thinking, her face has sunk back into wariness. Oh, she'll go for anything you dream up, but she won't give you the pleasure of thinking with you. She's hostile to sharing. Whatever happens, you'll see her alligator eyes watching you do it. Her last retreat is not joining you, letting it be done to her, so you do it alone. You could go mad trying to catch the spirit of that nymph; it's like a fish. But you will not scrape her image from your eyes.

Alma McCain was likely born in 1951, around Frankfurt, which is between Cookeville and Knoxville in eastern Tennessee. No one knows where or when for sure. Alma was ripe at eleven, so there could be plus or minus a year. She would have been born in a cabin up a dirt road, without a doctor. Her mother would look too old already and she had had seven children, and three of them lived, Alma and her brothers, Clay and Buddy. The mother died in 1962, along with the last baby. The McCains roamed the back country, doing a little work and some second-nature thieving, following the old local art of moonshining.

That's how Alma met Henry Tawse, sheriff of a town called Nameless in Jenkins County. She and Buddy had gone into town for twenty pounds of sugar which their father needed in the still. On the way back, she let Buddy drive—he was eleven—and the pickup was going all over the road. So Tawse put on his siren and went after them. Buddy took off and hid in the long grass, but Alma said she'd been driving, and oh no there hadn't been a boy, certainly wasn't a boy. That look then, I'm sure. And he saw it because he was moldy in his own dead life. But he saw all the sugar too, and he wondered. He let her off: he was a kind man, not yet aware that he would have kissed her bare, cut feet if she had asked.

A few days later she comes to his office and says she and Clay were going to the fair, but she had suddenly thought why not call in and say thank you to Sheriff Tawse, and Clay and his temper had said do it, you bitch, and put her out on the road by herself. So there she was, and she really was obliged to him for not making a thing about Buddy driving, and that's all. It was getting dark, and he said he'd take her home. She let him kiss her in the police car, and she slithered over onto its big back seat, drawing him after her and just marveling to find what a load he had on him for her. He wept with gratitude on her old dress when he was done. She had a soft spot for him, whatever happened.

Tawse lived with his wife, his daughter and his father in the sheriff's house. But he used to haunt the derelict country place where he had lived as a boy. He took Alma there and told her how his mother and his two sisters had been killed in a crash on the Nashville road. Alma never asked him about his wife. She had never seen a marriage that worked, and she didn't want to embarrass him. He seemed so happy playing in the deserted house with her.

There was a federal agent in Nameless out to make a reputation bagging stills. He had Honeycutt, Tawse's deputy, on his side. But the sheriff was not eager to disturb the McCains. He had a dream of going away with Alma, to Chicago in a plane, maybe. She had never flown. Or to California. But Honeycutt was pushing Tawse. He reckoned the McCains were up to something, and he had seen Tawse and Alma sitting together on the slope of the reservoir. He just casually let it out that Alma had a husband in the penitentiary. "Oh, that's nothing," said Alma, when Tawse hit her and raged at her. She had forgotten Clem, a dumb kid who had married her when she was fourteen or fifteen and had been caught driving illegal whiskey to Chattanooga. After all, crazy lovers like her and Henry forgot their old attachments.

Then Honeycutt went out to the McCain place. He shot their dog and was going after their still when Alma's father came up and clubbed him to death. The family was burying the deputy when Tawse found them. He told them to get out of town, dumped Honeycutt in the river, and went to the old house, where he was expecting to find Alma waiting for him.

But she'd gone on with her family: in danger, the animal goes back into the lair. Tawse went after them. He found them on the road and stopped them. He told Alma to come with him—he was desperate—and she said no just as blunt and factual as she'd ever said yes. He wouldn't have touched her, but he wanted to kill her. As if she guessed his confusion, she put a bailing hook in his upper arm, his gun arm, and ripped it. He lost his job; a sheriff takes a shooting test every year, and Tawse could hardly hold a cigarette, let alone a gun.

Alma went with the family, but she'd been upset. After a while she set off to see her uncle, her mother's brother, in Waco, Texas. He had a barbecue restaurant, and he hired her as a waitress. But she got confused in the busy times, and he took her off the job. He made love to her one night, in his trailer, but when he told her to give him a blow job, Alma set her uneven teeth and bit off the end of his penis. She just left him there, howling and bleeding, and spat out the last shred of family.

She went to Arkansas, to Fort Smith. Honeycutt, the deputy, had told her once that he thought she could have been Miss Knoxville. So she entered the Miss Arkansas contest in 1972, and she placed fourth. There was a young man in the audience, Lionel Leonard, and he wrote her poems, and asked to be allowed to see her. She dated him for a while, but then she left for Nashville and got a position there in a House of Pancakes as a hostess.

A soldier came into the place where she worked, Glenn Kelly. He had been in Vietnam, and he was discharged. But he kept in training and wore a laundered uniform every day. They lived together in Nashville until Kelly went out one day and shot and killed Barbara Jean, the singer. Kelly was tried and put away for life. The whole thing got Alma's picture in the papers. Lionel Leonard came to reclaim her. He was sure they were made for each other. He found her in her apartment one night and begged her to marry him. Alma was tired, laughing and screaming at him to get out. But he wouldn't go, so she herself ran out to the verandah straight onto the butcher knife in the strong left hand of Henry Tawse, a vagrant with a last mission. She gasped and fell, so that her falling made the wound wider. Then Henry thrust the knife into his chest and collapsed on her.

> *I shudder at the violence I am writing, as if I were inflicting it on myself. I can become these people, or let them fill my emptiness. In a sentence, I can change my voice and my life.*

DAVID JOHN LOCKE

Jack Nicholson in The Passenger, *1975, directed by Michelangelo Antonioni*

He was in a small hotel in Chad, in northern Africa, in the desert, in the heat. David John Locke—profession: reporter. He had forgotten what he was looking for—guerrillas, no doubt, but if the urbane French-speaking President had happened by, on a tour of hotels, why not find the casual way to ask whether this civilized man had indeed killed thousands of his opponents? A reporter will ask anyone the old questions that everyone has learned to answer. So the world goes on. The expected interrogation hovers over it like flies above a corpse.

He was thirty-three, born in London; to America, age two, when his father was attached to the embassy in Washington. In America,

1944 to 1960, when his father retired with a commendation and a dinner from Eisenhower. What had his father done? Intelligence. He was one of the few British the Americans trusted. Nineteen sixty to 1963, back in England, at Oxford, reading history. In 1964, he began as a journalist for the *Sunday Times* and the BBC, then the *Washington Post*, and so on, working on projects like Insight, Focus or Survey. A gang of bosses sent him to trouble spots to bring back fresh reports with the tang of danger and impudence—Beirut, Vietnam, Cuba, Djakarta, Bangladesh, Chad, Chad, Chad—he had become an expert there, despite broken French and frosted insight.

There was a wife in Dawson Place, in Bayswater; the wife in a desirable, three-story Victorian house, narrow but deep, newly painted white, a house to keep up, with an attic room called Chad; the wife named Rachel, a tawny, angry wasp in the house, buzzing against him and the walls; a reason to be away and something to come home to; in and out, for how many more years, dark fingermarks always having to be sponged away from the doorjambs. While he had stayed in five hundred hotels.

There was Delamere in London, his blind friend from Oxford who took pleasure in David's American voice. Then, at forty, Delamere's blindness became operable. The operation succeeded. He was elated. But the feeling did not last. The world looked drabber than he had imagined. With his white stick he had tapped out the world. Now he stood on street corners paralyzed by information. He stayed indoors, in the dark. David Locke guessed that Delamere might do away with himself.

The previous night in a Chad hotel, before one more day of futile leads, David Locke met another Englishman, David Robertson. They were alike: same height, same age, same receding hair, same sinking stance, weighed down by a forgotten danger. They drank together. But when David Locke went in to see him a second night David Robertson was dead on the hotel bed, as if crept up on by the sinister peace while taking a rest. No trace of pain or regret: siesta. It was as if his vehicle had taken a turning and David Robertson had been borne off on another trip without bump or sway. Sometimes the dead die where they are sitting.

David Locke worked out what he would have to say at the hotel desk: "Il y a un homme mort. . . . " It was too complicated. He studied the corpse, how much it was like him. He never noticed the idea, but he acted on it, taking the body to his room, putting it on his bed, dressing it in his clothes, a decent fit after all. A lot alike. He steamed their two pictures from their passports. It was a small, magical exchange, like lifting the film of tiredness from a soul. Robertson was an international businessman, that's all he had said. David Locke looked in the dead man's bag; he was curious. He found an air ticket for London and Munich, a key and a diary with a few jottings: appointments, women's names—Melina, Lucy, Daisy, Zelie—and a hotel like another name, Hotel de la Gloria.

Feeling excited, he went down to the desk and said that the man in 17 appeared to be dead. That must be David Locke, said the black man. "Ah," sighed the fresh Robertson.

He went back to London and from the pavement outside the white house he saw Rachel watching David Locke's obituary on television. But Robertson was thinking of the dark-haired girl he had seen sitting on a bench in Bloomsbury. He had always felt a lack of attachment or conviction in himself that could let a friend fade from his life while he followed a stranger. Strangers are more beckoning; they offer new lives. After I had written that, I heard Mary Frances's scolding voice, trying to keep me in Nebraska. "But I never leave the house," I said, and she looked at me helplessly, so that I couldn't stand her eyes. I need to be in the dark, unseen.

Then to Munich. The key opened the locker at the airport. A slender black case stood in the locker, and in the case he found an inventory of weapons. The men who followed him to the Zimmermann church—be a tourist, he had decided—gave him an enormous fifty thousand dollars for the inventory. They all had a friendly chat, agreeing not to cry over the spilled milk of the anti-aircraft guns. Robertson was a gunrunner.

He went on to Barcelona in a hired car. He picked the place from the list of Avis offices. Why there, though? If anyone had known his love of Orwell, and his month in Catalonia in 1962, it might have been surmised. Was the Avis list printed with Barcelona in bold? Or was it chance, a stroke that obviates all this circumstantial speculation?

He found the girl in Barcelona, at the Palacio Guell by Gaudi; there she was on another bench, reading the same book, *Architecture Without Architects*. She could have been the perpetual student. It could have been anticipated that a tourist in that city would seek out Gaudi.

It was not awkward picking up this girl; perhaps she was as ready to take him from his track to hers. They went together, pursued by a Rachel anxious to hear from Robertson about Locke's last hours. They shared hotel rooms and Locke imagined how Robertson would have made love—secretly, so as not to break the package, for he had a weak heart.

Locke and the girl went by way of Almeria toward Algeciras—the rendezvous in the diary was set for there, at the Hotel de la Gloria. They found the place, a white building by the road, with a large open space behind it. He and the girl were in adjoining rooms.

Locke lay down to rest and the girl went to her room. He could feel the steady motion of time, like the hurtle of the earth. There must be an engine or an author carrying it all along. From the bed he could imagine a part of him going up to the window and out into the courtyard where cars came and black men got out to talk and look at the hotel. He could imagine his senses reaching farther out into the yard, leaving muffled noises behind in his room, a door opening, a bump in the air. And left there like an old shell, behind his senses, Locke-Robertson, David, was quietly shot. By whom? The senses were too far away to know. When Rachel arrived, the men, the black men, had gone. The girl was still there, loyal . . . or appointed? Night fell on the Hotel de la Gloria and the lights burning in its windows were like the sad but accepting guitar played within. All the senses of Locke, free but lost, gathered in the warm night air and looked at the girl with love and suspicion, like a reader following a story, saying, "Where next?"

MAUREEN CUTTER

Lisa Eichhorn in Cutter's Way, *1981,*
directed by Ivan Passer

There were two movie houses in Bedford Falls then, in the summers when Harry's child Mo stayed with us. It was three summers she came, in the middle fifties, years as long as the cars, and they were the Dream and the Circle, each pretty in its way, the Dream built in 'twenty-one and the Circle going much further back. It had been a proper theater and an opera house, and it had the old painted curtain with a view of a fine house across a lake at evening.

"Will the film be about the people in the house?" I remember Mo asked me one afternoon.

I was taken aback: she asked with such a weight of need. I would have made up some story about that house, but she seemed too earnest to mislead. "Maybe them," I surmised. "Maybe." But she thought my vagueness was a touch of mystery. You can never put hunters off if they are determined. Even silence entices them.

"It must be," she said, fixing her dark eyes on the house. The curtain shivered at times in some stage draft, and Mo wanted to see if the curtains stirred in the windows of the house. It would have been proof that someone there was watching us.

My brother Harry had married a realtor, Ruth, and they lived in Seattle, where Harry worked for a car dealer. He made money in the fifties and in the summers he'd take Ruth off to Mexico, putting Mo on a plane to Omaha. Nineteen fifty-five, 'fifty-six and 'fifty-seven it was, until she was ten. What a solitary, thoughtful child, tired-looking so you wanted to take care of her. Maybe as she got older and became a woman she learned about that look, and used it. But the Mo I knew was artless and implacable in all she did or imagined.

By looking in my list of pictures seen I can discover what I took her to: *The Trouble with Harry* (we laughed to think it might be her daddy); *The Night of the Hunter* (her hard, hot hand held on to me for most of that; I could count the beat of her alarm); *Picnic* (she was bored, she couldn't know yet the appeal to a provincial girl of doing something awful); and *The Searchers* (we saw that twice—like a view you circle round on so you can look at it again before you have to move on—and you know it's still there, years later, eroded a little, if only you would go back. But you can't, you never do).

Mo liked the pictures, but Travis would never go with us. It wasn't that he didn't enjoy particular movies; he couldn't accept their being stories, not real and true. He cried so much you had to take him away from the place. But Mo took the pretense for granted, the way some children can sit on a horse and not be afraid. As soon as she arrived in the summer, she'd say, "Anything playing, Uncle George?" and I'd make a fuss about being caught unprepared. "Well, I don't know, Mo. I hadn't thought about that. . . ." Then she'd frown at me, trying not to smile. You never forget the light in a child if you've helped put it there. Or it's going out.

"Do you have to spoil her with pictures?" Mary Frances would ask, the dust of bread-making up to her elbows. It was her unsteady humor, and she'd wink at Mo, to grab an ally. But then it turned to rancor and Mo learned not to respond. She'd study her shoes solemnly, counting the cutout holes in the pattern of her sandals while I soaked up Mary Frances's discontent. Anger in others will silence a child, until the quiet makes anger more suspicious. "Well, Miss Tight-Lips?" Mary Frances would demand, and Mo sank into passivity.

The summers came to an end. I had letters from her sometimes: Harry must have told her to write. But when she was fifteen or so, their tone changed and then the letters stopped. She went to the University of Washington for a couple of years but dropped out in 1968, when she was twenty, and then drifted down to Berkeley to live, saying she was going to finish her degree. But she never did.

She sent me a long letter in 1971, nine pages, typed, done over a span of three months, in installments. She apologized for getting out of touch, and said she remembered me well and still liked to go to the movies. When she got to Berkeley, she found a job at the Pacific Film Archive. She was friendly with a man there named Luddy who'd given her books to read on film. But she thought the books spoiled the pleasure, and she didn't persevere with them.

At the time she wrote, she was working in a bookstore for an Elmer Bender and his daughter, Marge, who was married to the writer John Converse. I used to read him in *The New Republic*, and I'd thought he was fair then. You can never tell enough from reading. She sent me his photograph, and that put me off. He had dead eyes, and a level, dishonest face, like a face in a mirror. Mo was in love with him, and they were having an affair without Marge knowing—or speaking. Converse and Marge had a little girl, but he had promised Mo he was going to marry her, told her time and again, and she got used to deceiving herself about it. Until he went off to Vietnam to be a reporter, and she had to recognize that he was more interested in testing himself.

So Mo moved across the Bay. She worked with the Elster Corporation, and then she was taken on at San Francisco General as an orderly. She met Alex Cutter there. He was back from Vietnam, without an arm. I learned this later, from Harry, when I determined to put the bits and pieces of her life together. Cutter was luckier than many veterans, but filled with anger and self-pity, and looking for someone to be his one to blame. By then, perhaps, Mo was prepared to be a victim: it becomes a way of life for so many of us. You can count the broken faces wherever you look.

They were married. I have a picture of the wedding: Cutter in a bow tie, all askew, his black patch slipping off a drunken eye—I have never established whether that eye was damaged, or the patch swagger. Mo is next to him, on his sound arm, but looking alone, staring at the photographer as if he had just offered to shoot her. There's a handsome man on her other side—he seems asleep, propped up—Richard Bone, Cutter's one friend. His drowsy eyes are looking down at Mo's dark hair, as fine as chocolate lace. Is he smelling her?

They went to live in Santa Barbara, the three of them. There must have been good times, but Harry said it was always a wonder Mo stayed. He told her he'd have her back at home. But she didn't budge. She drank more year by year, vodka or rum, while Cutter talked about his loathsomeness. The police said she was drunk and had dropped a cigarette which set light to the house and she'd been burned to blackened bone. It was dry timber, with straw rugs, the house: it was consumed in fifteen minutes, and no one was there to drag her out. They knew her by the teeth.

I fretted over her years before that, and Mary Frances would look at me in disbelief. "Can't you ever care for your own children?" she said. "You dreadful fool."

"They don't want it," I explained.

"How would you know?"

"They hold me off."

"You'd do anything for a stranger." She was crying. "Those films. They make the strange so attractive."

This could be so. They are so full of hope and change. I remember, though, in 'fifty-six how Mo took me for an ice cream after *The Searchers* and recounted the story we'd just seen, about a search for a niece who did not know her uncle anymore. I have done what I can with Mo's life. Cutter died not long after her. He had needed her too much. He had gone to the house of this man named Cord, and become abusive. Bone was with him. It was some stupid quarrel: Cutter was always looking for grievances. I wrote to Bone asking him for information. But all I got was a handwritten page saying, "I let her down, like everyone else let her down. She was depressed that night, and for all I know she shut the door after I had gone and built a bonfire in the living room. We will never know for sure; she kept it her secret. She did not mention you."

How does anyone read that and not imagine more?

AL

Charles McGraw in The Killers, *1946,
directed by Robert Siodmak*

There's no more than "Al" to go on, the one surprised word uttered by his companion as the two men were shot by a policeman named Lubinsky and James Reardon, an insurance agent, in a bar in Philadelphia. There were no marks of identification on this Al, no family pictures, no driver's license, no names or initials sewn into his clothes. He was a man of about forty-five, in a dark suit, a white shirt and a plain black tie, with shoes that someone polished every day. He wore a gray hat with a black band, and the face beneath it was cut out of rock. There was a frown above and between his eyes, cold, hard eyes, but sensitive, or worried, too. He looked like someone who took care, yet he handed out pain without any weakening. Al was a professional killer. Or so they said. They said he had killed a man, "Swede" Lunn, in Brentwood, New Jersey, and that he had done it for money. He was a contract killer. You wouldn't reach him directly. If you wanted someone killed, you need never meet Al or ponder over his eyes. You put in a call, and a few more calls got to Al. The sum of money you had agreed would go down by maybe 60 percent by the time it reached him. Those are the eyes of someone who suspects he's being chiseled.

This was in 1946—I wonder if Als still work in the same way. This Al and the other one came into Harry's Diner in Brentwood just before six, just before dinner. They took over the place, they closed it up, they had Nick Adams stay where he was, and they waited for Lunn. They said they would be killing him for a friend. The other one was fat, aggressive and theatrical, but Al was lean and restrained. He said no more than he had to, and you could have fancied that he was bored by the other one's caustic and unnecessary talk. It was as if Al was the real thing, while the other was an actor horning in on a contract to get material for a picture. The other one was already thinking aloud in script lines—"They all come here and eat the big dinner." But Al saw no act in what he was doing; he did not enjoy the lip-smacking talk. He was worrying whether he could shoot Lunn correctly and get away without a trace.

Al hoped not to be noticed. Real hired killers must not look dangerous. They need a kind of meekness, a gray availability that no one remembers. There were no marks and no identification: in taking other lives safely, Als must surrender much of their own. They live in boardinghouses, moving on, their lack of Social Security, credit rating, tax base and driver's license excused by the propriety of their lives and the steady call for killings.

From my world of law-abiding wallets full of identity, I wonder how one contacts Al and buys the assurance of his unobtrusive craft? I have a job and I do not think I can do it myself. So I am on the lookout for him, patiently examining shamefaced men.

JOE GILLIS

William Holden in Sunset Boulevard, *1950,*
directed by Billy Wilder

Like many who made long journeys to Los Angeles, Joe Gillis had once meant to be a movie star. He never owned up to it; he sneered at actors and their emptiness. When he met them, he was reassured to find his superiority justified. None of this altered how as a youth in Ohio he had longed to be on the screen. It was not exactly that he wanted to be a picture actor. He wanted his life to take place *on* a screen, with all the enhancements of close-ups, dissolves and hushed music.

But one day in the house off Sunset Boulevard Joe Gillis looked at the empty pool and thought what a hole it was, where a drunken slip could smash a face. He thought of those movie moments when tuxedo pomp walks backward into the water, and hilarity soars on the splash. Feeling blue, and trying to organize good times, he told Max to have it filled with water. Should it be cleaned first? Max had wondered. What did Joe know about pools? He said he guessed not. Wouldn't the water clean it? A few days later, he toppled gracefully into that pool—it was his best moment, his starry fall—and, drowning and dying, he swallowed water and spewed out his story.

He had been born in Dayton, Ohio, in 1918. His father had a drugstore. Joe served ice cream and floats in summer and put out the magazines. He admired their pictures, and he had a collection in his room above the drugstore of *Photoplay* and the other picture papers. He sensed that the stories were less accurate than the pictures. The stories were so torrid, so sweet, so full of mood, like advertisements or letters of persuasion. When he grew older, Joe recognized that these stories about the stars' lovers and their pets had the same drama and atmosphere as the stars' movies. He could not be sure whether this was a trick, something no one else had noticed, or whether in Hollywood people did live out motion picture stories. He could believe the latter, for when he went to the movies himself he always wanted to be up there, moving, turning, waiting, watching, smiling on the screen. He practiced those faces in the mirror and he lived with the blessed momentariness of someone always being just noticed.

It hurt his face. He had been a good-looking boy, but in adolescence his features took on the folds and ghostly inside-outness of one of those paper toys that children fold. There were so many instants in Joe Gillis's face it was all he could do to hold the thing together. When he smiled, you felt the parts were going to come apart. So he had to settle for a grin, and that turned mean and sour. By the time he was twenty, he looked and felt unreliable. He could never do a thing without imagining he was being written. Joe did not like writing or reading, but he had announced that as his calling because he could not get the inward scrutiny out of his rattled, dishonest head.

He studied English at the University of Dayton, and he wrote a story in 1939, about a kid who helped the Wright brothers in their first attempt to fly. It was fiction, but it was carefully researched, and it soared on Joe's own wish to mingle with the famous. Paramount read the story—it was sent to them by Joe's professor—and they bought it for five hundred dollars. The studio told him it had been "an invaluable, background contribution" to the 1941 picture *I Wanted Wings*. Joe saw that movie three times, but he never found a trace of his story beyond the common theme of flight and the general emotional yearning for transformation.

He went into the army, determined to use all the idle time he had heard about to write more stories. But within a week of landing in Europe, he had been captured. No shots were fired. His detachment simply walked down a road and found itself among Germans. No one struggled or argued; it was like a journey reaching its appointed end. So Joe Gillis was sent to a prisoner-of-war camp, and there his face became gaunt but his fingers grew calluses as he wrote story after story in lead pencil on the gray paper that he managed to save. There was not one war story. They were all about happiness and success.

When he was released, Joe went back to Ohio, got his stories typed up, and sent them to Paramount with a letter of explanation that was already like a magazine article on how this young writer became a movie scenarist in a harsh, unfriendly stalag. A few days later he followed the registered package on the train, confident he would never see Dayton again.

From 1946 to 1950, Joe Gillis worked on seventeen pictures. He was on staff at Paramount for two years; he got a credit for the shared original story on *My Wife the Mailman* (which claimed to be set in Dayton) and another for a script on a quickie Western, *Canyon Fire*. Other scripts were bought and shelved, or passed on to other writers. He was paid for treatments. He lived well enough, but the insecurity and the lack of glamor sapped him. Studios got to know him, they anticipated his jaded face and anxious calls, and his reputation became that of a has-been. He hated stories now. He regarded the elements of fiction as the cards in a pack. They were always all there. There was no surprise; solitaire always came out if you cheated. He was a hack, and he hit the typewriter with the violence of self-loathing. Back in Dayton his condition would have been recognized as a mental breakdown. But this is harder to discern in Los Angeles.

Then one hot day he tried to get his car out of reach of the repossession men, and he drove it into that unexplained driveway off Sunset Boulevard. It could have been the beginning of a lane up into the hills, or the mouth of oblivion. It beckoned, just as if art directors and gardeners had plotted all morning over its open, sleepy abandon. The mansion was something out of a fairy tale, Joe told himself, and then Norma Desmond called to him from the balcony, the voice like a fingernail dragged across glass.

She took him in; she would not let him go. For she had never lost her love of stories, and she regarded him as a pilgrim, a pen and a fan sent by providence. She lavished clothes, love and her script upon him. He wore the clothes all the time—when they went out, when they stayed at home; he was her male model, with the whisper "gigolo" in his ear and sticking out in exactly the way an ivory-colored silk handkerchief protruded from his top pocket. He suffered her love—he let her clamber all over him, her fearful, sinewy heat and her precipitate orgasms, she was always so in love with love. And he took her pages and folders of script and hacked them down into a polished, lifeless work.

She shot him. He fell into the pool. The script had not sold. He had wanted to leave. And she had never told him that in all those love-stews he had put a child in her. It was as if she regarded the conception as hers alone. But if he had known, he might have shot himself. Joe

Gillis was a coward who was horrified easily. And he had ordered the pool filled so that the Chinese tiles on its floor shone and smiled.

MAX VON MAYERLING

Erich von Stroheim in Sunset Boulevard, *1950, directed by Billy Wilder*

Born in 1894 in Vienna, Max Meck; died in 1964 in Pasadena, Max von Mayerling. A man of many parts—military spy, fraud, illegal immigrant, military costume advisor to motion pictures, director, husband, failure, the humiliated one, guardian of unlocked doors, chauffeur and magician. If every previous generation of the Meck family had felt itself advancing with seriousness, then Max is the augury of modern times, forever stepping into greater implausibility but never losing his balance. As we drag our history forward, we seem able only to find more unbelievable lives. Yet Max never gave up the ghost. He dressed impeccably, and his pained eyes spoke of duty, honor and expectation. Just by glancing at chaos, he could convince his stepson, Julian, that there was still a notion of order, and a gulf between it and reality, a loss, the prevailing message of Max von Mayerling's eyes.

The Meck family was very poor. What did you expect? The father worked in a bottle-making factory in Vienna; the mother had seven children, all in three rooms on the third floor with only one window that admitted daylight. The others were trapped by wells, backs and the gloomy overlay of the bottling factory. All those nineteenth-century cities, filled with children and the memory of others who died in infancy; kids hungry and thin, with eyes burning in their scrappy faces; their heavy shoes clattering on the stone steps, their pale legs striving to carry the leadlike shoes; an era that seemed like a dingy, overcrowded tenement building where there was always someone ill, or dying, or being born.

The most natural mood of the tenement is a jittery, cheerful anxiety—like someone who expects bad luck. But at the age of twenty, Max Meck was already possessed of the grace that could have lived on a country estate. He alone knew how he had acquired it: he may have worked as a valet or groom; he may have read novels and visited the theater. But at twenty he knew accoutrements. He spoke like an aristocrat, and behaved toward women with that curt British-ness that was in fashion with gentlemen. As the war came along, so Max was the picture of a young Prussian officer, thoroughly versed in the history of battles, sentimentally drawn to the cavalry but up to date on artillery statistics.

When he joined the Austrian army, his superiors noticed this authority and extricated him from the ranks. They had his birth certificate, and they could measure how far his presence belied it. Some wise adjutant realized he had an actor on his hands, and so Max was drafted into espionage. He posed as a German flier, was shot down over France and imprisoned, but was taken into the confidence of his French brother-officers. When he had had his fill of their information, he escaped and hiked back to Germany. Of course, the information was trivial. But it delighted the Germans and the Austrians to hug such a trick to their hearts. Max could have been shot in the process, for those tricked must respond severely if they ever detect the trick. He took extravagant risks so his superiors could enjoy a sense of advantage. Espionage is a state of mind, like unfaithfulness; it is more a treasure to the imagination than a concrete advantage.

As the war ended, Max Meck took a ship to Mexico from Lisbon, hired as the ship's doctor. Thus, he came over the border to the south of San Diego, a sturdy, resolute man, dressed in rags he had purchased as adornment to the tan and the scars he had won to make up his peon look. Six weeks later, Max von Mayerling was working as an extra in pictures, and as a military costume expert on films showing the wickedness of the Hun. He watched the making of these movies and saw nothing he could not understand. The realization of plots was second nature to a spy.

He was a director by 1921—*Speckled Hens and Cockerels*, a sardonic portrait of the marriage-market in Granada, about which the legend endures of pornographic scenes shot for the delectation of a studio boss. In 1925, a mangled version of his *Death Valley Days* was all that Hollywood could divulge of an extravagant masterpiece. *The Honeymoon* was withheld; its symbolism was deemed too flagrant. And *Princess of the Micks*, with Norma Desmond, was so immediate a commercial failure that Miss Desmond, its spent owner, withdrew the picture and herself from public gaze.

Max was by then her husband, so she did not prevent his following her to Europe. She had forgotten how they came to be married. But her aberration was his tragedy, for he loved her. She teased him and

69

said he had fallen in love with her only to inspire masochistic ecstasy, a pressing strain in all his films. He replied that love was always absurd; the choice of whom one loved should be perverse. She hired him as her butler when she had divorced him. He could get no more work in pictures, so she kept him on an allowance. Max watched two other husbands come and go. The first was too proud to speak to a predecessor, but the second recognized tradition and liked to chat with Max.

Years passed. Back in America, living on Sunset Boulevard, Norma became more erratic. She tried to kill herself in 1940, and Max removed the locks from the doors so she could not isolate herself from rescue. And so he lived, with a beloved who did not consider him, and who sometimes beat on his chest with wrath. He did not sleep from imagining a suicidal leap in her. He was caught in a trap of frustration. Max wept for an hour every day until his black eyes had the luster of velvet.

Then Joe Gillis came along, offering the phantoms of a comeback and another lover to Norma. Max did all he could for Gillis; being polite to this jerk was a refined self-abuse. And at the time of the shooting, it was Max, a director still, who coaxed Norma downstairs and into the loony bin by conjuring up a camera to track back in front of her languid advance. It was as lovely as an Arab dance, he thought.

He visited Norma, and never mentioned the pregnancy that the star and killer ignored. She had no anesthetics in labor, but screamed at the mysterious pain. The son was born and Norma went back to eight years of asylum hours.

Max petitioned the state of California to be appointed the boy's guardian. He was accepted. He had the boy named: Julian Kay, he told the registrar, the first name that came into his head; he was an effortless inventor.

He took the boy to two rooms in Inglewood. Max worked as a chauffeur and as a magician who hired out for children's parties. He cared for the child in a doting and grim way. He looked after him physically so that he grew up soft and babylike. But he allowed his mind no innocence, and he taught the boy the proper spartan caress that a man must bring to women. So Julian grew up with an odd, unemotional expertise, as appealing and perverse as a mustache.

Max died in 1964. He was returning from a party where he had made pigeons fly in and out of reality. He had a heart attack at the wheel, and his car collided with a truck carrying beer. He was killed instantly, as he had always hoped he would be.

GUY HAINES

Farley Granger in Strangers on a Train, *1951,*
directed by Alfred Hitchcock

Perhaps it is all those gleaming whites stooping to the cunning of lobs and drop shots, not to mention the paranoia of disputed line calls, with smudged chalk, elderly judges set in cherry-colored silence, and the horror of a bad call marring the purity of the game. Still, tennis players are not easily trusted. Their elegant lines of movement succumb to forced errors or double faults. Tennis is a game for flawed saints. Its arrangement of white and green is like a cucumber sandwich in which, somehow, a virulent mustard has been smeared. "Anyone for tennis?" they are supposed to sing out in polite, middle-class theater; it seems an innocent game, a prelude to marriage, what with mixed doubles and the hints of love in the scoring. But it is often the tennis player who is the killer in that land of Agatha Christie.

Guy Haines was never quite in the front rank of players. He looked a little frail next to Savitt, Sedgeman and Schroeder. His backhand was unsound, not so much weak as snatched and evasive—a smile hoping to conceal a cavity. He had never spent a summer driving three hundred backhands every afternoon against an unbeatable wall; he never took his weakness and pounded it flat. Perhaps he admired his own little kink, and so his backhand was a wicked shot—sliced, cut, spun, dropping over the net and twisting back into the netting—but something that broke under pressure. At Wimbledon in 1949, Budge Patty so repeatedly attacked his backhand that Haines lived in the shaded corners of the court, a suspect under interrogation.

But Guy Haines was welcome on the court and in the clubhouse. He was the best-looking tennis player on the circuit. He had a gracious way of losing and a shy acceptance of victory that won sentimental support. He smiled a lot; he was courteous to umpires and pally with ballboys.

He was born in 1926 in Manchester, New Hampshire, with the real name George Hank, of German descent. The father had a laboring job in one of the mills in a town losing its eminence in that industry. Young George had no special talent, except for nimbleness at ball games. His schoolwork was always interrupted by practice. But he was slight and hurt easily. He liked the notion of being safe on his side

71

of the net—no matter that he was one of those who perfected the winner's easy hurdling of the net to land in the loser's lap with consolation and bravos.

During the war, Guy worked summers on Long Island as a ballboy, helping the pros and making himself available as a partner at country clubs. He was not drafted because of flat feet—marching would have crippled him. But he kept the lightest tread on the court, where he was known as a retriever.

He won some worthwhile competitions in New England in 1945 and 1946. Tennis was still an amateur game, accessible only to players of some means. Guy Haines (his *nom de raquet*) was eager to play in Europe, but he needed a patron. In Huntington, Long Island, he found and married Miriam Chitty, who had inherited money from her parents. She was willing to put these funds toward Guy's expenses, and she did understand that it would impede his plans if she accompanied him on the tour. So she kept a scrapbook at home, rejoicing when he won the Italian Open in 1948, and made the Wimbledon semifinals in 'forty-nine.

The marriage drifted. Absences grew into separation. Guy met Ann Morton, the daughter of Senator Morton of Pennsylvania. He was moving in society circles, telling the Mortons that Miriam was a spoilsport, one of the sluts of Long Island, waiting to be bought off with a good divorce settlement. "I could kill her," hissed Ann Morton one day, though never having met her. "Me too," said Guy, always eager to agree.

Their marriage conjured up a strange genie: Bruno Anthony, a tennis fan, who set out to meet Guy on the train from New York to Washington. This was achieved with the full effect of chance and surprise, and Bruno introduced the motif of "crisscross"—lines of force that meet and feel the knot of intersection. "Why sure," said Guy, almost to himself, "your father and my wife." "Exactly," said Bruno. Or something like that. Who can ever remember conversations on trains, with all the rattling of the machinery? Guy was a skilled player, and Bruno an overemotional fan, quick to jump to conclusions, and so touchingly ready to do something, to be as active as a tennis player.

So Bruno killed Miriam, strangling her on an island at a fairground in the town where she lived. And then, like anyone who believes in fair play, he looked to Guy to dispose of his own hated father. Crisscross? One good turn deserves another, the spirit of doubles—one at the net, the other taking the baseline.

Guy was embarrassed. The police could see how he had been freed by the death of Miriam; he had no satisfactory alibi; he did not tell the story of Bruno, that charming maniac, because he was afraid it would not be believed, or because he was guilty about a real pact. Had there been a moment when he had grinned at Bruno, said "Okay, pal!" and told himself, why not, if this idiot feels like it? He did not report Bruno; it was his backhand again, tensing and shrinking under pressure.

But it all worked out. Bruno was too unstable to make a case against Guy: he became obsessed with incriminating clues and some final fairground disaster. He died. Guy was cleared. He married Ann Morton and became an assistant to her father. He was himself elected to the Senate in 1964, representing Delaware, and he was not seriously damaged when Ann Morton divorced him, charging adultery with a woman or women on trains between the capital and the Haines home in Westchester.

Senator Haines became a confidant of President Nixon in the late 1960s, and so it was—crisscross, everything in meetings—that he was charged in the aftermath of Watergate with attempts to obstruct justice, convicted, and stripped of his office. He served eight months, and now runs a tennis school on Long Island where whites are obligatory. He has not temporized with the recent taste for colored shirts. Guy Haines wears long white trousers as he runs around his backhand.

PETE "SWEDE" LUNN

Burt Lancaster in The Killers, *1946,
directed by Robert Siodmak*

Peter Lunn was born in Bemidji, Minnesota, in 1908. His parents were both Swedish—his father from near Askersund—and they had made their way to America in the early years of the century. The mother had been married once before, but her husband fell sick and died in the terrible northern Minnesota winter of 1905. A year later she married Olf Lund, a dairy farmer on land to the north of Leech Lake. The family went by the names of Lund or Lunn, slowly yielding to American usage, not noticing as the lilt in their voices went flat.

like a dumb Swede

Peter was the largest in the family, a runner in summer and a football player in winter. He would have gone from school to the farm, but for the illness of his father in 1926–27. An uncle, Lars, came over from Sweden to help with the farm, and Peter reckoned that he was being edged out. So he left Minnesota and drifted down to Chicago. He was working in the stockyards when he read a notice in the paper inviting strong young men to come to a gymnasium. A fight manager was looking for new talent. Peter had grown up a gentle kid, extreme only in his taste for romantic gestures. He was amused at the idea of putting on boxing gloves and hitting another man, but in his trial he knocked out his opponent in the first round, and he was signed up on the spot. He took it as it came, reckoning that if he made some money he would send it back to his parents. The manager said he was going to change his name for fights to Ole Anderson—it sounded more Swedish—but he called Peter "Swede," and that stuck.

From 1928 to 1935 he had seventy-six bouts as a light-heavyweight; he won fifty-five, lost nineteen, with two draws. All the losses came in the first and last years of his career. In the times between, for five years, he went unbeaten, with twenty KOs. With better backing and promotion, he might have been a contender. But his manager was a mediocre guy, and Swede learned that Scandinavians were not a draw in the big Eastern cities where title fights were held. So he never got his chance, and that hurt him for, once he had been beaten five times as a novice, he stopped laughing at boxing and learned the craft. He wanted to be champion as much as he had ever wanted anything. In 1934, he beat Gunboat Smith in Detroit and fought a twelve-round draw with the Englishman Len Harvey.

He was making as much as two thousand dollars a fight, but he lost half of that to his handlers, and he never managed to control the costs of training and travel. Somehow he had the idea that a potential champion should be extravagant. He bought rounds of drinks and then watched the fun around him as he sipped a soda. Naturally shy with women, he would invite a couple of girls to have dinner with him and his gang. Then he'd see the girls go off with a sparring partner and a second, while he got to pick up the check.

Nineteen thirty-five was the bad year. In January he had promised himself he'd have a title fight that year. Then he lost six in a row, and in Philadelphia in October he broke his right hand on Tiger Lewis's head and stood up like a dumb Swede while Tiger beat him. His corner and the crowd were telling Swede to go down, but it went the full ten, and he was never the same young man again. One fight can age a boxer. If Peter Lunn had lived, chances are he'd have been punchy by the time he was fifty.

So he retired. He still had money and clothes enough in those years. Boxers and gangsters are drawn together. Boxers have grown up more than they know with gamblers and their most obvious chance of reemployment is as bouncers or muscle. For their part, gangsters like to tame tough men who have taken and handed out punishment without notice or much profit. They regard fighters as idiots, and gangsters are so insecure they keep themselves surrounded by foolish strength.

Lunn had known Jim Colfax, and he hung around with him without understanding what Colfax was up to. He had a detective friend, Sam Lubinsky, who warned him off Colfax, but by then Peter was crazy about Kitty Collins, Colfax's mistress. The Swede wasn't as smart as Colfax had been. He believed Kitty when she said she wasn't anything more than a friend of Colfax's; and he was impressed when she told him, "I hate brutality. I could never bear to see a man I really care for being hurt." That one comment finished boxing for Lunn; he saw how ugly he had been for eight years. He was madly in love, but he said nothing to anyone and he thought no one noticed.

Then one day in 1938, Peter Lunn was there when his old friend Lubinsky came into a Philadelphia restaurant and made to arrest Kitty because she was wearing some stolen jewelry. "Don't do that, Sam," said Swede, casual as could be. "I gave it to her. She don't know nothing about it." Kitty went along with the gallantry, Lubinsky had no option, and despite his years in jail Peter never asked himself how the stuff came to be around Kitty's neck and pinned to her sweet bosom. It had been a grand moment, stepping forward, like raising his arms and having the announcer call him the new champion.

Colfax and Kitty were still friendly in 1940 when Peter Lunn got out of jail, and he came back to the gang. Maybe Kitty was touched by him. Maybe Colfax got irritated. In any event, the two men fought over her, and Colfax learned just how hard you can be hit in real life by a hand that was broken so that its owner had to give up boxing. They made a sort of peace, and they got on with robbing the payroll from the Prentiss Hat Company in Hackensack. That was July 20, 1940—a quarter of a million. A champion's lifetime in a few minutes.

Colfax had planned to double-cross Peter, but Kitty warned him and the two of them went off to Atlantic City with all the money. She said of course she loved him, and the Swede was in glory and heaven. But she left him inside a week, took all the money and went back to

Colfax. Lunn was so sad he tried to throw himself out of the hotel window, and only a devout chambermaid stopped him and told him to be a man.

He went away, but not far, to Brentwood, New Jersey, where he worked at a gas station and lived in a room at Ma Hirt's on Spruce Street. He led an uneventful life, plain and straight, and he waited. One day in 1946 Colfax happened to drive by and stop for gas. They had a friendly talk, never mentioning the job. Then a few weeks later two men came to the diner just before six when the Swede normally ate. They waited, and then they went up to Ma Hirt's, found him in his darkened room and put eight shots in him where he lay. Swede must have heard them coming, big men on an outside wooden staircase, all creaks and their repressed breathing, but he never made a move to save himself.

> *I would like to be like Harry Dean Stanton in*
> *Paris, Texas, calling up the characters on a*
> *telephone. Yet I have never met him, and he*
> *seems utterly unmeetable. "How pitifully*
> *absurd!" Mary Frances said once when I told*
> *her I thought, perhaps, I resembled James*
> *Stewart in Harvey. She was right, is right, like a*
> *rope around my neck.*

KITTY COLLINS

Ava Gardner in The Killers, 1946,
directed by Robert Siodmak

"My word, sir, that's a lovely child you've got there," said the gunman to Christopher Collins, a while before he shot him. This was one night in August 1924, hot and humid, in a tenement house in the South End of Boston. Collins was a policeman home by eight for his dinner. Ten minutes later there was a knock at the door and three of them came in, leaving a fourth on the doorstep. Mrs. Collins was indignant and scared, the two feelings coming in rapid flushes, so she hardly knew what she was saying. But her Chris was not surprised, and that shocked her—he a policeman, apparently seeing nothing outrageous in three men coming in, in jackets too on that night, and shooting him. Without a protest. And a fond-faced smile when the man remarked on little Kitty's looks, as if the father had not noticed it before for himself.

This Collins had come out of Ireland in 1919, landed in Boston and joined the police. In 1920, he married Kathleen Carroll, whose father was in the railways. A year later, Kitty was born, and Donal, the next, and Cliona in 1923. Their house was noisy with argument, and because Collins had trouble sleeping he got a habit of cheap white wine. He didn't notice much, which no one found odd in a Boston cop. But it affected those near him. He might have Kitty on his lap, dark with lustrous eyes already at the age of three, yet her father wouldn't reckon he had more than the cat asleep there, something to stroke once in a while.

A week after the shooting, the *Globe* said aha, this Collins was a black-and-tan; and that explained why years later a party would come to his house and shoot off his face in front of the wife and kiddies. It was assumed that he'd done something bad in Ireland, and his colleagues in the police came to the realization that, why, yes, surely he'd been an anxious man. There was a police pension, and a collection in the city (which might have tripled but for the hints that Collins had deserved what he got). So the family lived on in the South End, looked after by the police, and once a year the recipients of a banker's order, out of Philadelphia, for three hundred dollars, never explained, but somebody's way of remembering Kitty's eyes, and allowing they shouldn't have had to see the blasting of her daddy.

Kitty grew up tall, slender and gorgeous, but always fighting with her mother. The mother had formed the opinion that her Chris had been a no-good—hadn't he let her down and ruined her life?—and she said Kitty was like her father, and a liar too. And just to show her mother, Kitty by the age of sixteen could tell sweet, polite lies to anyone with the look of a young nun on her face, and then a wink that was a startling thing, like the Virgin Mary giving you the eye.

She gave up school around then, and in 1937 she found a job as a waitress on the trains between Montreal and Washington. She liked the crowds of men on business, and she got nice tips. But best of all, after dinner, she went to the observation car at the back of the train to count her money. One night there she met a glib fellow, Dickie McCoy, who sat with her and picked her pocket without her feeling a thing. Then, on the spur of the moment, instead of going off with the money, he told her what he had done and won her with the magic of it. She laughed, and later that night he took her maidenhood with the same light touch. He was years older than Kitty, but she woke enchanted and in love. The lying had made her romantic.

McCoy taught her to be a dip, and she was fair at it. The railroad company got complaints, but they never thought it might be a woman. By Christmas 1937, Kitty was rich and happy. Then, one day, between Philadelphia and Baltimore, a man named Jim Colfax caught her hand inside his coat and said she was a wicked girl. He talked about turning her in, but he took her off the train with him and made her his woman in his house in Philadelphia. Colfax was big in the rackets, and he needed a pretty young thing around to impress people.

After she'd got over the humiliation of it, Kitty saw that Colfax was a dull man. She was bored without the motion of the trains and meeting all sorts of new people, joking with them and flirting, bringing them a Reuben and lifting the wallets from their inside pockets. Colfax took her to nightclubs and places but he was always leaving her on her own while he chatted with some men. Once or twice she asked about his business, but he was hard on women knowing anything.

One night at a club in Baltimore, she was on her own when Pete Lunn came over to ask her to dance. He had a hold like a bear, and she thought he was grand. They got close, but then Colfax turned nasty. Kitty liked having the two men growling at each other over her, and she led them both on. It was a change from getting up late and trying on all the expensive clothes Colfax bought for her. But boredom made her reckless. Without any need but sport, Kitty had taken to stealing again. She took some jewelry one night in a Philly hotel, and she was wearing a fancy brooch in a restaurant when a cop arrested her. But Lunn was there, and he knew the cop. With a radiant grin on his face he said *he* had stolen the stuff, and given the one piece to Kitty out of sentiment. So Lunn went to prison instead, and Kitty thought he was the sweetest dope she'd ever met.

Lunn was away two years, and Kitty sent him a few postcards in jail with harmless messages. Colfax never knew about it, and so when Lunn got out of prison in 1940 he was taken back into the gang as someone who was owed a turn. But by the time they did the Prentiss Hat job in July, the three of them were all suspicious of one another. Maybe Kitty never knew which side she was on: it was a lot for a nineteen-year-old, in love with Lunn perhaps, but softened by

Colfax's money, and still a liar. So she went off with Lunn and the money, and then back to Colfax. It had one result: everyone else on the job was cut out. Colfax and Kitty kept all the money—$200,000 to split, said Kitty with a grin.

It was 'forty-six when Lunn was found and shot. But that was the end for Colfax, for an insurance man named Reardon got interested in the case and he worked it all out and stirred up the members of the old gang so they came down on Colfax and shot him. There's always someone whose sole purpose in life seems to be to work everything out—geniuses with no lives of their own to live.

Kitty learned from it all. She decided the gangster life was exaggerated. She called herself Grace Devlin and dyed her hair blonde. So she went to Atlantic City—where she and Lunn had gone on the lam—because she had liked the air and the slow roll of the gray sea. In the summer of 1947 she came in second in a Betty Grable look-alike contest, and she met a handsome man who was bodyguard to all the girls, Lou Guarini, a swell talker. They had a fling and Kitty got a job as a receptionist in one of the hotels. She met Tim Reid, the house dick, and they were married in 1949. They lived in a set of rooms at the hotel until 1963, when Tim died. Grace enjoyed the hotel business, and she got to be an undermanager, friendly with all the people, making sure that Tim was one-up on the dips and grifters.

In 1965, she moved into a place of her own and went back to seeing Lou. Her health was going, or so she said, so Lou would go out for her medicine and her sherry. He moved in with her and they're there still, a well-known couple, devoted and bickering. Grace let her hair go back bit by bit, until she found it was quite white. She never looked better, and she'd had some money put aside, so they manage and feel superior to the way things aren't what they were.

AMY JOLLY

Marlene Dietrich in Morocco, 1930,
directed by Josef von Sternberg

The child christened Elise Rissient was born in Courbevoie, a suburb on the northwestern side of Paris, in 1905. Her father was a projectionist of moving pictures. As this man extended his influence—to the ownership of theaters, the publishing of film magazines, and at last the production of movies—the family became more prosperous, acquiring a summer house in Rozven, in Brittany. It was there, in the summer of 1922, when Elise was seventeen, that her intense love affair with a young man, Francis de Pene, was observed fondly but inquisitively by a neighbor, Colette, who took it as the inspiration for *Le Blé en herbe*.

Yet Colette was not just a voyeuse, feeding off the girl and the rapid flow of her enthusiasm and wretchedness. The novelist became her character's friend, taking her on picnics, showing her the wild flowers on the cliffs, describing the trial of Landru to her, and teaching her Burgundian cooking. The two women spent a summer in love and fragrance, celandines and garlic, exchanging confidences as if there were no difference in their ages. "Ma belle," Colette exclaimed one August evening, "quand t'es aimé, si jolie." The cascade of open vowels, in Colette's rough voice, was like the first drops of rain before a thunderstorm—Elise Rissient never forgot the sentence, and so it presaged her own next name.

It was Colette who encouraged her singing, and gave her lessons in how modesty could command a stage as surely as nakedness. In 1924, at nineteen, Elise left Courbevoie and took a room on the rue Jacob which Colette helped her find. She worked hard at her singing lessons and began to build an audience in the small left bank cabarets. She sang sweet songs, full of sentiment in a simple, child's way. Yet her modesty sometimes seemed to crack—like the shell of an egg as a fledgling stirs—and the glimpses of a darker wisdom were intriguing to men in the audience. Elise had several short affairs in 1925 and 1926, and in that time she grew into a mysteriously detached young woman, a little teasing toward men and love. In a way she never understood, but which was related to her spreading fame as the model for *Le Blé en herbe*, Elise was called a temptress and a femme fatale. This reputation, however she resisted it, did harden her a little. As a singer, she offered a sexual mischief resting within the fripperies of romantic convention, like a sword wreathed in tissue paper. She won a following whose cheers grew louder and more urgent as Elise declined to notice or be warmed by them.

This quality of perversity drew invitations from Berlin in 1927. Learning enough German for some songs, Elise went there. Whether stunned or indifferent, she responded to the greater salaciousness of German cabarets with a coolness that was all the more inflaming. She seemed untouchable, so corrupt she could resist every man's desire;

there was a clamor to lay hands on her. If she gave herself to no one man in particular, all of them felt her denial. In 1929, a distinguished official in the Ministry of Education named Janrath shot himself beneath a large photograph of Elise on which he had stuck feathers giving an extra sensual texture to her filmy skirt.

There was an ugly noise in the Berlin papers: Elise's foreignness was held to blame; she was called "a depraved nymph" and so on. Pictures of the Janrath wife and children—rather like a soccer team, so many and so glum—were printed in silent accusation, next to Elise's knife of a smile. She did not bother to defend herself. She went by train to Santander, and took a boat for Morocco. During that voyage, she changed her name to Amy Jolly, and elected to be as sinister as the world wanted to believe.

She had come to the land of the Foreign Legion with the same need as many of its soldiers—a new name, a chance to escape, and hardship of service to stand as a rebuke for the guilt she was too proud to acknowledge. The self-respect of the silent and ungiving made a pact between her and the legionnaires. For the first time in her life she was acclaimed but not pursued. The soldiers regarded her as a true myth, someone who would fade into ordinariness if one of them actually had her in love. She guessed this reasoning, and smiled through the loneliness it entailed.

But one soldier struck her. Tom Brown, an American apparently, was a laconic, long-limbed man, secretive yet mocking his own discretion. She felt weak whenever she saw him, grinning back at his grin, and wondering if she would faint. Her desire made her feel she would die without him. There was a dispassionate curiosity in her aware how mad she was for him. She was sensible, of course, at all times, never a hair out of place. But what fuller proof was there of madness when she was really wild with longing?

Brown may have thought of killing this woman: his bleak calm was so close to being ruined by her. He loved her, too, no matter that he had given up on that notion, and its concession to women. But he was not as resolute or hard as he wanted. Feeling would creep in: we cannot look at things, and see them, without giving vulnerability and surprise a chance. So he had to defend himself against her impact. He had an elaborate, insolent salute for her, a deprecating wave of the hand to indicate playfulness. Yet her straight glance cut through the ornate gesture so that he felt pierced.

He gave in to love. He said he would go with her, be with her. Then, out of some horror of the weakness it meant, he picked up a stick of her greasepaint and wrote on her mirror, "I changed my mind. Good luck"—with a slash and a scroll beneath the message, reasserting his salute. She read it, and when the day came for Brown's regiment to march south into the desert, she followed him through the ace-of-spades archway in the wall, kicking off her high-heeled shoes, pleased by the heat of the sand. It was 1930.

Amy Jolly grew dark from the sun. Tom Brown watched her become a Legion whore, taken by other men. He never protested or touched her himself, and he no longer saluted her. She believed their love could only be expressed by frustration; they never dulled in each other's eyes. Amy looked like an Arab, but the nomadic life did not spoil her. She was loved, and nothing else does so much for appearance.

A kind of mysticism settled on her, mixed with hashish and superstition learned from the other camp women. They had seemed impossible companions once, but Amy knew them now, especially Tanya, a Bedouin who taught her fortune-telling. Tanya told her she had innate feeling for the art—she only gave her timing and confidence, just as Colette had shown her how to hold a stage.

They traveled together in Africa and came to Cairo, where they opened a club in 1936. It was a haunt of Allied officers during the war. When Tanya died, Amy took her name and became sole owner of the club. She dyed her hair black, wore kohl and smoked cheroots. She kept girls for the soldiers, but no longer sold herself. In 1946, she took a boat to Mexico, anticipating disturbances in Egypt.

By 1950 she had reached Robles, where she opened her newest premises. It was a small place, but discerning customers sought her out. She served drink and chili, and she slowly acquired a few very young, outrageous girls. Tanya ran the club with a disdain that had become her public persona. She liked another American, a sheriff named Quinlan from over the border. He was a heartfelt detective, who could often tell her her own thoughts. Yet he was not afraid of asking Tanya's occult advice. They were lovers for a time, wearied by their own appetite. They watched their orgies with far-off, amused sympathy. She knew he was a dead man in whom talent was turning sour and fat. He gave her up and then a few years later came back on a case that was already ruining him. Tanya watched him die, like a weighted balloon, in the trash of the border. It didn't surprise her; she guessed Quinlan had chosen her as the person to utter his epitaph.

She closed her place and drank herself to death in a year. It was not hard for someone who still had the inner delicacy of the young Elise.

The most raddled whore can have the self-esteem of a child collecting wild flowers in Brittany, noticed by an author and set down in a freshness that never ages.

I am old, but I can still see myself as a loner not tired by the road and its endless motels. To this day, I would rather think of something out of reach than be emperor of what I know.

NORMA DESMOND

Gloria Swanson in Sunset Boulevard, *1950, directed by Billy Wilder*

You can look at movie magazines from the early 1920s, amazed at the faces of beautiful young actresses, stars then, but so little known now that their euphonious names sound concocted—Barbara La Marr, Lupe Velez, Agnes Ayres, Alexandra Laguna, Leatrice Joy, Norma Desmond, and so on. All brunettes, with black lips, curls stuck on their brows and eyes like bulletholes: they seem to cherish the pain of sexual exploitation by men. There is implacability in the faces, like a ship's figurehead battling into the elements. It comes from signaling feelings; those silent women are stranded in the impossibility of utterance. A few years later, after sound, women's faces softened. The loveliness grew quiet and intriguing. Words were put out, like bait on the threshold of their being. They smiled, where silent faces had had trumpeting frowns.

It must have been maddening. Not many of them lasted more than a few years; the business was exhausting, and that kind of beauty is our endless American resource. It was only will that made any of them famous, or put forbidding strength in their faces. Somehow, they all seemed overdone; no matter how hard they tried, they must have known the shame of feeling coarse or clumsy. You can imagine them killing even, at the end of their tether, laughing if the gun went off and there was only a small puff of light to show explosion. But the man aimed at was staggering, stupefied, his hands clutched to the hole where life was leaking out. The ladies could make you believe.

So many of their names were false. Norma Desmond was born May Svensson in Milwaukee in 1899. She was the daughter of Swedish immigrants, the youngest of five children. Years later, some version of Miss Desmond told *Photoplay*: "I had picked a good time and place to be born. The automobile was not much older than I was, so there weren't many of them. Trolleys and wagons were pulled by horses, and none of them went too fast. It was a safe, clean time. When you were thirsty in the summer, your mother made a pitcher of lemonade. And everyone did the family wash on Monday and hung it out in the fresh air to dry."

Charming, don't you think? But actresses are in love with such crystal-clear happiness. May Svensson's early life was not a pitcher of homemade lemonade or the bouquet of fresh laundry. Instead, she was taken by her father on his tours of Wisconsin and Minnesota, selling Bibles and being driven by penury into increasingly reckless confidence tricks in which the daughter was often the decoy. They lived in cheap hotels, or on the run: there were a few nights in town jails, the child in a cot next to the sheriff's desk waiting for her father to be released.

And so it was, in 1911, that May saw her father shot down by a man named Gregson, the victim of a small enough fraud, a God-fearing but choleric man who had pursued Svensson for seven months. May was holding her father's hand, and talking to him, coming out of a diner in Kenosha, when a pistol blast met them. She felt the pressure in the air and was dragged sideways by her father's fall, his dead grip on her growing tighter.

She had her picture in the Chicago papers, wide-eyed, floridly becurled and stricken. A manager at the Essanay studios noticed it, and his flabby head was so touched by her plight that he saw a way of making money. He found her and devised a series of one-reelers about a waif, "Sweedie" she was called, an orphan and an outcast who got into sentimental scrapes and comic adventures. The films were poorly made, but the child bloomed in them. The camera breathed in time with the rising beat of puberty; in a year of those short movies she became an object of furtive lust, her picture pinned in lockers. The movies learned early how to fashion an arousing innocence that inspires its own spoiling.

"Norma Desmond," as Essanay had called her, was married at fifteen to Wallace Beery, twice her age and the robust exponent of his own ugliness. It was like a virgin princess being taken by a barbarian. The public was thrilled with alarm. In reality, Norma scolded him incessantly, until he left her with the beach house, all but one of their cars and the vases filled with his cash. This was 1917.

She had an extraordinary career in silent pictures, earning as much as $15,000 a week, to say nothing of bonuses. She worked for Marshall Neilan, Cecil B. De Mille, Harry D'Abbadie D'Arrast and Allan Dwan. Her burning gaze played on audiences like the light of the screen. The industry romanticized her and her "enchanted" life. Perhaps she believed those stories herself—her image was over-powering. She had gone so swiftly from the sordid to the luxurious, from being abused to being worshipped. She was a Cinderella who became a tyrant queen, without time to clean the coal dust from her fingernails. An aura of transformation surrounded her. There was a famous portrait of her face staring through an embroidered veil, a celebration of beauty as a fatal delusion. She met the tycoon Noah Cross and he mounted a play with her as Salome, discarding hundreds of veils, while he sat on a stool in the wings to see her body emerge through the misty gauze.

Perhaps her conviction was too intense for the naturalism of sound pictures? Or were her demands for money more than the industry could endure? *Princess of the Micks*, her film for Max von Mayerling, her husband, was a disaster in which she sank one million dollars of her own money. And so she went to France, marrying a marquis whose name she never learned to spell. She made a film there, *Une Jeune Fille de campagne*, about Charlotte Corday, in which the character will not speak—to protect her excessive expressiveness or the actress's lack of French.

While in Europe, she married the German Baron von Rauffenstein. Mayerling had never really been given up during these other marriages. He simply went from being husband to personal manager; it meant he dressed earlier in the day. There was consternation in the press, but the three figures handled the "ménage" without dismay. Moreover, in 1931–32, Norma Desmond had an affair with Serge Alexandre, also known as Stavisky. To this day there is a rumor in France that she had a child by the swindler, a daughter, who was passed on to a simple farming couple on the estate of Baron Raoul, a friend of Alexandre's. (An unexpectedly striking face in an out-of-the-way place will often inspire such fancies. But suppose real foundlings are not especially pretty, what then?)

In 1934, she returned to the mansion on Sunset Boulevard (bought for her by Noah Cross), where she would remain until her removal, at the hands of the police, in 1950. Mayerling came back to America in

1939 and became her butler. Norma Desmond slipped from glory to oblivion, unaware in her retreat of any change in her power or her looks. She was so removed from public contact now, she may have thought herself divine.

She had only a monkey as an intimate until Joe Gillis strayed into her life. He seemed to offer the means of a comeback, but he was also a lover and a slave. When he thought to leave her, she shot him, in the belly, as yet unaware that her own body nurtured his child. In the asylum hospital, she never deigned to notice her swelling or the birth of the boy. She was officially insane, lecturing the other inmates and shooting them with imaginary guns when they ignored her. She died in 1959, still firing.

JULIAN KAY

Richard Gere in American Gigolo, *1980,
directed by Paul Schrader*

Critics of our educational system would appreciate Julian Kay, if they could stomach the squalid aspects of his success. They say schools are organized stagnation, where inept teachers confront the brutal young with dread and contempt. They say teaching is brainwashing; only learning counts, and in most of our schools those charged with education are indifferent to whether that occurs. And so, the claim goes, a growing body of young waste forms, overcast and unaware, with no role in society except to infect the educated with their resentment.

I don't know the answer. Some say all children should stay at home and learn from their parents. But isn't that a way of ensuring narrowness and the excess of shelter that leaves us tender? What would happen to business if parents were at home, practising cottage instruction? Yet I wonder, if I had had the time, whether I couldn't have kept my children in what I believed. They might have understood me, and Mary Frances, and that might have helped them in the world. As it was, they went out there and they suffered for it. People talk of change, and faster change too, as if to say parents must be resigned to a kind of knowledge redundant to their children. But I read to them, and all their later pain seemed to have the atmosphere of stories.

Julian Kay is a model of self-education, and survival. In all the gallery presented here, I doubt if another person has overcome such handicaps, or made so much of himself. Out of a tangle of grossness, he has grown smooth, acceptable and negotiable. There is already some talk of a political future for him. After all, he is rich, good-looking, well-spoken, and he has come from the world of the misbegotten. He has great appeal to a voter seeking miracles.

He was born in 1951, in an asylum hospital, taken with forceps from the small, irate body of his mother, Norma Desmond, the onetime movie actress. The father was Joe Gillis, a screenwriter who had become Miss Desmond's companion and paramour and then her victim. Even so, the birth certificate says "not known" in the matter of a father. And since the mother was a certified incompetent, Max von Mayerling, one of Miss Desmond's former husbands, was listed as guardian to the infant.

Julian never spoke to or was spoken to by his parents. Max von Mayerling told him that he was an orphan. Norma Desmond was dead by 1959; Max died in 1964, when Julian was thirteen. But Max left a letter of explanation with a lawyer in Santa Monica, to be given to Julian on his twenty-first birthday. That letter was sent to the last known address of Julian Kay; sent and not returned. Only Julian knows whether he saw and understood it, and his face is still lovely and unlined in its public appearances.

Mayerling took a small apartment in Inglewood, and lived there with the child he called Julian Kay. Long before Max's death, Julian had fallen into a pattern of truancy. Whenever Max had an engagement as a magician at a children's party, he would enlist Julian as his assistant. It was Julian he vanished from closed trunks and Julian he sometimes sawed in sections, only for the little boy, in mauve tights, to reappear as whole and bouncy as a rubber ball.

On other days, Julian was inclined to set out for school, then take some wrong turning and head north to explore Los Angeles. At ten and eleven, having purposefully grubbied himself beforehand, he collected quarters whistling up taxis for people outside big hotels. His special charm in this was his line of chatter to the ladies as they waited for the cab. Without ever being dirty, he was a sophisticated urchin, passing on the ornate words and saturnine wisdom he had picked up from Max. One or two of the ladies gave him presents or called him honey. One, on her own, asked him to ride out to Pasadena with her, and on the way she manipulated him and collected his first pearly semen in an Yves St. Laurent scarf. Julian had to walk back from Pasadena, fulfilled, striding on love's air.

Max von Mayerling had a collection of erotica, which he never hid from the boy. The old man would tell Julian stories at night about his own sexual adventures in Vienna, Budapest, Monte Carlo, and so on. He taught Julian French and German; he told him how to play servant or master; he gave him jokes, gestures, tricks and touches. He made an adroit gentleman out of him.

When Max died, Julian arranged the funeral and went on with his life as usual. There were no relatives to rescue him; no inspectors to make sure he was still cared for. He went to school no more often than before. He kept the apartment up, selling some of the more ponderous furniture Max had collected. As for money, he set out to offer himself and a taxi to single ladies. He was a strong youth, and he got a reputation. Women went in search of him.

One day in 1969, he was picked up by Anne Alexander, a resident of Malibu and the impresario for a ring of call girls. She had heard of this taxi stud, and she was impressed by his agility and courtliness in the confines of the cab. She took him home and questioned him about his life. Nearly twenty years his senior, she was more attracted to him than she could understand. Born in France, she was surprised by his fluent French, albeit in a slightly dated idiom that marked Max's days in Paris. Anne told him he was wasting his talent. Taxi trade was bound to be quick and cheap. Once she slept with him in the greater ease of a bed, she added that a cab could not let his range and diversity show. She proposed to manage his career. She would advertise him discreetly, and then send him out on assignments. She would take 20 percent of his earnings, and she would provide a new wardrobe for him. For the next three years they were lovers. On those rare nights when Julian needed anything like a home, he stayed with her in Malibu.

But in 1973, they ended their personal ties and settled for business. Julian had enough money to buy an apartment in Westwood. He branched out, and worked for other agents. His reputation as a hired lover increased. He took on a few missions in New York, and one in Rome. But he preferred L.A. He knew its attitudes and the spiritual bliss in skin and pleasure; and he had the California patter by heart.

Then in 1979, he drove out to the Palm Springs home of a couple named Rheiman. He relaxed the tense wife, and brought her to seven climaxes as her husband watched from behind an ivory-hued net curtain. But Judy Rheiman was found butchered, sexually abused, and Rheiman himself had an impregnable alibi. Just as Julian met Michelle Stratton, lovelorn wife of the California senator, just as he thought of marriage and happiness, he found himself under suspicion of murder.

The stress finished the Stratton marriage: Michelle could only save Julian by giving him an alibi—that they had been together. The scandal raged, but Julian acted like its press spokesman. He never hid or scurried; he let the cameras see his face. He gave short, lucid statements to reporters and he thanked them. By the time he was cleared, he was famous.

He and Michelle married. They live in Laurel Canyon and they run the Kincaid Gallery on Doheny—one of the most reputable purveyors of art objects for the home. They own a restaurant and a small art-movie house, the Dissolve on La Cienega, where they specialize in foreign films and do a Bresson festival every winter. They are a favorite couple around the town, and there is every prospect of their interests and power rising.

> *Is there no sure way of raising our young? Is parenting the tragedy that tears us from our hopes? "I am your father," you nag, talking to yourself.*

WALTER NEFF

Fred MacMurray in Double Indemnity, *1944, directed by Billy Wilder*

He was an easygoing kid, liked by most people, a boy strangers were ready to give a nickel to if he had any small talk. Walter Huff had all kinds of talk, and everyone agreed he would go far. "Out of Moline, anyway," said Walter one day when he was eleven. He spent a lot of his time watching the river's inexhaustible flow southward, imagining the places it led to. He put any bit of wood or paper on the water just to see it being carried away from Moline. He thought of the

Mississippi as a glossy, gray road on which he might glide into his future.

He had been born in Moline in 1901, his father a doctor, his mother a music teacher. She taught him piano, and he took to the banjo and the cornet of his own accord. When he was in his teens he used to go over the river to Davenport where he knew a younger kid, Leon Beiderbecke. They both played cornet, and Leon was the better of the two. But Walter didn't mind that. He learned from the kid, and he got into the habit of slurring notes together. It was lazy but it made the girls look up. Leon called him "Skid" because of it, and the name stuck.

In 1919, he got a job on a riverboat, and after a year he made it all the way to New Orleans. That had been his dream. He listened to all the jazz he could find, and he bummed around when he was out of work. Then, in 1922, he got a job on a liner going around the Caribbean, to Panama, and on to San Francisco. He was a year playing dance music on the boat when he dropped off in Panama for a vacation. Music began to bore him on the boat, and so on a whim in Panama he joined the Army and did a three-year hitch there as a sentry on the Canal.

The very day he got out of the service he met a blonde, Maggie King, a hairdresser on a liner. He showed her around and they got talking so that she missed her boat and moved in with Skid and a pal of his, a piano player named Harry Butterworth. They were soft on each other, and Maggie told Skid he should work as a musician again. She said she was a singer and that encouraged him. And she had a fair voice, soft and clear, but sultry. Together they got work at Murphy's, the best club in Panama, and they did a number together that was a sensation, she standing inside the curl of his arm, singing to his muted accompaniment.

They got married, and most of 1928 was as good as it gets. But Skid caught fire with happiness: agents from New York came down to check on him, and other women kept after him. There was a dancer at Murphy's, Anita Alvarez, who was hot for him, and first she took a New York offer and then six weeks later Skid got the call. It was what Maggie wanted for him, and they agreed that he could save money until they had enough for her passage.

It was a reasonable plan, but there are marriages that may need the remoteness of a Panama. Skid was a hit in the city. Everyone wanted to buy him a drink, and Anita slid into the empty place in his arm. Maggie came to New York on her own money, and she found that

Alvarez answered Skid's phone. They broke up. Once they got back together for a radio show, when Skid's lip was going—he had given up practising. They did their old number that once, and it was a heartbreaker, but Skid kept slipping. By 1932 he was on the street, selling pretzels.

Then, instead of folding up, Walter Huff realized that he was back where he started—no worse than that. His ease returned. He hitched west, and as he went he read a book about insurance. It seemed like a snap, and he knew he was good with people. So he went all the way to California, to Los Angeles, and the General Fidelity offices with Keyes, head of the claims department.

"You look used up," said Keyes.

"Yeah, but I'm resilient," Walter told him.

"What's your name?"

"Huff. Walter Huff."

"Huff? That's no kind of a name."

"No one told me."

"Makes people think you're in a bad mood."

"But I come as a pleasant surprise."

"Have to change it."

"Do I get the job?"

"Who do you want to be?"

"I kinda like the two *f*'s."

"I can see you might. Griffith?"

"That's a park. Cuff?"

"Could be ragged. Neff?"

"You got it."

"No, you've got it."

Keyes could tell he could talk, and he liked his quick grin—it was amiable, but it knew insurance was a play on weak nerves. Walter Neff was hired, and he worked hard to please Keyes. The two men never had a conversation when they weren't telling each other off, but they took it for granted they were friends and the point didn't need to be stated directly. Walter got in the habit of having vestas for Keyes's pipe whenever he seemed to have mislaid his. Walter rented a little bungalow in the Los Feliz hills.

It was February 1935 when he drove over to the Spanish-style house in Hollywoodland about a renewal and met Phyllis Diedrichson. She was wearing blue pajamas, and she kept him talking. She asked if Walter handled accident insurance, too—her husband was at the office—and that's when Walter started to get the chills from her

91

sidelong look. That was the start. Walter was always impressionable, and Phyllis Diedrichson got to him in ten minutes.

They fell into this torrid affair. Walter set up life insurance for the husband, with a double indemnity—twice the coverage if the death was by accident—and Phyllis knew already how it was going to be accidental. The husband signed it one night with a mass of papers. And they killed him; Walter was in the back of the car and he broke the guy's neck. Walter, a gentle man, agreeable too: that was the measure of Phyllis Diedrichson and what she could make you imagine.

Walter got on the train to San Francisco, pretending to be Diedrichson. Then he jumped off the train, and together they put the body on the tracks, as if the man had had a drink or two and fallen off the observation platform. It worked out fine, and General Fidelity was set to pay up. But Keyes knew it smelled wrong. He asked Walter what he thought, and Walter had to give back his ordinary professional skepticism. "Could be," he said.

Keyes worked it out. But Walter was shuffling snakes by then: that was Phyllis for you. He got scared of her, and he fell for Lola, Diedrichson's daughter. Then there was Lola's Italian boyfriend. Then there was the rendezvous in Griffith Park, and Walter picking up a bullet. He'd meant to get rid of Phyllis, but he'd never thought that you could spell Phyllis with two f's.

Walter spilled the whole story to Keyes. He assumed that he and Phyllis were set for the death house. But General Fidelity was cautious. They didn't like the idea of double indemnities getting so much publicity, so they let the two killers go. But they got them tickets on the same boat, going to Mexico. And Walter and Phyllis met on the deck, and it wasn't so romantic. For the first time in his life, Walter felt ruin. Phyllis was full of death, the same as always. They heard there was a shark following the boat and they waited till they saw its fin in the moonlight and they went over the side. With Walter's unhealed wound bleeding. Begging the shark to hurry.

PHYLLIS DIEDRICHSON

Barbara Stanwyck in Double Indemnity, 1944,
directed by Billy Wilder

I cannot better the last paragraph of Diane Johnson's fascinating
Phyllis (Knopf, 1983), an investigation carried out nearly fifty years
after the event, in which the author was regularly waylaid by
intimations of hitherto unheard-of iniquity. The paragraph in question concludes a postscript in which Ms. Johnson reports the discovery that a Phyllis Nirdlinger was registered at the St. Francis
Hotel, in San Francisco, over the Labor Day weekend of 1921—the
time and place of the prolonged party which brought about the death
of Virginia Rappe, and the downfall of silent clown Fatty Arbuckle.
This knowledge came in an anonymous letter delivered while Ms.
Johnson was correcting the proofs of *Phyllis*, but when there was still
time to give her book a last, prescient shadow:

"So we are supposed to believe that Phyllis slipped over the side of a
steamer bound from San Pedro to Balboa—this ship was called the
Miranda—fifty miles or so off Quinones. It would be comfortable to
think so. But isn't it more likely that that was the legend Phyllis
wished to establish before she started up as someone else? She was a
thirty-two-year-old mass murderess, in her prime. What reason is
there to take her sudden remorse and its impetuous suicide on trust?
Isn't it more credible that she let Walter Neff go first and then turned
away to a new alias and a fresh man already scouted out? She would be
eighty now, a little deaf, perhaps forgetful, but hardly less than
dangerous. Even allow that she took to the water, had she forgotten
how to swim? The suggestion is that a shark claimed her and the
already wounded Walter. I prefer to pity the fish."

The woman who officially met this watery death was Mrs. Phyllis
Diedrichson, widow and co-slayer of her husband, H. S. Diedrichson.
She was on the *Miranda* with Walter Neff, after they had both been
trapped in an investigation spearheaded by Wilson Keyes of General
Fidelity's Los Angeles office.

His report described how, in 1929, Phyllis Nirdlinger was hired as
assistant head nurse at Dr. Bruno Sachetti's Verdugo Hills
Sanatorium. Her credentials were borne out by scrupulous attention
to duties. No wonder, then, in 1930, when the head nurse died in an

automobile accident—a vacation mishap, in Salt Lake City, so for once Phyllis cannot be implicated—that she was promoted.

However, in the years 1930 to 1932 there were five deaths at the sanatorium in which Phyllis did appear to have had a part. All five involved elderly victims of pneumonia. Re-investigation traced the hand of the head nurse in every case, and disclosed the modest but touching legacies that went to her from two of the deceased. Of course, people die in clinics and hospitals, and head nurses have the authority of good first officers on ships with captains looking forward to retirement. Too many patients in sanatoriums have no relatives to ask awkward questions or act as likely heirs.

Dr. Sachetti was neither lazy nor inept. He had an excellent reputation, but it was shattered in 1933 when three children died of pneumonia in one week. In hindsight, we must conclude grimly that two of those deaths—Georgie Trescher and Cara Chacon—were extras to aid the impression of an epidemic, and to crowd the death of Dickie Graff, only four, whose one living relative was a Mrs. Lita Diedrichson. It speaks to the cunning of Phyllis that this Mrs. Diedrichson was so won over by the head nurse at Verdugo Hills that the two struck up a friendship.

The sanatorium had to close: child mortality knows no public relations. Phyllis Nirdlinger looked around for a new position and spent time with Lita and H. S. Diedrichson. The strain had been too much. The two ladies became so close that they went off to Lake Arrowhead in December 1933 for a vacation to plan the coming Christmas break. It was an early and severe winter at Lake Arrowhead. Lita, already suffering from lung trouble, caught cold in the high chilled air. Phyllis Nirdlinger went for help, but she took the long way, trudging twelve miles through snow around the lake. Locals wondered why she had not gone the mile and a half on the ice over the lake. It was strong enough to support a truck. But Phyllis said she had not known the ice was thick enough; she had meant to be safe rather than sorry. Yet she had to be both: Lita Diedrichson was found dead by the rescue party.

Christmas was a mourning feast, and Phyllis was the natural comforter for H.S. when he collapsed. Used to being looked after and having a comfortable home, Diedrichson proposed to Phyllis in April 1934. The former head nurse accepted, less for herself, she said, than for Lola, Lita's daughter, so much in need of a mother figure. And so Phyllis Nirdlinger changed her name and moved into the house clinging to the steep hillside beneath the Hollywoodland sign. She may not have been sure what she was waiting for, but Walter Neff decided her.

Because there was no trial, no one bothered about the facts of Phyllis Nirdlinger's life before 1929. Not until Diane Johnson undertook her research. She established that Phyllis Nirdlinger was born in Anaheim in 1903, the child of a German manufacturer of ice skates and an American, Anne Belden, who had been a high-school swimming champion. Kurt Nirdlinger died when Phyllis was eleven—of a fit of coughing brought on when a cod bone caught in his throat. Nothing Phyllis had done in the way of offering him bread to chew had averted the tragedy. The mother was away that day, swimming across San Pedro Bay to raise money for the Belgian atrocity victims.

Phyllis herself was such a swimmer that she became a member of the Mack Sennett Bathing Beauties. It was there she befriended Norma Desmond and Mabel Normand. Dry, too, in one or two one-reelers, Phyllis took on the roles of confidante and cocaine supplier to Miss Desmond. The details are still clouded, but the persevering Diane Johnson has made it clear that the long-held belief in Mabel Normand's part in the death of director William Desmond Taylor in 1922 might be opened up to include Phyllis Nirdlinger. Phyllis was a demure drug connection for the film community, an active agent in the decline of Taylor, and the last person known to have been with him at 404½ Alvarado Street, where he was found shot to death.

The case was confused. At Taylor's funeral, another movie queen, Mary Miles Minter, declared undying love for him. And Ms. Minter is alive still, a recluse, eighty-one or so as I write.

> *I can understand the wish to solve these old mysteries. Over the years, I have lain awake, a supine detective, sorting through the details. It is so like the approach of a killer planning a crime. But then Mary Miles died yesterday, fat and afraid, I hear, to leave her house. Now there is only the picture of her youth left, as white and frilled as a flower, and forever transient.*

WILSON KEYES

Edward G. Robinson in Double Indemnity, *1944,
directed by Billy Wilder*

In 1981 in Omaha there was a retrospective of the paintings of Wilson Keyes. It brought satisfaction to those who remembered him. The catalogue with the exhibit spoke of "this unhindered naive, a primitive from the American heartland who had a career of order and prosperity, except for one disaster and the passion evident in these pictures."

Odd to think of WK as a naive: he was our model of common sense and the deductive process. Harder still to call him primitive: none of us ever saw a discourteous act, or heard a reckless expression. In Omaha, he was regarded as sophisticated, as clever as anyone we had. But I suppose that's what the writer meant. There was something he could never let us see, nothing ugly, but an eye for danger. It's there in the portraits of women, wild smiles resting on folded, blatant legs; California houses with fire-colored roofs and snake-green cypress trees; and the drawings done at Belsen. It's there in the colors, blues that never dry, bloody skies and screaming yellows; and in the signature on all the canvases, the *X*, a flourish like crossed swords.

Keyes was born in Omaha, Nebraska, in 1890, one of five children, the son of the city's civil engineer. Young Wilson excelled in math and science at school, and from the age of ten he was helping his father in the execution of technical drawings. Indeed, Arthur Keyes's classic *The Building of Bridges* (University of Nebraska Press, 1905) contains a note of thanks to "my son, Wilson . . . for his splendid illustrations." In 1908, Wilson Keyes entered the university to study mathematics. He also involved himself in student dramatics, executing backdrops for *The Way of the World* (a production banned by the authorities after its bawdy opening—and still a legend twenty years later).

He graduated in 1912 and was sent to Stanford by his proud father to study business. With what seemed to everyone an equable temperament, Wilson Keyes adapted to his first experiences of California and maintained his high academic standards—but for the spring of 1913, when he suffered a breakdown of indeterminate nature. However, his recovery was as thorough and convincing as all of his performances, and no one had reason to worry about him. "All the worry goes inside with Nebraskans," as my father used to say. "Goes inside and builds, like a twister with no way out." I have seen Mary Frances, standing straight and thin against the sky, just leaning perhaps, and known she was curled and tortured, unable to cry out.

Keyes took his Master's at Stanford in the summer of 1915, by which time he had had several offers from San Francisco businesses. Instead, he took a trip to Paris. It was true to his sensible nature to admit the need for some relaxation, and a part of his conscientiousness to want to visit a city whose treasures were threatened by war. During the fall of 1915, Keyes explored the museums and galleries of the city, while renting a small room in Montmartre close to the Moulin de la Galette. He saw wonders and wounded soldiers, but Bonnard was his greatest discovery.

Not long after he returned to America, Keyes enlisted in the army, and in May 1916 he was commissioned as a lieutenant. Fourteen months later Keyes was in France, a captain. For five months he was in the front lines, playing a prominent part in the design and construction of trenches. The American claim to have drainage superior to that of the French or the British owed much to the resourcefulness of Wilson Keyes. Lives must have been saved in that more hospitable dryness. Elsewhere, some drowned in mud. They are still digging up skulls and bullets.

From 1919 to 1923, Keyes was restored to Nebraska, and to the university, where he taught Introduction to Business, Insurance and Actuarial Theory. He made some of those courses into institutions. Though his time at Lincoln was short, his influence there both as teacher and as friend to those not much younger was considerable. He was loved there, and it was hurtful when he moved away, to Los Angeles, to take up a position in the General Fidelity Insurance Company. People couldn't understand how he was not satisfied by teaching.

He served General Fidelity until 1940, becoming head of the claims department, famous for his instinct in detecting frauds. The Diedrichson case may have been his most secret success, for General Fidelity chose not to take legal action. It may also have been a crisis in Keyes's own life.

He was forty-five, he had been married ten years, he had a home in Glendale and two children. All seemed settled and normal. His co-workers assumed he was content. But Keyes worked hard. He had too little time for his family or his hobby of painting. Moreover, the realization that his trust in Walter Neff had been misplaced was a greater blow than Keyes ever indicated. Perhaps the last angry words of Phyllis Diedrichson lodged in his excellent memory and turned bad there:

"So what's in it for you, Mr. Keyes? You're not an empty man. You're not a machine. You go pale when I attack you. Your damned pipe goes out, and your mouth clamps down on it. So you caught our trick. You saved General Fidelity money. Does that satisfy you? Or tell me, Wilson Keyes, do you sometimes wonder what it's like to step out of line, to give up the rules for someone like me? Don't you wonder, Keyes, you liar? Know how you're a liar? Because you've such a busy little imagination locked in your briefcase. And someday it'll have to come out. Or kill you."

In 1940, Keyes was fifty. He had served his country well. Yet he heeded the invitation from Washington to serve again. Going east ended his marriage, but Wilson Keyes accepted a post in the secret service. He had an aptitude for decoding and his old skill as a detective. By 1944, he was attached to that section of the service tracing war criminals. He was in Europe late that year, and present at the liberation of Belsen in 1945. Keyes did not return to America until 1947, so extensive was his work for the Nuremberg trials.

It was no easy retirement. He came back a roundabout way, chasing Franz Kindler, one of the more brilliant of Hitler's young disciples. Under the name Charles Rankin, Kindler had begun a new life at Harper College in Connecticut where he was masquerading as a teacher and had married the daughter of Judge Philip Longstreet. Keyes was dogged in unearthing Rankin's true identity and in saving his new wife, Mary. Rankin/Kindler died, falling from the tower of the town church, and Keyes's mission was concluded.

Nearing sixty now, divorced in 1945, Keyes found that General Fidelity had no more use for him. A new generation had risen to power. And so he went to New York with a small government pension. He found work as a cashier, and he was picked up by a widow. Remarried, humiliated in his job, he resumed painting: his smothered life spilled out on the canvases.

Then, in 1950, he fell in with a floozy, Kitty Bennett, the kind of woman the insurance investigator had once recognized in an instant. He embezzled for her, he gave up everything for a night or so, and then he learned she was betraying him with her pimp. He painted her and killed her. Yet the pimp was executed, and Keyes became a derelict. He died on the Bowery in 1953, the first year in which his paintings began to climb in value. Today, a good Keyes—of Kitty or Phyllis, lounging in exultant carelessness—can sell for fifty thousand dollars.

DEBBY MARSH

Gloria Grahame in The Big Heat, *1953,
directed by Fritz Lang*

Kenport was the only world Debby Marsh knew. It was like so many of the cities in Ohio—dark gray in winter, pale gray in summer, solid by day, glamorous at night. Then the windows in the tower buildings could sparkle; the streets had a rosy wash, with traffic lights going red and green at every intersection. The night sky was an old mauve cloth draped over the buildings. In the dark, the towers and the streets seemed illusory. You did not have to feel the layer of scum waiting on every touch; you could believe the city was a creature from the lake, still damp and alive. Debby preferred the romance of the night, and she settled for it whenever she could, along with several other lies and half-truths.

She was born in the city in 1930, in the Woodland section. That was a joke, because there were no trees, just block after block of housing for the workers in the auto industry. Debby's father was a fitter and there were six children in the three-bedroom house, built to one of the two patterns available in Woodland—the two- and the three-bedroom units. There were houses where couples lived, without kids, who had a spare room and no use for it. And others where three kids had to share one room, growing up without privacy. Debby pretended to be sick a lot, so she could have days at home and be alone in the room, dreaming in the quiet and the space. Neither her parents nor the school took the illnesses or the truancy it veiled seriously. There wasn't time, or the hope. In the thirties, her father was out of work a lot, waiting around the house, getting drunk. To Debby's mind, it just showed you that people couldn't get along without money. Didn't it follow that they'd manage better with more money?

Then, in the war, Kenport grew rich again. There were military contracts. The factories needed more men, and as the city became more popular there were new, cheap apartment buildings out beyond

Woodland. They went up so fast that one of them fell down. So they built it back up again. The feeling of war brought energy back. A lot of gangsters came into the city. They seemed to have a great life, going out every night, eating at the Lakeside Manor, having cars in pretty colors. The women with them wore fur coats, even on warm nights. Debby liked to be out at night to watch them all go by.

That's how she got to know them. One night in 1948, outside the Blue Gardenia, a nightclub on Wisconsin Avenue, she talked to a group of them. There was one called Vince. He had a girl with him, but he just let go of her, and came over to Debby and asked how old she was. She lied, and he grinned. He gave her a pair of nylons right there on the street, and asked her if she knew how to put them on. Then he pinched her cheek, real hard, and went on into the Gardenia. The woman who'd been with him looked at Debby as if she were a rainy day.

His name was Vince Stone, and he worked for Mike Lagana, one of the most important people in Kenport. Vince took Debby over. He bought her new clothes and sent her to a hairdresser's where they made her look older. He took it for granted she was moving into his apartment, and he fucked her all the time like she was a heavy box he was moving upstairs. It was all right. Her mother had told her to expect this, and the clothes were more than she could have dreamed of.

One night Vince told her to go over to Lagana's house.

"What for?"

"Whatever he wants."

"What does that mean?"

"I don't know. Go on. Hurry."

So she went over to the house, and Lagana introduced her to his mother—who only spoke Italian—and then he took her upstairs and made love to her. "Very nice," he said. "Really quite nice." And he told her if she ever wanted a little more just to give him a call. When she got back, Vince beat her up, as if he'd never guessed. So the next day she called Lagana, but he reminded her that he was very fond of Vince and couldn't take her away. Loyalty was everything.

It could have been worse. Vince hit her some, and he had these foul tempers when he'd curse Lagana—until Mr. Mike phoned, and then he was sweetness, which was not pleasant in Vince. Debby shopped a lot. Sometimes she got to go to Chicago on business, and stay in the hotels. She preferred that: it was nice to stay in, order up cocktails and pastries, instead of having to cook, or go out the way they always did.

She got her mink, though, and she liked to snuggle in it. Vince liked her best naked beneath the coat, so she had a struggle watching it didn't get torn or stained.

Then all you heard from Vince was Bannion, some detective who was trying to shake up the world. It had to do with Tom Duncan's suicide, and how Bannion kept pestering the widow because maybe there was more to it. Then Bannion's wife got blown up in the family car. Debby ignored things like that. It was the only way.

But one night in the Retreat, Bannion was there when Vince put his cigarette out on the hand of the girl who was shaking dice at the bar. Bannion took her side and Vince backed down like a coward. He left the Retreat without Debby and on the spur of the moment she offered to buy Bannion a drink. But he said not on Vince Stone's money, and that stung. Debby never liked to realize none of the money was hers. So she went after Bannion, to be friendly. She knew straightaway she'd got to him. Because he stopped and grinned, a guilty grin. Why? His wife was dead, wasn't she?

They went back to his hotel, and Debby sat on the bed in case he was shy. But all he did was give her a drink and ask questions. So after a while she called it a night and returned to Vince's place.

He was there playing cards with a gang, including Higgins the police commissioner. She had blown him one night out of boredom. But Vince came after her about her being friendly with Bannion, and before she knew it he picks up a pot and throws scalding coffee in her face.

Higgins took her to the hospital. The doctors gave her something for the pain, but they said it would get worse. What about the scars? she asked. Some, they said, but not bad, and plastic surgery would handle it. So they put a bandage on half her face and the neck, which looked cool. So she went back to Bannion's hotel, since she'd got it for him. The two things throbbing in her mind were dread of the damage in her own face and desire for Bannion.

The detective took her in, and got another room in the hotel for her. So much for the allure of half a face! He talked about the case, how he'd realized that Duncan's widow had her husband's last letter—the dirt on Lagana—and how she had it in a safe deposit, where it stayed as long as she was alive, getting $500 a month from Mr. Mike.

Debby worked it all out. She took the gun Bannion had left her as protection. She went over to the Duncan house. Mrs. Duncan was about to go shopping. She was wearing a fur coat just like Debby's—"We're sisters under the mink, Bertha." Debby liked that line and then she shot Bertha. She went back to Vince's place and put a pot of coffee on. By the time he got back she had watched two pots boil away. But the third was ready to go. It slapped him in his ugly face, and he screamed. She had never known him so moved.

She told him about Bertha being dead, about how the heat was going to start. And he took out his gun and shot her. It surprised her. She reckoned that he would only whine and collapse. There had always been something more to Vince. Hadn't he noticed her and liked her on the silky street?

HARRY LIME

Orson Welles in The Third Man, *1949,
directed by Carol Reed*

For someone shot in a sewer, there has been such romancing of Harry Lime. I can never hear the name without thinking of that caustic compound in which English domestic murderers reckoned to have corpses devoured. But if you look at the Harry Lime stories—in their magazine originals, or in the long-running television series —why, Rollo Martins, their author, has made our urbane Lime out of the green fruit.

In fiction, he is tart but refreshing. Whereas, in life, he was poison. How are such tricks worked? It must be that we are fascinated by evil. The most horrible thing is how the world has turned out so close to Harry's cynicism about the ghost of decency having been given up some time ago. "In these days, old man, nobody thinks in terms of human beings." Always with an "old man," the lie in his own bland council. Maybe Harry wanted to think he was lying, so he pushed that fake bonhomie into every other sentence.

He was born in Balham in 1916, the only child of Constance Lime, the widow of George Lime, killed on the first day of the Somme, twelve weeks earlier. George was a subaltern from a well-to-do Streatham family that owned a number of electrical shops in South London. Married in 1914, George and Constance had been able to buy a small house in Balham thanks to money from his father. When George died, the Limes assumed that Constance and the child would move into the large house on Tooting Bec Common. But Constance was the daughter of a bus inspector from Brixton, convinced she would be uncomfortable in the big house with people whose distaste for her was allied to the condescension that falls on poor relatives. With a friend, she opened a ladies' hairdressing shop, Conita, at the top of Brixton Hill, and made a go of it.

It was a brave stand, by a cheerful young woman, so brisk at business that she was able to send Harry to Dulwich College in 1927. Some sons would have been proud. But Harry tended to side with his grandparents in thinking that a mistake had been made. He preferred the large house, the maid who brought him tea and the chauffeur outside the college in the afternoon to run him back to Streatham. He deferred to his grandmother, a petite snob with only three fingers on one of her hands, abhorred by his mother and cold to the child, but a model of odd learning, superior diction and polite sarcasm. Although a small woman, she did everything as if from a height.

Harry and his grandmother played a game in his childhood with a large collection of toy soldiers. It had belonged to his father, and his grandmother had kept it when George grew up. With Harry, she restaged the battles of Marlborough and Wellington. They deployed troops on the Persian carpets, and Harry marveled at how she would tip over the killed lead creatures with the cane she carried. Conferring death seemed so easy. Harry was left to guess how the Battle of the Somme had been managed.

He had too little of his mother's energy, and too much of his own cunning to need it. At school he got by, cheating or stealing others' knowledge, so glib in class it was hard for many masters to recognize his ignorance. He disdained his mother's shop; at least until he was fourteen, when he suddenly seemed to appreciate the bantering girls his mother employed who were always comparing themselves to pictures of Myrna Loy or Constance Bennett. Often with them, he put on fatherly airs, and talked to impress them.

Harry's strength at Dulwich was in theater. He seemed to lose his puppy fat on stage; he came to life, and gave his voice a walnut resonance. In truth, it was a very mannered way of speaking, as if his mother had tried to imitate his grandmother. But it carried in a theater; its bogusness seemed mellifluous. He played Romeo (with Rollo Martins, a pet crony, as his Juliet), the Chorus in *Henry V* and, in his last year at school, a Falstaff who seemed to have the genuine dropsy of alcoholic old age. Never quite a child, Harry was fascinated by the elderly; at the time no one realized how far this bred in him a premature insight into death and decay.

At eighteen, he was a hypnotic hulk: his charm matched his size. He was flat-footed and clumsy physically, but a hummingbird in chat and badinage. He liked to hide the one with the other, so he was often at Conita after school, slumped in a velvet-covered armchair, flirting with the girls or the customers in that languid, elaborate way of his that thrilled anyone with an insecure education.

His grandparents said he could go to Oxford. But armchair talk had made him lazy, and he needed underlings, people easily impressed with him. So he hung around the area and got a job as a salesman for H. O. Motors. He was very winning. He could rattle off a fine line of pastiche poetry about the cars, while his pinched breathless girth was a subtle suggestion that all movement should be by way of limousine.

This was 1935. Harry got a reputation in South London. He became a wrestling impresario—he discovered and promoted "Man-Mountain" Dean. He had a hand in the automobile business and he advised his mother and several other people in hairdressing. The police kept an eye on him, and Harry watched their attention with a mixture of pride and wonder just as, when on the stage, he had paused in a speech and felt suspense and need in the audience running like lucre into the palm of his hand. He knew some bad elements: he mixed with the Elephant & Castle gang, and he was on drinking terms with Moseley's assistant, Hamm. He was what was known as a "wide boy," and no one was a more amused model for the term, opening his fine coats to show that stretch of white shirt. He dressed fastidiously, and he usually had some dolled-up sharpie on his arm, a working girl to whom he was giving his quick shampoo-and-set Svengali act.

It was the war that Harry had been waiting for. He did fire-watch duty and he started up a salvage business during the Blitz that made him £100,000 in one year. It was not pretty: he and his gang cleaned out bombed houses for the survivors or the faraway relatives. He had an estate agency as a sideline, buying wrecked sites and reselling them. He learned fast and he knew as much about shattered structures as anyone around.

The London papers got on to him. He was attacked. And then, in a disarming gesture, he formed the International Refugee Office. It was a private organization, but it had several illustrious patrons on the letterhead—the Duke of Abercorn, Bud Flanagan, Roland Northover. It became an ideal way of absorbing money from the other businesses and it allowed Harry to present himself as a Santa Claus for bombsites and broken lives.

He became an international figure. For much of 1944, he was in

America, speaking about the plight of refugees, filling large halls with his orotund voice, moved by suffering he had never seen. I heard him speak in Omaha, and he spent a weekend with us, in the course of which he tempted my wife into a reading of part of *The Country Wife* that was too much for her. He had been traveling, and he was worn down, as lean and urgent as a tightrope. He was always watching her with his soulful eyes, and Mary Frances was flustered the whole weekend. "What an actress!" Lime said to me. "How can you ever trust her?" You can want to kill a man on Saturday, and be beaten down by Sunday, overcome by his awfulness, aware that you are not what killers are made of, not yet.

Harry Lime went to Europe in 1945. He was in Vienna soon after it was relieved, setting up his International Refugee Office. It was a tidy front for his rackets, the most lucrative of which involved medicines. He invited Rollo Martins over—it was Rollo who had done the press pieces on Harry when the IRO was formed, "little bits of rehabilitation," Harry called them. Now he wanted Rollo again, to polish up his image. But the police were on to him and Harry faked his own death. Only for the foolish Martins to appoint himself detective. It all came out, and Harry died in the sewers, larger than ever in a winter coat, sunk in the dark flow of sewage.

I nearly told Mary Frances, to reassure her. But she could have thought I did it.

KAY CORLEONE

Diane Keaton in The Godfather, 1971,
directed by Francis Ford Coppola; and in The Godfather Part II, *1974,
directed by Coppola*

A wife in the Corleone family had tasks and duties: to be available for her husband's lovemaking and to bear children; to suckle these children in plain view of the family so as to foster the fullest reverence for motherhood; and then to pass the care of the young children to nurses and maids, but to be an ultimate court of appeal and a source of intimate advice for the children; to lead visits to church, and to ensure that the children were nicely dressed and making progress toward first communion; to deal with the cooks in the choice and preparation of

He had a dark aura

family meals; to know the names of retainers and associates and greet them warmly; to shop and look decent; and to know when to speak and when to leave the room. In return for an exact performance of this role, the wife and mother received the unstinting adoration of all the men in the family. She should never remark on the inadequacy of the arrangement; she should not get drunk or curse in public; she should have no affairs; she should not have a loose tongue or inquisitive ears; she should never question her man; she should accept adoration modestly and wear dark and plain colors. And be above suspicion, like Don Vito's wife.

Kay Adams was born in Concord, New Hampshire, in 1921. Her father, Lawrence, was a lawyer; it was a family of four children, all close in age, in their quarrels and their firm affection. In the long winters they skated and tobogganed, and in the spring Kay developed as a track athlete. She was state champion at 220 yards in 1938, and there was some talk in the *Monitor* about her as an Olympic prospect. But no one knew then that there would be no more Olympiads for ten years.

She entered the University of New Hampshire at Durham in the fall of 1940, at which time she wanted to study law and then perhaps join her father in his practice. But in February 1941, she went up to Dartmouth with a gang of UNH girls for the Winter Carnival. During that weekend of parties she first met Michael Corleone, a pale-faced boy with eyes like black olives, a senior majoring in classics, yet seeming younger than she was. He was so hesitant Kay noticed her own moderate voice dropping to a hush when she talked to him. He had a dark aura that enchanted her. She fell in love with him in a quarter of an hour.

He graduated that spring, and went back to his home in Long Beach, Long Island. But they corresponded, he in his beautiful black script, she in her sprinting hand. He wrote to her in grave sentiments, and she answered as fittingly as she could. She feared that a real declaration of her feelings would have alarmed him. So she curbed her passion, and made herself a cheery girl, full of fun and optimism. From the outset she felt herself responding to him, never taking a lead.

In the summer of 1942, he took her on a trip to Nantucket, telling her he was going to join the army. He added that he loved her, and wanted to tell her as much. Kay was sure he would ask her to sleep with him; she was eager to be asked. But they only held hands and kissed. She noticed how cool his hands stayed and she wept in the

106

certainty that someone so meek would be killed in the war.

But he came back a hero, returning in time to attend her graduation at Durham in 1945—not late despite an illness the doctors could not specify, but which she knew was Michael's absence. They spent that summer together here and there, and in August Michael took her to the Corleone house for the marriage of his sister, Connie, to Carlo Rizzi. Kay understood they were in the olive-oil and groceries business. She was amazed by the scale of the wedding, and the old-fashioned affluence in the house.

Michael was changed. Still slight and reticent, when he did speak there was a new assurance, nearly an insolence. It was as if in disproving fear he had gained an edge of arrogance. This was there when he told her how his father had once freed Johnny Fontane from a contract—asking the bandleader for his signature or his brains on the legal document—so that she could not tell whether he was boasting or joking with her. But Michael introduced her to his parents in a formal way that bespoke his intentions. She was made welcome. Don Vito took her for a stroll on the beach the next day to ascertain she was not Catholic, but would convert. "Oh yes, of course," she said, wondering at her own hurry, knowing once and for all that she was a godless slut.

Then Michael's father was shot in the street: she had always hated New York. A little while later there were stories in the papers that Michael had avenged Don Vito, killing men called Sollozzo and McCluskey. Then there was no word of him. She went to the Long Beach house, and it was a grove of men in dark coats just hanging around. Tom Hagen, Michael's adopted brother, said he couldn't tell her where Michael was or whether he was alive. The only smile on his face was one of irrelevant, distant kindness.

Kay went back to New Hampshire and she taught school in Concord for two years. Then one day, as she was walking some of her children home, a black limousine stopped and a man in a black coat and a black Homburg got out. It was Michael, and he asked her to marry him.

He told her he had been away, but it was safe and necessary now to be back. She asked him about the killings. He said he would tell her one thing, one thing only, and then she was not to raise such matters again. Yes, he had killed them: he was proud to say as much about anyone who meant harm to his father. Would she marry him?

They were married in 1948, and their son Anthony was born ten months later, in 1949. Kay had never seen such contentment in Michael's eyes. They had another child, a daughter, two years later.

Kay had whatever she wanted. The wealth so hurt her New England soul that she taught herself never to want, like a visitor to Arab countries. She had a driver for trips to Manhattan, but she saw how she was never free. Michael had quietly discouraged all her old friends; and there were more men to make up for it; and the family, so often gabbing in Italian. She tried to learn the language, but Michael told her, "Kay, I don't want you ever to talk in Italian." So he whispered Italian to Anthony, like a hot, private joke.

She learned the family business, and realized that the houses—on Long Island, and then at Lake Tahoe—were havens that held her in the same mud, fed by corpses. The children were never close enough to her. All those intermediaries had bred a cold in Anthony such as she had felt early in Michael. There was nothing to do but brood. When she got pregnant again, she managed her own abortion—so badly that she could have no more children.

Michael was solicitous, like a medieval envoy. She knew as he bent over her in bed that she would have to tell him about the abortion. She reckoned he would likely kill her; or have her killed—he would stay impersonal. But he was crueller. He sent her away, keeping the children for himself. It was only later that her father explained how, technically, she had deserted him. Refusing a divorce, Michael could probably keep the children.

That was in 1960. For over a year Kay drank. Michael sent her money to live, but not enough to come to Tahoe more than twice a year to see the children. On every visit, Anthony was grimmer toward her. She thought of killing herself; she would never throw off Michael's baleful authority otherwise.

Then, in 1962, she was visited in her small New York apartment by George Locke. He was retired, he said, acting for friends. He seemed to know so much about the Corleones already. It was he who told Kay that Michael had been married once before, to a Sicilian girl, in the years he was away. She had been blown up in their car. Locke asked Kay how she felt about her children. Had she thought of seeking custody?

She said she had been told it was useless. Yet, their father's character was such that . . . who knows? said Locke. He went away, but he came back often. He let her guess that he was acting for the Justice Department, for Robert Kennedy. Would Mrs. Corleone sue for custody? For divorce? Her chances might be good, even in Nevada, if she could make the character of her husband an issue. What did she know? The administration was ready to help in any way, provide every protection, if only Michael Corleone might be nailed. What did she know?

So little, Kay cried. Michael had things done, at second or third hand. Locke told her they were certain he had had Hyman Roth shot. She told him that she was sure Fredo had not drowned in the lake. Kay searched her memory: it was like going through analysis. She laughed out loud when she remembered, Michael had owned up to killing Sollozzo and McCluskey. It might be enough, said Locke.

The hearings were eventually set for December 1963: Michael's lawyers managed so many delays. But before then John Kennedy was shot in Dallas. Locke came to her and explained Robert's distress and his suspicion that organized crime had been behind the assassination. "Going on will be harder," he advised. "The attorney general is not sure of his position. After all, we do not count on winning in Nevada. It is the appeals process that interests us. But now . . . we have to consider the danger, and the ordeal, for you." Kay looked at his kind eyes but knew such prospects were hers alone, like her thoughts of the children.

She went to live at a military establishment. She was escorted to Nevada, in and out of the courtroom. Michael's lawyers assailed her time and again, but charges were made in court and newspaper coverage spread as the media realized what was happening. The court awarded Michael custody. But he was already fearful of the appeals process and his lawyers met Kay's to propose a compromise—Anthony, now fifteen, should live with her half the year, and the daughter the other six months, her settlement to be generous.

Locke was very tactful. This proposal was in her best interests, he said. Fight on, and she might get far less. Stop the fight and Michael Corleone would escape the larger charges. He supported Kay's wish to accept the compromise without disappointment.

And so, in the fall of 1964, Anthony came to live with Kay. She was surprised that he was friendly, so devoid of bitterness. In the last two years, he had grown more antagonistic, but now he was sweet, obliging and considerate. At Christmas, he had his bodyguard rape his mother, saying she was a disgrace, not fit for the family. Then he told the man to beat her.

She woke up the next day, sure Anthony would be gone. But he brought her breakfast, and chatted with her, until he had her raped once more. He would not do it himself, but saw the rarer disdain in watching it performed. Kay began to drink again and died in June 1965, at which time Anthony told the press he was indeed grateful for the belated opportunity to get to know his mother. Then he closed up the apartment and went back to Tahoe.

SKIP McCOY

Richard Widmark in Pickup on South Street, *1953, directed by Samuel Fuller*

There she was, her face twelve inches away from his, their bodies bumping and swaying together, all those little enforced touchings —total strangers, so strange they didn't even need to talk or admit they had noticed each other. Touching, but not noticing, it was what he liked about city life and subway work.

There she was, this dame, this broad, in a white sleeveless dress. He could smell the cheap powder under her arms and see the stubble of black hair there, shaved in a hurry a day, two days ago. Her hair grew quickly. He could feel it stirring when he let the car's curve take him into her thigh. Her dress was made there so that it had a flap folded down like a lapel on her hip. She had one hand there resting on it with a noisy bracelet on the wrist, saying look, here it is, come and get it. You were meant to want to unpeel the flap, but he just wondered how he could slip his wafer of a clever hand inside it without her knowing or wanting it to stop.

So he looked at the flap on her right hip, and she noticed and looked at him watching and made sure he'd seen the sneer. She had big plum-colored lips he wanted to mash with a fork. Her eyelashes moved slowly because of the black gunk on them. He could smell the greasy cosmetics and he could smell her last meal—something with pickles. She had that sort of statuesque tasty look, the bracelet, earrings the size of spoons, her hair off to one side and all done, like a football, the touching flap and the big white plastic shoulder bag resting on her left hip.

As he looked at the flap and at the *Post* folded in his left hand, his right felt the bag. It was smooth but sticky with a cinch of a catch made like two big balls. The noise in the train ate up the click when he opened it. The girl sighed, as if she was thinking about her guy eating her pussy. She was a long way away.

He knew it: her handbag was a mess. There was a handkerchief and

110

several crumpled tissues floating on top of the deeper junk. He went farther and touched something moist and yielding. He looked at her, his hand between this alive thing and the sateen lining of her bag. Her sleepy eyes picked up his look and used him as a voyeur watching her get off on her lover's licks. It was a sandwich, half out of cellophane. She was eating again. Pastrami on his fingers. He smiled at her thick arms and their glossy pimples.

Deeper. There it was, a wallet flat and old like a used shoe. He held it in two fingers like tweezers. His one hand lowered the *Post*, held her pouty look in an insolent stare and lifted out the wallet until the *Post* covered it. The dip and the lift, fucking her in her sleep. He put the wallet inside the folded paper and shut her bag for her. Again, her features moved, smug and settled, taking a goodbye kiss, looking forward to a snack.

That was Skip McCoy, also known as Joseph McCoy, the son of Irish immigrants. Limerick people, born in New York City in 1923, raised in the Bronx between 169th Street and Cotona Park. Father a pickpocket, died inside. Mother an ironer and presser in a laundry. Skip one of five kids, taught the trade by his father. A natural for it, which is to say not just good at it technically, but fulfilled by it. Thieving is a sport of the soul, and a dip can only touch anyone without them knowing.

1938, the year his father died, Joseph "Skip" was sent to juvenile hall for three months. 1939, first conviction, sent to reform school. Refused for military service. 1942, for stealing on the subway, three years in Sing Sing. Out in 1944, after more lessons inside. For three years, then, no one could pin a thing on him, but Skip got rich and took himself a room in a Manhattan hotel for living in. 1947, police framed him on another job, five years in Sing Sing. Got out in 1951, went to live in a shack on the waterfront, Lower West Side. Always lived alone. Two-time loser, next time for keeps.

So, that day in April 1952, on the Lexington Avenue line, grinding against the broad, giving her the dead-eyed stare. Candy it turned out she was called: perfect! What he would have guessed. Into the shoulder bag, one shithole of a cunt. The wallet had nineteen dollars, old photographs, the cards of a pack of businessmen, and the pieces of film in a little yellow envelope. The film was pictures of pages in a book, as far as he could tell, full of printing and diagrams.

That was what it was all about. This Candy had been carrying pictures of secrets, atom-bomb stuff, getting it to the Reds. There'd been two FBI guys in the car following her. They'd seen what Skip was doing, but they didn't want to disturb anything and they couldn't lay a hand on Skip in the crush.

So Skip had the cops after him, this Candy *and* the Reds, all hot for the pictures. A dip had got himself into the spying business! But Candy hadn't known what she was doing, that dumb shit. She was just doing a favor for her creep Joey, and he slapped her around and told her to find the artist who had lifted her wallet. Cops knew it was Skip, but they were told to lay off. FBI wanted to get the foreign agents, too, big stuff. Which put Mr. McCoy in the best seat. They pay heroes, don't they?

Candy came around and Skip slugged her and felt her up while she was out. But he hated touching broads, so he hit her some more. And then Joey got into it, and wasted Moe, the tie lady, just to show he was serious. In the end, Skip played it out fine. He got off for handing back the photos. The FBI snatched the Reds and Skip got Candy to pour his beers. But she went all gushy for love on him. So he sent her out to work—hostess in a restaurant (so the slut could eat)—and then the second week he lifted her wages while they was lovey-dovey. And that taught her.

1954, beginning of the end, Skip McCoy arrested on the Seventh Avenue line. Twenty years for Skip. He laughs; this kid won't break. Up in Sing Sing his mind started to go. That's what they say—can't see Skip is out-thinking them. They let him out in '69. Skip still acting. He was simple by then, talking to himself. Losing his touch too, hands shaky. Hang in there, Skip! Died 1971, pneumonia, sleeping out. Never complained, though, not Skip. Happy thinking of the fine work he'd done. Champion.

> *This trashy monologue creeps up on me, just from thinking of Skip's snicker. I have been able to talk like movie people after one look at a picture. But I have had so little to say for myself. Even now I might slip upstairs to Mary Frances and be as gruff and as loved as Tracy in Adam's Rib. But my sincerity went to the movies, leaving a bereft mimic behind.*

CORA PAPADAKIS

Lana Turner in The Postman Always Rings Twice,
*1946, directed by Tay Garnett; and Jessica Lange, 1981,
directed by Bob Rafelson*

By the time she was fourteen, there wasn't a man didn't notice her. And almost before they knew it, or felt the new pressure in the air around them, she knew they were looking at her. Out in the street, she recognized the way they dawdled and maneuvered to get a clear view of her. She'd be headed for the store, and two guys half as far from it would suddenly see a butterfly on the ground, or something that they had to study, and she'd have to walk on past them with both of them crouched down admiring the butterfly and just happening to look up as she came by so they could imagine the airy glow under her dress. Cora put on an extra sway to make her skirts move.

This was in Des Moines, Iowa, where she was born Cora Smith in 1913. Her mother was a cook at a hotel, and her father was a farm laborer. He was a big, handsome man, as dark as Cora but more tanned from being out in the sun so much. He was a quiet, resolute man until he understood how other men were studying Cora. Then he got angry and uneasy, and he sneered at his wife, who hadn't let him sleep with her since the birth of Cora. She had been horrified by lovemaking and she turned all her attention to cooking for people she never met or knew. She grew fat, less from eating than from the idea of food and its steady company. Her husband went off every day on foot with a bottle of lemonade and a loaf of bread. But after Cora came of age he took wine instead, and he came home flushed and sour, too tired to play horseshoes.

For Cora, her father felt like other men, except that he looked at her with bitterness. Several times he'd blunder in on her in the bathroom, or while she was putting on her stockings, and he'd scowl as if it had been her fault. So she got casual. She let him see her dressing a few times and she left her clothes around the house. The kindliness in her father had vanished. He was a stranger to her, but he seemed to hate her for causing the new distance.

Cora was fifteen when she went all the way. She was itching to find out. There were boys in school who had felt her all over while they were kissing, and some who'd had their hands in her and even for a

113

second or two their things. But she knew they were ignorant. She wanted someone older who could take all the worry away and teach her. There was a stockman on one of the farms, one where her father worked sometimes, a big man with hands as rough as bark. He'd watched her for a year, until one summer evening she went into a barn with him and got it all over with. He was a demon lover and she was like a soft pillow for him, or like an empty barrel tossed in the air on a bull's horns. Cora got to be an expert that first time. She came five times before supper, every way he worked on her. She was soaked and battered and only wanted more.

But the stockman got bored after that. She would try to cross his path, but he was never there; and once she saw him start a conversation with someone just to avoid meeting her. Cora couldn't understand his caution. She'd have done it on Euclid Avenue at Sunday lunchtime if he'd wanted to. Yet he didn't, so she hunted for others and got the worst reputation in the school. All this while, her father's dark face took on a violent tinge, like smoke. Cora told him, "You're sickening for something. Ought to see a doctor."

Then, in 1930, she entered a beauty contest for all the high schools in Iowa. Which she won, with Cora herself the only one surprised or pleased at that. The prize was a trip on the Chief to Hollywood. When she got there, there were photographers to take her picture, and they all whistled at her, which made her feel happy. She was given a screen test, and apparently the studio people liked her looks. But she had to say some lines and it felt peculiar saying these emotional things without feeling them. So they told her no use. She could have gone back home, she had the ticket. But she stayed and she got a job as a waitress in a hash house near the railroad station.

It was a lousy job. The tips were small, and the men who came in thought they could wipe their hands on her. Some of them were good-looking, and she'd go with them to what they called parties but turned out to be her with two or three of them in a room with a lot of beer. Then one day a big guy came in, tanned like her father, and he told another guy off for feeling Cora's leg.

"You're a gentleman," she told him when she took his order.

"Golly," was all he said, big eyes stupid over her.

So he asked her to marry him. Said he had a diner and a filling station, the Twin Oaks Tavern. He needed help there, and he surely liked her. His name was Nick Papadakis: he was Greek and his hair was like crude oil, heavy and shiny. What decided her was when he said his place was in the country, a long way away, in the hills. She missed the country, so she said, sure, she'd marry him, but she didn't get off till six.

At the Twin Oaks Tavern, she cooked, she served and she pumped gas when he was away. There was just him and the cat, and the cat was a better lover. Nick was the clumsiest man she'd ever met, full of shame and respect for his own size and her "tenderness." Also people thought he was Mexican, and just because she had black hair they took it for granted she was too. She hadn't gotten married to be a Mex.

Then one day this bum came by, Frank Chambers, and he conned a meal out of Nick, and then as a topper Nick gives him a job helping out, mechanic and so on, which Frank says he's expert at. That made Cora laugh, but when she saw Frank noticing her she felt glad he was staying and she got wet watching his mean black eyes. A few days later, they made it and it was the best yet. He was like an animal and he kept up with her good. He'd known what to do from the look in her eyes. Cora never liked to talk while she was doing it.

He was all for them leaving, but Cora said what about the three years she'd put in? She said what was the point of going if it was only to another hash house? What then? he said. She never had to spell it out. He knew from her not having the words, and he was kissing her breasts all the time, working out how they'd kill Nick.

Which they did, in a fake car accident. Only Frank had cracked the Greek's skull first and they drove the car over a cliff. Then Frank messed her up so she'd look hurt too. Rip me, she told him. So he tore open her blouse from the throat to her stomach, and he slugged her in the face. She went down and looked at him and he jumped on her and fucked her once before the alarm. It was all neat, but the car went too far down the cliff, and with Frank pushing it he went too so Cora thought maybe he was dead.

In the hospital, he signed a confession to this eagle lawyer, Katz, who then proceeded to get Cora off but wanted half the insurance because of the confession. What an operation. Just a look at them both and he'd known. Cora wouldn't have minded making it with Katz. And she felt sick that Frank had betrayed her at the first pressure.

So they ran the tavern for a while, and business was good because people came by to get a look at the couple from the papers. But Frank stayed and he was good for her still. Then she got the telegram saying her mother was sick, so she went back to Des Moines and watched her mother die, with her father watching both of them. After she died, he told Cora how lonely he was going to be, and she said sure, she knew, and he cried and she had to comfort him, and then just the once they

115

were in bed and he was amazing. She told him she was proud of him, and he should get remarried quick.

Then Cora went back to California, and there was Frank to meet her, wide-eyed about her mother dying. She found out he'd been with a woman in a circus while she was away, and he was so miserable about it she wanted to laugh. It made her think he really loved her, and so they got married. There were a few weeks when it was fine, and she told him she was pregnant and he was chipper as a kid. They went to a beach up by Topanga, and it was all deserted. They swam and she thought, So, this is love—okay. But she strained herself: she could feel the load in her stomach shift. Frank got her in to shore, and carried her up the sand to the car. And he started to drive to Santa Monica on the coast road with all the curves and he was so worried that he never saw the truck coming.

FRANK CHAMBERS

John Garfield in The Postman Always Rings Twice,
*1946, directed by Tay Garnett; and Jack Nicholson, 1981,
directed by Bob Rafelson*

At Slapout, in Oklahoma, where the two panhandles bang together in the wind and sun, in 1911, the birth of Frank Chambers. (How many different sentences are there to set down the facts of beginning?) He was illegitimate. His mother, Eileen, nineteen when he was born, worked in a hardware store, and lived in an upstairs room. A lot of men, Slapout people and some passing through, got to go up Eileen's stairs, so Frank never bothered to wonder who his father was. But when he was a boy there were jokes that maybe it had been a nigger, which cut him hard because he didn't want it said his mother would have gone with a black.

His mother was a wild-eyed woman. She didn't seem to know if there was a smudge on her face or a rip in her dress. And if she discovered it, she had a high, what-the-hell laugh that troubled a lot of people. She told Frank she didn't know where she'd come from. When she was only a little girl, her parents had taken her to Oklahoma City and she'd gotten lost, as simple as that, and never found them. Nor they her. So she'd been put in an orphanage till she was sixteen, and all she'd known for sure was her name.

116

he blamed the poor paint

As Frank grew up, his mother made a separate part of the room for him out of packing cases, so she could have company at night. Frank's bedroom was dark and dry-smelling, and he kept a candle there to light when the wind was howling outside. His mother never treated him like a child. She would talk to him just as she did anyone else—offhandedly, laughing for no apparent reason, and quarrelsome with just the same suddenness. It made Frank alert, being with her. He never knew when she might whip her hand out and slap him, or draw him against her warm, shaking body. People in Slapout laughed at her, and they made out she was weird in the head.

Once, when Frank was ten, he woke up in the middle of the night. There was burning in the packing-case wall. He cried out for his mother and got out of bed. The fire was creeping across the floor of the large room, like honey spreading. His mother was nowhere. He ran down the stairs out on the street, shouting for help. But it was late, and the wind had gotten up. The hardware store was gutted before the firemen came. There was old wood in the building, and a supply of kerosene in the basement.

Frank watched the firemen, waiting for his mother. She never came, so the Moodys, the people who owned the store, took him to their place. Next day, it seemed Eileen had been out at a ranch all night. Frank couldn't understand how the town reckoned she had started the fire. Just the same, she was sent to the asylum in Norman, and Frank was looked after by the Moodys, who built a new store. Twice a year they took him to see his mother, but the hospital was no good. In a year she didn't know Frank, and she was scratching all the time.

He stayed in Slapout till he was seventeen and all the Moodys saw was that he should work in the store all his life. So he went down into Texas, to Pampa, and for a year he hung out with a kid, Woody Guthrie. Frank played washboard while Woody sang and played guitar. They made a little money, and they knew some girls. But Frank got into fights with them. He never knew how, but all at once he'd punch at the woman and she'd look at him like he was a monster.

So he took to the road in 1929 and became a regular bum. He passed through Bedford Falls in 'thirty-one and I gave him work painting the office. It was badly done; his lunch breaks got longer; and he didn't put sheets down, so he ruined the floors with drops of paint. I had to talk to him, but he blamed the poor paint and the customers being in and out. That downright angered me and I told him, "Just remember, fellow, I never needed this painting done."

117

"Never needed it?"

"Not really."

"I ain't working for no idiot, then." And he threw the brush on my desk.

He hitched to Los Angeles and started to ride up and down the coast on freights. He would stop off, do a few days' work, steal, get into the small jails on vagrancy charges, fight the rail police, pick fruit. He got hard and mean, hating the straight life of homes and jobs. He had a slingshot, and he liked to roam at night, find a window lit up, with a family inside, like an advertisement, and put a stone through the window.

In 1933, he tried Mexico; he'd heard it was easier there. But it was hot, the food sickened him, and he never trusted Mexicans. He came back and hustled tourists in Los Robles. Then he got on a hay truck and rode as far as Twin Oaks before they threw him off.

There was a diner and Frank tried the old free-lunch scam—some guy in a car who was to meet him and pay for the meal. But the dumb Greek served him enchiladas and swallowed the check. The guy even offered him a job, and Frank was trying not to laugh when he saw the woman in the kitchen. He wanted to work her face over then and there.

Cora liked it that way. The Greek husband did nothing for her. The first time, Frank bit her lip and tasted blood like thick sweat. She was a treat, and he got tired for the first time in his life humping her. Frank wanted the Greek to notice and fight him; he wanted to split his stupid skull. So he didn't need pushing when Cora walked around the idea.

"I don't care if I fry for it," Frank told himself. "It'll make trouble for them." *Them* meant that straight world in painted houses. He ended up in the death house, not for putting the wrench through the Greek's skull, but for killing Cora, faking a crash so she went through the screen and her blood fell on the hood like she was taking a leak. There was a priest in the prison, and Frank said for sure he hadn't done it. Then Frank talked to another prisoner, who said it was his subconscious. There were two people in him. It made Frank shiver to think about that. Cora was the only one he'd ever liked as much as he wanted to rip into her.

JIMMY DOYLE

Robert De Niro in New York, New York, *1977,*
directed by Martin Scorsese

"What sort of thing is that then?" asked Jimmy Doyle. He was eleven, but he had that Irish edge in the way he talked, like a chipped curbstone, that was never young.

"That's a saxophone," said Martin Dougherty. "Tenor saxophone. You seen Billy today?"

Jimmy whistled in perplexity, "Saxo—? What kinda name's that? Billy Phelan?"

"That's the one. Named after Adolphe Sax. He invented it."

"Pretty thing."

"It has a glorious tone, too. Billy playing tonight?"

"I reckon. So . . . do you use it?"

"The saxophone?"

"Yeah."

"Do you want it, Jimmy?"

"I might. I might."

That's how Jimmy Doyle got his first saxophone. He was born in Albany in 1920, and this was in 1931, the first year Billy Phelan got a name for himself in Louie's poolhall. Jimmy used to hang around Billy. He liked the snappy way he dressed and the way he got with the cue in his hands—like its long hard line was his gaze and his poking the balls this way and that was sorting out the world. Jimmy loved to sit on a high stool outside the light listening to the click of the balls: it was like tough talk jazzing away while pages of print bored the world.

Jimmy wasn't reading. It was a wonder, his teachers said, when he talked so well and when he could knock out any tune on a piano, the way some one-finger typists can race along. But Jimmy was afraid of the silence in reading, and he couldn't see how the shapes on paper stood for things, not when any shout or tune made everyone look up, as if Billy'd just walked in for a match.

After a couple of months with the saxophone, Martin Dougherty heard Jimmy playing. He said, "You should take lessons, Jim. You're not bad."

"Lessons!" scoffed Jimmy. "I worked it out."

119

That was that. For better or worse, Jimmy puzzled out a way himself, or he gave up on a thing. He couldn't sit still while anyone told him something for his own good. He learned to play well, but who knows if he might not have been better if he'd listened to Martin Dougherty?

"Won't be told," said Martin.

"Cold little fellow," said Billy Phelan. "Watches me play, but never says a word."

"Because you're better than he is," said Martin.

"Has a great respect for excellence, our Jim."

"Cut your throat if he could get it off you."

So Jimmy grew up proud, lonely and mean-tempered, a lean stick of a young man, hands full of the saxophone, like a priest holding a trollop—that's what Martin said once, and Jimmy flashed him that shark's grin, all teeth and hunger. But he got a job playing in a place on Clinton Avenue, in 1938, and they only threw him out because he played so hectic.

He went down to the city in 1940 and tried to hang out with musicians, but he wasn't relaxed enough. So he went into the army, and in 1942 he heard about a vacancy in the Glenn Miller band which he got for two months before Miller told him he had to go because he was a disruptive influence. "It's this sweet shit you play," said Jimmy on his way out.

So he went back to the infantry and he went to France in 1944, where he got a medal for taking a German machine-gun post outside Caen, all on his own. Still, the army sent him home later that year because he was against taking orders and got into a lot of fights. They sent him back to Fort Benning and he worked there on the camp radio station. He had a two-hour show in the early hours of the morning and he played a lot of jazz records. He got fired when he played Charlie Parker's "Tiny's Tempo" over and over for two hours.

He got out of the army in January 1945 and went back to New York, to Monroe's and Minton's, to listen to Parker, Monk and Gillespie in person. He tried to sit in with them but they wouldn't have anything to do with him. Some said it was because Jimmy seemed so hostile, but he thought it was because he was white. Still, his head was full of the spilling phrases played by Parker and the abrupt harmonic leaps. Once, just once, Parker sat back and listened to ten minutes or so of Jimmy saying why he should be allowed to play. "So?" said Jimmy, exhausted. "I just heard you, man," said Parker. "You can't be better on that horn."

On VJ day, Jimmy dropped by the Moonlight Terrace, where the Dorsey band was playing. He slid in and out of conversations, trying to pick up women. That's how he met Francine Evans, the singer. She thought he was crazy, but she couldn't stop him or stop listening to his tirades of wooing. The storm rushed past her ears, frightening and entrancing. She never got rid of him and next day he took her along to his audition at the Palm Club. He played so hard and fast, the manager there was ready to turn him off. But then Francine got up and started to sing and Jimmy fell in behind her, just like Lester Young's velvet cushion for Billie to loll on. The guy hired them both.

But Francine had to leave town with the Frankie Harte band, her real job. So when Jimmy finds out about this he follows her all the way to Asheville, North Carolina. They got married down there: she knew she'd never escape him. And Harte hired Jimmy so long as he'd keep it down a little.

They toured for a year until Harte decided to give it up and asked Jimmy if he wanted to take over the band. For a while it was a hit, but when Francine knew she was pregnant she decided to go back to New York. She had had an offer to do cover records and the traveling was too much for her. So Jimmy stayed on with the band for a while, just to prove it was his. But without Francine they soon lost their following.

Jimmy got back to the city furious. He laughed at Francine's records and dragged her out to Harlem every night when he sat in with Cecil Powell, the one black musician who took him seriously, even if Cecil had turned him on to marijuana. Also, Jimmy had the hots for this black girl singer, Lucy Wiley. The baby was born Jimmy, Jr., in 1948, but the marriage was coming apart to the sound of Jimmy's frenzied talk.

In the next few years, Francine took Jimmy, Jr. to California, where she was getting into pictures. Jimmy stuck it out in New York and he got some notice fronting a group with Miles Davis for a year until they had a fistfight on the stand. Jimmy was doing heroin by 1951, and he talked less. But his stuff was popular with college kids, and in 1953 he was set up in his own club, the Major Chord. People said they'd heard there was gang money in the club.

He lived alone, more reclusive. He didn't see his son for years at a time, but stayed in a room at the Carlyle Hotel, a room he had painted black. By 1960, he was in bad shape from the heroin, and he went into a clinic for a cure. It worked, but he was dead in 1966. There was a memorial concert where a lot of good players came out for him. When

Thelonious Monk played the finale—Jimmy's "Taxi Cab Blues"—he shouted out into the hall, "Fuck you, Jimmy!"

> *I might kill a man if the right music was*
> *playing, or carry Mary Frances over a snow-*
> *capped mountain, to happiness, sure thing. But*
> *stealthy strings hold sway in these narrow,*
> *italic passages, dark corridors where the*
> *storyteller lurks.*

FRANCINE EVANS

Liza Minnelli in New York, New York, *1977,*
directed by Martin Scorsese

If not quite born in a trunk, Francine Evans had a childhood in which it was her responsibility to keep her parents' dancing shoes bright and shiny. She was the daughter of the Mendozas, one of the best-known Latin dance couples in the West. Felipe was Mexican, and he had a brief career in movies around 1920 before he married Wilma Schuyler, a young dancer he met at Universal. They moved away from Los Angeles and went into business together as teachers of Latin dance. They had studios up and down the California coast, and they boosted their trade by winning several national contests. Wilma, of Dutch extraction, dyed her creamy hair black in order to enhance the image of Latin synchronicity. Francine (born Frances) came into the world in Santa Barbara (where the Mendozas had their home) in 1923. She had magnificent black hair of her own.

Always close to music, the young Frances began to sing as she watched her parents gliding or stamping their way across all the polished floors. She played the leads in several high-school shows —*The Pirates of Penzance, The Merry Widow, The Girl from Tijuana.* Her parents encouraged her musical aspirations, ensured that she had good technical training, and had the foresight to provide for proper orthodontry when she was still in her teens. It was in 1942 that Frances went to New York, with several letters of introduction to friends and colleagues of the Mendozas. One of these was Tony

Harwell, who became her agent, and came up with the new name Francine Evans. As such she made her first impact, winning a Carmen Miranda impersonation contest on the radio.

She was for a year one of the Peters Sisters, a backup group with a lot of studio work. In 1944, she toured with the Jimmy Dorsey band, and in 1945 she got a position as featured vocalist with Frankie Harte—it was then she had an affair with the band saxophonist, Georgie Auld, and made her first hit record, a song they wrote together, "Got a Thing for the Sax Man," a torch classic.

Then on VJ-night, not long after she and Auld had broken up, Francine was at the Moonlight Terrace when Jimmy Doyle approached her and started talking her to death. She knew inside the first hour everything that was going to happen. He had a nagging energy that was going to free her own repressed need to be a star. But he couldn't stand competition; he wouldn't want to see anyone else's fame. And while she knew that everyone had always liked her, she guessed that the streak of self-destructiveness in Doyle would keep him a minor figure. She would be transformed by him; he would barely notice her. But they fell in love like people going over a cliff hand-in-hand. It was the first time in her happy life Francine had felt the drive of compulsion. The new note of desperation in her singing voice came from Jimmy.

Touring with Jimmy was a nightmare. He lived only to be on the stand, and once there he would cut anyone, steal solos and scold the other players for any mistake. Francine tried to make every passing hotel room a version of home. But Jimmy regarded such rooms as anonymous, transitory bases. He passed through them, unaware and chaotic. But they married, she got pregnant and their music improved. For both of them, uneasy as it was, so full of arguments and silence, this period came to stand for "what it could have been like."

Francine knew the marriage wouldn't survive when she went back to New York to have Jimmy, Jr. She guessed that Jimmy had had an affair with Bernice Kay in her absence. When Jimmy saw his son, he looked at him with the amused superiority he put on when sitting through a drum solo. In two months, he moved out and was living in Harlem.

In 1949, they got a divorce and Francine moved with Jimmy, Jr. back to California. There had been movie offers. Her father had done a lot of talking with her and, together with Tony Harwell, he had been working for a year on Arthur Freed to consider Francine. She tested better than anyone suspected; the rather forceful nose photographed cute. Francine had only one song and fifteen minutes in *Would You Believe It?* (1950, Charles Walters), but it was enough. Metro put her straight into *The Girl from Hot Coffee* (1951, Stanley Donen) as a replacement for Garland.

Her movie career was established. She made *Shore Leave* (1952, Donen); *Vaudeville Family* (1953, George Sidney); and then the enormously successful *Happy Endings* (1954, George Cukor). Francine took Jimmy, Jr., east for the New York opening, and she met Jimmy again. He talked about seeing her another time, and they made an appointment. She was all ready to go when a premonition fell on her. She actually saw the tense figure of Jimmy waiting for her on a street corner, and she remembered the grinning scorn with which he'd warded off all her new success. She decided not to see him.

But ever afterward, she got calls in the night. Sometimes he said nothing; sometimes he blew a breathing tone on a mouthpiece; sometimes he started a huge speech, imploring yet blaming her. Jimmy, Jr., was troubled by the strange irregularity of his father's presence, and Francine sent him away to a private school. She made *Lady Love* (1956, Rouben Mamoulian), and then that adventurous failure, *A Virtuoso Personality* (1957, Vincente Minnelli).

In 1957, she married her longtime accompanist, Paul Wilson. It was a comfortable, unexciting marriage for two years, until the mutilated body of Wilson was found in their Holmby Hills mansion pool when Francine was on location in New England for *Labor Day Picnic* (1959, Nicholas Ray), her last film.

Francine was terrified by the murder. She refused to consider any more pictures; she sold the house without ever setting eyes on it again; and she moved to Santa Barbara.

She lives there still, in her early sixties now, seldom seen, one of the true reclusives of showbiz. Until his death in 1966, she was pestered by Jimmy, and she often gave him money to support his heroin addiction. All offers of a comeback were refused, though she did make one TV spectacular, "Francine," in 1963, remarkable for her undimmed vitality and the promise of Bob Fosse.

So optimistic in her films, so settled in her early life, Francine Evans has accepted tragedy. Still adored by the masses—her films are played more now than in the 1950s—she exists in a state of torment, unable to stop or deter the drive of her son to remind her of his father.

JOHN CONVERSE

Michael Moriarty in Who'll Stop the Rain, *1978,*
directed by Karel Reisz

Would it have occurred to me to pursue Converse if I had not been at the dentist's with one old copy of *Time* to help me wait? It was Mo's teeth that proved she had been burned down to the bone, and now mine guided me to a sleeping clue. The eyes, the mouth—our histories are stored there.

In a *Time* silky with use I found a review of a book, *Wounded Soldiers* by John Converse. It was a 1975 issue, and the book was an account of Vietnam veterans disabled by the war. It was based on interviews, and the review picked out one with "Alex Cutter, intent on finding an incident in his American milieu that will answer for his injury." I remembered Converse as Mo's half-hearted lover. But I had not imagined he would have seen her again, not after her marriage to Cutter.

Wounded Soldiers was in the library. It had been borrowed many times, yet it seemed to me meretricious. The material was full of pain, but the writing was artfully noncommittal: horror built up while the book assured itself that there was nothing else to do but recount these lurid events as meticulously as possible. A photographer who recorded them would have been called cold, but Converse was praised for what *Time* termed "cool lucidity." He could make his emptiness seem like helpless wisdom. Sometimes the book was mere unsentenced lists: ". . . Gangrene. Stench. Flowers by the roadside. Maggots in the flesh. . . ." In shedding grammar he had taken on the role of a torturer. The acid words dripped in my head; it was not reading, but being beaten, quietly, so that one would not cry out.

So I learned about Converse: born in 1941, the only child of a surgeon who moved every three or four years to a richer hospital, taking his son with him. The mother died when the boy was four—I could find no cause of death. "Oh, quite simply, she detested my father. She was worn out by him," Converse told me. His casual hands turned over in the air, like a life rolling aside. He had majored in communications at UCLA, and gone into the Marine Corps with a commission. Somewhere he must have taken a wrong turn, a dead end. You cannot always tell from brief biographies. They do not

125

include unhappiness or error. Everyone seems so confident and straight ahead in *Current Biography*.

He had married the daughter of a Berkeley radical, Marge Bender. He worked for her father, writing for his magazines and editing a little. It didn't seem enough for someone with his ambition. Perhaps he loved Marge: they had a daughter. But he wrote a play, *Under the Christmas Tree*, about a marine on furlough who rampages in his old home and kills his unavailing parents. It was successful off-Broadway; it was done often in the sixties, bought for the movies, but never heard of. When I read it, I could not credit its thrill at dreadful cruelty. You understand, I do not say such things cannot happen. We all know of massacres. But how can anyone treat them lightly?

I wrote to Converse's publisher; the letter never came back and never produced an answer. I would have let him go out of sheer inability: I do not know how one becomes an indefatigable inquirer. I grow tired waiting for chance's lead. No Marlowe.

Then three months after my day at the dentist's, I saw in the paper that John Converse would be lecturing at the university in Lincoln on "Conscience and Reporting." It was open and free to the public.

He was a tall man, thin and slack. As he lectured, the light fell on the bald peak of his head. His voice was languid and inexpressive, except when it tensed against giggling as he made a sarcastic remark. He talked about his "crisis" in Vietnam, and the call he had heard to write "not from the several, bogusly intelligent points of view of war's leaders, but in the impacted fear and degradation of those in the way of a war." As if real writing could be so bereft.

He spoke for an hour, with desultory questions for another fifteen minutes, and then there was cheese and wine in the Faculty Lounge. I sipped a cold claret, looking at the heartbreaking Wilson Keyes of a wild garden in Laurel Canyon. I waited for Converse to autograph his book, and to satisfy fawning, hushed questions. One young woman was possessively attentive, but he slid her aside when he realized I was waiting and would not go away.

"I wondered if we might have dinner," I asked him.

"Oh, dinner." His gaze drifted away to the young woman.

"I am Mo Cutter's uncle," I told him.

"Really?" Surprise made him stupid, until he grinned, and it was insolent. "Well, I never."

"I would like a chance to talk with you."

"Would you? Why?"

"I am so much in the dark over her death."

"I could do breakfast, I suppose."

"Tomorrow?"

"I have a ten a.m. flight. Can you come to the Holiday Inn?"

"Eight?"

"Eight-thirty, say."

I stayed in Lincoln, in a motel. Those places have not changed. I wondered if it might be the last time I ever tried to sleep in a motel. I cannot have many motel chronicles left, I trust. Yet I would linger on in the drab cubes a year if it meant another day of life.

He was late the next day and he had cut himself shaving. A year later he was made editor of *Newsweek*, but that morning he was soiled and hungover from the girl in his room.

"Old Mo then," he sighed, as he drank coffee with Tylenol.

"I know about your friendship," I said, to save time, I thought.

"You do? You think you do?"

"She wrote to me. She sent your picture. I don't mean to blame you."

"You're old Uncle George, aren't you? The sly one."

"Sly?"

"Took her to the movies."

"Yes, sometimes."

He looked at me and he forked hot cake in syrup. "Felt her up in the dark."

"I did not." I hated myself for blushing.

"She said so."

"It's not true." He had made me disavow her.

"Ah. . . . Well, Mo wasn't always too straight, was she? She did make things up. And then, once she'd started on heroin—"

"She took drugs?"

"An addict. Scag addict."

"When did you see her last?"

"What?" He began laughing, as if my ignorance had only just dawned on him. "That night!"

"The night she died?"

"Of course. I . . . fucked her. Excuse me. You know."

"I thought Richard Bone . . ."

"After him. I saw him leave. But it wasn't either of us."

"Wasn't what?"

He searched for a way of saying something he normally left unsaid.

"That made her do it—if she did it. Or maybe Cord had the house burned down. Cutter was after him. Had this crackpot theory that

127

Cord had murdered some girl he was involved with. Nonsense, of course. People don't do that."

At everything he said I felt the ground around me less certain. I wanted to be utterly deaf. He was so familiar with such black subtleties between people, and so indifferent.

There was a silence. "I made that up about you in the dark."

"Why?"

"She never said that. She said something about you—something pleasant, I think—but I don't remember. Why do you care?"

"I think about her. Isn't that enough?"

"No, not really. At least, I shouldn't think so. Look, I have to go. But supposing I was the last to see her alive—I may have been. There was nothing I noticed. Nothing. She didn't need other people, or wrongs, to do a thing like that. It was in her, that's all."

"But noticing depends on kindness."

Have you ever seen a younger man study something old, then wipe it from his mind, knowing he will live longer?

"Those who notice most are often good at hiding," said Converse. He got up and went away, leaving me to pay for his half-eaten breakfast.

JACK TORRANCE

Jack Nicholson in The Shining, *1980,*
directed by Stanley Kubrick

Born on October 4, 1938, in Bedford Falls, Nebraska. I should know. He went away from there in 1954, east, to the great cities, calling himself Jack Torrance. He would do nothing except the most menial and humiliating jobs, for he had made up his mind to be an artist. Every night of his life he spent in movie houses. Then he went home to his room and watched more films on television until he fell asleep on their copycat plots. Then he got up and went to his work. He had no friends and he never made contact with his family. People vanish in this manner every day.

By the time he was thirty, Torrance had decided to write. When he went to work, he took with him a black briefcase that contained the manuscript of all his writing. He was so unwilling to risk losing it. In time, he went back and forth from his job, operating copying machines, with two suitcases and a briefcase filled with paper. He had never shown any of his work to another human being.

Then in 1973, he met and married a woman named Wendy. "What you got in the bags, hon?" she wondered. "Oh," he said, rolling shyness and pride around in his smile, "just my books, my works." "Can I see, hon?" It was an innocent enough request—it would have been unkind not to ask. "Why no, my sweet, certainly not," said Torrance, smiling again at her crestfallen face. She looked like a little boy who had, all along, been pretending to be a grown woman.

But as this married life went on—Jack hardly knew how—Wendy grew large with child. "Maybe you should get a better job, hon." She had a way of almost talking to herself. "Now that we'll soon be three. Why, you could teach, dear, knowing as much as you know. Wouldn't you think?" And he simply watched her, letting his inner groan climb silently to where the gods of *belles lettres* could smile at it.

He found a job in a private school in Vermont teaching English, and their son, Danny, was born there in the middle of a blizzard so severe that it delayed the arrival of the midwife, thereby allowing the death of Danny's twin brother. "What do we call him, beloved? The better to distinguish him, I mean." "Who, hon?" asked Wendy from her bed of convalescence. "The boy, the other one." "I don't know. Do we call him anything?" "Ah," sighed Torrance, "shall we say Tony, then? I think it would make everything a little more meaningful." "Sure, hon," said Wendy, sucked at by Danny and overawed by Torrance.

Vermont was not good, not with six months of winter, then mud and sticky heat for the rest of the year. Moreover, Torrance had begun to send his works to publishers, magazines and literati. They all came back, with a speed shown by the postal service on no other occasions. He was drinking. In one bourbon temper he had seized Danny and made to demonstrate a Luis Tiant curveball with him, only for the boy's shoulder to be dislocated. In Dickensian contrition, Jack gave up drink, pouring eleven bottles of the amber out into the snow (keeping only a snifter for an emergency).

To smooth over the ugly incident, they all moved to Boulder, Colorado. There Jack would settle to write his masterwork. But awkward realities intruded—the friendliness of neighbors, the humdrum need to make ends meet, Torrance's own extraordinary laziness and the little chatter all day long between Danny and the imaginary being who lived in his mouth, Tony.

129

Therefore Jack answered an advertisement requiring a winter caretaker for the Overlook Hotel, deep, deep in the mountains. It was a large, old-fashioned luxury hotel, attractive and salubrious in the summer, but inaccessible from October to May. The management needed someone to be there, to answer the radio, maintain the heating and so on. It was an ideal job for a writer, and yes, of course there was room for Wendy and Danny, too. Room? Why there were 237 rooms, not to mention the variety of bars, restaurants, games rooms, solaria, ballrooms and hideaways.

Torrance bundled his work and his family into their yellow Volkswagen and headed into the mountains in the first somber chilliness of October. They arrived as the last of the summer staff were leaving the Overlook, including the black cook, Hallorann, who took a special shine to Danny. Torrance was reminded by those departing of how an earlier caretaker—named Grady—had been so weighed upon by the isolation and the eerie serenity of the Overlook that he had chopped up his wife and two children, in small pieces, as if preparing a ragout.

Life went on in the Overlook, Danny going up and down the monstrous corridors in his pedal car, Wendy making breakfast for three in a kitchen equipped for three hundred, and Jack in the privacy of an abandoned sun lounge conjuring up the mood and creatures of his fiction. He became a little more dreadful—I say this, and who could be more reluctant to admit it? He was churlish to his family, even while he was imagining going into one of the hotel's empty bedrooms to find a tall, Nordic nude (a woman) arising from the bath to give him a wet embrace. But even in his dream he hated himself. For this siren changed into a hag whose ulcerous sores set him screaming. "Don't whistle through your teeth, hon, puts my nerves on edge." "Does it, dunghill?" And so on.

What was he writing all the time, in those empty, sun-blanched rooms where the timbers creaked and the outer brightness of snow rose like a tide against the glass? All those years of solitary movie-going, a pastime that left him forever pale, had degenerated into a vast, God-forsaken novel (albeit masquerading as a work of reference) involving the characters from those movies, their lives enlarged beyond the scope of the films. A mad book, a unique book, but not his own book. And like all thieves, he went in dire terror of being stolen from. That was why he left a top-sheet on this pile becoming a book, covered with the dittos of one line, "All work and no play makes Jack a dull boy."

In his mania, Jack was meeting Lloyd, a barman, in the Gold Room, and coming back from those imaginary conversations drunk. He had encountered a butler, Grady, in the crimson-and-white gentlemen's bathroom, who had advised him to "correct" his family.

Far away in Florida, Hallorann picked up a telepathic call for help from Danny, and set out for the Overlook. Torrance became violent, and Wendy had to homer him with a baseball bat, a Carl Yastrzemski, as it happens. She shut him up in the food store, but someone let him out—was it Grady? could a ghost open a door? Hallorann arrived only to have Jack bury an axe in his panting parka! Wendy and Danny fled for their lives, out into the moonlit snow. In a maze without a center, Jack chases his child, driven back into boyhood, until he stops, numb and weary, the steam of his sweat turns to frost and the last grimace of Torrance becomes an ice entrance to his dead mystery.

Wendy and Danny make it away in the snowmobile that Hallorann has arrived in—that's why he was needed. And in the hotel, the aimless eye of patience, with months to go before the thaw, sees a group photograph on the wall, with a young Jack there, Jacko even, and the date: July 4, 1921—it's a holiday picnic, and isn't that Evelyn Cross in a burning white frock, and . . ?

But no human eye saw that picture, and in the May that came, Jack's stiff corpse was dropped in the earth, a bone for it, and Wendy was notified by letter.

Ah, you say, what happened to that work-in-progress?

> *I have a special fondness for Jack. He taught me that I might be mad, instead of just unhappy—quite a striking addition to my role. And then he sprang to life, so real a character that he chose to steal the half of the book already written and make off down the beanstalk. I had to give chase, of course, but through tears of love for him for seeing such promise in the story so far.*

VIVIAN STERNWOOD

Lauren Bacall in The Big Sleep, *1946,*
directed by Howard Hawks

Born in 1907, in the Sternwood mansion on Beacon Hill in Boston, Vivian was the first child of Colonel, later General, Guy Sternwood (1869–1941) and his new wife, Millicent Webster, a great-grand-daughter of Daniel Webster. Vivian's father was one of his country's most respected soldiers. He had fought in the Philippines against Aguinaldo, and although trained as a cavalryman he had written a short book, *An End to Horse Power* (1904), that predicted many of the military developments realized in the First World War.

During Vivian's childhood, the Colonel fought in Mexico with Pershing, and then in 1917 he went to Europe. He was instrumental in directing the strategy of the 1918 Meuse-Argonne offensive, one of the few decisive attacks of the entire war. However, in October 1918, he was seriously wounded when a shell hit his car. Both legs were broken and there was extensive damage to his hips. He endured seven operations, and managed to walk a little until 1922. But, thereafter, he was confined to a wheelchair. Rather than suffer the New England winters, the Sternwoods moved to Los Angeles, to 3765 Alta Brea Crescent, a property purchased for the General by Noah Cross, an old colleague from the cavalry.

Guy Sternwood's last great defiance of his disability was to have another child, a second daughter, Carmen, born in 1920. She was thirteen years younger than Vivian, who came to fill many of the roles of a mother to Carmen when Millicent Sternwood died in 1925. With the General incapacitated, and looked after by John Norris, his orderly from the Western front, the two sisters resembled mother and child. Yet there was no affection between them. Vivian was tall, sophisticated and ruthless when she had to be. Carmen was a gamine, a child-woman, helplessly cunning. The sisters disliked each other, and kept company as a way of practising their malice.

Vivian's own life centered on her friendship with Evelyn Cross, the daughter of the Sternwoods' benefactor, and a truer sister than Carmen. When Evelyn suffered her teenage breakdown, and had to go away to a family property in the redwood country, Vivian went as her companion. General Sternwood was happy that his family could repay the debt to the Crosses, but he was perplexed that Vivian would not tolerate the least mention of Noah Cross.

In 1928, Vivian married Esteban Hernandez, an actor brought up from Mexico by B. P. Schulberg in the vogue for "Latin lovers" that followed the death of Valentino. Hernandez made a few films, with some success, especially *Swords of Toril* (with Barbara La Marr), but his accent was too heavy for sound pictures. Vivian had met him in 1926, at the Hearst ranch. She enjoyed his cheerful indifference to his own career and his stamina in bed. But, out of work and money, Hernandez went back to Mexico, to Agua Caliente, in 1930. He kept in touch with Vivian, but he knew she did not want to live south of the border, and he was developing business interests that kept him occupied. Simple divorce proceedings took place in 1931.

By then, Vivian was keeping company with C. C. Julian, the Canadian entrepreneur whose fraudulent oil company had caused a scandal in Los Angeles in 1927. Divorced by his first wife, Julian was promoting mail-order schemes. He and Vivian were secretly married in 1932—for Julian had hopes of using her as a contact to the Cross fortune. A year later, Julian fled the country because of mail-fraud charges. Both Vivian and the thirteen-year-old Carmen went with him, by boat to Hawaii and then to Shanghai. Their revels came to an end in that city: Julian killed himself after a riotous party at the Astor Hotel. It was all Vivian could do to disguise Carmen's part in the orgy and to put blame on "an allegedly nineteen-year-old secretary," from Chifu, not seen again. Shanghai was Carmen's coming of age. After that, she assumed any man wanted her, and she asked strangers if they knew how the Chinese screwed.

Back in California, Vivian sent Carmen to the Rutledge school up in Mendocino. But no school could hold Carmen. She seduced those appointed to guard her, and then escaped while they slept. She came home on a truck she had picked up in Oakland and led out of its way by a day's journey. The driver was pale and anxious to be rid of his passenger. Vivian had Carmen examined by a specialist. He said she was calculating, not mad. A nymphomaniac? No, merely a wanton, without inhibition.

So Vivian got on with life and in 1936 she met Sean Regan. He was an Irishman, always spouting bits of Gaelic, an officer in the IRA, in America illegally, doing what exactly? Raising money, some said. But Regan was not energetic. He sat around, telling stories and drinking. He appreciated General Sternwood and he helped bring Vivian and her father closer together; she could be kind to her father when Sean was there. So she married him in a rush of gratitude. That was in 1937, a year when Vivian needed strong liquor or a man with the same effect. Evelyn had been killed on the streets, and nothing anyone could say altered the general opinion that she had been wayward and deranged, a discredit to her long-suffering and public-spirited father. We are in the hands of those who survive us.

It was a year of betrayals. When Carmen met Regan she asked him to go to bed with her, just like that, in front of Vivian, the General and Norris. "Not just now, sweetheart," Sean had said, and Carmen broke into peals of laughter as if they were all to take it as humor.

But later that summer, Carmen found Regan out in the garden doing a little target-shooting with a pistol. She asked him to teach her. So he showed her this and that and gave her the gun. She held it in her small white hand, the fingernails dipped in red.

"Will you now?" she wondered.

"Will I what?"

"What I asked."

He considered and he said, "You're too determined, Carmen."

So she turned the gun on him and shot him in the stomach. He died at her feet, raving idiotically at her composure, so she kicked at his wound with her bare feet until the toes were crimson too.

Vivian buried the body in an oil sump. She told Carmen never to tell their father, and the wide-eyed killer agreed. It was said that Regan had just gone away, as unexpectedly as he'd appeared. Vivian lived somewhere between widowhood and desertion. But then, in 1939, Carmen got into trouble again. A bookseller, Arthur Gwynn Geiger, sent the General several IOUs signed by Carmen. So the General hired a detective, a man named Marlowe, to clear it up.

Marlowe wanted it all out—how Regan had been killed, how Carmen had posed for Geiger in pornographic pictures, and so on. Vivian waited, until 1941, when her father died. Then she went to Noah Cross, told him what she knew and what she guessed, and asked him if he could get Carmen into an asylum and make sure she stayed there.

"At my discretion?" asked Cross, and Vivian was left to wonder what he might do, or have done, to establish Carmen's insanity.

"She's not to be hurt," she told him, and he sighed and smiled and said he'd never hurt a soul. Five weeks later, Carmen entered a hospital in Oregon. Noah Cross took care of the bills and arranged to have her watched night and day.

Vivian was the last Sternwood left alive and free. She was rich and nowhere near old yet. She lived in a strenuous active way, drinking too much and not taking enough care over whom she met. She was reputed to have helped back Bugsy Siegel in his Flamingo Hotel, the beginning of modern Las Vegas. She was said to be the mistress of Jonathan Shields, the movie producer. She was a close friend of Samson DeBrier, and a hostess at some of his gatherings.

Otherwise, she remained tall, illustrious and determined to get what she wanted. It was only that she wanted less, and was readier to seek the oblivion of drink, amusing company or sleeping in the sun. She died in 1972, of cancer. Her will and that of Noah Cross left provision for unending vigilance with Carmen.

L. B. JEFFRIES

James Stewart in Rear Window, *1954,*
directed by Alfred Hitchcock

It was the turning point in Jeff's life, and in the end nothing about it displeased him as much as that. He didn't believe in turning points happening to him. He had photographed plenty of them: a tidal wave shattering a building, a figure lifted off the ground by the bullet that was killing it, a racing car stuck in midair, life-and-death instants. But he had been the cool recorder of them all, and he lived by the principle of never getting into the picture himself. Now there he was on all the front pages, both legs in plaster, with a plan of the courtyard. He had even posed for one idiot, holding the telephoto lens up to his face. And the paper had gotten a picture of Thorwald and put it on the lens. "Peeping-Tom Pix Man Snaps Murder," was the headline, as if he were the only voyeur in New York, a city of windows and vantage points.

Was this what forty-two years of acquired craft had been leading to? He felt trapped, not just by another eight weeks in plaster—if there were no complications, and the surgeon had told him about what to expect at his age—but by the media, the phone and Lisa. Lisa Carol Fremont, a dame with class, turning on a light with each name. He had to marry her now. It was the will of the city and its newsprint love for a hero and a heroine. She could tell him she had proved herself in action, wriggling her hand at him to show him Mrs. Thorwald's wedding ring on *her* finger. Giving *him* the finger and letting Thorwald work out the dotted line across the courtyard to where Peeper Pix Man was sitting and waiting.

Lionel Bartleby Jeffries, born in La Crosse, Wisconsin, 1912. Graduated with honors in English/journalism from the University of Wisconsin in 1934, the first student to get photo projects accepted for credit. He'd stayed in the Midwest for two years working on papers, getting quicker, building his portfolio. He never did atmosphere or portraits, just hard news stuff. He got a jewelry-store robbery on the Loop in Chicago, and he sold those pictures in New York and Europe—with old ladies scattering, and the bag in one jittery thief's hand spilling open, pearls in midair like drops of milk. He was getting known.

In 1937, he went to New York, freelancing. An old La Crosse contact led him to Joe Losey, who was making documentaries for the Rockefeller Foundation. He hired Jeff and it was good work, but Joe had been full of political angles; he liked emotional pictures of poor people. But they got along, arguing all the while, and on the side Jeff had taken a series of pictures of the Mississippi in flood: houses floating, with people perched on the roofs, rowboats full of chickens, that kind of thing. *Life* had bought three of them—it was his first time in the magazine.

He banked on the war. He had no family ties, he'd go anywhere, and this was going to be the first war really photographed in action. Not just rows of Brady corpses and the generals smoking pipes under the trees, but the moments of action. He got *Life* to send him to London in 1940 to cover the Blitz. While he was there, he met some RAF boys who talked about photoreconnaissance. They took him up on a couple of the early bombing raids and he learned about the special cameras.

So he got into the air corps and was promoted and assigned to help set up the photorec. teams. That's how he met Tom Doyle, the best unblinking, blue-eyed pilot he ever knew, the man who was flying when Jeff got the D-Day stuff, the Arnhem pictures and the Dresden night-raid spread. All the while he was flying Jeff was selling pictures to magazines too. *Life* kept hold of him throughout the war, and just assumed he'd be on staff afterward. It was a pinnacle for Jeff, and he realized later that he should have had some other goals so he could keep moving.

From 1946 onward, it was one trouble spot after another: the fighting in India, the Berlin airlift, Trieste, Vienna, Perón in Argentina, Malaya, Korea, sweating with fever, freezing your butt off. Traveling, living in hotels, eating when he could, knowing every journalist in the world but having hardly any friends, except for Doyle, who'd become a New York City detective. No long relationships with women, but the political reporter in London, a translator in Buenos Aires, the hotel manager in Singapore. Women who were there when he passed through, women who didn't want explanations.

Then, in 1953, he'd met L. C. Fremont. She worked for a fashion house and she'd had this idea to pose six models in silk nightdresses up in the Bronx, and she'd wanted a "gritty, realistic" look to it, so she'd asked for Jeff, and as luck would have it, bad luck he told her, he'd been between planes. So he took those weird shots, and there'd been that secretive smile on Lisa's face, and the pictures were sensations. People were that foolish. He got a lot of the credit for them. They were exhibited in museums and later on Susan Sontag had written a piece about them in the *New York Review of Books*—which never had photographs anyway!

Lisa was after him. Not just for more assignments—she said they had to keep on with that "adventure"—but marriage. He liked her. But she was perfect, and he wasn't used to career women, not as people to know or go to bed with. If she came over to his place, she had her calls forwarded and tied up the phone. He wasn't the settling type, not even at forty-two. He'd be active for years yet.

Then the racing car hit him. In the picture it stayed stuck in midair, but in life a wheel had broken his leg. So, just as Lisa wanted, he was laid up, at her mercy. But he *was* lucky, or so it seemed to Jeff. For out in his own backyard something started to happen. The guy at 125 West Twelfth, Lars Thorwald, murdered his wife. Jeff saw it, or enough bits of it to piece the story together.

But that was what got *him* in the papers, and it killed his nerve. It had never happened before, but when Lisa was in the apartment over the way, and Thorwald found her and started in on her, Jeff didn't want to look. He wanted to go to the window and shout out to Thorwald, "Stop! I can see you!" But he hadn't done that. He'd covered his eyes, and then looked through his own fingers. He'd lost his confidence, and gotten a wife instead.

It changed his life. Everything else, up to the day he was killed in the Tet offensive of 1968, had come from that. He married her, and he stayed in New York. The fall had been bad. One leg was never as good again. He wasn't as mobile. Lisa said it was all for the best. She helped him open a studio in Manhattan. He did a lot of fashion work. She got him to call himself Lionel Jeffries, which he hated until LBJ came along and Jeff saw some remote benefit in it.

They got divorced in 1962, when he had an affair with a model. Damn it, how could you look at those broads all day without screwing them? Then when Vietnam got hotter, he came to a decision. He left his studio to his assistant and he went out there as a freelance. But he was fifty-six, and he limped, and the war he'd known before had fronts, fixed targets, things to photograph. In Nam, he was slow and the war was water running all around you. One day he got caught. He started to take a picture of a woman trying to stop the bleeding from her leg, but the woman took out a pistol and shot him. Jeff's last picture showed the flash of her gun, caught in midair. But the flash came all the way and got him.

LARS THORWALD

Raymond Burr in Rear Window, *1954,*
directed by Alfred Hitchcock

He was the son of Swedish dairy farmers who had come to Minnesota on their honeymoon with an intention of staying never divulged to parents back in Sweden until the young couple had their homestead and their first cattle. Lars, their oldest child, never met his grandparents, but he lived with their pictures on the wall, honoring them, and writing to them once a month until they died. He was born on the farm in 1902.

As a boy, home from school, he would go out to the fields and count the cows as they lumbered in heavy with milk. He learned to milk them himself and he walked among them when he was very small, his head no higher than their sad, bashful eyes. Lars liked the simplicity of those creatures, he liked the smell of their dung and the warmth of their milk. He gave the cows names, and he knew them all, so that he grieved if one of them died.

At sixteen, he left school and, without thinking about it, started to work for his father on the farm. He was twenty, when he went to St. Cloud and met Gunnel Strand, the daughter of another farmer, people who had come to America a year after his parents. He courted her and they were married in 1923. He and his father built another room onto the Thorwald farmhouse so that Lars and Gunnel could live there. As the oldest son, it was taken for granted that Lars would have the farm one day. He and Gunnel tried to have a child of their own, but although their love filled their resting hours, no child came.

Then, in 1928, on a winter night, Lars was driving Gunnel home from St. Cloud in a snowstorm. He would blame himself later for one glass of beer too many. But there was ice on the road. The car locked in a skid and the passenger's side struck a tree. Gunnel was killed by the force of the impact, and Lars had to walk the rest of the way home carrying her body.

He never recovered from that loss, he might have stayed happy all his life if Gunnel had lived. He had been brought up to live in slow, calm steadfastness, for good or ill. He remained on the farm until 1932, but then he left. Times were so much harder, the farm could not support as many people. His younger brother, Gunnar, was married with children of his own, so Lars left and wished him luck.

He went first to Chicago (who knows if he and L. B. Jeffries didn't look at each other from opposite sides of the street?), and he worked as a guard at the Art Institute, slowly putting on weight as he sat for so much of the day. Then, in 1939, he decided he would go to New York. He had a second cousin there who worked at Macy's and got Lars a job: a store detective. But it only lasted a year: Lars was not observant enough.

In 1943, he answered an advertisement for a traveling costume jewelry salesman. His beat covered lower Manhattan and Staten Island. With a suitcase of samples, he went on foot, calling at stores and those houses where previous customers had lived. It was a wearying job, but he reckoned he couldn't be choosy. He got used to it, he learned a little about the cheap costume jewelry he carried, about how to get a sale from being stubbornly boring. He learned shortcuts, he worked out the best places to eat, he passed the time of day with Moe Williams and bought a tie or two from her. And he picked up Anna Bryant as a customer.

She was a widow who lived near Willow Brush Park on Staten Island. He met her in 1948, when she bought a brooch in the shape of a rose. She was quite a handsome woman, he thought, and so talkative that his reticence didn't show as much. They went on a date, to see *Sorry, Wrong Number*, and when she had finished explaining its plot to him over their supper, she said, "You know, *we* could get married. We might do that. We both need someone to look after us."

He consented; he could think of nothing else to say. They married and moved into an apartment on West Twelfth Street. It was a little expensive, but he was ready to walk rather faster and she said she could probably get a job. But her health was not good. Not that doctors could put a finger on what was wrong, but Anna spent more and more time in bed. Lars would make dinner for her when he came home, yet she scolded him for being late.

Lars did all he could to interest or divert her. He told her stories about his day, but she said they were too mundane. He read cookbooks to make the dinners more appealing. He said he had heard that L. B. Jeffries, the famous photographer, had moved in across the way. And he used to sit in the dark smoking cheap cigars watching the life in the courtyard. There was a dazzling woman (she reminded him of Gunnel) living in the apartment above Jeffries. Lars decided to kill his wife. It was worth a try and he never appreciated that the whole world thinks of it.

Later, a lot later, when he was on death row in Sing Sing, Jeffries came to visit him. They were surprised to discover that they had been born within three hundred miles of each other. Jeffries had known several Swedes in his youth. He took some photographs of Thorwald and, before he died, Lars saw them printed in a magazine. He had not realized how heavyset and forbidding a man he was. No wonder Jeff had been suspicious.

> *This Thorwald is the best example I know of an unexceptional, downtrodden man, one of the quietly desperate, sucked into a drama against his will, and never acquiring the confidence or panache it requires. It was as if a mistake had been made.*

ALICIA HUBERMAN

Ingrid Bergman in Notorious, *1946, directed by Alfred Hitchcock*

Only children cannot help but see themselves as central figures in what is going on—even if they are outcasts. This is not to charge them with vanity. They may be passive observers or helpless victims, hubs of numbness, a vacancy around which all things revolve. Equally, the contest in large families may spur on remarkable self-centeredness in children. But the one among many *is* in competition. No matter how narcissistic, he or she regards life as a group performance, an ensemble. The only child has an intimation that he or she is the only person alive. His and her portrait of the world is an illusion that regularly taunts the solitary consciousness. Is it possible that the only child finds it harder to believe in things? Does he see all life as a mystery only he has noticed? And what of an only child born to an only parent?

Alicia Huberman was born in Vienna in 1919. She was the daughter of Reinhold Huberman (1889–1950), the physicist, and of his wife, Charlotte, who died when Alicia was two weeks old, of blood poisoning incurred in giving birth. Disappointed by the city, Professor Huberman left Vienna with his child and took up a position at the University of Göttingen. While there, he contributed to the experiments of Gustav Hertz and James Franck, involving the electron bombardment of gases to stimulate light emission. This won them both a Nobel prize for physics in 1925, from which Huberman's exclusion always rankled.

The professor doted on his daughter and was sufficiently alarmed by vulnerabilities in her health to take her to a doctor for a checkup every three months. No serious maladies were found, but the close scrutiny kept Alicia wary of her own constitution. She grew up timid, diligent and successful at school, yet threatened by the way her father, her everyday housemate, the god of her needs, assured her that his work was too complicated to talk about.

In 1934, when Alicia was fifteen, her father told her they were going on a trip to America. She asked why, and he said times were changing in Germany, several other scientists were departing, so why not? After all, he could probably get a respectable position in America. They might be glad to have him there. Alicia did not argue or think of the loss of friends. Her father had been her closest companion. She intensified her study of English and worried about the voyage and the chance of seasickness.

It was as her father had said; it always was, like being told a story. Soon after arriving in America, he was invited to join the faculty of Georgetown University, and they were helped in finding a pleasant apartment close to the campus. In due course, the professor told her, she would become a student at the university. Alicia's English developed very well; it made her more conscious of German being spoken in the house. Her father had colleagues in. They would shut themselves in his study and talk till the early hours of the morning, eating a cake she had made.

In 1938, Alicia entered Georgetown. Her father was still teaching there, and he surprised her by forbidding her to take any of his classes—she was not drawn to them, the subject seemed beyond her—and not to acknowledge him if their paths crossed on the campus. They were to behave "professionally." It seemed like a game, to ignore her father, and it perplexed Alicia. She had a dream in which he no longer spoke to her at home and then one morning asked her, politely, "Who are you, young woman, and why are you living in my home?"

It was in 1942 that Professor Huberman went away. She was not to be alarmed, but he could not tell her where. They could write to each other, of course, but not directly. There was an address in Washington they were to use as a clearinghouse. Alicia had the apartment to herself, and several of her friends from Georgetown made use of it as a place for parties. Sometimes they talked about her father, and one of them guessed that he must be in Los Alamos, New Mexico, the hush-hush research place in the desert. Alicia wrote to the professor asking if this was so, but he ignored the question. Then, when he came home for Christmas in 1943, he was more suntanned than she had ever known him to be. His health was garish.

In 1945, a man called on her with news. He said her father had been arrested as an enemy agent. A random watch on his movements had amassed much incriminating evidence. He would be tried secretly, and was already in detention in Washington. But they would arrange for Alicia to see him. She went, and her father was impenetrable. He talked of the old days in Vienna and what she would do with her life now. He never discussed the accusation, and she lacked the courage to refer to it.

A friend said Alicia shouldn't mope. Parties were arranged, and she learned to drink whiskey. In a few weeks, she was a drunk. Her apartment was one long party. Her father was given a ninety-nine-year sentence. She saw him the same day, and he said it was not unreasonable. She was not to be concerned. Her old fears about this sole relationship being lost were realized. One day a dark man, aloof and cold, was at her party. His name was Devlin. His air of anonymity seemed sultry to her. She let him make love to her. He didn't like her, she knew; so she fell for him.

He asked how she felt about her father. She didn't know the answer. He thought it was a shame and said she could help America. The government needed to know her father's contacts. There was a man in Rio de Janeiro, Alexander Sebastian, whom they suspected. As far as they could ascertain, she had met him once when she was a child. Would Alicia gain his confidence? Was that too much to ask?

They went to Rio together. Devlin would kiss her and then, between kisses, urge her to get closer to Sebastian. She felt like an instrument, without a will of her own. To please Dev she would do it. And Sebastian was kind. He asked her about things, and gave small, attentive laughs if she tried a joke. She relaxed in his company. She began to trust him. Then she remembered he was an accomplished deceiver like her father, someone who could do one thing but not refer to it, just like Dev in their contorted embraces. Then Sebastian asked her to marry him.

She reported this to Devlin, assuming he would overrule it. But he stayed professional, and said why not? To Alicia, it was not horrifying to marry Sebastian: he was entertaining and considerate. It was worse to betray what she felt herself. A spy had to be promiscuous, and she could not manage that. She didn't have the energy to lie. Her health began to deteriorate, and she hated the gloating way Sebastian's mother said, "My dear Alicia"—such a hiss there—"marriage seems to agree with you." The old woman, the authentic Mrs. Sebastian, made "agree" sound like the effort to gulp down something unpleasant.

Alicia had Devlin invited to a big party at the Sebastian home, and that's when he found the earth in the wine bottle. But to deflect discovery of his real search, Dev let Sebastian see him kissing Alicia. Every kiss was calculated. Of course, Sebastian was not fooled. He and his mother began to poison her, very slowly, at the frightful evening coffee rituals. She had claustrophobia. She felt sicker as the slow days passed. She could neither sleep nor concentrate. Something in the lethargy of the poison seemed to suit her fallen state. She accepted it.

Then Devlin came to the house one night, while Sebastian was in conference with the other Nazis. He went up to her room, picked her up and carried her down the stairs. Her weakness let her feel like a leaf swept forward by the wind. To be rescued, we need an inkling of death wish. In Alicia it was now a chain inkling. She went mad—she was not saved—and Devlin was able to go back to business thinking love was a pill.

ALEXANDER SEBASTIAN

Claude Rains in Notorious, *1946,*
directed by Alfred Hitchcock

The parents of Alexander Sebastian planned to meet on the island of Madeira, at Reid's Hotel, for the birth of their child. The mother, Grazina, went there three months ahead of her time to be in the best health. The father, Lorenzo Sebastian ("The Coffee King"), on business in Europe, set out from Lisbon in ample time. But his schooner foundered, with the loss of Sebastian and the crew of six. So Alexander was born in 1893 to a mother actually just widowed, yet unaware of the loss.

The mother moved her son to a home on Lake Geneva, where Alexander grew up. In those years, she handled the affairs of Sebastian Inc. with more astuteness than her husband had managed. She saw to it that their coffee penetrated the market of the United States, all the more significant when European sales were interrupted by the Great War. As a child, Alex had private tutors. In 1911, he entered Christchurch College, Oxford, to read Classics.

During the war, he lived in Switzerland, Brazil, America and England, conducting business under the tutelage of Mrs. Sebastian. He also made himself available to British Intelligence as a source of information picked up on his visits to Berlin. For Alex had secured contracts for delivery of coffee to the German Army. It was galling to mother and son that similar deliveries to France and England were made difficult because of the hostilities. As Alex said at the time, "War should not hinder the flow of necessaries, coffee or information. Only humorless puritanism impedes them."

After the war, Alex took increasing control of the business, and in 1918, aged twenty-five, he acquired the monies left by his father and prudently reinvested by Mrs. Sebastian. There was time for pleasure, too. Alex was a gourmet and a devotee of sophisticated company. He spoke five languages (French, German, English, Portuguese and Italian), and moved easily in and out of the great estates of Europe, bending to all politics, consistent in his charm and his faith in trade. In the early twenties, he was a close friend of King Carl II of Rumania and a go-between for him with his mistress, Magda Lupescu. When that couple was forced into exile, they found a home in the Sebastian mansion in Geneva.

Always interested in novelty, Alex went to Vienna in hopes of being accepted as a patient by Sigmund Freud. He was turned away because there were so many young women ahead of him on the waiting list, and because Freud quickly detected "the balance of a born yachtsman" in Alex. However, Alex liked the city and spent a good deal of time there over the next few years. Among many others, he made the acquaintance of Professor Reinhold Huberman, and one Sunday afternoon he taught croquet to the professor's exquisite but rather fragile daughter, Alicia.

It was in 1928 that Alex had an intense weekend of conversation with his mother. She estimated that Europe was in flux, that a new Germany would be born again soon, destined to engage in conflict with the Reds. Its natural ally in the crusade would be America, the land of capitalism and technology. England and France were finished. The allegiances that had been sensible in the Great War should be reassessed. It was up to Alex to identify the emerging forces in Germany and make contact with them. "I suppose so," he said wistfully, for he could never quite fathom such far-reaching motives, even if intrigue delighted him.

So Alexander Sebastian drew nearer than he felt was tasteful to the leader of the National Socialist Movement. He also devised a plan whereby, in the scuttle of prominent Jews to get out of the new Germany, a few spies might be passed along too. In particular, he advised Professor Huberman on getting to America, establishing a career there which who knows . . . ? "And Alicia will have so much more fun there, won't she?"

By 1937, Alex and his mother had shifted their base to Rio de Janeiro. This was not his inclination. Rio offered less than Europe in the way of society. But his mother pointed out that in an extensive and wide-ranging war it was imperative to be close to one's raw materials. Moreover, South America lay there on the modern globe, a monster asleep, so unknown that it had to become more important.

During the war, the coffee trade was a cover for a courier system that brought information down to Rio out of the U.S. and thence across the Atlantic. It was through Alex's small, adept hands that some of the atomic secrets passed. He did not understand what he was conveying, but he regarded espionage as part of a useful sharing. "In an age of such power as this, secrecy will only lead to undue advantage and precipitate action."

But in the middle of the war—torpid days in Rio, with guilt and shortages pressing on the neutrality—his mother fell ill. It had never

145

happened before. So it was food for his curiosity that he felt neither anxiety nor pity. He cared for her, in the usual ways, but he was indifferent to her fate.

He examined his own life: he was fifty, fit, prosperous, not cast down by the world's war, not spoiled by his advantages. He deserved better. He would make sure he got it. This ambition took precedence over Sebastian Inc. and the future of National Socialism. It survived his mother's recovery. He had at last picked up a proper sense of his own soul. It soared above Germany's possible defeat in the war. Who lost wars anymore? The victors would be obliged to prop up the vanquished.

In this blithe mood, his life welcomed back Alicia Huberman. He recalled the awkward child on a Viennese lawn, perplexed by the narrowness of hoops. He had made a joke about "Miss Hoop-erman" that had kept her laughing for ten minutes. What bliss that she should appear in Rio now a lovely woman. His mother warned him, but he was not deterred by the difference in age. He married Alicia and he was happy for five months.

Then his mother demonstrated how Alicia was an agent of the enemy. Nor did she shirk that task. She explained to Alex that he had put them both in jeopardy. She whispered that Alicia had used him, that she was nothing but Devlin's pawn. He slid back into middle age and he permitted the arsenic to put gradual rings of smoke around Alicia's sad eyes. They gave it to her every night, a drop in her coffee.

Alex had to keep the story from the others. His wife would succumb to her illness. Any other solution might point to the error he had made. And so when that suave thug Devlin came in and carried Alicia away, as if she were a rag doll, he had nothing to do but compose his parched face, go back into the house and admit failure. The silent, thrilled disbelief was his death sentence.

Alexander Sebastian passed away in 1946, in Rio de Janeiro, of a wasting illness that accomplished its end in eight weeks, the invalid meekly sipping coffee every night, watched over by his mother.

WALKER

Lee Marvin in Point Blank, *1967, directed by John Boorman*

He would be Walker still. Though he lay in an empty cell on Alcatraz, shot more times than he could count, looking up at the dahlia stain of rust and time in the corner of the wall and ceiling, he would fear no demise. He would survive, Walker still. There was a power of imagination that could melt away bullets and heal their wounds, as if the film of him being shot could be run in reverse, the bullets breaking out of skin which closed behind them, the slugs rushing backward to their guns and making the exact insertions no matter that the gun kicked just before they arrived or that a flare was sucked back into the gun just before the bullets.

In 1967, at the age of forty-five, with his wife, Lynne, and a wartime buddy, Mal Reese, he had carried out the biggest job of his career, of his life, on a Wells Fargo office. Afterward, they had gone by helicopter to the abandoned prison of Alcatraz, in San Francisco Bay. But instead of dividing up the money, as agreed, Reese had shot Walker, and Lynne, he realized, was party to the betrayal, not simply the beautiful young wife he had met on the waterfront on a rainy day, with the wet making her silk blouse cling to her body, with drops of water hanging on the lobes of her ears, with her brown hair sticking to her brow, but a liar, a traitor, a whore for jovial Mal Reese.

Lying in the open cell, crumpled in one corner, gazing up at the stain in the other, Walker estimated that they had cheated him of a ninety-three-thousand-dollar share. The sum was as odd, round and appealing as his dreams of vengeance. He would get them and count off the ninety-three thousand even if every dollar had to be a leaf of their fine skin. He would go after them. He would be Walker, thumping down however many corridors it took until they trembled at the sound of his coming. As he felt his blood knocking in his head, he heard his own hard shoes on the corridor, walking toward his victims.

He would raise himself from out of the corner and out of the cell, and he would go down staircases and corridors out onto the small island of rocks and brambles to what passed for a beach, and there he would let himself be carried out on the cold currents of water in the Bay. When Alcatraz had been a prison, it was said that no escapees had

147

ever made that swim. But the prison had had central heating and large meals, so that flabby, tender inmates became too soft for the water. The broken Walker was still hard and cunning. He would make no swim; he would let the current of desire carry him to shore.

He would survive. The bullets would be removed or his muscular insides would chew and digest them. They would be lodged there like knots in his wood. He would recover, and as his strength came back he would begin to look around for Reese. And one day he would be on a pleasure boat in the Bay, listening to the loudspeaker describe the impossible waters, when a man would approach him, a man who knew what had happened, a man who would tell him Reese had done what he did with the compliance of the Organization. But Walker could go after him if he listened to the man's advice. This man would be called Fairfax.

Walker would find Lynne, alone, abandoned by Mal Reese, awash on a sea of narcotics and melancholy. She would kill herself the night he came to her, as if she knew that was a traitor's only duty. And Walker then could go after Lynne's sister, Chris, a woman he had always liked, but he had met Lynne first and been lost in her rain-soaked attraction. He would find Chris, and she would agree to help him. There would be no need for explanations. Like two sleepwalkers they would share their dreams.

He would trace them and track them down one by one, the members of the Organization who had welcomed Mal in. There was Stegman, the car dealer. Walker would go to meet him, to try out a car. He would take Stegman on the trial drive, battering the car against walls and concrete posts until the story spilled out of Stegman. And there would be Carter. He would go to Carter's office, and push the man around past one Venetian blind after another, the plastic slivers rippling as the man's body went through them. And he would meet Carter in an L.A. storm drain, but a rifleman would pick off Carter, and Walker would find a parcel of ninety-three thousand cutout pieces of paper, not the money, and only a ribbon of credit cards in Carter's pockets, like an umbilical cord between him and the system.

And Chris would be bait for Mal. She would send word to him that she had always wanted him. And the bodyguards would pass Chris up to the penthouse in the outside glass elevator. Walker would watch her rise. And while Mal was slowly undressing Chris, he would come up too, overpower the guards, until he found Chris and Mal both naked. And he would lead the timorous Mal by a sheet wound round his nakedness to the edge of the roof and then, in panic, Mal would move. The sheet would unwind and his pale nude body would drop to the street. Avenged, but still minus ninety-three thousand dollars.

He would go on, as far as Brewster, the head of the Organization, the one man who could authorize his money. With Chris, he would go to Brewster's L.A. house, lie in wait for him and terrorize him. The flustered Brewster would say all right, all right, you know you're a very bad man, Walker, and Walker might smile to himself. No one would see. But the arrangements would be made, for a drop-off of ninety-three thousand dollars, on Alcatraz again.

And Walker would be there in the sepulchral galleries. He would watch Brewster in the spotlight in the courtyard as the helicopter came down with the package. And Brewster would call out to Walker to come and get his money. But Walker wouldn't go. Then a shot would ring out and Brewster would be dead. And Fairfax and the rifleman would walk down to the courtyard, like a couple of golfers coming up to the green. And Fairfax would say his plan had worked. He would have used Walker to clear a way to the top of the Organization. Then Fairfax would say that Walker could come down now. It would be safe now. Fairfax would open the package to show him the color of money.

But Walker would never go down. He would stay transfixed by the way the dried-out puddle in the courtyard had left a stain like a flower.

CHRIS ROSE

Angie Dickinson in Point Blank, *1967,*
directed by John Boorman

She might have been so many things. This is a country made for pretenders, with an art that tempts hope. She lost count of how many times people told her, "You could be a model, did you ever think of that?" And she made herself available. Born in San Diego in 1942, she moved up to Los Angeles when she was seventeen and tried to be noticed. She had boyfriends who knew people in pictures. And once she went for a weekend on Catalina with a photographer. He did a few poses of her, but he was more taken with the fog. She had been to some studio parties. Once an associate producer took her to dinner and a hotel afterward. He asked if she would fellate him, and she agreed if he would test her. "Shit, no," he said, plaintively, "this is personal." So she walked out. She had decided to be practical and she knew that someone who might become a star could still end up a hooker.

So she told herself pictures were corrupt. She ate health foods, she jogged, she went with a schoolteacher and she looked better than ever until a lifeguard at Venice stopped her and said, "You in pictures?" So she went with him and he was nothing but it was the best sex. It was a limited kind of paradise with him, but Chris was empty because what might have been still appealed to her more.

She had an older sister, Lynne, the wild one, who had gone to Alaska as a waitress and married Walker. Some people called him a psychopath, and Lynne regarded him with fear sometimes. But Chris liked him. Behind that craggy look, she thought, was a weird human who had decided achievement was foolish. They had odd talks in which she went with his silences. "Suppose you think you're good-looking?" he said once. Chris blushed and Walker studied the fire. "It's not worth much," he said. "Won't last."

"I know that."

"Yeah, but it's something," sighed Walker, as if he had thought about it a lot and come away with respect for transience. Chris looked at his sleepy face. He wasn't noticing her, but she felt a tugging at her spirit, as if he were imagining her.

Then one day her mother called from San Diego to say Lynne had phoned and apparently Walker had disappeared.

"What did she mean?" asked Chris.

"You know. Gone off. For good, I think. I think it's for good."

Chris called Lynne but there was only an answering machine. Four months later she bumped into Lynne at a Mexican restaurant on Fairfax. She was tanned and happy, and with another guy, Mal Reese. She told Chris they had been to Acapulco for a break.

"What's the matter?" said Chris.

"I'm doing cocaine," Lynne told her.

"What about Walker?"

Her sister's mood dropped. "What's it to you?"

"I don't know."

"You look good, Chris," resentfully.

"I do?"

"Yeah, bitch. You know it." They laughed and it was over.

That was the last time Chris saw Lynne. Lynne was found dead in her house two weeks later. She'd taken a whole bottle of antidepressants and she'd choked on her gray vomit. Two days later Mal Reese called her.

"Is that Chris?"

"This is she."

"I wanted to say this that time we met, you're a very lovely lady."

"Did you know Lynne died?"

"God no, I didn't know that."

"Tuesday."

"Jesus. Is that right? Are you free tonight?"

She didn't answer.

"We must get together so you can tell me about it."

So they had dinner, and then Mal suggested taking her back to his penthouse apartment for a brandy. He said he knew a man in casting at NBC. Chris went along with it; it held off the isolation. They hardly mentioned Lynne, and when Chris once talked about Walker Mal shut up completely. She went to bed with him, and in the night, as he rolled over on her for a third time, she felt a breeze in the room and she had a brief, untrusted vision of Walker coming to rescue her with a part in a picture. But nothing came except the morning.

> *The happiest man, the most settled and assured,*
> *is flawed if he cannot sleep. And the one to be*
> *tortured and shot the next day has mercy if he*
> *does not have to stay awake.*

MA JARRETT

Margaret Wycherly in White Heat, *1949,*
directed by Raoul Walsh

Born in 1881, in Telluride, Colorado, the daughter of a brothelkeeper, Kitty Reilly, she was named Lucy Gray. Her mother already had offspring—Alvin Brown, Sukie Black, Pence White—and gray was the next color in line. Unacquainted with her father, yet guessing he might still live in the vicinity of the silver-mining town, Lucy developed a forthright questioning manner; every man felt she had her suspicions about him. From the age of seven, she would trudge through the snow, the mud and the summer dust with a six-gun knocking on her slender hip. No one knew whether it was loaded until that day, in 1892, when two fellows held up the Sheridan Hotel and backed out onto the street. "Varmints!" Lucy cried out, to turn them, for she would not shoot a man in the back. Her first shot took one of the bandits in the kneecap, the second went through an onlooker's beard, and the third struck the manager of the hotel, coming in pursuit, between the eyes.

This was not good for the brothel business, already disrupted by Lucy's habit of wandering in and out of rooms looking for her mice. So Kitty, not without a tear, sent her daughter away. The pretext was the child's alarming cough. Common sense put it down to the cigars, but Kitty reckoned it was the altitude. So Lucy was sent to live with a cousin of Kitty's in McCook, Nebraska. She learned to ride there and worked at ranching. But she excelled in shooting competitions, and she was known for her way of aiming while smoking a stogie.

At seventeen, she met William Jarrett in Cheyenne, Wyoming, as Buffalo Bill Cody's Wild West Show played the town. Jarrett was assistant business manager to Colonel Cody, a scrupulous mathematician with a flair for the show business. Sixteen years older than Lucy, he was smitten by her spunk—they met when a mouthful of tobacco juice she had directed at a spittoon (nine feet away) landed on the shiny toe of his shoe. "Were you aiming at it, young lady?" he wanted to know.

"What's it to you, pisspot?" she gave back, not promising a love match, but William could smell out a tender heart, and he bought her a buffalo dinner straightaway. When he learned she was a shootist, he asked for a demonstration: Lucy was part of the Wild West Show before she'd finished buffalo farting. But it was hard for her because Annie Oakley—old souse—was the shooting star, except that she was often too drunk to hit a wall. Lucy was employed to do the real shooting that Oakley had once been capable of. A wagon would come into the arena with Annie up front blasting away on nothing, and Lucy under the canvas plonking the targets. It did not foster friendly feelings between the girls.

Lucy and Jarrett were married in 1898, and a son was born the next year—Cody, after their buckskin boss—in Casper, Wyoming, as the show toured. For the first five years of the child's life, they stayed with the show, roaming the West. But in 1904, they built a homestead in the part of South Dakota near Custer. It was a wild place, with Indians around, and Ma kept the child in one arm and a gun in the other.

Away from the show, William Jarrett was hardly able to chop a cord of wood, much less skin bears or make decent whiskey. So Ma took to doing a little holdup work in small banks in Nebraska. She would sometimes take Cody along, originally for luck, but once he cottoned on, he was cover for her. Ma had taught Cody to shoot as soon as she'd given him a pipe.

Ma never was sure about the death of her husband, on a camping trip with Cody. But there were things between men you shouldn't inquire into. William had been a worrier, and he was holding her and Cody back. They could get a gang together now. The automobile had put a fresh face on the holdup business, and while Ma had had to go into spectacles, so that her shooting slowed a touch, she was a merciless driver, so long as you had a strong car.

All through the 1920s, the Jarrett gang kept active. There was the bank in Chillicothe, Missouri (1922), the railroad holdup outside North Platte, Nebraska (1925), and the Wells Fargo job in Topeka, Kansas (1927). It happened that I was riding on the train they stopped near North Platte. I was fourteen then, and I had been visiting my grandmother. The train stopped and I could hear a lot of laughter and whooping down the line. I was able to watch out of the window, and I have never forgotten the jaunty wave Ma gave me as she strode around in boots and a cotton dress. She went on, then stopped, came back and handed me a chocolate bar out of her pocket. "There, son." She smiled. Her hand was small and bony; her nails were cracked. The back of her hand was dotted with freckles and she wore a thin gold wedding ring. There was a six-gun in the other hand; it seemed as big as a man's finger in a baby's fist. I kept that chocolate bar for years, till it was hard and black. It was the best story I ever had for my children—that and the one about Johann Tickle. I think Harry threw the chocolate bar in the fire.

Then, in 1928, outside Aberdeen, South Dakota, the gang was trapped in a motor court and Cody set off so as to let Ma get away. Cody was taken and, with a lot of bribing of witnesses and barefaced lies, they were able to get him fifteen years in the state penitentiary.

He was out in ten, but it was a bad time for the family and Ma was never quite the same again without her boy. She was reduced to typing envelopes and baking pies while he was away. What's more, Cody's headaches got a lot worse in prison. That was one of the reasons he was released in 1939, because the doctors suspected he had a brain tumor or something and didn't have a long way to go anyway.

Ma and Cody decided to head further west, and so they moved on into Idaho and Oregon, but it was cold and high there, and somehow Ma had gotten superstitious about living at altitude. She was sure it hurt Cody's head. They did a few jobs, but they lived simply and many a night in front of the fire they'd read Charles Dickens to each other. Actually, that was the period when Ma really mastered reading—and shot an owl to celebrate!

It was in 1942 Cody met the other woman—Verna, yellow-haired tramp. She was from Chico and said they'd love it in the south where it was warm. She got her hooks into Cody—always parading in her underwear and pouting at him—and they got married, damn it! Then in no time Ed Somers was coming by, an "old, old friend" of hers, full of ideas for a new gang. Ma could see Verna had the hots for Ed—greaseball hunk, he was—and she could tell that Cody didn't always catch on. He needed looking after still.

So, anyway, in 1945, the new Jarrett gang held up a train in the Sierras. Then all hell broke loose. Cops were out after them, and Cody said he'd had enough. He turned himself in on a smaller job (three-year sentence, he thought) just to get the heat off. But they gave him another fifteen in Folsom, so he knew he had to crash out. Ma looked after the so-called "gang": most of the time it was telling Ed and Verna to stop using themselves as mirrors. She went to see Cody in prison, and she'd heard that there'd been an attempt on his life there. Hell! If you had to be in prison, you expected security. So she told Cody she'd settle Ed—it had to have been his idea. But Ma was sixty-eight, and Ed worked out with weights. It was a real fight, but in the end Verna put a bullet in the back of her head to shut her up.

CODY JARRETT

James Cagney in White Heat, *1949,
directed by Raoul Walsh*

The headaches had begun as his trick, like a fingertip of grease put on a fastball so that it fell off the table as it neared the plate—a certain additive, a definite effect, illegal but winning. Whenever Cody Jarrett wanted his mother, and didn't want his father around in their precious air, he would curl up, with his hands between his legs, shudder and whisper, "Head hurts." Whatever she was doing, Ma would order his father away, she'd pull the drapes together so that the house became darker and more auspicious, and she'd come to his side, smelling of flour, tobacco and gunpowder.

"Head hurts, Ma," he'd say.

"I know it," she told him.

"You're with me."

"It'll pass, by and by."

As he lay there, letting her gnarled hand stroke the back of his neck, he was dizzy at the lack of pain and his own guile. But as the years went by, and he acted his heart out to hold on to Ma, he noticed that the strain of his belief in the play had begun to make his head throb. Then, once, in amazement, he realized that he was having a headache, unbidden, not ordered. It had stolen up on him, a pain imprisoned in his brow, so that he didn't dare move or open his eyes. "Ma!" he cried in a voice of such fear and agony that it startled the seventeen-year-old Cody and made him afraid of the force in himself. Ma came, and his father came too, two faces looking down into the cradle of migraine.

His father said that Cody was moping in the house. They should go off into the hills, get some fresh air and exercise. "That wood stove," his father explained, "makes the air go stale, and you spend all your time indoors reading comic books." So father and son packed a tent and put on boots. Ma watched them depart, and she told William to come back and get a gun in case of mountain lions. He took the pistol and a box of bullets and put them in the backpack. Cody stood watching, his shoulders hunched, a tense look on his face.

They didn't converse in the hills. His father cooked a meal the first night while Cody gathered wood. He watched his father at work and pretended to be a hostile tracking the white man. He thought how easily he could pick off his father.

"Hey, dreamer!" yelled William Jarrett. "What'd I ask?"

"All right, Pa." Ma would be baking now with a pot of milk and moonshine warming on the stove.

Three days later, Cody came back down the same path toward the house. He was carrying the pack and the same anxious expression.

"Howdy," said Ma, and then an hour later, "Pa coming?"

"No Ma, he's not."

"What's he doing?"

155

"Got hisself killed."

"How'd he do that?"

"Fell right off a cliff. Body landed in rushing rapids. Swept away."

"Damn it!" said Ma.

"I know," said her son in a heartfelt way.

It passed off.

But Cody had the headaches now like the color of his hair. It went from brown to gray but the headaches didn't grow older or weaker. Ma saw she should never let him off on his own.

It was while he was in prison the first time that Cody got teased by other men about Ma. These guys were always talking about the sex thing and they had pictures of cuties in bathing suits. When he came out of prison, Cody had worked it out that he ought to get himself that kind of woman so he'd be less odd. Verna looked exactly like the pictures, so Cody said he'd marry her. She laughed at him, but then he slugged her good and she got that wicked-bitch afraid look in her eyes. Ma couldn't understand about Verna. She said the girl wasn't good for him. But that wasn't the point. Just keep her around for appearance.

The new Jarrett gang did a lovely train as it came out of a tunnel in the mountains. But one of the gang used his name, Cody, and the driver heard. So Cody gave him one in the gut and the guy tipped over on a lever, and the engine gave off white steam right in the face of one of the gang. He was a goner—blind and helpless.

Back in the cabin, Cody got his worst headache yet; maybe it was Verna's powder-puff scent. Ma took him into another room. "Don't let them see you," she said as he curled in her lap. "Might give 'em ideas." Then she passed him a drink: "Top o' the world, son." That was saying it.

So Cody took a rap on a small job and in the prison he meets this Vic Pardoe, and they get along. One day at lunch someone whispers in his ear that Ma is dead. The head starts to burst. Cody Jarrett gets up ranting and roaring, Cody can see him, and he staggers along the top of the tables before four guards restrain him and carry him out. That guy's nuts, thinks Cody.

The doc is for putting Cody in an insane asylum. But he gets a gun and breaks out with Vic. Goes straight for the old house; it's night when he gets there. Cody gets to Verna; she's so scared she's wetting herself. But all she can do is set up Ed, and Cody plugs him at the top of the stairs so he goes tumbling down. What are stairs for?

Then the gang plans a new job, just to prove Cody's his old self.

Night before it, Cody meets Vic outside the house and they have a regular talk. Vic wants to get into L.A. to see his wife. "You're lonesome, like me," says Cody. "All I ever had was Ma. I was just talking with her. Always trying to put me on top, she was. . . . Maybe I am nuts."

But "Vic" was a cop, it turned out. Liar. Traitor. Knife in the back. Couldn't trust anyone. Cody ended up on top of the gas tank and one of the shots set it off, a column of fire and heat with Cody laughing in it. His headache had finally exploded the world.

BRIGID O'SHAUGHNESSY

Mary Astor in The Maltese Falcon,
1941, directed by John Huston

Everything visible was real: the long legs, her high breasts, the swimming-pool-blue eyes, and the waves of what we call red hair. But redness in hair covers a range of hues all unlike the smart red in a box of paints—there's rust, whiskey, dried blood, paprika and ginger, iron-strong earth, a claret where it meets the glass, one of the russets you find in a Cox's Orange Pippin (an English variety of apple), copperiness, a thin bitter red that could be sour or poisonous, a noble faded red like the red of Raphael. The red of red hair goes on forever, and you've never quite pinned it down. I always wanted a red-haired child, but Mary Frances and I were brown and brown, so it might have been strange and worrying.

Brigid O'Shaughnessy had the unequivocal body of a fine creature. But she was a frightful liar. If you asked her the time, and she looked at her little watch, with a face the size of a dime, instead of telling you it was 8:56 (and you had a train at nine), she'd say, "Oh, it's early yet, just after a quarter to" or, "Heavens, it's nearly ten past. You'll have to stay the night." She had a set of names for herself in the way con men keep a wallet full of cards—she could be Arlene Wonderly, or Stella Leblanc, Hope Middlewhich, Hermione Heigho, Winifred Wadman, Gwendolen Torrance—I don't know what!

She was born in Annamoe, Co. Wicklow, Ireland, the child of a professor of literature at Harvard who was teaching that year at Trinity College, Dublin, and was having a weekend walking in

Wicklow with his wife when—the rain falling—she said, "Horace, I would like us to hurry."

"How so, my love?" he enquired.

"I'm pregnant," she said.

"You didn't tell me," he complained.

Enough of that. There are childhoods so flat you can put a reader to sleep with a faithful account. If I was to tell you how thoroughly and religiously Brigid was brought up, you'd only say, "Well, how is it she turned out an incorrigible liar?"

Cut to when she's eighteen, with a shock of pimento hair only fierce brushing could tame. Straightaway, she carved up men with her falsehoods. She had a beguiling trick of dropping her eyes, lowering her voice and drawing muskily close to a man—all in the spirit of intimate confession—to say, "Dear heart, I have to say something. . . ."

The he in question was like a cork in a vortex. He listened and was moved a mile by her sad tale. Then time passed and he cottoned on that this revelation had been mist. He mentioned it, "I say, my dear . . ." And wham, her eyes were pools of remorse, the blush was raspberry and she came closer still, so that if he'd looked he might have seen the rising of her nipples beneath her blouse. "That *was* a fib, dearest, a half-truth really. I want now to tell you the hard facts. . . ." And so on, a little closer, a little more hushed and momentous, a better show every time.

To cut it all short, we come to 1930 and there she is—red head at morning, sailor's warning—in hot pursuit of the Maltese Falcon, a statuette stuffed with gemstones and a history harder to believe than it is to tell, and anyway who's seen the bird in the last century?

But we all need something to be looking for, and the falcon made a pretty trail by way of Constantinople to Hong Kong and San Francisco. It picked up colorful characters as it traveled: Casper Gutman, Floyd Thursby and Joel Cairo for starters, with Pacific voyages on boats called *La Paloma*—everything a romancer could wish for.

But then in San Francisco, looking for help, she'd gone to Spade & Archer, and in that alley off Bush Street, above the Stockton Tunnel, as Miles Archer came closer to swallow the next sotto voce untruth, she had put a bullet inside him. And later, Spade had worked it out, despite her holding her trembly body against his with that threat of ultimate coming clean in her eye. Imagine a milk-white body with that Titian hair, imagine that, Sam, you were saying to him without opening your mouth except to breathe and let him see the cooked lobster of your tongue.

It could have gone on forever, this farrago of lies and a falcon too heavy to fly. Yet Spade called it quits. Not that he wasn't impressed by the lies or the liar. But he came up with a stuffy quote about what's expected of a detective, how if your partner's bumped off and you know who did it why it's "bad business" to let the killer go. And, anyway, he knew enough to know he shouldn't trust her. He had seven or eight reasons for turning her in and, against them, only the vision of that hair on top of that pale body. So he turned her in, the sap. You know a man like that's a depressive and that one day he's going to come to a full stop, the end of his alley, and never say or write another civil word.

Spade didn't know if they'd hang her or give her life. He never bothered to find out. He was the sort who had read about Lot's wife. Well, they made it life, and who can say it wasn't because, there in the court, she gave the judge the impression of edging closer and looking up at him with the unadorned, woeful truth? "Your Honor . . ." did she begin?

She went to prison, and no one ever knew how, but after two years there, they suddenly realized she was nine months pregnant. She was delivered of a boy baby, named Sergius, but she agreed he should go to an orphanage and not know the glum truth about his real mother—unless she ever found herself in a position to reveal it. He did well, too, in the air force and Hollywood. But that's too much to get into here.

CASPER GUTMAN

Sydney Greenstreet in The Maltese Falcon, *1941, directed by John Huston*

THE BABY EATS HERE! said the sign, in bold red with the exclamation mark like a flame. The sign was attached to a playpen in the window of the best bakery in Mitcham. Mr. and Mrs. Gutman did cakes, pies and puddings, as well as a range of loaves. And they took no less care with those offerings than they did with their rotund infant, Casper, who sat, large, pink and glowing, in the playpen as an advertisement. He had been born in 1879, a thirteen-pound baby. The exertions of the delivery were such that his mother had to be kept on a diet of lard cakes for a year.

Casper's parents were German, and they had come to London fifteen years before his birth. I don't know why. I can't know everything. Look into your own family trees and try to account for all those jagged changes in direction.

As a boy, Casper kneaded the dough. He could crawl into the oven itself to retrieve loaves. He was the delivery boy, and he was always on show at fetes and faïrs with a sampling of the family eats. Still, it was his large, contented presence that spoke loudest. To look at Casper was to wonder whether one didn't have room left for just one more turnover, or another slice of crusty farmhouse.

He was spared most of the burden of formal education. Eating or urging others to do so took up much of his time. Yet, by the age of eighteen and at 270 pounds he had amassed a body of diverse knowledge. Without any central preoccupation, he had an archipelago of hobbies and subjects. They included card games, the Great Western Railway, Levantine history, the comic novel, horse racing, the grammar of Latin languages, food (of course), mental arithmetic, the Hanseatic League, bizarre murders, shaggy-dog stories, the life of Sterne, cricketing statistics, papal anecdotes, fire irons, Chinese tortures, the campaigns of Wallenstein, miniature gardens of the Japanese type, the history of puppets, culinary aphrodisiacs and those vagaries of fact that are often lumped together under the title "Believe It or Not".

He managed to be active without ever really doing anything, ubiquitous yet not there when a crucial question arose. His declared profession was stage conjurer, and he did manage the company that included Walter Little. He was sometimes quoted in the popular press, and he sold a few jokes to music-hall comedians of the second rank.

It was soon after 1920 that he became caught up in the quest for the Falcon. The object had first drawn his attention in the coincidence of two of his interests—Levantine history and papal anecdotes. The death of his father (from a surfeit of éclairs) enabled him to sell the bakery to an emerging conglomerate, lodge his mother in a nursing home in Middlesbrough and be off, around the world, following the savage-claw trail of the Falcon. "Ah yes, sir, the Falcon!" he would sigh, the comment coming out of him like a sweet zephyr.

Late in the 1920s, the search grew apace, crowded with competitors, not least Mr. Joel Cairo and Miss Arlene Wonderly. The lady was not anyone he knew, but Cairo and he had crossed paths before: a bridge problem that Gutman sold to the *Daily Mail* for a guinea had been solved by this same Cairo, writing from Tiflis. The trio had their meeting eventually in San Francisco in 1930.

"We begin well, sir and madam," said Gutman. "There is, as far as I can see, no trace of the ordinary among us."

Miss Wonderly began to tell the truth, and Joel Cairo said a modest "when" as Gutman poured jiggers of Wild Turkey.

"Ah, sir," creaked Gutman, "I trust a man who says 'when.' For isn't timing the essence of polite behavior and a good kill?"

Miss Wonderly again, blushing plum, begged to get something off her chest, but Gutman had spied a copy of *Tristram Shandy* in Cairo's morocco briefcase. There followed a digression on the book and its author. For this was one passion that united Gutman and Cairo. They to-ed and fro-ed about Eliza, my Uncle Toby and so forth, their voices making an exquisite harmony: Cairo soft, snakelike and begging; Gutman as boomy as far-off thunder.

A little put out, Miss Wonderly said, "I am afraid I do not know the book or its author." Like gentlemen, they turned the discourse to her and, among other pretty confessions, learned that she had first seen the light in a small Irish town, Annamoe.

"Oh, that is most remarkable," thrilled Cairo.

"Indeed," said Gutman, "for you will be delighted to hear that Sterne as a child fell into the millstream at Annamoe."

Miss Wonderly went ruby with pride and consternation: "Of course, you gentlemen must understand that I had nothing to do with it."

Their laughter had scarcely died away when the San Francisco episode drew to its close. But Gutman and Cairo were well met, and not inclined to trust one another to continue the search alone. Put it another way, the Falcon was probably a pretext. They became a team, doing their best to endure the thirties and the war in travels through Asia Minor, the Orient and South America. When Gutman's funds ran out, in Macao in 1945, he and Cairo took to bridge professionally. There and then, they whipped Bannister and Grisby in a challenge match for $3,000.

As they grew older, they did not think of the Falcon for weeks at a time. The sedentary satisfaction of bridge became more appealing. They made seven spades, doubled, on the Q♣ lead in this hand at Caracas in 1949:

161

Coata

♠K
♥J32
♦KJ862
♣KJ83

Gutman

♠Q109752
♥KQ86
♦–
♣965

N

W   E

S

Cairo

♠AJ43
♥A109754
♦Q
♣A7

Sternberg

♠86
♥–
♦A1097543
♣Q1042

Their last recorded hand was in 1951, in Marienbad. After that they fade away. But I am confident they went on to campfire soirées in the Matto Grosso, reading a little Sterne to one another, or yarning about the Falcon. It is possible that, independently, they had both reached the conclusion that the bird was too rare ever to be seen, let alone caught or plucked. Yet as I think of them, they would not have admitted that ultimate impossibility to each other. And so they would have gone to sleep blissful in their partnership, tricksters to the world but loyal to the game.

I wish I had time to write a dozen Gutman and Cairo stories, all bravado and vulnerability. They might be a great success—erudite, rather inefficient villains. There is no warmer myth than that of ill-matched friendships that go on forever, so moved by their dream that transport becomes their nature. Such creatures might be no longer sure whether they were huntsmen or quarries.

VICTOR LASZLO

Paul Henreid in Casablanca, *1942,*
directed by Michael Curtiz

Why does no one attempt a life of Victor Laszlo? Did he intimidate actors? He was a liar, of course, and a liar in life may be a bore to deal with. A sad abandoned bore. Every dishonesty betrays the fabric of discourse. We trust the cloth less, and perhaps we speak less when we remember lying. But put a liar in a framework that includes the pressures pushing him into falsehood, and he can become a whimsical hero. There is something redemptive in the honest portrait of a liar, and of why he tricked and cheated. His wretchedness falls away. As for being boring—he may reappear in magical hues.

The life would have scenes in Eastern Europe and on the eastern edge of the U.S.; it would insist on romance taking priority over politics; and it would have the consummate fraud being taken seriously, but declining to fall for the world's earnestness. It would be a black comedy and—as a now elderly but experienced moviegoer—I would like to see Robert De Niro and his freezing smile in the part.

There is no way of telling when or where Victor Laszlo was born, nor whether that is the name he was born with. 1909 to 1911 probably covers the moment itself. As for place, there are Hungarians who claim their nationality not by birth or parentage, but in cast of mind. We know Laszlo was in Budapest in 1919, a child in a suburban orphanage, the star inside forward of their soccer team—all this from a group photograph and one action shot of Victor, billowing shorts below his knees, taking a ball on his tiny instep where it seems as heavy as a cannonball.

By 1930, Laszlo was on his own in Horthyist Hungary, a land suspended in time, busy with its café life, with novels, gossip and theater, torn between old Hapsburg allegiances and the approaching Nazi blight. Laszlo had several occupations. He was an injury-dogged soccer player, written off as a sloucher in the sports pages, but as precious to some fans as Len Shackleton or Tommy Harmer, a man of languid brilliance and inspired passages. He was a cartoonist, a domestic ironist, his men having to balance harridans with gold rings against blondes in short skirts. He was an actor: small parts, handsome but unsound, seductive in the right role but not always audible.

163

And so the 1930s passed, leaving Laszlo a little puffier, a smoker and the husband of Magda Meszaros. He was content at first. Granted regular surprises in his life, he was not deep or demanding. He never disliked Magda. But he could not stop falling for any other woman he noticed. There were affairs, lies about having to see a man about a car, wrong numbers, and sick cousins in the country. This wore him down. The indignity of so many furtive ploys nagged at him. He needed a nobler part and great lines.

So, one day in 1939, he let Magda sniff out details of a liaison with Ivy Horvath, a journalist.

"It is as I suspected," said Magda. She always opened a conversation with drums.

"Do not be hasty," Victor advised her. He felt better already.

"What do you mean, swine?" Oh yes, this was the ticket.

"Have you noticed the state of the world?"

"Cabbage is very dear."

"And why?"

"There is a war coming?"

"And what happens then?"

"What?"

"Spying."

"With that Horvath tramp?" He felt like a comic with a new routine.

"She is a German agent—can't you tell?"

It struck home. "She *is* very jolly."

"I have been asked to see her. Required, really."

"For the country?"

"The Admiral himself requested it."

"You have a letter from him?"

"Would he put such things down on paper?"

His wife went quiet. Who can say she fell for it? She may have swallowed hard and eaten poison. She was dead a year later. But that last year may have been the happier because she credited Victor with a high duty. He sang when he washed up.

Wretched Hungary, leaned on by Germany. Unlucky Laszlo. For his wife could not keep quiet about his secret life. She was so proud, she talked, and talk spread as far as the Resistance. They reckoned this Laszlo must be an agent from another branch of the clandestine tree. So they employed him too, and had him run fearsome risks that he could hardly protest. The only benefit of this ironic plight was that fresh ladies flocked to him, all considerate of his "other" life.

Early in 1941, the "movement" instructed him to make his way southwest, out of Hungary on a long quest for America. It was that or a concentration camp. And so he made his way to Casablanca with Ilsa Lund, fond of her but infatuated with his story.

He arrived in America, and he spoke in large halls about the camps and the darkness in Europe. He went into antifascist raptures; he spoke with reverence about socialism. He thought this play would run forever, and wondered if one day he might be on a stamp. But after the war, he was ostracized. America was all fashion. In the late 1940s, the FBI came to him and said it would be easier if he talked of his own accord. If only they had known! Nothing now could stop his torrent. Still, the actor in him agreed to be reluctant. He let the perspiring government agents trap him in inconsistencies. He could make a cheek muscle flutter in panic. He was patient, letting them coach him into remorse and coming clean. Doctors told him he was ill, but Laszlo shone with the rapture of confession. He went before the House Un-American Activities Committee in a brilliant rendering of pierced shiftiness, correcting his deaf inquisitors on the spelling of names he was making up. Three years later, in 1952, he passed away, leaving as many mysteries as unpaid bills.

> *We are as pleased to see a sham swing through*
> *life in a book or a film as we are ready to enjoy*
> *the screen's smashing to pieces of one car after*
> *another. The wish to keep free from bumps and*
> *fibs in life is so nerve-wracking, do we need to*
> *let the forbidden force have a fling?*

RICHARD BLAINE

Humphrey Bogart in Casablanca, *1942,*
directed by Michael Curtiz

We used to tell stories about Rick. He was only ten or so years older than this writer, but can't you remember the luster that ten years has for a kid? Growing up near Omaha, I used to see him around the city. He seemed tall and unshaven, a wild fellow. But I find now that he never grew above five feet eight. In the few pictures I have of him later in life he seems to be making an effort to look dapper and impressive. In those early days, you heard stories about Rick "borrowing" someone's car for a night drive and outrunning the cops. He had girls hanging around him a lot of the time. He looked bored with them, but he'd let them kiss him sometimes. It was a privilege to catch the dime he tossed through the sunlight and hear the "Hey, kid, get me a Nehi, will you?" I did that twice, and the second time he grinned at me. I thought I felt the sun beaming. Yet I saw Rick's crooked teeth when his mouth bared.

He had been born in Omaha in 1900, the son of a pharmacist. (Later, I know, he said he was younger, and from big tough New York; forgive him—no one in this book has managed without a few lies.) If I remember him as a kid out of school, the figure in the best adventures, older-seeming than his peers, a boy's man, it wasn't that he neglected his studies. It surprised me, on going into it, that his grades were steady and high. He had an A– average, and he kept on working, trying to be better. The more I look at his record now, the more clearly I see a short, diligent man, whose amiability and natural bravery must have furnished his legend. Or was the legend just something I and others like me required? Was he only the conscientious boy who had to act up to it? When you think about how he turned out, you have to wonder whether his disillusion had something to do with that early feeling of inadequacy. Maybe I helped urge heroism on him and it became his curse. But was I supposed to look at the world and not use my imagination?

Richard Blaine went to Lincoln, to the university, in 1918. He majored in history, and he was especially interested in economics. He was one of the group that owed so much to Professor Wilson Keyes, though he and Keyes had heated arguments in class. Rick was already affected by radical ideas, and Keyes was a tough conservative who could never see past the sacrifices imposed in Russia in the name of communism. But that's how Rick grew in our eyes. He was quarterback on the football team his junior and senior years—which was a big thing in Nebraska then and now. But he had a reputation, too, as a red-hot debater and a guy who tried to read Lenin in Russian.

All the same, in those days he still helped out in his dad's pharmacy on Ames. He was generally ready to do a good turn for the old folks. He was best friends with Ralph Hunt, and he was godfather to Ralph's second daughter, Laura, born in 1920. Here's a picture of him outside the church, holding the baby. And Ralph's next to him, holding Mary

Frances's hand. She's gazing up at her younger sister with that fretful look on her face. So young, so worried. Rick looks as proud as can be.

It surprised everyone when he went to Detroit to work in the Ford factory. Rick could have been in management, I'm sure, but he stayed on the assembly line because he said he wanted to get to know the working man. He was there for three years, and he came back a lot harder and a sight less cheerful.

He lived in a room in Omaha then, full of books and Mitzi Glass. They had gone together a little at Lincoln, and she was the best-known radical in town. Because of her great red hair, and her severe looks, people used to call her "Red Mitzi." Now, I'm sure there were some who hated what she believed in, or were afraid of it, but I think a lot of people were fond of her really. Rick loved her. They never got married because they said it was an irrelevance, and that made for a gulf between Rick and Ralph. But Omaha could take him then, without spitting him out. There was never any of the outrage that got talked up later.

Anyway, in those years, Mitzi was organizing farm labor and Rick helped her; he was writing his novel about the automobile industry—*Drums of Steel*—and he was drinking. No one ever denied that. I know some people who'd admired him once gave up on him. They called him a layabout and a lush, and no one much liked his book: it's awkward and high-minded, but the stuff in the factories is good, I think. It was what happened to Mitzi that moved Rick on. In 1930, there was a strike up near Bassett. Strikebreakers came in and Mitzi got hit on the head with a fence post. It took her five months to die but she never regained consciousness. The word was that Rick went into the hospital one night and smothered her. If so, it was merciful.

He went out to California then and he did a lot of organizing with fruit workers. That was hard. The labor was poor, Spanish most of it, and itinerant, and the bosses were rough on union men. Rick stuck to it and that's the period when he joined the Party. But he got pneumonia in 'thirty-three, a bad case. He was always weaker afterward, and drinking still. Then in 1935 he went on a trip to Moscow. It was for students mainly, but Rick managed to go on it and he was there two months. From all I can gather, he came back redder than ever. But he returned by way of Africa, having gone on from Moscow to Abyssinia on some sort of mission.

It was no surprise in 1936 that he started speaking for Spain and the Republic and early the following year he was over there with the

Abraham Lincoln Brigade. He fought all through the war, at Madrid and then in Barcelona. He was a captain, and his health was finally shot by the experience. Worse than that, I think, he was disenchanted. That war, he thought, could have been won. He despaired not so much at the free countries staying neutral, but at the dissension in Spain itself among the various branches of the anarchists and the Communists. In addition, he didn't like anything he heard about the trials going on in Moscow. By the end of the war, he had given up the Party and he was looking for a different life.

Rick was in Paris for a time doing not much, except trading on the black market and carrying on with Ilsa Lund. He was regarded as a cynic by then. The drinking was constant, and not even Sam, a guy who had come out of Spain with him, could keep him cheerful. The affair with Ilsa was hopeless; she had all these causes, perhaps Rick used her to remind himself of all he'd lost. He wanted it to fail, he was dependent now on self-pity. So when the Germans came in, Rick got out. As I heard it from Sam, Rick was going anyway but later he persuaded himself that Ilsa had let him down.

He got to Casablanca and he opened the Café Americain, where anything was possible. You could buy or sell whatever you wanted —jewels, drugs, papers, lives—it was a rat-race of a market. There were people of all nationalities and persuasions. The war was held down by money, greed and fear. It was an ugly place, and the movie they made romanticized it and Rick. He was as vicious as he had to be by then, just taking his cut on whatever happened, OK-ing every kind of deal and arrangement.

The big new thing in his life was Louis Renault (1891–1964), the head of the Vichy police in Casablanca. Apparently he took one long look at Rick and knew he was homosexual underneath all the brooding and the sneers about women. He could see Rick was dying too, and he was decent enough to do what he could for him. After Strasser was killed and the weird but wonderful Victor Laszlo got away, Rick and Louis slipped off into the fog together. They went south, to Marrakech, and they lived there after the war, until Rick died in 1949. I can see him sitting out in the sun, slipping a coin in an Arab boy's hand in return for one of those sweet cordials. Louis took the best care of him, and at the very end they were laughing together over reports of the red scare in America.

ELSA BANNISTER

Rita Hayworth in The Lady from Shanghai, *1948,*
directed by Orson Welles

"You need more than luck in Shanghai," did she say? And more than one man to give you a name anyone would remember?

Is evil an unequivocal current in the world, a primary color in human nature? Is it useful or necessary to preserve the word? Was Hitler evil, was Noah Cross, was Elsa Bannister? Or should we rescue them a little and say they were disturbed, in the hope that actions such as theirs are automatically demented, quite outside ordinary human nature? If they were mad, then was all the harm they did meant in the hope of some larger good, and did madness blind them to the truth? Or were they just as deliberate and careful as an author, inventing a bad character, and then letting themselves slip into it, enjoying the wickedness as any child might? Is evil just a notion we share, a word in common, or is it a box that all of us must look into once at least?

I met Noah Cross once, in Omaha, at a party for Potter when he was ninety. Well, not quite met, I suppose. Saw him, asked him a question and got an answer. We say we have met the famous when they are unaware of us. We treat them like sites and wonders, and come away with snapshots. I knew some of the things he had done, and I think I regarded him as someone who just lost control. Not mad but weak, weak in a way that seemed to him like strength. But he proved a witty man, a man in control, capable of fine discrimination in cutting and eating a broiled sea bass, in recollecting a hand of bridge, or in describing the talk at San Simeon and judging whether Louise Brooks was to be trusted. He spoke in elegant sentences; his eyes twinkled over nice points, as if he were teaching them to good students; he declared himself a devotee of doubt and moderation. He seemed neither mad nor compulsive. He said to me, confidentially, "You see, Mr. . . . Bewley, most people never have to face the fact that at the right time and right place, why, they're capable of anything." It was a dark, brazen estimate, but he made it sound encouraging. I suppose we did meet, even if he fudged my name and offered that motto to any local building-and-loan man—dry sticks who deserved a shiver.

So Elsa was born in Chifu, in China, in 1918. Born in what was called a house of joy at that time and in that place, the child of a whore

169

named Poppy Munson, a Eurasian of a rare kind, I gather, with Oriental features and fair hair. "Blue, blue eyes, but slanted in their secret way," said Cross. He had been in the East at that time, and he declared—in a spirit of generosity—that he was the father of Elsa. I doubt that anyone could know that for sure. Poppy Munson had too many Caucasian clients. But Cross believed enough in doubt to use it.

Elsa Munson was brought up in her mother's trade, and she was famous as a child prostitute. Sailors told stories about her. We cannot say what she thought of this, whether she was hurt or complacent, whether the ordeal unbalanced her or seemed matter-of-fact. Whatever, she was a party to the orgy at the Astor Hotel in Shanghai in 1933 terminated by the suicide of C. C. Julian. Yet two healthy adolescent girls could surely tip a drunk out of a low-silled window if they felt the urge. If they were bored, horrified or out of their minds. If they were evil, or curious about evil's reputation.

Cross sent money for the girl to be brought to America. He put her in a boarding school in Connecticut, had her taught English, go to dancing classes, eminent doctors and fashionable priests, turned out a polished woman. Then he sent her one of his lawyers to arrange her adult affairs. This was in 1939, when she was twenty-one. The lawyer was Arthur Bannister, a lurching figure on two sticks, a crippled frog without the power to jump for himself.

Elsa married him, to get out of her finishing-school prison. Of course, he looked at her askance as any hobbling lawyer nearing fifty would wonder at a beautiful young woman picking him. But a lawyer is no novice with iniquity or compromise. He could see the liberty that Elsa was winning, as well as the sly jokes that would play to his back. But he would abide by the uncertainty and the jealousy. And if he ever felt shame, then he could contemplate the times when Elsa, like a dainty cat, would have to roam over his broken body at his instruction. A kind of usefulness held them together.

Bannister was transformed as a lawyer. He relished his ghastly lame-spider walk from table to witness. He extended it, sucking in attention. His strategies became bolder. An exhibitionist had always been masked by his crippled condition. Aroused by Elsa, he came into the open. His reputation and his income increased. He was talked about, and always the young, blonde, baleful-eyed wife was alluded to as the secret in his career.

Bannister took a partner, George Grisby, a brilliant, unstable man whose trial tactics were notorious. Their practice was based in San Francisco, on Montgomery Street, and their fame spread on a series of bizarre murders and society divorces. Elsa presided over one of the big houses on Washington Street, near the Presidio, keeping small dogs and romantic poets around the place, an icy hostess at dinners for other lawyers, a woman who seemed old already—never quite young or hopeful, never exactly American, never flawed by a single rash dream. Evil in idleness, perhaps, a lazy evil, too indolent to strike, bored evil, a variety that can float on unmotivated cruelty.

In New York on a summer night, she was riding in a horse-drawn carriage when hoodlums tried to rob her. A strolling passerby, Michael O'Hara, rescued her and drove her back to her hotel, yarning about China, Macao and sundry haunts. He had a half-caste look himself, high cheeks and narrow almond eyes full of self-love. He had a drugged face, and he was so large, so garrulous, so very innocent that Elsa thought to take hold of him like a balloon and make him squeak. She got Bannister to hire him as bosun on their yacht. Wasn't Michael a sailor, reeling along on dry land as if riding a swell?

Their yacht, the *Circe*, was headed down to the Caribbean, and then by way of the canal and back to San Francisco. It was the Bannisters' vacation, and Grisby was brought along to keep them amused. Elsa could see that Michael adored her; anyone could guess why she had had him hired. It inflamed him all the more that Elsa took their love for granted instead of letting him win her in his slow, romancing way. But she let Michael see Bannister humiliate her, and she was breathless with excitement the night Michael compared them all to a sea of sharks drunk on blood. It was like the stink of an orgy. Did she think she might destroy them all? Surely she never believed in going off with Michael to a house on a high cliff, called Nepenthe, where they would be happy. Happiness was not her thought. She was irked by existence, and wanted it to burn with the heat of the sun. Elsa was captivated by pictures of the new atomic explosions, a death by light.

The *Circe* sailed through fermenting seas, they picnicked on islands, dived from rocks and canoed on rivers filled with snakes, alligators and flamingos. In San Francisco, there were two killings and a trial where Bannister cross-examined himself. Elsa smiled at his mockery of the law. Finally, a bewildered Michael—a baby bull—ran away from the court. Elsa found him in a Chinese theater on Grant. There in the dark his hand felt the gun in her silk bag. "I was taught to think about love in Chinese," she whispered to him, her mind set on the Chinese show; but he had guessed the truth from the hard shape.

It all ended in the fun house with her and Bannister shooting at images of one another until all the mirrors were gone and only the real bodies stood up. And so they killed each other amid all the broken glass. Was she evil? Was she to blame, or did those early influences explain her malice? Is destruction an energy that takes us all at some time or another? Or is a woman as dark as that because so many men fear the way she provokes them? Elsa Bannister, dead at thirty. Evil's such a grand word, good's such a towering thought. I rule them out in favor of another pair—bored or hopeful, fatigue or life. As Bannister said himself in the fun house, "Of course, killing you is killing myself. But I'm pretty tired of both of us." That thing called "evil" has been through disappointment first. It thinks itself betrayed by life and wants revenge.

ADELINE LOGGINS

Tatum O'Neal in Paper Moon, *1973,*
directed by Peter Bogdanovich

In Bogue, Kansas, on a July day in 1936, they were burying Rose Loggins. Just the preacher, Rose's nine-year-old daughter, Addie, and a scattering of Bogue people including the man driving the car when Rose was killed, and his brother, for moral strength. Moses Pray came by as they were tossing in the earth. The noise of it gave him start number one. Number two was finding it was supple Rose turning stiff as the boards.

Moses was known a little in Bogue, but only a little because if you are in the business of selling Bibles to widows you have to keep moving; when customers see you it should be for the first and only time. So much acquainted with widowhood, Moses was especially sad to come upon a recently deceased lady, and a lady alone, for Rose Loggins had never obtained, or sought, benefit of clergy.

He had scarcely had time to put his hat back on at the close of the simple ceremony when those neighbors charged by Bogue with delivering Addie to her Aunt Billie in St. Joseph, Missouri, dumped the kid on him. He had a car and he had let on, while still distraught and before they had hinted at the child's destiny, that he was going in that direction. This Addie was a blunt little nut who looked like a boy and turned fiercer than a girl if you made that mistake. There was also the uncalled-for suggestion from those Bogue hicks that since Moses and Addie had such a resemblance . . . . How in the world anyone saw *that* Moses did not know; he could barely recollect now, all those years later, whether he and Rose had ever, even once, partaken in a way that would bring even the *chance* of truth to those coy, sidelong looks.

So Moses just took the dour child, with her belongings, to the Bogue depot to put her on a train. That was reasonable since he had, so to speak, been presented with $200 by the car driver's brother on account of the accident. Whatever was left from that after the one-way to St. Jo would be compensation enough to Moses for the good deed.

However, at the depot, Addie pipes up with the idea that the $200 is rightly hers since the brother had meant it for Rose's surviving child, and now Moses was stealing it. Furthermore, she was herself suspicious that she might be Moses's kid. You have to be so careful what you say in front of the young. Just to avoid an ugly scene, Moses sold back the train ticket and put the brat in his car.

So Moses set out for St. Jo reckoning to play the Bible game along the way and deposit the girl with as much of the $200 as she could count before he was off. The Bible game was very simple. You bought a paper with all the death notices. You saw that Pearl Morgan, say, had lost her hubby. You found where she lived, got over there and picked out a nice Bible in red or blue leather and you quick-printed on the front, "For Pearl." Then knock on the door and, "Good day, ma'am, I'm just delivering the Bible Mr. Morgan ordered. . . . Oh, no! He's dead? . . . Well, I am devastated. . . . Yes, that's right, ma'am. . . . 'For Pearl' it says. . . . Oh, *you*'re Pearl. . . . Now, you don't have to take it. . . . Well, it is $6.77." Whereupon Addie interrupted and said, "Oh no, Daddy, remember, this is the $9.54 edition." Just like that!

One way and another Addie got herself into the act. He didn't know where she'd learned some of her tricks, like the twenty-dollar-bill routine. She even outlived Trixie Delight, a vaudeville artiste Moses picked up in Cawker City. At first Moses had just thought Addie was downright jealous, but he took a better view of her when she alerted him to how Trixie was taking a little bit on the side from Floyd, the desk clerk at their hotel. After that it was just Moses and Addie getting on with the father-and-daughter show, though Moses was always careful to insist they were not kin.

The last bit of Kansas they took in a rush because some sheriff was after them: they had sold his own whiskey to a bootlegger who

173

a shithouse if we were kin

happened to be the sheriff's twin, yet more fraternal than identical. But they made it over the river into Missouri and thought they were safe in St. Jo when the sheriff turned up and just beat Moses black and blue. Moses took Addie to her Aunt Billie's and the child resigned herself to the new home. But in two minutes she knew how dull it was going to be, and before three she was running down the road after Mose. On those Midwest roads you can see in your rearview a mile behind you.

That settled the partnership; they got along very well for the next few years, without ever having to discuss whether it was business or sentiment that kept them together. We come to 1942, with Addie now fifteen, and a forward fifteen, showing just what can be done with good bone structure and a young woman with lipstick. They were in their hotel room in Ponca City, Oklahoma, when this conversation ensued.

"Mose?"

"Hmm."

"Mose."

"What is it, honey?"

"You're absolutely certain, are you, that you're not my father?"

"How many times do I have to tell you?"

"Hmm."

"Anyway, I'm only thirty-three, hardly old enough to be your father."

"No?"

"No."

"You'd have been seventeen. Couldn't you do it then?"

"Well, who knows? I wasn't doing arithmetic. I didn't do it, that's all that counts."

"Hmm. I think that's an excellent thing."

"Certainly is."

"Excellent."

"How's that?"

"Well, Mose, the way I'm beginning to feel about you, it'd be a shithouse if we were kin."

"What?"

"Oh come on, slowpoke."

"Button that up!"

"Mose!"

"What do you think you're doing?"

"Cuddling."

174

"Cuddling!"

"Seeing as we're not father and daughter, I think we should take advantage of all these shared hotel rooms."

The very next day Moses Pray joined the army and got off to war. It was one duty taking priority over another. The country was vulnerable, and he knew that Addie would get by.

JAY LANDESMAN GATSBY

Alan Ladd in The Great Gatsby, *1949,*
directed by Elliott Nugent; and Robert Redford, 1974,
directed by Jack Clayton

So much of it comes back to the mystery of being a Midwesterner. But in attempting to describe that, you must be able to say where the area is. There was a man once who said, without a flicker of irony, that San Francisco was the part of the Midwest he hailed from. Earlier today, doing a crossword, Mary Frances asked if Pennsylvania was ever considered to be in the Midwest.

Why not? The Midwest could be that mathematical center, a pinhole, or it could be all "the dark fields of the republic" between two narrow coastal strips, like the body inside its skin. Then there's that *New Yorker* cartoon, like the surrealist map of the world, warped by feeling, with desert prairie beginning on the other side of the Hudson, and stretching as far as the Pacific. When Americans use the term don't they think of a space of tranquillity or absence in the heart of the country, in the heart's heart? The ruffled dun-colored carpet across which coast-to-coast flights must pass, the uneventful land below while the movie plays at thirty-seven thousand feet?

I'm looking now at the Rand-McNally; it's one of my favorite books on America. I'm studying the two-page spread on Nebraska. That's Midwest to most people. It's a state determined by straight edges, except in the east, where the crinkle of the Missouri breaks the rectangle. And it's geometrical-looking inside the boundaries, with straight-line roads, the tidy blocks of counties, and so much white space to make the lines look bolder and more confident. Lines can go frantic there, the way taut wire curls up when it snaps. Up in the northwest of the state, there's Cherry County, "where the hay is so

175

fine," said Willa Cather, "and the coyotes can scratch down to water."
As far as I can tell, the county is ninety-five miles by sixty-two miles,
that's 5,890 square miles. Yet, really, on the map it's a picture of
nothing. There's a row of small towns in the north, along 20, and two
roads going north-south, 61 and 83, with hardly a notch on them.
There are a few lakes, the threads of rivers and the McKelvie National
Forest. But it's bare, flat and empty. Maybe the most interesting
thing in the county is the place where Mountain Time meets Central
Time, out there in the nothing, with an hour in a single stride.

There's so few people in Cherry County, and so few who'd want to
be there. If Nebraska means dullness in Manhattan or on Russian
Hill, then Cherry County is what Nebraskans regard as the back of
beyond. And in all the high-pressure places in America—where books
are published, movies produced, the country governed, the money
counted, TV generated—the Midwest stands for that sleepy space and
the anonymous audience. "The dark fields of the republic"—extensive, conservative, unenlightened, pastoral. A place where, if you
stay, you are seemingly content to be lumped in with the average, the
quiet and the normal. A part of the nation where all the writers on the
fringes imagine exists an archetypal uncomplaining Americana, like
Bedford Falls.

As if there isn't strangeness in Nebraska. As if the wind coming
across all that flat warm earth couldn't make a person feel the terror of
being fifteen hundred miles from sea in any direction, choking in the
dry aroma of wheat and dirt, until your head feels full of chaff. As if
the straight roads didn't have sudden, inexplicable kinks in them, like
the barbs in wire. The Midwest is taken for granted. It is not
glamorous or romantic; it is not noticed because the movie is playing
then, and because from that height there is so little to see. But don't
think the Midwest doesn't long to be in the movie. Let me tell you:
Marlon Brando, Montgomery Clift and Fred Astaire, all born in
Omaha; Robert Taylor in Filley, and Henry Fonda in Grand Island.
No, there's great acting and dreaming here, like barbed wire in our
heads.

James Landesman Gatz was born in Kulm, North Dakota, in 1890.
He was the son of poor farming people. Not much interested him
except the thought of getting away, improving himself, being popular
and successful. As a teenager, he set himself a schedule of exercise,
work, reading and elocution. He resolved to keep out of saloons, take a
bath every other day, save money and so on. He reckoned he could be
a hero and a famous man. He saw his task as having to find his

happiness and live with it. In America, the poor and the unknowns, some of them, quiver with impatience and humiliation.

When he was seventeen, he went off to St. Olaf's College in southern Minnesota, but it didn't work out and he took to beachcombing along the shore of Lake Superior. One day he saw a yacht at anchor, close to the land. The *Tuolomee*, it was called; its polished wood shone in the sun. There was a man on deck who saw Jim watching. He called out to him across the water, "What's your name?"

"Jay Gatsby," said Jim, just like that. He hadn't known he would say it, but it was all his hoping. The man on the yacht was Dan Cody. He owned it. He was rich from the gold rush and he called Jay on board and asked him to stay.

From 1907 till 1912, Jay lived with Cody, sailing to the West Indies and the Barbary Coast, working the boat and talking to Cody. He learned about the world, because Cody had had it by the tail for years. Jay got off the boat another man, smooth if not quite sophisticated, knowledgeable, graceful, and inwardly as empty as an actor has to be.

He made his way and he joined the army, so in 1917 he was training at Camp Taylor, near Louisville. The officers could meet the best young ladies of the town, and so it was that Gatsby and Daisy Fay fell in love, in the acutely romantic way that suited a man with his hopes for himself and the world, and which occupied her intensely for the moment. But he went off to the war. He brought great honor to himself in the Argonne offensive. He won medals and was made a major. After the war, he took the opportunity, offered to officers, to study at Oxford. He was at Trinity College only five months, but it was in that time he learned Daisy had married Tom Buchanan.

When he came back in 1919, he got a job with Meyer Wolfsheim, the gambler, in New York. Why a gambler and a racketeer? Gatsby was nearly thirty. He had to put away his uniform and his medals, and he had lost Daisy. If he wasn't to give up on his hopes he had to move fast. So he worked for Wolfsheim and happened to join him in the same year as Prohibition. In as hopeful and desirous a country as this there's always profit in short supply.

Gatsby got rich and famous, but he stayed mysterious. That's an actor's way, for if everyone hails his Hamlet he doesn't want to let on that only hours before "a little more than kin, a little less than kind" he was riding the subway to the theater. Gatsby bought a house in West Egg. From his terrace, he could look across the water at the green light on the dock of the Buchanan property.

He met Daisy again. He was sure they were still in love and she had been waiting to be reclaimed. A poor Midwestern boy who has waited that hard and long reckons the princess will be bound to recognize him. But Daisy was a coward. She couldn't quite make the break, and she couldn't own up that she had been driving Gatsby's car when it hit and killed Myrtle Wilson. So Gatsby took the blame, and the East slapped him in the face with its cold, hard hand. For the one and only time in that summer of 1926 he tried floating on the air mattress in his pool at West Egg. That's how George Wilson found him and shot him dead. Jim's father came to the funeral, but that was about all. The great crowd from his fabulous parties had melted away, the poor son of a bitch.

NORMAN BATES

Anthony Perkins in Psycho, *1960,
directed by Alfred Hitchcock*

This place where he lived was not a desert or a busy town. It was a small place, where at church, on Sunday, most of what had happened during the week was passed around. Life became plainer because of these dry accounts. People knew one another with the rather clinging loyalty of a community aggrieved by the building of a new highway. In its sudden obscurity, the place stuck together.

But it took ten years for anyone to realize that Norman Bates, out at the motel, had kept a version of the mother they had buried in reverent distaste, or that a few people who stopped at the motel, and the somewhat fewer still who went on up the road, had seen her, a prim silhouette in the window, sitting in the glow of a lamp, asleep or thinking. When it all came out they recollected how little they had seen of Norman in those years. He had come into town twice a month, maybe, for provisions. Otherwise he had stayed with mother, running the deserted motel, and the community had thought of him as a crooked tree, always there whenever you passed. No one thought to marry him, or cheer him up; he was a closed-off man, circumscribed by the tragedy. They never dreamed anyone so unobtrusive, so courteous, could have been fermenting in such a passionately crazy existence, and still reply with his boyish uncertainty when spoken to.

Everyone thought him straightforward and limited; then, afterward, they were merciless about his wickedness and dishonesty. Yet not to be open is not always lying; it can be no more or less than closed.

This was in Stanislaus County, east of where Route 5 now blasts along the San Joaquin Valley before it comes to Tracy, and the road goes right to Sacramento and left to Oakland or San Francisco. Modesto is the big city in Stanislaus County, but that's in the east. The west is just the Stone Hills and the northern end of that valley, an irrigated furnace where so much of the country's fruit and vegetables are grown. A mile or so to the east of 5 is the old 33, an important road in its day, but neglected now. Fairvale is maybe twenty miles from Crows Landing, and the Bates Motel was twelve miles from the town.

It's strange country, flat but rumpled like an unmade bed, where orgy or listlessness have an equal chance. It is a small town of itinerant workers, mistrusted by the natives. It is the "Golden West," yet so far still from San Francisco and the real flourish. There's suspicion there and resentment, a lot of isolated houses built on elevated ground, as if the owners wanted to see anyone coming. Henry Bates put up his house in the late 1890s. He was a builder, and his own place was meant as his advertisement. It was an imposing two-story wooden house with attic rooms above, like hooded eyes, and a deep fruit cellar. It was on a knoll with steps leading up to it from the path that stopped at the wide verandah. There were bushes around the house and a tree at one rear corner, but it stood out against the sky like a mask watching the land.

Henry Bates took a wife in 1930. By that time he was fifty-four, and his wife, Norma Ray, from Turlock, was only twenty-eight. She moved into the house and, they say, made it brighter and more agreeable. In 1932, they had a son, Norman. The house was large enough for a big family; maybe that's what Henry intended. But it had picked up an empty atmosphere from being the house of a single man, and not even the three of them could dispel the feeling of rattling in too spacious a box. The wide, steep staircases and the high-ceilinged rooms made Norman an anxious child, always on the edge of panic if out of sight of his mother.

In 1940, Henry built the motel. Twelve cabins on the flat ground between the house and the road. There was more and more touring then, but the war cut it back and Henry became depressed. He died in 1943 at the age of sixty-seven. The son was miserable, and it drew him and his mother even closer together. She often took him into her bed at night because he was nervous; she bought him records of the *post office on the dark stairs*

Beethoven symphonies to play in the evenings when the wind was beating against the exposed house.

Norman grew lean and tall, like his mother, a woman of nearly six feet. He helped a lot around the motel, because after 1945 its business picked up. Weekends they had all of the cabins taken sometimes, and Norman had charge of the laundry and the linen. He loved to help his mother; he hoped he was eclipsing the failure his father felt at the end. Norman got to be fifteen and sixteen, and sometimes his mother invited young people over to the house for a party. All the lights blazed and there was dance music on the phonograph. There were games of hide-and-seek, from the fruit cellar to the attic rooms, and post office on the dark stairs. But Norman never got fixed up, and after the parties he wanted to dance with his mother until she was tired. Norman sometimes watched her when she thought she was alone—in her bathroom, dressing, combing her long black hair. It's not that strange in an out-of-the-way place, and maybe if no one knows or is hurt, then it's not even so bad. But fathers push themselves on daughters and sons fall in calf-love with their mothers. Loneliness and need are the reasons and climate for it; and they are too strong to be denied. But sometimes they are forced into unexpected, alarming directions.

Then, in 1950, the work started on the new highway. A lot of men came into the area as labor, and there was a foreman, Juan Padilla, head of the Mexican crew, who used to call on Norma. He was younger than she, but he wanted an American woman. Norma was still handsome; perhaps romantic freshness had been kept alive by Norman's fondness. Padilla lived in a trailer on the site, but he would visit and stay late and he got into the habit of sleeping over. He scarcely spoke to Norman, but he grinned at him and made little kissing noises when they were alone together. Norma didn't seem to notice. Norman felt he was losing her just as the motel was losing its traffic.

So one night he got a bottle of cheap red wine for Padilla, and he put strychnine in it. His mother never touched liquor, so he thought it would be safe. Padilla would drink and she would stay sober. But he misjudged the strength of their love, and her wish to do foolish things for the Mexican. Padilla teased her, sang to her, and cajoled; he told her she would be crazy with love if she took some of the wine. So he taught her to drink and they both died, side by side in the old bed with the satin coverlet.

Norman wrote out a letter in the red pencil that Padilla used on his

180

work dockets, telling Norma he didn't want her anymore. He was thoughtful enough to add misspellings that might help identify the Mexican. But Norman was helpless with tears at the same time; he could not understand the overlap of cunning and disintegration in himself. When Sheriff Chambers got there Norman was incoherent. The sheriff had never had a case like it, but he worked it out that Norma had killed Padilla and then killed herself in what he regarded as the torment of a spurned lover. Looking at the naked Mexican's corpse, Chambers easily imagined melodrama. He felt a great pity for Norman, who had probably never in his life spent a night out of that house. He was really not fit to look after himself, least of all in that house. But he was eighteen, and it would be up to him.

For a time, Sheriff Chambers and his wife would call on Norman, but he seemed happier on his own. He stayed on the desolate premises; he went on changing the sheets on the motel beds and he cleaned the house so thoroughly that Mrs. Chambers always knew it by that sweet carbolicky odor. "What cleanser do you use, Norman?" she asked him, but he smiled and said, "Lord, I don't know," just like a man who didn't consider housework seriously.

What he had done, he had gone to the mortician's the night before the mother's funeral, and taken away the body in its periwinkle blue dress. He'd put rocks in the coffin, rocks and pillows so there was no rattling. That's what they buried. He'd kept the body at home and he'd done what he learned from a book on taxidermy to pump chemicals into it to preserve it. He invented a hobby for himself, stuffing birds, to explain the packages of chemicals he received from Toledo. Now, he was self-trained, and no book on preserving advises about human bodies. The corpse lingered; its perishing was too slow for Norman to notice. In love with someone, seeing them every day, you do not notice them growing older. And Norman talked to his mother as if she were alive still; as these monologues went on so, in his solitude, her answers crept into his head. Over the years, he became her: that's what the psychiatrist said later. But he had loved his mother so much that, once he had re-created her, she became stronger. There were times when the mother was more real than Norman, for instance on November 28, her birthday, when he celebrated the anniversary, alone, with Beethoven and an ordinary Californian wine.

And if those times of feminine arousal ever coincided with a single young woman staying at the motel, and thinking, Well, there's a kind man, so that she smiled at Norman's hollow, empty-eyed charm,

Mother's eyes saw and they came back later with a kitchen knife. A woman knows where her sharpest tools are kept.

Life can feel the same day after day, so monotonous it could crush you. Yet life, truly, is inoffensive; we feel ourselves collapsing. So people must make it different, if they are not to be depressed. Sometimes those who dread the steady state pick on death as a way out, and the deaths can be as unusual as the most unlikely murders in history. It's never too wise to linger with those humdrum smilers in country places. They give you the shivers, and they can be stranger than any city, professional crazy, without a hair out of place or a blown bulb in a motel sign, so that it still burns VACANCIES on stormy nights when the family that owns the place has had a row and would be best left alone.

> Haven't you *thought of murder*, looked at the kitchen knives or the power sockets and wondered how you could inveigle your dearest to try them? It is one invention to think of murder, and another—far larger—to find a stranger for it. So we murder those we know, and justify our laziness with the purgatory it is to live with those we never quite reach, wondering who will die first if nature has its way, and which fool will be stranded.

BRUNO ANTHONY

Robert Walker in Strangers on a Train, *1951, directed by Alfred Hitchcock*

What is that Tolstoy saying about families? I think it's the opening to one of his novels. Something about all happy families being alike, but every unhappy family finds a misery of its own. It always sounds so true; it's like the echo of a fatal shot at the start of a novel. An aphorism needs that air of encompassing wisdom in a few words, and the respectful silence that comes after a gunshot. But once, I remember, Mary Frances misquoted it, all askew in her helpless fury. It was in one of those day-long arguments, all over the house and on into the evening, desultory but still hunting for a way to wound. It was the way of our Sundays. She said—or rather she announced, letting the line spiral down from the top of the stairs, her voice so fine, quiet but penetrating, a voice in keeping with the day's gloom: "Happy families all go their own way, always valuable and personal; no one else could understand their pleasure. But unhappy families all act out the same tragedy."

Her error was poignant. It stilled all the bitter talk. I did not dare correct her; she would have lashed at me for pettiness, for always being right. And after all, she was right; there *is* that script in acrimony, that habit of walking in wounded steps. Then I thought about what she had said and it seemed just as true as Tolstoy's opposite conclusion. Was that just the resonance of an orderly sentence, or the grave voice of a former actress who has kept tragedy for home use?

I have another motto: all families seek to give the same image of health to the outside world, and yet all of them, alone in their own houses, exist in intimate, unspoken competition that would look like frenzy to outsiders. The Anthonys were once held up to the world as an example. There was a picture of the four of them in a 1933 *Vanity Fair*: Jonathan and Marion, and their two children, Bruno and Julia, nine and seven then. They were in the garden of the East Hampton house, enjoying a picnic, a god and his goddess, with two attendant fairies. There was a white tablecloth spread on the grass, with bowls of strawberries and champagne, and four thrilled smiles, the same defiant gaiety breaking out where four mouths opened to say "cheese."

In *Vanity Fair* it was a way of keeping faith with the idea of blissful summer, even in 1933. At the Anthony Agency, the company Jonathan had founded, one of his young managers saw the picture and said, why not? it has such real warmth, it's the very illustration we want for the life-insurance campaign. And so, for three full years, that lawn brimming with happiness was the emblem of prudent coverage for life, home and assets.

But in those same years, if you had come unannounced into their house on a Sunday morning—of course, this was scarcely possible to any invaders except readers, for they had solicitous servants—you might have found Marion in the drawing room sobbing incontinently over a painting she was unable to finish, Jonathan in his darkened room, stunned by his depression, Bruno spying on the servants, trying to lure them into his intricate booby traps, and Julia writhing and frothing on the stairs in a fit no one cared to notice.

There was a crack in the genetic structure of the Anthonys. Jonathan's father had killed himself, drowning in his own bath, sinking under the weight of despair. Jonathan had lived all his life under the same load. Marion had had seizures in her childhood that her parents had denied. It had been no more than childish excitement, they said. But Julia was an epileptic with fits once a week. Bruno did not show any such symptoms. But he survived in this household only by an obsessive attention to his own malicious plans. It was his way of not noticing the sister he loved. In a large house, he told himself, it is easy to miss those eruptions and instead find your sister so still and drained that she must be comforted. "Julia is not strong, like the rest of us," said Bruno.

Bruno in his teens seethed with clever ways to destroy the entire family. His own devout trait of speculation and the family's wretchedness came together in his mind as a subject for mass murder. He wondered how to arrange the four deaths so that the legend of the Anthonys' perfection would not be dented. He considered the car, with all of them in it, going over a cliff; he could see the front-page picture of the wreckage, and four overlapping bodies. Or a poisonous vapor to choke all of them in their separate bedrooms. Or lightning that hit the choppy blue surface of their pool while all of them were engaged in water polo.

But as the boy became the young man, such ideal dramas fractured in his head like the pieces of a broken plate, glued for a while, but then quietly freeing themselves in the hot washing-up water. Bruno was twenty and Julia seventeen: this was 1944, a year for invasion and liberation. Like prisoners, the two children had fallen into a pact against their parents in which their love for each other became confused with loathing of the elders. They did things to aid both causes. They would kiss and cuddle, sitting on the stairs, when their parents passed by—to be caught, to make their parents' lives and their own impossible. Every illicit caress was a stroke upon a genie's lamp called murder. They held their breath in the delicious, red-handed peak of danger and arousal.

Julia was sent off to an asylum. Her father said that her fits put her in peril. They were accelerating in frequency and delirium. She needed professional care. Bruno was not permitted to visit her. But he learned where the asylum was, from his father's canceled checks, and he could get there in a day's journey. He would howl outside the barred windows, like a wolf. Julia was moved to Arizona.

And so Bruno decided that he should kill his father. No need to touch his mother. She was so bereft he could handle her. But his father had taken away his most precious companion. With Jonathan dead, Bruno could assume control of the family affairs and have Julia released. The two of them could live together and play all the games they chose.

He had to discover a way of disposing of his father, and here Bruno's delicate genius—always derided by the father—came into its own. He dreamed up the principle of exchanged murders: two people, strangers, meet and offer to commit each other's murders. They will have an alibi on the crucial occasions. The police will see their motive, only to be confounded by the immovable explanations that on that night they were at dinner with the Carstairs in Connecticut or flying to Minneapolis. So long as the two parties stayed strangers, the arrangement would work. Bruno loved the simplicity of the plan.

Guy Haines was the ideal other, a semi-famous man, an athlete, such a good guy. Bruno hated him, and he could tell that Guy flinched whenever he touched him. No one would suspect them. So he followed Guy's cantankerous wife, Miriam, to the funfair, spirited her away from her hick beaux, took her on a boat ride to an island of love and strangled her there, squeezing until the fussy spectacles fell off her face. It was so easy. She thought he was a gentleman and was quite ready to be abused.

But Guy proved stuffy. He pretended to be horrified at the news, then he delayed over his part of the bargain. Bruno gave him a plan to the East Hampton house with his father's bedroom clearly indicated. But he could read Guy's lazy mind, and it was Bruno there in the bed (in one of his father's robes) the night Guy came to the house to warn Mr. Anthony. Oh, the foolish look on the idiot's face.

A little pressure was in order. So Bruno went back to the funfair to leave Guy's lighter there: it had crossed tennis rackets on it, ideal as a clue. He made the journey and stayed overnight in a not very prepossessing hotel to give Guy time to catch up. Best of all would be if the cops could nab Guy and the lighter in one swoop, with his guilty hand reaching out for the rackets. While he waited, he sent a postcard to Julia in Tempe: "Flying to you shortly, love. The world is slowly working itself out. There is a very loud amusement park right in front of my present lodgings."

Guy did follow Bruno. They met up on a carousel and as it whirled round, faster and faster, the calliope racing, the enameled plaster horses plunging up and down in their effort to get away, Bruno wondered if Julia's fits were like this. He was thinking of her, and of how soon he would be with her, in arid zona, when the whirlpool of noise, fun and happiness cracked and he became a dead man with the lighter there in his open hand. If the police noticed it, they would realize what he was trying to imply. Guy would *have* to kill his father, and everything would be all right. He would go all the way to Arizona and carry Julia out of her prison. Perhaps she wouldn't know him now. If it was madness, why, madness must have its advantages. In which case he would marry her.

DOLLY SCHILLER

Sue Lyon in Lolita, *1962, directed by Stanley Kubrick*

"Husband at home?" he croaked, fists in the pockets.

Thus reunion, not in the Indian Ocean and not a waltz into darkness, but at grimy Coalmont, the last house on Hunter Road, all dump and ditch, on September 23, 1952, he near the end of his journey, she frankly and hugely pregnant and exhaling "We-e-ell!" at the sight of him. HH meets Dolly Schiller, after all these years. She, the seventeen-year-old, had married Richard "Dick" Schiller, gotten pregnant and wanted to pay off their debts so they could move to Alaska, where he had been promised an opening in his very specialized corner of the mechanical field. It was the last time Lo and HH clapped eyes on each other. He gave her four thousand dollars to ease the way, he elicited the lowdown (it had been dramatist Clare on the QT who'd had his way with her), and then he drove off through the drizzle of the dying day noticing that the windshield wipers could not keep the moisture from his eyes. She was dead three months and two days later, during childbirth, on Christmas Day, up in Gray Star in Alaska, where not all facilities matched Dick's mechanical field. HH was dead too, of coronary thrombosis, in legal captivity just before the start of his trial for the murder of Clare Quilty. So the three of them were wiped off the board, without issue, in three months.

Dolores Haze was the daughter of Charlotte (née Becker) and Harold Haze, conceived on a 1934 honeymoon trip to Vera Cruz,

might as well have stayed in bed

Mexico, and born on January 1, 1935 (what a chance alighting on holidays) in Pisky, itself in a corn, coal and hog-producing area. At that time, HH was twenty-five, Paris-born and Lo-bound, still not quite married to Valeria Zborovski. How astonishing it is to look back on your life, busy and vital at the time, it seemed, and to realize you were still twelve years away from your date with destiny, and might as well have stayed in bed as gone to the wedding.

HH came to the U.S., after being divorced by Valeria, in early 1940. He wrote a history of French lit. for English students, he went on an Arctic expedition and he was in and out of asylums. It was in 1945 that the widow Haze and her Dolores moved to Ramsdale, New Hampshire. HH was then hot out of an asylum where he had contrived his own recovery by games of wordplay, dream-scheming and general storytelling (rather of the lo-and-behold variety). He too came to Ramsdale, looking for a summer's quiet concentration. He would have lodged with the McCoos, but their house burned down, and so, at a loss, he was sent to 342 Lawn Street, where Charlotte and her Lo resided. Who says there is not some omniscient author dealing out the hands? Where are we if those two do not meet? And what caprice is it that can say, "Why not in Ramsdale, New Hampshire?" with a straight face?

HH first saw her there, on May 30, 1947, feeling like the fairy-tale nurse to a lost princess, for she was the spitting image, the look-alike, of his childhood sweetheart, Annabel—hence HH's love of the moment of truth in a twelve-year-old girl.

Well, things moved fast, and so they must, for a nymphet's prime does not last long enough for a slow coach. On June 21, they had a tussle on the sofa, or—as it were—by just touching her HH set all paradise loose and let a happy hand slide up her sunny leg until she rolled off the sofa. Then Charlotte packed her off to camp and on the same day accepted HH's distracted proposal of marriage—legalized in a few days while Dolores was still away. Six weeks after that—talk about "Days of Our Lives"—Charlotte found the journal in which HH had been penning up a storm for Lo and ran outside in tumult, meeting a suitably swerving car. Kaput. The howl of brakes, the soft bump, and the renewal of summer's whispering silence.

So, on August 15, HH goes to collect Lo from camp. He takes her that night to a hotel in Parkington, The Enchanted Hunters, where daughter and stepdad share a room (342!) and the stark act of love, adding their names to a register that included Marie Samuels, Georges Beaulieu, Carl Proffer, Clare Quilty, and P. H. Vazak,

187

among so many others—such are the summery delights of Parkington.

They spent a year then exploring America, a year of motels—ideal places for slumber, argument, reconciliation and insatiable, illicit love that has no home—and travel among the wondrous places and place-names of the country, without a worry about the Mann Act. It was a year of Little Iceberg Lake, Hell's Canyon, Death Valley, Hot Coffee, the Grand Tetons, Mission Dolores, Milner Pass, Scotty's Castle, Goose Necks, Poker Flat, Phoenix, Arizona or Alex, Mississippi. They were insects, the two of them, endeavoring to crawl in and out of every tiny, exotic place, the happy-bored patrons of an endless drive-in, they always in the car, and it, the changing scene, dissolving in and out on the wraparound white screen. A movie tour, with all the setting suns and painted deserts bloody as fruit salad in the best flicks of 1947–48—*Duel in the Sun, Pursued, Out of the Past, Body and Soul, Lured, Kiss of Death, I Know Where I'm Going, Brute Force, Ramrod, They Won't Believe Me, Dark Passage, Red River, Force of Evil, State of the Union, A Double Life, Sleep, My Love, I Remember Mama, Unfaithfully Yours, A Foreign Affair, No Minor Vices* (I can't go on . . .).

Later: and so in the dying summer of 1948, Dolores Haze enters Beardsley College for Girls, where she is cast in the play *The Hunted Enchanters* by Clare Q——y. HH sniffs a rival, maybe the driver of the Aztec Red pursuer so much in the corner of his eye. He aims for a second transcontinental idyll (always HH's dream) with Lo. And on July 4, 1949, as epochal as a bomb test on Bikini, CQ makes off with Lo. Thus start the sad years of HH, the looking and the waiting, the searching and the hoping, until on September 22, 1952, he receives the Hello, Dad letter from Dolly Schiller in Coalmont.

I am not put off or shocked just because an older man, far older, should see and want to touch the firm, innocent beauty of a rosebud. No, and not surprised either that after bloom the rosebud falls away and there is as little left as there is on the blank page at the end of a book or the pale screen after a show.

BERNSTEIN

Everett Sloane in Citizen Kane, *1941,
directed by Orson Welles*

He had a law degree, the result of night school and toiling at his books till two a.m., then getting up at six to be at the factory by seven. It was a relentless routine for seven years, for Nathan Bernstein was far from brilliant. It took the edge off his youth, and made him seem ten or fifteen years older than his real age. But he never let himself be resentful. He didn't practice the law he worked so hard to master; he never turned into a smart Jewish lawyer. But he felt better for having the law degree, a little more worthy and safer if anything ever happened. And studying law had taught him to talk. The studies took away any social life; but he never complained, not even to himself. There are men who would as soon push themselves near death as risk the horror of being laughed at by a lady. Perhaps Bernstein looked at all the doubt and anxiety in courting, and gave it up for work. But a man like that, a man so caught up in business that he did not notice growing old, could harbor private visions of romance that never faded.

He was born in Hoboken in 1859, in sight of Manhattan but outside its privileged aura. He scanned the city's surface so many early mornings, the columns black but burnished by the sun rising behind them. Then, at the end of the day, the setting sun threw a low platinum light back on the city, which gave it depth and warmth. Its grays became mauve and the browns turned gold and ginger. Throughout the day and during his lifetime, Manhattan came to look more magical and exalted from New Jersey, more like an illusion. The increasing row of monuments loomed over the ragged Jersey shore, like civilization on the edge of swamp and wilderness.

Bernstein's parents were Austrian; his mother spoke no English; his father was a pawnbroker. Yet Bernstein became chairman of the board of Kane Enterprises, sitting in solitary splendor on top of the Inquirer Building after Kane had gone. Kane's will left instructions for Bernstein to keep the use of the office and the title for as long as necessary. The tycoon had always trusted loyalty; it was the surest kind of friendship. And Bernstein had never once picked up the cynicism to think badly of Mr. Kane, or regard him in less than the light in which Kane saw himself. Even when the boss lied or manipulated, Bernstein kept his eyes on the glorious career requiring the deceit. He loved Kane, and Kane knew it; but neither man ever spoke of it.

Bernstein was twenty-eight when he answered the advertisement in the *New York Chronicle*:

> Gentleman newly arrived from the West, possessing
> funds and ideas, requires general manager who will
> be tireless but amusing when tired.

The interview that followed a month later, when Kane returned from Lisbon, was not prolonged:

"Mr. Bernstein. . . ."

"Yes, Mr. Kane?"

"Ah . . . I was thinking. Have we met?"

"I answered the advertisement."

"Exactly, Mr. Bernstein. This . . . newspaper."

"Yes, Mr. Kane?"

"Think it might be fun to run a paper?"

"Well. . . ."

"Could you manage a paper, Mr. Bernstein?"

"I believe I could."

"Could you manage me?"

"Not if you noticed it."

"Mr. Bernstein, I believe we are going to be fine friends."

Nathan Bernstein was Kane's general manager when they took over the *Inquirer* in 1890. That meant he hired and fired people, handled contracts and parties, and generally oversaw the affairs of a man who reckoned he might, if he had to, lose one million dollars a year for sixty years.

In 1896, when he was thirty-seven, Bernstein was going over to Jersey on the ferry. It was a Sunday afternoon, but he had spent his morning at the office. It was a hot afternoon, and he felt sticky in his business clothes; not that he owned much else. He saw the other ferry coming in as his pulled out—two slow boats clanking and honking as they passed—and he saw a girl standing by its rail, all in white, carrying a white parasol, excited to be in the city for the rest of the day. Perhaps she was going to meet a boyfriend; she didn't look more than twenty. Bernstein didn't speak to her, and she never noticed him. For years afterward, he looked for her on the ferry, but he never found her. And he never forgot the smile on her face, a smile for the day, the old ferryboats, or a rendezvous twenty minutes away. In that moment, he had seen the years of his empty future stretched ahead of him, and he smiled with the sadness of a fulfilled man.

Nathan Bernstein died in his office in 1945, days after the news of victory in Japan. The obituary in the Kane papers misspelled his name.

SUSAN ALEXANDER KANE

Dorothy Comingore in Citizen Kane, *1941, directed by Orson Welles*

At eight o'clock in the evening, on West Seventy-fourth Street in New York, sometime in 1915. . . . It had rained hard an hour earlier, and the streets were still empty of people. There is all the poised tension of a trap in the air. Charles Foster Kane was on one of his nocturnal walks to the Western Manhattan Warehouse, going down to the waterfront with only a cane as company—perhaps he never intended getting there. But he set out on that walk often; it might have been established that he used Seventy-fourth Street. Then it would only need a fresh, muddy puddle, a passing carriage, and Susan Alexander, half-moaning with the pain of a toothache, half-laughing.

It sounds contrived, the kind of chance meeting to make a man of power suspicious. Did Jim Gettys construct the scene, guessing that it could grow into a "love nest," to destroy his best opponent's best chance? Or was there some more mysterious director of fate at work? It is not that Kane was a philanderer, likely sooner or later to get caught in an affair. He seems so timid with love, sex or women; they are all like statues he bought in Greece but never bothered to unwrap. No, he needed a special kind of sentimental occasion: the atmosphere of his mother and the presence of a novice; someone who would be entertained by his amateur magic without knowing who he was; someone with a career he could fashion. The arrangement is so astute. If Gettys was this clever, lucky New York to have such a boss. Only a great and important man would know how open he was to a nobody, a cross-section of the American public.

191

Alexander was not her name. It was the strong but romantic name she took for herself when both her parents were dead. She had the choice down to Alexander, Mallory or Rivers, all more musical than Stock. The Stocks were of German descent, born New Yorkers, who had been able to move up from the Lower East Side to Seventy-fourth Street. Susan was born there in 1894. But by the age of eighteen, she was on her own in the world, employed in the sheet-music department of Seligman's. She did not quite read music, but she had hopes of being a singer and it was a comfort to her to be in the music business.

Then, that wet night in 1915, she went down to the drugstore to get something for her toothache, and she met this large man dabbing at the mud thrown up on his face by a carriage. She offered him hot water and took him home; there was nothing seductive about that, not until her tender imagination asked to leave the door to her apartment open. That small ajar was like an idea occurring to the dirtied man. And because she had laughed—without any malice, women laughing do not have to be fearsome—he took it into his head to entertain her. He could waggle both of his ears at the same time; it was something he had learned at Harvard from a Venezuelan. He put his hands together and made shadow silhouettes of animals on the wall. Before long she sang for him, in that small salon voice, pretty, brittle and afraid of any larger hall.

A year later, the gubernatorial race was on, and Kane could not visit Susan as often as he wanted. If he had won the election, in all that euphoria and busyness, he might have dropped her—not without a generous gift, but still dropped her. Gettys could not let it go. He divined that all Kane needed to finish himself was a challenge; there was a ruinous need in the newspaperman for politics to be glorious, touched by honor and drama. He would be a terrible governor when the job bored him; it was a rare act of public spirit in Gettys to ensure that the state was spared Kane. He sent a simple note to Mrs. Kane, and on the night of the great oration at Madison Square Garden she invited her husband to go up to West Seventy-fourth Street with her.

The grim confrontation urged Kane to the abyss. All chance of doubt was sucked away in the roasting air of melodrama. He defied Gettys and Emily, he ignored the qualms in Susan. Let the loving people decide. Susan knew then and there that he would marry her, that she would be powerless, and that the marriage would be a disaster. She could see an avenue of pillared unhappiness ahead of her.

They married on the run in Trenton in 1917, and the honeymoon yielded place to singing lessons. Kane missed his son. He tried to squeeze love out of his life to reduce the pain. He treated Susan like a property that had to pay off. Even Matisti, her singing teacher, felt for her, the most forlorn student he had ever had. Matisti recognized her ordeal and fell in love with her, despite her strangled voice. Amid the horrors of the Chicago opening, he made bravura, restorative love to her; it was almost a teacher's duty. But Kane blamed him for her failure; Matisti was sent away. The mortifying tour of *Salammbo* continued and in 1920 Susan sought to kill herself.

Then, he relented, and in a matter of weeks it was as if opera had never existed. He removed her from it and put her down elsewhere, as the hostess of the growing Xanadu. So she lived in Florida, too pale-skinned for suntan, in a house too large for contentment. She became an expert on jigsaw puzzles, a listless center of picnics, a half-forgotten companion to a man who no longer thought of being funny. She left him in 1932, walking out on all of it with just a couple of suitcases.

She became a chanteuse, singing in small, smoky lounges, talking to an audience who had come to see notoriety and who were ready to needle her into gossip. For a few years she managed, and in 1938 she put her money into the El Rancho in Atlantic City. She sang there, but she was the show. She'd drink with the customers, or on her own. She was there in 1940 when Kane died, and there drunk when Thompson, the reporter, came to interview her.

It was easier after he died, like the light coming back at dawn after a sleepless night. She gave up singing and decided to make a success of the place in Atlantic City. She changed her name again, got rid of it all. Over the years she won respect on the East Coast, and she enjoyed hiring other, younger singers and running a clean house. She never married again. There were other men, but after Kane she did not trust real feelings. She could only wonder whether she wasn't just a figure in someone else's great drama. So she said who needs it? She died in 1978, in Atlantic City, an old lady known for her tough kindness.

RAYMOND

Paul Stewart in Citizen Kane, *1941,*
directed by Orson Welles

Anyone who ever went to Xanadu between 1927 and 1940 knew him. Sometimes guests passed their weekend there, or their week, without ever seeing Kane. But it was Raymond who greeted them, who made sure they were comfortable, and who saw to it that their car was ready and waxed when they left. They all knew Raymond's number on the house phone. It was Raymond who happened by in the rose garden to name all the varieties, he organized the menus for the picnics, and he personally put the catsup with the silver on the dining table. He was all-knowing, and he was discreet; he could hide a drunk or supply some cocaine. He ran the place. It was his kingdom. He even gave himself to rumor, chuckling if someone asked whether he was really a Cajun. "Just cagy," he answered, and the smile flattered the questioner. Far more than Kane, Raymond knew that Xanadu was a hothouse of unconfirmed possibilities.

But no one was sure if Raymond was his first or his last name, or whether he was Ray Raymond, or Ramon Ramone. Was he American or Italo-American? His accent slid and his complexion fluctuated, like a movie with replacement footage. He disappeared not long after the deal giving Xanadu to the nation. No one knew where he went, but who remembered where he had come from?

He had been hired personally by Mr. Kane. Yet no service contract was ever found. No one was sure how Raymond had been paid. His small room was stripped bare before he quit. The one personal trace left was the tidy circle of grease on the wall where he had sat up in bed doing whatever he did. He had handled all the petty-cash arrangements and he could have taken a small fortune out of the several household accounts without anyone knowing.

Afterward, people wondered. Had Raymond been a spy? Was he the plant of the government, the FBI, organized crime—or all of them? If someone really knew where the bodies were buried at Xanadu, wouldn't all those interests (and others) value a piece of his time? After all, everyone went to Xanadu; it was where show people sought privacy. That couldn't fail to make the world wonder and worry. Moreover, it had been palpable all along: Raymond ran the place. He was the one who said, "It was Rosebud," wasn't he? It was Raymond who presided over the burning of so much.

MARY KANE

Agnes Moorehead in Citizen Kane, *1941,*
directed by Orson Welles

There are mothers in a quiet stir of dementia because of the family's ruin, mothers moldy with decay propped erect at an upstairs window; there are mothers whose deaths allow the real story to grow; there are mothers waiting in breathless anticipation to know whether their lover is their son. An only child is a matter of choice or fate, but an only mother is an inevitability. The mother has this advantage over wives for any man—his way of selecting a wife makes him doubt the dream that there is a one and only true wife for him; yet maternity gives him that assurance with the first heartbeats of consciousness, or like the three beats on a stage before the play starts. We could marry anyone, but mothers are as fatal as character.

This is the most perplexing mother of them all, the mother who does not just explain a story but whose existence shows the need for story. We tell stories to clear away the darkness of family history and influence, things in life we are not brave or intelligent enough to explore. Every narrative utters the secret pain of family.

Mary Clay was born in 1832, in England. She came to America when she was eight, her own mother dying on the voyage. With her father, she went by wagon to St. Joseph, Missouri. They lived there for several years, during which he worked as a sign painter. In 1856, when she was twenty-four, Mary traveled to Denver, Colorado, to take up a position as housekeeper. In that city, she met James Kane, a saloonkeeper, and in 1858 they were married.

Since they both had some experience in running establishments, it seemed sensible for them to open a boardinghouse in New Salem, Colorado, in 1859. It was in the mining country and there was demand for a clean house where God-fearing miners and their relatives might stay, secure in the knowledge that the premises were not also a brothel. To that extent, the boardinghouse reflected the dominance of Mary in the marriage. There were those who saw Jim less as her husband than as the odd-job man she employed.

a rich young American

Fred Graves was such an observer. He came to New Salem in 1864, a year after the birth of the Kanes' son, Charlie. Graves was an attractive young man, limping away from the war, a jack-of-all-trades but a prospector for the moment, just bursting to shout "Eureka!" He had a room at the Kane boardinghouse, and he talked to Mary a good deal in the long winters. Graves may have been simply her companion, but there were suspicions in Jim's mind. He knew he was a disappointment to his wife.

Graves went farther west in 1868, worn out by mining and the hope of being lucky. He owed six months' rent at that time, and he had no money after he had bought his ticket to San Francisco. But Mary let him go and only half an hour before he left Graves thought to give her the deeds to his fruitless mine. He scribbled out the deed of sale and hurried away, jaunty with the prospect of change. Always change.

Once or twice Jim Kane went to look at the old mine. He kept his liquor in the shaft. And once, in 1870, Mary took young Charles to show it to him. They walked into the cold tunnel, hand in hand, talking about ghosts from the old Indian burial ground. They had a lantern and they saw the way blocked ahead of them. There had been a fall, recently it seemed. Charles asked his mother about the flickers he could see in the rock from the lamplight. She guessed it was nothing, but she came back later to look more closely. She carved out one piece of rock veined with glitter, put it in a bag and took it down to the assay office.

The Colorado Lode would be known by 1900 as the earth's third richest gold mine. Mary hired a geologist to examine it, and then in 1871, when she knew, she closed it down.

"What are you doing?" said a bewildered Jim. He thought the mine had been blessed by his booze.

She wrote a letter to Walter P. Thatcher on Wall Street and he wrote back saying he thought it could be managed. Mary Kane had proposed that a trust be set up by Thatcher to run the gold mine and hold it and its profits until Charlie's twenty-fifth birthday. At that time, the whole thing would be his, the capital and all the reinvested money. As part of the deal, Thatcher was to take Charles away to Chicago, to be his guardian, and to ensure that he had an education and upbringing that befitted a rich young American.

The boy would not see his parents, but he would only appreciate that absence gradually. In return, the Thatcher Trust would pay Mary and Jim Kane fifty thousand dollars a year until they were both dead. Jim argued it, but Mary was adamantine. Why, oh why?

The mine was hers. Jim was a waster. Maybe he loved Charlie, but he was a bad influence. Yet he was a weak man, and his son was strong enough to handle him. Mary might have left Jim fat-rich, drunk and happy in Colorado. She could have gone east with Charles. She could have guided his education. She could have lived with him and seen him. Did she think she would hinder him or make him ashamed? Or was Mary Kane not truly interested in her son? Did she prefer the freedom and the fifty thousand dollars for herself? Was there that dreadful loneliness in her of being mystified by family expectations? Couldn't she pretend for the boy?

She never saw Charles again. Jim didn't stay in Colorado. He went the way of Graves to California, and he was dead by 1874. Mary had bargained with him. He could have all the fifty thousand dollars of the first year and his liberty in return for leaving and abandoning his claim to all future moneys. It was so immediate a bounty, Jim could not resist it.

Mary Kane remained in Colorado, stayed on in New Salem. She did not appear to use or understand her own freedom. People said she was cold and miserable, but she may have wanted just to be alone. She did not look for a new man or change her ways. She died in 1888, having used her money to build a large hotel, the Overlook, on the site of the old boardinghouse. It would become a fine establishment in its day, a hotel fit for dreams.

All of Mary Kane's things were shipped east when she died, to a warehouse in New York—her clothes, her glass and chinaware, the wood stove and the sled her father had made for her with the painted rosebud on it still pink and fresh.

SALLY BAILEY

Susan Sarandon in Atlantic City, *1980,*
directed by Louis Malle

Not quite Miss America, maybe, but as lovely as you'd want to see, living in a shabby apartment, getting in at one in the morning, weary and afraid that she smells of the oysters she spends the night serving. This young woman has gone east out of an inexplicable desperation, or one that she has never paused or troubled to convey to those left behind. It was assumed, and so no one could deal with it; hopes are dreams, but so are camouflage and evasion.

She was born in what she thinks of as an unsophisticated fastness of the Midwest; she prefers to forget it now, and seldom owns up to it. I have heard she tells the story of being from Saskatchewan. No one says she has run away, or is missing. Her parents understand approximately where she is, and she assumes they have that rough idea. She counts on them not to ask questions. There's nothing to report to the police; nothing to hire a private detective for. But just suppose the father went after her, not chasing—just wanting to know, then she'd do anything to get away, go wild, run from her apartment leaving clothes, a hot iron and snapshots behind her.

When she gets home at night, she turns on one muted lamp—as if it were a signal, as well as tender golden illumination for what she has to do. She takes off her shirt and throws it on the floor. She has done that all her life, and she lives for the ideal of a new shirt every day. The old ones are shameful, tossed in the trash. Then she arranges herself in the mirror and slides the chemise off her shoulders, off her breasts. There, in Atlantic City, six nights a week, she cuts open a lemon and squeezes its juice on her arms, on her breasts, rubbing the juice between them, in her armpits and absentmindedly on her nipples. So as not to smell of fish, thinking that the place she comes from was so far from the sea.

Does she know the instant when the man across the way, Lou Guarini, an elderly dandy with silver-plate hair and a cautious walk, looks up from his dark to watch this young woman at her toilet? He is old enough . . . old enough, anyway. What a strange, circuitous route it is that she went so far away and yet is now willing to have an old man spy on her in this intimate situation, a lover if he was twenty feet closer. The shy are always exhibitionists in another part of their lives.

She was twenty-eight when she got to Atlantic City, not less than young but a little battered in her innocence, with startled eyes that had seen more than she could ever admit. She had hopes of becoming a croupier, wearing black and white and arbitrating fortune. There was a school of instruction at one of the casinos—the Alexander—with a genuine Frenchman imported to teach the talk, the ease and the sublime acceptance of chance. Sally met the old woman who ran the casino, not long before she died, and the raddled blonde looked her up and down.

"How old did you say you were?"

"I didn't say," said Sally.

"I didn't think you did. If you had, I wouldn't have asked you again because I'd have remembered."

"Twenty-five."

"You're old already."

"I want to learn."

"Yeah? What are you running away from?"

"Nothing."

"Like hell it's nothing."

"My mother. My mother, my father."

"Where?"

"Nebraska."

"Speak French?"

"Sure."

She had a few sentences rehearsed which came out fine, and the old woman grinned and told her okay. So Sally took the course, and she worked in the fishbar in the evenings to pay the rent. Then her sister, Chrissie, arrived, pregnant from Sally's ex-boyfriend, Dave. Somehow Dave had gotten hold of this cocaine, but the Mob came after him and they killed him. At least Chrissie's kid wouldn't have to bother with a father!

Sally didn't know how to handle the funeral and that's when this Lou character stepped in, Mr. Practical, Mr. Experience. But he had a lover's look in his old pink eyes, and he confessed to Sally how he studied her at night. She didn't know whether to be shocked or wise, so she reacted as if it were nothing much. She made love with Lou that night, and she knew enough to be kind and to enjoy her generosity. It was slow and then quick, but he was gentle and very eloquent. She felt safer with him than she had in ten years.

A couple of hoods humiliated him the next day in front of her, and she saw how old he really was. She wanted him to be able to melt away, he was so close to tears. But there was something about him, or about what she had done for him. A few nights later, he shot the two gangsters like someone in a movie. It turned out he had been dealing in Dave's cocaine. In a matter of a few days, magic had reached down and touched him, turning tarnish to true silver. He was rich, and he had won the love and respect of a young honey.

They went off together, saying they were going to Florida for a good time. The first night they stopped at a motel and they made love again. The next morning, while Lou was in the bathroom, she took some of his money. Did she mean him to see her? Kindness repaid kindness. It was his greatest pleasure just to watch her. This was the way of not saying outright she had to go her way. He declined to notice the theft. He let her take his car and he hitched back to Atlantic City.

Sally drove to Baltimore, she traded the car and she got a plane to Paris and then to Nice. She knew that was near Monte Carlo, and she was wondering how she'd look in a black croupier's suit with a white silk shirt, a fresh one every night.

> *Chrissie, Christina, she's still in Atlantic City.*
> *She writes often, long, placid letters on lined*
> *paper, telling me everything she's been doing*
> *(nothing much), and how my grandchild is*
> *(Albert). My eye flies through the letters. They*
> *are too detailed and calm for me, I suppose. She*
> *is a good girl, good but undemanding. That's*
> *what I want to say. She tells me her life is*
> *working itself out, and that she is full of great*
> *hopes. That's all very well. She has her own*
> *business, faith healing. Apparently she hears*
> *from the others, off and on. It seems she is our*
> *center now, poor thing. She says I must come to*
> *Atlantic City, and bring Mary Frances. But I*
> *flinch at the prospect of all the arrangements.*

GILDA FARRELL

Rita Hayworth in Gilda, *1946,*
directed by Charles Vidor

For something like twenty years, men she had just met were always telling Gilda, "You should have been in pictures. I mean that sincerely."

They were speaking their truth, but they were ill at ease because they knew the world took that line for a lie—being the sort of men they were. So they felt badly about themselves, and sometimes they went away thinking Gilda was a coquette who'd led them into it. But they weren't just telling Gilda she was sexy or beautiful. They felt something else—it might be the way the light picked up the back of her head, or her trick of looking past people, so that they felt unnoticed, like a movie camera. Or perhaps it was because with Gilda there was always what you heard—reputation—and her intense, impatient amusement when she was there with you, her presence.

People in movies have a sensational *now* about them and a mysterious past. That's what acting is: when Miss Julie first appears you have to hold your breath because of this sweaty, barefoot young woman wanting to dance *now*, on midsummer's night, with castanets in her nervous hand; but you have to see all the way back down an uncertain corridor to her past. Gilda was like that, as sexy as a photograph: she made you notice and left you wondering.

She laughed and tossed her strawberry-blonde hair when men wondered why she hadn't been in movies. And she never let on that she could have been. That was too much like boasting, and Gilda wanted presence to speak for her past. Explaining was so unglamorous. But one day in 1938, she could have been in a picture. Gilda was born in Santa Monica in 1921, and she was a girl who used to hang around the studios. She got noticed. One day a fellow asked her if she could dance, and was she old enough. "Sure," she said straightaway, never liking to be seen thinking. They were making *Strike Up the Band* at Metro and she was in the chorus if she wanted for the "Do the Conga" number, with Busby Berkeley as the choreographer.

And Gilda was there, waiting for wardrobe, when this other guy came by.

"Hi, doll," he said. "You sing a little?"

"Sure."

"One look and I knew it. Want to work?"

"I'm working here."

"Days, right? I mean a position."

"What sort of position?"

"I got a boat. Offshore. Nice class of people we have. I run a show and it's quality stuff. You know Errol Hill?"

"No."

"He produces for us."

"Singing and dancing?"

"Exactly."

"What would I make?"

"Why don't we talk on the way?"

The guy was Tony Cornero and he had worked out how you could get outside legal city limits off the Santa Monica beaches. So he had a big boat out there, the *Rex*, as a pleasure palace with gambling, and he had a ferry service—water taxis—going from the pier. It was a lot of fun while it lasted, and Cornero was soft on Gilda, which suited her. She did a couple of numbers every night, and then she'd circulate, talking to the customers. Tony was a very faithful guy. He never went with anyone else, and Gilda respected that. So she flirted, but she kept herself for him.

Well, Earl Warren, the California attorney general, got after the boat and when he busted them, Cornero took Gilda to Las Vegas. They stayed there for a few years, and in 1945 they went to Havana. But Tony had the notion to start up the gambling boat again after the war, and he went back to California. Gilda remained in Cuba because of Ballin Mundson. He was an older man, gray-haired with a scar on his face and a dangerous gentleman act. He had a casino in Argentina but he came to Havana several times a year for a "holiday." He spent a lot of his time there, with the Germans living on the island. In 1945, Mundson asked Gilda to marry him. He told her he would overlook her checkered past, hold no grudges or suspicions, and take her as she was. She never thought she was anything she shouldn't be. This tolerance was like iced water on your tummy as you soaked in the tub. It frightened her. But Mundson was attractive: the more condescending he was the more she wanted him. She wanted to be in bed with him so she could examine his scar.

They married and he took her to Buenos Aires. Mundson had a manager at the casino, Johnny Farrell, and Gilda could tell that he was jealous of her. He thought she had disturbed the nice arrangement he had with Mundson. At first she wondered if Johnny was in love with Ballin, but she never saw any evidence, so she decided it was just a money and power thing. She got used to Farrell being frosty with her; she enjoyed it. In return, she let Johnny see her talking to other men so he'd have to decide whether to tell Mundson or not. He got this constipated face and held his silence.

Ballin Mundson had a secret deal with the Germans in South America. Except that Ballin was cheating them, so some of them came to Buenos Aires to settle with him. He killed one of them and got away in a small plane, but the plane crashed in the sea and everyone assumed he was dead.

Johnny took over the club, and Gilda started to like him. He was more relaxed without Ballin and his swordstick. Gilda was always drawn to men who didn't like her; it made her feel the more seductive. But Johnny was angry with her, told her he was guarding her for Mundson. Keeping me prisoner? asked Gilda. Just to irritate Johnny, she did an act in the floorshow, ''Put the Blame on Mame,'' with a striptease that made him stiff with embarrassment. If Johnny wanted her, Gilda thought, why lie to himself?

Mundson wasn't dead, he was in Rio. He came back one night, and he just took it for granted that Johnny and Gilda were lovers. People always had their minds made up about her, as if she were their invention. But old Uncle Pio shot Mundson when he went after her. People she hardly thought of were often waiting to rescue her. This time Mundson was really dead.

''We should get away,'' Gilda told Johnny.

''The two of us?''

''Sure.''

''Why should I trust you?''

''Don't, if you don't want to.''

''Do you love me?''

''Sure.''

''How do I know?''

''Ballin knew.''

They went to Miami, and Johnny ended up working for Santos Trafficante. He and Gilda were married. But nothing worked out well for Johnny. The more he mistrusted her, the more she provoked him. And the Mob didn't appreciate a man who couldn't keep his wife under control. Johnny was found dead in the harbor in 1961. Gilda moved around. She had been Hyman Roth's mistress for a while in the 1950s, and she was with Fredo Corleone for a time. These men liked her because she had been with Tony Cornero. They loved her out of loyalty to the code.

Today, she's in a home in Pasadena. She has bad arthritis and needs constant nursing. A check for her bills comes in the first of every month from a Florida bank. That's why the nurses still gossip about her. They tell stories that awful gangsters are paying for her because of all she did for them. They've assumed that her disability is a reward for being so bad. So they chatter away in the gap between this sad old lady and her shady past.

HANK QUINLAN

Orson Welles in Touch of Evil, *1958,*
directed by Welles

On October 4, 1957, his sixtieth birthday, Hank Quinlan would be obliged to retire as police chief of Los Robles. How could that Libra keep calm at such a prospect? It was just as Tanya had told him, across the border, when he asked her to read his fortune: "You haven't got any. Your fortune is all used up." Quinlan knew that. He was clear in his mind that he would die anyway, from candy bars and corn chips, in his stinking house, if he didn't have to pull his terrible weight around on police business. So he acted accordingly. It had always been a likely conclusion.

He had been born in 1897 in San Diego, the son of an Irish-American stoker in the navy and a Mexican woman. He was a half-breed when the type was rare and the name damning. As a child, he had thought it was too much bad luck, and contemplated an adult life in which he moved away and opted for one race or the other. His name was American, and he could pass for white, but in his feelings he suspected he was more Mexican. He believed in horror, in the Church and in fortune-telling; he hadn't much faith in making money or being a success. Occasionally it occurred to him that there was a dark fate contained in his misfortune. For he had a mind that dealt in logic and intuition simultaneously, guessing a thing and working out how it might be so.

When he was seventeen, he married a girl, the only girl who didn't sneer at his mixed blood. She was a Danish blonde, Eva Anderson, and he was proud of her. He joined the city police force and enjoyed wearing the uniform. In 1916, Eva was murdered. She was strangled in their own home. There was blood in her blonde hair. There were a few things stolen and there were words in Spanish daubed on the wall in her blood. So the stupid detectives worked it out that Mexican thieves had done it. But Quinlan had a hunch it was another Dane who had been after Eva before Hank came along. He talked with the detectives. He even said, "Look, I'm half Mex. I think I know." But they told him he was distraught and he should leave the case to them. Everyone in the San Diego police felt good when they got a couple of Mexican kids and charged them. The two were executed, but Quinlan knew they were innocent.

Next year, the Dane enlisted in the army, so Quinlan followed him. They went to the same training camp, the same regiment, the same troop ship. Quinlan never talked to the Dane, never gave a hint of knowing who he was, and the Dane avoided him. But he watched Quinlan. Except that if you're fighting an enemy, it is hard to watch out for one of your own, too. One day in a Belgian trench, the Dane got it, a bullet in the forehead just below his helmet. Not in the back, that might have been noticed. Quinlan called to him, so the guy would turn around, the only time he ever spoke to the man.

When Quinlan returned from the war, he moved to Los Angeles and he was promoted to detective. He was on the William Desmond Taylor case, and he got to question Mabel Normand one sweltering afternoon in her bungalow at Sennett. He had another of his hunches, but then the word came down to go vague on the case. That sickened him. He didn't like the big cities and having to work with other cops and the D.A.'s office. Quinlan couldn't abide being denied when he was right; he looked for a smaller setup, one he could arrange in his own way.

So in 1925 he moved to Los Robles. He was an assistant at first, but he could see that in a few years he would make chief, and the place suited him. Los Robles was two small towns split by the border. Los Robles was American, and Robles was Mexican. It was the one place Quinlan had known where his own mixed blood felt natural. He spoke good Spanish, so he made useful contacts on the Mexican side. With that, he became an even better cop than just hunches and hard work could manage. From 1929 onward, he was chief and he ran things the way he wanted. There was action in a border town, of course—knifings, immigration matters, some gambling and whoring, a little drugs. The Grandis controlled most of it, and they came to an understanding with Quinlan. They kept things tidy, they stayed in business and he got the "license fee" every year. It happened everywhere, and there were no outsiders and no undue violence. The wrong people never got hurt or upset. Los Robles got a good reputation, and it became a favorite honeymoon spot. The town managers appreciated Quinlan, even if they didn't invite him to banquets. They gave him every latitude and kept out of his way.

There were two murders in Quinlan's time, and for one of them there was no evidence. Hank knew who the killer was, so he told his deputy, Pete Menzies, to keep riding the guy until his nerve cracked. One day in 1935 they went to call on the suspect, and he came out at them headlong with a gun. Menzies was dreaming. He slipped in surprise and Quinlan had to protect him. The guy fired his gun; Hank was hit in the leg. Menzies shot the killer dead. But Quinlan had a limp ever afterward, and he put on a lot of weight. Menzies was full of guilt and gratitude for Hank, and he swore he'd never desert him.

Quinlan didn't marry again. He was the recipient of pity; ladies in Los Robles baked pies for him and invited him to Sunday dinner. But, in truth, he hadn't enjoyed marriage much. Eva had always wanted to talk and Hank was a more reflective person; his hunches came out of being quiet and peaceful. Living alone didn't trouble him. Whenever he felt horny, he'd just stroll over the border and spend the night at Tanya's. She never talked when he didn't want it, and she could always guess what he was hoping for without him having to tell her. The two of them trusted instinct.

From 1950 onward, Quinlan saw retirement coming up. There was a deal of time still, sure, but he knew what he would have to do. He waited for the right kind of case. By 1957, he was restless because nothing had come along in his damned settled town. Hank had done what he could to stir things up. He'd spread talk that had Joe Grandi worried; Joe kept on coming to him with wild versions of his own rumors. Hank had told that Mexican shoe clerk, Sanchez, that Marcia Linnekar had the hots for him.

That did it. Just over the border, and on his side too, Rudy Linnekar's automobile was blown up. With Rudy driving and his latest girl friend on the blue leather bench seat beside him. What was left of the girl they could strain through a sieve, but they found one of Rudy's shoes on Main Street—with his foot still in it. Much too much dynamite had been used, an extravagant amount, suggesting spike and passion.

Quinlan knew that Sanchez had done it, just as he knew Rudy would warn a Mexican off seeing his daughter while Marcia would welcome sex with color. Hank planned to frame him as he'd done before with thieves, and then let Pete Menzies realize how he'd rigged the case. If that didn't quite work—because Pete might stay loyal— here was a bonus for fortune: a solemn Mexican narcotics man, Mike Vargas, who had just happened to be near the car when it blew, just about to kiss his new blonde American wife. Hank couldn't see how Mexicans were getting away with stuff like that with white women, even if this one was a thick armed tramp and Vargas too much a fool to see it.

Vargas tried to interfere. He thought Sanchez must be innocent, because the kid had appealed to him as a fellow Mexican. Vargas had seen the shoebox empty in Sanchez's house where later Hank had "found" the sticks of explosive. So Quinlan just tweaked his Mexican tail. He got a gang to go over to the motel where Mrs. Vargas was staying and they raped her some and shot heroin into her so she was a wreck. Of course, Vargas could never have worked it all out: he had lousy instincts. But Pete was around to help him and Hank let the trap close in like a warm sleep.

He knew Pete had a recorder on him, he was so jumpy but so awkward; he moved as if he had a boil under his arm. Quinlan let the whole story spill out down by the filthy river, and there was Vargas lumbering along behind them so dumb he couldn't even keep the reverb down on the player. In the very end, it was Menzies who shot Quinlan. But Hank plugged Pete, too, and the two old friends went within minutes of each other. Hank had a hunch that way they could be on the same troopship to wherever they were going. There was never any reason why a cop who could think for himself had to submit to retirement.

RAMON MIGUEL VARGAS

Charlton Heston in Touch of Evil, *1958,*
directed by Orson Welles

He was "Miguel" in Mexico and "Mike" in the U.S., a man of twin allegiances, a Mexican citizen, an investigator of unworldly talent and distinction, but someone not entirely trusted. It was said of him that Vargas could never turn a blind eye. It made him a liability, an earnest man in a land of necessary compromise.

Ramon Miguel was born in Mexico City in 1926, the son of Escobar Vargas, a teacher and writer of adventure stories, and Jane Shannon, an American woman of considerable private fortune who had come to Mexico to buy Aztec treasures for her father's museum. At their level of society, a mixed marriage was a mark of originality, so long as the couple lived south of the border. Miguel was born and raised in a lovely house in the mountains, with servants, horses and an extensive library. He spoke English and Spanish, he learned American manners and jokes, and his parents looked forward to him having an illustrious career.

In 1944, he entered the University of Mexico, where he studied history, captained the polo team and was a convivial member of a conservative dining club. Upon his graduation, he was awarded a scholarship so that he could attend UCLA for two years to study American government. While there, he wrote a thesis, *The Serpent and the Eagle: The Mexican-American Relationship*, which was subsequently published in both countries and reviewed by William F. Buckley as "political science waving the flag of Ouida . . . yet sound for all that."

Vargas returned to Mexico City in 1950 and was made an inspector in the Security Division of the police. In 1953, he was transferred to the Narcotics Division, and in the succeeding years he was prominent in a number of arrests and seizures along the border. By then, he had a reputation for diligence and probity not easily escaped; it made the government very content to confine him to the detection of drugs. It was in 1957 that he met and fell in love with a young American woman, Susan Benyon, who was working as a courier in the area of El Paso and Ciudad Juárez.

When their marriage was announced, a government official spoke to Miguel's father, intimating that possibly Susan was a risky consort to so promising a career. The official could not speak unequivocally, but Susan's father was under suspicion for involvement in drug trafficking, and there were unquenchable rumors that Susan herself transported drugs and might even have insinuated herself with Miguel to facilitate that work. Miguel was outraged by this devious manifestation of racial prejudice, but in view of the concern he did agree to marry discreetly and honeymoon in Los Robles. "It'll be perfect," promised the brave Susan.

The day before the nuptials, he dozed serenely after he and Susan had made siesta love. When he awoke, there was his betrothed, smiling at him, and showing him a fresh plaster cast on her arm.

"Michael, my dear one, guess what?"

"What?" Impeccable in English, but not supple.

"I broke my arm."

"As we made love?"

"No, you silly. I slipped out of bed and I fell on the bathroom floor. I actually heard the crack—I was afraid it might have woken you."

"I never stirred."

"No, I know. You had excelled. So I simply ran over to the hospital and they set me—all in an hour. Wasn't that splendidly efficient?"

"Perhaps you will not be fit enough for the honeymoon."

"Don't you dare to even think that!"

So they were married, with the train on Susan's dress draped very artfully across her fat arm in all the photographs. They made their way to Los Robles and got caught up in all the troubles of the Linnekar killing. Mike was so solicitous, he sent Susan off to a motel while he consulted on the case with the horrible, fat police chief who smelled of refried beans. How was Mike to know that the motel in question was out in the middle of nowhere, with a hopped-up jitterbug as the only authority in sight? It wasn't his fault that the gang of greasers had come by, with a boss woman who sounded like the Devil, and done such unspeakable things to her. No, she didn't want to talk about it, or care to remember the look in their bloodshot eyes.

At last they were reunited. Mike was vindicated. Susan's heroin addiction could be controlled. The honeymoon could resume. But then Vargas suddenly noticed the difference.

"Susie. What happened to your plaster?"

"Oh Mike . . . they took everything."

"They cut the plaster off your arm?"

"They must have."

"Such animals!"

"I know, dear, I know."

"But doesn't it hurt?"

"Not as much as I expected. It must be mending."

"We must immediately go to another hospital and have you replastered."

"I suppose you're right."

It was years before the whisper reached as far as Miguel's ears that the "plaster" had contained four kilos of cocaine that Susan had been smuggling across the border. By then, it was too foolish to discuss, and too ridiculous to have investigated.

Miguel Vargas has been for many years the senior official in that branch of the Mexican government in touch with the U.S. Immigration and Naturalization Service. He is experienced in all matters of the border and he has collaborated with Professor David Gregory in preparing briefs for new legislation. He is kept very busy and has probably not yet heard the reports that his wife is having an adulterous lunchtime liaison with a man close to the American ambassador in Mexico.

JEFF BAILEY

Robert Mitchum in Out of the Past, *1947,
directed by Jacques Tourneur*

When he was just a little boy in Bedford Falls, Jeff said, "I like the bad guys." We were alone, at the far end of the yard. The last clumps of old snow were still on the ground, gray and hard. I think he was hoping I would explain it to him. Jeff was the youngest of the three of us. It was only later that someone told me how, when I went into the water to rescue Harry, the brother in the middle, Jeff had just watched from the shore. He never moved. But he was only seven. Still, he went dull afterward with me the hero and Harry the lucky survivor. There was no role for Jeff. Maybe the watcher had begun to ask himself why he only watched.

I asked him, "How's that?"

"I don't know." He kicked a stone and it hit the watering can, a dead shot, twenty feet away. He stared at his own skill, without pleasure.

"You don't like what they do, do you?"

"I s'pose not."

"Suppose, Jeff."

"Oh, George!"

"I'm only helping you."

"Maybe it's because they're so alone."

"The bad guys?"

"Yeah. I feel sorry for them. I mean, everyone's against them."

"I know," I said. "You have to wonder about them."

"Right, you wonder why they're bad. You think it's because they're lonely. And things."

"What things?"

"Well, don't you ever wonder what it would be like to do a bad thing?" I was thinking how to answer him; he must have looked up at me. "No, I s'pose you don't, Georgie." The sneer made me angry. My hand came up and hit him on the back of the head. It made him stagger, and I saw tears he couldn't squeeze back.

We always ended up laughing about it, but he kept that dark, thoughtful expression. I never felt I'd shaken the idea out of his head. It wasn't loose in there, it was part of the way he saw things. Mary Frances was afraid of Jeff; she never knew whether he was laughing at her or waiting for her to make a mistake. "He's too quiet," she said. "And too smart. I get frightened watching him think. He's gloomy, George." Was she trying to signal me about her frailty when faced with that mood?

Jeff never said he'd been warning me, but I think it was what we both thought of before he left town. He had some feeling that I was too good to be true, too noble for my own sake, that I was stuffy, solemn, a dead weight. He never apologized or explained. He never said he'd loved Mary Frances, or hated me. I don't believe either would have been quite true, and Jeff never bothered to say anything for conversation or kindness. He was attracted to her, I'm sure—that wasn't hard—but it was more that he had glimpsed the outline of a trap and was too proud or too black to walk away from it.

It was almost as if I'd set it up by meeting Mary Frances and marrying her. Neither he nor she ever bothered with justification. It was not something put down to my being so lousy depressed and such a pain to be with. They didn't say anything. Jeff just told me to forget about it, it was nothing, and Mary Frances said, "Don't let's mention it." She stayed with me, and he went away—so action settled it, if you weren't disposed to go on thinking about where he was and whether they were communicating. It makes me feel helpless to remember it this way, like a train rumbling along and we're all passengers who get on and off, and the train never knows or notices. That's what Jeff was like. But he was wrong if he thought I was only good, or that good is not difficult too.

So in 1937, Jeff went away, when he was twenty-two. He went to New York, the city, and I'll bet he was in his element there. The cities are made for watching and not talking, so you pass through the crowds untouched by all the stories you see and hear. You have to be unmoved in cities; you have to be able to look at the bums and the hopeless cases and say, "So?" to yourself. Jeff could do that.

He became a private detective and he called himself Jeff Markham. I don't know why he picked that name, but I can guess why he wanted a change. In the city you are free to be whomever you want, a hundred people a day. It's like picking a name for a character. You make yourself up; you decide on this raincoat and that hat. So he was Jeff Markham, with a partner named Fisher.

They had a fair business, and Jeff lived in Brooklyn. Then in 1943 they were hired by Whit Sterling. He was a businessman of some kind, but it was crooked, even if you didn't know how. Fisher said to leave him out of it, but Jeff said no need, the case was just personal.

211

Sterling had had this woman, Kathy Moffat, and they'd lived together for a time. Then one day she had shot Sterling and vanished with $40,000 of his money.

"Why'd she do that?" said Jeff.

He grinned. "I don't know. I still don't know."

"What do you want back, her or the money?"

"I want it all."

Fisher told Jeff it was his case, and so Jeff started tracing her. He was good at it, I think, and not everyone is. If I look for someone, I don't know how to start. Jeff knew the system and he tracked her down inside three months. She was in Acapulco and he found her one day when she walked into the bar where he was waiting. Perhaps it was one of those moments when he looked at her and said, "I can't help it," to himself. Fate. He could pass by the bums, and harden himself to wrecks dying on doorsteps, but then there was a providence he couldn't resist.

So Jeff and Kathy started a love affair. I don't know what it meant to her. Jeff was handsome. Maybe she loved him. Or maybe she had the same kind of irresistible impulse. Maybe they were both people who trusted the smell of their own weakness, who felt temptation more than anything. They stayed down in Mexico. He told her about Whit Sterling and his assignment. She said that Sterling was a monster. She had shot him because he was so bad to her—yet from the way she said it, he could have sold her mother to a glue factory or just failed to notice her new earrings. That cool way of talking blurs all iniquities. But, no, she'd taken no money. That was her lie, the moment when coolness fell away and the eyes ached with sincerity.

They moved on to San Francisco, afraid that someone would be coming after them. It was Fisher who came, tickled to be dogging his own partner. Sterling had called on him and Fisher was upset that he'd not heard from Jeff. He saw Jeff at the races and he followed him back to a cabin up in Marin where he and Kathy were living. When he realized what had happened, Fisher asked for some money to keep him quiet. The two men fought, and from somewhere Kathy had a gun and she shot Fisher dead. Then she got in their car and drove off, leaving Jeff to get home on his own. The gun was one surprise. The other was finding a bankbook and seeing that Kathy had a while before deposited $40,000. There's always some $40,000 or other, as solid as a gun.

So Jeff buried Fisher up in the forest, and he moved away. He didn't want to go on being a detective, and he decided he didn't enjoy cities anymore. So he went to a place called Bridgeport, in California, up in the Sierras, and he opened a filling station there. He kept to himself, but he made a couple of friends: Dickie, a mute kid who helped at the station, and Ann Ferguson, the dentist's daughter.

She didn't have what Kathy had had—not the danger or the duplicity—but he might have married her. Then one day in 1947, a fellow named Joe Stefanos stopped off at Jeff's place. You don't have to be looking for someone to find him. Stefanos was an associate of Sterling's and he remembered Jeff. So he told Sterling, and soon Jeff got a call to come on up to Tahoe for a talk.

Sterling was all smiles. No problems, he said. "It's all in the past, and anyway, I got Kathy back. What else do I care? She's in the next room." She was, too, the same as ever, lovely but slinky, with eyes like beads you couldn't pick up. And Jeff was still hooked. So he went along with Sterling's suggestion that he work for him again, especially after a quiet moment together when Kathy tells him that she still loves him, that she only came back to Whit out of fear. That's when a man has to see there's nothing so stupid he wouldn't do it. There might be a last intelligence in recognizing that compulsion, when desire triumphs over all reason and honor, when it banishes the fear of wickedness or shame.

So Jeff got involved, and it gets worse, with him ready to wipe out strangers for a chance of holding her cold hand. A lawyer is killed in San Francisco, and he is blamed for it. He's on the run, and Ann is helping him but she knows he's still fixed on Kathy and he can't see what she's giving up to be with him. All that desperation. By now, Jeff has guessed Kathy's behind it all—he wants it like that—even if he can't always admit it. She has to be other than ordinary. He could have been something decent and valuable—a doctor, a teacher or a man who gave his life to the building-and-loan business, so that he had nothing for himself.

He went back to Tahoe at night and found Kathy had killed Whit. He never knew or bothered to ask why. Reasons and explanations were like aging; they would dull Kathy's shine. She told him they must go off together again, to Mexico, and it would be like it was before. Day after day, if he wanted, she'd come strolling into that first bar and it could start again. Jeff may have agreed. But as she packed he called the police. When the two of them set out, they drove into a roadblock. Kathy knew what it meant. She shot Jeff and the police shot her; the first shot condones all the others. The police pour in fire these days, they're so edgy. The chief there wrote me a well-meant

213

letter. He said that Jeff had gotten in with the wrong kind. For he had left a diary, with a clear, unbiased account and a note with my address and what the finder was to do in the event of his demise.

> *I could never believe a life like this in our family, only a few years away from me. I roughhoused Jeff and I could handle him then. But when I write about him I see the self-destructiveness we shared—he in Mexico, on the road, in the lap of a tramp; and I safe and sound in Nebraska, a little deaf and going to waste. Maybe he knew more and opted for quickness. I found Travis once pretending to be his Uncle Jeff, and Mary Frances vomiting with fear.*

BREE DANIELS

Jane Fonda in Klute, *1971, directed by Alan J. Pakula*

Those murders were bottomless holes they tried to walk around, always with a dread of falling. Yet the murders were also incidental to the uneasiness between the two of them. So, as they inched their way through the night they watched out for the murderer, but they waited for each other. There were moments when she lost sight of the two threats, the two men who wanted her, when Bree Daniels was not certain she could tell them apart in the dark with only sound, smell and touch to rely on.

She had been born in Los Angeles in 1941, the daughter of a doctor whose Camden Drive practice included several show-business luminaries. Bree grew up with an uncertain sense (for her father was proud but discreet) of movie stars having small holes or imperfections in their glowing looks, too humiliating to discuss in public, but attended to by her father. When Bree was a little girl, she sometimes woke up in the middle of the night, crying for help. She had a flaring appendix, a detached retina, a bone disease, a migraine, and so on. Her father came to her room to deal with her. The first few times, he carried the old stethoscope he kept at home and put the cold metal disc on the troubled parts of her body. Playing the game, he said to himself.

But he became bored with having his sleep disturbed. "You have hypochondria," he told her one night. "What's that?" asked Bree, hushed by fear. "Is it serious?"

"Who knows?" said her father. "It's when imagination makes up illnesses to get attention. Go to sleep."

It sank in slowly on Bree, only just before sleep; her father believed she was lying. But she woke up every time with the true throb of pain or worry. She could not believe she was acting. It *was* pain, something wrong, and her father's presence did ease it, as if that cold metal disc sucked the hurt out of her. But her father stopped coming. He shouted out in the dark house, "Stop it, Bree." And she lay there in terror that she was dying, forbidding sleep.

When she grew older she realized that many of her father's best patients had imaginary complaints too. He took them at their word, and he would not be her doctor. Bree broke her foot in basketball when she was thirteen. She limped home and her father said it was bruising, without touching the foot. In the middle of the night her mother had to rush her to the hospital. Her father never mentioned it afterward.

She went to UCLA in 1959, a theater arts major, and she fell in with a group of young film-makers that included Francis Coppola, Carroll Ballard and, the most original and interesting of them all, Dennis Jakob. He asked Bree to act in a film he was making. It was about a young woman who pretends to be a ghost every once in a while, goes out in the night, and finds some young man to haunt.

They shot the film late in the fall of 1962, during the Cuban missile crisis. As they worked, often at night, in a deserted house on Sunset, in Topanga Canyon, on the beach and by the Sepulveda reservoir, the student crew had a radio bringing in bulletins of impending war. Bree felt this might be the last film ever made, and she put the force of her life into it, exhilarated and emboldened by the crisis. She loved doing it, having the crew so quiet you could hear small creatures ticking in the undergrowth, having the passwords—Camera . . . Speed . . . Action—and then partaking of her passionate reverie, a mood of ghostliness or materiality, while the camera sucked on her. She felt as if she had had sex after every take. She looked at the camera, awed by its desire and the implacable composure marking it.

The film didn't work. It didn't all cut together; the transitions were jagged; people said Bree was riveting, but why was so much of the other acting stilted? Don't all actors inhabit the same story? Dennis told her she should use the footage to get real work in pictures.

She called on agents. Her father gave her one name—just one, to satisfy her mother. She carried around the sixteen-millimeter film. Some people looked at it, or said they had; they said it was interesting, or they could not recall the big scenes. But it was hard to have the picture synchronised in double system so that they could hear her breathy silences conspiring with the night. There were promises made, odd, strained meetings; she was invited to some parties, and to Mexico. She was asked to read a few times, but nothing transpired. She made it as clear as she could that she would go to bed if necessary. They said, "Oh no," with a smile. "What do you think we are?" Integrity smothered her every wile.

As she waited for calls, a friend asked her to be in a play. It was *A Doll's House*, a cold Norway Christmas done in the Valley in July, sweating in the flannel costumes, but loving to have the audience under her spell. It filled two months of her life, as good as the film, but she had not been paid for either. Then another company asked her to take a small part in *The Mousetrap*, and they would pay her. For a few years in California she was in theater. Everyone said she should try New York: her hard edge would go down well there.

She moved east in 1966, and she had to start again. She got a few parts, but people told her to go for modeling jobs as protection. They said she had a new look, California Kennedy. Another model, Arlyn Page, asked her one day if she wanted to make a hundred dollars. Arlyn had a job on Long Island and it clashed with a "date" set up in the city. "A hundred dollars for a date?" said Bree, and Arlyn answered, "Sure, you know." The date was a teacher from upstate New York in for a conference. He gave her five old twenties and all she had to do was fuck him once and stay the night. He was a sad optimist and it was easy making him feel better.

It got to be that it was always there if nothing else came along. There was no need to be poor. And if there wasn't an audience or a camera to command, then she could soak up the authority of providing fulfillment for some timid, inexperienced man. It was acting for an audience of one. After a few months, she realized she was good at it; people were asking for her. She had calls in a way she never had from producers or agents. She was something like a star, and she got a service. There were some bad times. Tricks who wanted her to stand on them and pee on them, one man who had beaten her up—but he'd paid her and paid her extra when he cut her. Apparently, there was a rate he knew for such mishaps. There were others who admired her, and told her she was magnificent. There was one gentle old man who just liked to meet her somewhere and watch her undress in as slow and thoughtful a way as she could manage. He told her she was a goddess, and he murmured to her in a language she did not know.

Then in 1971 she turned thirty, and there were more tricks than parts. One day a man came to her apartment, a John Klute from a small town in Pennsylvania. He was a cop, or an ex-cop, and he was investigating the disappearance of a friend. One of the things this man had left behind was a pornographic letter, never posted, but written to Bree Daniels. Had she known him well?

Bree told Klute to get lost; he had helpless, still eyes that frightened her. He was so passive it got on her nerves. But he stayed around. He got a room in the same building, and he started to watch her. Bree felt there was someone out there spying. One night she knew there was someone trying to make as little noise as possible on the roof. She screamed, and suddenly Klute appeared from nowhere to protect her. The tread on the roof was still there. Two people had been watching her, Klute and the other.

Klute said that his friend must have been murdered, and that the killer was sure Bree was a clue. It didn't help that she had no idea how. So Klute looked after her. Sometimes she thought he was as creepy as any killer could be. But it was better than nothing having him there at night when the house creaked and the water pipes groaned.

It came to a head. Arlyn Page was murdered; she had been involved, too. Bree became more frightened; whatever Klute expected seemed to occur, but still he looked hurt, helpless and out of it. She said he should see a doctor; it seemed ridiculous in the middle of a crisis, but he took the idea seriously. He told her never to take chances. But Bree was desperate to end the suspense. One day she had to go to the old man's garment factory. He called for her, he said some pleading words in his strange tongue over the phone. When Bree got there, after dark, there was no one in the place. She waited and she heard sounds. Then the killer arrived and told her he would kill her too now. Bree stifled a laugh. Amid the danger and the terror, she could not shut out the naughty glee that she might be imagining this.

Is there any crisis or epiphany now that we can take on its own terms? Or do we sidle through

> *life like private eyes, noting the echoes and the*
> *similarities, saying, "How like that story this*
> *is," chuckling and comparing, even if it is our*
> *death.*

JOHN KLUTE

Donald Sutherland in Klute, *1971,*
directed by Alan J. Pakula

"You want to go off on your own on the case?" the chief had said.

"Yes, sir," said Klute.

"Where?" It was always tiring talking to Klute.

"New York City."

"On your vacation?"

"No, sir. As long as it takes."

"John, listen. You're a fine cop. You have problems with some of the other men, but you do good work. Outstanding. I know you like to work on your own. I know you and Tom Gruneman were friends. I appreciate that. But he's missing, John. He's not murdered, not that we know. And he's been missing five months. Some people prefer to be missing. You with me?"

"Yes, sir."

"I can't afford to send you off on a missing persons until we know more. Now, the family could hire a private operative."

"They've done that."

"And nothing?"

"No, sir."

"Well, that's how it is. Do you know how many missing people there are, John, in all the U.S.?"

"No, sir."

"It's a lot. Plenty. Anyway, John, I can't let you go."

"Then I resign, sir."

"Goddamn, John. . . . I'm sorry."

So he traveled to New York City, thirty-two, a psych.-soc. major out of Penn State, a year in the military, eight years a detective, single, independent. He had always wanted to be a private eye; when this case came up he hankered from the start to go it alone. And he wanted to meet the woman to whom Tom Gruneman had written that dirty letter. Klute had never had a secure relationship with a woman, but he was frightened of hookers. On this case he would have to meet one. He could tell himself he had no choice.

The city horrified him, but he would not let that show. He kept looking straight ahead, he studied maps and guidebooks in his hotel, and he never asked for help. Like everyone else in the city, he thought, he began to be enclosed in his own intense purposes.

He called on Bree Daniels. She struck him as danger straightaway; it was like running across open ground under fire being with her. Her whole look seemed naked, like a young breast, taut and fragrant. But the danger attracted him. He did not so much want to touch her as watch her being touched.

Klute took a room in her building. He could see her window from his. He sat there in the dark and watched her come home, put on the amber light and change her clothes. He followed her around the city. The crowds and the straight streets were ideal for pursuit. He wondered if everyone in New York was following someone. She never knew he was tailing her. He watched her go to several clients; he saw her waiting at an advertising agency, in a row of younger women with more amenable faces. He saw her come home, alone, and he noticed another dark shape on the flat roof above her apartment.

He guessed that she was bait he could take advantage of. Suppose somehow the killer knew that he, John Klute, had come to the city with no other design than to find him, the killer. Then he might realize that Klute was following Bree Daniels—a woman the killer had known? That the killer might have introduced to the killed? She knew many men by their numbers. She might have a book of accounts.

Klute had seen Bree disrobe for the old man with the clothing factory. He had watched the garments fall away silently and the body, pale and distant in the lamplight. Anyone could have looked at that window at that moment; she and the old man were oblivious in their remote idyll. So he was familiar with the factory, and he knew where to be hiding when the willful Bree ignored his flat advice. The killer's name was Cable, a partner in Tom Gruneman's old business, so obvious a possibility Klute had dismissed him long ago, had even discussed the case with him. Klute came in just as Cable was about to murder Bree. He timed it perfectly, like a climax, but he felt no excitement, for he could see that the uneasy relationship with Bree might be over now. She lay there, drained by the imminence of her death, her fierce face looking up at him, trying to work out the story.

219

Her perfume stayed behind

He took Bree back to Pennsylvania, away from the scabrous city where men had her number. They were married for four years, from 1972 till 1976. Klute rejoined the force, and Bree prowled the home. She became restless in the marriage. She could never find a way of being in the country town. She tried to see the other cops' wives, but she was harsh to their small talk, and they began to be disconcerted by her. Nor could she shift the cold stare from John Klute's face. He smiled, he laughed, he looked down on her with the intensity of a lover, but the chilly gaze came back when he imagined her infinite experience. She noticed him watching her. One afternoon she went for a walk through the town, without shopping, plan or an errand, and she realized he was tracking her, his police car creeping along on its mission.

She left him, and went back to the city. At thirty-four, there was no further illusion about acting or modeling. She became a whore again, and she had to prove that she was tough and competent enough to make business in the twelve or so years left to her.

John Klute quit the force again; he returned to New York. Out of money, he lived on the streets. It was a small step down; how easily his plainness became derelict. We are only inches from the gutter; its smell will come as no surprise. He watched Bree as well as he could, but he was losing his quickness. He knows where she lives. He has seen her laughing at a restaurant table, while the flambée flared. He has seen her at the fights in Madison Square Garden, restless in a cheap fur coat as her escort talked with other men. And once, as she slipped from a limousine, he held the car door and got a quarter from the old man in a mohair coat who whisked her into his building. Her perfume stayed behind her on the winter night. But she never noticed the wreck he had become. Bree has given up watching, and lives for the moment.

> *Sherlock Holmes would occasionally spring out of the disguise of a street tramp to catch a thief, or goose Watson. It had the added effect of seeming to suggest that every bum was in disguise. I have thought of trying it, in a stained coat, with stubble on my face, booze in the eyes and a sack tied up with string, coming to the back door to see if Mary Frances has any old memories to spare. She might ask me in and*

220

say, absentmindedly, "My husband seems to
have gone away." I could wear his old clothes,
shave with his cutthroat, revive his crushed
wife. . . .

MARY ANN SIMPSON

Kathleen Turner in Body Heat, *1981,*
directed by Lawrence Kasdan

He was the one in the band not sweating. She chose him for that and for his isolation from the others. She could see he was Latin, but she counted on a minimal exchange over this delicate request. And it might be a perverse talent to determine not to sweat. Something thin and lethal in the trombone player made her guess it was his act of will. The way he held the trombone she could see it as a rifle or her own legs draped over his shoulder. On hot nights in Florida she did not stop imagining bodies touching. She craved the breezes of an island.

"Sometime while you're playing," she explained, "a man will come out of that bar over there. He will stop to listen."

"He likes this sugar shit?" His English was correct but the slang sounded stilted.

"He is sentimental."

"What's he look like? There are guys all over."

"He's tall, fair, with a mustache. His hair is combed back, like a . . ."

"Like a Latin."

"Why not?"

"And all I do is signal you?"

"That's all."

"Come up with the slide?"

She nodded. It was too hot for more assent.

He laughed. "Like it has a hard-on."

"You can manage that?"

"I try, señora." Now he sounded like a Cuban hustler from Miami, imitating Speedy Gonzalez to be cute.

She dropped the limp twenty into the bell of his trombone. It rose to swallow, like a fish.

221

"So much?" he said, but then, "Maybe so little?"

She took her place, six rows from the front on the end chair. In her white skirt and her white blouse the trombone player couldn't miss her. Mary Ann had learned that if you were very noticeable people never saw anything else about you. So she sat in her own steamy damp listening to one swing classic after another while Ned Racine assembled his frail will to go out in the hot night. To master patience, she recited her other name, Matty, over and over again, under her breath. The old man next to her looked up, as if his worn-out life depended on it. She smiled modestly, to confess that this half-uttered, half-felt Matty was her best beau. But the old man looked stricken because he had revealed himself. Even at the end of their tether, men lost their heads over her.

The music pushed aside the thick vapor of the Florida night. She felt her brow—hot as a saucepan beneath the skim of perspiration.

"You what?" Matty had drooled at Wheaton, the first time they met, freshman roommates in the fall of 1965. She knew then and there that Matty had a cavernous weakness: she had to be liked. Whatever she said, there was always that need in it: "Oh, please like me. I'll do anything for that." If she told a story it was so her telling would be pleasing. When she asked, "You what?," whiny-eyed and defenseless, it was an offer of servitude.

"My temperature runs high," Mary Ann had told her. "A hundred is normal."

Matty Tyler came from Santa Barbara. She had been sent to Wheaton because her mother had gone there. Matty had led a gentle life. She said how spoiling it had been and how much less virtuous than Mary Ann's harder time in Joliet, the southwest end of Joliet, near the canal. Mary Ann was at Wheaton on a scholarship because she was intelligent and because her father was in prison after he had been caught embezzling from the bank where he worked. He had found God in prison, and Mary Ann had stopped visiting him since it was all he ever talked about.

Matty and Mary Ann were inseparable: Mary Ann let the light-weight Californian stick to her, and let her pick up the checks. In return, Mary Ann figured the tip, as soon as she saw the total, without the tax; she never tipped on the tax. Matty was bothered by all calculations, preferring to pay with a flourish. "All set then?" she'd ask. And every time Mary Ann overrode the sly wish to answer, "No, bitch, just sit there until I say so."

Mary Ann had carried Matty through Wheaton. She had rewritten her papers, told her what to think and guided her into a lady's B. She had the time. Mary Ann had straight A's until her junior year, when she realized she was too obtrusive. So she worked for a B and a C. It was hard for her. The comparative religion teacher, a wistful campus guru named Rosenthal, watched her sink, suspiciously. He called her to his office one day and said he couldn't understand what was wrong. On the spur of the moment Mary Ann said it was because she was in love with him. Then and there she gave him an expert blow-job. He was demoralized at having allowed it—he had been like a man looking at an X-ray of himself—so he gave her a grim, castigating C and moved on to higher things.

Afraid to lose her, Wheaton hired Mary Ann as a West Coast fundraiser. She went to California with Matty, and she took an office for the job in Santa Barbara. They kept in touch as much as possible while Matty helped her mother plan parties. At one of those affairs, Mary Ann met J. J. Cord. He owned parts of Santa Barbara, and he sorted things and people into those he possessed and those that belonged to others. It was simple and direct, the way California had been carved up a hundred years before. He made Mary Ann his mistress. He got her an apartment near the water, visiting her two evenings a week, parking one of his old, dowdy cars in the alley. Mary Ann watched how he dithered over her body, happier to look and own than become enmeshed.

"What does the name Noah Cross mean to you?" he asked one night.

"I've heard of him."

"How would you like to be at his hundredth birthday party?"

"When?" she said, wrinkling her nose at the prospect of a hundred.

"He'll surprise you," said Cord, his voice like a banker's speaking of a great ballplayer.

"That'll be nice," she agreed, twirling Cord's soft, sticky rope around her finger.

"Careful, sweetie, with your nails."

"Sweetie!" She reproached herself, dipped her head and kissed it better in the fall of her auburn hair.

The party was in Ireland, at Noah Cross's estate, with chestnut horses in the meadow in front of the gray-stone house. Black limousines went between the house and Shannon all weekend, carrying pretty celebrities—Adolph Zukor, Picasso, Jacqueline Onassis, Norman Mailer, Barbara Hutton, Hugh Harkness, old European monarchs, Cher, Pélé and Bricktop, whores, dukes and poets,

Giancanas, Gores and Windsors, with their entourages, all expedited by Michael O'Hara, Cross's ebullient majordomo.

Cross was borne around the house by two rugby-playing farmers, sitting on a carved Indonesian throne, sipping champagne and conversation and then nodding suddenly asleep, only to wake and be as quick as a boy for two or three minutes. Gifts rolled off him like wrong answers. He dismissed them all, searching for the rare thing a man of one hundred might want or taste.

In the early hours of the next day, Mary Ann explored the house. She walked into a drawing room awash with moonlight, like a room in a black-and-white movie. She took off her shoes and pit-patted across a marble floor toward the French windows. They eased open at her touch, and she stepped onto the warm stone terrace. There was an odor of jasmine in the mild air and horses snuffling in the dark. She caught the whiff of hot hay where the sun had beaten on a field; a half-cooked grassiness was hanging in the night air. Then Mary Ann smelled man, ancient, close and musky.

"Well now, Mary Ann," the voice creaked. He had picked up every name that entered his house. "Mary Ann?—that's a smaller girl's name."

She did not answer; it was heaven to have him prowl around her with talk.

"Sit here on the stone." She did as Cross told her, leaning her back against his sparse legs.

"I fancy I've worked it out."

There was no need to prompt him or ask for his walnut hand to play in her hair. She felt like a treasured great-granddaughter.

"Cord did not come with a gift?"

She shook her head; it tangled his hand.

"Yet Cord is not, would you say, inclined to forget?"

"Oh no." Cord would know what was expected, and what would be a golden treat.

"I'm sure of that. Can you see the horses?"

She could. The longer she looked, the easier it was to pick out the phantoms strolling in the night, like Stubbs horses slowly composing themselves.

"So I have decided," said Noah Cross. "You must be my present."

She guessed this man had been prepared to die for eighty years or so. He had nothing left but life and candid pleasure. There had been little else for years. People were afraid of him but she was attracted to the tranquil practicality.

He wore a white suit of Indian linen. It picked up every drop of moonlight and was easy to unbutton. She let the top of her dress fall down and she pressed her breasts against his soft dick. Neither of them spoke. Perhaps an hour passed, an hour of the gentlest caressing, before it rose as far as it would go and pushed out its thin but still wicked juice on her breasts.

"Excellent," said the old man, and the respect in his voice fell on her like a cloak.

"I love you, Mr. Cross," she said, so wanting to convince him. She bent down with her mouth so that his thing would not disappear in the night. She kissed it and put it back to bed.

Mary Ann remained in Ireland. She rode horses and walked the dogs. She could telephone wherever she wanted and read any of the books. She picked raspberries and gooseberries in the garden, and blackberries in the hedgerows. For an hour every afternoon, she and Noah Cross took tea and he taught her his principles of triumph.

"Not to have done a thing you've thought of—that will mortify you," he told her. "You will be dead soon. How can you contemplate that and not *do* things?" He told her how they might be done. He urged her to make life her stage. They were as engrossed as children in a game, two people as bad as I have ever heard of. But the evil have their tenderness, and the virtuous cannot keep schemes of destruction out of their heads.

Cross suggested that she have a friend over, so she called Matty. Cross inspected the two of them together. "Like twins trying to be strangers," he noticed. Matty was flattered: she wanted others to see the resemblances. Mary Ann saw Matty relax, as if free of a lifetime's constipation. But what had Cross meant in it for her? She looked at him and saw only eyes painted with the enjoyment of an afternoon and two pretty girls.

"Isn't he a dear?" said Matty when Cross went in for his nap. "And he can't be too demanding. That's nice for you."

Mary Ann smiled through Matty and thought, I will have to kill you, dear heart, I will really have to.

For two years she lived in Ireland, sleeping with Noah in the bed as large as a ship, with two setters stretched across the end beyond their feet. Until one morning in June 1972, with sunrise searing the windows so the dogs looked like blood. He was awake before her, as always, watching her young struggles not to give up sleep.

"Would you, my darling?" he asked her, putting the words into her like eggs in poaching water.

225

They were both naked: summer was coming. One setter woke and grumbled when she tossed the sheets back and knelt beside him. It was an old, sweet twig in her mouth, but warm and supple. The phone rang.

"Ruination."

She drew breath. "Let it."

"I am."

But it rang on, and a last duty to importance drew Noah away. He went to the table, naked and gaunt, his old body and the older penis upright. As he talked, he beckoned to Mary Ann; she went nimbly across the carpet. She was never so expert that kindness deserted her. As Noah Cross heard the stupid news from Washington, he came in her hot mouth, a hundred and two, and gasped at the freedom in his collapsing chest. She looked up and saw his face being abandoned. Noah tumbled down, dead. Mary Ann swallowed as she felt for his pulse and heard the petulant voice on the phone still asking for Noah. . . .

The band started to play "That Old Feeling." Mary Ann looked down at herself. Her breasts pressed against the silk from thinking about him. When she looked up, the Latin trombone was lifting like a gun aiming at a duck. The guy winked at her. She stood, turned and strolled in a bored way up the aisle. She left an elderly man behind her, a sentimentalist, vanquished that she would not listen to the music.

There was Racine, dripping, silly and indolent. She saw him see her and she watched his mouth open. His moustache was like the embossed scar for a wound he had not yet suffered.

It would take time, she knew, so it was agreeable that he was attractive in a defeated way. But it would work. Seven years of planning would not be denied. When Cross died, she had used the press's hounding of her as a way of persuading Matty Tyler to change identities with her. Matty was only too happy. And once it had started, it was awkward to go back because the new Matty had met Edmund Walker, who was disposed to marry her. What would a big real-estate man think if his fiancée had an assumed name? "Go on," urged the new Mary Ann. "I want you to be happy. And the name suits you."

For five years Walker grew richer, more explanatory and more tedious, and then in Miami, where they lived, Matty heard of Ned Racine, this less than rigorous lawyer who had made a mistake on a will. She knew the bar where he went, the music he liked, the old movie talk he hoarded, and how vulnerable he was to femmes fatales. So she strolled up the aisle and let him examine her and she reckoned six months before she could make the change in Edmund's will, get Racine to murder him, let the investigation gather, have Ned take the fall and let "Mary Ann" do her one last best friend's turn, and then follow the money to Sulaco.

She had always wanted to be rich and live in an exotic land, and Noah Cross had helped her believe in it. In Sulaco, by the shore, she would write mystery stories and see if her spirit lapsed in the hothouse of luxury.

I have had only a glimpse of her there: a postcard, with a looming cliff behind her and a gigolo reflected in her dark glasses. She looked trapped and ill, despite her tan. She never had the love of life that let Noah Cross last so long. She will be back, driven to intrigue, and she will know where to stand for the moonlight to catch her ivory silk and for "I love you" to linger in the scents and stew of the night.

But perhaps she will come back better, too, more able to notice that the half-deaf elderly man next to her heard, "Daddy, Daddy," and looked up ready to be transformed. Just as some children suppose themselves foundlings, so there are parents hoping to be claimed, undeterred by a toothache frown of evil in the young.

> *Do the deaf make mistakes, or do they lip-read the story?*

JOHN FERGUSON

James Stewart in Vertigo, *1958, directed by Alfred Hitchcock*

Is there some construction or do we live in unshaped turmoil? Is the mass of human creatures just random contiguousness, an impossible tottering pile, or is there an elegant cellular pattern in human association, so that the numb crowd is inspired by eternal forms of feeling and relationship—love, jealousy, curiosity, vengeance, desire, incest, ambition and fear of falling—flexing and pulsing through time and space, like the brain waves of sleep? Can the whole show be held

227

together, or is it a collection of stories in which only stupid coincidence tempts the patternmaker? And similar concerns . . . etc. etc.

John Ferguson was a captain of detectives. He had flown in bombers in World War II from the flat eastern edge of England to the medieval cities of Germany. He had been the navigator of the leading plane in the formation, which is to say the pathfinder, surrounded by maps, calculations and the toilet-roll trail of the way to the target, which he unwound during a flight. Then he would slip down beside the bombardier and look through the blast of the open hatch to the scars and dimples of the ground below. He matched these with the lines and clusters on the map and told the bombardier when to let the bombs go. The dead weight fell away from the plane; it lifted like a mother free of pregnancy. And soon the land flared and blinked with golden markers of destruction.

Later, when he examined photographs of Dresden, he told himself they were the aftermath of other raids, for the ruined city in no way conformed with the descriptive rigor of the maps. Like all men in the service he was told that he might expect reaction, exhaustion and remorse after the war. For ordinary men, decent people, had been made destroyers of the world. But Scottie, as they called him, never faltered. It had been a just war, one that had to be fought.

So he returned to San Francisco, the city where he had been born in 1915, the place where his father had died, falling from the top of one of the towers on the Golden Gate Bridge as it was built in the 1930s. Scottie joined the police. He had not thought of that before the war. He had wanted to be an architect; his degree from Stanford was in that subject. But the war taught him the pleasures of maps, routing and calculation, of search and destroy. It seemed to him that police work would employ these preoccupations, for what was it but the wish to bring order to the map of San Francisco, so that its grid could function?

In that city more than most, the smooth regularity of the map is affected by higgledy-piggledy ground. The cloth of the map is draped over a hard and arrested upheaval. Thus, one night in 1957, John Ferguson was engaged in a rooftop chase; they never found out whether it was a cat burglar or a Peeping Tom. With another detective, Scottie went up and down over the roofs of Pacific Heights after the dark shape. But Ferguson slipped: the roof was slimy from the fog. He slid down the tiles and was left dangling from gutter no more secure than sleep after five a.m. The other detective came back to help him. But in reaching down he tipped over to his death. Ferguson was left hanging, too nauseous to look at the zooming ground and the ragged body lying there.

He developed chronic vertigo. He could not stand on a stool to realign a picture or change a light bulb. Whenever he looked down he swooned; if any kind of desire filled him he might faint. He had to give up the police force and dramatic excitements. There was nothing else to do but go into a private line of detective work. It was the only way he saw of conforming to his illness.

Not long after this decision, he got a call from an old Stanford friend, Gavin Elster, who owned a shipping line in the city. They met, and Gavin asked him about his vertigo and his life in general. "You never married?" asked Elster. "No," said Scottie. "Not that. I don't think I'm suited to it."

"You like women, though?"

"Oh, very much. Very much."

Then Elster told him about his own wife, Madeleine, and why he was worried about her. She was beautiful, she was wealthy in her own right. They had a happy marriage. But Madeleine harbored some inner anxiety that Gavin could neither pin down nor dissolve. She had become obsessed with an ancestor who lived in the Bay Area a hundred years before, a woman named Carlotta, who had killed herself.

"Doesn't your wife need a doctor?" said Scottie.

"She refuses. You know how it is. I want you to keep an eye on her. Tell me what she does. Don't let her know, but follow her and be close—just in case."

Elster said he could afford the open-ended inquiry. He was sure that Madeleine's mood was temporary. It would pass, but until then. . . .

Ferguson began to follow Madeleine Elster. She was a blonde who wore gray and lilac. He got used to looking for her colors; they led him on like a motif, or some instinctive déjà vu. She was not hard to follow. She went in obvious and apparent ways, like an actress in a play whose feet have learned the chalk marks of rehearsal. And she did not look around her much; she did not look behind her in even a casual way. Rapt in her own thoughts, she went straight ahead and seemed more beguiling because of this certainty.

It was just as Elster had said. Scottie saw her first at Ernie's, dining with Gavin. The two men had arranged this. She stood close to him that night, while Gavin paid, so he was able to take in her aura. Then in the morning he waited for her outside the Brocklebank Building, on Nob Hill, where the Elsters lived. She went to a flower shop on Grant Avenue, and took the flowers to the grave of Carlotta Valdes, 1831–1857, at the Mission Dolores. He watched her misty-morning reverence there, and then followed her to the Palace of the Legion of Honor in Lincoln Park, where she sat in front of a painting of a woman which Scottie found out was called *Portrait of Carlotta*.

Then she went to the corner of Eddy and Gough, to the McKittrick Hotel, where she had rented the upstairs front room, which was the last place Carlotta lived before she killed herself. And then—all this time Ferguson followed her by car, parking in a dream of available space—on by way of Presidio Boulevard to Fort Point, the foot of the Golden Gate Bridge. There, while he watched her, the gray-suited woman slipped into the fast, cold ocean: Scottie went in after her and pulled her out, water falling from her dark gray suit like the feeling of apartness. He was holding her, heavy, unconscious, but sentient.

He fell in love with saving her. He took her back to his apartment at Lombard and Jones. He took off the gray clothes while she was still unconscious. Or was she sleeping, dreaming of a romance? They talked; they became friends. Madeleine told him about her feeling that Carlotta lived on in her, urging her to replay an earlier life.

The next day he drove with her, out to see the redwoods in Marin. There was a tree trunk cut open, with the rings of age marked off in a concentric calendar of history. Madeleine found the place in the tree where Carlotta had been born and died, no thicker than veneer. That night, she dreamed of a tower in a Spanish village, with an intimation of falling. Scottie heard her story and remembered there was a place just as she had described, at San Juan Bautista. He decided to take Madeleine there to make a complete exorcism of this haunting nineteenth-century tale.

But when they got there, as Madeleine discovered the further real details of her story, she became agitated. She ran away from Scottie and started up the staircase inside the tower. The detective ran after her, as fast as penmanship in an author who sees the conclusion for his story and wants to get there before its twist slips his mind. But as Ferguson began to climb the stairs, his vertigo returned. He was in an agony of nausea, from giddiness and the fear of what Madeleine might do. He was halfway up the tower when he heard a scream above him and then saw a dark shape, a bundle rushing downward, fall past the window at his level. He looked down and saw the gray-suited, blonde-haired body spread-eagled and still on the Spanish tiles below.

In mystery stories, in film noir, *the spirit of the
story has a secret pact with the villain. It has to
be, for the construction of the narrative is like
the ingenuity of the plot. Is that why Jeff felt
drawn to the bad, because they are authors,
because the atmosphere of intrigue must
always honor its design?*

JUDY BARTON

Kim Novak in Vertigo, *1958,
directed by Alfred Hitchcock*

No one knows what a stripper looks like. He had seen her "dance" a
few times before this sank in. Peeling to the lethargic beat of
tumescent music, she wore vivid makeup, glitter in her hair and
crystalline clothes, all hooks, straps, sequins and secret snappers. The
stripper's art needs special garments made to tear away like the husk
of a pomegranate. So you do not notice the woman as she is, because
you are looking for fulfilment of the mind's eye. You are examining
an idea—depravity or pleasure, or their perilous symbiosis. The
woman is playing a character. Her self stays garbed. Gavin Elster
realized this when he saw Judy Barton leaving the club in Oakland
where she worked. For he did not notice her. She slipped past him. He
was still searching for the odalisque in the green spotlight. The real
woman was so edgy and unimpressive, such a mess.

But the area between her brow and her chin, and between her
ears—the stamp of her face—was so like Madeleine's. He had realized
this in the club, under the lights; that stare was imprinted on the wall
of his mind already. Seven years of reproachful, frigid Madeleine had
put it there. This Judy had the same insecurity, but she was coarser,
more carnal, a copperhead, not the ash blonde of Madeleine.

So he came back another night, to the dark part of Oakland, and he
spoke to her. She thought it was another pickup. His car, his clothes,
his voice alarmed her: how easily wealth seems sinister. How foolish
of the world not to understand that he was broke, that he depended on
Madeleine's money. Gradually he seduced her. He knew enough of
her anxiety to woo her with insights. More than that, he was himself

seduced by his wife's features so transformed by sensuality. A whore had taken over the chapel called Madeleine. He thought of his abstinent wife with vengeful disdain now that he rode on Judy's body and he could look down on the same face, unrestrained and heaving.

Judy believed this suave man loved her. She had never known such dulcet kindness, or such consideration. She appreciated that he could only meet her on the east side of the Bay; he understood her ambition to be a performer. He began to school her. They had bed games in which she was another person. He praised her ability to imagine herself as someone else, and he said they might marry if only Madeleine were dead. He was joking, of course, but the game might be fun.

He bought her outfits—gray suits, with mauve scarves. He had her dye her hair blonde (it was becoming), and when it had grown longer he taught her how to put it up in a special twist like a vortex. Then he mentioned his plan. It was daring; it was becoming. It would require her total belief as an actress. It would win him for her.

She was to come over to San Francisco in her new look—so like Madeleine's that only Gavin would know the difference. Then she was to let herself be followed by a detective hired by Gavin because of concern that his wife was going mad. Judy would play the part of the wife, entranced by the sad history of a relative from the last century, Carlotta Valdes, whose melancholy drew her toward a solemn but well-shaped suicide.

"What if Madeleine, your wife, sees me?" asked Judy.

"She never goes out, she's so . . . depressed."

And so Judy began to be followed. It was hard not to notice her devoted shadow. But it was easier if she remembered the morbid gravity of Madeleine's daily ritual. She led the detective from clue to clue, establishing the story. Although she never looked at him, she began to feel the weight of tenderness in John Ferguson, like a bomb begging to fall or a love aching for a beloved. The intrigue worked; the plot turned into a narrative, even to the most risky moment of all, when she dropped into the Bay gambling that he would follow.

She kept her eyes closed as he rescued her, as he put her in the back seat of his car, as carefully as if she were a bouquet, and she remained in her imitation of sleep as he fastidiously took off her wet clothes. She wondered if he would recognize a stripper's body. But her embarrassment was eased away by the care she could feel in him. Once, his hand brushed against her skin, and she knew he had done it experimentally, out of temptation. She knew this man she had not yet seen was in love with her, and she felt his attention falling on her like dew.

Judy fell in love with him as they talked: he so longed to deter her from her scripted "death"—it was as if a character somehow knew that the duke, say, was destined to be shot in 1914, unless he could rewrite his story. It was easy to provoke the trip to San Juan Bautista because Scottie believed he could rid Madeleine of her curse. When they got there, Judy saw the signal at the top of the tower telling her that Gavin was ready.

She ran slowly to the tower, so Scottie could think of catching her, but because she had already lost the excitement of the play. Regret had taken over. She knew she was inflicting this conclusion on him. But there was nowhere to go but up to the top of the tower. Gavin was there with Madeleine's unconscious body. It was the first time Judy had seen her; she had not expected such likeness. They were identically dressed—Gavin had planned every detail—and Madeleine was draped in Gavin's arms, a stand-in for the death scene. There was even zest on his face as he looked from one gray-suited blonde to the other. Judy believed that for a moment he was not sure which one to throw away. The thought made her scream, and then Gavin released Madeleine's body to the ground. And put the same arms around her.

Gavin had guessed they could get away because Ferguson would have passed out. Such yearning cannot stay conscious.

They drove back. When Gavin returned to the city he had the grim news of his wife's suicide, and the pitiful guilt of the detective he had hired to guard her. Judy went . . . to Omaha, let's admit it. Gavin had told her to go away for at least a year, not to contact him, then to return and call him if she wanted to. He paid her off.

But she was not comfortable elsewhere, and she would not work as a stripper again. She was a typist for a bank, the Potter Bank. The shyness Scottie loved in Madeleine soaked into her. After six months she came back to the Bay Area, and she lived in the Empire Hotel on Sutter Street. She planned to spy on Scottie, watch him from afar. But before that could be accomplished, he saw her on the street. He was transfixed; Judy hardly knew how not to notice him. It felt like a mortal sin to be so unaware.

He approached her and talked to her. He had altered. He was more irritable, less gentle; self-hatred lived in him, eager for more victims. But he courted her, looking past her red hair into the small window of her eyes. He loomed over her with his suspicious love. He asked her to dye her hair blonde, to wear clothes like Madeleine's. It hurt her. If only Scottie could fall in love with her, the unnoticed her, they could go away and forget Gavin Elster. But he saw Judy just as an actress who might revive Madeleine's role. She could not speak out. It would kill her to admit betrayal.

Judy came to Scottie in gray, as a blonde, as Madeleine. The man was moved to tears by the illusion. But Judy did not have to own up to all her lies. She had kept a necklace that Madeleine had worn, an heirloom of Carlotta's. Now she put it on and waited for Scottie to recognize it: it was an act of passive self-destruction, worthy of Carlotta.

She saw Scottie notice it and remember; then came his fury and the need for revenge. What would he do? She half-wanted him to kill her. She deserved it. But he drove them both to San Juan Bautista, to the mission tower. She was consenting but afraid, and though he had to drag her up the tower she was urging him on. When they reached the platform at the top, he looked at her, the image of his dead love, the dead love alive again, and disorder swept *him* off the roof to his death. God keep us from finding whatever we search for.

Judy Barton went away. She did not speak up. It was easy for the world to conclude that the tormented detective had killed himself, had succumbed to vertigo again as he relived his failure. Gavin Elster goes free to this day, a pillar of San Francisco society. I could correct that error, I suppose; I have worked the story out. But I have duties of my own before that.

> *Years later, I still wonder how good an actress*
> *Mary Frances was. When we say good do we*
> *mean a cool talent to pretend, or a helpless need*
> *not to be oneself? She was as good as I have*
> *seen, but I must have looked emotionally. Did I*
> *stop her acting, or save her from it? Or did she*
> *sink into her amateur play, loving it too much*
> *for only three hours a day? What was her role,*
> *then? Heroine or victim?*

SMITH OHLRIG

Robert Ryan in Caught, 1949,
directed by Max Ophuls

Leonora appreciated the psychological imponderable in the state of his health. That must have been why she went to work for a doctor when she left Smith.

It was Smith Ohlrig's curse that he had everything—in a way, possibly, *was* everything. His cold bravado boasted of this, when he really wanted rescue. The illnesses, the fainting fits, the sudden onset of angina were not only frailties that he had willed in himself, the ultimate fruits of hypochondria. They were the way he had found of asking for love. But since he had everything, he was not supposed to need anything else. The bravado amounted to cruelty sometimes. Anyone with Smith suffered from it. But his uncertain health insisted that *he* suffered most, more mysteriously than others, and that he was beyond remedy or treatment. In a doctor's office, Leonora rediscovered the dull ways in which people can be helped.

Smith clung to ordinariness, or so it seemed. He could be charmingly offhand about his wealth, his companies, his influence. He alleged he had forgotten what he owned. His absentmindedness tried to erode the awesome legend. That's why he spelled his name for people, as if it weren't printed on two or three things in most homes. That's why he repaired his own cars and so often took over driving from his chauffeur. He had his humdrum doctrine in eating: at the best restaurants, he ignored the caviar and the French ways of preparing fish. He ordered a sandwich, and made a radical show of preferring it. He drank milk and Dr. Pepper, at the same time. It was meant to be endearing, but the bland tastes were so rigid that they became famous and forbidding. Instead of appearing ordinary, he resembled someone in the early stages of craziness.

He seldom kept up with business, but he was always reading the sports sections. He would become a devotee of some ball team, an unknown intimate of its players. "Kipper went two-for-four today," he'd say. If Kipper slumped and the team slipped, he'd make a big show of worrying over it, putting in calls when they were on the road to see how the game stood in the fourth or the seventh. Then he bought the team, just to put it out of his mind. For once he owned a baseball team, he immediately developed a passion for tennis or horse racing. His new team went into a panic because he never called. They thought he was angry with them. Their game deteriorated and every player was certain he was being traded. They got presents at Christmas, but nothing else. He heard of their losses, on the field and at the bank, with a dry lack of interest. "They think I'm made of money?" he asked.

Childhood, romance and ambition—all those states of hope and desire—had been eclipsed in him just because of the money. He was no businessman; he was self-taught in a weird half-knowledge that no one liked to challenge. He was capricious, fickle and willfully uninformed. He was always doing several things to avoid one. If there was a crisis in any of his concerns, when its decision came to him (for he arranged everything to need his approval), he would announce that he was going to drive to Salt Lake City to break in a new car. Being always the person in charge may have impressed him as a measure of his concern—that common human touch persisting despite corporate hugeness. But it left the companies dangling on his whim. He always waited to be inspired, and he lost fortunes because of it. But there were more to make up the difference.

It was as if, being hailed as the richest and most powerful man in the world, he had to demonstrate his helplessness and his indifference to wealth—made of money, he never took it as nourishment. He had a vague longing, beyond his cracked reason, to mock money and its authority. He was an American; he wanted to be supreme but ordinary, a tycoon and a regular guy, an author and a reader.

It made him inaccessible. So full of oddities and eccentricities, he had no substance. People complained that there was no real man there, just an assortment of Smith Ohlrigs, ways of playing the part. He married Leonora, and then lost interest in her. She might have made a man of him only by refusing him. If she had declined becoming his possession, she could have had whatever she wanted and she might have organized his life. He was only aroused when she left him. For he hated himself and he was moved if anyone else could share that feeling. All his maladies aided his conviction that he did not deserve to live.

But he could not free himself, except by driving across the country alone, in search of a common American who had not heard of him. And so when Leonora left him, he went in upon himself and he made a firebreak around his last position. He ordered sterile chambers in the secure penthouse floors of hotels. He surrounded himself with cleanliness, and often that took the form of nothingness. He sat still for days on end, alienated from himself, a moldering wreck preserved in a vacuum, the ghost of a madman who might be driving across some nocturnal desert, uncertain whether he was a dreamer or being dreamed. The more nothing prevailed, the more legendary he became. Unseen, he was imagined. Nonexistent, he was omniscient. Dead, or inert, he could be everywhere. He made a rare journey: uncomfortable as an author, he became a character for everyone, like the bogeyman or Santa Claus.

HOWARD

Jason Robards in Melvin and Howard, *1980, directed by Jonathan Demme*

He was driving in his blue Chevrolet Caprice from Gabbs, Nevada, to Cypress, California, one night in January 1968. His name was Melvin Dummar. He worked in a magnesium mine in Gabbs and he was going to Cypress to see his daughter, Darcy, who lived there with his estranged wife, Lynda. He was on 95, somewhere between Tonopah and Beatty, when he pulled off the highway looking for a place to take a leak. He was driving on a dirt road when he saw a man lying on the ground. Melvin stopped and got out of the car. He helped the man to his feet. The guy was over sixty, tall, thin, bleeding from an ear. He wore sneakers, pants and a shirt, and his hair was ragged. He told Melvin he had been out riding his motorcycle and he had crashed.

So the man asked Melvin if he would take him to Las Vegas. They drove on together, and the man said he was Howard Hughes. Melvin got him to sing a song, and when they entered Las Vegas "Howard" asked if he could be dropped off at the back entrance to the Sands Hotel. Melvin gave him a quarter and they parted.

Melvin Dummar never said the man had *been* Howard Hughes, only that that is what he had claimed. Eight years later, an envelope was found on the desk of a public-relations officer on the twenty-fifth floor of the Church of Jesus Christ of Latter-Day Saints Building in Salt Lake City. Inside it there was a second sealed envelope that contained a three-page document handwritten on yellow legal paper.

It purported to be the will of Howard R. Hughes, "being of sound and disposing mind and memory." It was signed and dated March 19, 1968.

There were sixteen spelling errors in the 261-word will. To describe the Hercules flying boat, the will used the popular term "Spruce Goose," no matter that Hughes himself hated it. The handwriting resembled that of Hughes and the will left his estate as follows: a quarter to the Hughes Medical Institute, an eighth to be shared among the University of Texas, the University of Nevada, the University of California and the Rice Institute of Technology, a sixteenth to the Church of Jesus Christ of Latter-Day Saints, a sixteenth to set up a home for orphans, a sixteenth to the Boy Scouts of America, a sixteenth to be divided between Jean Peters and Ella Rice (the two wives of Howard Hughes), a sixteenth to William Lummis (a cousin), a sixteenth for a school scholarship fund, a sixteenth for his personal aides, and a sixteenth for Melvin R. Dummar (spelled DuMar). The remainder—an eighth—was to be shared among the key men of the companies he owned. Noah Dietrich, a longtime associate of Hughes, fired by him in 1957, and by then eighty-seven, was appointed executor. Dietrich said, "It's the real thing." Some smart handwriting experts said the will was genuine, but others declared it a fake. Eventually, the courts decided that it was not the true will of Howard Hughes.

Dummar later admitted he had put the envelope on the desk on the twenty-fifth floor in Salt Lake City. He said a man had given it to him at the filling station he then had in Willard, Utah. Yet Dummar still said he had had nothing to do with the writing of the will. He maintained that in 1968 he had picked up a man who said he was Howard Hughes.

As if authenticity counted in this country. We have all pretended we are Howard Hughes, and it was surely a game that could have occurred to him. After all, he loved to make movies: he made a film about Al Capone, but called the character Tony Camonte; and he made love to the breasts of Jane Russell with a camera in a way worthy of an imagination that could never meet or talk to the real Jane.

Driving across the desert at night, not that far from Beatty, I have pretended to myself that I was Howard Robard Hughes to keep myself awake. I have allotted the portions of my estate, I have recalled the great thrill of the air, and the line of dark-haired actresses that I knew . . . and my head has been filled with glory, hope, absurdity and violence. And when I looked out of the window at the night desert rushing by, I have seen old men, hermits and unfound Crusoes, waiting to be discovered, loping along with the jackals. In the desert, fancy soars and a wondrous resolution of all ills comes to mind. The car roars with my excitement.

EVELYN CROSS MULWRAY

Faye Dunaway in Chinatown, *1974,*
directed by Roman Polanski

Even in a book, I have kept them as far apart as possible. There are only darker stories still between here and the end. And no matter that the Cross always stuck in her, Evelyn Mulwray was never simply guilty. There were those who remembered her as a radiant woman, an emblem of Los Angeles in its best days, the 1930s. Some people sigh and say that anyone who saw that in her did not know the real woman. I am not sure. She was a terrible victim, if you like, a spoiled soul. But was the sin, or the mistake—the rape—was that central, or was it something she learned to accommodate? Those who knew her (so few) and those who have fed on the scandal since (so many) took it for granted as the critical incident of her life, the worst thing. I am not sure. It may be the thing of which her father was most ashamed; it may be what made him a monster. But Evelyn could have feared other things more.

Her first fourteen years are flawless, in the way some lives started just before the Great War strike us as being passed in the last poignant light of a confidence that would soon end. That is sentimental: the Cross family had made its assurance and its home from the best official brand of piracy the world has known—free-enterprise venture capitalism. But the same fraudulent fondness may have worked for that very generation. In 1919, Evelyn Cross, nursing her mother in the influenza epidemic, was old and young enough to know the damage done to the world and to look at photographs of family picnics in the Santa Monica hills when she was seven and eight and nine, a white iris in her picnic dress, and feel the recent, unrepeatable bliss. Her innocence coincided with the world's weary sinking into suicide. She was not sucked down, but she whirled around like a flower on top of the water.

lying on a sofa, reading?

At twelve, she had said goodbye to a dozen young men often around the Doheny house, not so much older, but Galahads to the "up-to-date" young lady. Eight of them never came back; only one of the others was not wounded, and he had a nervous deafness from which he never recovered. In the brief American war—nineteen months—California had not lost its weather or its charm. It was a small city then, Los Angeles, conscious of all its countryside. People rode and walked on the paths in the hills. There were painting classes at Malibu, and nature rambles on Cahuenga. This was not southern England, where you could hear the bombardments. America was so removed from the war whose peace it would direct, and California was four days away from Washington or New York. It was the last paradise in the modern world, and Californians still live in a state of loss.

Her mother died, despite her father's assurance that that would not happen. He had been talking to himself, I think. Noah Cross had a great fear of being alone. He loved a full house; he had wanted many more children. He may not have loved his wife, not once that first physical desire had been met, and he took that with him wherever he went, like a gun to be fired. So Evelyn's mother must have known about some infidelities; there was a whiff of sexual gunpowder to Noah Cross. He was a rogue, a user, a robber baron—all of that. But I'm not sure if his energy had been malicious before 1919. Quite literally, he did not know the damage he did. Afterward, he knew; and he acted with what had to be regarded as aim and accuracy.

Noah went to pieces when his wife died. He could not be bluff, sweeping, jocular and commanding. He wept, he could not drag himself out of bed for days at a time; he lapsed into the self-pity of a child. And he had only a teenage daughter to help him recover. What happened? The law says she was raped; she was too young to have a mind in the matter for it to have been anything else, under the law. And what pedantry it is to speculate whether a fifteen-year-old was willing with her father. Isn't it? But I am not sure that Noah Cross could have done it if his daughter had not, even secretly, been consenting. Suppose, out of some mixture of mercy and curiosity, she offered it? She would not have said anything, not have known how to be seductive; but suppose she merely elected not to get up some afternoon when her sad father came dangerously into the room where she was lying on a sofa, reading?

Evelyn Cross loved her father. She admired his flourish, his laughter, his ways of riding, eating and telling stories, his appetite for doing all at the same time. She was his spellbound audience, reluctant to go to bed because it meant giving him up, like a storybook. She wanted to ask him to stop, so she wouldn't lose her place. She loved him physically. He smelled of horses, tobacco and that sourness that clings to a man's body and which a lap-child follows like a trail. She loves and shudders at it as much as at her own excrement. It is normal for girls to love their fathers, and normal again for that love to be erotic at least for a moment as they grow up. For Evelyn that moment coincided with her mother's death and her father's crisis. But he should not have let it happen. He could have angered her, hurt her, by saying no. But he was a weak man, as well as a titan; he could not bear to show her his fear.

Perhaps her kindness settled it. Perhaps she drew her troubled father down to her, held his head against her small bosom, felt the quickening, heard him go silent and then knew her inner thigh was being felt by his warm hand. She would not know what to do. He did it. But so often the man thinks he does it, and blame was not in anyone's thoughts that afternoon. It was just a meeting of need and kindness, of ignorant wonder and weakness. He may have been more gentle and tender than he had ever been in love. He may have christened her, welcoming and guiding her, praising her startled excitement, telling her she was wonderful and beautiful. They may have slept in the deepest contentment of their lives. No one ever heard Evelyn hate the moment or the way it was done. Yet it may have been snatched, brutal and selfish; and he could have prevented it.

It was luck that her moment should be so dramatic, and luck or passion's forgetting that it made her pregnant. But bad luck or good luck? If bad, then it must have been good that Hollis Mulwray was around, willing and able to marry Evelyn and take her north for the birth of the baby, Katherine. But Hollis assumed that Evelyn meant to be sheltered from her father. Perhaps the two of them should really have talked more to each other, not less; and perhaps pain and guilt were their most likely starting points.

Hollis's generosity must have implied to Evelyn the guilt and horror she was expected to feel. It could not be missing if he loved her as he did. And being in love with Hollis was the best thing in Evelyn's life. He was older than she; he was not handsome, and next to her father he struck no one as brilliant. But he was discerning and kind, and I am trying to suggest that kindness was vital to Evelyn. They told Katherine as she grew up that she was Hollis's child by an earlier liaison. Evelyn looked after her like an older sister. Hollis made a good father. Seeing him with Katherine, Evelyn realized the ways her own father had failed her.

So she felt as much reproach as horror. As Katherine grew older, it became harder for Evelyn to consider a clean sweep of honesty. That's what Vivian Sternwood, her closest friend, urged on her; that's what Jake Gittes wanted, but he wanted to marry her too, while all she found in him was single-minded physical satisfaction, too blunt for his soft heart. But by the time Gittes came on the scene, Hollis was dead. Evelyn never had doubts about the murderer. There were business reasons for Noah Cross killing Hollis. They had made Los Angeles between them, in such a theft that they never trusted each other. But that wasn't reason enough. No, Noah was jealous of Hollis; he longed to be seen as the father of Katherine, fifteen in 1936, that precious age. By then, Noah Cross had come to terms with his badness. He almost boasted about the courage it took. It made him feel greater than other men. Just as it did when Evelyn shot him and he did not even fall from the wound. And he felt true power when the police shot Evelyn, right through her imperfect eye, and he knew only relief as he held on to Katherine.

Someone told me that the thing you want to know about people is what most frightens them. It is advice that could come from a writer or a secret policeman. I don't think incest frightened Evelyn Mulwray, at least not the hot act, not the part of it called rape. She had done it, and known the excitement. She may have engineered it out of a curiosity that would not be refused. She could not reject it out of hand when Katherine was such a happiness for her. So she hated her father—well, most people seem to need to do that, sooner or later.

No, what Evelyn Cross Mulwray feared most was telling Katherine, talking about it to her child. There is a part of us, so deep down and buried, that could sleep with our own children. But the soul, or whatever, then has to describe the act in language; and then the body writhes away from hearing in the worst tortures. The animal is on a leash to the mind that will not let it forget or use the excuse of vagueness or exaltation. Evelyn and Noah were alike in this: they could let action do the thing, but when the word had to be uttered they fell back in dread.

> *I can never get Noah Cross out of my head. He is a demon, utterly unlike the man I have wanted to be. But I am greedy for details about*

> *him. He monopolizes me. Some part of me I do*
> *not know must want to be a man of action*
> *striding across the world, laughing at the*
> *wreckage he leaves. Am I depressed because I*
> *will not allow Cross in my life?*

HARRY MOSEBY

Gene Hackman in Night Moves, 1975,
directed by Arthur Penn

Named Harry for my brother, and Moseby for the ancestor who fought at Antietam and the Wilderness. We had the Civil War sword; it is in the attic, still, somewhere. He was born Harry Moseby Bailey in 1940, our first child. But he dropped the Bailey, to obliterate or forget the family he came from. It was an unexpected evasion in a censorious boy, always going on about "getting to the bottom of things." Wherever he is now, I fear he rants to himself and others about control, "having one's shit together," reading his fortune when he stands up to assess what he has left in the toilet. I'm sure it's a sturdy python: he would eat sensibly and look after his body. But there's a dark room in his life that would turn his bowels to water if he admitted it. He keeps me in that dark room. He walks around it, never solving it or counting the weariness of walking so far.

His first two years he turned us into lovers, Mary Frances and me, asleep in a cot next to our inspired bed. He was happy until he was seven, growing up in Bedford Falls to news of the war. Harry kept the letters from his Uncle Harry; he was as conscientious about the war as only a child could be. One day he sat on my knee—this was 'forty-four, that June, with pictures in the paper of the beaches, one named after his favorite Omaha, bringing sea to our landlocked state—and he asked me whether my ear was adequate reason not to be there. I felt guilty, his manner was so demanding. I explained it again. Mary Frances came in and said, "We're both lucky to have him," a benediction over my head, so so serene. Then she altered. "Can't you get that into your stupid head?," and I knew she was going. From one phrase to the next, she could jump the tracks. Harry just stared at her in that little boy's way; she moaned and went away teary with

243

another failure. The moan, high and small, like a dying cat, stayed in the room. "There, Daddy," said Harry, to comfort me.

Nineteen forty-six and 1947 were the bad years for him, and for all of us: years of anxiety and smothered feeling with nothing to be sure of: his parents were frantic, eager and fearful, all at once. But it was a few years before we understood it was more than Harry could take. His younger brother was born in 1945. As soon as that happened I knew we had waited too long, let him be an only child imagining the world should be that way. Then in 'forty-six there was the problem of the bank, when it seemed that we would founder and close, and what everyone kindly agreed to call my "breakdown." God! and all the rest of it. Mary Frances out of her mind at my depression: I had guarded *her*. And then the trip I took to New York and all that followed from that. Mark's visit. Harry was too young to comprehend, so we told him nothing; we could not bear the thought of children picking up our dismay and anger. But he lived in his mother's moods as much as anyone. They were climatic, the air in the house vibrated with her frustration and I was a cellar of unhappiness. He heard his Uncle Mark shouting in the house, and he must have heard his mother scream, such a hideous cry and such a relic of the actress she had buried. Then later, when she visited, he saw how beautiful Aunt Laura's face had been spoiled. After that, she stopped coming. He adored her, too. Harry knew that the fabric around him had been torn in several places past repair. He hated disorder and, since I was the head of his household, he made me culpable. Did my deafness stop me hearing the first ripping sound in our family?

When he was fourteen, he asked to be sent to the military academy—to get away and to reproach me. I knew I had lost him, and I never said it was more than I deserved. But I feared for him. He was a boy still, despite being tall and strong, and having to shave; I wondered how he would deal with the rupture. Sometimes you can see a look in a tense face that says, "This is my tragedy, it will destroy me, but I will never give it up"—like someone who can't swim, clutching someone else, ready to drag them down.

He came home once again in 1958, before he went to USC. That was all. He didn't pack up his things; there was not that much warning. He simply left his childhood, an untidiness for us to clear up. It was a large family, and I still don't understand what bursting energy it had that so many of us flew away from it, like the pieces of an explosion.

I watched his life from afar; I wasn't told that he did write two or three times a year to his mother. He majored in psychology at USC, but his greatest achievement there was being free safety three years on the football team. He was a first-round draft choice in 1962, taken by the Detroit Lions, and he was All-Pro in 1964, 1965 and 1966. I saw him on television, but it's not a game of faces. It's all helmets and the huddled strategy. But he was good. You felt he had a passion about keeping his end zone intact. He was only 180 pounds, but he could stop much larger men inside the five-yard line when they were going at full speed. He absorbed their velocity, forced their momentum upward and crashed them down on their backs. It took the strength out of him. He retired in 1968, looking older than his real age.

He had met a woman in the Lions' business office, Ellen Pressmann, and they moved out to Los Angeles. Harry set up a practice as an investigator: it was his old, self-appointed role as the sorter-out of truth, a free safety who stopped the attacks. So much of what happened was his own fault, taking care of things, and looking away from those truths he could not settle. Harry was a problems man, but only for problems he could solve. The others he ignored.

By 1974, his marriage was coming apart. Ellen was seeing another man, Martin Heller. Harry went to challenge him. Heller was a cripple—from Vietnam, I think—and not much use to a woman, or not in the ways Harry was most afraid of.

"What does she want from you?" he asked Heller.

"Someone to talk to."

"Talk! Talk about what?"

"You mostly," said Heller. "She doesn't understand you."

"There's no mystery about me," Harry must have roared—the old horror.

About that time, he got a call from a woman named Arlene Iverson. She'd been in some pictures in the forties—she was a femme fatale in a few *films noirs*. She had a teenage daughter, named Delly, who had run away; would Harry find her? He always said he could find anyone—but only if he decided to look, of course—he never found me, though he used to tell maudlin stories about trying to see me.

Harry discovered that Delly had known a group of movie stuntmen. One of them, Quentin, had been her boyfriend. He told Harry she'd gone off with Marv Ellman, another stuntman. The leader of that group, a stunt designer and an agent for others, was Joey Ziegler, and he suggested that Harry look for Delly in Florida. Delly had a stepfather, Tom Iverson, an ex of Arlene's, and he ran a diving school down in the Keys.

He flew to Miami, and then he drove down to the Iverson place, between Long Key and Marathon. Delly was there with Iverson and his new wife, Paula, a tall, dark-red-haired woman who attracted Harry. It wasn't a very savory setup: as far as Harry could tell, Iverson was sleeping on and off with both the women, and no one was disposed to protest about it. There was a defeated air to the house, of freedoms turning to poison.

Harry tried to persuade Delly to go back home to Los Angeles; I doubt if he caught the irony in "home." He had a searching gaze, but he was always so sure he knew what he was looking for. Delly told him no, but Harry stayed around. One night he went out on a boat with Paula and Delly. He and Paula started arguing, the sort of fight when one person wants to be gentle but is afraid of seeming weak, and the other meets attack with counterattack. It reminded Delly of every parental row she'd ever heard, so she dived overboard to get away from it. Harry threw a searchlight on the water. Then Delly came up crying because she'd seen a dead man in a crashed plane on the seabed. She was overwhelmed, a child again. When they got back, Iverson assumed that his sleeping with her would be sufficient comfort. But Paula disallowed it at last.

In the middle of the night, Harry was awakened by Paula coming into his room. She wore her nightgown, old-fashioned and darned.

"How's Delly?" he whispered.

"Sleeping. You?"

"Thinking. What in hell is that kid supposed to do with this world?"

Paula crept into bed with him. They talked a little and then they made love. They slept and Harry woke when he heard Delly screaming; in his dream it was the cry of all lost children, but it was Harry himself who had been screaming. When he woke his mouth was stretched open, but his voice was strangled. The girl was screaming for him.

He went into Delly's room and he soothed her. He asked if she was sick. He told her he'd go with her back to her mother. He said he'd take her to a football game if she liked. The girl was calmed by his quiet voice and by his hand stroking her back. Then Harry looked up, and he saw Paula standing in the doorway. There was an expression of inexplicable distress on her face.

"You're a football player?" she wanted to know. "You were?"

Harry took Delly back to Arlene, and he wondered about his own marriage: Paula's warmth had shifted him away from Ellen. He was thinking of escape and a new life. Then he learned that Delly had been killed, in a car crash, with Joey Ziegler driving. He was suspicious, and he felt responsible for Delly. He met Quentin, and the young man told him it had been Marv Ellman dead in the plane off the Keys.

Harry flew back there. He discovered that the coast guard didn't know about the crash, though Iverson had promised to report it. At the Iverson place, he realized that Tom had killed Quentin too. Harry took Paula out in a launch and he forced her to explain. She said that there had been a gang—Iverson, Quentin, Ellman, Ziegler—flying stolen archaeological treasures in from the Yucatan. Harry said he was going to sort it all out, and would she marry him then?

"No, never," said Paula. "Do you know what I did? The night I made love with you? I did that to keep you occupied while Tom went to dive for the plane. There's a Mayan fertility statue on board, its belly is filled with heroin."

They reached the marker buoy, and Paula dived herself. She came up with the female statue Tom Iverson had never found. There was a ragged hole in the woman's abdomen—as if she had had a Caesarean—and there was nothing inside.

"Abortion," Paula shouted from the water. Then they both looked up at the sound of an aircraft. It dropped down toward them and a shot rang out. Harry was hit in the leg. As he fell over in the boat, he told Paula to dive to save herself. But the head of dark wet red hair just watched the small plane come back again, inviting it, and the brilliant pilot knocked it off, as if shooting a cabbage. But the impact shook the plane out of trim, and a wing tore the water. The plane cartwheeled; it snapped in two; Harry saw Joey Ziegler drowning in the cockpit, clinging to the last angle of air. The fine spray of Paula's head and hair blurred the sun.

I cannot write this in one night. It takes every night there is. So I have to leave it open in the day by the window, where anyone could see it. And I do that: I take that chance with Mary Frances. Not for me some top-sheet about work and play to divert prying eyes from knowing who's in bed with Jack. No, she has day after day to go through it all, finding and imagining references to herself. Leaving it there is my bravery, wondering if she can act every evening as if she has not read it or whether I will come

> *back and find the table bare and smoke rising*
> *from the chimney. But she can act, of course; so*
> *well, I am her fan as well as her fool.*

PAULA IVERSON

Jennifer Warren in Night Moves, *1975,*
directed by Arthur Penn

Two people do not remember all they shared, even if they were together one still summer night. There are several strands of talk in their memories, more and less than they really said, things they have tried to forget, and things they only said in their imaginations. There is what one meant and the other understood. Harry Moseby remembered lovemaking: it was the peak he had hoped for as soon as he saw Paula Iverson; so his mind smoothed away the slope of what led up to it. Paula had another version; it need not be correct, or his wrong. There are conflicting conversations in every dialogue. But it helps explain why she did not dive away from a plane intending to skim the surface of the water.

"Where were you when they shot Kennedy?" she asked him.

He knew instantly. "We were starting the afternoon training session. Karras was missing, and then he came out on the field. No one would believe him. He was crying."

"I was in L.A. It was my senior year in high school."

"What were you doing?"

"In bed with a boy. My first time."

Harry said nothing, and nothing is a part of talk.

"He kept the TV on and they interrupted the program. It was the morning still there."

"We won the game. Baltimore."

"You think it was Oswald?"

"Had to have been."

"Only Oswald?"

"Twelve years ago. We've had all the reports and do you think there hasn't been a thought in every journalist's head and every private eye's that if there's more to it he's going to find it out? Twelve years and what do we have as an alternative? Nothing, that's what we have. That and all the doubt."

248

"Yeah, that's what we got."

They lay side by side, touching slowly, their bodies were so suspicious.

"So you won in Baltimore?" she smiled.

"Right. I was supposed to meet my father there."

"Yeah?"

"I hadn't seen him for . . . five years. Haven't seen him since."

"Why not?"

"Family, you know."

"Same old thing."

"He was supposed to meet me, or we were going to meet. After the game. That was the plan. But I expect the Kennedy stuff . . . changed his mind."

"You call him?"

"Don't think so. He just didn't turn up."

"You waited?"

"Right."

"He lived in Baltimore?"

"No. This was at a hotel. He's from the Midwest."

"He never showed?"

"Suppose not."

"Did you ask at the hotel?"

"Can't recall."

"You should."

"You know . . . I was scared."

"Maybe he was there."

"Maybe."

They heard the cicadas, giving the night a serrated edge.

"You crying?"

"No sir!"

"You are."

They made love, touching each other as lightly as possible, for it seemed prudent not to make noise. She had only once before, at college, had to let her orgasm out in silent cries. She felt that she was dumb, or deaf. But she could hear the water lapping against the dock. Perhaps it was Tom paddling out into the stream. The crickets had stopped to listen.

Later, she woke suddenly, disturbed by his alarm. She heard the last of a cry from another room; in the dream, it had been the vagrant sound of her pleasure, looking for a home. She followed Harry into Delly's room and watched him talk to her. He was tender with her.

That gruff military air fell away; he seemed relaxed, as if he should have had a daughter. Then Paula heard him tell Delly that he had been a football player, and she knew she was going to be sick.

"You're a football player," she accused in horror.

"Oh, once upon a time," he grinned.

"What happened to your father?"

"He's alive still."

"You know?"

"He's fit. Has a deafness in one ear."

Paula turned away to look at the rims of light on the tide. Tears would not come; she did not deserve them. It was like the moment when fear finds its need, knowing there is a prowler outside, longing for him to show himself and end the suspense.

"Poor old man," she said, and went back to her room, her mouth full of vomit. I hope she said that.

I was her uncle; he was my son. But none of us saw each other anymore. She was the daughter of Laura and Mark McPherson, born in 1946 in New York. But her father left her and her mother when she was an infant over a drama she might have seen, but without understanding. Still, as she grew into childhood, she would talk to an imaginary friend.

"Who's that?" her mother asked.

"My little sister," said Paula.

"Nonsense," said Laura, laughing.

"No, Mother," said Paula with a firmness beyond her years.

She went to school, in New York, and then in Los Angeles. She was used to hearing nothing from her father, and she endured her mother's futile second marriage to Shelby. She disliked being an only child. She nagged her mother to tell her about her relations in Nebraska, but she did not dream of seeing them. They were not much more real for her than that imagined little sister.

Paula went to Smith in 1964, and she rode across country on the train. It went through Omaha in the middle of the night and she kept herself awake to look at the lights of the city. But the train did not stop. She studied English at Smith, and she wrote a good deal. Her final project was a research paper on Sylvia Plath, a Smith girl herself once, and a recent suicide. Paula herself was depressed at Smith. She found a psychiatrist and she was given drugs. The man said there were so many dark corners in her personal history. She should find her father, he thought. Nothing found could be as bad as not knowing.

She didn't tell her mother. In 1969 she took the job at ICM that her mother had arranged for her, and she did well there. Her script reports became famous for their prescience. She was given clients of her own. She packaged two successful movies—*Memory Street* and *Woken by Bleeding*—and she was not yet thirty. She might have gone far. She went out twice with Warren Beatty.

But she preferred Tom Iverson. He was a figure of imprecise power and wealth, on the fringes of the industry. He had been a stuntman and that loose coterie of individualists admired him. He had contacts high up in the Teamsters. He had been married before and he had been in jail once, for six months, for fraud. He was nearly twenty years older than Paula, but she planned to marry him and go to Florida, where he had a business.

Laura scolded her irresponsibility. All the planning would be wasted. Tom Iverson was no good; trust her opinion, she had seen that type before.

"My father?" said Paula.

"If you like."

"Where is he? I want to meet him."

"I don't know."

"You must know."

"I give you my word."

"I'll look for him."

"You mustn't."

"Why? Why?"

There must have been a lifetime's longing in that question, an awful vulnerability to the doubt. Laura made up her mind. It was the truth, she didn't know where Paula's father was, or whether he had changed his name. But her father had gone off with another child when he left.

"My sister?"

"Your half-sister," said Laura. "So I think."

It went on all night, the daughter preying on the mother's secrecy, the mother losing all the armor of her life. They both knew it was their last talk. A few months later, Laura killed herself. Paula had to take care of the funeral.

She married Iverson, and she went to Florida. It was hateful, he was loathsome. But she preferred it to Los Angeles. She liked the water and the colors at either end of the day. The racket was miserable. Every month she meant to leave, but then Delly arrived and Paula looked at her as a waif she might help. Harry Moseby came next. She never knew why he attracted her, for she didn't like him. It was

251

something deeper and more helpless. She betrayed him and seduced him; she thought that might help remove the mystery. And then she found the reason for her feelings.

Maybe a small madness overtook her. She was not pregnant. She imagined it, if you will, and took savage comfort in the cracked open womb in a Mexican stone goddess. She would have watched the airplane all the way into her head. How did we think we were safe from chance, when it was all that had brought us together once before?

TRAVIS BICKLE

Robert De Niro in Taxi Driver, *1976,*
directed by Martin Scorsese

I received it in June 1974, a postcard from New York City, a picture of Forty-second Street at night. The gaudy, not exactly registered colors show neon bubbles of pink and amber, the glaring marquees like flesh beginning to rot, and a sleek brimstone cab passing by. On the back, there was a stamp of the American flag, my name and address, and this poem, written in jagged black ink:

> here comes a little fellow riding his bi-sickle
> and all his inside thoughts are in an outsize pickle
> now, father of the family, please don't be fickle
> or else I'll come and tickle
> you—at least give a nickle
> to stout-hearted Travis Bickle

The Bickle was written in red.

It was the first we had heard from him since 1971 and the letter from the Marines announcing that, after forty-seven days' captivity under the forces of North Vietnam, Pvt. Travis Bailey had escaped and rejoined his unit. I wondered why the Marines wrote—out of strict duty? to help the letter-writers who had so many notices of death to convey? or because the corps knew that so many of their men no longer wrote to their parents? *Semper Fidelis.*

And I wondered how to read the verse. I realized I did not know my son's mind well enough to judge whether this was affected childishness, hostility, irony, scorn, disturbance or his true voice. Did he need money? Was that the point of the "nickle"? And why would he think I might be fickle? Had his name really changed? What was his outsize pickle? The grim chant to the verse jangled in my head, and I always saw his wolfish white grin. It was only later that I understood the picture was part of the poem: the city and the cab, like Sodom and Gomorrah and their approaching thunderbolt.

This was our second child, born on August 6, 1945, the day we dropped the atom bomb on Hiroshima. Yet he was a source of peace. I still remember the day in 1946 when he lay in his cot, twitching in a patch of sunlight, when I knew I could not leave him, and would stay with Mary Frances and Nebraska because of that. My decision was made above him, but he slept on, his small fists clenching and unclenching at his dreams. I wondered if my deliberation was just the drama of his sleep. I stayed. But in time the child left.

Travis was nine when Harry went off to military school. It was a severe loss for him, for he revered his older brother—not Harry simply, but the force of example in a brother bigger and stronger. Harry guarded Travis in boys' battles. He told him stories about armies and fighting. He showed him the difference between the ways Joe Louis and Marciano fought. It made Travis grow up on the alert for older models and advisors. Perhaps it persuaded him about God and all his duties.

As Travis developed, anyone could see the gulf between his need for conviction and his fear of uncertainty. He wanted to be a hero, but he needed someone to design the role for him. He had tantrums when he failed his own hopes, inaccessible bouts of recrimination in which he abused himself. There were early signs of violence. Once, in an argument over nothing, he hit a boy two years older and broke his jaw. He implored other kids to be his friends, but he alarmed them with his ugly need. Girls laughed at him, and he laughed back stupidly. There were occasions when I found him in the yard or on a street corner, alone and still laughing, but deserted by the objects of his mirth.

In 1961, when he was sixteen, he found God. The first discovery came at the church where we went at Christmas, and where Mary Frances sometimes spent hours at a time, sitting alone, muttering. But Travis gave up on the Church. He said it was hypocritical and out-of-date. There was a small temple in Wahoo—a cult, it would be called now. Its members lived in a commune. I picked up fragments of their

doctrine. They believed in missionary work: Travis was sent all over
the West, hitching and preaching. They insisted on peace, celibacy
and poverty as the ideal states and Travis became a disciple of them
all—learned but a crank, ragged, lonely and belligerent. He was
arrested in a demonstration at Offutt Air Force Base in 1964,
protesting some of the early troop movements to Vietnam.

The worst thing was the convert he made of his mother, her forlorn
attempts to show him her faith, and his rejection of her. The last thing
he wanted was company in his faith. It had to be alien to us. But his
mother's woeful instability heard his passion and thought it could aid
her. He laughed at her visions, beating her off. She looked at him as if
he had struck her. I only have plain words to tell you what happened.
But we lived in a madhouse, all of us unhealing wounds for each
other.

Then in 1968 he joined the Marines. For all I know, it was at the
instruction of his temple, the action was so contradictory to what he
stood for. He must have lied about Offutt to get in. He was sent to
Vietnam a year later. I don't know much about his time there: he is
like the unknown soldier. But he patrolled in the mud and the jungle,
and I imagine he shot some of the slim native people when he did not
know whose side they were on. Perhaps he preached to his fellows;
perhaps the bizarre faith failed him. He was captured. He must have
been tortured and degraded. But he escaped.

He left the Marines late in 1971 and then there was nothing until
that card in 1974 from New York. I don't know where he went or what
he did. He may have rested, traveled or settled somewhere; he may
have done all of those things. The temple denied knowledge of him.
He became the creature of my imagining. But when I received the
card, I knew he had altered in the empty years.

He became a cab driver. The rest is nearly famous. As he went from
Harlem to the Village, from Sutton Place to the piers, from Wall
Street to the Bronx, he began to loathe the city. He was looking for a
pretext, I think. He was in training again, buying guns, eating bread
soaked in brandy, testing himself in the flame, writing a journal to
himself, and becoming two men—the hard physique and the interior
monologue.

Then one day a child got in his taxi, a girl of twelve, only to be half-
pulled, half-seduced away by a man. He could not forget her age, her
high voice, and the debauched costume she wore. As he drove, he
searched for her. We may have hunted for a lost female child, he and I,
at much the same time.

Her name was Iris. He did find her again: it is the role of whores to be predictable, to use the same streets. She thought he wanted to buy her, like anyone else. He could not let her see that he needed to save her. But the more he talked to her the clearer he made it that she was in great danger. At about the same time, she decided that he was right, but mad. Simultaneously, she recognized her own predicament and the absurdity of his as a rescuer.

He prepared himself for the assault. He killed her pimp, the man who rented the room to her, and two of her clients. Four deaths, and he was shot himself, sitting in blood when the police arrived. The pictures were everywhere, with diagrams of the house and one paragraph saying that Travis Bickle, once a Marine, came from the Midwest and had been a religious fanatic.

I never understood why he was not confined for the rest of his life. But he went free. He had slaughtered known criminals, all of them armed; he had acted in self-defense, coming to the aid of a minor—no matter that he was himself heavy with guns and knives. He was a kind of hero, as frightening as those he had killed. They let him go. It was as if he had passed into a movie in which fact yielded to his fantasies, and the law became a pillow to his unhindered, unrestrained desire.

FREDERICK MANION

Ben Gazzara in Anatomy of a Murder, *1959,*
directed by Otto Preminger

In the beginning, I had supposed I would somehow find myself an Al, one of those reliable, businesslike, career killers, men who keep to themselves, looking like hundreds of others, men who render an uncommon service at competitive rates and then return to the crowd. Do you remember Al? He shot Pete Lunn in Brentwood, New Jersey, in 1946; and when he was shot himself he happened to be a man who had gone out that day without any identification. Was he the last of a dying breed? The last freelance killer? Was his profession co-opted by corporations and syndicates, taking all of the Als out of the way of private contracts? There must be many who, some time or other, want a sure killer all to themselves. An Al could be addictive, a permanent hiring. And Als might be a little less grim with health insurance and a company pension at sixty.

So I made up my mind to set out without an Al. I would wait for something to turn up. It was a strange, cheerful mood in which I believe I must always have been prepared to do it myself. But I knew I was too emotionally involved. I would bungle it, shoot an innocent bystander—if any such remained.

I set out from Los Angeles the day after the funeral, after a breakfast at the Chateau Marmont (another youthful ambition realized), where I read the trade-press paragraph on the funeral, with Paula's macabre tribute. I saw no reason to rush; I am never that confident driving a rented car, so I went patiently, giving myself the time to look at country that had been only names on the map. I had never been to Las Vegas, and I thought, Why not? I stopped there the first night, but I got in before dark, coming across the desert, seeing the fever of neon in the lapsing rouge daylight. It looked like a town painted in blood. I was intimidated by the big hotels, and I didn't have money to burn. How long might this business take? So I found myself a motel on Paradise Road called the Showdown, but I did visit the Sands that night just to look at the gambling.

There's no indication of night or day in those places, just the tables, with the croupiers in black and white, and people sitting or waiting for seats and the air of digestion that you get in a crowded cafeteria. I made one bet at blackjack, and I won. I felt perplexed at the omen and got up and went away, stepping carefully between the cowboys and the old ladies, suspicious of pickpockets.

The next day, I kept going northeast on 15, clipping the corner of Arizona. Around midmorning I got lost, and found myself in a haunted little town surrounded by dirt roads, but with made-up roads at its center: Colorado City, a place of many children in long dresses and shirts buttoned at the wrists, all with milky faces and a starched look in their eyes. It seemed to be the isolated home of a cult. I stopped at a store to ask the way and there were kids in silent clusters watching me. I drove on quickly, my back pounding from their eyes, afraid of breaking down. There are pockets in this country, laws to themselves, where anything could happen.

So on and on: to Grand Junction, Colorado, that night and a Best Western. The names change but the motels are alike; they have the same shape to their rooms, the same bed, the same pictures on the walls and TV sets showing the same old movies—*Night and the City* I saw there, falling asleep in *The Dark Corner*.

Going on 70 and 76 I was in Nebraska the next day. It was late October, and the sky grew darker. There was snow in the mountains

256

and the familiar hiss of cold stretching through the state. I didn't go home, though I could have made it. I went close, but somehow I felt safer not being known: Beaver Crossing, the Rendezvous motel, *They Live by Night* and *Farewell, My Lovely* on TV, stuff I can watch till the end of time.

In the morning, I drove through Lincoln and Omaha on 80, on to Des Moines, and then on 35 around Minneapolis, getting into Duluth after dark, stopping at the Detour motel. It was too cold for my constitutional, and *He Walked by Night*—which you don't see that much—was preempted for football, Green Bay versus Detroit. A dull game, the Lions have lost a lot.

And so it was the day after, the first Tuesday in November, that I got to Thunder Bay itself. The water of Lake Superior was the color of an old iron frying pan, and the sky was that scraped white when the wind has blown all day. You can feel the Arctic there. I could only think of bars and hotels as places to ask. It was a day and a night before I went in to an older inn, catering to sportsmen, and the man behind the bar gave me a beer—I was woozy from all of them—looked at the picture, turned away to scoop the head off my glass, looked again and said, "Older than that? Gray hair?"

"Very likely," I said.

"About fifty-five?" I love the way Canadians say "about." "Barney something or other. Used to work here. Moved down to Marquette, I heard."

About a year ago, he thought. I know, I know, you're wondering about Frederick Manion. Be patient. I was wondering too, wondering how such a man might materialize.

The next day, I drove back into America, along the Superior shore, through all the flat towns, hunched against the wind, and came to Marquette. As I drove in, I saw the lights of the Thunder Bay Inn, and I felt like Barney whatever coming to the place, and being struck by the coincidence.

I went into the inn: large, crowded, a lot of soldiers with noisy women. I sat at the bar and waited for the man to get to me. He had an embroidered name on his vest: "Alphonse, call me Al," it said.

"Thank you, Al," I said when the beer came.

He looked at me knowingly, the way barmen are always ready to say they remember you, and he grinned defensively.

"Barney around?" I asked casually.

"Mr. Quill? No, he's bowling tonight. Mary's here, though—in back." He nodded his head. I looked through the doorway at the end of the bar. It was open, and I could see into an office. A woman of maybe twenty-five was sitting there with a ledger and a calculating machine. I knew that face as well as I knew the name. I couldn't stay there, so moved but content with a beer. I left my drink and walked out into the blast of the night.

I had to work out how to do it. For all I knew, Barney Quill was someone else. I had to make certain. But the young woman . . . if there was no trace of him here in Marquette, how could I explain the way I felt I knew Mary's hunted look, the way she seemed to be staring at herself?

I moved into the Twilight motel, with a waterbed and *You Only Live Once* on the late movie, about a good man (Henry Fonda, no less) who becomes a killer. I enjoyed it again, along with the local ads—the car dealers peering at cue cards, the discount-furniture store with the owner in a Halloween mask (an old ad held over) and here, one for an inn, the Thunder Bay Inn, with its smug boss, Barney Quill, behind the bar, chatting to the camera about his range of beers and bar specials. It was him, Mark McPherson, gray now, but still dark and menacing. If I hadn't seen him, I would have known the voice and the slick, insolent way he had with the camera. I went to sleep happy at having found the man I wanted in this board game of motels.

The next night I went to the Thunder Bay Inn. It was crowded and I sat in an ill-lit corner. I was sure he wouldn't recognize me—it had been nearly thirty years, and we had met only once. The bar was full of soldiers again, and there was one man, a lieutenant, who caught my attention. He was in his late thirties, maybe, with very dark hair and sardonic eyes. His table included a younger woman, a flirt, touching all the men except the lieutenant. He watched her and the other men with a fixed, silky smile on his face. The more I studied it, the more I thought that man could be a killer. He was apparently sociable and amiable, but I felt the distance he was keeping between himself and his silly gang. The woman stood up and I heard some remark about the little girls' room. She walked away so that everyone could get a good look at her bottom. Everyone watched her go except the lieutenant.

Then he stood up and strolled over to a cigarette machine, collecting coins from the pocket of his uniform. I followed him, trembling with excitement and apprehension. Would I actually talk to him? What could I say? I saw his name tab: Lt. F. Manion. He pushed quarters into the machine, got a pack, opened it and put a cigarette in his white ivory holder: it was a sinister affectation. Then he realized I was standing beside him.

"Your turn, Pop," he said.

"Oh, thank you," I muttered, and he had gone.

I was mortified by my own feebleness. I had been speechless, helpless, a coward, sure the man would laugh at me or still the din and repeat what I had said, incredulous at my nerve. And what would I say? "I wonder if I can interest you in killing someone."

Back in the motel, I wept as I watched *On Dangerous Ground*. I had come so far, and promised this vengeance to myself for so long. Yet now I could not grasp it. I thought of going to a gun store, equipping myself, striding in tomorrow and killing him behind his own bar. But I have always abhorred violence; and always known that I would need an instrument. Yes, I have seen so many killings on film, but it is a fallacy that the viewer becomes more prone to use a gun himself.

One more night, I returned to the inn, resolved that it would be my last. Lieutenant Manion was nowhere to be seen. But Quill, or Quilty—whatever—was there again, applying liquor and bonhomie. The woman from Manion's party was there too. She was wearing a tight sweater and pants. When she danced with other soldiers near the jukebox, you could see she had no bra on. And you could see the outline of her panties through the sheer, synthetic material of the pants.

Then the woman left, and only a few minutes later Quill went out too, leaving Al to manage the busy bar. I had the impression that Quill followed her.

An hour passed. The crowd was lessening. I was blue and tipsy, sure I had failed, when Quill came back. I was sitting near the door that night, and I was no more than twelve feet away from him. He was an old man too, I could see, and he seemed out of breath. He went back behind the bar, whispered to Al, and I could hear Al's giggling above the talk and music of the bar.

I finished my last drink and got up. I took a final look at Quill. In stupid bravado, I waved to him. He paused, looked through the smoke and waved back: a tavern owner has to "know" everyone. I moved to open the door, but it was pulled away from me as Lieutenant Manion came in.

"Good evening," I said, but the man never saw me. There were tears in his eyes, and, I realized, a gun in his hand. He walked up to the bar and he put five bullets in Barney Quill, leaning over the bar and reaching down to make sure the job was done. My delirious laughter was the only sound in the raw silence of shock.

MARK McPHERSON

Dana Andrews in Laura, 1944,
directed by Otto Preminger

I walked out into the starry night jubilant. The breath of my song turned into mist in front of me. I stomped down to the water, thinking to crush the shingle with my amazed liberation. He was dead, and I had not had to lift a hand. Just as my weakness had sent me away, it seemed that the world had felt my desire and responded by sending forth a killer, driven by his own furious reasons—whatever they were—but I had seen tears springing in eyes that had been heartless the night before. Now I, the hopeful killer, found myself in tears that a miracle had lifted away the guilt I had not been brave enough to accept. It was as if a secret author had designed everything and let my despair and its mercy cross on the threshold of the Thunder Bay Inn. There on the narrow shore, I looked out at the steel glaze of Lake Superior in the moonlight and I howled at the moon.

"My dear fellow," said an elderly voice; I felt a gentle hand on my shoulder. I turned. It was a man of about my age, white-haired; I could smell whiskey, like sauce on the ice-cream night. "What's the trouble?"

I made an effort to control my laughter and my tears. The tension of the last week had made a wreck of me.

"A man was just killed in the inn," I explained.

"Good Lord," he said under his breath, looking at the inn's bright windows. "Was it murder?"

"A soldier," I said. "He shot the owner of the place. He seemed to be in a trance."

"You're shocked," he said. "You should take a little brandy. It's so cold tonight."

With that, he gripped my arm and I let him guide me to another tavern, quieter and still unaware of the sensation up the street. He sat me down and called for two brandies. He introduced himself as Parnell Emmett McCarthy. I said I was spending the night in town, on my way from Montreal to International Falls. Mr. McCarthy waited for me to calm myself, and then he extracted the whole story from me with a skill that belied my feeling that he was not far short of drunk.

I went back to my motel a young man again. I could not sleep, but stayed awake for *The Asphalt Jungle* and *Where the Sidewalk Ends*. As dawn broke, I went to my case and took out the letter given to me at the funeral by Paula:

> Dearest George,
> I have heard he is in Thunder Bay. This news is not fresh. He may have moved on.
> The other girl is or was with him. My dear, I do not think she was Mark's. I let Mark take her because he promised then to leave us alone. I have never forgiven myself, but I think the child was yours. Remember me.
> All my love,
> Laura.

The trial never knew of him as anything but Barney Quill, the deceased. The corpse has no history; it is enough that its violent coming into being initiates the trial. His whole shady past was covered by the revelation that Mary Palant was his daughter. There were lascivious gasps all over the courtroom: Marquette had thought she was Quill's mistress. Even now, they couldn't quite separate the old idea that he had been sleeping with her from the hot flash that he was her father. Suppose I had said she was not his, but mine, those gasps would have started tittering. The credulousness of that kind of audience can only be teased so far. Revelation is always close to the ridiculous.

The woman who had seemed like an army slut was actually a Laura, Laura Manion, the lieutenant's wife. They had been married a few years, since a time in Georgia when his and her first marriages had been broken apart by their affair. It was the contention of the defense, ably conducted by a Mr. Paul Biegler, backed up by none other than Parnell Emmett McCarthy, that earlier on the fateful night Laura Manion had left the inn. That Quill had pursued her and offered to drive her back to the trailer she lived in with Manion.

But he had driven off the highway into some woods—the place was found and avidly splashed in the local papers. He had hit Mrs. Manion, pulled off her pants, ripped away her panties and raped her. The abused woman had staggered home and told her husband. In his rage, he had gone straight to the inn and, under what Biegler called "an irresistible impulse," shot the innkeeper.

The state's case, conducted by a smart lawyer from Lansing, was that Laura Manion had been as willing to go with Barney Quill as she seemed happy to dance with anyone. They said that Manion knew his wife's looseness, and that it was murder plain and simple. For his part, the lieutenant remembered only a daze. I sat in the court (I could not miss it), tickled to think that a cloud of unknowing had met my need.

The case hinged on the evidence of Mary Palant. For the young woman had found a pair of torn panties upstairs in the inn, and put them aside. She had heard evidence in court and been reminded of them. They came into court, a tattered white flag of nylon, but with a label—the Smart Shop in Phoenix—that confirmed Mrs. Manion's memory of their purchase.

I looked at the two women, Laura and Mary. It still seemed hard to think of Laura Manion being raped. But if I thought that, why surely I would have to query all rapes—it is an old male humbug that women always want it. Mary Palant's face was more stricken. She had honestly given evidence that helped save a man for his wife. But it gave credence to the gossip that her father was a wolf. Her father? She had had to admit it in court: how Quill years ago had had an affair with a waitress in Blind River, Ontario, never married, then welcomed Mary when her mother died in a flood. But the constraint in Mary's face made me think she had lost not only a father, but her good opinion of him.

When the trial was over, I went to call on her. Yet again, I realized I was tongue-tied, weighed down with an awesome question too great to be asked. She was running the inn now, with the help of Al; it was the best way to fill the days.

I introduced myself; she was polite. I told her that I had talked to her father a few times before the shooting; that I had liked him, had been horrified by what happened, and a little curious to know more about him than had emerged in the trial.

"I felt he was a more private person," I told her.

"Yes," she said. "I think so."

The child has to trust what parents say about its origins. Suppose that waitress in Canada had been paid to look after Mary. Suppose Quill sometimes called on them. Suppose the little girl had wondered if he was her father, and claimed as much in her most ardent dreams. Then the mother had died. I grant the flood (I looked that up), but I wondered if Mark had not held the waitress under. She had no other kin; that is how Quill took the child. I checked: he had adopted her.

"Was he really your father?" I asked her, and I could not tell what answer I wanted.

262

"I thought so once," she replied, "but later . . ."

I might have prodded her. But I had reached the point of wanting to leave things alone, and there were tears in her eyes at least as honest as those I had seen on Lieutenant Manion's face.

"You have a fine inn here," I said, to change the subject.

"It is," she said, and I knew as if pierced that she and I had the same fondness for out-of-the-way places.

GEORGE BAILEY

James Stewart in It's a Wonderful Life, *1946,*
directed by Frank Capra

I was born in 1910: I will be seventy-five this coming February, and I will make it so that I can go to Marquette again in the summer. I was born in Bedford Falls, Nebraska, and I have lived there all my life. Nor do I have any intention of leaving the place; those hopes and fears have all gone. I was born conservative and local, and such a man can hardly deal with experience, take pleasure or accept tragedy, unless he abides by his nature. I have been away from Bedford Falls a very few times—I mean traveled away. But in my mind I have always ranged farther afield—not just to the West, or back to New York—but into possibilities, stories, other lives that I could not have. All my life, I have loved the movies, and they have a legion of slaves, pale, overweight and shy, but fantastic journeyers, of which I am one. We all of us have to be somewhere every moment: it is our dull duty, whether it's in Bedford Falls or the Pierre Hotel in New York. But the screen is like a map for our dreams on which we may always travel, without ticket, tiredness or pain. It is our greatest frontier, like a magic mirror.

Perhaps I am absurdly proud of Bedford Falls. I know when I was young I had a tendency to make myself sentimentally cozy about certain things: it was immaturity, I daresay, and I had to get as far as thirty-six before I learned anything different. Some days I see Bedford Falls as a nondescript town, a flat land with flat lives, small and small-minded, cautious, critical and piously inhibited. It may be so. Yet once I regarded it as ideal, like the small towns on Christmas

Lincoln to the university or running the company, I stayed in Bedford Falls. People said I was swell for letting Harry go two years later, but I was a coward too.

The 1930s were so hard. The Building & Loan went from trouble to trouble during the Depression. I was never home early. I could see people's pity at the haste with which I was aging. Faster than Mary Frances was growing up. I found reasons to be in Omaha, and I watched the Hunt girls, Mary Frances and Laura, attracting more and more attention. I was nearly a comic figure to the young set at their picnics. If Mary Frances did like me, it was because my image of premature failure interested her dramatic instincts. She was a fine actress. I couldn't deny it, but I was frightened by all the urging that she go on the stage. Not just because I would lose her then, but because I thought her parts acted on her like an illness. She had the nature of an actress—repressed in life, alive on the stage—but when she went back into life she was inflamed by what she had felt in the play. She was no longer satisfied or calm. With every play she became a little more disturbed as a person. Only I seemed to see this; but I loved her, and that made the difference.

Her mother had spells of melancholy or worse. There was some weakness in the family line, like an angle to the nose or a color in the eyes. There was the year when Mary Frances and her mother sank into crisis simultaneously. It was hot and windy and Mr. Jed Harris came by, proposing to make Mary Frances a famous actress. It jostled her terribly. For three days she had to be tied to her bed. Laura and I took care of it. Their mother was in another room, groaning so steadily that it got on your nerves.

Laura told me there would always be times like these, but I married Mary Frances in 1938 and took her to Bedford Falls. She cheered up a lot. We had Harry in 1940 and Bedford Falls had maybe its last great age during the war, dedicated to the soldiers far away and to self-sacrifice at home. I looked forward to the peace. I wanted to do my bit in ensuring that warriors coming home could have a house and a life to justify the fighting. But being left out of the war made me gloomy, and I had been a little influenced already by the dark holes of despair that overtook Mary Frances once or twice a year. We had another son, Travis, in 1945, but I could tell that Mary was near her brink.

The crisis came in 1946. Uncle Billy—my right-hand problem at the Building & Loan—lost a packet of money. It looked like ruin, prison and an end to everything. I was out of my mind. I thought of killing myself, and it taught me how troubled my head was already that there was no real stamina for life there to sustain me. I would have done something, and left Mary Frances, Harry and Travis. I could not trust or believe in myself. It was a dreadful discovery, worse than the loss of the money and the prospect of exposure.

Just before Christmas I went away for a few days to New York. It was subsequently called "the episode with the angel." That was Mary Frances's way of explaining it, the first sign of her refuge in religion. I went to see Laura, who had been in New York for several years. She was successful, it seemed, and I had a notion that she might loan me some money. I had never met her husband, Mark, before, and I was taken aback by the animosity between them. They had a daughter, Paula, but Mark paid no attention to her. He deliberately spoke of the ugliness he encountered as a policeman, and he brought unaccountably strange men to the house for beer and cards.

Laura wanted to help me. She had developed so much and so well, it made me suspicious of Bedford Falls. I did wonder whether Mary Frances might have dazzled Broadway if she had been able to accelerate as Laura had. Laura looked like a film star; she looked like a magical Mary Frances, the woman my wife could have become but for me, our town and her illness. But I had to consider whether the last might not be aggravated by the first two.

It was the last weekend before Christmas: Laura was buying presents, making arrangements, working at Bullitt's, and trying to get some money together for me. She knew Mark would forbid it if he found out, and most of her money, at her own early insistence, was in a joint account. There were secret meetings and complicated plans. She and I met at the Pierre Hotel and she gave me an envelope full of money. I could hardly speak, but when I looked up she was weeping.

"So you'll be going now," she said.

There was so much gathered but untouched sentiment in us—the dark clouds of Mark and Mary Frances—the air brimming with Christmas and the way in which Laura resembled the wife I had wanted. There were a few hours before my train. We never discussed it. Laura went away and came back with a key. We went up to a primrose-yellow room and made love in the winter light. Then we left. I went to the station, and Laura to her apartment, the two of us due at our family Christmases.

The Building & Loan was saved. Bedford Falls went on. We heard that Laura was pregnant again. Then in the spring of 1947, Mark McPherson came to town. He drove in, without warning. It all happened while I was at the office. He introduced himself to Mary

Frances, admired Harry and Travis, sent Harry out into the yard, and raped my wife, as quickly and brutally as he could.

I never saw him. Harry came to the office. He said, "Mommy's ill," very quietly, and took me home. Mary Frances was in the bathroom, naked, washing herself repeatedly. I never knew what Mark had told her, but she knew what he had done to her was for a reason, a rebuke. Harry may have understood more than she did, even if he was only seven. Travis was asleep in his cot. Mary Frances was demented, and an actress playing dementia. I have never known which for sure. The bad times come and go. She is like a character in a high-strung movie, like Olivia de Havilland as twins in *The Dark Mirror*.

What else would you want to know? I am seventy-four and Mary Frances is sixty-seven. We live in the same house; the crises now have more room to hide in. I sold the Building & Loan to the Potter Corporation, and I am what is called comfortable now. I have a video recorder and a library of films. In addition I have two sons who have changed their names from Bailey and who will not see me, a daughter in Atlantic City and another in the south of France. Among the four of them, my children have been in on the killing of over a dozen Americans. They all have their own nightmares.

I will go to Marquette again for a week in the summer, to the Thunder Bay Inn. I enjoy the lake, and the walks. There is a good library in the town and the people at the inn know me. Mary is married to Alphonse Poquette—Al, he prefers to be called—and they have two children, Tracy and Craig. Al is a little brusque. He finds me tedious, I think. Why not? I do not enjoy myself. But Mary invites me in to their part of the inn for tea sometimes. We talk, sitting there in the warm lounge, me with my uncertainty about who she is, never to be disturbed, she with her consistent, shallow friendliness, and both of us sitting beneath the glow of the lifesize painting of Laura that she inherited from her father.

A version of my early life is played on television every Christmas, but my country rumbles on in the darker pattern of my years since then, torn between Santa Claus and the bogeyman.

*   *   *

I sleep less and less. With so little to do now, why should I be given more time?

It was no longer night when I awoke, but there was still nothing but dark. The lights on our street go off at one in the morning. There is no sense of threat here. The night is a complete rest, or absence. So at five I can tell the several steps by which degrees of black are being withdrawn from the night. It is dark still, but a dark that has felt the first intimations of something else.

I lay in bed another half hour. It was not unusual that George was not there beside me. When I saw the first streaks of reflection in the oval mirror I got up and put on the scarlet dressing gown he bought me in New York, his one time there. It is threadbare, but it was a Christmas present and I will not give it up. He has told me that I look like Santa Claus in it. I am tall still, for a woman, and I have white hair above the red gown. Anyone without his glasses might make the same eager mistake.

Did he see that figure come down the stairs, stepping over those that creak, so the movement might look menacing, like a limp? I expected him to be asleep. I meant to shut the window and put a blanket round his shoulders. I have learned to do all that without ever waking him.

But he was sitting as if thrust back in his chair, his head twisted so that it was turned to look at the staircase and at me. Did he see me? Was he so wrapped in what he was writing that he wondered if he saw a specter on the stairs and had his heart quiver, just once, and stop? Did George die, frightened, seeing me, looking like a figure in a play come to rescue or rebuke him? The look on his face matched either prospect. The wanting to know and see was frozen, his mouth open and the last run of dribble was like a snail's trail on his chin. I saw the details, as if he had written me to be his discoverer.

His book, this book, lay on the table in front of him. The pages looked like stones in the coming light. They have lived on the table for years, defending it against polish. Perhaps I can save the table now, if I pack up the pages.

The book goes on and on about the actress I might have been, and the tragic player I became in this house instead. I have never understood such a waste of hope and worrying. I had none of the need to be an actress. I was only a girl with a certain cautious talent, and too much shyness in social situations. I acted, I daresay, to find a husband. It was the only way I knew of showing I was ardent and attractive. I found George, but he could never overcome the guilt that he had stopped me being an actress. It was one of his ways of ensuring unhappiness.

When truly he was the one of us who should have left. He had a chronic aptitude for the far-fetched stories of the movies. He was always seeing fatal nymphs in Tennessee towns, or hearing the engraved conversations that carry haunted lovers up to the screen, their faces torn by suspense. He could not look at anything without suspecting its capacity for story.

But he was afraid of that world, and so he remained here in Bedford Falls, saying he was deaf, needed, too prosaic, too ordinary to travel, a man with an unsound heart. But he traveled all the time in his mind. For years on end he was in the exciting motion of pictures, carried away, leaving his body in the chair by the window, but not noticing that real people growing up and growing sad were waiting for him.

The light now is pigeon gray. I will have to call the doctor, the mortician and the children, one after the other. There will be a quiet funeral in Nebraska, its plain loss not alleviated by long-lost daughters or the first rising notes of a rescue theme. We are all real here, and we have to bury the bodies when they have been abandoned.

Mary Frances Bailey
November 1984

HUNTS

BAILEYS

MARK McPHERSON

(1) LAURA = SHELBY (1920–72) CARPENTER (2)

MARY FRANCES (1917–)

= GEORGE (1910–

HARRY = RUTH (1912–

JEFFREY (1915–47)

PAULA = TOM (1946–75) IVERSON

MARY = AL (1947–) POQUETTE

MAUREEN = ALEXANDER (1948–78) CUTTER

TRACY (1976–

CRAIG (1978–

ELLEN = HARRY PRESSMANN (1940–

TRAVIS (1945–

SALLY (1951–

CHRISTINA = DAVE (1953– GRIMES

ALBERT (1980–

FILMOGRAPHY

American Gigolo (1980), written and directed by Paul Schrader.

Anatomy of a Murder (1959), directed by Otto Preminger; screenplay by Wendell Mayes, based on the novel by Robert Traver.

Atlantic City (1980), directed by Louis Malle; screenplay by John Guare.

Badlands (1973), written and directed by Terrence Malick.

Beat the Devil (1954), directed by John Huston; screenplay by Huston and Truman Capote, from the novel by James Helvick.

The Big Heat (1953), directed by Fritz Lang; screenplay by Sidney Boehm, from the novel by William P. McGivern.

The Big Sleep (1946), directed by Howard Hawks; screenplay by William Faulkner, Leigh Brackett and Jules Furthman, from the novel by Raymond Chandler.

Body Heat (1981), written and directed by Lawrence Kasdan.

Casablanca (1942), directed by Michael Curtiz; screenplay by Julius J. Epstein, Philip G. Epstein and Howard Koch, from the play *Everybody Goes to Rick's* by Murray Burnett and Joan Alison.

Caught (1949), directed by Max Ophuls; screenplay by Arthur Laurents, from the novel *Wild Calendar* by Libbie Block.

Chinatown (1974), directed by Roman Polanski; screenplay by Robert Towne.

Citizen Kane (1941), directed by Orson Welles; screenplay by Welles and Herman J. Mankiewicz.

Cutter's Way (1981), directed by Ivan Passer; screenplay by Jeffrey Alan Fiskin, from the novel *Cutter and Bone* by Newton Thornburg.

Double Indemnity (1944), directed by Billy Wilder; screenplay by Wilder and Raymond Chandler, from the novel by James M. Cain.

The Gambler (1974), directed by Karel Reisz; screenplay by James Toback.

Gilda (1946), directed by Charles Vidor; screenplay by Marion Parsonnet, from Jo Eisinger's adaptation of a story by E. A. Ellington.

The Godfather (1971), directed by Francis Ford Coppola; screenplay by Coppola and Mario Puzo, from the novel by Puzo.

The Godfather Part II (1974), directed by Francis Ford Coppola; screenplay by Coppola and Mario Puzo, from the novel by Puzo.

The Great Gatsby (1949), directed by Elliott Nugent; screenplay by Cyril Hume and Richard Maibaum, from the novel by F. Scott Fitzgerald.

The Great Gatsby (1974), directed by Jack Clayton; screenplay by Francis Ford Coppola, from the novel by Fitzgerald.

High Sierra (1941), directed by Raoul Walsh; screenplay by John Huston and W. R. Burnett, from the novel by Burnett.

I Walk the Line (1970), directed by John Frankenheimer; screenplay by Alvin Sargent, from the novel *An Exile* by Madison Jones.

In a Lonely Place (1949), directed by Nicholas Ray; screenplay by Andrew Solt, from an adaptation by Edmund H. North of the novel by Dorothy B. Hughes.

It's a Wonderful Life (1946), directed by Frank Capra; screenplay by Frances Goodrich, Albert Hackett and Capra, additional scenes by Jo Swerling, based on a story "The Greatest Gift" by Philip Van Doren Stern.

The Killers (1946), directed by Robert Siodmak; screenplay by Anthony Veiller, from the story by Ernest Hemingway.

The Killing (1956), directed by Stanley Kubrick; screenplay by Kubrick, from the novel *Clean Break* by Lionel White, additional dialogue by Jim Thompson.

The King of Marvin Gardens (1972), directed by Bob Rafelson; screenplay by Jacob Brackman.

Klute (1971), directed by Alan J. Pakula; screenplay by Andy K. Lewis and Dave Lewis.

The Lady from Shanghai (1948), directed by Orson Welles; screenplay by Welles, from the novel *If I Die Before I Wake* by Sherwood King.

Laura (1944), directed by Otto Preminger; screenplay by Jay Dratler, Samuel Hoffenstein and Betty Reinhardt, from the novel by Vera Caspary.

The Long Goodbye (1973), directed by Robert Altman; screenplay by Leigh Brackett, from the novel by Raymond Chandler.

Lolita (1962), directed by Stanley Kubrick; screenplay by Vladimir Nabokov, from his own novel.

The Maltese Falcon (1941), written and directed by John Huston, from the novel by Dashiell Hammett.

Melvin and Howard (1980), directed by Jonathan Demme; screenplay by Bo Goldman.

Morocco (1930), directed by Josef von Sternberg; screenplay by Jules Furthman, from the play *Amy Jolly* by Benno Vigny.

New York, New York (1977), directed by Martin Scorsese; screenplay by Earl MacRauch and Mardik Martin, from a story by MacRauch.

Night Moves (1975), directed by Arthur Penn; screenplay by Alan Sharp.

No Man of Her Own (1950), directed by Mitchell Leisen; screenplay by Sally Benson, Catherine Turney and Leisen, from the novel *I Married a Dead Man* by Cornell Woolrich.

Notorious (1946), directed by Alfred Hitchcock; screenplay by Ben Hecht.

Out of the Past (1947), directed by Jacques Tourneur; screenplay by Geoffrey Homes (Daniel Mainwaring), from his own novel *Build My Gallows High*.

Paper Moon (1973), directed by Peter Bogdanovich; screenplay by Alvin Sargent, from the novel *Addie Pray* by Joe David Brown.

The Passenger (1975), directed by Michelangelo Antonioni; screenplay by Mark Peploe, Peter Wollen and Antonioni, from a story by Peploe.

Pickup on South Street (1953), directed by Samuel Fuller; screenplay by Fuller, from a story by Dwight Taylor.

Point Blank (1967), directed by John Boorman; screenplay by Alexander Jacobs, David Newhouse and Rafe Newhouse, from the novel *The Hunter* by Richard Stark.

The Postman Always Rings Twice (1946), directed by Tay Garnett; screenplay by Niven Busch and Harry Reskin, from the novel by James M. Cain.

The Postman Always Rings Twice (1981), directed by Bob Rafelson; screenplay by David Mamet, from the novel by James M. Cain.

Psycho (1960), directed by Alfred Hitchcock; screenplay by Joseph Stefano, from the novel by Robert Bloch.

Rear Window (1954), directed by Alfred Hitchcock; screenplay by John Michael Hayes, from a story by Cornell Woolrich.

Rebel Without a Cause (1955), directed by Nicholas Ray; screenplay by Stewart Stern, adapted by Irving Shulman from a story by Ray.

The Shining (1980), directed by Stanley Kubrick; screenplay by Kubrick and Diane Johnson, from the novel by Stephen King.

Strangers on a Train (1951), directed by Alfred Hitchcock; screenplay by Raymond Chandler and Czenzi Ormonde, from the novel by Patricia Highsmith.

Sunset Boulevard (1950), directed by Billy Wilder; screenplay by Wilder and Charles Brackett.

Taxi Driver (1976), directed by Martin Scorsese; screenplay by Paul Schrader.

The Third Man (1949), directed by Carol Reed; screenplay and original story by Graham Greene.

Touch of Evil (1958), written and directed by Orson Welles, from the novel *Badge of Evil* by Whit Masterson.

Vertigo (1958), directed by Alfred Hitchcock; screenplay by Alec Coppel and Samuel Taylor, from the novel *D'Entre les Morts* by Pierre Boileau and Thomas Narcejac.

White Heat (1949), directed by Raoul Walsh; screenplay by Ivan Goff and Ben Roberts, from a story by Virginia Kellogg.

Who'll Stop the Rain (1978), directed by Karel Reisz; screenplay by Judith Rascoe and Robert Stone, from the novel *Dog Soldiers* by Stone.

A Selected List of Titles Available from Minerva

While every effort is made to keep prices low, it is sometimes necessary to increase prices at short notice. Mandarin Paperbacks reserves the right to show new retail prices on covers which may differ from those previously advertised in the text or elsewhere.

The prices shown below were correct at the time of going to press.

☐ 7493 9739 X	**Made in America**		Bill Bryson	£6.99
☐ 7493 9767 5	**A Good Scent From A Strange Mountain**		Robert Olen Butler	£5.99
☐ 7493 9628 8	**Faith in Fakes: Travels in Hyperreality**		Umberto Eco	£6.99
☐ 7493 9797 7	**Nude Men**		Amanda Filipacchi	£5.99
☐ 7493 9771 3	**Billy**		Albert French	£5.99
☐ 7493 9059 X	**Faggots**		Larry Kramer	£6.99
☐ 7493 9896 5	**Nothing But Blue Skies**		Thomas McGuane	£5.99
☐ 7493 9611 3	**Folly**		Susan Minot	£5.99
☐ 7493 9141 3	**Vineland**		Thomas Pynchon	£6.99
☐ 7493 3602 1	**The Joy Luck Club**		Amy Tan	£5.99

All these books are available at your bookshop or newsagent, or can be ordered direct from the address below. Just tick the titles you want and fill in the form below.

Cash Sales Department, PO Box 5, Rushden, Northants NN10 6YX.
Phone: 01933 414000 : Fax: 01933 414047.

Please send cheque, payable to 'Reed Book Services Ltd.', or postal order for purchase price quoted and allow the following for postage and packing:

£1.00 for the first book, 50p for the second; **FREE POSTAGE AND PACKING FOR THREE BOOKS OR MORE PER ORDER.**

NAME (Block letters) ....

ADDRESS ....

....

☐ I enclose my remittance for ....

☐ I wish to pay by Access/Visa Card Number

Expiry Date

Signature ....

Please quote our reference: MAND

Working It Out

Jo Platt was born in Liverpool in 1968 and, via the extremely winding route of rural Wiltshire, London, Seattle and St Albans, she is now happily settled in Bristol with her husband and two daughters. She studied English at King's College London before going on to work in the City for ten years. In 2000 she escaped into motherhood and part-time employment, first as an assistant teacher in a Seattle pre-school and then was a Bristol-based secretary to her husband.

Also by Jo Platt

JO PLATT
Working It Out

CANELO

First published in the United Kingdom in 2022 by

Canelo
Unit 9, 5th Floor
Cargo Works, 1–2 Hatfields
London, SE1 9PG
United Kingdom

Copyright © Jo Platt 2022

The moral right of Jo Platt to be identified as the creator of this work has been asserted in accordance with the Copyright, Designs and Patents Act, 1988.

All rights reserved. No part of this publication may be reproduced or transmitted in any form or by any means, electronic or mechanical, including photocopy, recording, or any information storage and retrieval system, without permission in writing from the publisher.

A CIP catalogue record for this book is available from the British Library.

Print ISBN 978 1 80032 476 3
Ebook ISBN 978 1 80032 475 6

This book is a work of fiction. Names, characters, businesses, organizations, places and events are either the product of the author's imagination or are used fictitiously. Any resemblance to actual persons, living or dead, events or locales is entirely coincidental.

Look for more great books at www.canelo.co

Printed and bound in Great Britain by Clays Ltd, Elcograf S.p.A.

FSC
www.fsc.org

MIX
Paper from
responsible sources
FSC® C018072

I

For Sharon, with love from your naughty little sister.

Prologue

'At a funeral, Jason,' I said, laughing bitterly and shaking my head. 'At your own aunt's funeral. Just when I thought I couldn't be any more appalled. You're so obviously beyond help and hope.'

I held the front door open and he exited without argument, before stopping on the top step, making no attempt either to walk away, or to come back inside. 'I can't explain, Edie,' he said quietly, his head bowed. 'It's a—'

I held up a hand. 'Well, you're in luck, because I don't want an explanation. I just want you to go.' With that, I closed the front door and returned to the living room.

Once there, I sat back down on the sofa and ran my eyes around the room, taking in our furniture, our photographs, our books, and desperately searching for something which hadn't been shared with, or touched and tainted by, Jason; something which was wholly mine.

At last, I found it lying on the coffee table, just an outstretched arm away.

Leaning forward, I picked up the large, leather-bound notebook I used to jot down project thoughts and ideas, whenever inspiration struck away from the office. And as a sudden sense of purpose halted the tears which had been flowing, unconsciously and unchecked, since closing the door on Jason – and on our relationship – I reached for a pen, dried my eyes and set to work.

Chapter 1

June 2018

I gazed for a moment longer at the late-spring rain streaming down the floor-to-ceiling windows behind Roger's desk, before pivoting slowly in my chair and scanning the large white-walled, open-plan office: my safe space.

Ruby and I were currently its only occupants. Luke's workstation, and Roger and Cameron's long white desks and drawing tables, sat empty, while behind the glass walls of her office, Alison talked intensely into the telephone.

'It's going to be very male out here when you go,' I said, concluding my rotation with my chair facing Ruby.

She looked up briefly from the printed drawings of a 1930s terraced house over which she was hunched. The design, for a basement excavation and rear extension, would be her last for Alison Gerrard Ltd before she took up her new post at Lovelock McCormick Architecture in Bath, in just one week's time.

She lifted her head, shaking her blunt-cut, white-blonde bob out of her eyes and away from her sharp features. 'It'll be fine, Edie,' she said, picking up a piece of sushi from a black plastic tray on the edge of her desk and popping it into her mouth.

'But who's going to supply me with emergency feminine hygiene products and tell me when I've gone too far with my colours?' I glanced down at my orange shirt and wildly patterned, navy and orange A-line skirt. 'And remind me when it's time to get a cut and foils?' I added, pulling absently at a length of hair, which had fallen from my messy updo.

She paused to chew and swallow before answering. 'You can carry off colour – it's your thing. Just like gloom is my thing,' she said, glancing down at her short, grey shift dress, which she'd teamed today with heavy-soled black brogues. 'Plus, I like your hair naturally mousy. Oh and I'll gift you half a dozen boxes of Tampax before I leave.'

'Thanks, but it's a feminine, listening ear I'll miss most.'

'Well, there's always—' she began, inclining her head towards Alison's office, before stopping short as the woman herself made an entrance.

'Edith,' she said, patting the side of her steel-grey chignon, her burgundy-lipsticked mouth hauled upwards into a tense smile.

'Yes?' I hurriedly picked up a stylus in a wholly unnecessary pretence of professional activity. It was a guilt-spurred response developed as a teen under the tuition of Mrs Skinner, a fine-boned, stick-thin geography teacher who dealt mercilessly with anyone found guilty of *distracting chatter*. And although Alison had no problem whatsoever with a conversation-filled workplace, her physical resemblance to said Mrs Skinner always provoked a look-busy reaction from me – as well as occasional unpleasant flashbacks to glaciated uplands and chalk escarpments.

'That was Mick Jarvis on the phone. The drawings went down very well with everyone yesterday,' she said in the clipped tone she always employed, irrespective of topic or mood. '"Bold, yet sympathetic" was some of the feedback.'

A sense of fulfilment and well-being washed over me. 'That's so great to hear.'

She nodded stiffly and withdrew into her office, adjusting her perfectly fitted charcoal jacket, before sitting back down at her desk. At sixty-one, she was still an undeniably attractive woman, her attention to detail regarding her personal appearance as fastidious as it was in every one of her drawings. And she was as formidable as she was fashionable; highly respected within the industry of which she had been part for over thirty years, with a reputation for prioritising the pursuit of architectural perfection above all else – including personal relationships, never having been married and, as far as I knew, socialising only on a professional basis. But while she had, for the past two-and-a-half years, been a scrupulously fair, generous and straightforward boss – one whom I hugely admired – female best-bud material she most certainly was not.

I turned back to Ruby. 'I think there's more chance of Roger sympathising with me over my PMT than of her lending a listening ear, don't you?'

'She'd listen to anything you had to say. She thinks you're great. Case in point are those warm words about your design,' she added, reaching for another piece of sushi. 'Well done with that, by the way.'

I smiled, a little sadly, knowing that the conversion of a listed pre-war substation into several homes was a project that Ruby had been rather keen on herself – something I hadn't realised until Luke, our loose-tongued office administrator, had let the fact slip. 'Better check Ruby doesn't poison your coffee,' he had sniggered, after Alison had approved my pitch. 'She thought she had that one in the bag.'

I'd been surprised because Ruby had never hinted either her interest or her disappointment to me, and still hadn't for that matter. Instead, she had stuck to perusing my ideas and being quietly supportive. It was that kind of support – as well as the workplace female camaraderie and gossip – which I knew I would miss.

'It's just nice to have someone relatable around,' I said, turning my chair towards my desk.

'You get on really well with Roger and Luke,' she murmured, frowning thoughtfully at the design in front of her.

'They're great,' I acknowledged, 'but they're not hugely relatable, are they? Roger's old enough to be my dad and Luke's a decade younger than me, lives with his mum and takes selfies to check his hair. He's not going to empathise with my late-thirties cankle-angst and cellulite battles. I swear my bum is relocating into my thighs,' I said, twisting in my chair to look. 'I think it needs a sling, or a bra, or something. Do they make bum-bras?'

'Mid-thirties.'

'What?'

She glanced up at me. 'Your *mid-thirties* cankle-angst and cellulite battles. You're thirty-five.'

I tutted and then, seeing that she looked genuinely concerned, added, 'You know I'm only joking, don't you? I mean, I'll definitely miss having you around and my bum is genuinely melting into my thighs, but I'm fine.'

At that, she stood up and came to stand beside me, placing a hand on my shoulder. 'I know you are,' she said gently.

I reached up and patted her hand. 'Like you say, Luke and Roger are great. Plus, there's always the new guy. He's quiet, but seems nice. I feel really bad that I haven't made more of an effort with him, actually.' I looked guiltily past Ruby towards Cameron's empty desk on the far side of the office, reflecting that I had said little more than 'Hi' and 'Bye' to him each day since returning from my Italian break. 'I haven't had one proper conversation with him yet.'

'He's hardly the new guy,' said Ruby, following my gaze. 'He's been here almost a month.'

'That long?'

'He started two days before you went away.'

'Wow, you're right, he did,' I said. 'I guess I've just been completely wrapped-up in this since I got back.' I jerked a thumb over my shoulder towards the drawings currently on-screen. 'You know what I'm like once I get my teeth into something. But I must find time to ask him how he's getting on.'

'Hmm…'

I looked up to find her still staring at Cameron's desk, her smile now replaced by a very definite frown.

'What?' I nudged her with my elbow.

'Nothing, it's just that he's not the easiest guy in the world to connect with, so I wouldn't feel too guilty about not getting to know him if I were you. I made a real effort and asked him to come for lunch a few times while you were away, but he said no. And I heard Roger offering to take him for a pint in one of those pensioner places he hangs out in, but again it was a no.'

'So not a fan of socialising with work colleagues?'

'I guess it depends on the colleague.'

I waited for further explanation, but all she offered me was a shrug. 'Oh, come on,' I wheedled, tugging at her dress. 'Don't leave me hanging. I hate being out of the loop.'

She hesitated for a moment, before bending down and, despite a total absence of eavesdroppers, lowering her voice. 'It's just that he's keen enough to make a *friend* of Alison,' she said, with a disdainful emphasis on the word. 'While you were away, he was in her office more times than the rest of us put together, and an awful lot of their conversations out here were *sotto voce*.'

I laughed and reached up, placing a hand on each of her shoulders and giving her a gentle shake. 'You're not seriously trying to suggest that there's something going on between them, are you? He's only a couple of years older than us and, even if the twenty-year age gap between them wasn't an issue, this is Alison you're talking about.'

'God, I'm not saying they're having sex, Edie,' she said, with a slight shudder. 'I'm just saying that he has no problem chatting to the boss and, I might add, going out for a drink with the boss after work.'

I felt my eyebrows rise involuntarily.

'Aha, yes,' she said triumphantly, pointing at my wrinkled forehead. 'Interesting, isn't it? He's happy to schmooze the woman who holds the purse strings and hands out promotions, but he won't have a pint with the hoi polloi.'

'Oh don't be so cynical,' I tutted. 'There are always loads of things to go over with the boss when you start a new job. You know that. Maybe Alison is trying to help him settle in. God knows *I* haven't tried very hard,' I added, experiencing a fresh wave of guilt.

'This is different,' she insisted. 'I honestly think he's best kept at arm's length.'

But displaying equal stubbornness, I shook my head. 'As much as I would love a bit of office intrigue, Alison is nobody's fool and doesn't like suck-ups. If she's going for drinks with him, then it'll be strictly business, and maybe he was genuinely tied up when Roger invited him to the crumblies' pub.'

She opened her mouth to object, but I got in first. 'Give the guy a chance. I bet he'll come out for a drink if I ask him.'

'Maybe he will,' she shrugged. 'Maybe he'll see you as useful – as someone with the boss's ear – as opposed to me and Roger: a woman on her way out of the door and Mr Ilkley-Moor-bar-t'at, not far off retirement.'

I pulled a disapproving face, more at her description of Roger than her continued cynicism. 'OK then,' I said, 'I bet he'll come for a drink with *us* if I ask him.'

Her eyebrows arched sceptically. '*Us?* With you and me, you mean? How much do you want to bet?'

'Fiver,' I said, holding out my hand.

She stared down at it. 'That wasn't a literal challenge, Edie. Take my advice and let it go.'

I thrust my hand further towards her and, after a moment, she sighed and then shook it, just as Cameron re-entered the office, clutching a coffee in one hand and a soggy, brown paper bag in the other. His thick, mid-brown hair had been darkened and plastered to his head by the heavy rain, and he looked weary, as well as wet, as he placed the bag and cup down on his desk and hung up his sodden navy blue raincoat. A twitch of his dark eyebrows and an upward tilt of his broad, stubbly chin in our general direction, was his only greeting, as he sat down heavily and removed a wrap and a banana from the bag.

I wasn't sure whether it was because Ruby had just moments earlier shared her rather negative assessment of him, but his wordless, barely-there acknowledgement of us felt distinctly on the chilly side. Nevertheless, turning to Ruby, and determined not to let her detect any newly sprung misgivings, I smiled brightly. 'No time like the present,' I whispered and rose to my feet.

She placed a hand on my arm and shook her head. 'Let's talk about it first,' she said.

I frowned, bemused by her concern. 'Why are you being so intense about this? It's just a drink,' I replied quietly. 'Just have the cash waiting when I get back.' Then, allowing her no time to raise any further objections, I strode purposefully across the office to where Cameron sat with his back now to us, apparently engrossed in a table of figures on his screen.

However, when I cleared my throat and he swivelled slowly in his chair to face me, his unsurprised, neutral expression was that of someone who had actually been fully aware of my arrival, and perhaps not entirely delighted by it either.

'Hi,' he said, a nod of his head making the word sound like an indication that I had permission to speak, rather than a greeting.

'Hi.' I managed a small smile, whilst attempting to suppress an early and uncomfortable suspicion that Ruby's stated opinion of our newish colleague might not have been entirely wide of the mark. But anxious not to let my doubts take hold, I stretched my smile to breaking point and decided to get straight to it.

'I tend to get rather absorbed in my projects and, since I got back, I haven't taken the time to say a proper hello. I was just saying to Ruby that I feel really bad about that,' I began apologetically.

At the mention of her name, his grey-green eyes narrowed, flicking quickly left and past me, towards Ruby. I turned to see her sitting at her desk, leaning over her work, her hair falling forward and obscuring her face from view.

'So anyway, the pair of us are going out tonight,' I continued a little uncertainly, turning back towards him, 'to a wine bar, if you fancy coming along. Fingers crossed you'll have dried out by then and, if not, we'll just sit you next to a radiator and let you steam.' I laughed lightly and waited for him to join in.

There followed a silent and mildly uncomfortable pause, during which, if he smiled, I missed it. Instead, he simply stared up at me, before at last taking a deep breath and picking up his wrap. 'It's fine. I know from Alison how focused you are,' he began, his tone low and deeply serious, which did nothing to lessen a growing tension in my spine. 'I'm afraid I'm busy tonight, so I'll have to say no to a drink. But thanks for asking.' And with that, he offered me a nanosecond of a smile, glanced briefly again in Ruby's direction and then swivelled in his chair to face his desk.

I stared at his broad, white-shirted back, experiencing a combination of mild indignation at his rather curt rejection of my invitation, and resentment that he had apparently been discussing me with Alison. The fact that his current clipped manner wasn't at all typical of his interactions with Luke and Roger – his *male* work colleagues – did nothing to quell my fledgling feelings of negativity towards him.

I frowned down at him, only a reluctance to hand over a fiver to Ruby preventing me from throwing in the towel just yet.

I cleared my throat for a second time, prompting him to drop his wrap from a height of several inches onto his desk before turning, with renewed and undisguised weariness, to face me once again.

'Sorry,' he said, running a hand through his wet hair and then shaking the drips onto the floor, 'I didn't realise there was more.' He looked up at me resignedly from under heavy brows.

'Won't keep you a moment,' I said, with forced cheeriness. 'I just wanted to remind you that Ruby leaves us for her new job next Friday. Hopefully you can find a gap in your schedule to come along to her leaving drinks. It'd be great if we were all there to say goodbye.'

I continued to smile, whilst noting that he appeared increasingly tense. At the best of times, his build made him look like a man in danger of being strangled by his own work shirt. But now, at the mention of drinks with his colleagues, he seemed to expand somehow, like Bruce Banner about to transition into The Hulk.

He eyed me unblinkingly for a second or two and then, without comment, picked up the remains of his wrap, replaced it in the precariously soggy paper bag and stood up, causing me to take a step backwards.

'Thanks for the reminder. I've a lot on but, yeah – thanks for the reminder,' he repeated, in an accent which now had just a hint of Danny Dyer about it.

I looked steadily up at him, refusing to acknowledge his width and height advantage. I didn't know what the newly adopted, tough-guy tone was all about, but I had encountered enough ridiculous displays of workplace machismo in the past that if he was attempting one now, it wasn't going to faze me.

I folded my arms and nodded, but didn't reply.

He looked pleasingly uncertain for a moment and then reached for his coffee cup, holding it up. 'They've given me a flat white, instead of a cappuccino,' he said darkly, now quite unmistakably channelling *EastEnders* and dropping consonants like confetti at a wedding. 'I'm gonna have to go back to Costa.'

I smiled acceptingly, genuinely amused by his bizarre, mockney-based attempt to assert himself. 'Cor blimey,' I said casually, 'that's a shime.'

He blinked in apparent confusion, before his expression hardened. Then he unhooked his dripping coat from the hatstand and brushed past me, exiting the office with a mumbled and gravelly, 'Back soon.' A second or two later, I heard the lift doors hiss open and shut.

'Did you really just say *cor blimey* and *shime*?'

I turned to find Ruby standing behind me, smirking. 'And what's with the folded arms and legs astride?' she asked, looking me up and down.

'Didn't you hear him?' I gestured towards the corridor. 'He suddenly started putting on a Cockney accent for some ridiculous reason – so I just joined in. And, even if I do say so myself, my effort was *way* better than his. He sounded like Prince William crossed with a Kray twin. Oh and he was trying to play the height card with me too. Amateur,' I huffed.

'He's over six foot tall, Edie,' she said, 'and from Hackney.'

'So?' I made my way back to my desk.

'So, short of shuffling around on his knees, he's always going to be taller than you.'

'You know exactly what I mean,' I said, pulling out my chair. 'It was his body language.'

'And as for the accent,' she continued, ignoring the interruption, 'the clue is in the word Hackney.'

After a brief pause, I turned my head slowly towards her, my eyes widening as the significance of the location dawned on me. 'Oh God, he's from East London,' I murmured, putting a hand to my mouth and recalling the details of Cameron's CV: Hackney born and bred, UCL educated. I glanced uncertainly towards the corridor. 'I'd forgotten. I thought he was trying to assert himself. You know, like when David Turner from planning makes eye contact and does that twitchy thing with his pelvis just before he sits down.'

'Nope. That's just how the guy talks.'

'So why haven't I noticed?' I said, biting my lower lip.

She shrugged. 'Well, you haven't really had much to do with him, have you? And to be fair to you, the accent doesn't often surface. I've noticed that it's definitely *way* more pronounced when he's stressed and on the back foot. Day-to-day he sounds pretty Home Counties.'

'Oh no,' I groaned, the thought that I had somehow managed to stress him out making me feel even worse. 'He's going to think that I was mocking his roots now, isn't he?'

'Yes, he is,' she replied matter-of-factly. 'Unless, of course, he thinks that was your Kylie Minogue impression. But either way, don't feel bad about it,' she continued, returning to her desk, 'because it was really funny.'

Deciding to ignore her remarkably poor attempt to make me feel better, I flopped down onto my chair. 'In my defence, his manner was really abrupt,' I said quietly, gazing unseeingly at my screen. 'He really needs to work on his body language and communication skills.'

'Well, I hate to say I told you so. Now, when do I get my five quid?'

'Hey, not so fast!' I exclaimed 'He may still come to your leaving drinks. I hope he does, actually, because it'll give us a chance to start over. Or perhaps I should say something as soon as he gets back with his coffee. What do you think?'

'He won't come to my leaving drinks,' she said flatly, ignoring the question. 'So you may as well just hand over the money right now.'

'What makes you so sure? I know he was a bit gruff, but he had just got absolutely soaked.' I looked at the rain still beating against the windows, whilst reflecting on the fact that I perhaps hadn't chosen the best moment in the world to pounce, or to make a joke about him steaming next to a radiator. '*And* they'd given him the wrong coffee.'

'My heart bleeds.' Ruby threw her empty sushi tray with unnecessary force into the stainless-steel bin next to her desk and refocused on her drawings.

'I don't get why you seem to have totally written him off.'

She didn't look up or reply and, still sitting in my chair, I scooted the short distance to her desk.

'Is there something you're not telling me?' I asked on arrival. 'And, if so, do you ever plan to tell me?'

At that, she leaned back in her chair and sighed. 'I'll tell you later.'

'Tell me what later?'

'Edith.'

I snatched up a pen from Ruby's desk and spun round in my chair to see Alison standing in the doorway of her office once more. 'Yes?'

'My apologies, I know it's your lunch break, but can I borrow you – just for a minute or two?'

'Sure, just give me thirty seconds.'

'Perfect.' She nodded and returned to her desk, leaving her office door ajar.

I turned back to Ruby. 'Tell me what later?' I repeated quietly.

'Everything,' she said, reaching for her mouse. 'But right now, you'd better go and see what the Iron Lady wants.'

Chapter 2

'Thanks.' Ruby reached up from the large, leather, wing-back armchair, to take one of the two glasses of wine I had just bought. 'God, that felt like a long day.'

'It's almost eight,' I said, checking my phone and then placing it on my lap as I sank down into my own armchair opposite hers. The chairs were just one of the pluses which made The Hayes a favourite post-work stop-off for us; its low lighting, quirky nooks and cosy niches also adding to its appeal for one-to-one catch-ups.

She ran a hand through her hair. 'Eight? Wow. I can't remember the last time I worked past seven. Sorry for keeping you hanging around, Edie.'

'Not a problem,' I said, struggling to remember the last time I'd actually left work *before* seven, other than to go for a drink with Ruby, Roger or Luke. Nor, for that matter, could I remember the last time I hadn't immediately started reviewing drawings, or checking emails, once home; although I had a sneaking suspicion that it may have been 19 October 2016 – the day before I threw Jason out and told him never to come back.

'Time's racing,' sighed Ruby, 'and I've got so much to sort and only a week left to sort it.'

I shook my head. 'The rest of us can mop up. You mustn't go nuts trying to get everything done.' I took a sip of wine and stared contemplatively into my glass, my mind still half on Jason.

'Why so maudlin?' asked Ruby.

'I'm just tired,' I replied. 'Like you say, it's been a long day. But this is helping.' I held up my glass.

She lowered her drink, studying me for a moment. 'Is everything OK? You seemed a bit flat after your chat with Alison at lunchtime. Hope there isn't a problem with the project.'

'No, it's all great,' I said, confused by the comment.

'Good. I was only asking because you looked a bit more intense than usual this afternoon, that's all. And then again, just a moment ago.'

'Oh, that. That was just Jason,' I said dismissively.

She stiffened and placed her glass in a slow, deliberate manner on the low table between us, while I immediately regretted mentioning him.

To the casual observer, she and Jason had got on fine when he and I were together. But I had always been aware of a slight tension on her part and, although Jason was an expert at hiding his feelings, I could tell that he was never entirely relaxed in her company either. I wondered later if he'd sensed disapproval in her even then, because there was certainly no missing it now, and ever since his multiple one-night stands had come to light, she had been anything but restrained in her opinion of him.

'What's he done?' she asked, her voice, for the moment, as controlled as her actions.

I took a breath. 'Look, I'm not upset, so there's no need for you to be upset on my behalf.'

'What has he done?' she repeated.

'Nothing more than remind me of the past.'

'How so?'

'It's really no big deal. It's just a practicality,' I said, leaning back in my armchair. 'You know how much I've hated renting since we split and sold up.'

She nodded.

'Well, there's still absolutely nothing on the market to buy, the service charge on my flat has gone up *again* and soon I'll be facing another rent increase too. So basically, I'm left flushing money down the drain, and when I thought about it this afternoon, I realised that I've been in that situation for well over a year now. I'm definitely going to have to think about a flat-share,' I said resignedly. 'But the idea of living with a stranger, even short-term, isn't great.'

At that, she looked relieved and her tone softened a little. 'So you're fed up because of a consequence of the break-up? Not because of something Jason's done?'

I looked at her and toyed with the idea of simply nodding and changing the subject. But deciding that, fireworks or no fireworks, I would feel better for getting the matter off my chest, I opted for the truth. 'Actually, he's started texting again and he sent a couple this afternoon. That's what got me thinking about everything.'

'What?' she exploded, throwing up her hands and leaving me silently thankful that she'd had the foresight to put down her drink. 'What's he texting you about?'

I held up a hand. 'Calm down. I'm quite capable of being appalled all by myself.'

'But *why* is he texting you?' she pressed, her cheeks flushing. 'Does he say he's missing you? Because I sincerely hope you're not swallowing any of his crap, Edie. Does he want to get back together?'

I shook my head. 'The texts are just about what he's up to; the kind of day he's having, plus a little bit of soul-searching.'

'Honestly, the nerve of the guy,' she said quietly, her complexion beginning to cool. 'How can he think it's OK to contact you?'

I retrieved my drink from the table. 'I don't know. He's probably bored of whoever he's with right now.'

'He's seeing someone?'

'He mentioned a movie he'd watched on Netflix last night. I don't think he was alone because it wasn't remotely his kind of thing.'

'You didn't ask him?'

'I haven't replied to any of the texts.'

'You're not curious who he's with?'

'Maybe a little,' I admitted. 'But mostly I just feel genuinely sorry for whoever it is.'

'Sorry for her?' Ruby's scepticism was obvious. 'No resentment? No wanting to punch her repeatedly in the kisser?'

'Definitely not,' I said resolutely. 'Why would I? I don't want him, and either they're in a relationship, in which case I sincerely doubt he's being faithful to her, or she was a one-off, unknowing bit on the side. Either way, I feel sorry for her.'

'*Unknowing* bit on the side?'

'Well, who would knowingly put up with that?'

'You always think the best of people,' she sighed.

'You're not exactly making that sound like a compliment.'

She shrugged. 'I just think it can leave you a little vulnerable sometimes, that's all.'

'Are you implying that I was naïve about Jason?' I asked, irritated at the thought.

'Oh, of course I'm not, Edie,' she said, gently. 'I never for one moment thought he was sleeping around and neither did anyone else.' Her expression hardened momentarily at the thought. 'He hid that side of himself brilliantly.'

'He did,' I nodded grimly. 'But while I accept that there will always be people, like Jason, who will let you down, I still believe that if you expect the best *of* people, you get the best *from* people – *most of the time*,' I said, emphasising the caveat.

She smiled. 'OK, you stick with that approach, if it works for you. But it's not for me.'

'That reminds me,' I said, reaching across the table and prodding her knee. 'What's your beef with the Cockney sparra that is Mr Cameron Grange? Did you see that he left a coffee on my desk after lunch, before he went off to his meeting? How magnanimous was that? I'm going to make a real effort with him starting Monday. I hate the thought of there being any tension in the office, don't you?'

I smiled questioningly at her, but her expression darkened and her mouth flatlined resolutely. 'Look, Edie, I've been wondering whether to tell you about something ever since you got back,' she began, so quietly that I had to lean forward in my chair to hear her above the noise of the increasingly busy bar. 'I don't want to make things difficult for you but, on the other hand, I think you should know.'

I stared at her, feeling slightly anxious but mostly intrigued as to what the gossip might be. 'What? What? What?' I breathed.

She looked at me over the top of her glass. 'If I tell you, you must keep it to yourself. If you talk to Alison about it, it'll just stir things up and you'll make things really difficult for me – and you could get Luke into trouble too. I'm telling you only so you know to be on your guard.'

'Solemn oath,' I said dramatically, placing a hand on my chest. 'Hand on heart.'

She rolled her eyes disapprovingly and then, after pausing to take a deep breath, said, 'Luke told me, when he was tipsy, that Cameron is apparently prone to varying his fees according to gender.'

'Meaning?'

'Meaning that he'll build you an erection in exchange for you helping him to get one.'

'Ruby Blair!' I laughed explosively. 'You,' I jabbed my wine glass towards her, 'are dreadful. What a completely outrageous thing to say.'

'It's not completely outrageous, Edie; it's completely true,' she said calmly, relaxing back into her armchair and crossing her legs, as if settling in to present an episode of CBeebies Bedtime Stories. 'Luke is aware of professional services going through at greatly reduced cost – no project name and no mention of it in any of the shared files – for a close and very buxom female friend of Mr Grange. It started immediately after he joined the firm.'

I tutted dismissively. 'You know what Luke's like. He'll have got the wrong end of the stick.'

She shook her head in a determinedly slow manner. 'He asked Cameron about it and Cameron was very frank apparently. Luke said he was...' She paused and looked thoughtful. 'I think the word he used was *laddish*.'

'But nothing could be going on without Alison knowing about it. She wouldn't allow anything dodgy,' I said adamantly.

Ruby shrugged. 'I'm not saying dodgy, I'm saying tacky. No doubt Alison knows all about it.'

'It just doesn't sound like something she'd OK,' I said doubtfully.

'Doesn't it? Cameron came with a reputation as someone who gets commissions and gets things done. Alison's not stupid. She knows how useful it is to have a networker at the table, a man's man, and Roger's never ticked that box, has he? He's about as macho and charismatic as a block of Wensleydale.'

'Alison's not the kind of woman who needs a willy in the room to cut a deal,' I insisted, shaking my head. 'She's a feminist.'

'No. She's a pragmatist,' retorted Ruby. 'She'll give him what *he* wants in order to get what *she* wants – and I don't have a problem with that. It's just that what he wants makes him a creep,' she added, shuddering.

'Luke could be muddled,' I said, still not convinced. 'You said he was drunk.'

'I said he was tipsy. He saw the woman when she met Cameron from work – a brunette with a boob-job and a low-cut top, apparently. They were all over each other by the lifts, and you know what Luke's like; he just *had* to tell someone. But,' she added a little anxiously, 'he's now terrified of anyone finding out that he blabbed. So you mustn't say anything, OK?'

'Of course I won't.'

'Cameron's not in a serious relationship with the woman,' she continued, her lip curling. 'He was very clear with Luke about that. The arrangement is casual and, apparently, not the only one he has going on. Mind you, not all of them involve a low-cost extension. So this woman must be particularly *giving*.' She shivered a second time and drank her wine.

I frowned into my glass, mulling over what she had said and accepting that the facts, as related by Luke, didn't reflect at all well on Cameron. But while I was positive that Luke was an honest, well-meaning kind of guy, he could easily have misunderstood the situation. That, coupled with a conviction that Alison's principles were pretty unshakeable, made the scenario an unlikely one. So either Cameron's actions had somehow been misinterpreted, or Alison somehow knew nothing about them.

I looked at Ruby. 'There's info missing. I'm certain of it.'

'Because you're just *so* in tune with Alison?' she sighed, her disapproval unmistakable.

'Well, yes, actually,' I said, feeling a little stung. 'I think I do know Alison pretty well professionally and in the past two-and-a-half years she hasn't done anything which I couldn't get on-board with. I'm not saying that Luke has deliberately misled—'

'Edie, listen to me,' she interrupted, her tone now irritatingly maternal. 'How do you think Alison rose to the top of the tree? A woman in a male-dominated profession, who started out with no connections or financial backing, now heading up her own architectural firm? Do you honestly think she got there without ever bending the rules, manipulating people or capitalising on situations to get what she wanted?'

'What I find difficult to believe,' I said steadily, 'is that any rule-bending or manipulation would involve her being complicit in a man taking advantage of a woman. In any way.'

'Maybe she thinks the woman getting the low-cost extension has the advantage,' she said. 'And maybe she does. But I still don't like it and I still think it makes Cameron a creep.'

'Only if it's true,' I pointed out, leaning back in my chair. 'There's still room for doubt about who's done what and who knows what.'

'Not in my mind.' She looked at me and hesitated for a moment before continuing. 'But in any case, I don't hate him for the discount pricing in exchange for sex, Edie. That just makes him a shallow prick. I hate him because...' She paused. 'I hate him because he came on to me and then didn't like it when I made it clear that I wasn't interested.' She spoke quietly, her voice now calm and steady. 'And he was...' She raised her hands, 'handsy. *That's* why I hate him. *That's* why I'm angry. So just be on your guard.' There was a catch in her voice as she concluded her speech with a wobbly smile.

'*What?*' I exclaimed, horrified. 'Why didn't you tell me that right away?'

'Because it all happened when you weren't here,' she began, looking suddenly tearful, 'and it was dealt with. I didn't want to drag you into it, but I do want you to be wary of him.' She looked up at me. 'I'd hoped him being aggressive towards you when you suggested a drink, and then me telling you about the sextension thing, would have been enough to do that. But you're always so bloody determined to see the best in people. You're too nice, Edie.'

I stared at her, momentarily lost for words, before managing, 'What do you mean, it was dealt with?'

She lowered her eyes. 'I spoke to Alison and she spoke to him. He insisted it was accidental contact. But he said he regretted that I'd been made to feel uncomfortable and would be more spatially aware in future, and I decided to let it go.'

'Why? And *why on earth* did you let me invite him out for drinks?' I put a hand to my forehead, remembering the way Cameron had looked at her that afternoon, and the tension that had seemed so inexplicable to me at the time.

'I did try really hard to tell you that he was someone to avoid,' she said, still addressing the floor. 'I told you not to worry about the fact that you hadn't got to know him *and* not to ask him for a drink. But then you pressed it,' she continued, finally looking up at me. 'I'm leaving in a week and I don't want this made into a big deal. I just want to go now.'

'He's not a reason for you being so determined to go, is he?' I asked, angry at the thought.

She hesitated and then shook her head. 'No, no. Of course not.'

Unconvinced, I dug my nails hard into the arm of the chair. 'But he's hardly a reason for you to stay.'

'Edie,' she leaned forward and placed her hand gently on my knee, 'this is exactly what I didn't want to—'

She was interrupted at that moment by the buzzing of my phone on my lap.

'Sorry.' I looked down at the screen. 'It's Giles – my cousin,' I murmured, declining the call. 'He rang earlier and I forgot to call him back.'

'Call him now,' she said.

I shook my head. 'It can wait. This conversation is more important.'

She stood up. 'This conversation is over. I don't want my last week at work to be all about some bastard who's used to getting his own way. He's not worth it. I just want you to keep him at arm's length. Literally. No matter how many coffees he buys you.'

I turned in my chair, reaching for her arm, but she shook her head and smiled. 'I'm going to the loo and then I'll get us another drink on the way back. Call your cousin.' And with that, she turned and made her way to the back of the bar.

I sat motionless, gazing after her and thinking about everything she'd said. There was a lot to take in, but one thing was clear: sextension or no sextension, Cameron Grange was a grade-A shit. OK, so Luke, especially under the influence of alcohol, might easily fail to grasp the nuances of a situation, but Ruby was an intelligent, clear-thinking, determined woman, well used to dealing with male attention. She was certainly not someone who would mistake accidental contact in a confined space for workplace harassment.

A text from Giles interrupted my miserable train of thought and, without pausing to read it, I picked up my phone and called him.

'Edie!' His greeting was as deafeningly exuberant as ever. 'How marvellous of you to call me back.'

I paused to lower the speaker volume before continuing the conversation. 'Hi, Giles. Sorry I didn't call earlier but the day ran away with me a bit. Can you talk now? Are you at home?' I imagined him sitting in his favourite armchair, slippers on, feet up and Anthony, his small, scruffy and incurably smelly rescue dog, curled up on his lap. It was Giles's favourite way to spend a Friday evening and I suddenly wished that I was there with him, rather than in a busy wine bar, learning unpleasant and upsetting facts about my new work colleague.

'I wish I was,' said Giles, sighing. 'But sadly, I'm not at home at all. I'm actually at Bristol airport.'

'Really?' I said in surprise, checking my watch. 'What are you doing there? I didn't know you were going away.'

'Me neither, and that's precisely why I'm calling you, Edie. Do you have time to listen to the tale, or shall I just cut to the chase?'

I leaned to one side, looking over my shoulder towards the busy bar. There was no sign of Ruby and she would have to queue for drinks when she reappeared. 'Tell me the tale,' I said.

'Right, well, first things first. Do you remember my old Eton chum, Tubby Bothwell?'

'Er...' I thought for a moment. 'Was he the guy who drank a pint of Bailey's at your birthday party last year?'

'Yes! That's him! You do have such a remarkable memory for names and faces.'

'Hmm,' I said, 'he was kind of hard to forget. He was carried out unconscious, wasn't he?'

Giles chuckled. 'He was, he was. Dear old Tubby. Always such good fun, with his gung-ho approach to life.'

'Yes, I seem to remember him being extremely gung-ho at the buffet and on the dance floor,' I agreed. 'Anyway, are you on your way to see him? How is he?'

'Well, here's the thing, Edie: he's dead.'

I lowered the phone and frowned at it for a moment before returning it to my ear. 'Dead?' I queried. 'But he's the same age as you, isn't he? Wasn't he?'

'A year younger, in fact,' said Giles, sounding under-standably subdued. 'Thirty-five. Dropped down dead of a heart attack in an all-you-can-eat Chinese restaurant last

Thursday. Coronaries were completely blocked, apparently. Who'd have thought it? Apart from absolutely everybody, of course,' he added quietly.

'I'm so sorry, Giles.'

'Yes, all very sad and, thanks to a miscommunication, I've only just discovered that the funeral is tomorrow in Edinburgh. Hence I'm at the airport.'

'I see,' I said, finally understanding. 'And do you need my help? Would you like me to pick you up when you get back?'

'You are so kind, but no, thank you. I actually have a quite different favour to ask of you.'

'Fire away.'

'Well, it's Anthony, you see. I've had to come away at such short notice that I was unable to make entirely satisfactory arrangements for his safekeeping and care.'

'You'd like me to pop round and walk him?' I asked, reaching for my bag and delving inside. 'I'm not at home, but I think I have your keys with me.'

'There is no need to trouble yourself tonight. Kerry, my wonderful neighbour at number 21 – you've heard me talk of her – has taken Anthony in. However, she is taking her son to a rather wonderful animatronic dinosaur event in Taunton tomorrow at nine a.m., so I was wondering if perhaps you could walk Anthony then? Would that be possible?'

I smiled to myself, always entertained by any mention of Giles's neighbours in the north-west Bristol avenue he had called home for a little over two years. Although I had never actually met any of them, their habits and foibles were, thanks to his affectionate anecdotes, increasingly familiar to me and it was obvious from the incidental details of his stories, that his neighbours were just as fond of him as he clearly was of them.

Mind you, I'd never actually met anyone who *didn't* like Giles. My cousin or, more accurately, my step-cousin, was as affable and easy going at the age of thirty-six as he had been when we were first thrust together as children, when my aunt had married his widowed father in 1993. From then onward, I had spent at least part of every one of my school holidays with Giles, in his large Cotswold country home, enjoying surroundings and a lifestyle which were in considerable contrast to those I experienced in my parents' comfortable, but modest, suburban Oxford semi. Giles Tripp was, my adolescent self had quickly decided, one of the poshest and, more importantly, one of the kindest people I had ever met. And my opinion of him hadn't changed at all in twenty-five years.

'That's no trouble at all, I'd love to walk Anthony,' I said, my nose wrinkling involuntarily in anticipation of the stench. 'When are you home?'

'My flight lands at around eight thirty tomorrow evening. I have hand luggage only, so I should be home at nine thirty, or thereabouts.'

'I'll stay with him until then. I know he's not a fan of being alone in the evenings.'

'Thank you, Edie, you are kindness personified. I must go now because they're calling my flight, but I shall text you all the details regarding collecting Anthony and – here's an idea – why don't you stay over tomorrow night and we can stride out for a walk and pub lunch on Sunday? My treat, to say thank you. I should love that, if you're not too busy.'

'That's sounds great, but I do have quite a bit of work to get through over the weekend, Giles.'

'Oh, come now,' he said, jovially. 'I bet you could see off most of that tomorrow afternoon if you bring your laptop. You know Anthony; he does nothing but sleep and break wind between ten a.m. and six p.m. It would be so wonderful to spend a little of Sunday with you, after what I daresay will be a rather sad Saturday for me,' he added plaintively.

I hesitated for just a moment. 'You're right. I can work Saturday. I'll pack my PJs and my laptop.'

'Marvellous!' he replied, his bounce returning. 'Bye, Edie. See you tomorrow.'

'Bye. Safe flight.'

I ended the call and relaxed back into my chair, enjoying the sense of contented calm which always followed any conversation with Giles.

'I'll pop your wine down here.'

I looked up, slightly startled to see Ruby back at my side and stooping low to place the glass on the table. 'Thanks,' I mumbled, disappointed to discover the glass to be such a large one and then experiencing an immediate sense of guilt at the realisation that, for whatever reason, all I wanted now was to go home.

'All OK?' she asked, sitting down. 'Did you call your cousin?'

'Yes and everything's fine. Well, not one hundred per cent fine, because an old school friend of his has died and Giles is on his way to Edinburgh for the funeral.'

Her face fell. 'Oh, I'm sorry.'

'Yes, I only met the guy once, but he was good fun. Anyway, Giles needs me to walk his dog tomorrow. I'm going to stay over and it'll be nice to see him – Giles, I mean, not the dog so much. He *really* stinks.'

We exchanged small smiles and then nursed our drinks as we fell into a subdued silence.

'Look, I'm sorry if I've ruined everything by telling you,' said Ruby eventually.

I looked across at her, feeling the last drops of my post-Giles peace of mind ebbing away and being replaced by a cool, steadily rising anger. 'The very last thing you should do in this kind of situation is apologise or blame yourself,' I said firmly, draining my first glass of wine and placing it heavily on the table before reaching for the second. 'There's only one person who's ruined everything, and that's Cameron Grange.'

Chapter 3

I was still yawning as I pulled off the Downs and onto the avenue of Victorian semi-detached houses where Giles lived. Aware that the neighbour who had Anthony was planning to leave home at nine, and not wanting to be late, I had set my alarm for seven thirty – an hour which, on a Saturday, definitely fell into the 'ungodly' category.

Parking outside Giles's house, I peered out of the car window, first at his small, gated front garden with its neatly trimmed low hedge and perfectly symmetrical display of shrubs and flowers, and then at the altogether more wild patch of ground which fronted number 21. Untamed fuchsia and rosemary spilled over a low stone wall and an enormous bush of some sort grew to the right of the front door, the longest of its lower branches extending across the path, narrowing it to around a third of its original width.

Climbing out of the car, I crossed the pavement and made my way up the cracked and aged redbrick path which led to the front door. The absence of a knocker left me hunting for a bell and after a few moments I spotted one – a butler's bell – hiding behind the foliage of the monster bush. I smiled as I pulled it and heard the satisfying tinkling of the pulley-operated bell in the hallway.

The response was an immediate and combined cacophony of dog-barking, manic childish laughter and an indistinct, but stern, female voice. A couple of seconds later the door was pulled ajar by a petite woman with shoulder-length, red-brown hair, whom I guessed to be in her mid-thirties. She wobbled as she crouched down and repeatedly flapped an arm behind her in an apparent attempt to deter something – I assumed either a dog or a child – from escaping into the street.

'You Edith?' she gasped.

'Edie, yes. Are you Kerry? Giles told—' I got no further as her arm shot out and she pulled me hastily inside the partially open door, before slamming it shut and leaning against it to catch her breath.

'So sorry about that, Edie,' she said in a strong Bristolian accent, her hair falling across her face as she leant forward, hands on thighs, and took several deep breaths. 'Just didn't want either of these two little—' She stopped short and straightened up. 'Just didn't want Harry and his friend, Ollie, running into the road with Anthony.'

She nodded over my shoulder and I turned to see two small boys, one blonde and slight, the other dark and decidedly chunky. Both were liberally spattered with mud and next to them, bouncing around their knees, panting and tail wagging violently, was Anthony. He also was muddied and very, *very* wet.

'Mine's the dark-haired one,' said Kerry, through a clenched smile. 'They've been watering the garden. And watering Anthony too, haven't you, boys?'

'We used a green hose with a yellow end. You twist the end and the water sprays,' grinned the blonde, for whom detail was clearly important. Harry nodded along, whilst eyeing Kerry warily.

She looked at him, her eyes narrowing, and a tense silence descended, before her frame suddenly relaxed and she sighed wearily. 'It's fine. It's only a bit of mud,' she said, as if to herself, before adding more loudly, 'But neither of you can go out looking like that, can you? So, Harry, take Ollie upstairs and find him some clean clothes from your floor. He can wear a pair of your joggers. Go on. Hurry up or all the dinosaurs will be dead.'

'They're already dead,' said Ollie. 'A meteorite may have killed them. Or volcanoes. Or climate change.'

'You're so clever, Ollie,' smiled Kerry, before turning to me and adding in a quiet mutter, 'His mother force-feeds him kale and David Attenborough.'

I took a step back as the two boys swept past me, whooping at nothing in particular and jostling for the lead as they galloped up the stairs on all fours.

'Not you, Anthony,' said Kerry, swooping down and grabbing the wiry grey-haired little dog by his collar as he made to follow them. 'We need to towel you down.'

'It's OK. I know you're in a hurry and I can sort him out when I get him next door.' I bent down to stroke Anthony and was immediately hit by a wall of halitosis as he panted up at me. 'Oh God,' I choked, instinctively but pointlessly covering my nose and mouth with one hand in an attempt to stem the stench, whilst patting Anthony's wet head with the other.

'Bad, isn't it?' said Kerry sympathetically. 'The vet has given him some new chews for his bad breath, but I reckon they've made it even worse. It's like he's eaten shit for breakfast.'

I nodded and stood up. 'Just like that,' I gasped. 'But if you let me have his lead and his basket, I'll take him, and his breath, off your hands and you can be off.'

She glanced up the stairs and then shook her head. 'We'll be lucky if we're away before midday,' she sighed. 'Ollie stayed over last night and the pair of them were still pelting each other with Lego and Haribo at two a.m. I know what'll happen; they'll run riot on empty all day and then cry all the way home. I just love motherhood.' She turned towards me and winked. 'How about a cuppa? The kettle's just boiled.'

'But I…' I checked my watch, keen to walk Anthony and perhaps fit in some work before lunch. 'I really don't want to make you late.'

She smiled up at me. 'There's always time for a cuppa.'

'Well, if you're sure.'

'Sure and desperate,' she said, walking down the hallway. 'Come on. You too, Anthony.'

We obediently followed her through into the back room, with its fireplace and alcoves which, I noticed, were identical to Giles's. But while Giles's mantelpiece and bookshelves resembled the inner pages of a John Lewis catalogue, Kerry's looked like a branch of Argos had thrown up on them.

Felt-tip pens, action figures, toy cars, cuddly toys and cereal packets – painted to resemble God-knows-what – occupied every inch of child-accessible space. The more usual reception room décor of three framed photographs, a bronze abstract and a vase – the latter containing a bunch of red gerberas – were relegated to the topmost shelves.

'My favourite flower,' I said, pointing up at the gerberas, as we made our way into a galley kitchen which, I guessed, had been tacked onto the back of the house at some point in the Seventies. It was long and narrow, with a small, metal-framed window over the sink and two Velux windows in its sloping roof. A half-glazed door at its far end opened out onto an ageing patio covered with potted plants and yet more toys.

I glanced around, contrasting the limited light and space here with Giles's considerably bigger kitchen-area extension, which ran across the entire width of the house to create a large, square single space. By force of habit, I found myself thinking about the ways in which Kerry's kitchen might be transfigured to lighten the back room and provide her with more useable space.

'The flowers are from your cousin,' she smiled, 'to say thank you for having Anthony last night. I told him there was no need. Harry loves him to bits,' she said, looking down at the little dog now sitting at her feet, 'and what are neighbours for?'

'Giles loves this neighbourhood,' I said. 'Although, I think he rattles around a bit in that house.'

She nodded, holding up two storage tins, one labelled coffee, the other tea.

'Tea, please,' I said, pointing at the appropriate tin and then watching as she returned the coffee to a cupboard, the chipped door of which hung slightly on its hinges as she closed it.

'Yeah, the house is a bit big for us too, now that it's just the two of us. And it always needs stuff doing to it.' I followed her eyes up to a damp patch and cracking around one the Veluxes. 'But I wouldn't want to move and mess Harry around, and we've got the Downs on our doorstep. He would really miss that. Plus, there's stamp duty and moving costs, and Giles is right, the neighbours are great. I mean, some are nuts, obviously. Patrick is *obsessed* with parking, and poor old June *literally* speaks her mind – but they mean well. And that's all we can ask of ourselves and anyone else, isn't it? Best intentions.' She picked up the kettle and poured water onto the teabags she had placed into a couple of mugs. 'Milk? Sugar?'

'Neither, thanks,' I said, as she scooped out the bags, tossing them into a composting caddy.

'Come and sit down,' she smiled, handing me a mug and picking up her own.

Anthony and I followed her back into the dining room, Anthony flopping happily into his bed as he passed, and me taking the opportunity to look again at the photographs on the bookshelves. Two appeared to be recent shots of Kerry and Harry and the third featured a beaming, wild-haired man in an Aran sweater. He was standing on a windy-looking beach, one hand held aloft, waving to the camera as his dark hair stormed around his face. Friend? Brother? Ex-partner? I wondered. Possibly the latter, if they had parted on good terms. I made a mental note to ask Giles.

Walking to a pine table for four, positioned in a bay which overlooked the garden, we each pulled out a chair and sat down. A sofa and armchair, covered in throws of varying but co-ordinating colours, and a large wooden chest took up the rest of the space.

'Sorry about the mess,' said Kerry, nodding towards the toys and various items of dress-up, littering the sofa. 'I bet your place is immaculate. Giles mentioned that you don't have kids.'

I blinked and felt myself redden. 'Oh, yes, that's right, I don't. I'm single,' I said awkwardly.

She put a hand to her mouth, now looking a little pink herself. 'God, that sounded awful – the way I said about you not having kids – like Giles had been discussing you and you know he's not like that at all.'.

'It's OK, I know he's *really* discreet. Hopeless at gossip, actually.'

She smiled, as if relieved. 'Yeah, the thing about kids just came up when we were talking about family one day. But when he texted last night to say you were coming to get Anthony, I thought, *Jesus, she'll think a bomb's gone off in here.* In my defence, it's not usually quite this bad, but they were getting stuff out as fast as I was putting it away last night and sometimes you've just got to say stuff it, haven't you? It won't take long to sort out when we get home this evening and I'd rather have them being Batman and Wonder Woman than staring at a screen.'

'Definitely,' I agreed, wondering whether it was Harry or Ollie who was the cross-dresser, 'and if it makes you feel better, I've left laundry hanging from every radiator in my flat this morning.'

She made a so-so gesture with her hand.

'But anyway,' she said, leaning back in her chair, pulling a scrunchie from her wrist and piling her hair on top of her head, 'what's it like having Giles for a cousin? Don't take this the wrong way, but you don't seem quite as posh as him.'

'Is anyone as posh as Giles?'

'Excellent point,' she laughed, picking up her mug and saluting me with it.

'We're not actually related,' I said, drinking my tea.

'You're not?' She lowered her mug to the table and leaned towards me, clearly interested. 'Really? So why does he call you his cousin, then?'

'I do the same, just because it's easier, but we're actually step-cousins. Giles's mum died when he was still in primary school and, a couple of years after that, Giles's dad needed someone to sort out their huge garden and my aunty was a landscaper – the rest is history.' I smiled at the thought of the romantic tale of love blossoming with the roses, recounted to me so often by my mother. 'Giles and I are both only children and we used to spend a lot of time together in the holidays, so we're very close; closer since we each lost our parents. His stepmum – my aunty – was the last to go, and she died three years ago.'

Kerry nodded and looked thoughtful, as if mulling something over. 'So how come you're both in Bristol now?' she asked after a moment. 'Is that deliberate?'

I shook my head. 'It's great that it's worked out that way, but it wasn't planned. He just happened to get his professorship a couple of years after I started my first job here.'

'And what do you do?'

I smiled at her interest, wondering whether I might at any point get a chance to find out something about her. 'I'm an architect.'

Her face lit up, before immediately falling again as she looked at something over my shoulder.

'Dear God,' she murmured, closing her eyes and rubbing her forehead.

I turned in my chair to discover that we had been joined by Harry and Ollie; Harry now wearing a *Lego Movie* T-shirt, green football shorts, matching football socks and a single orange shin pad. Ollie, meanwhile, was sporting a button-through *Star Wars* pyjama top and grey jogging bottoms, the latter accessorised with a white towelling belt which had been wrapped around his waist several times and secured with a large drooping bow.

'OK,' said Kerry quietly, her eyes still closed, 'so we're nearly there with the clothes. We just need a couple of quick swaps.' She opened her eyes and arranged her features into a patient smile. 'Get Ollie a T-shirt, Harry. There's a blue one on your beanbag. And I'll—'

'Ollie wants to wear the *Star Wars* top,' said Harry, wiping his nose on the back of his hand and then wiping the back of his hand on his shorts. 'Don't you, Ollie?' He turned to Ollie, who nodded vigorously.

'But that's a pyjama top,' said Kerry.

Both boys looked at her in a what's–your–point kind of way.

'It's best to wear outdoor clothes to go outdoors,' persisted Kerry, her voice calm and quiet, as if negotiating a hostage situation. 'We can find Ollie a fun outdoor top. It doesn't have to be the plain blue one.'

Ollie turned to Harry. 'Will it have *Star Wars* on it?' he whispered.

'I don't have a *Star Wars* T-shirt, Ollie,' said Harry apologetically. 'Only pyjamas.'

'Oh.' Ollie's lower lip protruded and his head drooped.

Kerry sighed audibly. 'You know what, as it's the weekend, I think it'd be OK to wear indoor clothes outdoors today. I'm just having a cup of tea with Edie and then we're off. So go and have a pee and find your shoes. And if you want to wear a belt, Ollie, I'll find you one because that's actually my—'

'Ollie wants to wear the white one,' said Harry. 'Don't you, Ollie?' Cue more nodding from Ollie. 'It goes around and around like a Jedi's and also he is practising his bows,' added Harry, indicating Ollie's waistline.

Ollie looked down at the belt, while raising his arms above his head, so as to better display his handiwork.

'Fair enough,' said Kerry, with the air of a woman who knew how to pick her battles. 'Nice knotting, Ollie. Now, off to the loo, you two.'

She looked at me as the boys disappeared back into the hallway. 'His mother'll go mental if I can't talk him out of that little lot before I take him home. He turned up here yesterday looking like Prince George at a polo match, and this morning he's a walking jumble sale.'

I laughed and put down my mug. 'I should probably let you go and sort things out,' I said, standing up.

Kerry heaved herself to her feet. 'Yeah, I'd love to chat, but the chances of either of them coming down with matching shoes on the right feet is practically nil. Now,' she continued, pointing to the hallway, 'I've already put Anthony's bowls and his squeaky duck thing in a bag for you. It's all out there. You just need to grab his bed, while I put him on the lead.'

A minute or two later, Kerry was holding the front door open as I squeezed through it, slightly damp dog bed and a Tesco carrier bag in one hand, and a lead, with Anthony on the end of it, in the other.

'Great to finally meet you,' she said, as I stepped out onto the path. 'Giles mentions you a lot. Just sorry we couldn't chat for longer.'

'Hopefully another day,' I said, feeling like I meant it.

'Yeah,' she smiled. 'Next time you're with Giles at the weekend, the pair of you should pop in for a drink. I'd really like to hear more about your job. A friend of mine is an architect and I think that creative, mathsy mix is really interesting.'

'I love my job, and the people I work with. Mostly,' I added, after a slight pause.

'Ooh,' she laughed. 'I like the sound of that *mostly* you stuck on the end there. Nothing I love more than a bit of workplace beef.'

I pulled a face. 'I'm just hoping it's not all about to go downhill fast,' I began, before turning as Anthony started to tug. 'He's telling me to quit talking and move,' I said, beginning to walk away down the path. 'You enjoy those dinosaurs.'

'Nah, it's gonna be hell, Edie,' she said, raising a hand in farewell, 'but at least I'm ready for it.'

Chapter 4

Feeling both relaxed and refreshed after a long soak in Giles's enormous claw-foot bath, I made my way downstairs to the living room. Once there, I switched on a lamp, further illuminating a room impeccably furnished with the antique bookcase, occasional table, piano and reupholstered sofa and armchairs which had once graced the drawing room of Giles's childhood home.

Pulling closed the heavy curtains and adjusting my voluminous dressing gown, I plonked down on the sofa, thumping some scatter cushions into submission behind me, whilst wondering whether to do some more work, or watch *Bake Off* on catch-up.

I smiled to myself, sinking further into the sofa and closing my eyes as I reflected on what had been a rather lovely Saturday afternoon spent strolling through Leigh Woods with Anthony, late-lunching in Ashton Court and then making our way home across the Downs in warm sunshine. It had been the kind of loosely scheduled day I had rarely enjoyed since Jason and I had—

I was grateful to be rescued from the thought by Anthony who at that moment appeared at my feet, tail swishing furiously from side-to-side, like a windscreen wiper in a monsoon.

'OK, then,' I said, bending down and picking him up, 'but just make sure you're facing the telly.' I placed him on my lap and after three stumbling rotations, he settled – with a sad inevitability – facing me, his panting breaths wafting up at me in wave after stinky wave.

I tilted my head upwards in search of fresher air, and stroked his head, waiting for it to droop onto his outstretched paws. 'Good boy,' I said softly, focusing on the ceiling and gently rubbing a forefinger between his small, grey ears.

He was asleep within minutes and, realising that I had left my laptop beyond reach on my bed upstairs, I leaned cautiously to my left, stretching to retrieve the TV remote from the arm of the sofa, whilst taking great care not to wake Anthony.

It was about an hour later and Paul Hollywood – arms folded, legs akimbo – had just finished insulting some poor bloke's rough puff, when I heard Giles's key in the lock. Anthony heard it too and was off my lap and whimpering with excitement in the hallway before the front door had clicked shut.

Turning off the TV, I hauled myself to my feet and followed the little dog into the hallway. There I found Giles on his knees and ruffling Anthony's head, whilst the latter repeatedly licked his face.

'Well, if you think I'm kissing you hello after he's had first dibs, you've got another thing coming,' I said.

Giles looked up, his grin broad, his pale blue eyes wide with fun and his round face slightly pink. 'Edie!' he beamed, standing up and sweeping back the unruly blonde hair that had fallen across his eyes. 'And aren't you the very vision of loveliness in your – or should I say *my* – dressing gown?'

I looked down at the blue and green tartan robe. 'Forgot mine,' I said simply.

'Not a problem,' he replied. 'You look ten times better in it than I do. Keep it, if you like.'

'If you're implying that this even remotely fits me, I'm insulted.' I undid the blue tasselled belt and pulled a significant quantity of excess fabric more tightly around me before retying it.

'Of course I don't think it fits you,' he beamed. 'Because I'm a chubster and you, dear Edie, are a sylph.' He patted his slightly rounded stomach, which was at that moment encased in a red checked shirt. A pair of dark denims, brown brogues and an unzipped, ancient and battered Barbour completed the look.

'You're an Adonis,' I said. 'And I want to hear all about your trip. Shall I put the kettle on?'

'Oh no, no, no.' He shook his head and wagged a forefinger at me. 'There is no need for a kettle when one has been to Edinburgh.' He reached into a green plastic bag at his feet and extracted a bottle of Scotch. 'Can I interest you in a wee dram?'

I wrinkled my nose. 'Hmmm. Sorry to rain on your...' I paused and squinted at the bottle, 'forty-six per cent proof parade, but I might opt instead for a glass of red, if that's OK,' I said. 'Not a huge fan of whisky.'

'I was aware of that, actually, which is why...' He smiled, dipping again into the bag and this time taking out a tartan tin. 'I got you this.'

'Aw, that's so kind,' I said, taking the shortbread and hugging him, despite the lingering whiff of dog slobber on his cheek. 'Thank you.'

'You're most welcome. Now how about I get us each a drink?'

I took the whisky from him. 'You go and flop. I'll fetch the drinks.'

'And a piece of shortbread each?'

'And a piece of *my* shortbread each.'

'Quite so,' he nodded. 'And then we can sit with our feet up on the living room pouffe and update each other regarding the weavings of our tangled webs since last we met.'

'Sounds perfect,' I said, turning and walking towards the kitchen. 'Go and position the pouffe.'

—

'There were actually quite a few of the chaps from school there. Batty Bately, Tiddler Salmon and Gracie Fields all turned up,' said Giles, picking up the bottle of whisky from the piano and pouring himself a second generous measure before returning to sit next to me on the sofa.

I shook my head. 'I can't believe that you know grown men called Batty, Tiddler and Gracie. That's just so disturbing, Giles.'

He looked at me solemnly and held up a hand. 'Confession: I made up those names solely to offend your left-wing sensibilities.'

I rewarded him with a theatrically heavy sigh and a second shake of the head. 'But Tubby really was called Tubby, wasn't he?' I asked, sipping my wine. 'He introduced himself to me as Tubby at your party.'

Giles smiled. 'Yes. That was fact. But he was the only one of us with a till-death-us-do-part nickname. Poor Tubby.'

His face fell and I reached out and took his hand. 'I'm sorry. It's such a tragedy that he died so young.'

'It is, it is,' he sighed. 'But come on. Enough about funerals. Tell me about you. How has your day been? Was

Anthony a good boy?' he asked, his face brightening at the thought.

'He was great company,' I said, 'depending upon wind direction.'

'The chews didn't help?'

'Afraid not. He smelled worse than ever when I picked him up from Kerry and she blamed the chews, so I haven't let him have another. And his breath does seem to have improved during the day. Marginally,' I added. 'It's all relative, obviously.'

'Obviously.'

I looked down at Anthony, who was now once again on my lap. 'But he is lovely.'

Giles reached across and patted his head. 'How was Kerry? Did you get a chance to talk to her?'

'We had a quick cup of tea,' I said, turning towards him, 'and I really liked her.'

'You know, I felt sure you would. She's just so very straightforward and no-nonsense in an enormously refreshing kind of way, don't you think?'

'I do. I would have liked to ask more about her, but she was too busy firing questions at me. I'm assuming she's a single mum?'

I had been focusing on Anthony, but looked up when I felt Giles's frame sag slightly. 'What is it?' I asked.

'Kerry's partner died in a car accident shortly after they moved into the avenue,' said Giles quietly. 'That was three years ago now. Harry was just two at the time.'

'Oh no, that's so awful, Giles,' I said, placing a hand to my mouth. 'When she said it was just the two of them in the house, I assumed it was a divorce, or a separation.'

'Same,' he said, nodding slowly. 'I lived next door to her for many months before I realised that wasn't the case.

We had chatted over the garden wall but, of course, these details don't tend to come up, do they? It was June across the road who told me the truth of the matter at one of the avenue wine and cheese evenings. Of course, Kerry has talked to me about it since, as we've become more closely acquainted.'

He sipped his drink, falling silent, whilst I thought about his over-the-wall chats and avenue wine and cheese evenings, and contrasted his home-life and neighbourhood relationships with my own. We were, I decided, worlds apart, despite being separated by just three miles of A-road.

'But how are *you*?' he asked suddenly.

'Oh, I'm OK,' I said, looking away and returning my attention to Anthony.

'Are you certain of that?' he pressed gently.

I took a moment before replying. 'Relatively certain,' I said, continuing to focus on Anthony.

Giles nudged me. 'Out with it.'

'Are you sure you want to hear it? It's really unpleasant workplace stuff,' I warned.

'Work?' he frowned. 'I can't remember you ever having a problem with work.'

'Me neither,' I agreed. 'But I do now.'

In response, he tented his fingers, pressing them thoughtfully against his lips. 'Lay it on me.'

When I finished my grim account of events several minutes later, Giles's expression was uncharacteristically stern. 'My advice would be to discuss the matter with your boss when Ruby has gone,' he said. 'It would provide an opportunity for you to clarify exactly what happened and to express your reservations regarding working with your new colleague.'

I shook my head. 'I promised Ruby I wouldn't mention it to anyone. The whole thing was supposed to be entirely confidential.'

'And yet Ruby chose not to keep it confidential.'

'Only for my sake,' I pointed out.

'I accept that, but my advice would nevertheless be to talk to your boss. You might find hiding your feelings more difficult than you think.'

'OK, I'll give it some thought.'

'Are your other colleagues aware of the situation?' he asked.

'I'm guessing not. I haven't noticed any tension between them and him. Mind you,' I ran a hand through my hair, 'I hadn't noticed any tension between him and Ruby until yesterday. I think I've just been so focused on keeping my current project on track that I've been in a bit of a bubble. And then, on top of that work worry,' I continued miserably, 'Jason texted me again yesterday.'

'*Again?* I didn't know he's texted you at all.' There was anxiety, as well as surprise, in his tone: Jason Hume was not an easy topic for either of us. He and Giles had become good friends during the time that Jason and I had dated, and as far as Giles was concerned, Jason's betrayal of me had also been a betrayal of their friendship.

To make matters worse, Giles maintained a wholly misplaced sense of guilt for not, as he put it, *spotting the monster* in Jason. I had tried many times to set his mind at rest on the matter. Ruby had been absolutely right when she'd said that no one had had Jason pegged as the kind of man prone to shagging strangers at Paris conferences, Prague stag nights and Ipswich funerals. But the fact that Giles was just one of a multitude of friends and family members who had failed to *spot the monster* in their midst did nothing to ease his sense of guilt, and he and Jason had neither met, messaged nor talked since the day I had asked my ex to leave our home, over eighteen months earlier.

'Don't worry, there's no drama,' I said, waving away Giles's concern. 'The texts are just accounts of his attempts to understand his own behaviour, plus a few details of what he's up to now. But yesterday, he mentioned our house in Hotwells, and that obviously didn't make me feel great about stuff – including not being able to knock a nail into the wall without permission and hearing techno through the floor at three a.m.' I rolled my eyes and then rested my head on his shoulder as he placed an arm around me in gentle support.

'So, why don't you move in here?'

I lifted my head and frowned up at him. Giles sipped his whisky and shrugged. 'Well?'

'You're not serious.'

'I'm perfectly serious,' he said. 'I've got three spare bedrooms. *Three*, Edie.' He held up the appropriate number of fingers to further emphasise the point. 'Plus the study. It's a disgrace of space for a single fellow. It would save you money while you house-hunt and you could have a whole floor to yourself if you wanted to. What's more, I never play my techno past midnight.'

I opened my mouth to speak but, unsure exactly what to say, I closed it again.

He smiled. 'Too suburban for you? Too *Terry and June* – or rather, too June and Stan?' he asked, gesturing towards the window with his tumbler. 'I understand and that's perfectly fine. I just thought I'd offer.'

'And it's a really kind offer, Giles. But it would be such a big change for you. You've never shared this house with anyone,' I said, looking around the sentimentally furnished living room and comparing it with my own, somewhat more functional, living space.

He shifted on the sofa, turning towards me, his eyes narrowing slightly. 'So, to clarify, your equivocation is entirely on my behalf, not your own?'

I thought for a moment. Giles was right, his location did seem terrifyingly suburban to me at this point in my life and career. But hadn't I, only yesterday, been confronting the possibility of having to move from Harbourside and share a home with a stranger? With that possibility, or inevitability, in mind, the offer of sharing a four-bedroomed period home with my best friend was a godsend, and one which I would have had to be an absolute idiot to refuse.

'I suppose it is,' I said.

'Well, in that case, it's settled,' he said. 'Because I am experiencing no feelings of equivocation whatsoever. Move in whenever suits, stay for as long as you like, and knock in as many nails as takes your fancy.'

'Are you sure?'

He looked thoughtful. 'Maybe restrict it to three nails per wall but, with that sole stipulation, yes.' He held out his almost-empty glass towards me. 'Let's do this thing, as the kids say.'

I smiled up at him and clinked my glass against his. 'OK,' I said, leaning sideways to kiss his cheek and then bravely bending low to kiss Anthony too. 'Let's.'

Chapter 5

'You're moving to Henleaze?' Luke leaned back in his chair and looked up at me, his slim, pale features crumpling in confusion. He was clearly having difficulty grasping the concept. 'From Harbourside?'

'Yes.'

'To Henleaze?'

'*Yes*,' I said. 'And I don't understand what your problem is,' I added, whilst actually knowing exactly what his problem was, but choosing not to acknowledge it.

'Hey, no problem at all,' he replied, holding up his hands. 'I just hope your mobility scooter is fully charged, that's all.'

'That's so very funny that I'm not sure whether to give you this now.' I held up the coffee I had picked up for him on my way into the office, an occasional habit I had fallen into over the past year, now that he and I were almost always the first to arrive each morning. Luke's early start time was due to the fact that he still lived with his parents and was dropped off at eight a.m. by his father on his way out of Bristol each morning. My altogether more pitiful reason was that, now that I was single, there really wasn't an awful lot to hang around my flat for after breakfast.

When Jason and I had been together, we would both linger as long as possible at the breakfast bar, having a second cup of coffee or an extra croissant, playing work-run chicken and seeing how late we could leave home and still be in on time. But these days, things were different. As soon as I had downed my OJ and Weetabix, I couldn't wait to quit the solitude and minimalist décor of my two-bed, one-person apartment, in favour of the Costa queue and the camaraderie and busyness of the workplace.

'I'm just winding you up,' said Luke, reaching up and taking the coffee from me. 'I'm sure Henleaze is great – and I bet my nan is wrong when she says she's always the youngest person in the veg shop.' He removed the lid of his coffee and blew on it. 'Except she isn't,' he added under his breath. 'Cos I've seen them all queuing for death in there.'

'Shut up.' I leaned over the desk and tapped the top of his head.

'Hey!' he cried, putting down the coffee and gently patting his highlighted, immaculately styled hair to check for imperfections. 'Be careful or I'll have you for harass-ment.'

He began to laugh and then stopped abruptly, looking up at me uncertainly. It was a reaction which made me wonder if he knew what had happened between Cameron and Ruby after all.

I said nothing, merely raising an eyebrow.

'Thanks for the coffee, Edie,' he mumbled meekly, picking up the cup.

'You're most welcome, Luke.'

He offered me a strained smile and, with neither of us willing to acknowledge or address the sudden slight chill in the atmosphere, an awkward silence ensued.

I was just beginning to wonder which of us would crack first – with my money being on Luke, who had resorted to anxiously chewing on a fingernail – when Roger walked in, carrying a black portfolio case in one hand and his much-dented silver flask in the other.

'Morning,' he said, in the no-nonsense, northern grunt which always left me waiting for him to conclude his sentences with either 'Mr 'erriot' or 'Gromit'.

'Morning, Rog,' said Luke with way too much enthusiasm, clearly hugely relieved by his arrival.

I offered Roger a small smile and a raised hand.

He glanced at us each in turn and then placed both the case and the flask down on his desk. 'Well, *you*,' he began, pointing a finger in Luke's direction, 'look like you're on amphetamines, and *you*,' his finger moved towards me, 'look like you've got a Monday mard on. What's up?'

'She's moving to Henleaze,' said Luke, clearly believing that to be all the explanation necessary.

Roger, however, looked confused. 'Henleaze is all right,' he said, frowning at me. 'I've got a friend in one of the retirement places there – the one on the Downs. He's only got the one leg, but they run a minibus to the supermarket every Monday, and put on plays in the home and suchlike. He's contented enough there. We go to that cafe next to the hospice shop when I visit. Nice range of jacket potatoes and no gluten-free, vegan nonsense.'

I glanced at Luke, who smirked at me in a point-proven kind of way.

'I just wondered, Rog,' he said, 'whether the Harbourside location might not be better for Edie... at her age... and with both legs.'

'Is the Harbourside rent cheaper?' asked Roger, sitting down and turning his chair toward me.

'No.'

Roger looked at Luke. 'It's not better,' he said flatly.

'Well, thanks so much for clearing that up,' murmured Luke.

'I'm really looking forward to it *actually*, Roger,' I said pointedly, with a sidelong glance at Luke. 'I'm moving in with my cousin who lectures at the university. He's single, so it'll just be the two of us in the house.'

'I'm liking all that.' Roger nodded approvingly, in the manner of a farmer who had just watched his dog successfully pen a flock of forty sheep. 'Lower rent, known landlord, quiet neighbourhood. All the pubs in Henleaze are as silent as the grave come ten p.m.'

'It just gets better and better,' said Luke.

'When do you do move?' asked Roger.

'Middle of next month, hopefully,' I replied. 'I've just got to sort out my current tenancy with the agency. I haven't got much to move, because most of my furniture is still in storage.'

'Let me know if you need a hand with shifting and the like,' said Roger gruffly. 'Don't struggle on your own.' He didn't look at me as he made the offer, but instead unzipped his case and peered inside in an attempt to distract Luke and myself from the fact that, despite a decidedly crusty exterior, he was a very lovely man with a very warm heart.

'That's really kind of you.' I placed a hand briefly on his shoulder as I walked past him to my desk. 'I'm going to hire a little van and I think Giles, my cousin, will be around to help. But I'll definitely take you up on the offer if he's not, so thank you.'

'No bother,' he said.

'And *of course* I'm happy to help too,' Luke chipped in. 'No matter how much I disapprove.'

'Thank you, Luke,' I said. 'And if you do find yourself in Henleaze on that or any other day, let me know and I'll stand you a pint in one of those pubs.'

His upper lip curled slightly. 'Yay.'

I tutted at him and was rewarded with a wink as he spun round in his chair to face his screen.

I smiled to myself, reflecting on the fact that Ruby's loss notwithstanding, I would still be part of a caring, if somewhat quirky, team of co-workers.

Regrettably, my sense of cosy camaraderie proved to have the longevity of a gnat. Because just as I was about to embarrass both Luke and Roger by telling them how much I genuinely appreciated them, Cameron swept into the office, his unbuttoned blue raincoat swishing behind him, like a villain in search of a nightie-clad woman to tie to the nearest set of railway tracks.

'Cam! How did the weekend go?' asked Luke, in a manner so cheery I could only conclude that either he didn't know that the man he was addressing was actually a bit of a bastard, or that he was capable of overlooking that fact in a way which was impossible for me. It was a confusing choice because, instinctively, I didn't really believe either to be the case.

Cameron said something about a weekend of DIY – a comment that clearly harked back to a conversation in which I had played no part – before answering a question from Roger about the central valley guttering on his butterfly roof. I, meanwhile, shifted my attention to Roger himself, wondering if I would be able to guess anything about his attitude towards Cameron from their exchange. But Roger's manner was as impenetrably deadpan as ever and, as for Cameron, he seemed completely at ease.

Until, that is, he looked at me.

'Hello,' he said, clearing his throat before adding, 'Edie.'

Unable to smile, or even to continue looking at him, I instead reached down to pick up my satchel from the floor. 'Hi,' I said.

I didn't know what his reaction was, but it was negative enough for Luke to say, 'It's not you, Cam. She's grumpy 'cos she's moving to Henleaze.'

I felt the blood rush to my face and, raising my head, glared at Luke, causing him to flinch slightly, like a dog being shown a rolled-up newspaper. 'OK, OK, no more jokes about Henleaze,' he said, turning away to face his screen. 'But they are only jokes. You're just so touchy this morning.'

I didn't reply, silently returning my attention to my bag.

'You're moving?' asked Cameron.

Having no choice but to engage, I looked up. 'Yes.'

I was aware that the monosyllabic response had the air of a challenge about it, but I didn't care. I met his gaze, daring him to take me up on it.

He looked at me blankly for a moment and then nodded. 'Well, I hope that goes well,' he said, taking off his coat and sitting down.

Roger stood up and walked over to Cameron's desk. I couldn't hear what he said, as he bent over and began talking quietly, but I did witness a rare smile from him as he patted Cameron's shoulder and then walked back across the room. He didn't make eye contact with me before he sat back down, and as I looked from him to Cameron to Luke – who was now head-down and typing rapidly – I realised that I had somehow gone from feeling an integral and protected part of a happy workplace family, to feeling completely marginalised in the space of less than five minutes.

I looked again at Cameron and felt my upper lip curl. It was all his fault.

'Hi, all.' Ruby bounced into the office, her eyes hidden behind by one of the many pairs of sunglasses she wore all year round, regardless of season or time of day.

'Hey,' said Luke, his mood now sufficiently dampened so as to restrict any further acknowledgement of her to a brief smile and a nod.

'Morning,' said Roger.

I didn't hear Cameron say hello. Nor did I see him look up, turn in his chair or raise a hand. But no one, other than me, seemed to register his ignorance.

'Hello, Ruby!' I said brightly, determined to compensate for everyone else's lack of enthusiasm. 'How are you? How was the weekend?'

'Great, actually,' she replied, removing her sunglasses and smiling broadly. 'I felt like I got a lot of things sorted, and,' she added quietly, 'thanks for Friday night. I know I crashed the mood a bit, but it was such a relief to share…' her eyes flickered momentarily towards Cameron, 'everything with you. I felt like I'd been hiding something from you and I hated that.'

'Absolutely,' I said.

'Oh, but how about you?' She lowered her voice to a whisper, her expression suddenly serious. 'Any more texts from Jason?'

Deciding not to dent her mood by telling her that, yes, I'd had two on Sunday evening, which I had ignored, the first reminiscing about the old days and the second asking me how my weekend had been, I shook my head. 'Nothing.'

She smiled again, seeming satisfied. 'Good. Because you can do without that.'

I nodded and turned to see Alison, pressing her shoulder against the glass door of the office and pushing it open. 'Good morning,' she said, sounding a little breathless and struggling to manage a leather tote, a laptop case, two poster tubes and a Marks and Spencer carrier bag. I made to stand up, but Roger got there first.

'Unload,' he said, striding towards her.

Saying nothing, she handed him the M&S bag before turning her left shoulder towards him. He slid the tote down her arm and then, carrying both it and the plastic bag, followed her into her office.

I lowered myself back into my chair, switched on my desktop and then ignored it, looking around instead at my work colleagues. Luke was frowning in concentration while still tapping away furiously at his keyboard; Cameron was sitting in profile to me, a stylus pressed thoughtfully against his stubbly chin as he studied a tablet on the desk in front of him; and behind the glass walls of her office, Alison was nodding slowly, while Roger spoke, addressing the floor, hands in pockets. Neither her expression, nor his, gave any hint as to the subject matter, but I could tell it wasn't cheery chit-chat about the weekend just gone, and as Alison glanced briefly in my direction, I had a horrible feeling that I myself had just featured in the solemn topic under discussion.

Fighting an increasing and completely unfamiliar sense of workplace isolation, I turned at last to Ruby, suddenly finding myself envying her escape from Alison Gerrard Ltd, and wondering whether I shouldn't perhaps grab a shovel and start digging a tunnel myself.

She looked up at me questioningly. 'All good, Edie?'

Unable to reply immediately, I nodded rapidly, hoisting my mouth up into a smile. 'Yes,' I managed after a moment, as inner Edie's lower lip trembled and she considered bursting into tears, 'everything's great.'

Chapter 6

I put enormous effort into hiding my feelings during Ruby's final week at work, not only to keep things positive for her, but also because I knew that, for the most part, said feelings were unreasonable. So I hid from Alison my resentment that she had failed to take action against Cameron, and I hid from Luke and Roger my distress over the warmth of their relationships with him and, of course, I hid from Ruby my increasing misery over her looming departure.

However, the *pièce de résistance* in terms of masking my feelings, was, without doubt, my success in concealing from *absolutely everyone* the fact that I despised Cameron Grange and wanted him to disappear, not only from the office, but also from the face of the earth. It is true that I achieved this primarily by simply avoiding his company whenever possible – including, on one occasion, resorting to answering emails and taking calls in the loo. But my simplistic approach to the problem seemed to work, and by the time Friday lunchtime came around, I congratulated myself on having contributed in no discernible way to any sense of disharmony within the workplace.

However, as Ruby and I sat opposite each other in The Florist on her final day, lunching on chicken katsu and sesame salmon respectively, she presented my feelings with a challenge that I feared might prove a bridge too far.

'I almost forgot,' she smiled, putting down her fork and reaching into the pocket of her coat, which hung over the back of her chair. 'There's something I've been meaning to give you.' She took out her purse and extracted a ten-pound note, holding it out to me across the table.

I shook my head. 'We've already agreed that lunch is on me.'

'I know,' she said, flapping the note, 'and I'll need some change from you. I just haven't got a fiver.'

I took the note. 'I don't get it.'

'The bet. You win. Cameron is coming out for a drink with us – with all of us – tonight.'

I stared at her for a moment and then laughed. 'You're joking.'

She shook her head and then rolled her eyes as my face dropped. 'Don't be angry.'

'I'm not angry, I'm appalled.'

'OK then, don't be appalled.'

'I don't understand why *you're* not appalled,' I said, working hard to keep my voice light. 'And angry, for that matter.'

She reached for her glass of water and took a sip before replying. 'Alison and I talked it through yesterday and she has discussed it with Cameron too. He's going to come along for one drink, and then leave.' She put down the glass, picked up her fork and scooped up another mouthful of rice.

I looked down at my salmon, having suddenly lost all appetite for it. 'So this is Alison's idea?' I asked, my buried resentment towards her in imminent danger of exploding to the surface.

63

'Don't stress about it. He's not going to be there for long and if he didn't come out with us, Roger and Luke might—'

'I don't care what Roger and Luke *might*,' I interrupted. 'And I'm not sure why you do either.'

'Look, they're not the only ones on Alison's mind,' she continued after a slight pause. 'You are too. She doesn't know that I've confided in you – and she mustn't know that,' she added hurriedly. 'We'd all agreed to keep this confidential, OK?'

I frowned angrily.

'Promise me you won't ever mention it to her, Edie,' she said pleadingly. 'It could reopen a whole can of worms for me.'

'Of course I won't mention it. But it's hard to sit by and witness all this crap. It's so unjust.'

'No one thinks that more than me, but I have to be pragmatic about it and I just want everything and *everyone*,' she said pointedly, 'to calm down and move on. It's in my best interests.'

'How is it in your best interests?' I exclaimed. 'I can see how it might be in *his* best interests, but our office politics isn't your responsibility, or even relevant to you after today, and *none* of this is your fault. It's *your* last day and *your* leaving drinks and *you* should decide who's invited and who isn't.'

'Agreed,' she said simply.

'So why on earth are you inviting *him*?' I asked, losing the battle to remain calm and throwing up my hands in exasperation. 'He hasn't admitted his guilt and apologised, has he? So you can't be up for forgiving and forgetting.'

'I'm not,' she said, 'but I am up for not making a difficult and potentially damaging situation any worse than it already is. It does me no good to gain a reputation for being difficult to work with. I need to maintain networks and focus on avoiding any negative impact on my career. Cameron and I both know exactly what happened; he's nervous about that and that's enough for me.'

I stared at her, not knowing what to say in response. She had told me a week earlier that she admired Alison's career pragmatism but, until that moment, I hadn't realised that she shared it to quite such a degree.

'Besides,' she continued, 'I'll have a much better evening having not kicked off about him showing up for half an hour. I don't want to waste my last day on that kind of negativity. Plus, he'll have to buy me a drink, of course,' she added, now sounding less political and more like herself. 'Let's not forget that vital point. Obviously I'll be choosing the most expensive cocktail on the menu.' She winked at me and returned her attention to her lunch.

I looked down at the money still in my hand and then placed the note on the table, sliding it towards her. 'OK, but I genuinely don't want this,' I said quietly.

Ruby sighed. 'Him joining us is honestly the best decision all round, Edie,' she said, taking the money and returning it to her bag.

'If you're happy with it, then it's fine,' I shrugged.

She put down her fork. 'You know, you don't sound like you really mean that.'

I shook my head. 'I'd rather he wasn't coming, but I meant it when I said: your evening, your choice. I'm just amazed he wants to come. He didn't seem remotely keen last week.'

'Not turning up wouldn't look great for him, though, would it? He wants to win friends and influence people – to be seen as part of the team, *one of the lads*.' She tutted at the phrase and my heart sank at her use of it, as my sense of exclusion increased.

Dejection must have been plain on my face because she reached out and patted my hand.

'I'm sorry. I'm so grateful to be able to confide, but I feel like I keep making things worse for you,' she said gently. 'You were so happy about everything when you got back from your wonderful holiday, and so over the moon about getting the substation project. But now, with all this Cameron crap, and having to rent a room from your cousin, and Jason thinking you'll come running whenever he snaps his fingers, I feel like I've never seen you so low.'

I stared at her hand, resting on mine, and marvelled with dark fascination at the way in which she'd inadvertently managed to sum up my life in just a few, incredibly depressing, facts. Even in the immediate wake of Jason's betrayal and departure, I was pretty sure things hadn't felt this bad. At least then I'd had a sense of relief that I was escaping a deeply dysfunctional relationship. That, combined with the comfort and distraction of a career which I loved, meant that I had never entirely lost my sense of optimism. But right now, as I sat opposite Ruby and she gazed pityingly across the table at me, I realised that I couldn't envisage any escape from my current miserable situation any time soon, and that I had absolutely no sense of optimism whatsoever.

'Sometimes, I think I shouldn't have told you about Cameron,' she said guiltily. 'I keep asking myself whether I did it to protect you or to make myself feel better. I like to think I wanted to stop you finding yourself in the same situation as me, but I can't deny that it felt good to get it off my chest.'

I took a deep breath and attempted to pull myself together. 'Don't be silly, I'm grateful to you.'

'Really?' She sounded doubtful.

'Really,' I insisted. 'Ignorance isn't bliss with men like Cameron. And as for your leaving drinks, I understand your reasons and I can always take my bitterness to the other end of the table until he's gone. I'll sit next to Roger and let him explain to me, *again*, the difference between boules and bowls. That'll keep me out of trouble for half an hour at least.'

'Thanks, Edie,' she said quietly, sounding suddenly emotional.

I smiled. 'No problem, Ruby.'

We looked at each other for a moment and then she cleared her throat. 'Well, Roger will be over the moon to have your ear tonight and, as for Cameron, you're absolutely right,' she said briskly, stabbing a piece of chicken aggressively with her fork and raising it to her lips, 'you don't have to go anywhere near him.'

Chapter 7

'So there it is, Edie, the difference between rugby union and rugby league is as much a matter of class divide as it is of mauls and play-the-ball restarts,' said Roger, concluding his detailed account of the respective origins and rules of the two games and reaching for his beer.

I nodded thoughtfully, having been genuinely interested in his monologue, as well as extremely grateful for it. It had kept me fully occupied and engaged for the half hour he and I – along with Alison, Luke, Ruby and Cameron – had been sitting at a table in the expansive bar on Portwall Lane, which served some of Ruby's favourite cocktails.

We had adjourned there following fizz, light bites and gift-giving in Alison's office, during which time it hadn't proved difficult to avoid a one-to-one conversation with Cameron. And having managed to secure an, admittedly rather cramped, spot on a padded bench between Roger and Luke immediately on arrival at the bar, I felt pretty confident I wouldn't have to engage with Cameron there either. It was a situation which left me free to relax into Roger's sports history lecture, interrupted only by the occasional dig to my ribs from Luke, as he twisted in his seat to contribute his own sporting observations, which inevitably included numerous double entendres about ball size.

Thus, by the time the clock above the bar showed seven, I realised that, firstly, I was actually quite enjoying the evening, and secondly, I had managed to entirely avoid interacting with Cameron since switching off my desktop at 4:50 p.m.

'Can't deny I miss my rugby days,' Roger sighed. 'Now it's all golf and watching cricket.' He picked up his pint glass by the handle, lifting it to his lips and tipping it back, only to discover that it was in fact now empty. 'By, you knocked that back quickly, didn't you?' he murmured to himself.

'I'll get you another,' I said, standing up, only for him to place a gentle hand on my arm and ease me back down onto the bench.

'No need,' he said, gesturing up and over my shoulder. 'He's back with the round.'

At that, I turned to discover Cameron standing next to me, Luke having at some point moved to sit next to Alison on the other side of the table.

'Is there room for me here?' he asked rhetorically, lowering himself into the space vacated by Luke and simultaneously placing a crowded tray of drinks on the table in front of me. 'Gin and tonic,' he said, handing Alison a glass, 'cider for Luke, bitter for Roger...' He reached across me. 'Tall green thing with an umbrella...' The extraordinary-looking cocktail was passed down the table to Ruby, who received it with a 'ta' and the briefest of smirks in my direction. 'And I know you said you didn't want a drink, but you seem to have finished that one.' He gestured towards my all-but-empty glass, whilst placing a large white wine in front of me.

There followed a general murmur of gratitude which, after spotting Ruby looking at me anxiously, I was careful to echo. Then I turned to Roger, with a query about golf clubs at the ready, only to discover that he was now quizzing Ruby about the flat she was renting in Bath.

Aware that Luke's relocation to the other side of the table had been at least partly strategic, as he was now discussing his future career hopes with Alison in a low murmur, I realised, with a crushing sense of defeat, that there was no alternative but to talk to Cameron.

I glanced again at the clock above the bar and then down at the drink that he had just bought for himself: half a pint of beer. That was good. He clearly didn't intend to hang around for too much longer.

Picking up and drinking my wine as a delaying tactic, I racked my brains for any topic of conversation which wouldn't make me want to chuck it all over him and ruin Ruby's evening.

It wasn't easy. I quickly dismissed as too emotive any reference to Ruby's departure, or to how he was settling into the office, and I certainly didn't want to delve into his dodgy private life. But just as I felt my face beginning to break out in a soft sheen of social panic, he took the initiative.

'How's the substation going?' he asked, focusing determinedly on his beer. 'All plain sailing?'

I looked at Ruby, who widened her eyes at me over the top of her cocktail, as Roger turned the topic to the structural underpinning of Bath. I couldn't tell whether she was indicating boredom or attempting to signal a note of caution regarding Cameron, but I offered her what I hoped was a simultaneously sympathetic and reassuring smile and then turned to Cameron and said, 'The project has been trouble-free in terms of client relations. They've been enthusiastic about everything so far, but it's early days. As far as the build goes, it's the existing structure that's the challenge: new windows, lowered windows... We're digging down and going up as well, but obviously we want to keep it all as true to the art deco original as possible.'

He nodded. 'Maybe you could talk me through the plans at some point. When you're not so busy.'

I stiffened at the suggestion and offered a non-committal, 'Mm,' before adding, 'So what are you working on? Got your teeth into anything yet?'

'Two pitches last week and we just heard this afternoon that we got at least one of them,' he said, picking up his drink and saluting me with it.

I managed a smile, despite my irritation at his use of *we*, a pronoun which he no doubt thought wonderfully team-spirited and inclusive, but which for me was just another reminder that, professionally at least, I was currently bracketed with an aggressively entitled chauvinist.

'OK,' I said neutrally.

I felt his posture sag and, despite the circumstances, I couldn't entirely suppress the feeling that I wasn't being the best version of myself right now. My determined froideur towards him, no matter how justified, didn't feel like a particularly professional response to the situation.

'What was your last project before moving?' I asked, for no other reason than to avoid another awkward silence.

'Converting light industrial units to residential. It was made more interesting by the fact that the building was listed – like your substation.'

At that, innate curiosity superseded my reluctance to engage. 'Was that in London?'

'No. I haven't lived or worked in London for over ten years. Still got the accent, though,' he said, picking up his drink, and sipping it unhurriedly, 'which some people seem to find entertaining.'

Startled by the pointed add-on, my drink went down the wrong way and a choking fit ensued which drew the attention of the whole table, Ruby and Alison murmuring their concern, Luke letting out a delighted guffaw and Roger commencing thumping me with great enthusiasm between the shoulder blades.

'I'm fine, Roger,' I gasped, holding up a hand and twisting away from him. 'It was a drop of wine, not a brick.'

'Welcome,' he said.

Alison extended her arm across the table towards me. 'Can I get you some water, Edith?'

'Thanks, but I'm good,' I said, shaking my head and patting my chest. 'Honestly.'

She nodded her acceptance and then returned to her conversation with a still-grinning Luke. Cameron, meanwhile, was calmly drinking beer and gazing around the room, showing neither concern nor amusement over the coughing incident. In fact, he didn't even seem to have registered it. I looked at him and wrestled with whether to explain and apologise for the misunderstanding over his accent, or simply take advantage of the break in the conversation and move on.

I knew that in any other circumstances I would have laughed, apologised to him and started afresh. But the matter was rather complicated by the fact that he had recently groped a woman without her permission, and therefore saying sorry and starting afresh simply didn't seem to be an option in this case.

'I've forgotten what we were talking about,' I said, 'before I nearly asphyxiated.'

He hesitated before replying, and I wondered whether he was toying with pressing the mockney matter. I braced myself for the possibility.

'Work,' he said.

'Oh, yes,' I replied, grateful for his decision to move on, whilst simultaneously resenting the fact that I should feel grateful to him for anything. 'You said that the listed building project wasn't in London. So where was it?'

'Mind if I switch seats with you?'

I turned at the sound of Ruby's voice to find her looking down at Cameron and offering him a smile which appeared impressively genuine, if a little wobbly; the cocktails were clearly hitting home. 'I haven't had a chance to chat to Edie yet and,' she gestured at his leg which, thanks to his width and the limited length of the bench, was pressing against mine, 'you look like you could do with more room. You'd be better off on a chair, wouldn't you?'

I felt him shrink away from me as Roger leaned across to address him. 'We thick-sliced lads are making poor Edie the Spam in the sandwich,' he laughed. 'Sit there,' he continued, pointing across the table at the empty chair opposite. 'I want to talk to you about the warm-up game tomorrow.'

But Cameron checked his watch and stood up. 'Sorry, Roger, I have to go.'

Luke pulled a face. 'Nah. Stay a bit longer. I fancy that chat about the game too.'

Ruby took a slightly unsteady step backwards as Cameron edged out from behind the table. Then she lowered herself carefully down onto the vacated spot on the bench, placing a steadying hand on my shoulder as she did so. 'Roger's talking about rugby, Luke, not Fortnite,' she said.

'Seriously, Cam,' continued Luke, ignoring the dig, 'at least finish your half.'

I frowned at Luke and looked at Alison to see if she approved of his efforts to make Cameron stay, despite her agreement with Ruby that he wouldn't linger this evening. But her habitually tense expression gave nothing away.

Cameron walked around the table and retrieved his jacket from the back of Luke's chair. 'It's been great,' he said, 'but I didn't realise the time. I'm meeting a friend and I don't want to keep her waiting.'

'Oh, well, in that case,' said Roger, 'don't let us keep you from your lady-love.'

Cameron smiled. 'She doesn't quite fall into that category.'

I put my glass to my lips in order to hide a sneer, as I wondered into which of Cameron's grubby little categories this particular woman might fall.

'You enjoy her. Sorry, I mean enjoy *that*,' said Ruby, digging me hard with her elbow.

Cameron turned to her as he put on his coat. 'Thanks,' he said. 'And good luck in your new job.'

She offered him a pursed smile as she sucked on the long red straw in her cocktail. 'Cheers,' she said, clenching the straw between her teeth.

He looked at her for just a moment longer and then raised a hand to us all. 'I'll see the rest of you on Monday.'

My mood dipped further at the thought, as everyone said goodbye and then fell silent, watching as he made his way across the bar. He exited without looking back and, as he disappeared from view, I returned my attention to the table.

Ruby was now, once again, fully focused on her cocktail, apparently intent on downing the remainder of it in as short a time as possible. Alison, meanwhile, was busy relocating the delicate, silver-spiral brooch on her grey silk scarf, while Roger looked on, offering murmured advice on the process. And as for Luke, well, he remained turned in his chair, staring at the door via which Cameron had just left, with the air of a faithful hound, longing for the return of its master.

I leaned back on the bench and took a large gulp of wine, aware that, after a promising start, these were suddenly shaping up to be possibly *the* most personally depressing set of farewell drinks I had ever attended. I mean, I had expected to feel a bit down at the prospect of saying goodbye to Ruby, but right now, my glumness levels were fast approaching funereal and, on top of that, I was again battling a confusing sense of disappointment in myself. What's more, as I looked disconsolately around the table, I couldn't help thinking that there didn't seem to be anyone in the immediate vicinity particularly qualified to help me make sense of that.

Ruby signalled the end of her cocktail by loudly sucking up the remaining dregs through her straw and then placing the empty glass heavily on the table.

Luke started slightly and turned towards her. 'Still working towards AA membership, Ruby?'

She hiccoughed quietly. 'Still working towards your boy scout badge in basic, Luke?'

He laughed, but didn't seem quite as entertained by the banter as usual and offered no comeback.

I nudged Ruby and, for her sake, dug deep for some party spirit. 'How about another?' I asked, pointing to her empty glass.

She tipped her head sideways, resting it on my shoulder for a moment, while patting my hand. 'Lovely Edie. Lovely, lovely Edie,' she sighed. 'Isn't Edie lovely, Roger?' She leaned in front of me to gain sight of him.

'She is that,' said Roger. 'And it's grand of you to notice, Ruby, but I am wondering if your next drink shouldn't be a soft one, so as you can keep on noticing things and not black out.'

'Everybody thinks the world of you,' said Ruby, laying her head once again on my shoulder. 'Don't they, Alison? You do, don't you?'

Alison shifted awkwardly in her seat, clearly uncomfortable at the request for an insight into her personal feelings. 'Everyone thinks extremely highly of Edith.'

Luke leaned across the table towards me. 'Just for the record,' he whispered, 'I think you're great too but, more importantly, I'm seconding Roger's soft drink proposal. Not sure what was in that green thing, but...' He jerked his head sideways at Ruby and pulled a face.

'Lovely Edie. Always thinking the best of everybody...' she murmured.

'That's very true,' nodded Roger. 'Although there's some as might say that's a fool's trait.'

Alison frowned.

'But not me,' he added, supping his pint.

'Nice catch, Rog,' said Luke, winking. 'Think you got away with it.'

I laughed and rested my head against the top of Ruby's. 'You're going to have to sit up if I'm to get another round in.'

Roger rose to his feet. 'I'm getting these. You get the next lot, Edie. Same again, everybody?'

Alison held up her gin and tonic. 'Thank you, but I've barely touched mine, Roger.'

'No problem,' he said, edging his way from behind the table. 'I'll just get you a shot of gin. Have a gulp to make room for it in your glass. Luke? Apple juice for you again?'

Luke raised his glass. 'Cheers.'

'House white for you, Edie?' Roger pointed at my glass. 'No point in wasting money on fancy fluids when they all taste the same, is there? And what was that concoction you had, Ruby?'

I felt Ruby shrug against me. 'Dunno. I just picked the most expensive one.'

Roger's eyebrows twitched in mild horror. 'Well, let's try something else this time, as I'm not sure that kind of cocktail agrees with you.'

'Or with Roger's wallet,' murmured Luke.

Roger said nothing but delivered a light cuff to the back of Luke's head as he passed, which prompted a number of hair-related protests from Luke, and a decision to retire to the loo to fix the damage.

Alison too, rose from her seat. 'I'll go and help him with those drinks and hopefully persuade him against buying that gin for me,' she said, walking away.

I watched her go. 'They're a nice bunch.'

Ruby heaved a sigh and sat up. 'I know,' she said, a little sleepily. 'Just a shame about Ca—'

She stopped abruptly, making a valiant attempt to censor her own negativity, despite an obvious blurring of brain function.

'About…?' I raised my eyebrows questioningly.

'Just a shame about the evening going so fast,' she said.

My initial thought was that the real shame was that Luke wasn't around to congratulate Ruby on the nice catch, but I just smiled and let her brave, but hopelessly inadequate, attempt at a cover-up go.

'Yes, but the good news,' I said, gesturing towards Roger, who was at that moment looking appalled as the barman placed a sparkler in Ruby's next cocktail and held a lighter to it, 'is that it's not over yet.'

Chapter 8

'Giles?'

Giles and I turned towards the small voice to see Harry standing on the road next to the open rear doors of the rental van, hired to transport my possessions from Harbourside to Henleaze. He was wearing a red and gold bodice and knee-length blue swim-shorts, over a black T-shirt and jeans. In his left hand, he carried a skipping rope.

'Good morning, Harry,' said Giles, appearing impressively unfazed by his young neighbour's attire. 'How can we help you?' He put down the plastic crate of shoes he was holding and straightened up as much as was possible in the cramped interior of the van.

'Your door is open,' said Harry, pointing to his right.

'Yes, that's because Edie and I are moving all her belongings into the house today,' said Giles. 'You've met Edie before, haven't you?' he added, smiling. 'She's going to be your new neighbour.'

Harry looked at me and nodded shyly.

'Hi,' I said. 'I like your costume. And your rope. Have you been exercising?'

Harry looked at the skipping rope. 'It's the Lasso of Truth. If I put it round you, you have to tell the truth.'

'How absolutely marvellous,' said Giles. 'I think we should all have one of those and wear them constantly. It would remove so much daily confusion and uncertainty.'

Harry looked both confused and uncertain for a moment and then, clearly keen to spare himself any further philosophical ramblings from Giles, he cut to the chase.

'Can I go in your house and get a biscuit from the jar with a fox on it?'

Giles laughed. 'Of course. You know where it is; help yourself,' he said, bending again towards the crate of shoes, before quickly looking up and adding, 'Oh, but do ask your mother first. We don't want to upset her.'

Harry looked down, shifting from foot to foot. 'I've asked her,' he murmured, 'and she said I could have one. Or five.'

Giles rubbed his chin thoughtfully. 'Is that right? Well, I suppose it must be, because I'm assuming that it would be impossible for you to tell a lie whilst holding the Lasso of Truth.'

Harry gazed at the skipping rope for a moment, and then reached through the open doors of the van, placing it carefully on the floor. 'She did say that,' he said softly.

'Off you go and fetch a biscuit then,' said Giles. 'Just one for now, and then maybe have some more later. Don't let Anthony out of the utility room though, will you?'

'No,' said Harry and, after grabbing his rope, was gone.

I looked at Giles and shook my head.

'What can I say, Edie?' he sighed. 'He's just too cunning for me.'

I smiled and then pointed at the crate. 'I'm taking that. You bring the bag of jumpers. I'm worried about all the heavy lifting you've done this morning.'

'I haven't lifted anything particularly heavy; I just make things *appear* heavy because I'm so very unfit.' He tilted his head upwards and stroked his neck. 'Do you know, I was horrified to spot the unmistakable beginnings of a double chin this morning. A double chin! At my age! My father didn't get one of those until he was sixty. I'm thinking of hiring a personal trainer.'

I gave him a playful shove. 'You are not.'

'You see,' he winced, rubbing his shoulder, 'I could never muster anywhere near the upper body strength which you have just exhibited. And besides, Tubby's passing has given me much food for thought regarding my eating, drinking and couch-potato tendencies.'

'You're seriously going to hire a personal trainer?'

'Well, I've got to do something,' he said. 'I may be thirty-six, but this body looks well on its way to fifty. Look at all this excess flesh,' he continued, pulling at his cheeks. 'My early-morning look is that of a man whose face has been kneaded by a crazed baker.'

I was about to shove him again but stopped myself.

'Well, I always think you look great,' I said. 'Not that I want to put you off getting fit, but you certainly have nothing to worry about in the looks department: thick hair; bright eyes; great teeth.'

He held up a hand. 'I know you're trying to help, Edie, but you are simply describing the characteristics of an averagely healthy dog, so best stop there. Now, let me take this,' he said, reaching for the crate of shoes. 'It's a tiny step on the long road to fitness.'

He picked up the crate with a grunt and, hunching slightly, made his way to the end of the van before stepping out and disappearing from view. I looked around at the dwindling number of boxes and bags, picked up the jumpers and some books, and then followed.

I emerged into the warm July sunshine of the avenue to discover that Giles had made very little progress and was now chatting with Kerry at the foot of her path, a sheepish-looking Harry at her side.

'So you see,' Giles was saying, 'it's entirely my fault. I saw him and I said, "Harry, would you like to come into my house for some biscuits?" He really didn't want to, but I insisted.'

I frowned, slightly concerned at the picture Giles was painting of himself as a man who attempted to lure small children into his home on the promise of baked goods, and who wouldn't take no for an answer.

Kerry turned as I approached, her face transforming from stern to warmly welcoming in a flash. 'Edie!' she exclaimed. 'I thought you were indoors. Great to see you again. And you're moving in! Brilliant.'

I smiled and put down my bag of jumpers. 'Yes, poor Giles has been exhausting himself helping me.'

'It's OK,' she said. 'Cos he's just taken a breather to feed me a load of…' She hesitated, looked down at Harry and took a deep breath. 'He's just been telling me that it was all his idea that Harry should help himself to biscuits. Apparently, Harry had nothing to do with it.'

Harry's head, already hanging, drooped a little lower. Giles, meanwhile, looked up at the cloudless sky. 'You've got to admit that it is a lovely day for a biscuit, though, Kerry,' he said.

She looked at him for a moment and then laughingly shook her head. 'I dunno, Giles,' she sighed, looking down and ruffling Harry's hair. 'Harry, what do you say to Giles for asking to go into his house before you're invited? And for asking for biscuits before they're offered?'

'Sorry,' murmured Harry, reaching into the pockets of his swim-shorts and removing two large handfuls of crumbs. He held them out towards Giles. 'Here.'

'Give me strength,' muttered Kerry, before continuing more loudly, 'Giles can't eat those now, can he? He'd need a spoon. Go and scatter them in the front garden for the birds and then wash your hands. But you're not to ask for biscuits again, Harry Baker. Wait to be offered.'

He nodded up at her and then walked slowly away, a perfect picture of penitence as he scattered his fistfuls of crumbs, like ashes after a cremation, and disappeared into the house.

Kerry watched him go and then rolled her eyes. 'Sorry about that,' she said. 'One minute he was playing in the lounge, the next he was gone.' She looked towards her open front door. 'I'm gonna have to have a serious chat with him.'

'He's just curious,' said Giles.

'That's one word for it,' she said, glancing across the road. 'Oh look, here comes June.'

I turned to look as the sea-green front door of the house directly opposite opened and a small, slightly stooped, elderly woman emerged. Despite the warmth of the day, she was wearing a beige trench coat and light-brown hat, and was wrestling a blue tartan shopping trolley down the single step onto her garden path.

'You all right there, June?' called Kerry. 'Need a hand?'

June looked up, apparently confused for a moment before spotting Kerry. 'Oh, there you are!' she said, smiling broadly and waving. 'Didn't see you at first in between that white van and your little red car.'

She made her way to the edge of the pavement, looking both ways to check the road for traffic. 'Be careful, June, because they race down here,' she said, stepping out and walking towards us. 'That's it. Carefully does it.'

Kerry gave me a sidelong glance. 'June has a tendency to think aloud,' she explained quietly, her mouth barely moving, 'a lot.'

'I think I'm just going to pop this down on the wall for a moment,' murmured Giles, lowering the crate, 'because June doesn't do brevity.'

'Well, good morning, everyone,' said June cheerily on arrival, looking first at Kerry and then at Giles, before finally affixing me with a prolonged, but not unfriendly, stare.

'Well, I wonder who this is,' she said.

I smiled down at her, forcing myself to maintain eye contact and not be distracted by the 'hat', which I now realised was, in fact, a shortish wig, worn at a rather jaunty angle and therefore affording only about eighty per cent coverage of the snow-white hair beneath it.

'This is Edith, June,' said Giles, placing an arm around my shoulders and giving me a squeeze. 'She's moving in today.'

'In with *you*? Into *your* house, Giles?' June let go of her trolley and clapped her hands together in obvious delight, beaming as she looked me up and down. 'Look at those big brown eyes and button nose – like a doll. Lovely. Even in those clothes and with that hair.'

On balance, I was rather pleased with the compliment, but still unable to resist checking my red T-shirt and yellow shorts for stains, whilst tucking various loose strands of unwashed hair back into my ponytail.

'How lovely! I always knew that you would find your-self a young lady-friend one day, Giles,' said June. 'And there was everyone else insisting that he didn't want a young *lady*-friend,' she continued, at barely reduced volume.

Unwilling to look at either Giles or Kerry, and refusing to dwell on June's unmistakable emphasis on the feminine noun, I said, 'Giles and I are cousins. He's kindly said that I can stay with him while I look for somewhere to buy.'

June's face fell. 'Cousins?'

Kerry put a hand on her arm. 'Step-cousins, to be precise, June. Isn't that right, Giles?'

'Quite right,' he beamed.

'Sorry, I always say cousin,' I chipped in, 'but we're not actually related. My aunty was Giles's stepmum.'

June nodded along, looking at each of us in turn. 'Not actually related,' she echoed.

'That's right,' said Giles.

'Good, good,' she murmured. 'Nothing against nature.'

I looked at Giles. He had gone decidedly pink.

'Getting anything nice at the shops, June?' asked Kerry brightly.

'Brazil nuts and avocados,' she replied. 'Doctor McMasters wants me to put on some weight, but she doesn't want me eating too many cakes.'

'Ooh, I do love an avocado,' said Kerry. 'Nice in a salad, or you can smush it up and have it with a poached egg and bacon on toast for breakfast. Lovely.'

June adjusted her wig with two hands and zero self-consciousness. 'Sounds delicious. I shall have that for my breakfast tomorrow.' She returned her gaze to me once more and I braced myself for whatever new thought she might be about to articulate.

'Well, June,' said Kerry, 'we had better let Giles and Edie get on with getting on, hadn't we?'

June started slightly, as if waking from a dream. 'Oh yes. Yes, indeed we must.' She smiled up at me. 'It's so lovely to meet you, Edith, and welcome to the avenue,' she said, taking hold of her shopping trolley and making as if to leave.

'Lovely to meet you too,' I replied. 'Hope to see you again soon.'

At that, she stopped short and turned, resting her hand thoughtfully against her chin. 'What about the wine and cheese?' she asked. 'I do hope you will be coming along *with Giles.*' She paused, looking from myself to Giles. 'It's at my house, on Friday 17 August, at 7:30 p.m.'

'Well, I'm not sure,' I said, taken by surprise. 'What a very kind invitation. That sounds lovely. I'll check if I'm free.'

June nodded. 'And I'll be sure to call round on the night to remind you.'

'Ooh,' I said, attempting a smile, 'that's very…' I hesitated and turned to Giles, 'thorough of you. Will you be going, Giles?'

'Yes, I will be there,' he replied solemnly, now looking pained as well as pink.

'Great,' I said, trying not to sound too disappointed, but aware that Giles's reaction was more that of a man confirming his attendance at a murder trial than a drinks party.

'Yes,' said June, clapping her hands lightly, 'and you can come along on his arm, Edith, and then everyone will see that he isn't—'

'Are you getting your avocados from the veg shop or Waitrose, June?' asked Kerry.

June looked at her blankly, clearly requiring a moment to compute the swift change of topic from Giles's sexual preferences to fruit and veg. 'Greengrocer,' she said eventually. 'They're certain to be cheaper.'

'Bound to be,' agreed Kerry. 'I get all my veg there.'

'Very wise of you, dear.' June patted Kerry's arm and then, after briefly taking my hand and Giles's in her own and pressing them together, she reached for her shopping trolley once more and walked slowly away in the direction of the High Street. I, meanwhile, made a mental note to tell Luke on Monday that I knew someone very attractive, and under forty, who shopped in the Henleaze veg shop.

'Well, that's you two married off then,' said Kerry.

I laughed a little awkwardly, while Giles tutted and picked up the crate of shoes. 'Good to know that the entire neighbourhood has been debating my sexuality for the past two years.'

'They're just confused by your new-man sensitivity,' said Kerry. 'They can't relate, that's all. Anyway,' she sighed, placing her hands on her hips, 'as I'm out here, can I do anything?'

'Thanks,' I smiled, 'but we're almost done, I think.'

'Well, if you're sure,' she said. 'But if I can't help you now, how about coming round for a drink tonight once you've finished unpacking?'

'That would be absolutely smashing. Thank you!' exclaimed Giles, his colour deepening further under the weight of my shoes.

I pictured my laptop sitting unopened on my bed and the column of unanswered emails which had been growing in length throughout Friday while I'd been at home packing.

'Edie?' Giles looked at me questioningly.

'Sorry, yes, that's so kind, Kerry. So long as you're not changing any plans for us,' I said, reassuring myself that Sunday would be free from well-meant neighbourly invites, and mine to schedule.

'I'll be grateful for the adult company,' she said, turning and walking up her path. 'Shall we say eight, then? Don't bring anything – just yourselves – and if you're lucky, I'll crack open some crisps.'

Chapter 9

Later that evening, I pushed the one suitcase I hadn't yet finished unpacking under my double bed, before flopping down on said bed and surveying my new room.

Giles being Giles, he had given me the pick of all the bedrooms, including his own – a genuine offer which had caused me to roll my eyes, tell him what an idiot he was and love him more than ever. In the end, I had generously opted not to turf him out of his bedroom, instead requesting the third-floor room, which had a rather lovely view of almost the entire avenue. The choice also enabled Giles to retain as much privacy as possible on the floor below.

What I hadn't expected, and what I discovered only on moving-in day, was that Giles had cleared the top-floor box room – which had, up until then, served as storage space in a house with no loft – and had installed a desk and shelving, thus presenting me with my very own study.

It couldn't, I told Giles, have been more perfect. And while in other circumstances, I might have found the transition from sole occupier of a newbuild Harbourside flat to lodger in a shared Victorian house a depressing or demoralising one, I actually felt completely at peace about it. What's more, I realised that, thanks to Giles, I had a sense of being domestically appreciated for the first time since my split from Jason.

'Edie!' called Giles. 'Just to let you know that we are due at Kerry's very shortly!'

'Coming!' Hauling myself off the bed, I made my way down two flights of stairs to find him waiting for me in the hallway, coat on and checking his reflection in the large, circular mirror which hung on the wall next to the vestibule. Anthony was stretched out across his feet, a habitual and occasionally successful tactic, employed to encourage Giles to take him with him whenever he went out.

'Sorry,' I said. 'I'd have been ready ages ago but these jeans were in the only bag I hadn't unpacked. I've also put my phone down somewhere, so I lost track of time a bit. I plugged it in to charge after lunch, but can't remember where. I'm just not used to so many room and socket options.'

Giles continued to gaze into the mirror, running a hand through his hair and then pulling a foppish wave or two to one side. 'We're fine. It's only just gone eight and your phone is in the kitchen – by the wine rack,' he murmured, without turning round. 'Oh and can you grab a bottle to take to Kerry's while you're there?'

'Will do.' I squeezed past him, heading for the kitchen. 'And don't worry, you look beautiful,' I added, entertained by the uncharacteristic interest he was taking in his appearance.

He didn't reply and when I returned with my phone and the wine a minute later, he was still staring at his reflection, although now somewhat disconsolately, I thought.

'Something the matter?' I asked.

He shook his head. 'No, no, it's just what we were talking about this morning. I really must lose some weight and sort myself out in general.'

I placed a concerned hand on his shoulder. 'Is this all because of Tubby?'

'In part,' he acknowledged, attempting to turn to face me and shuffling his feet awkwardly under the deadweight of Anthony as he did so. 'But I have to admit that there's also a little bit of vanity involved.' He tugged at his waxed jacket. 'I discovered yesterday that my nickname amongst the current cohort of students is Farmer Giles, and God only knows how the neighbours see me.'

'Oh, come on,' I laughed, handing him the bottle of wine. 'You're not upset because June thought you were gay, are you? Some of the most stylish and attractive men in the world are gay. It's actually a huge compliment.'

He looked at me blankly. 'I believe June is the one person in the avenue who *doesn't* think I'm gay.'

I thought for a moment. 'Oh yes, sorry, it's everyone else, isn't it?'

'It is.'

'Well, then!' I exclaimed. 'That's an even bigger compliment!'

He heaved a sigh. 'Yes, I suppose it is,' he said wearily. 'Thank you for helping me to see the uplifting truth of the matter, Edie.'

I nudged him. 'Are you regretting inviting me to come and live with you?'

He nodded vigorously. 'Not one iota of regret.'

I laughed again and gave him a gentle shake. 'Honestly, Giles, if I thought you were even slightly unattractive, I'd tell you.'

'You wouldn't.'

'I know. But you're not, so it's not an issue. And before you say anything, we all know that that's not just my opinion,' I continued, my hands still on his shoulders. 'It's not like you've ever been stuck for a girlfriend, is it? And not a dud one amongst them. All very gorgeous.'

I smiled up at him, secure in the knowledge that there was not a word of a lie in my pep talk. He had dated some very attractive women over the years, albeit all of a very definite type.

'They're always English roses,' my Aunty Isobel had sighed, during one of my last visits to her Cotswold home, before she passed away. 'The women he's drawn to are just so delicate, aren't they? Wouldn't-say-boo-to-a-goose types. I often wonder if he needs someone to challenge him, shake him up a bit, take him out of his comfort zone. What do you think, Edie?'

I hadn't thought much at the time, being far more concerned with my aunt's increasing frailty than with Giles's love life, as she succumbed to the cancer which had stalked her for so long. But now, as I stood looking up at him, I gave some consideration to the subject. As far as I was aware, he hadn't dated anyone – boo-to-a-goose types or otherwise – since moving to Bristol, and that did seem a bit odd.

He could, I supposed, be still hung up on Polly, his most recent girlfriend. They had split amicably, and remained good friends, when he had relocated from London. So it wasn't impossible that she might be behind his apparent lack of interest in finding a new special someone.

'How's Polly?' I asked.

Giles's response was to close his eyes very slowly, as if in mild despair. 'I'm not pining for Polly, Edie,' he said patiently. 'My mood is dampened only by my increasing resemblance to the man in the moon.'

Deciding not to pry further, I instead gave him a second shake. 'Well, snap out of it, because we're off out on the razz.'

He opened his eyes, smiling down first at me and then at Anthony. 'I don't think Kerry would mind if we took him along.'

Anthony looked up, as if sensing victory, before licking Giles's face, as the latter crouched to scoop him up.

'Oh God, Giles, that's *sooo* disgusting,' I said, making a retching noise and reaching into my bag on the end of the bannister. 'Personal hygiene is just as important as personal appearance, you know.' I took out a packet of wet wipes, removed one from the packet and rubbed his left cheek. 'What will Kerry think when she kisses you hello?'

He screwed up his face as I continued to scrub. 'It's OK,' he said, 'she's not a kisser. Oh, except when it comes to her good friend, Ronald. I've noticed that he always gets a peck and a *very* warm embrace.'

'Ooh,' I said, ceasing wiping and sensing gossip. 'Who's Ronald?'

'He's a friend of Kerry's,' he said, tucking Anthony under one arm and gesturing me towards the vestibule with the wine bottle. 'An architect, actually.'

'An architect? I might know him – or his firm. I know a Ron Chorlton.'

'I don't know his surname.'

'Well, what does he look like?'

Giles adjusted his hold on Anthony and shrugged. 'Just your typical alpha male: tall; broad; toned; strong jawline. Doesn't look at all like a Ronald, actually.'

I blinked. 'God, I don't know any architects who fit that description – but I wouldn't mind an introduction to one,' I laughed.

He didn't join in. 'You won't know him. He's not Bristol-based,' he said. 'He's with a firm in the Midlands somewhere. Birmingham maybe? I forget where Kerry said,' he continued, now applying gentle pressure to my back to ease me towards the front door. 'But I'm sure she'll be delighted to apprise you of all his particulars and I have little doubt that he'll come up. He usually does.'

———

Kerry, it turned out, had done rather more than open a bag of crisps. We arrived to find blini, crostini, olives and various crisps and dips waiting for us on a large coffee table in her front room, as well as a bottle of Prosecco, chilling in a blue plastic mixing bowl full of ice.

'There's beer too,' she said, as she ushered me into the living room. 'I just got fizzy stuff 'cos I thought you should celebrate moving in.'

'I'd love some,' I said, looking around the room, which was tidier than, but just as determinedly child-focused as, the dining room, with naïve clay creations and framed poster-paint artwork crowding out more traditional ornaments and pictures. Photos of Harry, from newborn to the present day, were dotted around the room, many of them, I noticed, featuring his father as well as Kerry.

'Anthony has curled up in the kitchen,' said Giles, entering from the hallway.

'He can come in here with us if he wants,' offered Kerry.

He shook his head. 'He's happy just to be in an occupied house. And I really don't want to risk him scoffing any of this delicious–looking fare,' he said, gesturing towards the table. 'This really is so very kind of you, Kerry.'

'It's nothing,' she said, dismissively. 'Have a seat while I sort you a drink.'

We sat down on a throw-strewn sofa, and I watched as she began to twist the cork, before shouting, 'Yay!' to applause from Giles as it finally popped.

As she smiled and poured three glasses, I thought again what an attractive woman she was. She was pretty even when dressed in sweats and wearing no make-up, but this evening, she had swapped the grey T-shirt and black yoga pants of the morning for a tea dress, patterned with small red and yellow flowers. She was also carrying off some startlingly bold red lipstick, which complemented her generous mouth and her energetic personality brilliantly. In short, she looked lovely in an undeniably striking kind of way, and I felt touched that she considered our visit occasion enough to dress up a little.

I thanked her as she handed me a glass. 'This is a great way to end moving-in day.'

'You all settled in, then?' she asked.

'I am. I'm on the top floor and I love it already.'

She nodded and sat down on one of two aged, beige velvet armchairs positioned in the bay, the seat cushions of which were balding and indented with use. 'I love my top floor too,' she said. 'We have a bit of a no-toys rule up there, so whenever I can't face the chaos down here at the end of the day, I run up with a glass of wine, flop down on the beanbag in the front bedroom and pretend the rest of the house is just as tidy.' She raised her glass of Prosecco and took a gulp. 'Works a treat.'

'I never ventured up there much, truth to tell,' said Giles. 'So it's wonderful that it's now being put to use. Why ever didn't I suggest you moving in months ago, Edie? As soon as you and Jason...' He hesitated awkwardly, clearly deciding that he had said too much.

Kerry looked at me over her glass and raised an entertained eyebrow.

'Jason is my ex,' I explained. 'We split up two years ago in October, sold our home in Hotwells and I've been renting in Harbourside ever since. I came close to buying a place in March, but the sale fell through when the owner decided he didn't want to sell after all.'

'House-buying is a bugger,' said Kerry grimly. 'We were so lucky to land this place, even if it was moth-infested and falling down. Still is falling down, for that matter.' She pointed to a narrow but lengthy gap between one of the window frames and the wall, which I now saw had been plugged with newspaper.

'Kitchen plans still going ahead?' asked Giles, sipping his drink and leaning forward to scoop up a blini.

'Yeah,' she replied. 'We've worked out what I can afford and it's all sorted, but the work won't start till next Spring. I don't mind the delay. I didn't fancy the idea of being roofless at Christmas and it gives me a chance to save up a little bit more.'

'What are you having done?' I asked.

'Not a lot,' she said, 'because I can't stretch to a lot, but it'll make a big difference. We're knocking through from the dining room and there'll be a lot more glass, so it'll be lighter. I'll have to show you the plans sometime so you can give me your expert opinion.'

'Edie is a wonderful architect,' said Giles, with heart-warming pride.

'I must introduce her to my Ron,' said Kerry, nodding.

'Ah yes,' he replied, his elbow digging into me lest the significance of the reference pass me by.

'He's coming to June's wine and cheese,' said Kerry.

Giles's eyebrows shot up in surprise. 'Out of choice?'

'He had a chance to get us some cheap tickets for something,' explained Kerry, 'but I told him I couldn't miss June's, so he said he'd come along – if it was OK with her.'

'It'll be super to meet him properly,' said Giles, picking up a cocktail stick and skewering an olive. 'I've only spoken to him in passing a few times to date, Edie, but he seems like an all-round nice chap. I'm sure the two of you will have lots to talk about.'

I shifted a little in my seat. 'Well, I'm not sure I can actually make it yet, Giles. I must check my diary.'

'Oh, of course, of course. I know what a busy work and social life you have, and the wine and cheese evenings do tend to be a little elderly. You mustn't feel under any obligation to come.'

He smiled reassuringly, whilst sounding a little deflated, and I felt suddenly guilty that my lack of enthusiasm for hanging out with his geriatric neighbour might be to blame for that. Giles, along with June and Kerry, had gone to an awful lot of trouble to make me feel welcome that day. The least I could do was appear grateful.

'Actually, I could check right now,' I said, taking my phone from the back pocket of my jeans. 'It was the seventeenth, wasn't it? And yes, I'm free!'

'Marvellous,' said Giles, now grinning broadly. 'June will be over the moon.'

'I just hope that I don't feel like too much of an interloper on the night,' I said.

Kerry took another large gulp of wine. 'Ron's an inter-loper but you're not. You're a resident. So you'd better get your speech ready.'

I laughed, but stopped short when I realised that neither Kerry nor Giles was joining in.

Giles gave Kerry a sidelong glance before returning his attention to the table. 'Hadn't actually planned on mentioning that just yet,' he murmured, his lips barely moving.

'Ooh,' she said, her face falling. 'Sorry.'

I laughed again. 'Stop winding me up.'

'So are you going for grey-green or grey-blue kitchen units?' asked Giles.

I held up a hand. 'Whoa, just a minute,' I said, turning to him. 'What's with the rapid subject change? Am I seriously expected to make a speech?'

He hesitated for a moment and then shook his head. 'Well... no... not as such.'

'Not *as such*?'

'All it is—'

'Oh my God, I have to make a speech.'

Kerry shook her head. 'Nah – it's nothing. Honest. I swear to God, mine was three sentences long. Besides, everyone's so pissed that no one cares or remembers. The ones without kids to get up for the next day are the worst. Like Patrick. He downs a beer a minute. And Stella's always out of her box by nine and heads home across the back walls.'

'Kerry's right,' said Giles 'It's all a bit of a blur for most of them and a fair few of them are totally deaf to start with anyway.'

'Across the back walls?' I queried, my horror at the thought of having to give a speech, for the moment supplanted by curiosity regarding Stella.

Kerry leaned in for a breadstick. 'The first time she did it, it was for a bet, but now it's her *thing*. She even left the back way when I had it here, didn't she, Giles? She lives on the other side of the road, Edie, so that was *really* weird.'

'You know you're quite right, she did, Kerry,' he agreed. 'Do you remember that I found one of her clogs in my roses?'

'Yep.'

I looked at Giles and my expression must have registered some concern.

'Oh don't worry. She's a retired PE teacher, very physically fit and has, to date, sustained no injuries,' he said happily, saluting both Kerry and myself with his glass.

'You know, I bet you and Ron will be talking shop all night,' said Kerry, prompting Giles to elbow me for a second time. 'I'm sure you'll get on. He's a brilliant architect and really into his work.'

Giles emitted a strange sound; part sigh, part cough.

'Did you meet him through work, Kerry?' I asked, keen to discover more about the potential new contact. Maybe Ron and his connections could be the answer to my professional prayers.

She shook her head. 'I work part-time, doing admin and reception at Warwicks.' She gestured towards the window. 'They're the solicitors on the High Street. Before Harry, I was in insurance, but I don't miss it. It wasn't exactly a laugh a minute.'

'So how did you meet Ron?' I persisted, determined not to be sidetracked.

'He's Mark's friend from way back,' she began, before pausing, obviously noting my confused expression. 'Mark was my partner. We lost him three years ago. Sorry, I thought Giles might have filled you in.'

'I mentioned to Edie that Harry had lost his father,' said Giles quietly. 'But that was all.'

Kerry smiled sadly. 'Well, Mark and Ron were friends for almost thirty years. I met Ron ten years ago, when I first started seeing Mark. Since Mark passed, Ron's been great – really supportive. He's fab with Harry and he's practical too, which is a bonus when you've got a house like this. I don't know what we'd do without him, really,' she finished quietly.

Giles cleared his throat. 'I wonder if you and he know any of the same people, Edie.'

'I'd put money on a ten-minute chat at work throwing up some connection.'

'Hey now, the last time I saw you,' said Kerry, smiling mischievously at me, 'it sounded like there might be something dodgy brewing in your office.'

'Did it?' I asked, my willingness to share gossip about the practice, even in vague terms, significantly lessened by the discovery that one of Kerry's best friends was an architect. 'I think maybe I was feeling a bit low about a friend leaving. I knew I was going to miss her.'

'Ah, that's a shame. Were you very close?'

'Yes, we joined the practice at around the same time, so we found our feet together, which was definitely a bonding experience. And it was nice to have a woman in the office I could confide in.'

She nodded sympathetically. 'What about the blokes you work with? Can you offload onto them?'

'Oh yes, they're really kind and supportive. It's all fine, honestly,' I added hurriedly.

'OK,' she said, with undisguised scepticism.

'Brace yourself,' said Giles, nudging me. 'She'll be reaching for the thumbscrews.'

'Well, if there is a pair of thumbscrews available, I'd love to use them on you some time, Giles,' I said, determinedly shifting the focus. 'Trying to get anything out of you is impossible.'

'Really? I always think of myself as an open book,' he replied, sounding a little hurt.

'You're a closed book and your pages are stuck together with superglue,' I insisted. 'You didn't tell anyone about being mugged in Hyde Park, or about having your appendix out, and we only found out about your house fire when Aunty Isobel asked if you still had a spare telly and you told her that it had melted.'

'What?' exclaimed Kerry.

'Small blaze, minimal damage,' said Giles airily.

I looked at Kerry. 'Closed book.'

She laughed. 'That's OK, I love a challenge. And, with loosening tongues in mind,' she said, reaching for the wine bottle and topping up my glass, 'get that down you. You'll need to spend the next month building up your tolerance if you're going to survive June's wine and cheese.'

'I'm looking forward to it, and to talking shop with Ron,' I smiled, leaning back into the sofa and stretching out my legs as the bubbles began to work their magic on my moving-in-day muscle fatigue. 'And to seeing Stella scale a wall. I really hope she's there.'

'Well, I wouldn't worry,' said Kerry, refilling her own glass and raising it towards me in a brief salute before necking half of it, 'because even if she isn't, something else'll kick off. It always does.'

Chapter 10

I hadn't been stretching the truth too much when I told Kerry that everything at work was fine. Because the fact of the matter was that very nearly everything had been fine in the weeks following Ruby's departure, with most things continuing just as before. Luke's sarcasm and hair were still firmly in place, Roger was still the dry-stone-wall voice of rock-solid reason and Alison still toiled, and intermittently enquired after our well-being, with her habitual lack of visible emotion.

The only obvious changes to the office environment were, therefore, Ruby and Cameron; Ruby because she simply wasn't there and Cameron because he was increasingly relaxed and upbeat.

I had detected the first whiff of change on the very first Monday after Ruby left, when I had walked past his desk on my way to lunch and caught him quietly humming 'Mr Brightside' as he sat, phone pressed to his ear, waiting for someone to pick up. He had stopped abruptly as I crossed his field of vision, but I had heard the humming start up again as I headed out of the office and into the corridor.

Just over two months post-Ruby and the character change was no longer a whiff but an unmistakeable stench. The tense, taciturn, shirt-strangled hulk in the corner was no more, having been replaced by an occasional T-shirt wearer, who oozed bonhomie and walked with a relaxed spring in his step. Of course, the transformation could have been attributable simply to settling in and having proved his worth. But personally, I had no doubt whatsoever that the rapid shift in his demeanour had more to do with relief at the departure of Ruby, his thorn-in-the-side accuser.

Luke and Roger seemed more than willing to take his altered work persona at face value, and I tried not to resent them for that, making a conscious effort to divorce my relationship with them – and with Alison – from their relationship with him. After all, Cameron was, on the surface, a supportive and amiable team player, and I was desperate to give Luke and Roger the benefit of the doubt that they knew nothing of how he had behaved towards Ruby.

As for Alison, I could see how, by applying her usual dispassionate, entirely professional approach to the matter, she would be able to maintain both a clear conscience and a highly effective working relationship with Cameron, untroubled by doubts as to whether or not the incident with Ruby had been a genuine misunderstanding. Moreover, when Ruby had declared that she didn't wish to pursue the matter, Alison would no doubt have simply accepted that decision on the basis that, firstly, it was Ruby's to make and, secondly, that it was impossible for her to categorically determine what had actually gone on between them.

And I might have been able to adopt the same approach as Alison, had I merely been Ruby's colleague, and not her friend. However, *as* her friend, I had no trouble whatsoever in determining what had gone on and consequently I didn't want to be any closer to Cameron Grange, either ʉratively or literally, than I absolutely had to be. I didn't seek his professional opinion, I didn't go for drinks if I knew he would be there and, whenever he tried to talk to me about any subject other than work, I kept my answers brief and closed-ended.

If my other colleagues noticed this reluctance to engage, they didn't mention it, and my relationships with them continued much as they always had. So yes, I hadn't told Kerry a barefaced lie; work was largely fine, with Luke, Roger and Alison, plus the enjoyable challenges of the job that I loved, providing me with a welcome daily distraction from the loss of Ruby, and the presence of her far-from-satisfactory replacement.

It was upon precisely these positives that I was reflecting while sitting at my desk one Friday evening, about a month after moving to Henleaze, when I was disturbed by Cameron saying goodnight. I had, until that moment, been in a perfectly good mood, having just received a text from Giles, reminding me not to work too late because we were going to June and Stan's that evening. I had smiled at the thought. OK, so it might not be an evening of cocktails or haute cuisine, but I was interested in putting some faces to names and genuinely looking forward to meeting, and swapping business cards with, Kerry's architect friend.

I glanced up and raised a hand to Cameron, affording him as little time and attention as possible, before fishing a Twix from my top drawer, with a view to redressing the mildly negative impact a renewed awareness of my creepy colleague had had on my mood. I then returned my atten-tion to my phone as it pinged, heralding the arrival of another text, this time from Ruby. Cameron, meanwhile, moved on to Luke – the only other person still in the office – from whom he elicited a much more enthusiastic and longer-winded response than he'd received from me, as the pair of them began to compare weekend notes.

I remained determinedly focused on my phone and reminded myself, yet again, that it wasn't Luke's fault that he didn't know Cameron was a bastard.

Ruby was as upbeat as usual in her text; her new job was still great, her new colleagues were still great, and Bath was still great.

Great.

I leaned an elbow on my desk and rested my chin heavily on my hand as I munched on my Twix and read through the rest of her one-hundred-per-cent positive update. It was hard not to be just a tiny bit jealous – Giles and three-quarters of my work colleagues notwithstanding. But my spirits lifted as she ended the text with the surprise news that she would be in Bristol for a lunchtime meeting on Monday, and the suggestion that we should meet up for mid-morning coffee – after-work drinks being impossible as she had to lead a p.m. meeting in Bath.

Feeling immediately brighter at the prospect of an in-person catch-up, I was just about to reply when a fist knocked lightly against my desk, causing me to start slightly and look up. Luke, coat on and messenger bag slung across his body, was grinning down at me.

'So, wotchu got going down this evening in Henleaze?' he asked. 'Beetle drive? Choir practice? Sweet sherry and bed?'

'Avenue wine and cheese.'

'Good one!' He laughed loudly, pointing at me, and then cleared his throat. 'No but seriously, whatever you're up to, enjoy.'

'I'm seriously up to a wine and cheese party. June and Stan are hosting.'

His nose wrinkled. '*Seriously*, seriously? People *seriously* do that kind of thing in real life? Not just in *The Archers*? Jesus, Edie, get out before it's too late.'

I took a final mouthful of Twix and swivelled to throw the wrapper into the bin. 'I'm fine with Henleaze,' I mumbled. 'I mean, I wouldn't want to spend every minute of every day there, but Giles is just so great and the neighbours are… well, I guess I'll find out what they are tonight. Don't worry, I'll be sure to report back on Monday, so you can take the piss more thoroughly then.'

'You do know I'm only messing with you, don't you?'

I looked up to find him looking a little anxious. I reached across the desk and rubbed his arm. 'I do, Luke.'

'Phew. 'Cos it felt like you were coming over all earnest with me there for a minute – what with *Giles* being *just so great* and all that,' he said, offering me a wink.

I tutted and rolled my eyes.

'Don't worry, I'm gonna stop annoying you now and let you get back to that.' He pointed at my phone. 'See you on Monday.'

'It's a text from Ruby,' I said quickly, as he made to leave. 'She's coming to Bristol on Monday and wants to meet up for coffee. Fancy coming along for half an hour?'

'Er… not sure. I'll have to check. Wouldn't you rather it was just the two of you?' he asked, noticeably lowering his voice, anxiety again clouding his expression, as he glanced over his shoulder towards the door.

'What's wrong?' I asked.

'Nothing. Why?'

'Don't give me that,' I frowned. 'I just asked you if you wanted to come out with Ruby and your response was to look panicked.'

'Panicked?' He laughed nervously. 'I'm not panicked.'

'Well, you look it,' I insisted. 'And now you sound it too. What's with checking the room to see if anyone's listening?'

He didn't reply, instead attempting a casual smile while adjusting his bag and shifting his weight from one foot to the other.

Did he know about Cameron and Ruby? He was behaving as if he might. But if that was the case, then I would have to screw up everything I thought I knew about Luke into a tight little ball and throw it into the bin along with my Twix wrapper. Because the Luke I knew – or thought I knew – wouldn't buddy up to someone who harassed his female co-workers. My Luke would have distanced himself from someone like that.

'Do you know?' I asked quietly, afraid of the question to which I was pretty sure I already knew the answer.

'Know what?'

'About Cameron and Ruby,' I replied quickly, without giving myself a chance to change my mind.

His expression became uncharacteristically serious. He looked, I thought, about ten years older.

'I don't want to be unprofessional,' he said.

'I already know. Ruby told me.'

'What did she tell you?'

'I promised not to discuss specifics. But I know about the accusation and I'd like to know if you do too.'

He looked pained. 'Edie, I can't even be sure what you're actually talking about.'

'I know about the harassment complaint and I know about the mutual decision to let it drop.'

'She told you all that?' he asked, looking appalled. 'And you've known about it all along?'

After a moment, he nodded miserably and I felt the blood rush to my face.

'Obviously, I couldn't talk to you about it,' he said quickly. 'Aside from all the confidentiality stuff, I wouldn't have wanted to upset you.'

'I don't care about you not discussing it, Luke!' I exclaimed. 'You were right not to discuss it. I just can't understand…' I gestured towards the corridor and took a deep breath to calm myself. 'I just can't understand how it hasn't affected your relationship with Ruby and, much more importantly, with *him*.' I jabbed a forefinger towards Cameron's empty desk.

'Of course it affected how I felt – about *both* of them,' he said, appearing confused. 'How couldn't it? I've just tried to be professional and not let it show. That's what Alison recommended and I definitely think it was the right thing to do – especially when it was agreed by everyone to let it go as a misunderstanding.'

'Do you *honestly* believe it was a misunderstanding?' I asked, offering him one last opportunity to make his behaviour towards Cameron more explicable, if not more palatable, to me.

He looked at me uncertainly, his expression changing by the moment. It was clear that there was some sort of internal battle raging.

'Look, if you want me to be completely honest with you, Edie,' he said at last, 'I don't think it was a misunderstanding. I wasn't there when it happened – or didn't happen. I wasn't a witness or anything, and neither was anyone else. As Alison said, it's crucial to remember that,' he added quickly. 'But while you were away, I saw enough to…' He shook his head. 'I shouldn't be saying any of this. It's unhelpful and unprofessional conjecture. I don't know what happened and I'm definitely not judging, or taking sides.'

His voice faded to a whisper and I blinked rapidly, uncertain whether to burst into tears or throw my pencil pot at him.

He slid his hands into his pockets and gazed at the floor. 'I know I'm a dick sometimes, but I'm not stupid. I get how upsetting this is for you. Like I say, that's part of why I didn't talk to you about it – that and the fact that absolutely *everybody* would have killed me, and I really don't want to lose this job.' He smiled sadly. 'But I'm glad she told you. I think that was brave of her and will have helped her a lot.'

I felt angry, disappointed tears beginning to well and, deciding that I'd better stem those before pelting him with pencils, I pushed back my chair and bent low, reaching into my bag for a tissue. It took only a matter of moments to fish one out, but by the time I sat up, Luke was turning to leave.

'OK, well, enjoy the wine and cheese,' he said, sounding subdued and waving to me over his shoulder. 'I'll see you Monday.'

'Wait! I was just getting a—' I began, before being interrupted by the buzzing of my phone which lay face down on my desk.

Luke nodded towards it. 'No worries. I know you're busy. You get that and I'll leave you to it.' And with that, he turned and left the office.

I looked after him and, the threat of tears having now receded, I screwed the tissue I was clutching into a tight little ball and threw it into the bin.

My phone stopped buzzing and I turned it over to see who had called: Jason. My God, there were spineless men at every turn tonight.

I leaned back in my chair and stared miserably upwards at the ceiling. The weight of disappointment I felt in Luke was crushing. He might have succeeded in selling his lack of moral fibre as fair-minded professionalism to himself, but it didn't wash with me. I would have had less of a problem had he simply maintained a polite working relationship with Cameron – I could have even coped with cordial. But their relationship went beyond that. There was a warmth to it, a black-slapping camaraderie and, worst of all, a nudge-nudge, wink-wink acceptance. Cameron was well and truly one of the boys.

My phone pinged and I glanced down at it: Jason again.

Resisting an urge to sweep it off the desk and into the bin, along with the tissue, the Twix wrapper and all respect for Luke, I picked up the phone and opened the text.

> I'd really like us to talk. Do you think that's ever going to be possible?

I considered the question, re-reading it five or six times, before placing the phone gently back onto the desk and bending forward to reach once again into my bag. I was going to need a tissue after all.

'Forgot this.'

I sat up quickly at the sound of Cameron's voice to see him standing at his desk on the dimly lit far side of the office and holding up a clear plastic wallet.

'OK, bye,' I muttered, looking down and allowing my hair to fall forwards across my face, as I reached for the scribble pad on my desk, picked up a pencil and began to draw. A moment later, and to my horror, I became aware of him crossing the office towards me.

I had no choice but to look up as he reached my desk, quickly removing the top sheet from the pad and adding it to the growing contents of my bin, lest Cameron recognise himself in the leering caricature, with enormous hands and a cuboid head, which I had drawn.

'Creative block?' he asked, smiling and looking towards the bin.

'I was just… er… thinking about some windows – trying to get an idea straight before I went home.'

'Anything it would help to talk through? I'm not in a hurry.'

I clenched my hand into a fist under the desk. 'No. I'm heading off in a moment.' To my annoyance, I heard a wobble in my voice.

He clearly heard it too and pounced on the vulnerability. 'Have you got time for a drink? You could talk windows and I could run some fibre cement façades past you.' His expression was warm as he again held up the plastic wallet and I wondered exactly how hard I'd have to hit him with my bag to knock a couple of teeth out.

'I'm going out tonight,' I said, making no attempt to sound regretful.

'Me too. I just meant for a quick—'

'I don't want to go out for a drink with you,' I said firmly, this time with no hint of a wobble. 'Not because I'm unavailable, but because I don't want to go out for a drink with you. I should have been clearer about that, so that there was no misunderstanding.'

He looked at me, clearly and satisfyingly taken aback. 'Right. Well, thanks for clarifying that,' he said, with just a hint of the East End; his version, I thought, of a wobble. We were even.

I stared him out for just a moment longer and then picked up my pencil, pulled the pad towards me and began to draw again. I didn't see him go and I didn't look up until I heard the lift doors open and close and I was certain that he had left the building.

Chapter 11

After spending the thirty-minute bus ride home lost in miserable analysis of my conversation with Luke – and reaching the unavoidable conclusion that he was, at best, a pathetic appeaser and, at worst, a sexist, morally bankrupt co-conspirator – I didn't at all feel in the mood for a chatty get-together with the neighbours. Giles, of course, was typically understanding; acknowledging my distress, handing me a large glass of wine and reassuring me that, in the circumstances, it would be perfectly acceptable for me to skip June's party, if that's what I wanted to do.

But not wanting to let him, or anyone else, down, I had insisted that going out would be a welcome distraction and do me good. Obviously, I hadn't really held out any hope of that actually proving to be the case, and yet remarkably, by the time June opened her front door to us, approximately an hour and a half after my doom-laden journey home, I was already feeling very much better. This was admittedly thanks in part to the large glass of red, but also to the unfailingly uplifting company of Giles. He was someone who seemed to emanate an aura of positivity and calm, and I marvelled – not for the first time – at what a near-impossibility it was to remain anxious or upset for long in his company.

'Come in, come in, Edith and Giles,' beamed June as she ushered us inside, the sound of lively conversation immediately reaching us through the half-open living room doorway. She was, I noticed, wigless this evening, her wonderful, slightly bouffant, snow-white hair fully revealed as she looked me up and down.

'Like a rainbow,' she murmured, gazing at the swirling pattern of my dress before more loudly, and quite directly, telling Giles that he had lost weight.

He laughed at the comment, but as I turned to look at him, I saw that she was right. The double chin, which he had so lamented a month earlier, was now nowhere to be seen and only the slightest hint of a rounded tummy was detectable beneath his blue-check shirt.

'June's right, you have lost weight,' I said, nudging him.

'It's only a few pounds, but thank you for noticing. Oh, but you didn't notice, did you, Edie? It was June who noticed. Thank you, June.' He offered her a small bow, whilst handing over a bottle of red wine.

'Have you been lifting dumbbells in a gymnasium, Giles?' she asked, taking the bottle from him.

He nodded. 'I have indeed been pumping the iron, June. As well as eating fewer biscuits.'

'You've been working out? When?' I asked, hugely intrigued, but he didn't seem to hear.

'You should eat avocados and nuts,' said June.

'Mental note duly made.' He tapped his left temple.

She looked pleased and there followed a pause in the conversation.

'So, June,' said Giles after a moment, 'shall we perhaps join the throng?' He pointed towards the open door.

'Oh yes! I must show Edith to everybody!' she exclaimed, making me feel like a newly purchased pair of shoes.

Taking my hand and placing an arm around Giles, she steered us both into what would, in his house, have been the living room, but which in hers was a long through-room heavy with lace. There were lace curtains, lace antimacassars, lace doilies and, the *pièce de résistance*, a long lace tablecloth covering a mahogany dining table positioned in the centre of the room. On it were a couple of large ceramic platters, bearing cold meats and cheese respectively, together with plates of varying pattern and size, laden with breads and savoury biscuits. Centre stage were two pale-green, gold-rimmed serving dishes, piled high with cherry tomatoes – so high, in fact, that I wondered whether cocktail sticks or glue might be playing some part in holding it all together.

Tearing my eyes away from the tomato mountains, I scanned the room, estimating a gathering of around thirty, some of whom I recognised as nodding acquaintances from my Monday-to-Friday walks to the bus stop. Heads turned as we entered and hands were raised in greeting but, to my relief, there was no pause in the general conversation.

'How delicious, June,' said Giles, gesturing towards the dining table and then rubbing his hands together. 'I do love a nice tomato.'

'Philip at the greengrocer's gave them to me,' she said. 'They're closed tomorrow for a staff treat-day and he said they'd go soft over the weekend. Do help yourself, and to the wine over there.' She indicated a lace-draped sideboard, on which sat a dozen or so wine glasses, plus a large number of bottles, to which June now added our own. 'There's white wine in the kitchen, as usual, so help yourself to that. Giles can pour you a glass, Edith, while I show you to Stan.' And with that, she once again took my hand and pulled me towards the garden end of the room.

I glanced a little anxiously over my shoulder at Giles. I hadn't anticipated being separated from him quite so soon. 'Red would be great,' I said. 'No need to disappear into the kitchen on my behalf.'

His response was to point and silently laugh at me before, to give him his due, immediately reaching for a bottle of red.

'Excuse me, gentlemen, but this is Edith, who *isn't* Giles's cousin,' said June a little breathlessly, as we came to a halt next to a group of three men, one of whom I judged to be in his eighties, and the other two their mid-sixties. June gently pushed one of them aside and, as a pair, we eased our way into the circle.

'Hello and welcome to the avenue,' said the oldest member of the group, a slight man with thinning white hair, whom I'd seen a couple of times at a distance but never spoken to. I remembered him because his resting face was particularly grumpy, like that of a disgruntled garden gnome. But as he smiled at me now, it was, as my mother used to say, like the sun coming out from behind a cloud.

'Great to meet you…' I paused, waiting for him to tell me his name.

'That's Stan,' said June quickly, with the slightly dismissive edge to her tone which people reserve for family members. 'And this is William, from number 40. He's in a band,' she added proudly, extending her hand towards a tall, slim, bearded man. His wavy, surprisingly thick, grey hair fell just below his collar, and he was dressed entirely in black.

'Call me Bill,' he smiled, peering down at me through tinted aviator specs. On closer inspection, I decided that he was well into his seventies.

'You're in a band, Bill? How exciting,' I said. 'What do you play?'

'Bodhrán and penny whistle.'

'Folk music?'

'Reggae mainly, but also a bit of Meatloaf, Belinda Carlisle – that kind of thing.'

'Wow, well, that's… that's just so… eclectic. I'll have to come and hear you play sometime.'

'We're playing Clifton in October,' he said, offering me a kindly look. 'I'll push a ticket through your door over the weekend, and some extras for your friends. How does that sound?'

'That's so kind of you,' I said. 'But let me know the date and I'll double-check if I can make it first. I'd feel terrible if the tickets went to waste.'

He shook his head. 'It's not a bother. Just pop the money to me in the next couple of days – no rush – and sell the tickets on if you can't make the date.'

'Oh… right,' I said, wondering exactly how much *not* listening to Celtic reggae was going to cost me. 'Thanks.'

'And this is Patrick.' June concluded the introductions by indicating the greying, ruddy-faced man standing to her left, currently flying in the face of wine-and-cheese convention by nursing a beer. Judging by his florid complexion and slight sway, it wasn't his first of the evening.

He wordlessly raised his glass to me in lieu of a 'hello', and there then followed a conversational pause, during which I smiled inanely and willed Giles to hurry up and bring me a drink.

'Have you got a vehicle?' asked Patrick, so suddenly and loudly that I started at the question. He raised his beer slowly to his lips, whilst narrowing his eyes and sizing me up over the top of his glass.

'Me? Yes, I do, thank you,' I said warily, afraid that, after the ticket hustle, he had me pegged as a sucker and was hoping to offload a used car onto me.

'A big one?' he pressed.

'Now, now, Patrick,' said Stan gently, 'we don't have to get into parking right away. There's plenty of time for that.'

Patrick frowned. 'Best to be clear from the start, Stan. We don't want a repeat of Angela and the Frontier Comanche fiasco, do we?' This question was, for some reason, addressed to me.

'Ooh, now, I haven't actually met Angela. Is she here?' I asked, looking anxiously over my shoulder, lest the woman herself should be listening in.

'Her nephew and his wacky-baccy mate lived in that behemoth outside my house for a month. *A month*,' Patrick repeated, his eyes widening and locking onto mine, clearly desperate for me to join in and acknowledge the full horror of the situation. 'Angela said the smell was Marks and Spencer potpourri.' He laughed scornfully. 'As if.'

'I'm not sure I actually know what a Frontier Comanche is,' I said uncertainly, looking around the group. 'Is it a camper van?'

'It's a ruddy juggernaut, that's what it is,' snapped Patrick. 'Outside my house. *For a month*. With a drug lord in it.'

'I think Angela said the boys were trainee accountants, Patrick,' said Stan. 'It was only for a week or so,' he continued quietly, leaning towards me and shaking his head, 'while the boys tried to find a flat. Although, I can see how it might have been annoying for you, Patrick,' he added in a placatory tone.

'Couldn't park my own car outside my own house,' he seethed.

'Well, you're safe with me. I've only got a Mini and there's barely room for a travel mug in that, let alone a meth lab,' I said, with a light laugh.

Everyone joined in, apart from Patrick, who instead muttered something about *thieving bastard accountants* under his breath.

'Getting to know everyone, Edie?' asked Giles, now, to my huge relief, joining the group and handing me a perilously full glass of wine, from which I immediately took a large gulp. He raised his own glass in the air. 'Cheers, everyone. How are we all?'

Positive murmurs followed, before June said, 'I've explained to everyone that Edith is *not* your cousin, Giles.'

'Oh,' said Giles, blinking a little, 'well, that's… good.'

'So lovely that a young woman, to whom you are *not* related,' she said with emphasis, looking around the circle, 'is living in your house. With you. Just the two of you. Together.'

Giles raised his glass and his eyebrows. 'Hmm.'

'Yes, I'm really enjoying *lodging* with Giles,' I said, with emphasis.

'There now,' said Patrick, in gruff approval. 'That's what normal people do. They lodge *in a house*. They do not sleep in a truck, on a residential road and smoke crack.'

'You're his lodger?' said Stan, looking first at me and then at June.

'Don't pry into people's private lives, please, Stanley,' said June. 'Many young people choose to pay rent in kind, these days. It's deemed perfectly acceptable. I read all about it in *The Times*, just last week.'

'So, Edie,' said Giles quickly, clearing his throat, 'shall we get some food and top up our drinks?'

I looked down at my glass, surprised to discover that I had somehow managed to drink over half its contents during the brief exchange regarding my landlord–tenant relationship with Giles. He, meanwhile, seemed to have downed his drink in one.

'Those tomatoes do look lovely,' I said.

'Go and fill a plate,' said June kindly. 'And then Giles must introduce you to everyone else, before you make your speech.'

'Oh yes, my speech.' My stomach lurched and I took another gulp of wine. 'I'd forgotten all about that.'

'Come along then.' Giles placed a guiding hand on my elbow, gently turning me towards the table. 'Let's get you something to eat and you can go over your notes.'

I attempted a withering look and he grinned in return.

'Such a lovely couple. And it's not at all going against nature,' said June, as we headed, by mutual unspoken consent, straight past the food and back to the bottles of red wine.

'Talk about a baptism of fire,' I hissed, when we reached the sanctuary of the sideboard. 'They really know how to lull you into a false sense of security with their grey hair and watery eyes, don't they? I reckon I'm going be at least twenty quid out of pocket to Billy Bodhrán over there for gig tickets, and thank God I've only got a two-door car.'

'Patrick mentioned parking to you, I take it.' Giles took my glass from me and filled it to the brim.

'Yes, he did. And hey, careful,' I added, nodding at the glass. 'I need to pace myself.'

'Because of the speech?'

'Oh God, the speech. I keep forgetting. Give me that.' I took the glass, drank a third of it, and then held it out to him. 'Top me up. I'm gonna need it.'

Chapter 12

By nine thirty, I had once again entirely forgotten about the speech and was, against all expectations, unequivocally enjoying myself. The number of wine-and-cheesers had increased by around a dozen and Giles told me that he reckoned about half of the avenue's adult residents were now in attendance at what was an increasingly lively and noisy event.

Almost all of the new arrivals were in the same age bracket as Giles and myself, and included several mums I'd spotted going into Kerry's house with their children. One in particular, Nicky – mid-thirties, with a newish baby boy and a daughter in Harry's class at school – seemed to be very interested in me, and even more so in Giles.

'So, you're *not* his girlfriend, but he *is* straight,' she said, slurring slightly on account of having been out for happy-hour cocktails with girlfriends before returning to meet her husband at June's. 'See, I told you he was straight, Andy,' she said, slapping the hand of her husband, who was standing quietly at her side, contributing little to this particular thread of the conversation.

'I don't recall ever telling you that he wasn't,' he said, calmly sipping a fizzy mineral water, it being his turn, he had confided earlier, for *Sober Saturday*. 'It's hell if you're both hungover,' he had explained. 'Last time that happened, we fell asleep on the sofa mid-morning and when we woke up, our eldest was styling Nicky's hair with Weetabix. Only about a third of it had set solid but, you know...' He shrugged. 'It still wasn't the best.'

'So *who* was it who told me Giles was gay?' persisted Nicky, her brow furrowing as she eyed Andy accusingly.

'And again,' he said, now sounding tense, 'that someone was not me, Nicky, as I have no interest in, or information regarding, the personal relationships in which poor Giles chooses to engage.'

'Poor Giles's ears are burning,' said Giles jovially, now joining the group.

Andy smiled and held out his hand in greeting, whilst Nicky's response was altogether more vocal.

'Can I set you up with my friends, Giles?' she asked. 'I've got two who are great, but I'm thinking maybe just one at a time, eh?' She laughed loudly.

Andy, I noticed, had begun to rub his forehead.

Giles looked at me questioningly. 'Well, that's a very kind offer, but—'

Nicky held up a hand. 'Let me stop you right there because I know *exactly* what you're going to say. But don't worry, both of my friends are *women*.' She winked at him and tapped the side of her nose.

Giles frowned and his eyes narrowed slightly, a clear indication that he was attempting to fill in the conversational blanks. After a moment his expression cleared. 'That's right,' he said. 'Because I'm not gay, Nicky. And thank you, Edie,' he added, turning towards me, 'for setting the record straight, so to speak.'

I focused on removing a stray hair from my dress, in preference to making eye contact with him. 'Welcome,' I murmured.

'*I* never thought you were gay, *obviously*,' said Nicky, placing a hand on her chest, 'and absolutely everyone I told you *were* gay was really shocked too. I can't think *who* started the rumour. Can you, Andy?'

Andy turned and placed his glass down heavily on the sideboard behind him. 'Let's go and get you some water.'

'Why?' she asked. 'I haven't finished my wine.'

All eyes turned towards the completely empty wine glass in her hand. It appeared to have been licked clean.

'Oh, God,' she gasped, looking first at the glass and then down at her feet. 'Did I spill it on June's carpet?'

'You spilled it down your throat, Nicola,' said Andy quietly. 'Along with two other glasses and lots of cocktails. Come on, let's go and find a tap.'

She beamed up at him. 'OK,' she said. 'And I forgive you.'

'Very gracious,' he sighed. 'I'll catch up with you later, Giles.'

'Super,' said Giles.

'Yeah, later, both,' said Nicky, grinning and wiggling her fingers over her shoulder at us in farewell, as Andy began to lead her away.

I waved in return and was just about to ask Giles for a bit more background information on Nicky, when he said. 'I wonder where Kerry and Ronald are.'

'Oh yes, that's right,' I replied, as he scanned the room. 'I'd forgotten they were coming. You're not worried, are you?'

'No, no.' He shook his head. 'I had just thought that, bearing in mind how you're feeling about work, Ronald might be a handy bit of networking for you.'

'Definitely,' I said, smoothing my hair and straightening my dress. 'But do I look professional enough? I'm probably on my second bottle of wine by now. Hope I don't talk bollocks and embarrass myself.'

He laughed and then turned as his name was called. It was Kerry, weaving her way towards us, wine glass in one hand and several cherry tomatoes in the other. She popped one of the latter into her mouth as she approached.

'Hello,' she mumbled through a mouthful of tomato. 'What time did you guys get here?'

'Yesterday,' said Giles. 'You?'

She chewed some more. 'Been in the kitchen for ten minutes with June talking me through her veg drawer. You enjoying *the do*, Edie?'

'I am *loving* it,' I said, my enthusiasm for the event growing with every successive sip of wine. 'Can't remember the last time I enjoyed myself so much.'

Kerry nodded. 'Knew you would. I could tell you were a people person from the off.'

I grinned, feeling hugely complimented.

She stood on tiptoe and looked towards the back of the room. 'Hey, I've just realised, I've lost Ron.'

'Where did you last have him?' asked Giles.

'In the kitchen,' she said, remaining on tiptoe. 'He was talking to Bill about Rick Astley. I should probably go and rescue him. I'm such a bad friend.'

'I'll go,' said Giles, already walking away. 'You stay and chat to Edie.'

Kerry smiled after him and then turned to me. 'He's a bit keen to see Ron.'

'Keen for me to meet Ron,' I said. 'I had a pretty crappy day at work and Giles thought it might help talking to Ron – you know, a little bit of networking in preparation for quitting on Monday.' I laughed, but knew that I'd said way more than I would have if I'd been sober.

'That bad?' she asked, looking concerned.

I shook my head and held up my glass. 'I'm exaggerating because I've had too much of this. I shouldn't have even mentioned it. It's all confidential, so don't worry about me droning on to Ron, or crying on his shoulder or anything.'

'Bloody hell, I wouldn't worry about that,' she said, rolling her eyes. 'He's more likely to blub all over yours.'

'Really?'

She glanced over her shoulder and then leaned in conspiratorially. 'Well, he probably won't let on, but he's not happy,' she said, lowering her voice. 'We went for a beer and something to eat first, 'cos he was so uptight, which just isn't like him. He's seriously, *seriously* fed up, Edie.'

'Wow,' I said, aware of my mood lifting, and only slightly ashamed that news of another miserable architect was making me feel better. 'What's happened? Or can't you tell me?'

'It's not confidential, like your thing,' she shrugged. 'Just someone being an arsehole. And Ron doesn't need to put up with that kind of hassle. He could have his pick of jobs,' she added, draining her glass and popping another tomato into her mouth. 'Doubt he'll mention it to you though, 'cos he's not gobby like me. Plus you're an architect and might know the person. He won't even give *me* a name.'

I pulled a face. 'Wow, that's so discreet. What are the chances of you knowing them? He's based in the Midlands, isn't he?'

'The Midlands?' she frowned. 'No, no. He *used* to work in Birmingham, but now he's in Bristol.'

'Oh, right,' I said, experiencing a sudden sense of prickling disquiet, my brief moment of uplift now dissipating. 'So he's in Bristol? I guess I might know the guy he works with then. How bad is he?'

'She,' said Kerry, raising a finger. 'He is a she – and she is *really* bad. You couldn't meet a nicer guy than Ron, but she's made him feel unwelcome from day one; cold-shouldering him, barely saying hello. She sounds like a complete cow, and it's really grinding him down.' She chomped angrily on her last tomato. 'Anyway, he offered to help her with something this evening and she just threw it back in his face. Basically told him to get lost. Why? Why be like that?'

She seethed on and, as she spoke, I listened and nodded along, repeating her words slowly back to myself, trying to divine the hidden meaning which I sensed was there, but which, thanks to God knows how many red wines, was currently eluding me. Meanwhile, the prickling disquiet had now been joined by a growing, and unmistakeable, sense of impending doom.

'I know I shouldn't get so wound up about it,' Kerry was saying, tutting at herself. 'He's a grown man and can handle his own problems. But it's the same as if someone was picking on Giles. Ron is *so* lovely and he's made a real effort with this woman – same as he has with everyone in the office – and to think that she's just being so horrible to him, day in, day out…'

'Awful,' I murmured absently. 'Poor Ronald.'

Her frown lifted and she laughed explosively. 'Ronald? Where did you get Ronald from?'

'Well, Giles…'

She placed a hand on my arm, still laughing. 'Ah, bless. Is that what Giles thinks his name is? That's so funny. Wonder if he's called him Ronald to his face yet.'

She looked towards the kitchen and then back at me, at which point her smile vanished. 'God, are you OK, Edie?' she asked anxiously, gently touching my cheek with her hand. 'You're not going to throw up, are you? Can I get you some water? Do you want to sit down?'

Ignoring her increasingly panicked enquiries, I instead gazed blankly at her, as the facts buzzing round my inebriated brain finally managed to arrange themselves into a logical conclusion.

'Is his name…' I began quietly, before taking a sip of wine as my dry mouth refused to co-operate further. 'Is his name Cameron? Cameron Grange?'

She stared up at me and I watched as the same realisation which had dawned on me just moments earlier, now dawned on her.

'Shit,' she breathed.

'I found him! Here he is!' Giles bounced up to us. 'The evening is complete!'

Kerry and I gazed at each other, saying nothing.

'What's happened?' asked Giles. I felt his hand on my shoulder. 'Edie, whatever's wrong?'

'Nothing,' I murmured, turning slowly towards him, 'but I'd like to leave now.'

I was aware of Cameron standing to his right, but I couldn't bring myself to look at him. Instead, I watched as Giles turned to him and spoke. 'I'm so sorry, Ronald, I don't quite know…'

'His name's not Ronald,' I said, lowering my eyes and addressing Giles's brogues.

'Kerry, we should go,' said Cameron, his voice low and steady.

'Jesus, Ron,' she exclaimed. 'Tell me she is *not* the woman at work?' She sounded incredulous. I was grateful for that, at least.

'One moment,' said Giles. 'Edie, you mean you work with Ronald? Surely, he's not the colleague who…'

'His name *isn't* Ronald, Giles,' I repeated firmly, now looking up.

'Let's go,' said Cameron.

'No,' said Kerry flatly. 'I'm not going anywhere. I want to know why she's being a cow to you. Why are you being a cow to him?' she asked, turning to me.

'Your name isn't Ronald?' said Giles, looking at Cameron. 'Is it simply Ron on your birth certificate?'

I turned to Kerry. 'I'm sorry, but he's clearly a very different person in the workplace,' I said, battling the effects of alcohol, shock and emotion to keep my voice calm.

Her upper lip curled, revealing even, white teeth. 'No one else has ever said that about him.'

'That doesn't make it not true,' I replied, aware of my heart rate increasing.

'Now, don't get angry, Edie,' said Giles. 'I think Ronald, Ron, is right. We should probably all leave at this point.'

'I'm not going to be chased away from a fun party by this bully,' I said, jabbing a forefinger in Cameron's direction. 'He can leave. I'm going nowhere,' I added, folding my arms.

'But I thought you *wanted* to leave,' said Giles, somewhat desperately.

'*Ron* a bully? That's rich, coming from you. And why should *he* leave?' growled Kerry. 'Or isn't it enough that you make his working life a misery? Do you have to piss all over his social life too?'

'Kerry,' said Cameron quietly, 'this isn't helping.'

'Yes, Kerry,' said Giles gently, 'please don't rush to judgement. I've known Edie an awfully long time and I can vouch for the fact that she is—'

'I couldn't give a flying f—,' she began, before stopping short. She took a breath and, blinking up at Giles, began again. 'I don't care how long you've known her, Giles,' she said, now sounding emotional as well as angry. 'I've known Cameron a long time too, and Mark knew him for decades. He loved him to bits and so do I.'

Giles appeared confused and hesitated briefly before his expression cleared. 'Oh, I *see*. Came*ron*,' he said, smiling faintly, enjoying the fleeting pleasure of understanding the abbreviated name, before his smile faded and he returned to the sad matter in hand. 'And you're absolutely sure that he's the one, Edie?' he asked.

'Well, of course I bloody am!' I exclaimed. 'It's not like I'm picking him out of a police line-up, is it, Giles? I see him every day: Monday to Friday.'

'Look, this situation isn't great for any of us,' began Cameron calmly.

'Oh, you shut up,' I exploded, at last turning to face him and discovering, to my surprise, that his expression was more injured puppy than angry Rottweiler. I had to hand it to him – he was playing this brilliantly. The man was pure, evil genius.

'Look at you, standing there, the dignified victim,' I said scornfully, looking him up and down. 'Well, let me tell you, *Ron*, that act of yours may go down a treat with

Kerry and all your other lady friends, but it doesn't work with me! I know what you are and what you've done. *I,*' I concluded dramatically, tapping my chest, 'know everything.'

'Come on then,' said Kerry. 'Spit it out. What do you know?'

I whirled round to face her. 'He's a—'

'No more, Edie,' said Giles firmly.

'Why shouldn't she know? Maybe everyone should know.' I looked up at Giles defiantly, but even when enraged and intoxicated, I trusted his judgement. 'It's not OK, Giles,' I said. It was a final, barely audible, verbal stamp of my foot.

'What's she talking about, Ron?' asked Kerry.

'I don't know, but we need to leave,' he said, taking her arm and turning away. 'Now.'

'Oh, but you can't leave just yet,' said June, smiling and placing a hand on his arm, as she walked past us with a bottle of white wine.

He looked down at her. 'I'm afraid—'

'Quiet, everyone, please!' The words reached us, at shocking volume, from the other end of the room, where Bill was now addressing the crowd through a wholly unnecessary microphone and speaker combo, the intermittent feedback from which was excruciating. 'Quiet, please,' he repeated, despite the fact that the entire room had been traumatised into complete silence several seconds earlier.

Cameron again moved towards the door but June was adamant. 'No, no,' she laughed, pulling him back. 'You sit tight, just for two more minutes. Please, dear.'

He looked, to my satisfaction, supremely uncomfortable and embarrassed, but he submitted to her request, returning to his spot beside Giles. Kerry moved to be at his side and, as they turned away from us and towards Bill, she placed a hand around his waist and hugged him to her. I watched, my anger towards him and my enormous pity for her, increasing, as he put a reciprocal arm around her shoulders.

My body drooped along with my spirits as I turned to Giles who, with an expression of what looked like utter despair, was now staring at his feet, his hands in his pockets.

I knew, without a doubt, that I had not only ruined his evening, but also done considerable damage to his friendship with Kerry. Why hadn't I just left? OK, so the evening was never going to end on a high, but maybe if I'd shut up, kept my cool and gone home, Giles and Kerry could have decided that my relationship with Cameron need have nothing to do with their relationship with each other. But there was no hope of that now. They had each taken sides, the battle lines were drawn, and two wholly innocent parties were caught up in the war.

Meanwhile, Bill was busy promoting his upcoming Clifton gig at one hundred decibels from the other end of the room, prompting some sporadic, drunken whooping and lots of ear-poking. Under cover of the deafening promo, I reached out and took hold of Giles's arm, forcing him to remove his hand from his pocket so that I could hold it.

'I'm so, so sorry, Giles,' I said as loudly as I dared, whilst standing on tip-toe, resting my chin on his shoulder and speaking directly into his right ear.

'It's just a series of extremely unfortunate events,' he sighed.

I shook my head, feeling boozy tears begin to well. 'I know I handled it really badly.'

'You were taken by surprise,' he replied. 'I would have been exactly the same.' He let go of my hand and placed his arm around my shoulders. 'Come on,' he said, as I leaned into him, 'let's sneak off while everyone's looking at Bill.'

'Yes, there they are, the two love-birds!' boomed Bill. 'Canoodling at the back!'

I raised my head from Giles's shoulder to find that all eyes were upon us.

'Don't worry, folks. They're not full cousins!' said Bill, an announcement which, after a moment's complete silence, prompted a single 'Hurrah!' and some scattered applause. 'So come on, Edith, come up here and get your flowers.'

A sorry combination of alcohol and distress meant that I didn't remember walking to the other end of the room. But nevertheless, a moment later, there I was, being presented with a huge bouquet by Stan, whilst Bill tapped his foot and played the opening bars of *Electric Avenue* on a penny whistle extracted from his back pocket.

There was more clapping and then Stan handed me the microphone, saying, 'Your turn, Edith.'

I looked around the room and saw that Giles had followed me and was now standing just a few feet away, smiling encouragingly. I bit my lip.

'You're just so lovely, Giles,' I said quietly, except not quietly at all, thanks to Bill's mega sound system. Cue yet more applause and a wolf-whistle.

Giles rolled his eyes and laughed.

I dabbed at my eyes with the back of my hand and sniffed loudly into the microphone, creating a noise not unlike a leaf-blower and causing the entire gathering to wince as one.

'Thank you so much, June and Stan,' I began hesitantly, the wobble in my voice amplified for all to hear, 'for welcoming me into your lovely home this evening, and thank you, everyone, for welcoming me so warmly to—'

I paused, aware of a loud tapping sound behind me and, turning, saw a dishevelled-looking, middle-aged woman, standing on the patio outside the French windows. Some sort of vegetation seemed to be hanging from her hair and she had one hand pressed flat against the glass whilst waving a wooden clog with the other.

June bustled past me. 'You carry on, dear,' she said, placing a hand on my arm and leaning in. 'I'll just let Stella back in. I think the new trellising has defeated her.'

I nodded, joining in the general acceptance of the situation, and as I turned back to face the room, I saw Cameron and Kerry slip away.

More thrown by their exit than by Stella's unconventional entrance, I lowered the microphone and was just about to return it to Stan, when I spotted Giles. He was still smiling at me and, on catching my eye, immediately added a supportive double thumbs-up to his visual pep-talk.

I swallowed hard, offered him a watery smile and then, raising the microphone and taking a deep breath to steady myself, said, 'I love my job. But work isn't great at the moment, so having somewhere to escape to – a home – is more important to me than it's been for a very long time. And I'm grateful to you all for making me feel so at home tonight.'

There followed a collective 'Aaaw', and as I, somewhat tearfully, turned and handed the microphone back to Stan, Giles offered me a congratulatory hug.

Then, as Bill once again struck up on his penny whistle, and June took Stella into the kitchen to look for a Band-Aid, we said our goodbyes and headed home.

Chapter 13

By the time I woke the next morning, Giles had already headed off to attend the seventieth birthday party of a family friend in St Albans. There was to be a lunch on the Saturday and then drinks the next evening, and although Giles offered to cancel his plans to stay overnight on the Sunday, I asked him not to.

We had talked briefly when we got home from the wine and cheese, with Giles being typically calming and also making me promise that I wouldn't do anything hasty on Monday, regarding either quitting my job or killing Cameron. But there had been no time or inclination for heavy analysis of the situation and, to be honest, I was happy to defer the discussion. Aside from anything else, I didn't want to embark on it with the mother of all hangovers. All I wanted to do was swallow Nurofen, drink water and hide from the outside world – and, more specifically, from Kerry – as much as at all possible until Monday.

The latter I largely achieved, with the exception of a few commiserative nods to fellow dog-walkers, during several hooded-shuffles across a rainswept Downs with Anthony. Those damp encounters aside, my only other weekend near-brush with humanity took the form of Bodhrán Bill, ringing the doorbell and then – apparently – running away as fast as his septuagenarian legs could carry him, but not before stuffing four tickets for *An evening of reggae 'n' rock with The Henleaze High Notes at The Eldon House*, through our front door.

As a result of having managed to get through the weekend in relative solitude, free from any awkward neighbourly encounters, I was pleased to find myself feeling pretty OK as I boarded the bus to work on Monday morning, and even in possession of a faint, but very welcome, sense of relief.

However, the traffic was heavier than usual and the journey particularly slow, and as the bus hiccoughed its way along the Downs, there was more than enough time for my focus to shift from a weekend which could have been worse, to a Friday night from absolute hell. Consequently, it wasn't long before my fragile sense of relief had had the living daylights kicked out of it by much stronger, unequivocally negative, emotions.

For a start, I felt physically sick whenever Kerry crossed my mind. Because although I still felt only anger and resentment towards Cameron, my thoughts regarding her were heavy with guilt and regret that she, and Giles, had become embroiled in a drama which would inevitably cause them both embarrassment and hurt.

Secondly, a return to work of course meant a confront-ation of some sort or other with Cameron and – as someone with a preference for sidestepping confrontation wherever possible – I was absolutely dreading it.

It was therefore with no sense of relief, faint or other-wise, that I stepped off the bus at College Green and trudged the short remaining distance to work. Instead, I was accompanied by doom, gloom and nausea, which were still determinedly clinging to the tails of my pink raincoat, as I finally pushed open the glass doors of the office at 8:50 a.m.

Cameron's desk was nearest the door and he looked up as I walked in.

'Hi,' he said, before immediately returning his attention to his screen. He sounded and appeared perfectly relaxed. The bastard.

'And what time d'ya call this?' chimed Luke, peering at me over the top of his screen and then swivelling slowly in his chair to track me to my desk. 'Still hung over from the wine-and-wine thing?'

'Morning, Luke,' I said, trying not to add a recollection of our Friday home-time conversation to my list of current stress factors. 'Morning, Roger,' I continued, turning to my right. 'Get up to anything interesting over the weekend?'

He frowned and cleared his throat. 'Oh, y'know, this 'n' that, this 'n' that,' he replied, offering me the same response he'd volunteered almost every Monday morning for the past two-and-a-half years – the only exceptions being when he had attended a sporting fixture or a funeral.

'No matches this weekend then, Rog?' asked Luke.

He shook his head. 'No, although I did have a couple of pints at the rugby club. Saw old Dave there.'

Luke nodded. 'He's your oldest member, isn't he?'

'He is that,' replied Roger. 'Ninety-three and living in Henleaze now, actually. Not far from our Edie,' he added, turning to me. 'In that care home at the end of your road. They've just had new bath hoists fitted throughout.'

'Oh, right,' I said uncertainly, switching on my desktop. 'That's nice.'

'Great that you won't have far to move when the time comes, eh, Edie?' Luke gave me a thumbs-up, without looking up from his screen.

I said nothing, acutely aware of how much his digs now irritated, rather than entertained. Roger, meanwhile, was now talking to Cameron, showing a kindly interest in how a client meeting had gone on Friday. I listened in as he offered encouragement and advice, and I found myself hoping desperately that his warmth was founded on ignorance. Because had I discovered at that moment that Roger knew the truth about Cameron, I would have marched straight into Alison's office and resigned. Roger was, I decided, the only thing actually worth staying for right now.

I turned in my chair and gazed at Alison as she sat frowning at her screen. Was Ruby right? Had she got to where she was not only through talent, self-reliance and single-mindedness, but also by ignoring inconvenient truths and prioritising professional progress over personal principles?

'Alison wants to see us. She asked me to tell you.'

My stomach lurched at the sound of Cameron's voice and I looked up to find him towering over me beside my desk. He appeared as untroubled and unsmiling as when I'd first arrived, and if he was at all anxious about the events of Friday night, he was hiding it brilliantly.

'When?' I asked.

'Midday.'

'Why?'

'I thought you might know.'

'Well, I don't.'

The terse exchange was enough to cause Luke to glance over his shoulder at us and, as I turned to pick up my bag, I saw that Roger too had shown an uncharacteristic interest in our conversation. Neither said anything though, and the silence, before I spoke again, was arctic.

'OK,' I said, beginning to unpack my bag.

Cameron didn't move and, after a moment, I looked up at him. 'Was there something else?'

He hesitated and I was conscious of my heart rate upping to a rapid thud. 'No,' he said at last, 'that's it.'

I offered him a coldly dismissive nod and returned my gaze, if not my thoughts, to my bag. There then followed another second or two of near unbearable tension, before he turned and walked away.

Had I been alone in the office at that point, I would no doubt have collapsed in a relieved heap across my desk. But being in the company of colleagues, I instead remained rigidly upright, staring at my screen and attempting to appear immediately engrossed, determined to avoid both conversation and eye contact with either Luke or Roger for at least the next half hour.

That plan, however, was immediately scuppered by Luke.

'Ruby left a message for you,' he said quietly and with uncharacteristic solemnity, as he approached my desk and placed a yellow Post-it in front of me. 'She said she'd messaged you a couple of times but hadn't heard back.'

'Oh, yes,' I said, checking my phone, 'she has. I've had it on silent. I wonder what she wants,' I murmured absently.

'Maybe checking about coffee?'

I looked up at him and frowned, before my expression cleared and I slumped in my chair. 'God, I completely forgot,' I said wearily, keen to see Ruby but completely lacking the energy for it, or for anything else other than breathing and remaining conscious. 'Thanks, I'll message her.'

He nodded a little anxiously and then returned quickly to his desk, fearful, I assumed, of a renewed invitation to join us.

For a moment I considered telling him not to worry, because I certainly didn't want to spend time with anyone who was such an ardent admirer of Cameron, either now or in the foreseeable future, and I couldn't imagine that Ruby did either. But in the end, I decided that the fewer words Luke and I exchanged that day – or any day, for that matter – the better.

Chapter 14

After delivering a crushing hug, Ruby sat down opposite me at one of the blue, Formica-topped tables, located towards the back of the small, bordering-on-gloomy, cafe, which was just a few doors down from the practice. The food wasn't great, the staff were miserable and the ambience was dire, but the unpopularity of the place had always made it our cafe of choice whenever we fancied a quiet, unobserved coffee and conversation.

'Sorry I couldn't make drinks,' she said, placing her cappuccino on the table and slipping out of a bright red jacket to reveal a leaf-green dress, both of which represented a surprising departure from her usual fashion palette of greys and black, 'but things are full on at Lovelock's and I have to be back for a meeting. I've been handed way more responsibility than was originally planned, which is great, obviously, but at the same time… well,' she shrugged and smiled, 'it's full on.'

'It's fine,' I said, shaking my head. 'We can arrange a drink when things ease up for you.'

'Hmm,' she said, her smile broadening, 'well, here's the thing. I'm not sure they're going to ease up any time soon, because Vincent – Vincent Lovelock – has already started talking pay rises and promotions!'

'Wow,' I said, desperately trying to inject some energy and excitement into my tone, whilst actually wanting to put on my pyjamas and cry myself to sleep. 'So soon? Congratulations! That's marvellous. You must have made a real impact.'

'Don't like to blow my own trumpet,' she laughed, 'but when Vincent and I went for a drink the other night, he said he was surprised that things had kind of stalled for me with Alison. His theory is that she feels threatened by any woman with potential but,' she wrinkled her nose and flapped a hand, 'forget I said that. I don't want to go there, because I know we feel differently about her.'

I reached for my coffee, pausing for a moment to summon the strength to pick it up. I had started the working day on a low and every successive development – my exchange with Cameron, the prospect of a meeting with him and Alison, and now even a coffee with Ruby – seemed to be further draining me of any remaining light and optimism.

'I'm so pleased things are going well,' I said, managing the positive response thanks only to a huge effort of will. Sadly, I couldn't quite muster a smile to go with it. So instead, I lifted my coffee to my lips and blew, in an attempt to hide my less-than-ecstatic reaction to Ruby's news. She was just so obviously happy and completely lacking in any regret about leaving Bristol and, as much as I hated myself for it, I couldn't help resenting her that, as I floundered around in a quagmire of crappy colleagues and neighbourhood angst.

'Edie?'

I looked up, as she placed her hand lightly on mine.

'Edie, has something happened?'

'I'm fine.'

'You're clearly not,' she said gently. 'You look like death and you're staring at your coffee like it's a bloody van

Gogh. What's wrong? Is it a hangover? Or,' she paused, her expression darkening, 'is it Jason? Because, if he's still messaging you, I'll—'

'Ruby.' I held up a hand and then, fearing that a conversation about Jason at this precise moment would tip me over into tears, I decided to lie. 'I haven't heard from him in weeks.'

'Good,' she said, her relief obvious. 'But if it's not him, what is it? It's not that bastard, Cameron, is it? Because if he's causing you any problems, I'm happy to go back there with you and sort him out. I'm valued and supported enough at Lovelock's to be able to speak up now and I'd do that for you. You do know that, don't you?'

I nodded, feeling extremely close to tears. Maybe a conversation about Jason would have been the better option after all. 'It's all OK,' I said, my voice catching slightly. 'He knows exactly how I feel about him. I've made that very clear.'

Her eyes widened and she blinked rapidly. 'Did you mention me?'

'No. But he's in no doubt that I despise him and want as little to do with him as possible.'

She flopped back in her chair. 'How so? What did you do?'

'I said no to an offer of help, no to an offer of a drink and then…' The room felt suddenly airless and I inhaled deeply. 'And then I made it very clear that I absolutely hate him. I won't go into the details because, quite frankly, I resent him even as a topic of conversation.'

'Wow,' she breathed, her expression one of grim fascination, satisfaction and approval. 'Bravo, Edie,' she said quietly, and for the first time that morning, I felt a little better.

'I miss having you around,' I said. 'I knew that I would.'

'And I,' she leaned forward, reaching again for my hand, 'miss you too. But there's a lot of stuff I don't miss. You know what I mean?'

I nodded. 'I so do.'

'Well, if you know that,' she said, releasing my hand and picking up her coffee, 'you'll also know that you need to get away.'

–

Having stayed with Ruby until the last possible moment, I made it back to the office with just minutes to spare before my meeting with Alison and Cameron.

'Take a breath, take a breath,' said Roger, looking up from a drawing, as I threw my jacket and bag on my desk and grabbed a scribble pad and pencil. 'You're not late.'

'I didn't think I was either, Roger,' I said, glancing towards Alison's office, where she and Cameron were already seated at the conference table. 'But I see Cameron decided to go in without me just the same.'

Luke laughed. 'Hey, steady your machete, girlfriend,' he said. 'He was in there from eleven fifteen to discuss a pitch, so chill.'

Ignoring him, I walked to Alison's office and tapped lightly on the door.

She looked up and beckoned me in.

'Could you please close the door behind you, Edith? And then take a seat,' she said, gesturing to the chair opposite Cameron.

I turned and pushed the door shut, taking the opportunity to close my eyes momentarily and catch a calming breath: in through the nose, out through the mouth. I was feeling much more energised and empowered than I had when heading off for my coffee with Ruby, but I was still far from my usual level of confidence and calm.

'Good weekend?' asked Alison, as I settled myself into my chair. She folded her hands on the table in front of her, her expression as tense as ever.

'I managed a few rain-walks,' I replied, offering her a smile only marginally less strained than her own, 'with Anthony, our dog.'

'How lovely,' she said. 'Cameron went walking in The Mendips.'

'Did he?' I looked across the table at him and rested a finger against my lips in order to suppress a sneer. He glanced at me and, just for a moment, the mask slipped and I saw in his eyes a resentment – an acknowledgement of what had happened between us. A second later it was gone and he relaxed back into his chair.

'I was going over a few things at the weekend and I would like you to work more collaboratively,' said Alison.

The swift change of subject and tone – from polite personal chit-chat, in which she had zero interest, to the business of the day – was typical Alison, but I still felt thrown.

'More collaboratively?' I queried.

'Yes.'

'Me?'

'You and Cameron. Both of you. With each other.'

She glanced over my shoulder and I turned to see Roger watching us from his desk. He looked down sharply as I caught his eye and when I turned back to Alison, her lips were pressed together in a thin, red, horizontal line.

'I do not mean an official collaboration,' she continued. 'But as a team we work best when we share and sound out our ideas. I think that was something which occurred naturally between yourself and Ruby, Edith. And I believe it's working between you and Roger, Cameron, but it needs to be across-team.'

I looked at her, wondering what had prompted this start-of-the-week, highly uncharacteristic lecture on teamwork. Had Cameron perhaps sidled into her office before nine a.m. and expressed his disappointment at my refusal to take him up on his selfless Friday-night offer to *share*? Or maybe he had called her over the weekend. Maybe their relationship was as close as Ruby had suspected.

'Of course,' said Cameron. 'That makes sense.'

He really was something else. But two could play the I'm-not-the-problem-here game.

'Absolutely,' I said brightly. 'In fact, Cameron suggested that we swap some ideas over a drink last week, but unfortunately I was time-poor that day. But point taken, Alison. I've been working in a bit of a bubble recently and, from a creative point of view, I know that's not great.'

She nodded. I didn't look at Cameron.

'Good,' she said. 'I want us to gel and sometimes, when dynamics change, that can take a little effort. I don't want either of you to feel that you don't have time to come up for air and conversation.' She hoisted her mouth back up into a smile. 'I'm pleased we all agree on this, and, of course, if you have any concerns, or if you feel there is anything which can be done to better facilitate integration and teamwork, do let me know.'

I nodded as it occurred to me that this new, out-there HR approach from Alison might have been prompted by more than just a moan from Cameron. Perhaps she'd taken legal advice after he groped Ruby and was now trying to head off any accusations of managerial culpability, or complacency, at the pass.

She pushed back her chair and stood up. 'Thank you, both.'

Cameron and I rose and headed for the door. He got there first and held it open for me.

I waved him through and, following him out, headed for my desk, before changing my mind and diverting instead to his, arriving just as he sat down.

'Sorry I wasn't free to go over things with you last week, Cameron,' I said, oozing regret, whilst ensuring that I was visible to Alison and audible to both Luke and Roger. 'But it would be great to discuss my project with you when you've got a moment.'

Cameron, with his back now to the room, looked up at me impassively. 'OK,' he said.

'And maybe I can help you with the cement choices you mentioned,' I continued. 'After all, we want to make sure that those boots fit you really well, don't we?' I laughed lightly, walking away.

'Hey! Don't let her get away with that kind of cheek, Cam!' called Luke, laughing along. 'Give her an inch and she'll take a mile.'

Reaching my desk, I sat down and looked unhappily across at Luke, still resentful of him, but also nostalgic for the pre-Cameron days, the Ruby days, when my colleagues were my friends and I didn't have to play anyone at their own grubby little games.

Then turning to my screen, I pulled my keyboard towards me and, with grubby games, Ruby's escape and the prospect of future collaboration with Cameron uppermost in my mind, I tapped out my letter of resignation.

Chapter 15

Giles had texted mid-afternoon to apologise for *radio silence* over the weekend and to ask if I fancied meeting him in town for a drink after work. He suggested The Cheshire Cheese, a favourite haunt of his, conveniently located for both my office and my former Hotwells home, and somewhere he and I had met often when I was still with Jason.

I had replied with an immediate 'yes', despite feeling as anxious about seeing him as I was eager. Because although I now felt ready to talk through Friday evening – and was keen to find out whether he thought his relationship with Kerry might be salvageable – I was not at all looking forward to telling him that I planned to resign. I knew he'd try to talk me out of it, but while I respected him way too much to hand in my notice before updating him, I was nevertheless determined to go through with it. As far as I was concerned, my relationship with Alison Gerrard Ltd was broken and irreparable and, that being the case, I felt that the sooner it was over and I could pick up my career elsewhere, the better.

Cameron was out of the office all afternoon, making the day not quite as unbearable as it might otherwise have been. But it was still grim enough for me to be heading for the lifts by five fifteen, to the obvious, but silent, surprise of Roger, whose eyebrows were slightly more raised than usual as he waved goodbye. Luke, meanwhile, paid more vocal attention to my early and rapid departure, yelling various quips after me about getaway cars, hot dates and an appointment to view a retirement home – all of which I ignored.

In terms of meeting Giles, I had no need to dash off so early. He had already told me that he was unlikely to be at the pub much before seven, and that six thirty would be the absolute earliest he could get there. But Cameron or no Cameron, I needed to get away from the office and I had judged that half an hour or so on my own with a glass of wine before Giles arrived would be no bad thing, as I braced myself for a post-mortem of Friday and for his reaction to my decision to resign.

However, within mere seconds of entering the pub, it became horribly plain that that plan was not going to pan out.

If only I'd spotted Jason before he'd spotted me, I could simply have legged it out of there and texted Giles to rearrange. Unfortunately, however, my ex saw me first and, judging by his relatively unsurprised expression when he did finally catch my eye, his time advantage over me had been long enough for him to pull himself together and adapt to the awkward situation. I of course had no such luxury, and my expression upon seeing him, as reflected in the mirror on the wall behind his head, was unblinking and bordering on lobotomised.

I froze: physically, emotionally and intellectually. So much so that I was unable even to raise a hand in response to his tentative wave – let alone leg it. It was the first time I had set eyes on him in the flesh since a near miss in a Clifton cinema, almost a year earlier. On that occasion, I had dodged into the loo after spotting him in the foyer, but tonight there was no escape, and to be so wholly unprepared for the encounter was nothing short of devastating.

In the end, taking matters into his own hands, he stood up from his table for two by the wall and walked to my position of petrification just a few feet from the bar.

'Edie,' he said, offering a smile as he reached me.

I looked him up and down. Everything about him, from his casual black sweater and jeans to his sleepy blue eyes and carelessly slicked-back, dark hair, conveyed a sense of charmingly effortless cool, even if at this moment it was tinged with uncertainty.

He cleared his throat before speaking again. 'It's great to see you.' Wisely, he made no attempt whatsoever at physical contact.

Movement being no longer beyond me, I could have managed a nod. But I chose not to. 'I'm meeting Giles,' I said.

At that, he lowered his eyes. 'Oh, yes,' he murmured, having the decency to look uncomfortable. 'He likes it here, doesn't he?' He looked back to his table and his drink. 'I'll get my jacket and go. I'm assuming Giles is just about as eager to see me as you are.' He attempted to resurrect a smile, but achieved only a grimace.

'You don't have to leave. I'll text Giles. He's running late. Finish your drink.'

I turned to leave, at which point he reached out and placed a hand on my arm. 'Edie.'

My head whipped round and I glared down at his hand. He withdrew it slowly, placing both hands into the pockets of his jeans. 'Sorry... sorry...' he said quietly. 'But look, if Giles isn't going to be here for a while, why not stay, just for five minutes, while I finish my drink? Then

I'll go. Five minutes and I'll be gone. I promise. Please, Edie.'

But there was no doubt or debate in my mind.

'No,' I said, walking away, leaving the pub and not stopping until I had turned the first corner. Then, feeling strangely numb and unexpectedly in control, I texted Giles, explaining the situation and suggesting that we meet at home. We could decide then, I told him, whether to go out or stay in.

Text sent, I began to walk, refusing to think about Jason and instead focusing on whether to catch a bus, call an Uber or just keep walking. As the evening was dry, and as Giles wouldn't be home for some time yet, I decided on the latter.

Determinedly focusing on putting one foot in front of the other and nothing else, I had just reached the top of Park Street and crossed to the Wills Building, when my eye was caught by the swish of a white-blonde bob and the flash of a red jacket on the opposite side of the road.

I stopped walking and turned quickly, standing on tiptoe and craning my neck in a failed attempt to catch a second glimpse of scarlet amongst the rush-hour pedestrians, sidestepping each other on the packed pavements.

'It can't have been her anyway,' I murmured, sinking back onto my heels. My mood dipped, as I imagined Ruby's afternoon at her Bath desk, surrounded by pleasant work colleagues who weren't competing with her for the boss's attention – or trying to cop a feel.

Still, I told myself, as large drops of forecast-but-forgotten summer rain began to splash down upon me, at least Ruby's career contentment had hardened my resolve that it was time to effect a similar change in my own life. That was something.

And clinging to that one tiny positive – and deciding not to let a drenching add to the misery of my day – I pulled up the hood of my raincoat, took out my phone and summoned an Uber.

Twenty minutes later, I was crouching on Giles's doorstep and rummaging through my bag for my keys. A search of my pockets had so far yielded nothing and I was just beginning to wonder if the keys had fallen out in the Uber, when I saw a pair of small grey-trousered legs, splashing up the newly puddled path towards me.

'I've been to Ollie's and made this,' said Harry, a little breathlessly, as usual foregoing any needless preamble. He held out a shoebox with some squares of bubble-wrap and a couple of corks stuck to it.

'Wow! I love that,' I laughed, standing up and enjoying a brief moment of uplift, it not yet having dawned on me that if Harry was outside my house, his mother would probably not be far behind.

'We always have to sit down at Ollie's, in case we break stuff,' said Harry, providing just enough information for me to deduce that Ollie's mother was precious about her possessions and preferred to operate a system of containment during playdates.

'Well, I love making models and drawing things,' I replied. 'It's actually my favourite thing to do. And that,' I pointed at the shoebox, 'is great. It looks like a computer.'

He looked at it for a moment. 'I think it is a computer.'

'Come on, Harry,' said Kerry, walking past without stopping and causing my smile to drop and my stomach to somersault. 'Let Edie get inside. And how many times have I told you not to run too far ahead? Hello, Edie,' she added, with obvious reluctance, as she turned to walk up her path.

'Hi,' I said, peering through the latticed twigs and branches of the various bushes which marked the boundary between Giles's front garden and her own.

'Is Giles in?' asked Harry hopefully.

I looked down at him. 'Afraid not.'

His shoulders drooped in disappointment. 'Oh. I wanted him to come for a play-date. Or I could come to your house.'

'Harry. Now,' said Kerry firmly.

'I'll ask him tomorrow,' shouted Harry as he ran back out onto the pavement, up his path and into the house without stopping.

Kerry didn't follow him inside, but instead looked after him before turning her head half towards me. 'Is there anything you want to tell me?' she asked quietly, her face largely obscured by the mesh of twigs and leaves. She looked, I thought, like a priest in a confessional.

'Don't be angry with Giles,' I said. 'None of this has anything to do with him.'

'I meant,' she said slowly, her voice uncharacteristically monotone, 'is there anything you want to tell me about you and Ron?'

I shook my head. 'No,' I replied 'there isn't.'

She turned away and went to step inside.

'Kerry.'

'Yes?'

'I hate confrontation and all this is making me so unhappy. I love my job and I just want to get on with it and the people I work with. I've always tried really, really hard to do that.' I hesitated, aware that this might be my last opportunity to state some sort of case. 'I'm honestly not a bad person,' I concluded, somewhat desperately.

She paused for a moment on the threshold and lowered her head. 'The thing is, Edie,' she said, quietly, 'in this situation, one of you has to be a bad person, and I know it's not Ron.'

And with that, she disappeared inside, gently closing the front door behind her.

–

'She thinks I'm a bad person, Giles.' I finished my miserable account of the day with a despairing sniff, whilst dabbing at my eyes with one of Giles's monogrammed hankies.

'I cannot deny that that is rather the implication.' He removed his arm from around me and leaned back on the living room sofa, adjusting his tartan dressing gown and offering me a wearily sympathetic smile, in the manner of a stoical, but put-upon, Arthur Dent. 'But you do have to remember that Kerry is going to be every bit as defensive of Ronald as I am of you, Edie,' he said gently.

'I know.' I took a sip from the mug of tea he had made for me and rested my head gratefully on his shoulder. 'I've just never felt quite this hopeless before, Giles. You know how much I love my job. It's been a daily constant, no matter what other crap was going on in my life. But now everything is a mess and my hands feel tied.'

'They feel tied because Ruby asked you to keep your conversation with her confidential. But that was *not* fair, Edie,' he said with emphasis, 'and now I feel that you must give serious consideration to advising Alison that you are aware of the accusations made against Ronald. How else do you propose to respond to her request that you work more closely with him?'

I mumbled into my wine glass.

'I'm sorry, I didn't catch that.'

'I'm going to resign,' I repeated, at barely increased volume.

He sighed heavily. 'That is entirely your prerogative. But please allow yourself a week to reflect upon the decision. Do not rush into something which you might come to regret.'

I looked up to discover his expression uncharacter-istically troubled and I knew that I was to blame. 'I'm so sorry to burden you with all this, Giles. Of course, I will give it very careful thought. I'll wait at least a week before handing in my resignation and I promise not to do anything rash.'

I felt his frame relax and, after a moment's comfort-able silence between us, he said, 'Why don't we watch one of your life-enhancing TV shows? Isn't there's usually someone baking, being arrested or displaying their poorly genitals to a medic around now?'

I sniffed, laughed and then reached for the remote. 'There is,' I said.

'Perfect.' He raised his mug, clinking it against mine. 'Here's to us switching on and switching off.'

Three hours later I headed upstairs to bed, grateful to the happy combination of *Embarrassing Bodies*, *Cops with Cameras* and – most of all – Giles for keeping me distracted from thoughts of the less-than-perfect day just gone, and the unpromising week to come.

Sadly, however, that peace of mind was not to last because the moment I climbed into bed and plugged in my phone to charge, the twin notifications: *Text message Jason* and *Text message Ruby* appeared onscreen, delivering an unwanted, last-minute reminder of a day best forgotten.

I sighed, wishing that I could ignore at least Jason's text. But, with the damage to my mood already done, I felt that I had no choice but to read it – and to read it first. Because while Ruby's text might inadvertently make me feel like a personal and professional failure, it would still be less depressing than whatever Sir Shaggalot had to say, and I wanted to save the best, or at least the best-intentioned, for last.

Propping myself up on pillows, I began to read, immediately interested to note that, in contrast to Jason's other recent messages, in which his tone was meanderingly reflective and regretful – like Winnie the Pooh with an undercurrent of Eeyore – this one was direct and to the point to an almost clinical degree.

> Would like to say it was good to see you tonight, but it wasn't and, believe it or not, my evening only got worse. There are things I need to tell you. I'd rather explain face-to-face, but if you prefer, I'll put it in an email tomorrow. But in-person would be better – for you, not for me. I'm sure you'll have questions. Let me know. And I'm sorry – still. J

I frowned at the screen, surprised to discover that, on this occasion, curiosity was my overwhelming response, way ahead of frustration, irritation or exhaustion. And it came as a further shock to realise that I was actually toying with the idea of meeting him.

I wondered for a moment about consulting Ruby. But I knew that there would be little point in that, other than to share the intrigue. She'd only explode, either by text or, worse still, by phone and I just wasn't up to that conversation right now.

I closed Jason's text and opened hers.

> Great to see you today but was sad to find you so low. I hope it's nothing to do with Jason. Don't waste any time on that bastard, Edie. He's so not worth it and remember, you can call on me any time. Tell me if he bothers you again. You don't have to handle him, or that creep Cameron, on your own. xx

After a moment spent gazing at the screen, and aware of an undefined, embryonic anxiety, I reopened Jason's text and replied.

> Tomorrow after work – 6pm? Cheshire Cheese again?

His reply arrived within seconds.

> See you there.

I inhaled deeply and, as I let the breath go, I felt my anxiety subsiding and being gradually replaced by something else. Whether it was a sense of calm or delayed shock kicking in, I wasn't sure, but as I switched my phone to silent and placed it face down on the bedside table, of one thing I was certain: I didn't want to reply to Ruby just yet.

Chapter 16

I didn't tell Giles about the arrangement to meet Jason, deciding that I'd caused him quite enough anxiety over the past four days and that he deserved some time off. So instead, I spent breakfast time on Tuesday asking him about his ongoing fitness programme, which would, that evening, see him running around the Downs, whilst being yelled at by a former army corporal. Determined to keep the mood upbeat, I didn't voice any of my concerns regarding the possibility of torn ligaments – or the much greater one of doing a press-up in dog poo – and I congratulated myself that, despite everything, he headed off to work that morning displaying greater levels of equanimity than at any time since ten p.m. the previous Friday.

My equanimity levels, on the other hand, had remained resolutely at zero since waking, a situation which manifested itself from 8:30 a.m. in a complete inability to focus on work. Instead, I found myself inescapably preoccupied with examining and re-examining the events of the past few months. In particular, as I watched my work colleagues going about their daily business, I found myself questioning my dramatically changed opinion of them.

Did, for example, my past experience of Luke *really* bear out that he was an unreconstructed chauvinist?

Had Alison *always* behaved like a ruthless pragmatist? Was Cameron actually a…?

What was Cameron? Processing my feelings towards him was particularly challenging, as I struggled to reconcile three primary, inescapable facts: firstly, that he had harassed Ruby; secondly, that Alison had rated and employed him; and thirdly, that Kerry loved and trusted him – completely. And as I noticed him that morning, talking respectfully to Alison, listening with apparently genuine interest to Luke, and bringing a Lemsip to Roger, who had been coughing and sneezing practically non-stop, it felt as if trying to make sense of Cameron Grange might cause my head to explode.

I did my best to hide my inner turmoil, primarily by making copious notes about nothing, in between staring thoughtfully at my screen and saying 'Hmm' a lot. But I realised that my subterfuge had failed utterly when Roger, of all people, suddenly asked me if I was OK.

'Hope I haven't given you my bug, Edie,' he said nasally from his desk at lunchtime. It was just the two of us in the office, Alison and Cameron having left for a site meeting and Luke having popped out to pick up a sandwich.

'I've got numerous medications if you need anything.' He extracted an enormous handkerchief from his trouser pocket and blew his nose loudly. 'Far too many, in fact,' he added, sighing and opening his desk drawer, peering inside and then holding up a bottle of Day Nurse and several packets of pills.

I turned to him, puzzled by the offer. 'I'm fine, but thanks, Roger.'

'You don't look fine,' he said, pushing shut the drawer. 'You look completely out of sorts.'

'Do I?'

'You do.'

I didn't reply, but nodded acceptingly, realising that *completely out of sorts* was exactly how I felt and, moved by Roger's gruff, fatherly concern, I found myself wondering whether I might feel better if I had a little cry.

'Client being reasonable and co-operative?' he asked, now with the air of a no-nonsense protector on the lookout for anyone in need of a good kicking.

More silent nodding.

'Well…' He cleared his throat. 'That's grand. But if the situation should change and I can be of any help, just say. Oh and tonight,' he cleared his throat for a second time, 'provided I haven't keeled over by then, I'm taking Cameron for a pint at The Port of Call if you'd like to join us. I think I heard you say you wanted to talk some things over with him yesterday.'

I continued to nod but didn't look up.

'He's a nice lad, you know, Edie.'

I stopped nodding, feeling as if I was walking an emotional tightrope and about to lose my balance. 'Is he?' I murmured weakly.

'He is,' replied Roger emphatically, apparently judging the question to be unrhetorical.

'I'm out tonight,' I said quietly, after a moment. 'But thanks for asking.'

'Exciting. Where are you off to then?' called Luke, as he barged his way through the glass double doors, making a typically crashing return to the office. 'Somewhere in Henleaze? Bingo? Bowls? Bridge?'

'Just for a drink.'

He grinned. 'She's being suspiciously vague, don't you think, Rog?' he said, flinging a *Pret a Manger* bag down on his desk and then reaching inside. 'Here, got you this,' he continued, throwing me a piece of plastic-wrapped banana cake, "cos you've been even less smiley than Roger lately.'

I looked at Roger who raised his eyebrows at me. 'He's not wrong.'

'Yeah, so cheer up,' said Luke, sitting down and taking his lunch from the bag. 'No excuse now,' he added, pointing at the cake.

I stared down at it, as my emotional tightrope swung precariously from side-to-side. 'Thanks,' I murmured. 'And, you know, I'm sorry if I've...' I stopped, unable to finish the sentence, not wanting to think too deeply about what I might actually be apologising for.

When I raised my eyes, Luke was looking at me questioningly.

I heaved a sigh and then managed a smile. 'Maybe I do have your bug coming on, Roger.' I turned towards him. 'My head feels like someone has poured concrete in my ear. Is that how yours started?'

He shook his head. 'I was coughing up large quantities of green phlegm from the off.'

'You know, on second thoughts, maybe I'll save this smashed avocado thing for later,' murmured Luke, sliding a box back into the bag.

'Are you going to go home, Edie?' asked Roger.

'No.' I shook my head. 'But I think I probably need some fresh air,' I continued, standing up and reaching for my coat. 'I'm sure that'll help. Can I get anything for anyone while I'm out?'

'Very kind, but no thank you,' said Roger.

'You couldn't get me a smoothie, could you?' asked Luke. 'I forgot to pick one up.'

'Sure,' I said, walking towards the door. 'What flavour?'

'Anything,' he said, before looking towards Roger as the latter began to cough loudly and productively, 'so long as it's not green.'

Chapter 17

That evening, as I walked into The Cheshire Cheese following a day of emotional confusion and nervous anticipation, I wondered if my meeting with Jason might prove to be an anticlimax. In fact, a significant part of me was hoping that it would be exactly that. I hoped that he would turn up, repeat his spiel of twenty-two months ago, about his feelings for me being completely separate from his addiction to sex, and then bugger off; forever, this time.

Instinctively, however, I didn't feel that that was going to happen. The tone of his text had been so different, so to-the-point and so wholly devoid of bullshit, that I was pretty sure he had something new to say. That being the case, I felt I had no option but to listen to whatever that might be – no matter how much I might not want to.

So I bought myself a glass of wine, sat down at the same table for two he had been occupying the night before, and I waited.

He arrived at just after six and spotted me immediately, raising a hand before going straight to the bar and buying himself a lager. He didn't, I noticed, smile once. And he still wasn't smiling as he walked towards me, placed his bottle on the table and sat down.

I watched as he removed his jacket, twisting in his seat to hang it with excessive care on the back of his chair. I knew him well enough to realise that the prolonged lack of both eye contact and conversation were a sign of significant nerves. Friends I'd introduced Jason to had usually included 'laid-back' in their initial assessment of him. It didn't matter whether he was stuck in traffic, delivering a report or chatting over dinner, he habitually appeared relaxed, whether in fact he was or not. So for him to appear even slightly uncomfortable, as he did this evening, meant that internally he was a churning, chaotic mess.

I had seen such unease only a couple of times in the past: first when his mother died and then again when I refused his appeal to give our relationship a second chance. So whatever information he was now about to impart, I realised that it had to be pretty big and pretty grim. What I didn't yet know was whether that information was stressful to him alone, or whether it was also about to impact on me.

I waited for him to settle himself and then, determined to get straight to the point and to remain as dispassionate as possible, I asked, 'What is it you want to tell me?'

He folded his hands on the table and looked at me expressionlessly. 'I'm getting help,' he said.

Relief flooded through me and I relaxed back in my chair. 'Well, congratulations. But is that it?' I demanded, my sense of relief almost immediately displaced by a rising tide of irritation that he had dragged me here solely to boast about his efforts to be a better person.

He shook his head. 'No. But part of the process involves being honest with myself and open with you about what I am and what I have done. I need to take ownership of that.'

I widened my eyes, his statement of intent only adding to my annoyance. 'Well, that's great if it makes *you* feel better, but what if you being open and honest makes everybody else feel like crap? Personally, I don't feel like I need any more details, courtesy of you. The ones I discovered all by myself were quite enough.'

'You have every right to be angry.'

'Kudos for accepting that.'

'But this isn't about the past, it's about now, and it's not just about me, it's about you too.'

'About me now?'

'Yes.'

I picked up my drink. 'Go on.'

'When we were together—'

'I thought you said this was about now,' I snapped, anxiety rather than anger causing me to lose my cool. 'Let's skip the historical background, Jason. I was there throughout, remember?'

'Please, Edie...' he said quietly. 'I wouldn't have asked you to come here if I didn't think you needed to hear what I'm *trying* to tell you.'

I took a deep breath and gestured with my wine glass for him to continue.

'When we were together, whenever Ruby was around...'

I closed my eyes and exhaled slowly at the mention of her name, realising that I had been unconsciously holding my breath.

'Whenever Ruby was around, she made it clear that she was attracted to me.' He delivered the information with no apparent emotion.

I opened my eyes and stared expressionlessly at him. 'But isn't *everybody* attracted to you?' I said, trying to sound bored. 'I'm pretty sure that's why we're no longer a couple.'

'Then, one weekend, when you were away, she turned up at the house,' he said, maintaining a level tone and attempting no rebuttal. 'At first, she claimed that she'd forgotten you were away and had been passing and thought she'd stop by. I made her a coffee and then she admitted that she'd known you wouldn't be there, but felt that there was a mutual attraction between us which needed to be addressed. At that point, I said I thought she should leave. She was your friend and that made me uncomfortable,' he added, lowering his eyes and addressing the table.

'You were uncomfortable because she was my friend…' I said slowly, as if considering the point. 'So, can I just clarify? Your moral code is that friends are out of bounds, but absolutely anyone else is fine?'

'When you and I split up,' he said, continuing to ignore my increasingly bitter interruptions, 'she began calling and texting regularly, suggesting we meet up, offering to talk things through, if I thought that would help. I agreed, and when we met, she immediately told me how angry she was at what I had done to you, her friend. But as we talked, gradually her emphasis changed, and it became clear that she felt I had hurt *her* too. I had rejected her but slept with other women and she was upset by that.' He paused. 'I'm sorry, Edie,' he said, now looking up.

'Why?' I asked, with a nonchalance convincing even to myself. 'So far, you haven't – in this particular fantasy – done anything to apologise for.'

He looked at me steadily. 'I met with her a number of times and on the fourth occasion I slept with her. It was some months after you and I had split up. I don't know why I did it. I don't remember wanting it to happen.'

'The fourth occasion? Well, thanks for being so specific.' I placed my elbows on the table and rested my head in my hands. 'But is there much more? Because I'm so, so tired of everything to do with you, Jason.'

'I knew that I'd made a mistake, so I called her and apologised and said that I was really mixed up and in therapy and didn't want another relationship, casual or otherwise, for a long time. She seemed to accept that. I think the truth was that because you had no interest in me, and I – as far as she knew – didn't want a relationship with you or with anyone else, she was no longer interested in me.'

'Deep,' I murmured, focusing entirely upon my resentment towards him and an impatience to be gone.

'But then, after hearing nothing from her for months, she suddenly got in touch again, about three months ago. She said that she knew that I'd been texting you and that I was seeing someone – I'm not, by the way,' he added.

'I really, *really* don't care whether you are or not,' I said, still leaning on the table and feeling as if its support was the only thing preventing me from collapsing to the floor, curling into the foetal position and relying on the kindness of strangers to roll me into taxi. 'Just, for God's sake, finish your story.'

'Edie…' he reached across the table towards me.

I sat upright and glared at him. 'Just finish it,' I snapped.

He slowly withdrew his hand.

'I replied to her, confirming that I wasn't seeing anyone. I had hoped that would be it, especially when she told me that she was moving to Bath, but her texts and calls just kept coming. Again, at first, she was telling me not to hurt you any more than I had already, and about how much she cared for you, and that I had to stop contacting you. But then the tone changed and she wanted to meet up again and said that she thought maybe we'd missed an opportunity. In the end, I knew I needed to put a stop to it and I agreed to see her. We met for a drink – here – last night.'

I looked steadily at him, but said nothing.

'When you walked in,' he continued quietly, 'I wanted her to be early – to walk in too. At that moment, I didn't care about the consequences of that, I just realised that, one way or another, I wanted you to know everything.'

He paused and I picked up my wine glass – ignoring the shaking of my hand – and took a gulp. 'Yay for your epiphany. But don't stop now,' I said, 'you've got me gripped.'

He lowered his eyes to the table. 'When she arrived, I apologised for treating her badly. I told her again that I knew I had a problem and that I was dealing with it and that I couldn't see any kind of relationship working with her, either now or in the future. She asked if I still loved you and whether I wanted a relationship with anyone else, but I told her that I didn't think it would be helpful to discuss that. Then she accused me of using her and of being a misogynist and various other things, and I left.' He looked around the pub. 'Suffice to say that it wasn't great and I'm slightly surprised they've let me in here again tonight.'

He picked up his lager, indicating that his account was at an end.

I threw my hands up. 'Why are you doing this, Jason? What exactly do you think the point of this is? Other than to anger, irritate and hurt me?'

'I care about you,' he said, emotion evident in his voice for the first time that evening. 'In my own twisted, unhealthy, desperately sad kind of way, I actually love you.'

Not trusting myself to speak, I simply shook my head.

He heaved a sigh and, when he spoke again, his tone was even once more. 'I'm sorry. Forget I said that. That's not why I'm here. I'm here because I need you to know what she is. She genuinely believes that you and she have a wonderful friendship, and that you are some sort of affable ingénue who needs her protection. But there's also a rivalry there, a jealousy of what you are – of whatever you have and she hasn't. I don't know whether you see that now, but you certainly didn't see it when we were together.'

He took another swig of lager, appearing suddenly exhausted. 'I don't know whether she plans to tell you she's had contact with me,' he continued more calmly, 'but I wanted to tell you the truth before she spins it into something it wasn't and isn't. She doesn't take rejection well and in trying to hurt me, I have no idea whether she'll hurt you too – even if she doesn't mean to.'

As he finished his speech, his voice broke and it was a moment or two before he spoke again.

'I'm sorry,' he said, 'but everything I've told you is the truth. I hope you believe me.'

'Believe you?' I stared at the table and took a deep breath, attempting to compose myself. 'You mean like I believed you every time you told me that your train/plane/taxi had been delayed?' I began quietly. 'Or when you told me that you were working late? Or that the conference had been extended by another day?'

Still not looking at him, I reached down for my bag before standing up and snatching my coat from the back of my chair. 'I don't believe any of it, Jason,' I said, walking towards the door and not looking back.

I exited the bar, throwing on my coat as I headed for home. Tonight, I decided, I would definitely walk all the way. Then maybe by the time I got there I would feel less desolate, less desperate and less village-idiot-stupid than I did right now. Because no matter what I'd told Jason, the truth was that at that moment I did believe him. I believed every single word.

Chapter 18

Thankfully, Giles was still out doing star-jumps and poo press-ups on the Downs when I arrived home from The Cheshire Cheese. I wasn't in the mood for conversation and, more importantly, I didn't want to worry him by appearing anything less than completely fine. His absence therefore came as something of a relief and, after making myself a quick sandwich, I left him a scribbled note saying that I could feel a cold coming on, and hurried upstairs to bed.

Having already told Roger, Luke – and now Giles – that I was ill, I was perfectly placed for calling in sick the next morning, so when I woke before six and found myself unable to get back to sleep, I decided to do just that. However, my plan was scuppered less than an hour later, when Giles himself woke up *genuinely* unwell and unable to go into work.

The first indication that there was a problem was a range of disturbingly loud anatomical noises coming from the middle-floor bathroom at around six forty-five. When I went down to investigate, a very green-looking Giles shared his suspicion that the mussels he'd had for supper the night before had been off. To my credit, I simply patted him on the back, nodded sympathetically and made no reference whatsoever to the ninety minutes he'd spent rolling around in shit.

Of course, the upshot of Giles being at death's door was that it just didn't feel right for me to stay at home all day faking it. So, having placed as many meds, drinks and electronic gadgets by his bed as I thought he might need, I headed off to work, leaving strict instructions for him to call me if he didn't improve.

From a selfish point of view, Giles's stomach bug at least provided me with an unlikely, but very welcome, distraction from my woes. Until I stepped out into the bright morning sunshine of the avenue, I hadn't had a second to think in any detail about my distressing evening with Jason. In fact, it had barely crossed my mind at all. However, once away from all the heaving, retching and playing Florence Nightingale, I didn't even make it to the end of the road before my focus turned once again to dissecting his deeply depressing pub monologue.

At times, I found myself pulling back from my early, wholesale acceptance of his account. My gut instinct may have been to believe him, but then my gut instinct had been to believe him when he said he was re-parking the car at his Aunty Pam's wake, when in fact he was having sex with his cousin's wife in the cupboard where they kept the Toilet Duck. So what did I know? And while it was undeniable that the timeline he had provided regarding Ruby's calls and texts did tie in with her various discussions with me, that didn't mean that his entire account was accurate. Maybe, I reasoned, Ruby had contacted him only to warn him off, and maybe she had decided not to tell me about it because she didn't want to worry me.

But it didn't matter how many times I told myself all this, I still couldn't completely silence the voice in my head which repeatedly whispered, barely pausing for breath, that Jason was telling the truth. Because, why would he lie? What possible advantage was there for him in telling me that he had managed to resist sleeping with my friend only until we'd split up? It hardly made him shoot up in the perfect partner stakes. All it did was confirm him as the despicable low-life I already knew him to be, and make me doubt Ruby – and he had been perfectly upfront about the latter being his intended purpose.

In this way, I spent my entire morning alternately running towards, and then stepping back from, the emotional precipice of accepting that a woman whom I had called a friend, in whom I had confided and had total trust, was actually as duplicitous as the ex with whom I had felt secure enough to purchase a three-bedroomed terrace in Hotwells. To sum up: I felt as confused, as conflicted and as far from my happy place as it was possible to be, a situation which did not go unnoticed by Luke.

'You look *even* worse than you did yesterday,' he said quietly, as he returned a drawing to me at the end of the morning. 'I've scanned that in again for you,' he added.

'Thanks and thanks.'

He nodded and then, after glancing at Cameron and Roger, both of whom had their backs to us, he said, 'Do you fancy lunch out? Might be a nice break.'

I pointed at the scribbled calls-to-make list on my desk and the plan now in my hand. 'I've not made much headway with these this morning.'

'That's why I thought stepping away from them might help – seeing as staring at them hasn't.'

I looked up at him again and then, realising that he was right, I nodded and reached for my coat.

Luke sat down opposite me and gazed around the deserted cafe. 'I know this place is a favourite of yours and Ruby's,' he said, with a slight shiver, 'but God knows why. It really gives me the creeps. I notice there's no hygiene rating on display.' He raised a hand and indicated each of the walls in turn. 'Look, look, look.'

'Shhh,' I said, pushing his hand to the table and glancing over my shoulder at the cashier, who had greeted us with a grunt and undisguised disdain on entry. 'She'll hear you.'

'Well, maybe she should,' he said, glancing down at his wrap and then picking it up and taking a bite. 'Is beige a flavour?' he asked, chewing hard. ''Cos this is so beige.'

'I've only ever had the coffee here before,' I admitted, looking down at the rather sad excuse for a coronation chicken sandwich I had selected. 'And I'm not sure I've really got that much of an appetite today.'

'You're not ill, are you.'

I had just picked up my sandwich, but paused before taking a bite. 'I can't tell if that's a statement or a question.'

'I'm not sure either,' he acknowledged. 'But you don't look classically sick.'

'Classically sick? Is that a look?'

'You know, green, or white, or yellow, or spotty, or snotty.'

'Oh, I see. In that case, no, I don't think I'm classically sick.' I bit into my sandwich.

'So, what's up, then?' he asked. 'It's me, isn't it?'

I looked up, expecting to find him smirking, but instead his expression was uncharacteristically serious. 'What? No, don't be silly. Of course it's not you. Why would you think that?'

'You've been fake-smiling at me since first thing Monday and I just wanted to make sure that wasn't because of what I said on Friday. You know…' he added a little awkwardly, 'when we talked about Ruby.'

I put my sandwich back down on its chipped, white plate and heaved a sigh. 'Look, I had a really, *really* bad Friday night and not a great weekend. Monday evening wasn't much fun and then last night, just when I thought things couldn't get any worse… guess what? They did.'

He looked relieved. 'OK, so it's not me, then. Great. Let's talk about *Game of Thrones.*'

I smiled, while at the same time feeling completely wrung-out and desperate to offload about the wine and cheese, and about Jason, and about Ruby. Sadly, I was all too aware that any explanation of my life traumas of the past five days would extend way beyond what was left of our lunch hour. Besides, I reminded myself, my smile fading, Luke was firmly in Cameron's camp over all this.

But there was one issue which I thought we could adequately cover over a sandwich, and to leave Luke in the dark over my intermittent moodiness towards him – something which he had clearly picked up on – didn't seem fair to either of us.

'It's not *entirely* you,' I said.

'I bloody knew it,' he sighed, pulling a face, throwing down his wrap and pushing his plate away from him. 'Come on, then. Out with it.'

'OK.' I took a deep breath. 'It's just that, I'm coming at the Ruby and Cameron thing as a woman…'

He frowned. 'Er, yes, obviously.'

'And as a feminist.'

'Obviously again.'

'Whereas—'

'I am not a woman.'

'Nor are you a feminist,' I said, picking up and taking a second bite from my sandwich.

He raised his eyebrows. 'I'd dispute that, actually.'

I looked at him doubtfully. 'I know everyone agreed to let it drop, Luke, but we both still know what actually happened and, because of that, your relationship with Cameron bugs me. I'm sorry if you think that's not fair, but I can't help it.'

'It's not remotely fair,' he said, frowning. 'And if we filled this cafe with fair-minded feminists, they'd pelt you with those crappy muffins over there for claiming that it is.' He gestured towards the selection of lacklustre cakes on display behind me and I turned in time to see the cashier throw an offended scowl in our direction.

'They look really yummy to me,' I said loudly, as she began wiping down the counter whilst muttering something about *entitled pricks*.

I sighed and turned back to Luke. 'Look, I'm not saying you shouldn't be professional,' I said, keeping my voice determinedly low. 'I'm not saying shun Cameron like he's an Amish with a button-fetish. But do you have to be so matey with him? You seem to positively admire the guy.'

He was now no longer frowning, but his expression was still about as far from acceptance as it was possible to be. His jaw twitched as he clenched and unclenched his teeth, and I noticed a growing pink tinge to his cheeks.

'You're angry,' I murmured, realising with some fascination that I had never actually witnessed that before.

'I can't believe what I'm hearing,' he said, his hardened tone as unfamiliar as his stony expression. 'Imagine if the tables were turned and it was a woman in Cameron's position. Would you still be sitting there, calling me out for being *matey* with her?'

'Of course!' I exclaimed. 'Cameron's sex has nothing to do with this. If it was a woman we were talking about, I wouldn't want you to be unpleasant to her, but neither would I expect you to fawn over her and look up to her as if she was some kind of role model. It makes me think that you think what Cameron did was OK.'

'It was OK.'

My jaw dropped. 'You don't mean that.'

'Of course I bloody do. What is *wrong* with you, Edie?' he asked, now sounding exasperated. 'I've always thought that we were on the same page about all the important stuff. But you've lost me on this one,' he said, looking at me with obvious disappointment as his face began to cool. 'I'm sorry if you're upset about what happened. Maybe you think Ruby left because of it – and maybe she did – maybe she would have changed her mind and stayed if this hadn't all kicked off. But you're letting your friendship with her get in the way here. Cameron is a good guy who, in my opinion, handled a difficult situation in the right way. And you know what, I *do* admire him for that, even if you don't.'

I stared at him, seriously considering ending the conversation there and then, gathering up my things and going back to the office. But then, what was back there for me? I no longer related to any of my colleagues except Roger – and the only reason that he was still on my list of relatables was because I hadn't actually discussed this particular topic with him yet.

My shoulders sagged at the thought and, dismissing the idea of storming out – which would, in any case, have required the summoning up of far more energy than I was at that point able to access – I instead closed my eyes and allowed my head to droop. 'I can't believe you're standing up for him, Luke. Can't you see how wrong that is?' I asked weakly.

He didn't reply and after a moment or two it crossed my mind that maybe he'd gone. But when I opened my eyes, he was still sitting there, the only difference being that he was now looking at me with obvious concern.

'Edie, is everything OK?' he asked gently. 'Only you really don't seem yourself right now.'

'No, everything is not OK!' I snapped, anger now superseding exhaustion. 'I've had enough. I've already drafted my resignation and I'm handing it in as soon as we get back to the office. And in the meantime, Luke, don't you dare try to gaslight me into thinking that harassment in the workplace is acceptable. Because it's not. The only twisted thinking here belongs to you and your new best bud, Cameron – not to me.' I stood up, grabbed my coat and reached for my bag.

But then Luke was on his feet too, my satchel in his hands. 'What? Whoa, Edie.'

I made a grab for the bag, but he leaned away from me and hugged it to his chest. 'Of course I don't think harassment in the workplace is OK. But isn't that exactly why we *should be* supporting Cameron? Telling Alison what was going on was the right thing for him to do. Ruby had to be made to understand that her behaviour was unacceptable and he clearly wasn't getting through to her. And having got Alison to intervene, he then let Ruby off the hook. He didn't have to do that, did he?' he asked, his tone a gentle appeal for understanding. 'I know she's your friend, but that kind of thing is not OK on any level. You didn't see it, Edie, but I did. She was persistent and full-on and, maybe because no one's ever objected before, she didn't seem to pick up on how uncomfortable he was with it.'

I blinked up at him, my mouth opening and closing but no sound coming out.

He placed my bag on the table and laid a gentle hand on my arm. 'OK, so now you look classically sick. Sit back down for a moment.'

I lowered myself slowly onto the chair and sat motionless, staring at him.

'You OK?' he asked.

'So it was *Ruby* who harassed *Cameron*,' I murmured.

He appeared puzzled for a moment and then suddenly his eyes widened and he put a hand to his mouth. 'Bloody hell. Did you think it was the other way round?' He threw his head back and laughed loudly. 'Well, thank God for that, because I thought you'd gone insane!'

I continued to stare at him and his face immediately dropped. 'Shit. Sorry, Edie, but I'm just so relieved. You know, I seriously thought you'd turned into some sort of… Never mind, God, I am sorry,' he said, clearly having some difficulty pulling himself together. 'So why did you think…?' He looked at me, with a mixture of horror and excitement. 'You're not saying Ruby told you that?'

I attempted a nod, but instead found myself rocking, as my upper body insisted on moving backwards and forwards along with my head. It was a strangely comforting motion.

'Shit a brick.' Luke slumped back in his chair and looked dazedly down at the table. 'Why would she do that?' He addressed the question to his beige wrap, rather than to me – presumably because he felt it would be more likely to provide him with a coherent response.

After a moment or two with no reply from either myself or the wrap, he looked up, reached across the table and patted my arm. 'Look, it's not a great thing to have happened, but at least she's not waiting for you back at the office. You'll have had a chance to think it all through and calm down before you see her again. Although, to be fair,' he added, 'you seem pretty calm right now – in a catatonic kind of way.'

When I still didn't reply, he said, 'And now you don't have a problem with Cameron, which is really, really great. We can all be best buds!'

I stopped rocking, covered my face with my hands and let out a groan.

'Edie, honestly,' he said, 'don't let this make you feel bad. She was a bitch for doing that to Cameron, but he knows nothing about it, and he doesn't know that you were angry with him, so just forget about it. Hey and I know it's not funny right now, but we'll be wetting ourselves about this tomorrow.'

I slowly lowered my hands from my face and stared miserably up at him.

'OK,' he said, hurriedly taking one of my hands and giving it a squeeze, 'maybe not tomorrow, but in a few weeks' time you'll be all, "Remember when I thought you and Cameron were complete sexist bastards?" and we'll be all, "Yeah, how weird was that?" and we'll have a right laugh about it.' He grinned at me and nodded rapidly.

'Luke, does Cameron work for sex?' I asked quietly.

At this point, he stopped nodding and his expression bordered on fearful. 'Does he work for…?' He hesitated for a moment. 'I'm sorry, what did you say, Edie? Only it sounded an awful lot like you were asking me if Cameron

183

is a sex worker. Not that I'd judge if he was, of course. I'm sure he'd be very popular with both sexes.'

'Does he provide architectural services at reduced cost in exchange for sexual favours?'

His face contorted into an expression midway between laughter and panic.

'She told you that too?' he asked, pursing his lips as the corners of his mouth twitched uncontrollably upwards, the urge to laugh clearly winning the day. 'And you believed her?'

I closed my eyes and decided that this time I might not bother opening them until tomorrow. 'She said you told her that Cameron was putting work through at reduced cost for a woman he—'

'Now that bit *is* true!' exclaimed Luke excitedly.

I opened my eyes, experiencing a microscopic surge of hope that I might have been just a tiny bit justified in believing Cameron to be a bastard. Admittedly, it was a hope which didn't do me a huge amount of credit, but if he could be proved to be at all sexist or misogynistic, then that might at least slightly alleviate the enormous burden of being completely and utterly in the wrong, under which I was currently being crushed.

'He brought the project with him from his last practice. It's only a small build,' said Luke. 'Barely a build at all, really.'

'That's OK,' I said, not caring about the value of the project for which Cameron was accepting payment in kind. It was the principle that mattered.

'It's for a Bristol client. She lives in Henleaze, actually,' continued Luke. 'Single mum – a widow – big house, tiny income. On a very tight budget basically, but still wanted to pay for everything. So Cameron doesn't charge her his going rate and he makes up any shortfall to the business for work carried out in office hours. He's covering part of the build-costs too. The client doesn't know anything about that, though. We invoice both her and Cameron for the practice costs and, when work starts, the contractors will invoice the practice, and then those costs will be split between Cameron and the client. It was all agreed with Alison when she offered him the job. Not sure that there's any sex involved – although I guess there might be. They're certainly very close… Edie? God, Edie, you're just looking worse and worse.'

It was at that point that I decided to stop grubbily scraping around for any mitigating circumstance which might even partly excuse my behaviour towards Cameron. The man was clearly a saint.

'I'm not going back to the office,' I said hoarsely. 'Can you tell Alison that I'm classically sick? Please don't say anything to her, or Roger, or Cameron about any of this.'

For a moment, he looked like he was about to argue but then, instead, simply nodded. 'Shall I sort a cab?' he asked.

'No, thanks. You stay and finish your lunch.' I pointed at his untouched wrap. 'I'm going to walk for a bit and then catch a bus. And Luke,' I added, standing up, 'I'm so sorry for, you know, thinking that you…' I wobbled to a halt and decided against a second attempt at the sentence.

He waved a hand. 'Hey! I'm a renowned dick. Anything is believable!'

I smiled and walked around to his side of the table, bending low to give him a hug.

'Wonder why she lied like that,' he said, as I straightened up to put on my coat. 'I mean, I always knew she was a bit tricky, but that's above and beyond. She could have just said nothing and you would never have known. So why lie?'

I buttoned up my coat and shrugged sadly. But as I offered him a wave and made my way towards the door of the cafe, I was pretty sure that I already knew at least part of the answer to his question. Because Jason, I decided, had been absolutely right: Ruby Blair did not take rejection well.

Chapter 19

I spotted Nicky as soon as I turned the corner into the avenue. She was coming out of a house just a few doors down and looked to be in a hurry, as she pulled the door shut and made her way quickly down the path. I slowed my pace and then, as she paused to close her garden gate, I stopped walking altogether and turned to examine a shrub in the front garden next to me. My conversation with Luke hadn't left me in the mood for neighbourly chit-chat and, besides, Nicky didn't look as if she was up for any either.

But I was wrong.

'Edie!' she exclaimed.

I turned to find her smiling as she stooped to retrieve a set of keys from the pavement. 'Just throwing away my keys,' she laughed. 'Are you a bit of a gardener?' She stood up and nodded towards the bush.

I stopped fingering the twigs of the leafless plant. 'Oh, hi. I was just…' I looked at the bush, 'wondering what this is.'

'Dead,' she said, matter-of-factly. 'But I'm glad I've seen you. You on your way home?' She nodded over her shoulder. 'I'm walking that way.'

'I'm going…'

I hesitated and for a moment I considered claiming to be heading in the opposite direction. But in the end, I decided that I didn't have the energy for a detour. 'I'm going home.'

'Great,' she replied, as we started to walk. 'I'd actually been hoping to run into you or Giles because...' She paused and pulled a worried face. 'Andy told me that I was really loud and out of order at June's – especially about Giles. I just wanted to say sorry to you both and check that he wasn't upset.'

Despite the unwelcome reminder of Friday night, I managed a smile. 'Not at all. He was fine.'

'Are you sure?' she asked, looking doubtful 'The thing is, I haven't been out for cocktails in a very long time and they're like milkshakes, aren't they? I had three and they hit me all at once. And then I had all that wine on top of them at June's. Urgh.' She shivered and placed a hand across her mouth at the thought. 'I was good for nothing on Saturday, but at least I had a bit of a lie-in. Not much of one, though. Amelia did my make-up while I was asleep and then I had to get up because I couldn't leave the mascara in my eyebrows. You know how it is.'

I nodded sympathetically, whilst thanking God for the small mercy of not actually being able to relate. 'Well, don't worry about Giles,' I said, slowing as we reached his gate. 'He isn't the kind of guy to take offence. Besides, you said some very flattering stuff about him.'

She looked relieved. 'Thanks for being so nice about it. But do say sorry to him anyway.'

I pushed open the gate. 'I will.'

'So how come you're home so early?' she asked, checking her watch. 'Half-day?'

'Bit under the weather.' I continued through the gate.

'Oh, I'm sorry,' she said, sounding guilty. 'I'm keeping you talking when I expect all you want to do is get home.'

Yes, that is all I want to do, I thought. But aware of the effort that she was making to be both friendly and apologetic, and aware also that I was actually lying about feeling unwell, I turned and said, 'It's fine. Just a headache. I could have stayed at work but I'll get more done away from the buzz of the office. Plus, poor Giles is properly unwell,' I looked upwards to his bedroom window, 'so I thought I could check on him at the same time and then take Anthony for a walk. Giles usually takes him to work with him on a Wednesday, so no dog walker.'

'Poor Giles,' she said, following my gaze to the first-floor bay.

I nodded and, by way of making at least some reciprocal effort to be neighbourly, asked, 'Where are you off to? Have you got a child-free afternoon?'

'I wish. My mum's got Arthur, but I'm going into school to help with Amelia's class for an hour. Kerry and I go every Wednesday. Harry and Amelia are in the same class.'

At the mention of Kerry's name, I felt my few remaining dregs of positivity drain away like bathwater down a plughole. 'That's lovely,' I said. 'Have fun.'

'Unlikely. You never know what they're going to throw at you – literally,' she laughed.

'I bet. I know I wouldn't cope. Anyway, I'd better not make you late.'

'No, no. I'm just glad I ran into you. And I was serious about putting Giles in touch with my friend – if he's up for it. Tell him to let me know if he'd like more details.'

'Will do.' I turned away for a second time, just as Kerry emerged from next door. I began my walk up the path, pretending not to notice her, but Nicky scuppered the ruse.

'Here's Kerry now,' she said. 'Sorry, Kerry, did you wonder where I was? I got chatting to Edie – apologising for Friday night.'

I cringed at the reference.

'Oh, right,' said Kerry, locking her front door and walking down the path. 'We're not late, Nick. You're always early.'

'Always desperate to get out of the house,' said Nicky. 'But poor Edie's not well, Kerry.'

They both looked at me, Nicky with motherly concern, Kerry with an expression I chose not to analyse.

'I'm fine,' I said. 'It's Giles who's the real patient.'

'What's happened? Is he OK?' Kerry asked, her concern now matching Nicky's. Clearly, she still cared whether one of us lived or died.

'He thinks it might be food poisoning.'

'Plenty of fluids and tell him to stick to dry toast for today and then nothing fatty tomorrow,' she said.

'Thanking you, Nurse Kerry,' laughed Nicky. 'Come on, we'd better go. Enjoy your break from the office, Edie, sounds like you need one.'

Kerry turned and eyed me stonily.

'Oh no, actually,' I said hurriedly, anxious to make it clear that I hadn't been complaining about Cameron to Nicky, 'I'm feeling really good about the office and all my work colleagues. They're really nice people and I'm lucky to work there and I'm looking forward to us all working together more closely as a team.'

'Oh… well…' began Nicky, smiling a little uncertainly at the sudden expression of corporate peace, love and understanding. 'That's so… nice.'

Kerry's face, meanwhile, would not have looked out of place on Mount Rushmore. 'We'd better go, Nick. Bye,' she said, raising a hand in my direction, as if waving away a wasp.

'Bye, Edie,' called Nicky, as they began to walk.

I waved and then, unsure whether I wanted Giles to be awake or asleep, I walked to the front door, opened it and stepped inside.

—

I tapped gently with a single fingernail on Giles's bedroom door and waited.

In response to a rather feeble-sounding, 'Come in', I pushed open the door to find him semi-recumbent, propped up on three pillows, his dark blue paisley pyjamas buttoned, as always, to the collar.

Anthony, meanwhile, was curled up and fast asleep on top of the duvet, taking full advantage of his master's weakened state and in direct contravention of Giles's one and only Anthony-related house rule (*No Anthonys allowed on any beds, at any time*). The jug of water I had left on the bedside table was still three-quarters full and the medication apparently untouched.

'How are you?' I asked, placing a fresh glass of water and a plate of toast on the table before sitting down on the edge of the bed. I placed a hand on his forehead, as he looked sleepily up at me. 'You don't feel as if you've got a temperature.'

He shook his head and yawned. 'I swear it was those mussels. Dear God, is that Anthony?' he added weakly, lifting his head. 'Get off the bed, Anthony.'

Anthony half-opened his eyes and then flopped onto his side.

Giles sighed despairingly and lowered his head back down onto the pillow.

'I'll take him with me when I go,' I said. 'How are you feeling?'

'Better. I fell asleep just after you left. What time is it now?' He glanced at the window. 'Is it after six?'

'It's two thirty. I took a half-day.'

'Not for me, I hope.'

I picked up and proffered the plate of toast. 'Too soon for this?'

'Not at all. I'm starving. Thank you,' he said, taking it from me, before eyeing the single, dry slice of wholemeal with obvious disappointment.

'Kerry recommended dry toast only, and she's a mum, so…'

'You've had a conversation with her?' he asked, appearing immediately brighter.

'That might be overstating it slightly. I was talking to Nicky at the gate and Kerry came out. Nicky told her you were ill and she offered some advice.'

He bit into the toast.

'I could tell she was worried about you, Giles.'

He offered me a half-smile and continued to chew.

'Nicky wanted me to apologise to you for being loud on Friday night. Sounds like Andy had a go at her for it. I told her it was fine and not to worry.'

'I wasn't at all offended,' he said, taking a second bite of toast.

'That's what I said. She also asked if you'd like to hear more about the friend she mentioned to you at June's. I think she's pretty keen to get the pair of you together. I know that's not top of your list today, but I wanted to tell you before I forgot,' I added.

He put down his toast and twisted to reach for the glass of water.

'Here,' I said, passing it to him.

'Thanks.'

'So, are you interested?'

'In what?' He looked at me over the top of the glass as he sipped the water.

'In Nicky's friend.'

'Oh,' he let out a breath. 'You know, I'm not sure that I am just now. I'm a bit busy.' He tapped the side of his head. 'Up here.'

He said nothing more, and if he hadn't been unwell, I would have pressed him for an explanation. But in view of the day he was having, I decided it would be best to save that particular interrogation for another time. So instead, I rose to my feet and picked up the jug. 'I'll refill this and then come back for Anthony. Can I get you anything else?'

He didn't reply, but instead gazed down at the plate of half-eaten toast on his lap. 'Good that Kerry is talking,' he murmured.

He didn't look at me and his expression was so glazed that I wondered if he even realised that he'd spoken aloud.

Still holding the jug, I sat back down on the bed.

A moment or two later, he turned towards me, appearing mildly surprised to discover me still there. 'Sorry, I missed that, Edie,' he said, rubbing a hand across his face. 'What did you say?'

I looked at him, wondering how much to tell him. I wanted to set his mind at rest about Kerry's taste in men, and also to assure him that I was going to do absolutely everything in my power to ensure that neighbourly relations were fully restored. But at the same time, he looked absolutely exhausted and, on top of that, I was terrified of being judged, no matter how fairly and gently, by Giles.

Uncertain whether concern for my feelings or his health was my primary motivation for wanting to delay any discussion regarding Cameron, I decided to give Giles the final say in the matter.

'Would you like me to stay and chat?' I asked. 'Or would you rather sleep? Or listen to the radio? I don't expect you want me to stay and chat after the night you've had.'

He looked at me thoughtfully for a moment. 'Would *you* like to stay and chat?'

'Well, I would and I wouldn't,' I began hesitantly. 'I mean, you're not well. But, on the other hand,' I continued, heaving a sigh, 'I think I have something to say which will make you feel better about Kerry – as well as making me look like a complete idiot. But there's not a lot I can do about that and, on balance, I think there's stuff you need to hear.' I shrugged to indicate the conclusion of my list of pros and cons.

He remained silent and motionless for several seconds and then nodded. 'OK – tell me the stuff.'

'Right…' I cleared my throat and took a deep, fortifying breath. 'Well, advanced warning: I'm going to précis wildly, because otherwise I won't get through it without sidetracking and possibly tears. Questions will be taken at the end.'

He nodded again. 'Always a fan of a précised approach when it comes to personal problems.'

'I met Jason for a drink last night,' I said without further hesitation, 'and he told me that after we split up he slept with Ruby.'

Giles's eyebrows rose slowly to maximum height. 'Ruby, your work colleague and friend?'

'Yes.'

'And you believe him?'

I grimaced. 'I haven't talked to Ruby about it yet.'

'But you do believe him,' said Giles.

'Can't think of a self-serving-bastard reason for him to lie.'

'I'm sorry, Edie.'

'There's more.'

'I'm braced.'

'Today, I went for lunch with Luke,' I continued, now turning my head away, choosing to deliver my summary of events to the water jug, in preference to maintaining eye contact with Giles. 'He told me that Cameron had not at any time harassed Ruby. In fact, it was quite the reverse.'

'I see. Crikey.'

'Luke also told me that Cameron does not get women into bed by offering them reduced-cost architectural services.'

I now forced myself to look at Giles and saw that his mouth had formed the stern moue he usually reserved for politicians on *Newsnight* and Anthony's toilet-time accidents.

'I don't believe I was ever made privy to that particular gem of supposition,' he said solemnly.

My shoulders sagged under the almost physical weight of his disappointment, a burden which increased when I thought about all the people made miserable by my unprofessional and ultimately unhelpful approach to supporting a female colleague in the workplace. Cameron was unhappy in his new job; Kerry had witnessed a vague but unmistakable character assassination of her dead husband's best friend; and Giles had had a wonderful friendship with his neighbour firmly kicked into touch. And all thanks to me.

'Are you certain that Luke is certain?' asked Giles.

'He wouldn't lie about something like that.'

His eyebrows rose again, this time questioningly.

'I should talk to Alison,' I said meekly.

He nodded slowly. 'You should.'

'I should have done that weeks, months, ago,' I said quietly, hanging my head. 'I'll text Alison and ask for a meeting tomorrow morning. Then, depending upon the outcome of that, I'll talk to Cameron and also to Kerry. I'll make sure she knows that it was all my fault and nothing to do with you. Hopefully, the fact that you and I share no genetic material will make it easier for her to accept that it's entirely possible for you to be a measured, rational person, whilst I'm a total moron.'

Giles sighed. 'Edie, my main concern at this moment is for you. You find yourself in a difficult situation, which is not, as you seem to think, entirely of your own making. If what your colleague told you today is true, then Ruby is guilty of Iago-like duplicity and malice which you, as someone devoid of those characteristics, failed to anticipate. She is the guilty party here. You and Ronald are victims.'

'Whatever Ruby may have kick-started, I perpetuated,' I said miserably, not looking up. 'I dragged you and Kerry into this. I'm just clinging to the hope that she thought I was completely off my face at June's, and that she hasn't started harbouring any doubts about Ronald – I mean Cameron.'

'I'm certain she hasn't,' he said reassuringly. 'She will undoubtedly have written you off as the kind of drunk who embarrasses herself at parties and whom it is always best to ignore.'

'Thanks, Giles. Sort of.'

'You're most welcome. And now,' he said, 'let us hope, for Kerry's sake, that Luke's account pans out. You must keep me posted.'

'I will,' I replied. 'And if it does, I won't waste any time in sorting everything out, or at least trying to sort everything out. I'll be happy for Kerry if Cameron is after all a nice guy.'

Giles yawned. 'He has always looked and sounded like the perfect male companion to me: good listener; proficient plumber; stubbly, but not unkempt.'

'Do you think he moved to Bristol to be closer to Kerry?'

'I assume that to be the case.'

I stood up. 'Well, the sooner I can confirm to her that he is the man of her dreams – and not the stuff of my nightmares – the better. I'm just going to take Anthony for a quick trot around the block.' I bent down to scoop him up, lifting my chin as I did so, in an attempt to avoid any face-licking. 'Then I'll message Alison.' I shuddered involuntarily at the thought of the conversations to come.

'Well done,' said Giles.

I looked down at him. 'You know you still don't look well. In fact, you look worse than when I first walked in.'

'Really?' he said, sounding puzzled. 'How strange that your cheery tale of malicious falsehoods, ruined reputations and a tortured conscience should not prove just the pick-me-up I required.' He frowned up at me for a moment and then laughed.

I tutted. 'I know I'm ruining your life, Giles, but you're saving mine and that's what counts here.'

'Delighted to be of service,' he said, easing himself back under the covers and closing his eyes. 'Delighted to be of service.'

Chapter 20

After arranging a first-thing meeting with Alison for the next day, the intervening hours served only to ratchet up my anxiety. The consequence was a largely sleepless night, spent running through a series of hypothetical conversations with Alison, all of which ended with her screwing her thin features into an expression of utter disbelief. When I did eventually drop off, at around four a.m., my sleep was fitful and disturbed by dreams of bedding down in a potpourri-filled Mini, whilst neighbour Patrick plastered the windscreen with parking tickets.

It was no surprise, therefore, that as I entered Alison's office at eight forty-five the next morning, the first thing she said to me was, 'You don't look very well, Edith. Have you slept?'

Luke had asked me the very same thing – although with a higher expletive content and a reference to drug addiction – fifteen minutes earlier, and I was just grateful that no one else was yet around to echo the sentiment that I looked, as Luke had put it, like shit.

'I'm fine,' I said to Alison, as I joined her at the conference table. 'It's just a cold, or an allergy, or something.'

She didn't question the explanation, instead merely extending her hand towards me, palm upwards, as an indication that I should continue speaking.

Alison being neither a touchy-feely nor a chatty person, I judged it best to spare her any mention of the personal distress which was at that moment welling up inside me; the pain of having misjudged and hurt others, the fear of being judged irrational and unprofessional. Instead, I inhaled deeply and cut to the chase.

'Before Ruby left the practice, she confided in me, as a friend, that she had made a complaint against Cameron regarding inappropriate workplace behaviour,' I began, reciting the opener which I had mentally prepared between the hours of midnight and four a.m. that morning. I had no clue what I was going to say after I had finished said opener, nor what Alison's response to it might be, but I comforted myself with the fact that, for the time being at least, I sounded relatively calm and in control.

'Ruby told me that, after talking to you, she had accepted an apology from Cameron and, despite still feeling aggrieved, had decided not to take things any further. She asked me to keep the matter confidential – which I did – but it has inevitably impacted negatively on my attitude towards Cameron, both professionally and personally,' I continued, the steadiness of my tone belying an internal gastric and emotional churning. 'I thought it best, therefore, to share with you how I felt, with a view to finding a way forward regarding my working relationship with Cameron, which is currently not, as I think you have realised, as effective as it might be.' I concluded my speech, clenching and unclenching my shaking hands beneath the table.

Alison leaned forward slightly, folding her hands on the desk in front of her. She appeared no more or less tense than usual and it was a moment or two before she spoke.

'No complaints of any nature have been made against Cameron,' she said eventually. 'I am not aware of him behaving improperly in any context. He is, in my experience and opinion, honest, personable and professional, and a significant asset to the practice. He merits respect. I hope that clarifies matters for you, Edith.'

I stared at her and nodded slowly, grateful like never before for her lack of sentiment and her rigid professionalism. Because I knew that if I had been sitting opposite anyone just a smidgen more prone to displays of empathy or curiosity, I would have crumpled. A simple, '*Are you OK, Edie?*' or '*What has actually happened here, Edie?*' would, at that moment, have reduced me to a hysterical, snotty heap.

'That's very clear,' I said. 'Thank you, Alison.'

Then, afraid that an embryonic twitch at the corners of her mouth might actually evolve into something approaching a kindly smile, I looked away and rose to my feet. 'I won't keep you any longer,' I said, walking towards the door.

'One more thing before you go.'

I turned reluctantly, but was relieved to find no hint of a smile, nor warmth of any kind. Instead, she was wearing an expression constructed of tempered steel.

'My description of Cameron…' she began.

'Yes?'

'It applies equally to you, Edith.'

I managed to meet her gaze for a moment with one which I hoped conveyed the gratitude I felt towards her, unable as I was to stretch to a verbal expression of thanks.

Then, turning silently away, I opened the door and, without stopping at my desk or to say good morning to

Roger who was now installed at his own, I headed straight for the loo. Because I was, I knew, about to crumple.

–

Thankfully, an onsite meeting with a surveyor and a construction engineer kept me out of the office for most of the day. Heavy, unseasonal rain meant that I was able to keep my puffy eyes and washed-out complexion – now completely make-up free, thanks to the earlier crying session – largely under wraps beneath a hard hat and the drawstring hood of my waterproof. As a consequence, the only concerned, bordering on horrified, looks I received were as I pulled down my hood and returned the hard hat, ready for the drive back to the office at around three p.m.

Of course, I didn't want to go back, and I was pretty sure that everyone there, with the obvious exception of Cameron, who had barely made eye contact with me since Monday, would tell me to go home. But I didn't have a choice. I couldn't let the awkwardness between Kerry and Giles rumble on any longer and, in order to sort that, I had to talk to Cameron.

I arrived back at the office shortly after four p.m. and, after receiving gruff kindnesses from Roger, teasing concern from Luke and no acknowledgement whatso- ever from Cameron, I spent the next hour or so moving between my desk and my drawing board, annotating designs based on that day's site meeting.

What I needed, I had decided, was to get Cameron alone – even if only for a few minutes. I had no doubt that he would respond civilly if I asked him for a meeting in front of our colleagues, but at this point I didn't at all trust myself to keep it together. A rising anxiety regarding the encounter, coupled with physical exhaustion and waves of depression over Ruby's duplicity, were taking a significant toll on my ability to think straight and function. If I was going to have difficulty using my words or, worse still, cry my eyes out in front of anybody, I would rather it was just Cameron, instead of the entire office.

My plan, therefore, was that if he decided to work late, I would wait with him until everyone else had gone, and talk to him then. Alternatively, if he left early, I would follow him to the lifts and ask for a meeting to discuss everything – either at work or in the pub. I honestly didn't mind which he plumped for; the prospect of either made me feel equally sick.

By five thirty, everyone was still at their desks. By six, Luke had gone but Roger was looking like he was in it for the long haul, having gone to the previously unheard of lengths of purchasing himself a coffee from Costa after his flask ran dry.

At six fifteen, my stomach lurched as Cameron rose to his feet and unhooked his coat from the hatstand. Standing up, I prepared to follow him. However, a moment later, having retrieved something from his coat pocket, he was back at his desk and facing his screen.

I lowered myself slowly back into my chair with some difficulty, thanks to a whole-body tension which seemed to extend even to my eyeballs, making blinking an effort of will. I attempted to relax, stretching my arms upwards and then leaning forward in my chair, rubbing my lower back and catching Roger's eye as I did so. He shook his head at me and then stood up and walked to my desk.

'What on earth are you still doing here?' he asked quietly. 'You're pushing yourself towards influenza, without a doubt. Especially after that soaking this afternoon.' He nodded towards my sodden coat, which I had hung over the back of a chair to dry.

I smiled at his kindness. 'I'm fine. My coat kept me dry. I just didn't sleep very well last night.' I put my hands to my face and rubbed my eyes.

'So go home and get some sleep, then. That's the answer, isn't it?'

Cameron stood up a second time and I looked anxiously past Roger and towards him. I really didn't want to miss him leaving.

Roger glanced over his shoulder, as Cameron picked up a roll of drawings and unfurled them on his board.

'Well, it's time for me to be off,' said Roger suddenly, checking his watch.

I frowned up at him. 'Really? You've just got yourself that coffee, haven't you?'

'Aye,' he said wearily, 'that was stupid of me, wasn't it? Never mind, eh? I'll just take it with me.' He returned to his desk, switched off his screen and began gathering his things. 'I reckon Alison's forgotten that she's meeting with Richard Webster tonight. Last-minute arrangement to discuss the park development.' He looked towards her office. 'She's making no sign of moving.'

I turned in my chair as he walked towards her door and, lightly tapping, entered. I heard 'drinks' and 'Webster' before he pulled the door shut behind himself.

I sighed and went back to my screen, feeling completely drained and wondering how much longer I could last. Staying awake was becoming a genuine concern.

However, at that moment, both Roger and Alison emerged from her office, the latter hurriedly putting on her coat as he held her bags. 'Thank you for reminding me,' she was saying. 'I would have completely forgotten. Goodnight, Edith, Cameron.'

Roger raised his coffee cup in silent farewell, and they were gone.

And then it was just us.

I inhaled and exhaled deeply three times and then, unwilling and unable to think the situation through any more than I had already, I rose to my feet and slowly crossed the office, coming to a halt beside Cameron's desk.

His back was to me and as I stood, dry-mouthed and preparing to attempt speech, I was transported back to that similarly rainswept day, when I had invited him to come for a drink with Ruby and me – for a bet.

In hindsight, the circumstances of that invitation now seemed less than ideal. I liked to think that I had meant well at the time, but my motivation, my hasty assumptions and my stubborn persistence for him to comply did me no credit. I should have taken into account his relaxed manner and warm approach with everyone else and given more thought as to what exactly might have made him so reluctant to engage with the idea of going for a drink that evening. On reflection, it hadn't been the most auspicious of starts to a workplace relationship, and, like it or not, I had to shoulder some of the responsibility for that.

This evening, he was seated in exactly the same spot, and hunched over his work in exactly the same way as he had been then. The only differences today were that he was wearing a relaxed-fit grey jumper, rather than a fit-to-bursting white shirt, and that I was the one who was weary and rained-upon.

'Yes?' He turned suddenly in his chair and looked up at me.

Taken by surprise, I opened my mouth to speak, closed it to swallow and then found myself unable immediately to open it again.

His expression remained neutral as he waited for me to say something. There was no air of patience or impatience about him, no hint of interest, or boredom, or frustration. There was nothing. I merited, it seemed, no reaction whatsoever.

Fair enough. If I were him, I'd have set me to one side too. I'd have placed me way beyond contempt in the of-no-relevance pile.

Despite his apparent lack of eagerness for me to speak, I realised that I had to say something, or I'd never get home and to bed – and I was now desperate to go to bed.

'I'm not sure what order to say things in,' I began.

He made no response, but that was OK. There was no need for him to articulate the fact that he couldn't care less: it was obvious.

'Do you have time to talk?' I asked. 'Here? Or we could go for a drink. Whatever is best.'

'About windows?'

I frowned, not understanding. 'About windows?' I echoed quietly.

'Do you want to talk about windows and concrete and design in general, so that you can claim to Alison that we are working more collaboratively?'

'Oh, I see. No,' I said, shaking my head. 'I wanted to talk about what happened on Friday night – at June and Stan's. I wanted to explain and to apologise. But the thing is,' I put a hand to my forehead, 'it's not just a one-line kind of thing. There's quite a bit of history and explaining and it's actually quite difficult...' I pressed my lips together as I fought an urge to give in to tears, '...for me,' I managed eventually.

At that, emotion was finally detectable in his expression, and suffice to say that it wasn't compassionate understanding. 'As difficult as Friday night was for Kerry?' he snapped.

I blinked rapidly. 'I know. That was awful and I'm going to talk to her. I—'

'Don't talk to her,' he said flatly. 'You've upset her enough.'

I nodded. He was right. I should just leave Kerry to Giles. I should go back to Henleaze, explain things to him and then start looking on Rightmove. There were always flats to let in the Harbourside complex. I could be back there within a couple of weeks.

I looked at Cameron. 'I'm sorry,' I said quietly. 'I know you've done nothing wrong. That's probably the only important thing I actually have to say. Explaining everything would just be for my benefit. You'd still be pissed off – even more pissed off – so perhaps it's best that you're not very interested.' I shrugged, feeling increasingly dazed and suddenly beyond tears. The latter was at least an upside, admittedly a rather bleak upside, but an upside nevertheless.

'But even if I don't go into the details, I do want you to understand that I am genuinely and unreservedly sorry,' I continued, now on some sort of a grim, but surprisingly cathartic, roll and unable to shut up. 'I made a huge mistake and I hope we can get past that – not right away, obviously. But I hope you can start enjoying working here in the meantime. Alison thinks you're great. Everybody thinks you're great, actually: Luke; Roger; Kerry. Even Giles, who doesn't know you that well, is really impressed by your kindness and your plumbing. And I know you must be really angry with me and I'm not sure I could ever completely stop being angry with me if I were you, but I think you're probably a much better person than I am.'

He looked up at me and I saw that he was back to not caring. My mistakes, my distress, my apology, my admiration for him, meant absolutely nothing.

But Kerry clearly meant a great deal. He cared deeply for her, more than he did about himself, in fact. It was the anger he felt on her behalf, not his own, which he couldn't hide. It was a realisation which, at that moment, I found strangely comforting, and one which I decided I would pass on to Giles, so that he, in turn, could pass it on to Kerry. I was happy for her, and I just hoped that she cared as much for Cameron as he obviously did for her.

With a lengthening silence between us, I came to the unavoidable conclusion that our conversation, such as it had been, was at an end.

'OK, then,' I said, turning away. 'See you tomorrow.'

Walking slowly back to my desk, I set about collecting my things and switching off my desktop. It only took me a minute or so, but by the time I had put on my still-damp coat and turned to smile at Cameron, he had gone.

Chapter 21

I leaned my head against the rain-lashed window of the bus and decided to text Giles. He was at home, having taken a second day off work to avoid passing on his bug, and I knew that, even with heavy traffic, I'd see him within half an hour or so. But the idea of updating him at a distance appealed. I really didn't want any more upsetting conversations that evening.

Sitting up, I began to text, opting for a no-edits, stream-of-consciousness approach. It was, to be honest, all I was capable of.

> Spoke to Alison. Cameron hasn't done anything wrong. I said sorry to him and he didn't get angry, but it's still a mess. Can you explain things to Kerry? Tonight? I hate the thought of her maybe doubting him. He cares for her a lot and doesn't want me talking to her and I get that. It's best if you and she mend fences and I go back to Harbourside. Sorry for the screw-ups xx

I sent the text, returned my phone to my bag, and leaned my head back against the window. For the rest of the journey, my entire focus was on staying awake. It was quite an effort and when I stepped off the bus and onto the Downs thirty-five minutes later, I felt grateful to the cold drops of rain hammering down on my head, both for waking me up and for providing me with an impetus to hurry home. Otherwise, I may simply have sat at the bus stop for another half an hour, wondering what on earth Ruby and Jason, and Cameron and Kerry, and work and life, were all about.

I was a couple of houses from home when the sound of something being banged hard against glass caught my attention. The banging was urgent and prolonged and, despite the rain, I stopped walking and peered at the nearby living room windows, in an attempt to locate the source of the noise. It took me just a second or two to work out that the sound was coming from higher up and I eventually spotted Harry waving frantically from a first-floor window, whilst banging what looked like a toy truck against the glass. When we finally made eye contact, he grinned and turned away from the window. Just too late, I raised my hand and managed a smile.

Slowly lowering my hand, I stood for a moment, letting this latest regret, and all my previous ones, wash over me along with the rain. Then, heaving a sigh and dragging one foot in front of the other, I continued my walk up the avenue.

My hand was on Giles's gate when Kerry's front door opened wide to reveal herself and Harry standing just inside the vestibule.

'There she is!' shouted Harry triumphantly.

Kerry placed a hand on his head. 'Edie,' she said, 'have you got time to come in for a cup of tea?'

I stared at her for a moment. 'I don't think—' I began, before she interrupted me.

'I've spoken to Giles,' she said gently. 'I'd really like you to come in. It's all fine, honestly.'

I looked at Harry and, feeling grateful for the rain yet again, I wiped a hand across my damp cheek. 'I told Cameron that I wouldn't—'

'Oh, stuff Ron,' she said. 'Just come in and have a cup of tea. Or maybe something stronger? Up to you.'

'We've got biscuits,' said Harry.

I smiled at him. 'That does sound nice,' I said. 'Thank you.'

Opening Kerry's gate, I walked slowly up the path, as she and Harry stood back to let me inside.

'Let me take your coat,' she said, pushing the door closed behind me. 'It's soaked.'

'I've been outside most of the day.'

'Why didn't you put your hood up?' asked Harry.

I put a hand up to my dripping hair. He had a point. 'I must have forgotten to put it up when I got off the bus.'

'You look really sad,' he said. 'Have you broken something? Are you in trouble? Did you get told off?'

'That's enough questions, Harry,' said Kerry gently.

'Have you fallen over? Did you spill red paint on the carpet?'

Kerry's eyes narrowed and she turned towards him. 'Have *you* spilled red paint on the carpet?'

His mouth widened and turned down at the corners. 'Yes,' he said quietly, addressing his feet.

'Where?'

'In my room. But I cleaned it up.'

'With what?'

'Toilet paper and the cream you clean your face with. It made the paint go pink,' he said, before adding in a murmur, 'and big.'

Kerry's eyes closed slowly.

'I'll let you clear up and come back another—' I began.

She opened her eyes and placed a hand on my arm. 'Hang on just a moment, Edie. How long has the paint been on the carpet, Harry?' she asked.

'I spilled the paint at quarter to…' He paused to study a chunky blue plastic watch on his wrist and ran his finger thoughtfully around the dial. '…yesterday.'

Kerry heaved a sigh. 'Right, go and get into your pyjamas.'

He nodded and turned to go up the stairs. 'I'm not cross about the spill,' said Kerry, placing a hand on his shoulder. 'I'm sure it was an accident, but it's the kind of accident you need to tell me about right away.' He nodded again. 'And well done for spotting Edie,' she added. 'I'm very pleased you did.' At that, he grinned at me through the bannisters and then raced the rest of the way up the stairs.

Kerry turned to me. 'You're a beautiful woman, but today you look like shit,' she said quietly.

'You're not the first to have noticed,' I replied.

Smiling, she beckoned me to follow her and then installed me in one of the back-room armchairs, placing a multicoloured throw over my knees, while she went into the kitchen to make the tea. It was, I reflected, only a puréed meal and a box of dominoes away from nursing care. Not that I minded. Together with the low, warm light from a slightly bedraggled patchwork lamp, Kerry's kindness had sparked a tiny but distinct sense of well-being of the kind I hadn't experienced for several days.

A few minutes later, she returned, carrying two mugs. 'Here you go; black no sugar. That's right, isn't it?' she asked, handing one to me.

'Yes. Thank you.'

'Are you hungry? I've got biscuits and cake.'

I shook my head. 'Nothing, thanks.'

'OK.' She sat down opposite me.

'I'm sorry,' I said, 'about Friday.'

She rolled her eyes. 'What an evening.'

'What has Giles told you?'

'Well, he's told me about the bitch who lied to you about Ron,' she said sternly.

'I thought she was telling the truth,' I said quietly.

'Of course you did!' she exclaimed. 'And so you should. Women need to be believed over stuff like that and why would your first thought be that your friend is a liar? Nice people judge other people by their own standards. *You* wouldn't tell terrible lies about the new bloke at work, so you don't think anyone else would either.'

I looked at her, aware that if I'd had just an ounce more energy, I would have got up and flung my arms around her in silent gratitude for her kind-heartedness and above-and-beyond understanding. However, in my enfeebled state, I could offer her only a wobbly smile and a whispered, 'Thank you.'

'I was so relieved about it all when Giles told me. I knew in here,' she continued, patting her chest, 'that you were a good person. There's no way Giles would love you as much as he does if you weren't. My only real worry was whether you might have told anyone else what she'd said. But Giles said that he didn't think that you had.' She looked at me anxiously.

I shook my head. 'The only person outside the office I'd mentioned it to was Giles, and I didn't name Cameron, even to him. The only other people who know anything

about this are my boss, Alison, and our office administrator, Luke. And they both know the truth of the matter.'

Kerry heaved a sigh and looked relieved. 'No harm
done then.'

I looked at her incredulously. 'What?'

'Well,' she waved a hand, 'no *lasting* harm done – not
to me or Ron, anyway.'

'I'm not sure Cameron quite sees it like that,' I said
despondently.

'Look,' she said, placing her mug down on the wooden
trunk beside her, 'Ron will have been more upset that
you were being difficult with him at work than he will
to discover that some bitch has been lying about him. He
won't give a damn what someone like her thinks of him.
But he's seen you getting along with everyone else and
he'll have been wondering what he's done wrong. He'll
be relieved now, once he comes out of his strop.'

I nodded, despite not sharing her confidence that
Cameron would brush the matter off quite so easily. 'I
think what he was most angry about was that I'd upset
you.'

Her cheeks coloured a little. 'He's a lovely man,' she
said.

'Our boss thinks so highly of him.'

'He's like Giles; not a bad bone in his body. So anyway,'
she picked up her mug, 'what are you going to do about
this woman? Anything?'

I shrank into the armchair at the thought.

'I'm sorry,' said Kerry. 'It's none of my business.'

'I think it is kind of your business, actually,' I said,
staring into my tea. 'It's certainly Cameron's business.'

'You're going to talk to her?'

'I've got to think about what's best… for everyone. A lot has happened.'

'Yes, Giles gave me that impression. Obviously, he didn't actually tell me anything which it wasn't absolutely necessary for me to know. He's so flippin' cagey,' she tutted. 'But he said things were complicated.'

'He's right – they are,' I agreed wearily. 'So I'm just going to take one thing at a time, and today I had to apologise to Cameron.'

She saluted me with her mug. 'Well done for getting that sorted.' She was about to say more but at that moment, Harry ran in from the hallway.

'I'm in my pyjamas,' he said, turning towards me and indicating the grey jersey pair, emblazoned with black sharks.

'They're great,' I said. 'I bet Giles would love a pair like that.'

'My mum will get him some for Christmas.'

I looked at Kerry and she winked. 'I'll make a note of that.'

Harry went over to her and climbed up onto her lap. 'What shall we get Edie for Christmas?' he asked, a question which made me want to cry all over again.

'We'll have to have a big think,' said Kerry, kissing the top of his head. 'But we can't talk about it right now, can we? Or it'll spoil the surprise for Edie.'

At that, Harry cupped his hand to his mouth and whispered something in her ear. 'Great idea,' she said. 'Now go and clean your teeth and I'll be up in a bit to read and tuck you in.'

He slid from her lap and walked towards the door, raising a hand to me as he went.

'Night, Harry,' I said, removing the throw from my lap and making to stand up.

'No rush,' said Kerry, gesturing for me to stay sitting, whilst getting up and taking my mug from me. 'He'll faff around forever up there, so we've definitely got time for a top-up. Oh and if you're wondering what you're getting for Christmas,' she added, as she headed for the kitchen, 'it's a towel.'

Chapter 22

On Giles's recommendation, I took the next day off work – not that I had needed much persuading. I had come home from Kerry's feeling exhausted in every sense possible, and after attempting some food and enjoying a brief and uncontroversial conversation with Giles, I had gone straight to bed and, thankfully, straight to sleep.

Friday was therefore my own, and a day which I filled with reorganising my home-filing and with walking Anthony, whom Giles had left at home to keep me company.

But even though I was busy, that didn't stop my thoughts occasionally straying to my as yet unresolved personal problems. On the upside, there was no doubt that I was feeling much better about Kerry and, therefore, about Giles. I even occasionally dared to trust Kerry's conviction that Cameron would in time stop thinking of me as unpleasant, unprofessional and unthinking, and allow himself to recognise some of my better qualities, whatever they might be.

Of course, the one person I couldn't begin to feel even slightly better about was Ruby, and whenever she crossed my mind, I was immediately thrown into a purposeless chaos of hurt, anger and bewilderment as to why anyone would do what she had done to Cameron and, in the process, to me too. At times, I considered picking up the phone and telling her exactly what I thought of her. At others, I hovered over blocking her calls, texts and social media posts and having no further contact with her whatsoever. And in calmer moments, such as when strolling with Anthony on the Downs, I imagined sitting down with her, in our favourite wine-bar armchairs, and simply asking her to explain what our workplace friendship, which had been of such value to me, had actually meant to her.

But mostly, I tried not to think about her at all, focusing instead upon more immediate matters – such as tracking down and bagging Anthony's poos, which he would insist on doing on the run.

However, my ability to ignore the matter of Ruby came to an abrupt end at eight p.m. that evening, when I received a text from the woman herself. Giles had just gone upstairs for a post-run shower and I was settling down on the sofa to read *Factfulness* – a book all about the importance of forming fact-based, rather than bias-based, opinions – when my phone pinged.

It was with some reluctance that I opened the newly delivered text.

> Hi! Out with boss/friends from work – knackered, but they insisted. Worried because I haven't heard from you and you looked so wrung-out on Monday. How are things? There's a job coming up here so let me know if you want details. The office is totally creep-free, I promise! Hope all creeps staying away from you and that includes Jason. Is he hassling you? x

I read her text twice, acknowledging it to be actually a rather impressive composition; fewer than one hundred words and with more triggers than a rifle range. In just a few short sentences she had managed to highlight my dodgy physical appearance, emphasise her own personal appeal, contrast her fun-loving colleagues with my pervy one and sneak in a last-minute reference to my faithless ex.

I read it just once more before, with preternatural calmness possibly borne of mild insanity, composing one of my own.

> Hi Jason. Sorry for my reaction on Tuesday. I know telling me about Ruby wasn't easy. I'd really appreciate another opportunity to talk, now that I've calmed down. Are you free tomorrow or Sunday? Or another day? Just let me know. If you don't want to, that's fine – I understand. E

I pressed 'send', just as Giles entered, now in his pyjamas and dressing gown and carrying a mug. I watched as he settled himself into an armchair and placed his slippered feet on the velvet pouffe. 'Cocoa and slippers,' he sighed contentedly. 'Just like the dorm days, except without the beatings.'

'How was your run?' I asked, picking up my book.

'Knackering. No other word for it.' He placed a hand on his midriff. 'Just hope it's doing some good.'

He flopped his head back in the chair and stared upwards at the ceiling. I studied his profile, including his increasingly well-defined jawline.

'Your face has changed shape,' I said.

He eased his head upright and looked at me. 'For better or worse?'

'Well, you were very handsome anyway…'

'Goes without saying.'

'But you're looking especially fine today.'

'Clearly a dose of dysentery was just the ticket,' he said. 'Now, are you planning to watch TV or read your book? Or check your phone?' he added, nodding towards my lap as my mobile pinged.

I checked the screen: a text from Jason. I didn't open it, but when I looked up, I saw that Giles was watching me and frowning slightly. 'It's nothing,' I said breezily.

He nodded acceptingly and sipped his chocolate.

'It's from Jason,' I clarified. 'I texted him, asking if we could meet up. I think we need to have another conversation before I decide what to do next.'

'You must forgive me for wringing all that out of you,' said Giles drily.

I smiled and opened Jason's text.

> All good. Tomorrow better than Sunday. Morning/pm coffee?

'He's suggesting coffee, tomorrow,' I murmured. 'I wonder where we should meet.'

'Why not here?'

'Here?' I looked up, surprised by the suggestion.

Giles raised his eyebrows questioningly. 'Well, why not? It's your home and it would be preferable to discuss personal matters in private, rather than in a coffee shop, would it not?'

'And you wouldn't mind?'

He shook his head. 'I shan't make a point of seeing him, but if our paths do cross, I should be as civil towards him as his behaviour towards you currently merits. And, from what you say, he is at least *attempting* humanity.' He leaned forward and picked up his Kindle from the edge of the pouffe. 'I'll let you reply.'

'OK,' I said, tapping the screen. The message confirming an afternoon coffee in Henleaze took only a matter of moments to type and send.

My reply to Ruby, however, despite being approximately the same length as that to Jason, took considerably longer to compose. Determined to remain true to myself, I didn't want to imply a closeness which I no longer felt and, for the sake of my own ego and self-respect, I wanted to make clear that my career wasn't in the toilet and that I wasn't totally friendless. But at the same time, I was anxious not to sound so changed as to provoke any questions from her – texted or otherwise – before I had spoken to Jason. It was therefore several minutes before I had produced a text with which I was, if not exactly happy, then at least satisfied.

> Sorry for slow reply – hectic week at work. With friend atm, so will be quick. Cameron isn't causing me any problems – so don't worry. Work is full on, but good. Relax and enjoy your evening!

I took a deep breath and sent the text.

'All done?' asked Giles, looking up as I laid my phone down on the arm of the sofa.

'All done.'

He returned his attention to his Kindle, a slight frown of concentration forming on his brow.

I looked at him for a moment, aware that it was entirely thanks to him – to his quiet understanding, moral strength and reassuring presence – that I had managed to reply to Ruby's text with relative calm and that I didn't feel quite as terrified as I might otherwise have done at the prospect of a second conversation with Jason. Giles really was, I thought, *the* best friend and an unequivocally lovely man.

'Are you sure you don't want to find out a little more about Nicky's friend?' I asked, my mind making the small leap from consideration of Giles's personal appeal to the possibility of him finding someone to appreciate it.

He looked up and blinked, clearly puzzled. 'Sorry? What are we talking about now?'

'Nicky's offer to set you up. You didn't dismiss the idea just because you felt so ill on Wednesday, did you?'

His confused expression didn't lift. 'No.'

'OK. Just thought I'd check. Don't want your charms going to waste.'

He leaned back in his chair. 'I could say the same about you, of course.'

'Except that I haven't just been offered the chance of a date – *of course*.'

He returned his attention to his Kindle. 'I'll give it some thought.'

'Can't hurt,' I said. 'And what with your stylish night-wear, expert cocoa-making abilities and limitless patience, who could resist?'

'I could name a few,' he murmured.

'Really? Who?' I asked, intrigued.

'Oh…' He waved a hand airily. 'I was referring to my adolescence. I wasn't always the hunk of beef you see before you today, you know.'

'Come on, Giles,' I persisted. 'Why don't you text Nicky for some more info? Or is there someone at work I don't know about?' I asked teasingly.

In response, he sighed and placed his Kindle and mug on the table beside him. 'You have absolutely no interest in poor Hans Rosling's excellent book, do you?' he said, gesturing wearily to the book lying next to me on the sofa.

'What?'

'You've done what you always do. You have chosen a book with an impactful cover, which you think will make you appear intellectual on the bus, but which you do not actually wish to read. Tonight, for example, you would much rather torture me with enquiries regarding my arid love life.'

I thought for a moment and then nodded. 'That's true.'

He placed a hand on either arm of his chair and heaved himself to his feet. 'That being the case and as I have absolutely nothing of romantic interest to convey – no hidden lovers, no illicit affairs, no workplace shenanigans of any description, in fact – I shall go and return my mug to the kitchen and treat myself to a consolatory biscuit whilst I am there,' he said, retrieving his mug from the table. 'In the meantime, why don't you select something the opposite of erudite for us to watch on television.' He rolled his eyes at me and headed from the room.

I smiled and picked up the remote. 'Well, if you insist,' I called after him. 'I suppose I can always save my book for the bus.'

Chapter 23

When the doorbell rang at one forty-five the next day, fifteen minutes earlier than Jason's agreed arrival time, I was grateful that Giles had already headed out on a walk with Anthony. I knew both he and Jason well enough to be confident that they would have been civil to each other, but I also knew that, beneath the surface, they would have found an encounter difficult, especially with me in the room, and I wouldn't have wished that on either of them.

However, after taking several deep breaths and arranging my features into an expression of polite welcome, I was disappointed to find the effort had gone to waste, as I opened the door not to Jason, but to Bodhrán Bill.

'Afternoon,' he said, smiling broadly, his aviator specs glinting in the sunlight. He was, I noticed, wearing the same black shirt and jeans he had worn to June's party. An aged black leather jacket was the only add-on.

'Oh, hello,' I smiled.

He nodded but said nothing more.

'Is there something I can help you with?' I asked. 'Are you after Giles? Because I'm afraid he's out with Anthony.'

'No, no, it's you I'm here to see. I thought I must have missed you when you called round.'

I frowned, feeling totally lost. 'But I didn't call round.'

'Just as well that I'm here then,' he said. 'To save you the trouble.'

'The trouble of what?'

'Of coming round.'

I maintained a smile, although I suspected it was starting to look a little strained. 'Sorry, Bill. Why would I be coming round?'

'Well,' he laughed, 'you haven't paid me for the tickets yet.'

'Oh, the tickets, yes,' I said awkwardly, turning to look at the four blue oblong pieces of card lying face down on the small vestibule cupboard – exactly where I had placed them after discovering them on the doormat a week earlier.

'The thing is,' I said, picking them up, 'do you remember that when you invited me along to the gig, I said I needed to know the date because I wasn't sure that I'd be free to come?'

He looked thoughtful. 'Did you say that?'

'Yes, I did, and the thing is, I'm not,' I said, extending the tickets towards him. 'Not free to come, I mean.'

'Do not worry, do not worry,' he replied, gently clasping my outstretched hand, tickets and all, between his. 'The main thing is that there is someone sitting in those seats.'

'Er...' I looked at him, hoping that he wasn't going to say that responsibility for the latter fell to me.

'So, you just pass those on to four friends.' He let go of my hand, pushing it away from him and taking a step back as he did so. 'And pop the money through my door.'

Damn it.

I studied him for a moment, trying to decide whether he was a guileless geriatric with deteriorating insight, keen for as many people as possible to enjoy his wonderful music, or a ruthless salesman out to take advantage of a thirty-something woman with assertiveness issues.

I checked my watch. 'How much do I owe you?'

'Thirty-five quid.'

My eyes narrowed, as I performed a quick mental calculation. 'So they're... £8.75 each? That's a very unusual figure.' I glanced at the tickets. No purchase price was shown.

He didn't miss a beat. '£10 each, full price. £1.25 discount for friends and family.'

I heaved a sigh. 'OK, I'll push the money through your door this evening.'

'Much obliged,' he said, raising a hand in victorious farewell and making his way down the path. On reaching the gate, he took a step back, holding it open for Jason, as the latter stepped into view and paused on the pavement. 'Piccadilly Circus here today,' said Bill and then, as Jason thanked him and began to walk up the path, he closed the gate and was gone.

'Who was that?' asked Jason, tilting his head in the direction of Bill's departure.

'A ruthless salesman,' I replied. 'But hello, and come on in. I'll make us some coffee.'

-

I joined Jason at the grey, ceramic-topped dining table and handed him a mug. He seemed, I decided, more genuinely relaxed than he had at the beginning of our Tuesday conversation, although perhaps even more subdued.

He thanked me for the coffee and looked around the room. 'I see Giles has redecorated. Even changed the table and chairs,' he said, sounding strangely nostalgic as he patted the blue acrylic dining chair on which he was sitting.

'There are biscuits, if you'd like one,' I offered, instinctively ignoring his reference, however oblique, to the past. 'Giles is very good at buying biscuits, although not actually that great at eating them these days.'

'No?' He looked surprised.

'He's dieting and getting fit.'

'Brilliant. Is he well? All good at work?' The enquiries were tentatively made, as if he wasn't quite sure whether he had a right to ask.

'He's fine,' I said. 'He's just taken Anthony for a walk. You might see him later.'

He nodded, but knowing exactly what Giles's feelings were towards him, he looked neither hopeful of, nor happy at, the prospect. It was Jason's ability to read people that made him such an expert manipulator and liar; something I was now always very careful to bear in mind.

However, when it came to our current shared person of interest – Ruby – I could see no reason for him to lie, either about the fact that she had pursued him or that he had slept with her. The latter in particular was something which in the past he would have worked hard to keep tightly under wraps. What's more, the suggestion that Ruby was ruthless and self-serving was now entirely believable to me in a way it simply wouldn't have been three months earlier.

'So how are you?' I began. 'I don't think I managed to ask you that last week.'

'I'm OK,' he said. 'Work is fine and the rest...' He picked up his coffee. 'The rest will take time. The therapy is painful and slow-going, but I haven't tried to shag my therapist yet, so, you know,' he shrugged, 'small steps.'

I didn't reply.

'Too soon?' he asked.

'*Never* would be too soon.'

'You're right,' he said, addressing the quiet response to his mug as he replaced it on the table in front of him. 'I just thought I'd see if a bit of black humour might improve our relationship, because saying sorry to you doesn't seem to. But maybe I just haven't said it enough.' He paused, looking up at me. 'I'm sorry, Edie. So, so, *so* sorry. In the past, I've apologised because I wanted forgiveness from you. But now, I don't expect it and I don't need it. All I need is for you to *believe* that I *am* sorry. Don't forgive me. I wouldn't forgive me.' He paused for a second time. 'Just believe me.'

'I'll think about it,' I said.

'Thank you. Oh and my therapist is a bloke by the way. So those steps I was talking about: *really* tiny.'

I smiled in spite of myself and saw him relax a little.

'But how are *you*?' he asked. 'Or is that a stupid question after I ruined your week? Go me,' he said, punching the air weakly with his fist and adding a feeble, 'Yay'.

'To be fair, it wasn't going great, even before your intervention.'

'No?'

'I've had some problems with a work colleague.'

His eyes widened slightly. 'That doesn't sound like you. Which one?'

'New guy, you don't know him. It was my fault, not his.'

'Is this the big guy Ruby mentioned? Joined four or five months ago?'

'That's him,' I said, interested in what she might have had to say. 'Was she positive or negative in her assessment?'

'Negative,' he said. 'Very. But she was ranting at me for messaging you at the time, so he might have just got caught up in the all-men-are-shits storm.'

'No,' I said, 'she really doesn't like him.'

'Because…?'

'I have been told that he resisted her charms.'

'Ah,' he said, nodding slowly. 'Well, tell him from me, to watch his back.'

I considered explaining that it was actually a bit too late for that. But, for whatever reason, telling Jason anything more about Cameron felt like a betrayal of a colleague whom I had already let down quite enough.

'I'm going to have to talk to her, of course,' I said instead.

Concern and something akin to fear flickered across his face. 'Wow,' was all he said.

'What?'

'Well, I just think you'd have to have a bloody good reason to put yourself through that.'

'I do, don't I?'

'To check whether I'm telling the truth?'

I shrugged. 'Leopard, spots and all that.'

He attempted a smile, but I knew that he was hurt and I regretted the faux-flippant reply as soon as it was out.

'I'm sorry,' I said. 'That was unnecessary. I just mean that I have to be sure of the facts, and that would be the case no matter who was involved.'

He picked up his mug and saluted me with it. 'It's fine. You're right to be sceptical and I accept your scepticism completely. When you've told as many lies as I have, it'd be unreasonable to expect anything else. But if it's of any

229

comfort, I lied to myself at least as much as I lied to you – so much so that I can barely recognise my own truth anymore.'

'That's of zero comfort to me, Jason,' I sighed.

'I know, I know…' he said, running a hand through his hair. 'And I wish to God I could stop saying stuff like that out loud all the time. I drone on and on to anyone who'll listen about re-educating my drive and not turning my anger inward and reconnecting with my sense of self. I'm just so therapied-up, Edie, I can't help it. It's as if I have to constantly remind myself and everybody else of what I am and where I'm at.'

He took a gulp of coffee and cleared his throat. 'But anyway,' he continued, suddenly brisk and businesslike, 'something which may be of genuine *practical* help to you, is that I still have all the text messages Ruby and I exchanged. We've used them in therapy, but they also back up my version of events, if you want to see them. Although, I should warn you that the most recent ones contain a number of rather disturbing threats involving my nads and a stapler.'

'Well, as agonising as that sounds,' I said, pulling a face, 'I probably should look at them.' I dreaded the prospect, but was also relieved at the possible existence of evidence which would remove the need for me to make a judgement call between the word of a lying, cheating ex and that of a possibly psychopathic friend.

'Look, is your mind made up about us, Edie?' asked Jason suddenly. 'Forever and completely, I mean. I'm sure it is, but I have to ask.'

He offered me a look, heavy with regret and resignation. Jason being Jason, I was pretty certain that he already knew the answer to his own painful question. But

I understood why he had chosen to ask it and I wasn't sorry that he had. I was as in need of clarity and closure as he was.

'I couldn't go back, Jason, no matter what you said or did. I'm sorry.'

He shook his head. 'You've nothing to apologise for, Edie.'

'It's not that I think you're incapable of change, because I'm sure you are,' I said, keen to inject a level of positivity into the conversation, despite its grim content and circumstances. 'And I'm certain that, eventually, the new you will find someone to start over with.'

'But it won't be you.' He didn't make eye contact, focusing instead on his coffee with brow-furrowed intensity.

'No. I'm afraid you look way too much like the bastard I used to live with.'

He stared into his coffee for a little longer, before smiling up at me. 'I'll tell my therapist you said that. He'll be proud of you.'

We sat in silence for a moment and then I asked, 'If I call or see Ruby, how do you think she'll react?'

'Denial,' he said flatly, drinking his coffee. 'Undoubtedly.'

'And if there's no room for denial? If your texts are incontrovertible?'

'Well, when I told her something she didn't want to hear,' he said with a grimace, 'she chucked a gin and tonic over me. But I don't think she'd do that to you. She genuinely likes you and admires the fact that you have principles, even if they're nowhere near Machiavellian enough for her. Plus, she craves your approval and it bothers her when you don't agree on things.'

'She told you that?'

'Yes. Something which particularly irritated her was your relationship with Alison. She couldn't understand why you liked her so much. She wanted you to approve of all her choices and share all of her opinions. She needed that, for some reason – as well as everything else you had in the world, of course. But whatever,' he shrugged, 'by her standards, she likes you – loves you even.'

I heaved a sigh, feeling my anger towards her dissipating into pity. 'Strange way of showing it.'

'Yes, well,' he murmured, 'I'm not throwing any stones here.'

I watched as he slumped slightly in his chair, as if guilt was a physical burden. 'I believe you, by the way,' I said.

He looked at me over the top of his mug. 'About Ruby?'

'About being sorry.'

'Oh.' He cleared his throat. 'Thank you. I'll tell my therapist that too. God knows we need some uplift in our sessions. I thought he was going to cry when I told him about Ruby throwing her drink over me and then followed that up with the news that you still despised me and hadn't believed a word I'd said. But he's helping me a lot,' he continued quietly. 'He's a good guy; reminds me of—'

He stopped short and we both looked towards the hallway as the front door slammed shut.

'Giles,' said Jason, the colour draining from his face.

I nodded and, as we listened to the clinks and rustles of a lead, coat and boots being removed, I looked questioningly at him.

'If he's OK with it,' he said, 'it'd be good to see him. If not, I'll go. It's fine.'

I hesitated for a moment and then, taking a deep breath, stood up. 'OK,' I whispered, 'I'll go and talk to him and, in the meantime, you show some optimism, and put the kettle on.'

Chapter 24

'For you.' I placed the cup of coffee on Luke's desk and smiled.

'Wow, thanks,' he said, turning in his chair. 'Haven't seen you here this early for a while.'

'I know. Mornings are a lot slower since I moved to Henleaze,' I said, walking to my desk.

'So why so early today?' He glanced up at the large clock which hung on the wall at Cameron's end of the office. 'It's only just eight.'

'I've got a bit of catching up to do after last week.' I sat down and placed my satchel on the desk in front of me. 'It was my least productive four-day week ever.'

He prised the lid from his coffee and blew. 'How are you? You look way better than you did on Thursday.'

'To be fair, the only way was up really, wasn't it?' I smiled. 'And I got a few things sorted over the weekend.'

'Did you, er…' he leaned low across his desk towards me and glanced left and right, checking for eavesdroppers in the completely deserted office. 'Did you get in touch with… you know… with *her*?' He offered me a slow wink.

'You mean Ruby?'

'No, Mary Berry,' he tutted, sitting up. '*Of course* I mean Ruby. I'd have been straight on the phone to her Thursday afternoon, if I was you.'

'Would you?' I asked, surprised.

He laughed. 'No way! Who in their right mind prods a snake? And there's more than a hint of snakiness about our Rubes. I'd stand well back, Edie.'

I slid my laptop from my bag and placed it on the desk in front of me. 'Don't worry. Now that I'm in possession of the actual facts, I'm not in a hurry to see her,' I said, keeping my voice determinedly calm, whilst searching my bag for my phone. 'There's no excuse for what she did and I don't particularly want to watch her trying to come up with one.'

'Well, if you change your mind, you know I'd come with you. You only have to ask.'

I looked up to find him completely in earnest.

'Thanks for the offer,' I said. 'I'm genuinely touched.'

He sipped his coffee. 'Obviously, I was only offering because I know there's no chance of you recording the conversation for me.'

'Obviously,' I said, recommencing the phone search. 'This bag,' I muttered, 'has more pockets than a snooker table. Ah, here it is!' I continued triumphantly, holding up the phone before opening a text from Giles asking if I'd put any of his burgundy, monogrammed socks in my sock drawer by mistake, as he was unable to locate a pair. I glanced down guiltily at my blue boots, inside which my feet were currently encased in a pair of burgundy, monogrammed socks, and I wondered whether I should break it to Giles that I didn't actually have a sock drawer, but had simply co-opted his, his socks being so irresistibly silky-smooth – not to mention, clean, paired and always good-to-go.

'Morning, Cam,' said Luke.

I looked up sharply from my feet.

'Hi,' said Cameron, raising a hand to Luke and placing his bag on his desk. 'Edie,' he added, nodding civilly but stony-faced in my direction.

'Hel-hello,' I said, attempting *bright* and achieving *strangulated*. I cleared my throat and then smiled as broadly as possible by way of compensation.

He looked at me in the same way Anthony had looked at the bowl of supermarket own-brand dog food which Giles had begged from a neighbour at ten o'clock on Sunday evening, having realised that he'd run out of Anthony's usual high-end variety.

I suppressed a sigh. Clearly a miracle transformation in Cameron's opinion of me hadn't occurred over the weekend after all. What a shocker.

I glanced at Luke, who was looking between Cameron and myself with an enjoyment he was clearly incapable of disguising. If he hadn't picked up on the tension before, he was onto it now, and he couldn't help loving it.

He jerked his head towards Cameron, who was now sitting with his back to us, and mouthed, 'How was your weekend?' at me.

I rolled my eyes but acted on his cue nevertheless. 'Good weekend?' I asked, adding, 'Cameron', when he showed no sign of responding.

He turned in his chair. 'Yes, thanks. You?'

'Me? Oh, well, erm…' I began, unprepared for the immediacy of his reciprocal enquiry and now racking my brains for weekend news. 'A friend – well, no, not a friend – my ex, actually… I mean, things are OK, so he's sort of a friend, I suppose. Anyway, he came round for coffee. And I bought a ticket for a gig, which I don't think I'll go to, because it's not really my kind of music. I bought four tickets, actually – long story. So, y'know, as weekends go, it was… interesting.' I tacked on a light laugh, which went on just a little too long to remain the right side of sane.

Cameron nodded impassively. 'OK.'

'What's the gig?' asked Luke. 'I might take the tickets off your hands.'

'They're for my neighbour's reggae and rock band. He plays the penny whistle.'

'Damn it,' said Luke, shaking his head. 'If only he played the kazoo, I'd have bitten your hand off.'

I laughed and noticed Cameron smile, which made me feel a little better. Shared amusement was, I reflected, at least a start.

'So how did you end up buying so many tickets?' asked Luke, as Cameron turned towards his screen.

'My neighbour is *really* pushy.'

'Nothing to do with you being a soft touch, then?'

'Hey,' I protested, 'I knocked him down from £10 to £8.75 a ticket, *actually*.'

'£8.75?' he echoed, as if impressed. 'Well, that certainly doesn't sound like a figure he snatched out of thin air when he saw you coming.'

I bent down and placed my bag on the floor. 'I wonder if Roger would like the tickets. I don't want any money for them and it might be a fun night out for him and a few of his friends.'

'Provided there's wheelchair access and it doesn't clash with *Countdown*,' said Luke. 'Oh and so long as you don't actually mention to him that it's a gig.'

'You're right,' I sighed, 'it's not really Roger's thing, is it?'

'To be fair to Rog,' said Luke, now tapping at his keyboard, 'I don't think it's anyone's thing. Apart from the desperate and the tone-deaf.'

'Don't suppose you know anyone who fits the bill?'

'Not outside of this office, no,' he murmured absently, staring intently at a document onscreen. 'But why not ask your professor cousin? Bet he knows loads of saddos at the uni who'd just love to go.'

'Why didn't I think of that?' I exclaimed, brightening at the thought of a possible out from an evening of sitting through a penny whistle version of *Like a Virgin*. 'Giles is always saying what a complete bunch of weirdos his colleagues are.'

Luke didn't reply, being now too engrossed in work to look up. But I was pretty sure I heard a quiet laugh from Cameron's end of the office, and that, combined with the prospect of not having to go to Bill's gig after all, made it by far my best start to the working day in a very long time.

Chapter 25

The next few weeks progressed, if not brilliantly, then at least without disaster, which in the context of my recent past actually felt like a win. Workwise, it was a highly productive time and, in terms of personal relationships, my good-mornings and good-nights to Cameron became daily less self-conscious, as did all our admittedly brief interactions in between.

This upturn in workplace productivity and relations had the very welcome side effect of edging almost everything to do with Ruby from my thoughts. Just occasionally, I had a nagging doubt that ignoring my outstanding issues with her might not perhaps be the healthiest of approaches. But as a highly distressing read-through of her texts to Jason had freed me from any obligation to sit through her version of events, simply refusing to think about her remained an attractive and effective option.

Of course, the flaw in my approach to the situation was that it was entirely unilateral, as a text that I received while at work one mid-September morning made abundantly clear. In it, Ruby apologised for being out of touch, 'due to shadowing Vincent' (whether this was with or without his knowledge and a pair of binoculars wasn't clear), and then announced that she would be making 'a surprise visit to Bristol very soon'.

It was a text that left me staring wide-eyed and open-mouthed at my phone, as I wondered exactly when the unspecified visit might take place. Next week? Tomorrow? *That afternoon?* The uncertainty sent my anxiety levels through the roof and, from that moment on, Ruby monopolised my thoughts, her spectre looming larger than it had at any time since I had read her disturbing correspondence with Jason.

Not surprisingly, by midday I was a bit of a wreck, my focus being constantly interrupted by imagined conversations with Ruby, all of which concluded with me wearing a glass of red wine.

But just as I was contemplating a lonely, Ruby-obsessed lunch at my desk, rescue came in the completely unexpected form of Cameron.

'Are there any areas of work you'd like to discuss?' he asked, stopping at my desk as he left Alison's office. 'I've got a few and I thought maybe we could talk them through over lunch today or tomorrow.'

'Today would work best,' I replied quickly, pouncing on the opportunity of company and distraction, and reaching for my coat and bag.

'What? Right now?' he said, apparently a little taken aback by my speedy uptake of his offer.

'Sure, if you like,' I replied, standing up.

'But I have to send an email first.' He looked back towards his desk.

'No problem, I'll go and call the lift,' I smiled and, keen to be gone as soon as possible, I headed for the door.

–

As I took my seat in the soulless cafe, with some delayed but undeniable nerves, it was hard to believe that just a few weeks had gone by since Luke and I had sat at the very same blue Formica-topped table and I had discovered that Cameron Grange was an innocent man. It felt like a lifetime ago.

'Luke told me that you come here a lot,' said Cameron, surveying the deserted space with an obvious degree of not unreasonable confusion. He frowned down at the wholemeal sandwich he had chosen from the meagre selection on offer. It appeared to have been run over.

'Yes, I really, really like it here,' I said loudly, smiling over my shoulder at the cashier. She was the same woman who had served Luke and me, and had greeted me with a look of contemptuous recognition on entry. She now stared stonily at us for a second or two before returning to chewing her nails.

I sighed and turned back to Cameron. I hadn't been over the moon when he had suggested the cafe for lunch, but thanks to Luke he'd seemed very keen to give it a whirl and, bearing in mind the current fragile state of our relationship, I hadn't wanted to argue the point – or any point, for that matter.

'We tend to come here more for the privacy of the place,' I said, lowering my voice and leaning across the table towards him, 'rather than for the food or the atmosphere. There's never really anyone else in here.'

'No kidding,' he said, picking up half of his flattened sandwich and watching as its ends drooped slowly into an upside-down smile.

'We can go somewhere else, if you like,' I said quietly, although clearly not quietly enough for the bat-eared cashier, as a loud tut and the word *dickheads* reached us from the counter.

I winced and Cameron smiled, not at me, but over my shoulder at our accuser. 'Here is just fine,' he said, returning his attention to the sandwich and biting into it.

I looked down with zero appetite at the possibly-blueberry muffin I had purposely chosen in an attempt to make up for the disrespect shown to the cakes by Luke several weeks earlier.

'So, how is the church project going?' I asked brightly, attempting to kick-start the conversation. 'Roger said there was a decision to be made over parking.'

He nodded. 'We're going underground, so we can have a garden. We hit a grave, but we're back on track.'

'Yes, Roger mentioned the skeleton too. I had that on a previous job years ago. It was a London office block development and I was still training. We uncovered graves and various artefacts. It set everything back by twelve months.'

'Difficult.'

'It was.' I picked up the muffin – an ancient artefact if ever there was one – peering closely at one of the supposed blueberries, distracted for a moment by the fact that it appeared to have legs. I returned it to the plate and pushed it away from me. 'So, did you make up your mind about the façade?' I asked, aware that a silence was extending between us.

'Yes.'

I looked across at him, waiting for something more, and as he questioningly met my gaze, I leaned back in my chair and said, 'I don't have any design or build issues at the moment. Do you?'

He hesitated for a moment and then shook his head. 'I do not.'

'Did Alison ask you to suggest lunch?'

'No.'

'So why did you? Because it's pretty obvious that you'd rather not be here.'

He placed his barely touched sandwich back down on the plate and studied it for a moment. 'I suggested lunch because we currently work together and, unless you're planning to quit, we're going to have to work together for some time to come. That being the case, the sooner we can achieve a productive working relationship free from suspicion and resentment, the better.'

'But I'm honestly not at all suspicious or resentful,' I smiled.

'I wasn't talking about you.'

I placed my hands under the table, clenching them into tight fists. 'OK, but I have apologised,' I began, my smile now fixed and my voice even and controlled, 'and I have admitted that I made a mistake. I am not by nature a confrontational or judgemental person and in the past I have enjoyed amicable, productive, mutually supportive working relationships with all of my colleagues. I prefer to work *with* people, not in competition with them. I'm neither calculating nor manipulative and I am not a threat. I made a mistake based on misinformation, and that is it. I'm as eager as you are for us to move on from that.'

He picked up his sandwich and took a second bite.

I watched him unhurriedly chewing the mouthful and felt a resentment, of the kind I had just denied, begin to bubble up inside me. He was giving me nothing here.

'And,' I added, 'I would just like to say that although I accept full responsibility for the current situation between us, your initially brusque and negative manner towards me did not get our relationship off to a great start.'

He stopped chewing and stared across at me. 'What?'

'There wasn't a whole lot of warmth or enthusiasm on show when I first asked you to come for a drink after I got back from Italy,' I pointed out.

'Well, I'm so sorry if I appeared less than enthusiastic,' he began, sounding mildly incredulous. 'But at the time, I was soaked to the skin and aware that I had just been the subject of a whispered conversation between yourself and not-my-biggest-fan Ruby. It crossed my mind that your invitation to go for a drink might be some sort of joke at my expense. Then, of course, you appeared to confirm that to be the case by taking the piss out of my accent – like I was the Pearly King.'

'Ah yes, now,' I held up a finger, 'I'm actually *really* pleased you've mentioned that, because it was a complete misunderstanding,' I began a little uncertainly. 'You see, I thought you were trying to assert yourself by pretending to be tall and Cockney. I had forgotten that you're from the East End which, in my defence, isn't hard to do because your accent comes and goes a bit with your nerves. So when I did my Cockney impression, I was trying...' I hesitated, unable to recall at that particular moment what on earth I had been trying to do. 'I think I was trying to level the playing field and also lighten the mood a bit.'

He had shown no emotion throughout my little speech but now sighed heavily and ran a hand through his hair. 'You know, I don't even know where to start,' he said wearily. '*Pretending to be tall?*'

'The thing is, I had just been told that you weren't a very friendly person,' I said desperately. 'Something which, by the way, I was initially unwilling to accept. But when you were standing over me, all huge and gangland, I thought, *Ooh, maybe it's true. Maybe he isn't a very friendly person after all.* Your body language and your... your...

surly diction made it much easier for me to make the mistake I then went on to make.'

He nodded. 'Fair comment. You're not the first person to mention my surly diction.'

'Really?' I asked, experiencing some relief that my perception of him hadn't been entirely left-field.

He looked blankly at me for a moment before answering. 'No, Edie, not really,' he said with exaggerated patience. 'No one has ever described my diction as surly, or my posture as gangland, or questioned whether I'm actually as tall as I appear to be.'

He shook his head despairingly and I forced myself to pause and take a breath, conscious that my panicked attempts at an explanation were only making things worse.

'Look, do you know what I thought you had done?' I asked hesitantly. I wasn't sure whether Alison had enlightened him, and I still had my doubts that putting him fully in the picture would make anything better, but I knew that continuing to acknowledge a mistake, without explaining what that mistake was and how it came to be made, wasn't going to lay this to rest.

'Kerry told me,' he said.

'OK. Good.' I felt myself relax a little, confident that the information would at least have been imparted with an emphasis on forgiveness and moving on. In fact, I now strongly suspected that she might be the reason that we were sitting there having lunch. 'She's so lovely, isn't she?' I said.

'She has a huge heart,' he replied, the statement somehow all the more endearing for being delivered gruffly and with a slight awkwardness.

I gazed down at the sorry excuse for a muffin. 'Well, I feel better that you know the background. I mean, I know it probably doesn't make you feel great, and God knows it doesn't reflect well on me.'

'Yeah, well, some of all this doesn't reflect well on me either,' he said, now more weary than gruff. 'Even if I couldn't help the diction, I could've ditched the cynicism when you suggested a drink.'

'That's a very generous thing to say.'

He stared at his sandwich. 'We need to start over.'

'Oh, I would *really* love that,' I said, aware of a hint of desperation from my voice.

He looked up and smiled a little sadly. 'Let's do that then,' he said quietly.

He extended a hand across the table and I reached out and shook it, managing a small smile in return. Then we sat, each contemplating our unappetising plates of food, neither of us eating or speaking, but both, I assumed, feeling a little better than when we walked in.

After a moment, I cleared my throat and said, 'I'm happy with my windows but, thinking ahead to another pitch, I do have an internal courtyard and a curving light-well idea to show you.'

This time, his smile was broad and relaxed with interest. 'Sure,' he said, bending down to retrieve his laptop bag from the floor. 'And after that, if you're up for it and there's time, I'll show you some stained glass.'

Chapter 26

'Thanks again for coming with me, Giles.' I sat down on the bottom stair and pulled on a boot, as Giles bobbed and weaved his way out of the living room, desperately trying to avoid Anthony, as the latter alternately bounced up and then flopped down in his path.

It was the night of Bill's gig and I was still feeling guilty about dragging Giles, not to mention two of his work colleagues, along with me. He had been an absolute rock for me over the past couple of months, keeping me focused on the positives in my life – not least my improving relationship with Cameron – and it didn't feel great to be repaying that kindness by forcing him to endure three hours of Bill banging his bodhrán to a load of Eighties classics.

'No problem, I'm actually really looking forward to it,' he said, so brightly that I almost believed him. 'But I wonder if I should just take a quick peek at the Eldon House website to see if it allows dogs...' he added in a murmur, a statement which caused Anthony to sit bolt upright and wag his tail furiously.

'Even if they do, do you think he'd be OK with the noise?' I asked doubtfully. 'Remember what Kerry said happened when he was in her kitchen and Harry suddenly turned the volume on the radio up to max?'

Giles pursed his lips. 'Excellent point,' he sighed, bending down and picking up the little dog. 'I'm sorry, Anthony, but we just can't risk a toilet-time accident in the pub, can we? Let's pop you in your bed.'

I reached for my other boot and was just zipping it up when he reappeared, closing the back-room door behind him.

'Have you arranged to meet your friends at a certain time?' I asked, as he walked past me to the vestibule and unhooked his waxed jacket.

He shook his head. 'I just said we'd be there from seven. It's not a huge place, so I'm sure we'll spot them.'

'And their names are Joe and Florence? Is that right?'

He peered into the hallway mirror and ruffled his hair. 'I know this jacket has seen better days, but how about the rest of me? Do I look gig-appropriate?' He glanced down at his jeans and then turned towards me, pulling open the jacket in flasher-fashion to reveal a grey V-neck sweater over a white T-shirt.

'Gig-appropriate?'

'I am aiming for a little more casual than usual with the T-shirt. But now I'm not so sure it's entirely me.'

'Well, I think it's very you – especially the new gym-honed you,' I said, looking up at him approvingly. 'But you're not on the pull, are you? It'd be so much easier to ask Nicky for her friend's number. She offered it to you weeks ago.'

'Funny you should say that.'

My eyes widened. 'You haven't.'

'I have.'

'When?' I exclaimed.

'I texted Nicky earlier in the week and she sent me...' He paused, taking his phone from his jacket pocket and tapping the screen, 'Melissa's details.' He turned the phone towards me, displaying a photograph of a fine-featured redhead, with glowing, freckled skin: just his type.

'Wow,' I said. 'Tell me more.'

'She's a radiologist and also an exhibiting sculptor in her spare time. She enjoys playing the cello, parapenting and kick-boxing.'

I wrinkled my nose. 'Sounds a bit ordinary.'

'Quite. And what she'll see in me, I'm not sure.'

'You're loaded,' I pointed out.

'True, true,' he said acceptingly.

'So have you arranged a date yet?'

He extended a hand and hauled me to my feet. 'Let's talk about it later, or we'll be late. Oh and you look very lovely in your purple boots and fetching floral blouse, by the way.'

'Why, thank you,' I smiled. 'I was wondering when it was my turn for a compliment.'

'I know you were,' he said, opening the front door and waving me through. 'And now that all boxes have been ticked, let's go.'

–

The bar area immediately inside the entrance to the pub was already crowded when we arrived, with people standing in small groups chatting and about half a dozen or so waiting to be served by one of three bar staff.

'Can you see Joe or Florence?' I asked, standing on tiptoe in an attempt to view the whole room.

Giles pivoted and then shook his head. 'Can't see anyone I recognise, although I suppose they may already be in there.'

I followed the nod of his head and, through open double doors, saw a second area, less densely packed than the bar but busy nevertheless. Along the far wall I could see the tops of four microphone stands and, behind those, a drum kit on a raised platform.

'Ooh,' I said, nudging him. 'Exciting. Hey and you know what? Bill's band must be OK for all these people to have bought tickets. I thought it might be just the four of us.'

'Yes, I must say I'm rather surprised about that too. Shall we attempt to buy some drinks and then go through?'

'I'll get the first round,' I said, squeezing past him and heading for the bar.

Giles followed and it wasn't long before my order was being taken.

'We didn't know the band was quite so popular,' I said to the barmaid, as she handed me half a cider and began to pull a pint for Giles.

She flicked a blonde plait over her shoulder and smiled. 'Well, we're lucky that it's always quite busy on a Saturday night,' she said. 'But yes, the live music nights do pull in a few more punters. I've never heard this lot before, have you?'

'No, but a neighbour of ours plays with them.'

'Aw, it's nice that you've come to support them,' she said.

I reached into my bag for my purse, taking out the tickets as I did so. 'Is anyone checking tickets in there?' I glanced towards the other room.

'Tickets?' She placed Giles's pint on the bar and turned towards the till. 'There aren't any tickets. It's a free event.

So that's six-ninety, please. Contactless?' She held out the card reader towards me.

'But I paid...' I looked down at the tickets in my hand, whilst imagining myself snatching Bill's penny whistle from his grasp, snapping it in half over my knee and then putting the boot into his sound system.

'Is your name Edith?' I looked up to find a white-haired barman, I assumed the landlord, smiling at me.

'Yes,' I said, tapping my debit card aggressively against the reader.

'The reserved table is right at the front. Just make your way through. It's got your name on it.'

'What reserved table?'

He reached under the bar and took out a glass, continuing to serve another customer. 'The one you paid for,' he said. 'So just go on through. Anyone else sitting there, ask them to move. Come back if there's a problem.' And with that, he walked to the other end of the bar, with the drink he had just poured.

I frowned angrily and turned to Giles, handing him his pint. 'Apparently, I paid over thirty quid for—'

'So I heard,' Giles chuckled. 'That Bill, eh? He's a little bit tricky, isn't he?'

'A little bit tricky?' I exclaimed. 'He's a conman! I'm really pissed off and will be demanding a full refund.'

'Will you indeed?' said Giles, making a start on his pint.

I looked at him and sighed. 'Oh, of course not,' I admitted. 'And I'll probably buy tickets to his next gig too.'

'And that's what makes you so charming.' He put his free arm around me and gave me a squeeze. 'In any case, we've got a table out of it, which is great, isn't it? Come on, admit it, you love a table. You hate it when we can't get a seat.'

I smiled. 'You're right. I do.'

'Well, then,' he said. 'Cheap at twice the price. Shall we go and find it?'

We wound our way through the open double doors into the second room, which was about twice the size of the bar area. Once inside, our table for four wasn't hard to spot, it being the only table in the room and situated front and centre, just a couple of metres from the band – or from where the band would be, when they finally appeared.

'This feels so odd,' I said, as we sat down, drawing a number of confused glances and smirks from those nearby. 'It's like we're in the royal box – or the disabled section. I feel like a fraud.'

'What time do they start?' asked Giles, clearly way more at ease with privilege than I was.

'I'm not sure,' I replied. 'How about I check my fake tickets?'

'Excellent idea.'

I reached into my bag and took out a ticket. 'Seven thirty,' I said, handing it to Giles. 'Do you think your friends will be able to find us?' I swivelled in my chair, scanning the increasingly crowded room. 'We're very low level.'

'Don't worry, I've texted them,' he said. 'They'll find us.'

'Great. Joe and Florence are both historians, aren't they?'

'No,' he shook his head. 'Or rather, yes, they are, but they couldn't make it this evening.'

'Oh,' I said, still looking round. 'I clearly haven't been paying attention.'

'My fault. I didn't update you.'

Something in his voice made me stop searching the room and focus on him. 'So who is coming?' I asked.

He didn't reply, but instead looked over my shoulder and pointed.

I turned and saw Kerry walking towards us and looking questioningly at Giles. When I glanced back at him, I caught him shaking his head and mouthing something at her, actions which he then hastily and unsuccessfully tried to disguise as a yawn and a stretch.

'What's going on, Giles?' I asked.

'Hello!' beamed Kerry, on reaching us. 'You got us a table.' She looked around the room and then pulled out a chair and sat down. 'You got us *the only* table. How the hell did you manage that?'

'At huge expense,' I said, rolling my eyes. 'Giles didn't tell me you were coming. What a nice surprise!' I smiled and stood up. 'Let me go and get you a drink.'

She took my arm and gently pulled me back down. 'No, no, Ron's getting them in.'

I turned to Giles who was now blinking anxiously. 'Cameron's here?'

He nodded whilst hiding most of his features behind his pint glass.

'Oh, that's really nice,' I said, trying hard to mean it.

'I know,' said Kerry. 'Great, isn't it?'

There followed a slight pause, before I asked, 'Does Cameron know that we're here too?' I wagged a finger back and forth between Giles and myself.

'He will do any minute now,' laughed Kerry. 'So, have you heard Bill's band before, Giles? I've only ever heard him play his recorder at the wine and cheeses.'

Giles replied in the negative and then asked Kerry whether she knew why Jeanette and Cormac's house at the far end of the avenue was up for sale. I listened for a moment to her explanation of how a top-floor refurbishment had slowly but surely descended into mental and marital breakdown, and then I made a decision.

'I'm going to help Cameron with the drinks,' I said, standing up and walking hurriedly away, not bothering to wait for acknowledgement or approval of my plan.

Once back in the bar, my colleague wasn't difficult to spot, being taller than the vast majority of his fellow drinkers. An additional aid to locating him was his thick mousy hair, which was today far more bed-head than usual, standing on end and adding to his height. He appeared to be next in line to be served and was tracking the bar staff intently, ready to catch an eye at the first opportunity.

I took a deep breath, affixed a smile, and then made my way towards him, tapping his back on arrival.

He turned with some reluctance away from the bar, his surprised expression immediately confirming that he was as uninformed as I had been about us spending the evening together.

'You?' he said.

'Yes, it is me.'

He frowned, clearly confused and also slightly flustered. 'Are you here for the band too? And hello, by the way.' He patted down his hair and glanced over my shoulder into the other room. 'Is this a coincidence?' he asked.

'Apparently not.'

'And you didn't know either?'

'Nope.'

He rolled his eyes.

'I still would have been very happy to come, though,' I clarified, 'even if Giles had told me that you were going to be here. So I'm not sure why he didn't.'

He looked down at me for a moment and then smiled. 'Same here,' he said. 'But Kerry does love a bit of drama.'

'Giles, not so much. So I'm not sure what his excuse is.' I looked over my shoulder. 'But I'm definitely going to ask him,' I added, with a certain amount of menace.

'What's this band, then?' he asked. 'Kerry was a bit muddled about their music.'

'Reggae and Eighties pop and rock. Our neighbour plays the bodhrán and the penny whistle.'

'Oh, OK. So she wasn't muddled then – apart from that she thought he played the recorder.'

It was at that point that the noise of a soundcheck, including a guitar being tuned and a shrill blast on a penny whistle, reached us. This was closely followed by Bill shouting, 'Hello, young lovers!' and making a reference to 'Giles and his cousin', which I was very grateful not to be able to entirely make out.

'Drink?' Cameron was looking at me, clearly amused.

'No, thanks, we've just got one.'

I turned my head as Bill boomed something about 'cousins' and 'blood relatives'.

'Are you sure about that drink?' asked Cameron. 'Sounds like you're going to need at least a couple.'

I turned back towards him and laughed. 'You're right,' I said, 'and thanks, a pint of cider for Giles and a half for me would be great. We'll get the next round.'

Chapter 27

Having said goodbye to Kerry and Cameron at the garden gate – Kerry hugging us twice, Cameron raising a hand – Giles and I made our way up the path and into the house, where we were immediately greeted on entry by the sound of Anthony whimpering excitedly in the kitchen.

'I'll let him out,' I said, as Giles crouched and began to tug at his laces. 'Cup of tea? I'm having peppermint.'

He didn't reply and I paused with my hand on the back-room door. 'Giles?'

'What? Sorry?' He let the laces drop and looked up at me, blinking at half speed.

'Cup of tea?'

'Oh yes, of course,' he said. 'I shall make a pot momentarily.'

'No,' I tutted, 'I'm offering to make you one. Go and relax in the living room and I'll put the kettle on. Peppermint?'

'Super, smashing, marvellous,' he grinned, and then, abandoning his efforts to untie his shoes, he stood up and, steadying himself against the wall, eased them off his feet. 'Must've done double-bows,' he muttered, before meandering into the living room.

I released Anthony from the kitchen and watched as he immediately raced off, presumably to cover Giles in slobber, and then I set about making the tea.

It can't have been more than five minutes later that I entered the living room to find Giles fast asleep in an armchair, feet outstretched and head resting on the back of the chair. Anthony was also out for the count, stretched across Giles's lap.

I smiled, placing Giles's tea quietly on the table next to him and then sitting down on the sofa with my own. It had, I decided, been an unexpectedly fun evening, due in large part to the pleasure and relief I had felt at seeing Giles and Kerry so apparently at ease with each other once again. But that aside, I had also, I admitted to myself, very much enjoyed Cameron's company – after a slightly awkward and guarded start. OK, so alcohol had undoubtedly helped, but I felt that there had also been a genuine, grass-roots improvement in our relationship. And that made me feel better about him, and about us, and about life in general.

Anthony sneezed, waking Giles with a start. His eyes opened wide and he slowly lifted his head to look at me.

'I'm so sorry, Edie,' he said, rubbing his eyes. 'Did I drift off there?'

'You did, but I forgive you and your tea is next to you,' I said. 'But wouldn't you rather just go straight up to bed?'

'No, no.' He leaned to his left and picked up the mug. 'I'd like to drink this first. You know, I really shouldn't have had that final half. It's done for me.'

'Well,' I shrugged, 'you don't do it very often, and I don't know about you, but I thought the alcohol really improved the music.'

'Yes, that early cover of *Heaven is a Place on Earth* really was hellish, wasn't it?'

'I was just relieved that Bill didn't get us up on stage,' I said. 'Do you think he felt guilty about taking money from me for the tickets? I can't think of any other reason for all the *kissing cousins* shout-outs.'

Giles yawned. 'What an evening.'

I looked up from my tea to find him frowning down at Anthony, as he stroked the small dog's head with a single finger.

'You did enjoy tonight, didn't you, Giles?'

He looked up but didn't reply, instead gazing at me wordlessly for several seconds.

'Giles?'

'Oh, yes, sorry, I did have a very nice time. Sorry, Edie, I was rather lost in contemplation there for a moment.'

'And what were you contemplating?'

'Relationships. Cameron and Kerry seem so very happy in each other's company, don't you think?'

'I do. There's clearly a strong bond there.'

'Yes, a very strong bond,' he murmured. 'That's very important, isn't it? Do you know, I'm not sure that I've ever quite had that in a relationship – with a partner, I mean.' He looked down and resumed stroking Anthony's head.

'Oh, come off it,' I cajoled. 'You've had some lovely girlfriends and some very happy partnerships.'

'Admittedly, but I've never felt a connection snap – or my heart break – at the end of a relationship,' he replied, his frown deepening. 'One would expect to experience that if one had a deep affection – a bond, as you put it – with one's partner. I do sometimes wonder whether my heart has ever really been touched, romantically speaking. And maybe that is preferable: no gain, but no pain either.'

I said nothing, taken aback by his sudden decision to share his feelings. Of course, I assumed that three and a half pints of cider was playing a part in that, in the same way that booze had made it much easier for me to talk to Cameron about my university days and for him to tell me about his childhood in Hackney. But Giles had just made an unprompted reference to his love life and he'd never done that before, even when drunk.

He sighed and replaced his mug on the table. 'So, I'm thinking of texting Melissa tomorrow.'

'Oh, wow, that's a brilliant idea!' I exclaimed, surprised but relieved by the positivity of the suggestion, hot on the heels of such uncharacteristic, bordering-on-gloomy, introspection.

'Is it?' he asked.

My smile faded. 'Isn't it?'

He shrugged. 'It all seems a rather more difficult decision this time, more of a *big deal*, as my students might say. But I do think, on balance, it's probably for the best. What do you think?'

'Er...' I hesitated, increasingly aware that we were now in uncharted territory, something which I would have thought near-impossible in a close relationship spanning over two decades. '*For the best* is a bit of a weird way of putting it, if I'm honest, Giles. I'm not sure I'd want someone asking me out on the basis that they had decided it was *for the best*.'

'I see,' he said, his eyes unfocused as he mulled it over. 'I suppose what I meant was that contacting Melissa would, on balance, make me feel better.'

I sighed. 'Well, it's still not *Casablanca*, but I do think you should do whatever makes you happy, or happier, if that's what you're saying.'

'I don't know what I'm saying.' He yawned for a second time. 'I'm just wondering if it is acceptable for me to ask Melissa out, if my attention is...' He ground to a halt and, evidently feeling no need to complete the sentence, gently eased Anthony from his lap and stood up. 'I am off to bed.'

'Oh… OK,' I said, as taken aback by the abruptness of his decision to end the conversation, as I had been by his initiation of it. 'Night, then.'

'Goodnight. Thank you for your company this evening and every evening, Edie,' he said, disappearing into the hallway with Anthony at his heels.

I gazed after him, thinking about what he had said. Such emoting seemed wholly out of character, but then, I reminded myself, I had never previously been on-hand to witness the birth of any of Giles's relationships. Maybe pre-date agonising and soul-searching was standard, and he had just never been drunk enough, or geographically close enough, to share it with me before.

I really hoped that was it. But as I hauled myself to my feet and headed out of the room taking my peppermint tea with me, I couldn't shake the unsettling feeling that it wasn't.

Chapter 28

October rolled into November and Ruby's threatened surprise visit to Bristol – the prospect of which had so traumatised me a couple of months earlier – thankfully failed to materialise. What's more, her messages – although still packed to bursting with her successes and my misfortunes – gradually decreased in frequency, and even when I did hear from her, the negative impact of her updates was so diminished that I found myself more fascinated than distressed by them.

All of which tied in rather nicely with my preference for letting our relationship fizzle, rather than nuking it with a dramatic confrontation. After all, I told myself, lots of friendships faded and to seek out conflict when my life was so nicely back on track, would be a pointless backward step. The power station project was going well and, more importantly, my relationship with Cameron had continued to steadily improve, to the extent that a chat over lunch or a drink with Roger and Luke after work no longer felt forced or uncomfortable. In fact, my conversations with him were now something I very much enjoyed.

For Jason too, Ruby's departure appeared to kick-start a period of sustained improvement. True, he suffered the occasional worry that he might one day return home to find a bunny boiling on the hob, but on the whole his texted updates revealed an increasing optimism for a future in which he did not need to sleep with every willing woman in order to achieve emotional and sexual fulfilment. An additional point of happiness for him was that he and Giles had now managed to have a beer together. Their conversation had admittedly been entirely cricket-based – but it was at least a start.

As for Giles himself, my fears that he was about to enter a period of introspective gloom and self-doubt following Bill's gig proved unfounded. He had awoken the next morning displaying his usual bonhomie and, with no apparent hesitation, had texted Melissa to arrange to meet for lunch the following week; a lunch which had since been followed by multiple dog-walks, an evening at the theatre and dinner at a Clifton restaurant.

Thus, it seemed, for the time being at least, that all was well. And it was with this significantly improved sense of well-being, coupled with a weekend spring in my step, that I turned the corner into the lamp-lit avenue one Friday evening to see June making her way slowly towards me from the opposite end of the road.

She raised a hand, I waved back, and a minute later we met at Giles's gate.

'Oh it *is* her. She looks so wide in that coat,' she murmured, before continuing more loudly, 'and how are you, Edith, and how is your Giles?'

'We're both really well, June,' I said, looking down uncertainly and wondering if double-breasted might not be working for me after all. 'How are you?'

'Good, good.' She smiled, putting a hand to her head and adjusting the blonde, Margaret Thatcheresque wig which was perched there. 'We were in Eastbourne with friends last week. There's a hotel there which puts on dinner dances. We visit every year at this time. It's quite lovely.'

'Sounds it,' I said. 'I'd love to see pictures of that, if you have any.'

She beamed, clearly delighted by the suggestion. 'I could show you the ones the official photographer took. I'll bring them to the wine and cheese. Remind me of the date, dear.'

'The date of what?'

'Of the wine and cheese. You're hosting.'

'Am I? Are we? Giles didn't tell me.'

June put a worried hand to her mouth. 'Oh dear, I do hope he hasn't forgotten. They are so hard to rearrange, because everybody is so very busy, you see.'

I placed a hand on her arm. 'I'm sure he hasn't forgotten. Giles is very organised about such things. I bet he's mentioned it to me and I just haven't been listening properly.'

She looked thoughtfully up at me and I instinctively braced. 'So very scatty,' she said quietly.

I suppressed a sigh. 'Well, like I say, I'm sure it's all fine, but I'll mention it to Giles when he gets home.'

'Ah, yes, and how is he?' Her eyes twinkled impishly. 'William tells me the two of you were holding hands in the very front row of his concert.'

'We weren't holding hands, June,' I said, politely but firmly.

'And canoodling.'

'And we were *definitely* not canoodling. Giles and I are *not*—'

'Oh and here's Kerry,' she said, leaning to look past me and waving, 'in her pyjamas.'

I turned to discover Kerry now just a few paces from us. 'Hello, both. Sorry about the loungewear,' she said, brushing down her navy hooded sweatshirt and joggers, 'but I've been stripping wallpaper all day.'

'Loungewear,' echoed June, looking Kerry up and down. 'Well, I do like the sound of that. It looks ever so cosy.'

Kerry pointed to my bags. 'Just home, Edie? Bet you can't wait to get inside and offload that little lot.'

'I must get inside too. I have Stanley's liver in here,' said June, holding up a Co-op carrier bag.

'I expect he'll be wanting that back!' I exclaimed, laughing.

'Oh my goodness, it's not *Stanley's* liver, dear,' she replied, at first horrified and then reaching out with kindly pity and touching my hand. 'It's from the butchers – where they sell meat,' she added helpfully, clearly now doubting my grasp of the basics.

'Yes, I was just—' I began, but she didn't pause for breath.

'Stanley's slightly under the weather, so the iron will do him good.'

'Ah, wish him well from us,' said Kerry, as June turned to cross the road. 'Let us know if you need anything.'

'Will do!'

Kerry watched until June was safely up her steps and inside and then turned back to me. 'Long day?' she asked.

'They're all long,' I said. 'But I love it, so no complaints. How about you? Is there much more scraping to be done?'

'Oh, loads,' she laughed. 'Maintaining that house is like painting the Forth Bridge. But I'm taking the night off! I just nipped out to drop Harry's things at Nicky's. He's having a sleepover.'

'Sounds good. Are you going out? Or having a quiet night in?'

'Well, I was supposed to be going out with some mums, but that's fallen through thanks to an outbreak of chicken pox,' she said ruefully. 'A couple of the kids are sleepless with it and their mums are knackered. And another of the mums is pregnant and has never had it, so she's a bit worried about catching it. But it's fine, we'll just save our night out for a couple of weeks' time.'

'Well, if you fancy a drink, I've got a bottle of red doing nothing and I could do with unwinding,' I said.

Her face lit up, but she hesitated nevertheless. 'Are you sure? I bet you're knackered, aren't you? I know how busy work is.'

'Honestly, it'd be really nice. I've hardly seen you since Bill's gig and it's tricky to talk when Harry and Giles are around.'

She laughed. 'Yeah, men, eh? Well, so long as you're sure, that'd be fab. I'll just take this inside,' she held up what I presumed to be Harry's school bag, 'and then I'll be right round.'

–

'So where's Giles tonight, then?' asked Kerry, leaning towards me from her position on the sofa and refilling, for the second time, the glass I extended towards her, before pouring the last dregs of the bottle into her own.

'Date night,' I replied, relaxing back into my armchair. 'With Melissa,' I added significantly.

Her eyes widened and she flapped a hand, as she hurried to swallow a mouthful of wine. 'Ooh, yes,' she rasped, coughing slightly, 'Nicky said he was seeing her friend. Melissa, eh? What's she like? Sounded nice, the way Nicky described her.'

'Haven't actually met her yet, but I've seen a photo and heard a description and, based on that, she's his usual type.'

'Which is…?' Kerry pulled the pouffe nearer and plonked her feet down on top of it.

'Highly accomplished English rose.'

She nodded. 'Could've guessed that.'

'Yes…' I sighed. 'My aunty always wanted him to branch out a bit, but you know…' I shrugged, 'you like what you like, don't you?'

'And what does Edie like?' she asked, winking.

'God, I haven't thought about men in a long time. I'm just really focused on my job and that's making me really happy right now.'

'No one you're interested in *at* work?'

I choked on my wine. 'At work? Has Cameron told you *anything* about Luke and Roger?'

'A bit. But nothing about whether they're sexy or not. So come on, fill me in.'

'In a nutshell… Luke: mid-twenties, wouldn't look out of place in a boy band. Clinically obsessed with his hair and I'm *definitely* not his type.'

'Fair enough. Next!' shouted Kerry, waving her glass.

'Roger: sixty-something. Hobbies include bowls and being Northern.'

Kerry laughed.

'I actually love them both to bits and I couldn't work with nicer people,' I said, smiling at the thought. 'If they were my age – and I was their type – I'd definitely be hankering after one or both of them.'

'And your boss?'

'Alison's scary, but doesn't mean to be. Definitely married to the job and not touchy-feely *at all*, but tries really hard to relate and act normal. She's very straightforward. You know that if she's got something to say to you, she will say it *to you*.'

'Yes, Ron likes that about her.'

'Me too. Talking of Cameron, where is he tonight?'

'Haven't the faintest.'

The response surprised me and sparked a renewed interest in their relationship. But Kerry's widowhood somehow made even gentle nosiness feel inappropriate. So I reached for my wine, pressing my lips firmly together until the drink reached them in order to keep all tipsy enquiries at bay.

'It's good that you and Ron are getting on so much better now,' said Kerry.

I looked up from my glass. 'Has he said that?' I asked, delighted by the possibility.

'Well, no.'

'Oh, OK,' I said, immediately deflated.

'He doesn't actually say, "*I'm getting on much better with Edie*",' continued Kerry, 'but I can tell he is because he talks about you now – by name – whereas he didn't before. Now, he says things like, "*And I said to Edie…*" and "*Edie suggested…*" and "*Edie really liked this… this doughnut thing I've added to my staircase.*" That kind of thing.'

'That makes me feel really nice,' I said, with a childlike simplicity borne of booze. 'Thanks for telling me.'

'And you feeling really nice about it makes me feel really nice too,' she replied huskily and with some emotion, a reaction, I assumed, also attributable to half a bottle of red wine.

We sat for a moment, smiling inanely and enjoying the shared sense of well-being, before she said, 'Tell me to piss off and mind my own business if you want to, but did you ever have it out with her? You know, the woman who lied about Ron.'

I took a deep breath and shook my head. 'I did not,' I said solemnly.

'And you're OK just leaving things like that?'

'I think so,' I replied uncertainly. 'I mean, sometimes I think maybe I should have said something. But then I think, what would that actually achieve? Things are really good at the moment; I'm back to loving my job and looking forward to going to work. So why make myself all stressed and miserable for nothing?'

'I suppose I get why you wouldn't want to rake it all up again. And if she's leaving you alone…'

'Hmm, well, there you go.' I mumbled the response into my glass, ignoring a nagging sense of disquiet and deciding not to mention Ruby's occasional texts.

'Just the same, a sorry from her would have been nice, wouldn't it?' frowned Kerry. 'I mean, God knows I've said and done enough things I regret. But saying sorry, *being* sorry and trying to put things right – that's the important thing. I really respect a person who can do that. It can tear a person to pieces sometimes, admitting to themselves and to everyone else that they were in the wrong.'

I nodded, feeling suddenly emotional, as Jason inevitably came to mind.

'But whatever,' said Kerry, waving a hand. 'I'm just sorry about what happened to you and Ron and that you lost a friend.'

'She wasn't a friend to me,' I said quietly. 'And it's just weird and a bit pitiful that she thought she was, despite everything she did.'

Kerry smiled sympathetically, hauling her feet off the pouffe and shifting to the edge of the sofa to lean forward and rub my arm. 'I reckon that for people like her, friendship is all about control and needing to be needed. They're threatened by the idea that their *friend* might be able to get along just fine without them, or might want to have other friends. So they try to make that person feel bad about themselves and about other people. But if they can't be made to see how wrong that is, then we just have to let them get on with it and move away.'

I nodded, unable to fault her uncomplicated wisdom.

'The only thing is, of course,' she continued, plumping a cushion and then settling herself back onto the sofa, 'it's chuffin' hard to spot a nutter like that from the off.'

I laughed, in spite of the sombre topic. 'You're absolutely—' I began, only to stop short, as we heard the front door creak open and then click shut, closely followed by the sound of voices and of Anthony skidding on the wooden hallway floor as he rushed from his bed in the kitchen to greet Giles.

I widened my eyes at Kerry.

'Is Melissa with him?' she mouthed, hurriedly sitting up and adjusting both her hair and her loungewear.

I nodded excitedly. 'I think so,' I whispered, putting a hand over my mouth to prevent a snigger.

A moment later, Giles entered the living room and – no two ways about it – his face fell like a brick down a mineshaft when he saw us sitting there. Kerry clearly spotted the reaction too.

'Hiya,' she said cheerily. 'I just popped in for a glass of wine with Edie, but don't worry, I'm off now.'

He stared expressionlessly at her. 'Oh.'

I waited for him to add a smile and a request that Kerry shouldn't rush away, but instead he simply nodded his comprehension and then transferred his solemn gaze to me.

I threw him a dissatisfied look, followed by a slightly tense smile. 'We haven't quite finished our wine yet, Giles,' I said, with exaggerated cheeriness, holding up my glass. 'Why don't you grab a drink and come and join us?'

He hesitated, looking out into the hallway, as we heard the flush of a loo.

'I tell you what, why don't you *both* come and join us?' I pressed.

He didn't reply.

'Or even just come in and say a quick hello?' I was no longer smiling and there was an obvious frustration to my tone. Was he always like this with his dates? Over protective? Not wanting anyone to even set eyes on them until he was sure?

He glanced across at Kerry, his shoulders sagging minutely as he bit his lip. It was a fleeting reaction, and one that I hoped Kerry hadn't spotted. But as I turned, I saw her look self-consciously from Giles to her loungewear and then back at Giles, and I knew, without a doubt, that she thought he was ashamed of her.

'Giles,' I said, hearing the loo door open and reaffixing a smile, in order to fend off a snarl, 'do you have Melissa with you? We'd *love* to say hello.'

At that, he turned to his left and beckoned. 'Melissa, do come in and meet my cousin – my step-cousin – Edie...' He extended an arm in my direction.

Melissa entered stage right, looking willowy and slender in a black shirtdress, patterned with small red roses. A pair of long, high-heeled black boots put her at just a couple of inches shorter than Giles. 'Hello, Edie,' she said.

'...and our next-door neighbour, Kerry,' concluded Giles quietly, swinging his arm towards her, whilst still looking at me.

'Hello, Kerry,' said Melissa.

'Hello!' Kerry and I responded in unison.

'I'm so sorry I'm such a flipping state,' said Kerry. 'I've been decorating.'

'Don't worry.' Melissa smiled kindly. 'I was in my sculpting dungarees ten minutes before I set off to meet Giles. They redefine being in a state. I wash them about once a year.'

I welcomed her warm attempt to make Kerry feel better and I only wished that Giles, who was currently standing next to her and looking about as warm as one of her sculptures, could put in the same level of effort.

'Can I get either of you a drink?' I asked, standing up.

Melissa smiled. 'Ooh, that sounds—'

'No, no,' said Giles quickly, holding up both hands as if fending off a mugger, 'thank you. I think we're... we're just going to...' He inclined his head towards the hallway.

'Oh, OK,' I nodded. 'Well, lovely to meet you, Melissa. Even if only ever so briefly,' I added pointedly, directing the comment at Giles.

'Hopefully I'll see you again soon,' said Melissa as they exited, with Giles closing the door firmly behind them.

Instead of returning to my armchair, I walked the few steps to the sofa and flopped down next to Kerry. 'Well, that was weird,' I murmured.

'I think he was a bit embarrassed of me,' she said softly, confirming my worst fears.

'God, no. Take it from me, he was terrified of me saying something to embarrass him in front of her.'

She didn't argue, but looked unconvinced.

'He just didn't seem himself, though, did he?' I said.

She shook her head. 'To be honest, I felt like I hardly recognised him. He's had his hair cut, hasn't he?'

'Yesterday,' I nodded.

'Suits him. I bet all the women at work fall over themselves for him,' she said quietly. 'But I should be going,' she continued quickly, keeping her voice low, 'do you think they've gone upstairs yet? Don't want to crash anything.'

We sat in silence for a moment, listening intently, and once we were certain that the hallway was empty, I walked her to the front door.

'We should do this again,' I said, 'the next time we can shake off the blokes.'

She laughed. 'I think the chances of Giles wanting to hang around for a drink and a natter with me at the moment are slim to nothing.'

I laughed along, whilst feeling hurt on her behalf. I couldn't be sure that Giles had a problem with introducing her to Melissa, but the fact that Kerry thought he did was enough to make me irritated with him. 'I'll keep you posted,' I said.

She reached up to give me a hug, before turning and walking away. I waited until she had reached her front door and, after smiling and waving at her through the now largely leafless bush, I turned and went inside.

Chapter 29

The next morning I was sitting at the kitchen island, mid chocolate croissant, when Giles walked in, still wearing his dressing gown and slippers.

'Morning,' I said, tucking my hair behind my ears and straightening my bathrobe, lest Melissa should be in his wake.

'Morning,' he replied, offering only a faint smile as he schlepped past me.

I watched out of the corner of my eye as he bent down to take a bowl, spoon, knife and side plate from the dishwasher. He looked absolutely knackered. It had clearly been a busy night.

A moment later, he returned to the island, carrying his crockery and cutlery, plus a box of muesli under one arm. A two-pint carton of milk hung from his right index finger and he was holding a chocolate croissant between his teeth.

'Neat trick,' I said, as he offloaded onto the granite surface of the island and sat down. 'You could be in a circus.'

'Aren't I already?'

I frowned, not understanding, but deciding to let it pass. There were more important, less existential, matters to discuss.

'No Melissa?' I asked softly.

'What?' he stopped pouring milk over his muesli and looked at me blankly.

'Melissa,' I repeated in a whisper. 'Where is she?'

'At home,' he said, in an of-course kind of way.

'Oh, OK. Early bird.'

He picked up his spoon and started to eat. When he still hadn't spoken after another two mouthfuls, I decided to try again.

'So, did the two of you have a nice evening? What did you do?'

'We went to Wilson's.'

'And was it good?'

'The food was delicious,' he said, not looking up.

'I've never been. I must give it a whirl.'

'You should.'

'And how is it going generally? With Melissa, I mean.'

'She's a very nice person.'

'Giles.' I put down my croissant and waited for him to stop eating and look at me.

'Yes?' he asked, frowning. 'What is it?'

I studied him silently for a moment, remembering what Kerry had said the night before about not recognising him and I now knew exactly what she meant. Even his Arthur Dent dressing gown and his jolly-old slippers couldn't disguise the transformation. He was toned, handsome and miserable.

'What is it, Edie?' he repeated, his tone uncharacteristically impatient.

I reached out and laid my hand gently on his arm. 'Is everything OK?'

He put down his spoon with a clatter. 'Everything is perfectly fine. I just want to eat my breakfast.'

'In peace, you mean? Without the third degree?'

He picked up his spoon, his expression serious. 'Yes, that's exactly what I mean.'

'No problem,' I said with faux brightness, removing my hand from his arm and sliding off my stool. 'I'll just go and unpack the dishwasher... *in complete silence.*'

I walked away, taking my breakfast things with me, now feeling as miserable as Giles looked – maybe more so. Because in all the years he and I had been friends, I couldn't recall us ever once having an argument, and yet I was pretty sure that we were about to have one now.

He finished his muesli and moved on to his croissant, while I put the kettle on the hob for a second cup of tea, and still neither of us spoke. I heard a scratching at the bifold doors and saw Anthony requesting to be let in from the garden. I opened the doors and he scampered in, running straight to Giles, bouncing around the foot of his stool, desperate for acknowledgement but getting precisely nothing. I knew how he felt.

I unpacked the dishwasher, made my cup of tea and decided to take it back up to bed. As I walked past Giles, Anthony, who had now given up bouncing and was instead sitting quietly under his master's stool, looked up at me mournfully. I bent down, patted his head and then continued towards the door.

'I'm sorry, Edie,' said Giles quietly.

I turned towards him. 'For upsetting Kerry?' I asked, without pause for thought.

'What?' He turned sharply. 'What do you mean?'

'Well, you weren't very polite to her when you got home last night.'

'I was impolite?' he said, looking so stricken that I began to regret my bluntness – but there was no going back now.

'When you came into the living room, you looked at Kerry as if… well, as if you were embarrassed of her.'

'I did?' He both looked and sounded horrified. 'Is that what Kerry thought?'

'You know what she's like. She made light of it but yes, Giles, that's what she thought. Of course I told her that you weren't, but I saw it too. You didn't look at all pleased to see her. And then you so obviously didn't want to introduce us to Melissa.'

He tilted his face upwards and closed his eyes. 'I see.'

'It just wasn't like you.'

'No.'

'So what's going on?'

He lowered his head, opened his eyes and dropped his half-eaten croissant into his empty cereal bowl. 'I like Melissa very much, but we're not going to see each other again.'

'Really?' I walked back to the breakfast bar, pulled out a stool and sat back down next to him.

'She didn't stay last night. In fact, she left before Kerry did and we then spoke at length on the phone.'

'Oh and what have you…' I stopped mid-sentence, reminding myself that I had no experience of Giles's preferred handling of personal relationships. Just because I had chosen to share all the gory Jason-details with him did not mean that he had an urge to reciprocate. 'OK.'

'I hate the thought of upsetting Kerry,' he said, his eyes fixed on the remains of his croissant.

'It'll be fine,' I said, waving a hand, sad to see him troubled, but also relieved and reassured by his concern. 'You know how laid-back she is. The next time you see her, you can explain that things weren't quite working out with Melissa and that's why you didn't rush to introduce her. In fact,' I added, 'I bet Nicky will tell her about Melissa, and then Kerry will work out for herself that your awkwardness was nothing at all to do with her.'

Giles continued to stare unblinkingly at his bowl. 'But it was to do with her,' he said quietly. 'It was everything to do with her. Clearly I'm now completely incapable of hiding my feelings.'

I gasped and put a hand to my mouth as the pieces fell into place. 'You fancy her!'

'It all seems so ridiculously complicated, Edie.' He lowered his head and ran a hand through his newly-cropped hair. 'One moment, someone is the friend they have always been; the friend one has known for… well, years in our case. And then the next moment, one is hit by the realisation that they are something more to you.'

He turned towards me, with apparent reluctance, as if afraid of what my reaction might be. 'I know I'm behaving like an adolescent. But I do feel that matters have come to somewhat of a head.'

'I'm just so sorry I didn't realise, Giles,' I said gently. 'But look, why don't you text her later today, go for a drink and talk it all through?'

'Good God, I can't do that!' he exclaimed, clearly appalled at the idea.

'Why not?' I asked, frowning and picking up my tea.

'Because we are next-door neighbours and she has given no indication of being even remotely attracted to me. Additionally, she is in a relationship with Ronald.'

I took a deep breath. 'So firstly, his name is *Cameron*, Giles,' I began, my tone patient and controlled. 'Or Ron, or Cam, if you prefer. But *not* Ronald. And secondly, if there's one thing I've learned this year, it's the importance of getting your facts straight. In this case, you do not know how Kerry feels about you, and you also know next to nothing about her relationship with Cameron. I mean, are they even a couple?'

'They spend much of their time together and have an exceptionally strong bond, as you yourself have pointed out.'

'OK, but so do we,' I pointed out. 'And when I asked Kerry what Cameron was up to last night, she said she didn't have a clue. That doesn't sound like the response of someone in a committed relationship, does it?'

He shrugged.

'Well, it doesn't to me,' I said emphatically. 'So stop being pathetic and moping over your muesli and go and find out the lie of the land. And can I just ask,' I added, placing my mug down heavily on the breakfast bar, 'whether you are always this traumatised when you realise you fancy someone?'

'I assure you, Edie,' he sighed, shaking his head, 'that I have never felt like this before. I have no concentration; I am dithering over basic decisions and I am having difficulty sleeping. In addition, I realise that I have changed my hair, my attire and my physique for Kerry.'

'Like Sandy, in *Grease*.'

He squinted, as if trying to compute. 'Er…'

'What I mean is, you fancy her and you want to please her. That's wonderful, Giles – and also a tiny bit needy and lacking in self-respect, admittedly – but mostly wonderful,' I smiled.

'But it's having a negative effect on my behaviour and on my ability to function, and I don't believe that I can correct the situation whilst living at this address.'

'Oh don't be so melodramatically clinical,' I tutted. 'You can fix all this with a simple conversation. After that, if Kerry doesn't feel the same way, you go out with friends and drink far too much, and then come home and eat far too much, and then you rinse and repeat until you feel better.'

'And in the meantime, I will have caused Kerry deep embarrassment and be thought of forever thereafter as the creepy chap next door,' he said. 'I simply don't feel comfortable about approaching a woman who is currently in a caring relationship with a man who is building her a new kitchen. Kerry has lost her husband and has a young son to care for. She does not need some stuttering fool rocking the boat when things are going well for her.'

'But the whole point, Giles, is that you do not have the first idea how things are going for her!' I exclaimed exasperatedly. 'She could be sitting just feet from us, sobbing into her cornflakes because she adores a neighbour whom she thinks has issues with her loungewear! Or yes – maybe she would rather just keep you as a friend. I don't know. But neither… do… you,' I concluded, prodding his arm to drive the point home. 'Talk to her.'

'No.'

'Then I will.'

'No.'

'Yes, I will.'

He pointed a finger at me. 'Edith Whitmore, I am serious now,' he said, looking appropriately stern. 'Promise me that you will not mention one word of this matter to Kerry.'

'Let me just explain to you exactly what I'd say to her…'

'No,' he said flatly. 'Now, please promise me that you will not.'

I heaved a sigh. 'OK, if you insist. But how do you feel about me asking Nicky? I wouldn't mention your name, *obviously*, I would just ask her whether Cameron and Kerry—'

'I don't want you to mention anything to Nicola, either.'

'Giles…'

'Edith.'

My shoulders sagged. 'Oh, all right. But don't be afraid to change your mind about this when you've had a chance to think. A little digging would be so much more sensible and straightforward than moving out for six months.'

'But you're not going to dig with either Kerry or Nicola?'

'I've said I won't, haven't I?'

His frame visibly relaxed. 'Thank you.'

'For what?' I exclaimed. 'You won't let me do anything!'

'For listening,' he said. 'And for understanding. A little bit.'

I leaned towards him, giving him a hug. 'Don't mention it,' I said, patting his back. 'It's been a long time coming, but it was definitely my turn to listen.'

Chapter 30

I didn't see much more of Giles over the weekend, spending the rest of Saturday and half of Sunday in Hungerford at a small meet-up of university friends. When I did finally see him, he appeared fine and, as for his heartache over Kerry, he didn't raise the subject and neither did I.

While I had little doubt that his silence on the matter was due to a wish not to be a bother, my reasons for an uncharacteristic display of discretion and self-control were quite different. Having agreed not to discuss Kerry's relationship status with either herself or Nicky, I was desperate to avoid giving Giles any opportunity to extend the moratorium on discussion to include anyone else – such as Cameron's friends, for example. And having succeeded in that aim, I arrived in the office at eight fifteen on Monday morning with a steaming cup of coffee in my hand and a determination to grill the hell out of loose-lipped Luke.

'Morning!' I said brightly, placing the coffee on his desk before staggering to my own to offload my multiple bags.

'You're a Monday marvel,' he smiled, picking up the cup and saluting me with it. 'But why the early start today? Playing catch-up again?'

'No,' I said, sitting down. 'I just thought I'd get going and make the most of the day. Maybe leave on time for once.'

He looked at me with something approaching suspicion. 'Well, thanks for this,' he said, blowing on his coffee.

'You're welcome.'

'Where's yours?'

'My what?'

'Your coffee.'

I glanced around my desk. In my haste to get to the office before Cameron arrived, I'd forgotten to buy myself a cup.

'Didn't want one,' I said quickly. 'So anyway,' I glanced up at the office clock, 'how was your weekend? I met up with my old uni flatmates. Wonder what everyone else was up to. Wonder what Roger did. And Alison.' I laughed lightly and shook my head. 'She's such an enigma, isn't she? And Cameron, he's a bit of an enigma too. I wonder who he sees and what he gets up to. I wonder...' I looked at Luke. 'Any ideas?'

'About what? That was a very long sentence,' he said, sipping his coffee, 'with a helluva lot of wondering in it.'

I clenched my teeth into a smile. 'Start with Cameron. What kind of thing do you think he does at the weekend? And with *whom*,' I added significantly.

Luke shrugged. 'Well, he went to that gig with you, didn't he? So that's that one answered: he listens to shit music with needy types. Alison's *way* more interesting.'

I looked again at the clock. Cameron would be in soon and if we sidetracked onto Alison, I'd have to take Luke to lunch to get anything useful out of him before home-time. 'Yes, yes, she is an interesting character.'

Luke reclined in his chair, slowly swivelling back and forth whilst tapping his lower lip with his pen. 'Do you reckon she has a partner?'

'Don't be silly,' I said dismissively.

'It's just that I've—'

'Hey, but do you think *Cameron* has a partner?' I asked.

Interrupted mid-sentence and with his mouth still ajar, Luke frowned. 'Sure. But I think that Alison—'

'Do you *think* he has a partner?' I interjected. 'Or do you *know* he has a partner. *Definitely* know?' I pressed, leaning towards him across my desk.

He continued to frown. 'He hasn't said, "Luke, I've got a girlfriend" and provided photographic evidence of the fact, if that's what you mean.'

'So you don't *definitely* know.'

'No, Rumpole, I don't *definitely* know,' he said, putting down his coffee. 'What's with all this sudden interest in Cameron's private life anyway?'

'Not just Cameron's,' I said defensively. 'I'm interested in Alison's and Roger's too.'

His frown lifted and a slow smile spread across his face. 'Edie, have you got the hots for him?'

My jaw dropped. 'No, I have not!'

'You do-oo,' he said in a sing-song voice. 'I knew you did. All that "anger" towards him.' He drew the inverted commas in the air. 'Anger, my arse. That was pure sexual tension. Soooo obvious.'

'It was not!' I exclaimed, feeling myself blushing. 'It was *absolutely* not. I want to know whether he's single or not because…' I hesitated, trying to decide whether or not it was OK to confide. 'I'm asking for a friend.'

'Oh, *for a friend*,' he said, winking and tapping the side of his nose. 'I get it. Yeah, yeah, *for a friend*. Your little

283

fluttery friend in here, is it?' He asked, placing a hand on his chest.

'Luke,' I closed my eyes and took a deep breath, 'I promise you that I am one hundred per cent enquiring about Cameron's relationship status for a friend. I promise you.'

'So you're saying someone has asked you to enquire?' He picked up his coffee and took a sip, studying me over the top of the cup. 'Interesting…'

'Well, not exactly,' I said. 'It's more that I'm investigating the situation because they're… a bit shy.'

'A bit shy?' He sounded incredulous. 'Your friend is over twelve, right?'

'It's OK for a man to be shy, Luke.'

He spat his coffee out onto the desk. '*A man?*' he spluttered, bending down, opening a desk drawer and taking out a packet of wet-wipes. 'Look, Edie, I may not be totally sure whether Cameron is seeing a woman, but I promise you that he has not, and will never have, a male partner.'

'I know that,' I said, 'it's just… Oh look, it's a long story and I don't think I've got permission to tell it. I just need to know whether he has a girlfriend and, if so, who she is.'

'Well, I'm afraid I don't know – not for sure anyway,' he said, mopping up the coffee spray. 'I just assumed that he was seeing the woman he's drawn up the kitchen plans for: Kerry. He talks a lot about her and they're obviously very close.'

I slumped in my chair, staring at my desk, feeling disappointed for Giles. 'They are,' I said quietly.

'Hey, but don't give up hope until you're certain.'

I looked up at him and nodded slowly. 'You're right. We have to test the information and verify the facts. Otherwise, we're just guessing, aren't we?'

He shrugged. 'Well, you're the one actually doing all the guessing here. I'm not really that invested in—'

'So, will you find out if he's seeing Kerry or not?' I interrupted, leaning forward and lowering my voice. 'You know, do a little digging. Covert ops. Report back to me later in the week?' I smiled winningly at him. 'Will you?'

He stopped mopping, looked up and grinned excitedly, leaning towards me across his desk. 'No.'

'What? Why not? That's so unhelpful.'

'Ask him yourself,' he said, tossing the wipes in the bin and returning the packet to the drawer.

'I can't ask him,' I said.

'Why not?'

'Because he'll want to know why I'm asking.'

Luke shrugged. 'Tell him it's because your friend fancies him.'

'But that's not true.'

'Aha!' He whirled round in his chair. 'Well done for admitting it,' he said. 'And in that case, just tell him that *you* fancy him. It's 2018, Edie, not 1818. You're an empowered woman. You can make the first move. I don't understand why you're turning this into such a project. Just tell it like it is.'

'But that's *not* how it is,' I groaned, just as Alison walked in.

'Good morning,' she said, making her way briskly towards her office.

'Morning, Alison!' I said, hurriedly turning to my screen and switching it on before beginning to unpack my bags.

'Hi,' smiled Luke, raising a hand. 'Good weekend?'

She paused with her hand on the half-open door and after a moment she let it swing shut and turned to face us. 'Yes, I did have a good weekend, thank you,' she said. 'And how was your weekend, Luke?'

'It was great, thanks.'

Alison nodded. 'Good. And yours, Edith?' she asked, turning towards me.

'Mine was also great,' I said.

'Good.' She nodded again, and then turned and entered her office, closing the door behind her.

'Hey and here comes the artful Roger. Hi, Rog!' said Luke, turning in his chair.

'Morning, both,' he replied, walking to his desk and banging his silver flask down onto it.

'Hello,' I said. 'How was the weekend? Get up to anything interesting?'

He removed his coat and scarf, hung them up on the black metallic hat stand behind his desk and sat down. 'Oh, this 'n' that,' he said, with his usual gruff good humour. 'This 'n' that.'

'Nope, sorry, Rog,' said Luke, shaking his head. 'Edie needs more information than that this morning. She's info hungry. She's already interrogated me, it's your turn next, and then Cameron's when he gets in. Isn't that right, Edie?'

I continued to unpack my things, without looking up. 'Yes, I'm in nosey mode, Roger.'

'Oh… well… I…' Roger cleared his throat. 'I don't rightly know that I… that I have any very interesting information to impart, as such, Edie. But I did, amongst other things, enjoy a bracing walk with a friend and then we ate a lunch of ham, egg and chips and chicken salad respectively,' he added in a rush before, clearly embarrassed and several light years out of his comfort zone, turning to face his drawing board.

I looked at Luke who in turn looked at Roger and then back at me, his eyes widening slightly. He took a breath as if about to say something, but I shook my head and put a finger to my lips. He nodded acceptingly and picked up his coffee and we sat in bemused silence until Cameron arrived just moments later.

'Morning,' he said.

Luke and I said, 'Hi.' Roger silently raised a hand, keeping his back resolutely turned to the room.

Cameron frowned and looked questioningly at me. I mouthed, 'Not sure,' and Luke offered him a shrug.

Cameron tried again. 'Good weekend, everyone?'

We all looked at Roger, who gave a thumbs-up, without turning round.

'Well, I met up with uni friends,' I said, 'in Hungerford. We had a really nice time.'

'And I was at a birthday party,' said Luke. 'Probably best not to go into details – not that I can remember many. But Cameron,' he continued, with a side-long glance in my direction, 'whatever were you up to?'

Cameron, who had by now settled himself at his desk, switched on his screen. 'I was at a wedding in Stratford.'

Luke looked at me. 'With whom?' he mouthed, jerking his head towards Cameron.

I rolled my eyes. 'How lovely,' I said. 'A winter wedding.'

Luke made a chicken gesture and I was just reaching for a Post-it note to scrunch up and throw at him when Ruby walked in.

'Morning, everyone!' she said brightly, casually removing her sunglasses and bright yellow coat and striding across the office. It was as though she had never been away.

I had no clue as to my own expression, but when I looked at Luke, I saw that his was that of a man attempting to smile through the pain of having caught his penis in his zip.

I didn't have time to check out Roger and Cameron before Ruby was at my desk. She threw her coat across it and bent low to envelop me in a crushing hug, which I returned on a reflex.

'God, your face, Edie!' she laughed, straightening up and pointing at me. 'You look like you've seen a ghost! Oh and Vincent is on his way,' she said, throwing the comment over her shoulder at Luke. 'He stopped off to get some pastries, after I told him how much Alison likes them. I think we're running early, so I hope that won't be a problem. To be honest, I wish I hadn't mentioned the pastry thing now.' She ended the explanation with an eye-roll.

Luke, still not having fully regained his composure, nodded rapidly. 'OK. Yes, that's fine. No worries.'

'So, how are we all?' asked Ruby, looking around the office before settling her eyes on Cameron. 'Everyone behaving themselves?'

The enquiry was made with an intonation and body language so unexpected that I couldn't immediately place it. However, a few seconds later it dawned on me that she was attempting to flirt with him.

He looked at her expressionlessly.

'Why are you here?' I heard myself say.

She turned to me and laughed again. 'I know! I nearly texted you last night, but in the end I thought it'd be fun to surprise you. And it *so* is!'

I felt my face begin to burn as I blinked up at her.

'Edie's not the only one rather flummoxed to see you, Ruby,' said Roger, suddenly at my side. 'To what do we owe the pleasure?' he asked, with uncharacteristic jollity.

She turned her head towards him, her eyes remaining fixed on me for the first few degrees of the rotation, before she looked at him and sighed. 'Oh dear. Alison's obviously not keeping you updated, Roger,' she said despairingly.

Roger cracked a rare smile. 'Alison is a quiet one and no mistake,' he said. 'But, er,' he cleared his throat, 'no. I knew that Vincent was coming here this morning, but there was no mention of you. And I reckon Alison is as surprised as we all are, judging by her rather nonplussed expression.'

I turned to see Alison looking out at us from her office, her brow furrowed and her mouth fixed in a thin, red, deeply unimpressed line. 'Maybe,' continued Roger quietly, returning to his desk, 'Vincent forgot to tell her you were tagging along. Still, I'm sure she'll enjoy the catch-up.'

Ruby waved a hand. 'Never mind,' she said, with impressive nonchalance. 'I suppose it was rather a last-minute decision, wasn't it, Vincent?' she added, as a tall, lean man in his early fifties, with a greying buzz-cut and small round glasses, entered the office. A black messenger bag was slung across his body and he was toting a white cardboard box containing, I assumed, the aforementioned pastries.

'Vincent, this is Luke, Edith and Cameron,' Ruby said, nodding at each of us in turn and smiling lingeringly at

Cameron. 'And Roger, you know,' she said as an apparent afterthought, gesturing towards him.

'I do indeed,' said Vincent, smiling at us all and walking towards Roger, his hand outstretched. 'Good to see you again, Roger.'

'Aye,' said Roger, shaking his hand. 'How are you? And how are Harriet and the children? There are three of them now, aren't there?'

'All well,' said Vincent. 'Although the youngest is quite a handful.'

Ruby placed a hand on his arm. 'Oh come on, he's gorgeous. They all are. Harriet was telling me *such* funny stories about them when we went for drinks last week. She's such a wonderful mother.'

Vincent looked at Ruby with an undisguised admiration which, I suspected, might not have been entirely professional. I sent up a silent prayer for Harriet.

'I tell you what, Roger,' said Vincent, apparently unable to tear his gaze from Ruby, 'I hope Alison has no hard feelings about me snatching this talent from you.'

She lowered her head, tilting it to one side and smiling coyly up at him. I looked past her to Luke, who appeared transfixed, watching the scene with an expression of horrified delight. All he needed was some popcorn.

'No hard feelings at all, I'm sure,' said Roger, 'from any of us. Not a bit of it.'

'Careful,' laughed Vincent. 'Don't be too understanding, or I'll be after Edith as well. Ruby is forever telling me how brilliant she is.'

'Well, she is,' said Ruby.

Struck dumb by the impossibility of making any sort of sense of Ruby Blair, I simply stared at her.

'So, can we go straight in?' asked Vincent, turning to Luke.

Luke stood up, hurrying from behind his desk. 'Yes, of course.'

'Oh, Vincent,' said Ruby, her hand still on his arm, 'would you be very cross if I took just another few minutes or so to catch up with everyone? I know you wanted to talk to Alison about...' She hesitated and widened her eyes significantly. 'About *the thing*. So how about you discuss that first and then I'll join you. What do you think?'

'I think you're incorrigible, that's what I think,' he said, causing Luke to put a hand to his mouth and me to shudder involuntarily. 'But that's fine. Join us in a minute.' He turned to Luke. 'Shall we?'

'Of course, of course,' said Luke a little breathlessly, ushering him towards Alison's door. 'Can I get you anything to go with those Danish, Vincent? Regular tea, herbal tea, coffee? Or we have...' The rest of the drinks options were lost to us, as he closed the door.

'I see my desk and table are still here and that Cameron's desk is still all the way over there,' said Ruby, turning towards him. 'I thought things might have been rearranged to bring you in from the cold, Cameron. Or can't you be trusted? Do you need to be kept at arms' length?' She glanced over her shoulder at me and delivered an almost imperceptible wink.

Cameron's expression remained unchanged, save for the addition of a slight flicker of his eyebrows as he focused on an area of floor a few metres from his desk. 'Hope you're enjoying the new job,' was all he said, and I found myself strangely relieved that he stopped there. I didn't, I realised, want to hear a Cockney lilt and have his anxiety confirmed.

'Oh, I just love it,' she said casually, walking towards him. 'I mean, of course, I miss people; people I didn't even think I was going to miss,' she added, her tone oddly intense. Her back was to me now, but as Cameron looked up at her and frowned, I saw a discomfort too obvious to ignore.

'So, Ruby...' I rose to my feet and hurried towards her, linking my arm through hers and turning her away from Cameron, 'what's your schedule? Are you in Bristol for the whole day?' I asked, finally managing to rustle up a smile.

'Yes, all day!' she exclaimed happily. 'I thought we could have a drink in The Hayes when you've finished here. I'll tell Vincent to head back without me. I'd invite him along, but I want you to be able tell me...' she glanced over her shoulder at Cameron, '...*everything* that's gone on since I last saw you.'

'Vincent would like you in there now, Ruby,' said Luke, emerging from Alison's office. 'There's a coffee on the table for you.'

Ruby ignored him. 'Does six o'clock work for you, Edie?'

I stared at her, desperately trying to come up with a believable excuse for ducking out. But as I caught a glimpse of Cameron's profile, jaw set and brow still furrowed in either anger or anguish, I knew that ducking out was no longer an option.

'Yes.' I nodded slightly manically, aware that my forced smile and cheery tone were in danger of disintegrating into a grimace and a groan at any moment. 'That works.'

'Can't wait,' she beamed, bestowing another brief hug and then heading for Alison's office, entering without knocking and closing the door behind her.

I stood for a moment, not moving, focusing instead on regulating my breathing and slowing my heart rate.

'Want me to come along?'

I turned towards the quietly made offer to find Luke looking up at me from behind his desk, his expression as downcast as I felt.

I shook my head. 'No, but thanks,' I replied. 'I think it's probably best that I go alone.'

'You know, all that talk of pastries has made me right hungry,' said Roger, reaching for his coat and pausing next to me to put it on, 'so I'm going to go out and get some for us all. What type for you, Edie? Chocolate, custard, or one of those red jammy ones? They're your particular favourite, aren't they?'

I smiled at him, resisting – only for his sake – a sudden urge to take his hand in mine and press it to my face. 'That's such a nice idea, Roger. Yes, red jammy, please.'

'Righty-ho,' he said cheerily. 'Luke?'

'Chocolate, please, Rog,' he replied, looking rather emotional at the prospect of a pain au chocolat.

'Grand choice,' Roger nodded. 'And what about you, Cameron?' he asked, walking over to him and laying a fatherly hand on his shoulder.

Cameron tore his eyes away from his screen and smiled up at him. 'Chocolate would be great,' he said quietly. 'Thanks, Roger.'

Chapter 31

Roger's treat notwithstanding, the rest of the working day felt intensely serious. Because although I managed to avoid any further encounters with Ruby, the effect of the first one lingered, and not just with me, but seemingly with everyone. Consequently, the atmosphere in the office could be described as flat at best.

Not that Ruby had been a topic of discussion between us. I had no doubt that if Luke and I had been alone at any point, her name would have come up, but clearly neither of us felt able to mention her in front of Roger or Cameron. And they didn't refer to her visit either, other than obliquely, when I overheard Roger telling Cameron that Vincent was one of many architects keen to maintain ties with Alison, primarily with her retirement and the possibility of taking over the practice in mind.

Of course, this wasn't news to me. Alison had been welcoming – or perhaps tolerating – a steady stream of sycophantic professional suitors the entire time I'd worked for her. But Vincent's visit had unsettled me in a way the others had not, and Roger's reference to Alison's retirement had rattled me even further – enough that I made a mental note to raise the matter at my upcoming appraisal. If there was the possibility of finding myself with a new boss any time soon – especially one with a particular fondness for Ruby Blair – then I wanted to know about it and consider my options.

It was a thought which had made a difficult day dire, and as I shifted uncomfortably in one of The Hayes's large leather armchairs and awaited Ruby's arrival later that evening, my ability to think calmly and rationally was demolished by a wrecking-ball of anxiety regarding my long-term professional future and my scarily imminent, and highly personal, meeting with Ruby.

Staring down at the two small glasses of red wine I had bought and placed on the low table in front of me, I found myself unable to think through what I might say to her or to guess at what she might be about to say to me.

Fighting a new and rising sense of panic, I closed my eyes, inhaled deeply, exhaled slowly and forced myself to focus and take stock of the situation.

However, as just three seconds of 'taking stock' officially confirmed the situation to be, as I had suspected all along, *absolutely bloody awful*, I decided to ditch cool analysis in favour of the rapid consumption of alcohol. Sadly, I had managed just two mouthfuls of wine, neither of which had hit home, when Ruby arrived.

'Oh my God and I thought *I* was early!' she said, appearing at my side and dropping her bag to the ground. 'What time did you get here?' she asked, bending low to kiss my cheek.

'Erm,' was all I managed, as she flopped down opposite me.

'For me?' She leaned forward and picked up the glass of wine. 'Bit small,' she laughed, 'but thanks and cheers.' She raised her drink in my direction and downed half of it. 'I so need this. Haven't stopped today.' Letting out a contented sigh, she leaned back in her chair. 'So, how are you? What's the gossip? You always say everything is fine, which is great. Just hope you're being truthful with me.'

'I am,' I said, tensing slightly at her hypocritical and hugely ironic expectation of honesty. 'How is Bath?'

I posed the question wondering whether it might be possible to get through the evening without reference to either Cameron or Jason, because there was still a small but significant part of me that felt just fine with that option. After all, what was so wrong with letting a toxic relationship gradually fade, rather than squeezing it to the point of explosion, like an angry zit best left alone? No messy public confrontation, no distressing unpleasantness, no red wine all over my favourite pale-blue silk shirt... No closure either, of course, but then maybe closure was as overrated as taking stock.

I picked up my glass and drained it.

'Bath is great,' she declared. 'I just feel so... appreciated, in a way that I was never appreciated by Alison.'

'She appreciated you,' I said, twisting in my chair and looking towards the bar, wondering about the possibility of getting another drink.

She smiled and shook her head. 'You are lovely, Edie, but she definitely preferred your style to mine. In fact, she just plain preferred you to me. We both know that. And now that Cameron has arrived, she's moved on to being head-over-heels about him. But you're better at shrugging off that kind of snub than I am. I need to work in an environment where the boss doesn't let personal stuff get in the way of appreciating creativity. That's what's so great about the Bath practice.'

She paused and looked around the room. 'It's quite busy in here for six p.m., isn't it?'

I didn't follow her gaze, but instead kept my eyes firmly fixed on her face, knowing that, however much I dreaded confrontation, I couldn't let the implied and wholly unjust criticism of Alison go unchallenged. Neither, I realised, could I let this relationship, with its huge burden of unowned and unacknowledged betrayal and lies, keep limping along. I needed closure after all – or, at least, a shot at it.

'I think you're wrong,' I said.

She blinked slightly, before turning towards me, her smiled fixed. 'Sorry? Wrong about what?'

'About Alison,' I began, taking a breath. 'I think she has likes and dislikes and not a lot of charm, but I don't think she has favourites. Certainly not to the extent that it influences her creative or professional judgement.'

After the most minute of hesitations, she laughed. 'Now, don't go getting all affronted on me. I know you think I've got her all wrong.'

'You're right. I do think that.'

Her smile disappeared. 'Why are you being so serious? What on earth's the matter?' she asked, studying me with apparent concern and then leaning forward in her chair. 'You know, I've been so worried about you, Edie. You've sounded so flat in your messages over the past few months. I honestly think that job is sucking all the confidence and fun out of you. You're a brilliant architect and it really pisses me off to think that slowly but surely your talent is being undermined.' She shook her head. 'God, and you're too nice even to see it happening. You should do like I did and get the hell out.' She relaxed back, assuming, I could tell, that hers was to be the closing statement on the subject.

But she was wrong again.

'I can't see it happening because it's not happening,' I said. 'Not to me, anyway. I feel very appreciated and highly supported and I'm really sorry that you didn't feel the same way. You should have said something.'

She didn't immediately reply, having clearly gone into momentary shock that I hadn't let the matter lie. But it took just seconds for her features to relax back into friendly compassion.

'I'm sure you're right,' she said, with the kindly condescension of a psychiatrist addressing a delusional patient. 'I should have talked to Alison. I suppose I just didn't have the energy for that – not with all the Cameron crap and a move to Bath on offer. But don't forget that you have options,' she continued gently. 'There's a job coming up with us soon and the starting salary would be great; not far off mine.'

I took a deep breath, surprised at how angry I was becoming.

'Thanks.' I tried to smile, but couldn't even come close. Instead, with my heart thumping in my chest and feeling too breathless for wasted words, I got to the point. 'Alison told me that you didn't make a complaint against Cameron.'

'What?' The question was out before I had finished speaking. Her colour rose and she glared furiously at me. 'What did she say about me? That woman so resents me. She wouldn't think twice about misrepresenting me.'

'She didn't say anything about you, other than that you hadn't made a complaint against him,' I said, working to keep my voice steady. 'I don't understand why you told me that you had.'

She took a moment before replying, her complexion gradually cooling. 'Well, put yourself in my place,' she said. 'If I'd told you I'd done nothing about it, you'd have never shut up. You'd have dragged me kicking and screaming into Alison's office, or you'd have told her yourself. All I wanted was for you to know what a shit he was, so that you didn't get hurt. I didn't want to kick-start a complaints procedure – not when I was leaving anyway.'

I stared at her, grudgingly impressed by her quick thinking, as well as frustrated that the only way of contradicting her would be to drop Luke in it. And I had no doubt that she would make trouble for him over a breach of confidentiality if I did that.

'Actually, I'm really hurt,' she continued quietly, her head lowered and her voice now heavy with disappointment, 'that you're sitting here, berating me for trying to protect you.'

'There was no need to lie to me,' I said, 'about anything. I would always prefer to hear the truth – no matter what it is.'

She looked up and her expression softened further. 'OK, so maybe, in hindsight, that was wrong of me. But I hid the truth from you with the best of intentions. Anyway, look,' she said, heaving a sigh, 'I've been really looking forward to seeing you and we've got all serious and – once again – it's that bastard, Cameron, at the root of it. Let's just forget about him and talk about something or someone else. How is life outside the office?'

She smiled affectionately and enquiringly, and I felt my anger begin to cool and harden. Even when directly confronted with her lies about Cameron – something which would have reduced anyone with any kind of conscience to a quivering, apologetic wreck – she still felt in control. She believed that she had me, and our relationship, in the palm of her hand.

When Jason had told me how much she had valued my friendship, I had pitied her. I had wondered whether she, like him, would acknowledge and take responsibility for her mistakes, enabling us to perhaps salvage some sort of new relationship from the wreckage of the old.

But Ruby, it seemed, wasn't in the same place as Jason when it came to a desire for redemption. She simply didn't share his need for it. For now at least, Ruby just wanted what Ruby wanted, and she was clearly prepared to trample anything – including the truth – which threatened to get in the way of that.

And so, with little expectation of or desire for a future friendship, and now simply in search of an end, I decided to send some more truths Ruby's way.

'Things feel a lot more settled. Giles is great to live with and Jason and I are building bridges.'

At the mention of Jason, her expression of friendly interest remained unchanged, but her knuckles whitened as she tightened her grip on her glass. I wondered how much pressure would be required to shatter it.

She shook her head despairingly. 'Y'know, you're *way* too nice, Edie.'

'Am I?'

'Well,' she placed her drink on the table, 'after everything Jason did to you, how can you possibly have anything at all to do with him? I admire your ability to forgive, but I also find it a bit frustrating at the same time. I can't help it.'

'He's in therapy and seems to be taking it seriously.'

'Therapy?' She rolled her eyes. 'OK, but don't let him get close enough to hurt you again. We know what he's like.'

She took a breath and I thought for a moment that she might be about to go further and offer me a justification of her use of "we". But instead, she simply exhaled and shrugged, apparently ready to let the subject drop.

I hesitated for a moment, weighing up whether to confront her and end our relationship with an angry and very public exit – either hers, or mine – or to move on and save that final confrontation, that explanation of why I never wanted to see her again, for an email when I got home.

'Tell me about Bath,' I said. 'Are you house-hunting?'

'No,' she said dismissively, clearly with no interest in the subject. 'Are you? I really hope Jason's soul-searching isn't distracting you from that. How often is he in touch?'

I had, I realised, been wrong; she clearly couldn't move on from the topic of a man who had ultimately rejected her. Her pause had merely been for thought.

'How often does he message you?' she pressed, picking up her drink, her eyes narrowing as she waited for my reply with an impatience she couldn't hide.

'Message me?'

'All these bridge-building messages you're exchanging.'

'Oh, I see. No,' I shook my head and then, with a lack of hesitation which surprised even myself, I lit the fuse. 'The bridge-building has taken place in person.'

'You've seen him?' She was clearly appalled – and outraged. In the past, I would have mistaken that for the righteous indignation of a protective friend. Now I recognised it as the jealous rivalry of a woman who saw me as competition.

I pretended not to notice. 'He's talked to Giles too, which I'm pleased about. I never wanted their friendship to end because of me. But what are house prices like in Bath? They're pretty comparable to Bristol, aren't they?'

Fury and disbelief still etched across her face, she ignored the real estate enquiry. 'Does he want to get back together with you?'

I frowned at her for a moment and then said, 'Let this go, Ruby. Stop worrying about it.'

At that, and with obvious effort, she managed a smile. 'What do you mean? I can't help being worried for you. You're my friend.'

I was tempted to ask her for a definition of the term, but resisted. 'Don't worry,' I said, 'I'm not as fragile as you think.'

'Of course, I know how strong you are. But spending time with him must still be upsetting for you. It makes me really angry to think that he even wanted to see you.'

That at least, I thought, was the truth.

'I'm past being upset,' I said. 'He's got a problem and he's trying to sort himself out by confronting what he is and what he's done. Obviously, it's a lengthy process,' I added with a sigh, 'due to the fact that he's *done* quite a lot. By his own admission, most of his encounters are a bit of a blur.'

'Bastard,' she murmured.

'I think you're angrier with him than I am.'

'I'm as angry with him as you *should* be,' she snapped, looking up sharply. 'I don't think you know just how awful he is. No one was off limits, Edie. Even...' She hesitated theatrically.

'Even you?'

She blinked in confusion. I guessed that she had been anticipating a lengthier, more drawn-out conversation on the subject; one that involved lots of anxious questioning on my part, before she finally revealed, reluctantly and with some distress, that Jason, just like Cameron, had burdened her with unwanted attention.

'What?' she said, clearly thrown.

I shrugged. 'Don't worry about it. I think we'd be hard-pushed to find a woman Jason knew and *hadn't* tried to get into bed, don't you?'

'But, doesn't it—' she began.

'Bother me? No, it doesn't, not anymore. So don't let it bother you. He told me what happened and said that he felt bad about it and I believe him.'

'Jason told you about me?' she asked uncertainly.

'Mmhmm.'

'What did he say?' she asked, clearly on edge.

'That he regretted his behaviour and that he had apologised to you for it.'

She appeared to think for a moment and then bit her lip. 'I should have told you that he kept hassling me.' She closed her eyes and shook her head. 'But how do you tell a friend that without hurting them? So, I just made it clear to him that there was no way I was interested.' She opened her eyes and looked at me appealingly. 'If I'd known that it was all part of a bigger pattern of behaviour, then obviously I would have told you.'

'Like I say, I'm not angry with Jason anymore. I just hope that he can sustain a change. He says he wants to.'

She smiled sadly, leaning back in her chair and visibly relaxing, clearly judging – not unreasonably – that Jason had decided against telling me the whole story. 'After all he put you through,' she said, her tone now warmly maternal. 'I just don't know how you can believe a word he says, Edie.'

And that, I decided, would be the last condescending thing she would ever say to me.

'I can believe him, Ruby,' I began steadily, 'because he has kept every single text the pair of you have exchanged since I first introduced you to him three years ago. I haven't read them all, just enough to get a very clear picture of timings, of his desperate squirmings, and of your absolute determination to bed him as soon as he was my ex – having failed, of course, in your impressively persistent attempts to bed him while he was still my partner.'

Her expression rapidly transitioned through shock, disbelief and rage, before cooling into what appeared to be a hardened, icy acceptance of the facts. She then stared impassively at me for what felt like a lifetime, before picking up her bag and rising slowly to her feet. She didn't make eye contact with me again after that, and 'I never liked this place,' was all she said, as she turned and walked away.

I watched her go, my body rigid as I focused exclusively on her receding figure and then on the doorway through which she had exited. Only when, after several minutes, I felt certain that she wasn't coming back to order a second glass of wine and throw it all over me, did I collapse back into my armchair and close my eyes.

Chapter 32

How long I remained unseeing, unmoving and unthinking, with all the remaining fight or flight capabilities of a washed-up jellyfish, I wasn't sure. But when I opened my eyes a short time later, it was to the sight of a wine glass of being placed on the table in front of me.

'For you, if you want it,' said Cameron, indicating the glass of red. 'And I'm happy either to stay and keep you company, or to go away and leave you in peace. It's up to you.'

I stared at the glass, slowly dragging myself back to the moment. 'Thank you,' I murmured. 'That's really kind of you, and some company would be great.' I gestured to the armchair opposite. 'I expect that's still warm – and possibly smelling of sulphur.'

He sat, placing a bottle of beer on the table as he did so.

'Have you been here long?' I asked, resting my head against the back of the chair and wondering how much of my encounter with Ruby he had witnessed, if any.

'Only as long as it took to buy the drinks,' he said. 'I didn't see her,' he added, as if reading my mind.

'Lucky you.'

'You OK?'

I picked up the wine and took a large gulp. 'It didn't feel great but, you know, at least it's done now. There's some relief in that.'

He nodded. 'I wanted to say thank you for this morning.'

'For what?'

'For taking the pressure off me,' he replied, 'and piling it onto yourself in the process.'

'I didn't do anything noble. If I'd confronted her about everything over summer – like I should have done – she wouldn't have even turned up this morning.'

He raised an eyebrow and reached for his beer. 'Wouldn't she?'

I paused, considering the question. 'You're right, she'd probably have turned up anyway,' I said wearily. 'She's not one for letting the dust settle.'

'No.'

He smiled and I heaved a sigh, slumping again in the chair and rubbing my forehead. 'I'm just so sorry about everything, Cameron,' I said quietly.

'There's really nothing left to be sorry for.'

I laughed humourlessly. 'Nothing except being unwelcoming, unco-operative, insensitive to your heritage, passively aggressive, actively aggressive and generally ruining your first seven months in a new job.' I shook my head despairingly. 'And now, in response to all that, you turn up with a glass of wine and the offer of your company, when most people in your position would think that sitting here miserable and alone is exactly what I deserve at this point.' I blinked back a tear and quickly leaned forward, reaching for my bag with the dual purpose of hiding my face and locating a tissue, just in case.

'I take your point,' he said, sounding thoughtful. 'But, to be fair, you only ruined about three months of my new job. Because, you were away for the first two weeks, didn't really speak to me for the next two weeks and, since August, you've actually been pretty OK.'

I looked up to find him grinning. 'It's water under the bridge for me, Edie,' he said. 'And I'd really like it to be the same for you. Deal?'

He held up his beer and after a moment I raised my glass in response. 'Deal,' I said huskily, making use of the tissue. 'I'm sorry for being emotional. It's just been...' I took a breath, 'a lot.'

'It's not a problem,' he said, shaking his head. 'Despite my gangland appearance, I'm surprisingly in touch with my emotions.'

I laughed, wiping away a couple more tears as I did so. 'Oh, don't,' I sniffed. 'I'm feeling bad enough about being deliberately mean to you, without being reminded of all the unintentional stuff.'

'It's fine, I'm actually OK with gangland.'

I looked across at him, his height and width making the armchair appear half the size it had when Ruby was sitting in it. He was, I decided, a much better fit.

'Me too,' I murmured and then, aware that I was beginning to stare, I blinked and cleared my throat. 'I still can't believe that Vincent brought Ruby along today without telling Alison.'

'Yes, well, I'm not sure Vincent's brain had much to do with that particular decision-making process.'

'I know, I'm surprised he could stand upright.'

Cameron laughed loudly.

'Sorry, but it's true,' I said, laughing along. 'The guy made my skin crawl. Did you hear him call Ruby incorrigible? He sounded like a lecherous Edwardian uncle.'

'Maybe Alison should have a word with him about never mixing the personal with the professional.'

'So you've had that lecture too?'

'More than once,' he said. 'But it's fine, because I can see where she's coming from.'

'Same here,' I nodded. 'I always think it must be a bit weird being in a relationship with a work colleague. I mean, when do you get a break from work? How do you avoid bringing your domestics into the office?'

'I think it'd take real determination.'

'So you've never dated anyone you worked with?' I asked, sipping my wine, my interest in the topic increasing as I remembered that who Cameron was currently dating was actually a matter of significant interest to me right now. It would be a much-needed, feel-good end to a very crappy day if I could go home to Giles with the good news that Kerry was single after all.

'No, I haven't', he replied.

'OK...' I leaned my elbow on the arm of the chair and rested my chin on my hand, wondering how best to approach the subject of his love life. On another occasion, after a different kind of day, I might have possessed the energy, wit and will to do it with sensitivity, subtlety and tact – or I may have judged it best simply to avoid the subject altogether. But on that evening, feeling emotionally, physically and intellectually drained by my encounter with Ruby and emboldened by alcohol on an empty stomach, I made the decision to be direct.

'Are you seeing anyone at the moment, Cameron?'

He paused mid-sip and frowned at me as he lowered the bottle, replacing it carefully on the table. 'Well, that was to the point.'

'I know. But I'm so wrung-out that I haven't got it in me to be anything else. Plus, your answer might make me feel a whole lot better and *couldn't possibly* make me feel worse, so I thought, *For goodness sake, Edie, just ask the guy.*'

'Not an unreasonable approach,' he said, adjusting his position in the armchair. 'But you do know that I didn't come here looking for a date, don't you?' he asked quietly and with some awkwardness.

I gasped and put a hand to my mouth. 'Oh, I'm so sorry, yes, of course I know that. That's not what I meant.'

'Phew,' he said, clearly and visibly relieved that I understood he had no interest in dating me. 'You had me worried there,' he added, laughing.

'Well, relax,' I said, attempting to match his upbeat tone, despite the very definite knock to my ego. 'I tend to go for leaner, fine-featured types, rather than guys who are, you know, bigger and more earthy.'

'OK, so not feeling *hugely* complimented by that.'

'You know what I mean, you're just more...' I hesitated. 'Well, you're quite *grrr*,' I growled, holding out my arms and sticking out my lower jaw, in an attempt to convey breadth and masculinity. 'You're sort of—'

'It's fine,' he said, holding up a hand. 'I'm happy to leave it there.'

'Well, anyway, I was asking whether you were single for a friend.' He raised a dubious eyebrow and I held up a finger. 'And before you repeat the phrase *for a friend* in a sceptical tone, I promise you that I am, quite genuinely, asking for a friend.'

His mouth twitched but he nodded acceptingly. 'OK.'

I relaxed back into my chair and focused on my wine, very much enjoying Cameron's company and just wishing that I could find the fact that he wasn't at all attracted to me as inconsequential as he did.

As I'd said, he wasn't my usual type either, but you could always acknowledge potential in a person, couldn't you? He may be a bit of a monolith, but I was still willing to accept that his broader, more masculine build could – especially when coupled with nice eyes and an attractive personality – prove just as irresistible as a stringy Tom Hiddleston or Eddie Redmayne. Even that bit of stubble he always sported – his facial hair apparently being too much of a challenge for any cutting edge currently known to man – was actually rather nice, in a ruggedly unselfconscious kind of way. It drew attention to his mouth, which was also…

'I'm not,' he said.

I started slightly. 'Not what?'

'Not seeing anyone.'

'Oh!' I clapped a relieved hand to my chest, my mood instantly lifting. 'That's *such* lovely, lovely news, Cameron.'

'For your friend, maybe.'

'Seriously, you don't know what a relief that is. I feel emotional all over again,' I said, flapping a hand in front of my eyes.

'Again, not quite so many happy tears flowing over here.'

'Hang on,' I said, a potential problem suddenly occurring to me. 'You're not attracted to a long-term friend and on the brink of telling them, are you?'

He screwed up his face. 'What? No.'

'Good. And none of your female friends are attracted to you?'

'Well, if they are, they're keeping it to themselves.'

'Brilliant,' I said, raising my glass in salute.

He stared at me, saying nothing.

'*Obviously*,' I said, returning my glass to the table, 'I don't mean it's brilliant that no one fancies you. I just mean that you being single, and not fancying anyone, is very good news for my friend.'

'You know, Edie, at risk of sounding entitled,' he said, drinking his beer, 'if you're planning to set me up with someone, I'd really appreciate being given some choice in the matter.'

'Oh, God, yes, of course,' I said. 'But I promise that I have absolutely no intention whatsoever of introducing you to any of my female friends and, if I ever did, I would be very clear with you about everything and, of course, ask your permission first.'

'So why all the questions?' He put down his beer, leaned back in his chair and folded his arms.

I hesitated for a moment. But as we had already established that he and Kerry were not an item, I couldn't see a reason not to be straight with him. I believed him to be discreet enough and caring enough not to make things awkward for Giles, and certainly not for Kerry.

'Giles really likes Kerry,' I said. 'But he thought that you two were together and didn't want to spoil things by telling her how he felt. And because he wouldn't let *me* talk to her either, I decided to find out what the situation was from you – hopefully without making things tricky for anyone.'

'I see.'

'I understand if you feel you should tell Kerry. But, if you do, can you let me know, so that I can prepare Giles for that – by text, obviously. Because he *is* going to kill me,' I added, biting my lip at the thought.

He shook his head. 'I won't mention it to Kerry. The timing is up to Giles.'

I breathed a sigh of relief. 'Thank you. I didn't want to make things difficult for you and Kerry if you were a couple. But at the same time, I thought it would be a real shame for Giles not to try and find out.'

'It's OK,' he said. 'I understand and I think it's good to get things straight. I just hope it works out for them.'

'Me too.' I gazed into my glass of wine, marvelling at the fact that in spite of Ruby's visit – or perhaps somehow because of it – I actually felt surprisingly good. Cameron's company, and the news that he was a single man, had lifted my mood to a wholly unexpected degree. 'Thanks so much for coming here tonight, Cameron,' I said quietly. 'I *really* appreciate it. You've made me feel so much better.'

'Same. We should do this more often.'

I realised that it was a suggestion I wanted to hold him to. 'Definitely,' I said, offering him a smile which, after a moment or two of comfortable silence between us, I suspected might be edging towards happy-fool territory. So I drank my wine to give my mouth something else to do.

'Another?' asked Cameron pointing at my glass.

'No, thanks. If I have any more than this, I'll spend the rest of the evening either laughing or crying hysterically. But let me get you a beer,' I said, putting down my glass.

He shook his head. 'Thanks, but I'll get it. So long as you're happy to make that last.'

'Very happy.'

'OK then,' he said, making to stand up.

'Ooh, but before you go and while I think of it,' I began, holding out a hand. 'Did Kerry tell you that Giles and I are hosting the next avenue wine and cheese? We'd love it if you could come along.'

'She might have mentioned it,' he smiled. 'How are you feeling about that level of neighbourhood responsibility?'

'Not remotely bothered,' I replied emphatically. 'I'm going to leave all the logistics and planning to Giles. My role is simply to shop and skivvy as requested. So you'll come along with Kerry?' I asked. 'Unless, of course, you're still suffering PTSD from the last one?'

'The flashbacks have been decreasing steadily.'

'Good to hear.'

'But if the invite is genuine…'

'Of course it is!'

'In that case, thank you and I'd love to come. Kerry promises me that something always kicks off. And hopefully this time,' he said, standing up and turning towards the bar, 'it won't be us.'

Chapter 33

'And you are absolutely certain that this doesn't look at all fuddy-duddy?' asked Giles, presenting himself for inspection in front of my armchair, as I sat with Anthony sprawled and snoring across my lap.

'Giles, as I have already told you several times, you look great,' I replied, without looking up from my book. 'The trousers are perfect and that is my number one favourite shirt on you. You know how I love red stripes,' I murmured absently, whilst adjusting my towelling turban and bathrobe.

'It's blue check.'

'That's right and I really, really love it.'

He let out a sigh with just a hint of whimper about it, causing me to close my book and place it on the arm of my chair.

'Why not sit down for a moment?' I said, pointing at the sofa.

He shook his head. 'No, no, I'm disturbing you. You read your Hans Rosling book. You must have nearly finished it by now.'

'I'm on page eleven.'

'Well, jolly good for you for making it to double figures.'

I laughed. 'Sit down. You'd be doing me a favour.'

He sat with obvious reluctance, perching on the edge of the sofa.

'Now, just take a few deep breaths and try to relax,' I said gently. 'You and Kerry know each other *very* well and like each other *very* much. There are probably fewer uncertainties surrounding this first date than any you've ever been on before.'

'True, true.' He nodded, adjusting the collar of his shirt. 'But it also feels so much more important than any other first date.'

'I think that's a good thing.'

He looked at me and frowned slightly. 'Yes, I think it probably is,' he agreed after a moment.

'And I was teasing about the shirt,' I said. 'You look genuinely, *genuinely* handsome, and I'm not just saying that because you're my cousin and I love you.'

'Step-cousin.'

'That too.'

He smiled across at me. 'Thanks, Edie.'

'Thank *you*,' I said, wanting to give him a hug, but not enough to disturb Anthony and shift from my rather comfortable armchair. It had been another busy week at work and I was looking forward to a Saturday night in, consisting only of Anthony, my book and early bed.

'Now,' I said, reaching behind me for the curtain and twisting to peer out into the darkened avenue, 'hadn't you better be going, or Kerry will be knocking on our door and, relaxed as the woman is, I'd rather she didn't see me in my pygmy PJs.' I looked down regretfully at the shrunken, unironed legs of my hitherto favourite rainbow-stripe pyjamas; the most recent victim of my refusal to take care-labels seriously.

Giles took his phone from his pocket. 'She intended to text when the sitter arrived. Oh and she has texted,' he said, checking the phone. 'Oh… oh, dear. Oh… OK…'

'Problem?'

'A slight one,' he replied. 'Kerry's sitter has had to cancel. She's got cover, but not until seven forty-five at the earliest.'

I pulled a face. 'What a pain. The table's booked for seven thirty, isn't it?'

'Yes, but it can't be helped. I'll just call the restaurant,' he said, tapping the screen, 'and see if I can move the booking to eight, or maybe eight fifteen, to be safe.'

'Hang on,' I said. 'Is Kerry ready to go?'

He looked up from his phone. 'Yes, but—'

'OK, then.' I eased a reluctant Anthony off my lap and stood up. 'I'll pop round and stay with Harry until the replacement sitter gets there.'

I walked past Giles, as Anthony staggered the short distance to him and flopped down prone across his feet.

'Are you sure?' asked Giles, attempting to shuffle after me into the hallway.

'Of course,' I said, swapping my slippers for a pair of pumps and grabbing my keys from the vestibule cupboard. 'It'll save you the faff of changing your dinner arrangements. I'll send Kerry round to you right away.' Opening the front door, I stepped outside and slammed it shut before Giles could raise an objection.

I scurried down the path, out onto the pavement and then up Kerry's path to her front door, all the while keeping my head low and shielding my face with my hands, lest a neighbour should spot me. Then I pulled the bell and waited, shivering a little.

A moment or two later, Kerry opened the door, looking beautiful in a dark blue, fit-and-flare dress patterned with grey leaves.

'Edie!' she exclaimed, obviously surprised to see me but, to her credit, resisting any urge she may have been experiencing to look me up and down. 'Come in, come in,' she beckoned. 'You must be frozen. What's going on? Are you locked out?' she asked, ushering me into the hallway and closing the front door.

I laughed. 'No, I've come round to sit with Harry until the official sitter gets here, so that you and Giles don't miss your dinner reservation.'

'Oh,' her expression went from confused to delighted in an instant. 'Are you sure? You look ready for bed.'

I waved a hand dismissively. 'I was just flopping, so I thought I may as well flop here with Harry. If he's OK with that, of course.'

'He'll be over the moon,' she smiled. 'He's in the bathroom at the moment, but we've just popped *Megamind* into the DVD player and the plan was to start watching that now and then finish it with Ron when he arrives.'

'Cameron's coming?' Shock was evident in my voice.

Kerry's face fell. 'Is that a problem? I thought you two were getting along really well.'

'Oh, we are, we are,' I said, trying to smile. 'I...' I hesitated, reluctant to appear vain. 'I just look a bit, you know, not very...' I pointed up at my turban and then down at my bathrobe and crumpled, calf-length pyjama bottoms.

She laughed and waved a hand. 'Now let's be honest,' she said, 'you couldn't look bad if you tried. And as if Ron will care.'

I nodded, feeling simultaneously complimented and crushed. 'Yes, I'm being silly. He won't notice, will he?' I said weakly.

'Nope.' She turned to look up the stairs. 'You ready yet, Harry?' she called, at a volume that caused me to wince and take an involuntary step backwards. 'There's a surprise visitor for you down here!' She turned back towards me, looking down at what she was wearing. 'Is this all right?' she asked uncertainly, brushing off the dress. 'Do you think it fits OK? I did think about asking if you'd come round this afternoon and give me your opinion, but then I felt like a bit of a tit for fussing.'

'You look great,' I said, now feeling wholly complimented. 'I really love the dress. Where's it from?'

'Nicky,' she said. 'It's all from Nicky: the dress, the bag, the shoes.' She pointed towards a navy blue shoulder bag and matching heels on the floor next to her. 'Do you think it's OK?'

'It's a perfect look,' I said, 'and besides, Giles got flustered when you were wearing your decorating gear. I don't think you should try too hard to make him feel any more unworthy than he already does.'

Appearing a little emotional, she threw her arms around me in a crushing hug. 'Thanks, Edie.'

'Edie!' cried Harry, running down the stairs. 'You can watch *Megamind*.'

'Hey, now listen, you,' said Kerry, placing a hand on his head as he came to a halt by her side. 'Edie's going to stay with you until Ron gets here and I want you to be really good for her. You're not to ask her to make, paint, kick or throw anything. You just sit quietly and watch the movie, OK?'

His eyes slid away from hers. 'I was going to do that anyway.'

'That's good. And I love you very much.' Kerry crouched and opened her arms for a hug.

'I love you,' he said.

She kissed him and stood up, unhooking a black coat from the end of the bannister, before stooping to pick up the shoulder bag and slip her feet into Nicky's heels. 'Thanks again, Edie. There are Wotsits and wine in the kitchen if you fancy them. You've got my number. Any worries at all, just call me.'

'We'll be fine,' I smiled, as she opened the front door. 'Have a great evening. Relax and enjoy.'

'I'll try!' she called, pulling the door shut behind her.

I looked down at Harry, who was now staring with some concern at my head.

'Everything OK?' I asked.

'Is that your towel?'

'Yes,' I said, bemused for a moment, before recalling his planned Christmas gift to me.

'But I really do need a new one. This one's so old.'

He nodded. 'We can't set it on fire with matches because that would burn the house down. But we *can* put it in the bin,' he offered helpfully.

'Well,' I said, placing a hand to my mouth in order to indicate thought, 'what I might do is put it in the bin when I get home, because it's keeping my wet hair out of my eyes at the moment.'

'OK,' he said acceptingly, taking my hand and leading me into the kitchen. 'Now, let's get Wotsits and watch *Megamind.*'

'This is Ron's other favourite bit!' said Harry, pointing at the screen with one hand and cramming Wotsits into his mouth with the other. 'Ha! Ha! Ha!' He laughed explosively, sending a geyser of orange crumbs over both my white bathrobe and the sofa.

I laughed along, while dusting off my robe and acknowledging *Megamind* to be a genuinely entertaining movie. I had been a little sceptical at Harry's repeated claim that it was Ron's favourite film in the whole world, but by the time we were twenty minutes in, I could easily believe that, even if *Megamind* didn't quite top, say, *Saving Private Ryan*, *Moonlight* or *The Theory of Everything* for Cameron, it could certainly be up there.

'Do you think Ron will mind that we've started watching the movie without him?' I asked, reaching into the large communal bowl of Wotsits which sat on the sofa between us.

Harry shook his head. 'He knows all the words off by heart.'

'That's good.'

He gazed at the screen.

'What's your favourite part?' I asked.

'I like it when Megamind flies on his motorbike. But I don't like it when he's in school,' he murmured, standing up to retrieve his glass of water from the large coffee table in front of us.

'Because he's sad at school?'

'The others don't pick him to play and won't be his friend,' he said, sitting back down, 'and that's not kind.'

'It isn't,' I agreed. 'But I know that you have lots of lovely friends at school, like Ollie and Amelia.'

'Yes,' he said absently, staring fixedly at the screen, 'and Harvey and Brody and Betty and Tom and George and James... And Giles is my friend and yours and Mum's.'

'That's right, he is.'

'And Ron is your friend.'

'We work together,' I replied, a little taken by surprise.

'I worked with James yesterday. We made flags. Is Ron on your table? Does he sit next to you?' he asked.

'Not quite next to me, but not far away.'

'He said you're his friend,' he said, turning back to the screen. 'He says you let everyone join in. We should shush now and watch *Megamind*.'

'OK.' I took another Wotsit and relaxed back into the sofa, feeling unexpectedly moved that Cameron had described me both as inclusive and as a friend. His opinion of me, I realised, really mattered, and to know that we had, it seemed, turned things around so completely, after such a disastrous start to our relationship, made me happier than anything had in a very long time.

Unfortunately, that happiness was extremely short-lived, being immediately snatched away by the jangling of the butler's bell and replaced by a renewed awareness of my less-than-glamorous appearance. The latter had, thanks to the recent Wotsits shower, deteriorated significantly over the past five minutes – something which, until that point, I hadn't actually thought possible.

'It's Ron!' yelled Harry, leaping up and tipping the remaining Wotsits over me in his eagerness to get to the front door.

Putting *Megamind* on pause, I hurriedly picked up as many Wotsits as I could, throwing them back into the bowl, before following Harry out into the hallway. By the time I got there, Cameron was already inside and bending low to hug him.

'Edie,' he said, standing up, removing his jacket and smiling at me in a way which made me feel more self-conscious than ever, despite the fact that he looked only slightly less dishevelled than me. His crumpled grey shirt was half-untucked and his thick hair was wet and standing on end – the result, I assumed, of a hasty towel-dry – and yet somehow, I reflected, he was still managing to look rather good.

He pointed at my turban. 'A last-minute call-out for you too?'

'How can you tell?'

'And I see we have Wotsits for snacks,' he continued, his eyes moving down to my bathrobe.

'Not many,' I said. 'I'm wearing most of them.'

'We're watching *Megamind*, Ron,' said Harry, taking his hand and then mine.

Cameron smiled at me for a moment longer, before taking a breath and looking down at Harry. 'Great!' he said, as all three of us walked to the living room. 'That's my favourite.'

–

I waited for Cameron to return from putting Harry to bed and then stood up as he re-entered the living room.

'Oh,' he said, looking from me to the two glasses of wine he was holding, 'do you have to go?'

'Well, I…' I looked down at my orange-stained bath-robe and shrunken nightwear, 'I feel like I need a change of clothes. I smell like the Sainsbury's cheese counter.'

He laughed. 'Not from where I was sitting,' he said, looking again at the wine. 'But it's fine if you need to head off.'

I hesitated for just a moment and then held out my hand. 'Well, if you don't mind, then I don't mind.'

He handed me a glass and I settled myself into one of Kerry's beige armchairs, while he sat back down on the Wotsit-strewn sofa.

'I hear you're going to put your smelly old towel in the bin,' he said, glancing at my turban, 'setting fire to it not being an option, since the candle incident.'

I frowned. 'I haven't heard about the candle incident.'

Cameron grimaced. 'Harry and Ollie put a bagful of birthday-cake candles they'd been collecting, into a plastic bowl and then they threw in a few of the matches Ollie had brought with him from home.'

'No,' I gasped.

'Yes. The idea was to create a giant candle from all the leftover ones. Fortunately, Kerry came upstairs to see what was going on, because there hadn't been any banging, crashing or screaming for a couple of minutes and that made her suspicious.'

I laughed and removed the towel from my head, running my fingers through my hair in lieu of a brush.

'So why are you binning the towel?' asked Cameron.

'Because I suspect I might be in line for a new one at Christmas,' I said, glancing towards the hallway and keeping my voice low.

'Oh yes, that's right, you are. But I won't entirely spoil the surprise by telling you which members of the *Marvel* universe it features.'

'I wonder if I can get a bathmat to match,' I said, turning my head at the sound of footsteps on the pavement outside.

'I don't think it will be them yet,' said Cameron.

'I really hope not. It's barely nine.'

'So how was Giles this evening?'

'Is it too disloyal to tell you that he was a complete and utter nervous wreck?'

He shot me a conspiratorial look. 'Kerry too.'

'Really?'

'Really,' he said quietly, his gaze turning to a gilt-framed photograph of Mark and Harry which sat on the mantelpiece.

'Has Kerry dated at all, since...' I began, but found myself unable to complete the question.

'This is her first date since Mark.' He smiled, but his sadness was unmistakeable.

'You know, whatever happens, Giles will protect her feelings,' I said. 'And Harry's too.'

'Yes, I get that impression.'

He looked at me with an expression which, just for a moment, made me wish that I was sitting close enough to comfort him somehow. Perhaps I could place a hand on his arm, whilst further reassuring him of Giles's intentions. Or perhaps I could place my arms around his neck, rest my head on his broad chest and ask him why he didn't find me at all attractive.

'You OK?' asked Cameron. 'Only you've stopped blinking.'

'What? Oh... it's the, er, smell of Wotsits,' I said, closing my eyes and taking a deep breath. 'Bit much.'

'I can only smell your usual perfume – which is great, by the way,' he added casually.

I felt a need to take a large gulp of wine. 'It's Clinique,' I said, aware of sounding slightly hoarse. 'I've got the body-wash and moisturiser too, so I'm drenched in it right now.'

'Well, it's all winning over the Wotsits, and I meant to ask you,' he continued without pause, leaning back on the sofa, 'was Giles OK with you asking me about Kerry?'

'Never had to tell him,' I said, whilst making a mental note to place an online order for a new tube of body-wash; my current supply was running perilously low.

'You didn't?'

'No, because I didn't see him when I got home from The Hayes on Monday and by the time I did see him, he'd already spoken to Kerry. Or rather she'd spoken to him. She didn't tell you?'

'All she said was that they were going out tonight and that she was really happy, but totally terrified, about it.'

'I should have updated you at work.'

'Or over a drink,' he said. 'But update me now.'

'Well, apparently,' I began, relaxing into a comfort zone of feel-good gossip, 'Nicky told Kerry that Giles had decided not to see Melissa again and so—' I paused, as Cameron looked confused. 'Do you know about Melissa?'

He shook his head.

'OK, so, quick recap: Nicky offered to set Giles up with her friend, Melissa. She was very lovely, but Giles was only interested in friendship because, as we now know, his affections lay elsewhere.'

Cameron nodded. 'With you so far.'

'Next, Nicky tells Kerry that things haven't worked out between Melissa and Giles and that Giles has gently let Melissa down. When Kerry hears this, she realises that Giles hadn't been embarrassed of her loungewear. He'd actually been uncomfortable because of the situation with Melissa.'

Cameron looked at me blankly. 'You lost me at loungewear.'

I drank my wine and flapped a hand. 'Forget the loungewear. The important thing is that when Kerry found out about Melissa, she guessed that Giles might be feeling a little bit low and so suggested a coffee to cheer him up. That's when she prised open his glued-together pages and made him talk about relationship and *that's* when they sorted everything out.'

'So you didn't have to drop yourself in it for meddling.'

I frowned at him.

'I meant "for *helping*", obviously. I misspoke.'

'Hmm.'

He smiled. 'Well, I'm pleased there hasn't been any awkwardness.'

'Yes, me too,' I replied, placing my empty wine glass on the coffee table. 'And talking of awkwardness, I'd better head next door. I want to be out of the way and in bed if Kerry comes back for coffee. The last thing they'll want is me hovering in the kitchen.'

I stood up and Cameron stood too. 'I'm not planning to get in Kerry's way either. I'm staying over, so I'll be heading upstairs soon myself.'

He walked ahead of me into the hallway, stepping to one side to let me to the front door.

'Thanks for keeping me company,' he said, as I turned the latch.

I smiled at him over my shoulder. 'No problem. Loved *Megamind*.'

'It's my favourite, you know.' He scratched his jaw. 'Although, strangely, I don't actually own a copy of it myself.'

I laughed, stepping outside and beginning to walk away. 'See you Monday.'

'How about a drink next week?' he asked suddenly.

I turned and then hesitated, slightly thrown by the proposal. 'A drink?' I asked a little breathlessly, shivering and pulling my bathrobe more tightly around me.

He propped his shoulder against the doorframe, leaning casually. 'Yes, I feel a need to know more about the loungewear, and Luke pointed out yesterday that we haven't all made it out for a while.'

'Oh yes, sure. That sounds great. Bye!' I said hurriedly, scuttling away while feeling slightly ridiculous that I had been on the verge of mistaking Cameron's suggestion for anything other than after-work drinks with our colleagues. After all, I reminded myself, this was a man who had made it very clear, less than a week ago, that he had no interest whatsoever in dating me.

I frowned slightly at the recollection and tried hard not to be bothered by it as I completed the short but freezing journey home. But as I reached Giles's front door, and raised a hand in response to a final, smiling farewell over the hedge, I had to admit that the prospect of *never* dating Cameron Grange actually felt like rather a shame.

Chapter 34

Thanks to a broken-down bus, I was last into the office on Monday. However, a broad grin and a 'Hi, Edie,' from Cameron, as I made my slightly frazzled entrance through the glass double-doors, immediately improved my mood to a surprising degree.

I smiled back at him, thinking how nicely the shirt he was wearing that morning picked up on the grey tones of his eyes. 'That's such a good colour on you,' I said before I knew it, and then hurried to my desk, complimenting Luke on his suit and Roger on his sweater as I went, just to keep things even.

I was rewarded with a confused frown from Roger and a smirk from Luke. 'Why thank you,' he said. 'And I love that…' He looked me up and down as I hurriedly removed my coat and threw it over the back of my chair, '…that highly colourful combination of clothing you're wearing today. Now, when you've had a moment to settle yourself down, Alison would like to see you.'

'OK.' I began unpacking my bag. 'What's the subject under discussion?'

'Nothing project-related,' he said. 'Just a general check-in with you. And with Cameron.'

I looked up and Luke mouthed a silent, 'Ooh', for my benefit alone.

I turned questioningly to Cameron but he just shrugged. 'Let me know when you're ready,' he said.

'Well,' I looked around my desk, 'I'd prefer now, before I get into anything else.'

'Fine by me,' he said, standing up and picking up a scribble pad and pencil.

I did the same and then walked ahead of him to Alison's office, knocking on her door.

She beckoned us in. 'Good morning,' she said, standing up and waving us towards the conference table. 'How was your weekend, Edith?'

'It was great, thanks.'

'Good. And how was your weekend, Cameron?'

'Fun,' he replied.

'Good,' she said, placing her hands flat on the table in front of her and momentarily glancing over my left shoulder. I resisted an urge to turn, instead looking down at my pad, pencil poised. 'I have a few things to say regarding the future of the practice.'

I looked up sharply, aware of a sudden and uncomfortable increase in my heart rate. Her face gave nothing away; she looked as steely and as uncomfortable in her own skin as she always did.

Cameron was studying her with apparent calm, but I knew his face well enough by now to recognise tension in his jaw.

Alison fell silent, with neither Cameron nor I offering her a prompt. She was, we knew, selecting her words with a view to conveying her thoughts in the shortest time possible, ideally leaving no room for ambiguity, doubt or questions. The woman was as efficient as any computer programme and she was currently loading.

'I am sixty-one,' she said eventually. 'Over the next two years, I plan a staged withdrawal from the business and thereafter the eventual transfer of the practice to new ownership. I have been presented with numerous offers from various parties which would enable me to do that.'

My pulse increased further, as a feeling of breathless anxiety was joined by one of nausea. I wondered how soon we would feel the influence of new management and whether Vincent Lovelock or, God forbid, Ruby Blair might one day be sitting behind Alison's desk. I put down the pencil with which I had been unconsciously doodling and moved my hands to the arching metal arms of my chair, gripping them tightly in order to stop myself from getting up and walking away.

Alison, meanwhile, was still talking.

'We are a practice renowned for an unfettered style and an ego-free, collaborative approach. Those who do not share our ethos find themselves uncomfortable and go elsewhere. The only way to identify whether an architect is a good fit is by working alongside them, and this applies also to identifying professionals whom I feel sufficiently share my philosophies and values to take the practice in a direction of which I can continue to be proud. This being the case, the obvious solution is to transition from within.' Having addressed her opening remarks to the surface of the desk, she now looked up and eyed us steadily. 'So I should like you, Edith, and you, Cameron, to think about whether you can work together to take the practice forward, following my retirement. We have two years to assess whether this can work. I believe it can. However, that does, of course, depend entirely upon your ambitions and your ability to work together. Personal conflict hinders the pursuit of professional harmony and is not conducive to a creative, efficient workplace. Any questions?' she asked, bringing her speech to an abrupt and wholly unexpected end.

Momentarily struck dumb, I looked at Cameron and saw that he had made almost a full page of notes. I, meanwhile, had drawn two windows, each with a distinctly ecclesiastical edge to them.

'I'd like to go away and consider what you've said,' said Cameron.

She nodded. 'Any questions, Edith?'

'Not immediately,' I murmured, still feeling shell-shocked.

'Excellent,' said Alison, clearly judging it time to smile. 'Let's meet again in one week's time, when you have had a chance to reflect further on the idea of running the practice in partnership.' She stood up. 'Thank you, both.' And with that, she returned to her desk and we silently rose from our seats and exited.

Neither Luke nor Roger looked up as we emerged. In fact, no one said anything at all until a minute or two later when Cameron came over to my desk and, pointing at my scribble pad and offering me a smile, said, 'Mind if I take a look at those windows?'

–

There was never any question that Cameron and I would be able to discuss Alison's proposal during office hours. An open-plan office and no time for a lunch away from my board made that impossible. So despite my eagerness to share my thoughts and to hear his, I waited patiently for the end of the working day – and for Alison, Roger and Luke to say goodnight – before packing up my things and making my way to Cameron's desk.

'Still busy?' I asked, as he pored over multiple drawings. He looked up. 'I am.'

'Will you be long? I was wondering if you fancied discussing Alison's offer over a drink? It's all a bit of a bolt from the blue, isn't it? I mean, it's an exciting bolt, but a bolt nevertheless.'

He leaned back in his chair. 'I've got to think it all through,' he said quietly.

'Of course.'

I waited for him to go on, but he said nothing more.

'Oh, I see,' I said, after a moment. 'You mean that you want to think it through before discussing it with me.'

He nodded. 'I don't think I'd make much sense if I tried to talk it through with you right now. I may need to talk to Alison again too,' he added after a slight pause.

'One-to-one?' I asked.

He shifted in his chair. 'There's a lot for us to consider,' he replied, shamelessly dodging the question.

I pursed my lips, resentful that in the space of less than thirty seconds he had managed to put a dampener on *the* most exciting day of my professional life to date. With just a few short sentences, he had left me feeling excluded, untrusted and irrelevant.

'OK,' I said, not at all keen to prolong the current topic of conversation, but unable at that particular moment to think of an alternative one.

With an obvious effort, he managed a smile. 'Kerry had a great time on Saturday night, by the way.'

'Giles too,' I said, assuming his comment to be his way of ticking a conversational box and preventing me from suggesting a Giles-Kerry update as a pretext for a drink.

'It's good that it seems to be working out for them.'

'It is,' I replied, hitching my bag further up onto my shoulder. 'Anyway, I'll let you get on. Bye.' Then, without waiting for a reciprocal farewell, I headed for the lifts.

Chapter 35

I wondered at first whether, having turned down an initial opportunity to talk through Alison's offer, Cameron might undergo a change of heart and suggest a drink another evening. But as Tuesday and Wednesday came and went with no further mention of the matter, my hopes gradually faded until they were completely snuffed out on Thursday evening when Giles told me that, according to Kerry, Cameron wouldn't be coming to the wine and cheese the next day after all. After that, I was in no doubt whatsoever that he had zero intention of sharing his concerns or opinions with me and, what's more, was keen to avoid putting himself in any situation where doing so might be unavoidable.

Of course, I would have loved nothing more than to tell Giles all about Alison's exciting offer and Cameron's crushing reaction to it. But fortunately for Giles, he was spared any Monday and Tuesday moans, thanks to consecutive evenings spent with Kerry. And by Wednesday, when the pain of Cameron's snub had dimmed to a dull ache, I realised that the last thing in the world I actually wanted was to drag Giles down from his romantic high with my cheery tale of shattered career dreams, courtesy of a man whom I had come to trust and admire.

So I said nothing to Giles, nor to anyone else for that matter. I had considered requesting a further meeting with

Alison, but the only purpose of that would have been to wring my hands and beg her to tell me what, if anything, Cameron had said about the idea of working with me. So instead, I had put my anxieties to one side and attempted to carry on as usual. And I think I must have managed that pretty well if Luke's behaviour towards me was anything to go by, because he showed absolutely no awareness that I might have been feeling anything other than completely chipper, as his teasing banter continued at full throttle all week.

'Skiver,' he said, tapping his watch, as I switched off my screen and buckled my satchel at one minute past five on Friday evening.

'I've got to go and help Giles get ready for the party,' I replied, standing up.

'A party?' he exclaimed, looking hurt. 'And you're not inviting me?'

'It's the avenue wine and cheese. I thought I'd mentioned it.'

'Oh, OK, yeah, you did,' he said, turning back towards his screen. 'I just got confused when you said "party".'

I tutted and stopped at his desk as I made my way to the door. 'You're more than welcome, if you'd like to come. Giles has bought some unsurprisingly posh food and wine and you'd reduce the average age to around sixty.'

He grinned up at me. 'Tempting, but no. Hey, Cam might take you up on it though,' he added, raising his voice. 'Eh, Cam? Fancy going to Edie's wine and cheese *party*?'

Cameron turned in his chair. 'Sounds about my required level of excitement,' he said.

I forced a laugh and turned back to Luke. 'Can't quite believe the extent to which my Friday night is being dissed here.'

'Ah, shaddap,' he said. 'You know you're the coolest person in the office.'

I smiled at him, grateful for the easy affection and not caring whether the compliment was a serious one or not. 'Have a good weekend and say bye-bye to those two for me when they come out of there.' I motioned towards Alison's office, where she and Roger were seated at the conference table, clearly in deep discussion.

'Will do. Go easy on the Emmental.'

'I'm more of a Gruyère girl,' I said, heading across the office and tacking on a 'Night, Cameron,' as I walked past his desk.

'Edie,' he said, quickly standing up and glancing towards Luke, who at that moment was knocking on Alison's door with a bundle of files under one arm.

'Yes?' I paused, disappointed to find myself appraising and approving the fit of his navy blue shirt as he approached.

'This evening…'

I shook my head. 'Don't worry, Giles has already told me that you can't make it and to be honest it's just as well. People might have to share glasses as it is. Apparently, double the numbers are coming to the parties this year compared to last. Something to do with austerity, Giles thinks.'

'Austerity?' Cameron frowned. 'Really?'

I didn't reply or turn away, deliberately allowing him an eleventh-hour opportunity to make some reference, no matter how small, to our looming meeting with Alison. Even a tiny hint as to why he felt unable to discuss any of it with me would be something, because his failure to do so to date was bound to set alarms bells ringing for our boss regarding our ability to maintain an effective working partnership in the future. Didn't he see that?

Or maybe he did see that. Maybe he wasn't actually interested in a partnership and maybe, for all Ruby's lies and misrepresentations, she had been right about one thing, namely Cameron's preference for a uniquely privileged, one-to-one relationship with the boss, rather than a shared one.

I looked up at him, reluctant to believe her analysis and willing him to say something, anything, to confirm himself as the uncomplicated and – OK, yes – increasingly attractive man of integrity I had believed him to be less than a week ago. Because, at this point, there was no denying that the hurt I was experiencing was much personal as it was professional.

But he said nothing more, instead offering me a brief smile before returning to his desk and sitting back down in front of his screen.

I turned away. 'Well, don't work too late,' I said, with surprising calm and taking cold comfort from the fact that I had at least now moved beyond resentment to a point of acceptance. There was, after all, nothing I could do, except cross my fingers and focus on the meagre hope that Alison's Plan B would somehow include me.

Chapter 36

'Say when, June.' I smiled brightly, topping up her glass from a bottle of red, as I continued to focus upon fulfilling my role as co-host to the increasingly large crowd of wine-and-cheesers now packing Giles's kitchen area. I was determined not to spoil things for Giles and was aware that showing or sharing any Cameron-related anxiety would almost certainly create awkwardness between himself and Kerry, as their respective best friends – yet again – prepared to lock horns.

June stared at the slowly rising level of alcohol with the intensity of a surgeon performing keyhole surgery, before shouting, 'When!' so loudly and suddenly that Bill and Patrick visibly jumped and Stan put a hand to his heart.

'Edith is not hard of hearing, June,' he said gently.

She laughed, putting her free hand to her head and patting the black bob, with blunt-cut fringe, which was perched there. A bright red dress and an out-there pair of yellow Mary Janes completed a startling, but joyous, new look. She had the appearance this evening of Miss Marple after a Mary Quant makeover.

'Well, it's so busy and noisy in here, isn't it?' she said, looking around the tightly packed room. 'I was afraid Edith wouldn't hear me.'

'Are we sure all these people actually live in the avenue?' asked Patrick. 'Who's that bloke by the fireplace with the black eye, for example? I've definitely never seen him before.'

'You know him, Patrick,' said Stan, glancing over his shoulder. 'That's young Cormac, from number 47, who's married to Jeanette with the red hair. Although, sadly, they are getting divorced. He just doesn't look himself tonight because he's been in the wars.'

'Yes, a pan fell on his head again yesterday,' said June, looking across at Cormac with kindly concern. 'That's the second time in a month that's happened.'

'Because what we don't want,' continued Patrick, refusing to be sidetracked by Cormac's unusually bad luck, 'is people taking advantage of our homes and hospitality the way they do our parking spaces. I counted twelve vehicles parked in the avenue today, which were not registered to residents or their regular visitors.' He drained the bottle of beer which Giles had handed him less than ten minutes earlier.

'How do you know who the cars are registered to, Patrick?' I asked, with genuine interest. 'I thought only the police could run that kind of check.'

'I have a compiled a list by means of house-to-house enquiries,' he said, with obvious pride, 'and I have patrolled the avenue, recording number plates, daily, for six weeks. I shall shortly be presenting my findings to Bristol City Council, in support of my repeated requests for the introduction of residents' parking.'

'Oh… OK. Well, that's very… focused of you.' I glanced around our small circle for any shared concern over Patrick's obsessive tendencies. Unsurprisingly, there was none. June and Stan were gazing benignly at him, and Bill, for reasons which would soon become apparent, appeared to be far more interested in me.

'So, Edith,' he said, leaning in whilst pushing his aviator specs further up the bridge of his nose, 'we have a gig coming up in two weeks' time.'

I offered him a polite smile, my grip tightening on the wine bottle, as I determined to be nobody's patsy tonight. 'How very lovely. Is entry free of charge?' I asked through clenched teeth. '*Like it was last time.*'

'That's right,' he said smoothly, without any hint of conscience. 'Unless you'd like to reserve a table for you and your young man, of course.' He pointed towards Giles who was, at that moment, chatting with Andy and Nicky.

June let out a gasp and placed a hand on my arm. 'You must excuse William, Edith. He doesn't know.'

'Doesn't know what?' he asked, turning to her.

'Why, that Giles is no longer courting Edith.'

'Oh.' He shrugged, apparently unmoved by the fake news.

'It's fine, June, Giles and I were never...' I hesitated for a moment, 'courting. I'm very happy for him and Kerry.'

'Brave, broken-hearted girl,' she murmured. 'Back on the shelf.'

'Are you moving out?' snapped Patrick. 'Where are you going to live now?'

I looked at him steadily. 'Not in my car.'

He nodded as if satisfied. 'Sorry for your loss,' he said.

'Well, looking on the bright side,' chimed Bill, 'it'll end all those concerns about him being your cousin. I know you think it was OK, but a doctor friend of mine wasn't so sure.' He raised his wine glass. 'It's for the best. And, here's an idea, you can bring a different young man to the gig. Someone you're not related to. I'll set a table aside and maybe add a couple of chairs for your friends. That'll cheer you up. I'll pop the tickets round over the weekend.'

I took a deep breath and held up the wine bottle, resisting an urge to whack him with it. 'Thank you, but no table this time: we'll stand. Now, I'd best get on and fill some more glasses,' I continued hastily, denying Bill a chance to continue the hard sell. 'I'm not being a very good hostess, am I? Patrick, help yourself to another beer. They're in the bottom drawer of the fridge.'

'You're an excellent hostess,' said June, not letting go of my arm but instead squeezing it gently. 'And very stylish.' She looked me up and down, her eyes settling approvingly on my dress. 'Marilyn Monroe was buried in green.'

'Ooh, that's... interesting,' I said uncertainly. 'But thank you, June, and you're looking really fabulous tonight. I love that dress and those shoes. They really pop.'

She smiled happily. 'Well, I'll let you into a little secret. I saw you the other day, walking up the avenue in your smart blue boots and flowery coat, and I thought, "Why do I always wear boring colours, rather than cheerful ones, like Edith?" and so I bought these,' she added, looking downwards.

Feeling hugely complimented and not a little moved, I bent down to give her a hug. 'Thank you for noticing. I'm so flattered. That's a real boost to my self-confidence.'

I straightened up and she let go of my arm, giving it a gentle pat. 'I'll let you go and be a hostess,' she said.

I bade farewell to the group, pretending not to hear Bill's last-minute offer of *a special discount for singles*, and worked my way towards the kitchen area, chatting and topping up glasses as I went. After a few minutes, I spotted Nicky, who had now moved on from Giles and was filling her wine glass with water from the tap.

'There's fizzy water and white wine in the fridge, you know,' I said, placing my near-empty bottle on the counter next to her. 'Or I'm just about to open another red.'

She shook her head sadly. 'Thanks, but it's my turn not to have a hangover.'

I patted her shoulder sympathetically. 'Is Andy taking full advantage of that?'

'He was, up until about five minutes ago. Not sure where he is or what he's up to now.' She scanned the room. 'You know, I can't believe how popular these things have become. No offence,' she added quickly. 'Of course any party hosted by you and Giles would be popular.'

'It's OK, I know what you mean. When Giles first mentioned the avenue wine and cheeses to me, I thought I'd rather stick needles in my eyes.'

'But they're actually OK, aren't they? Certainly never boring.' She gestured over my shoulder towards Giles, who was now talking to Angela, Patrick's next-door neighbour and aunt to an alleged crack addict. 'I love that he's with Kerry.'

'Me too.'

'How about you? Are you interested in anyone right now? Or are you ecstatically single?'

I laughed at the suddenness and bluntness of the question and she bit her lip. 'God, I'm so nosey, aren't I? And I haven't even got the excuse of being drunk. Don't worry, you don't have to answer.'

'It's fine,' I said, thinking about her question and experiencing something painfully close to regret, as an image of Cameron – his hair damp and standing on end, his smile broad and unselfconscious – came to mind. I blinked and took a steadying breath. 'Ecstatically single would be pushing it, but, you know, I love my job, and that's where my focus is for the moment. I'm at a crossroads career-wise and it's such a busy time that I just couldn't commit to anything or anyone else right now.'

Nicky sighed. 'I've been there with work. But, you know,' she sipped her water, 'if things change, I have a friend I think you'd get on really well with.'

I smiled. 'Are you the avenue match.com?'

'Yep, that's me,' she said, a mischievous glint in her eye. 'Sad, stay-at-home mum, craving romance and so seeking it out for others. And talking of romance,' she added dryly, nodding over my shoulder, 'here comes my husband: Mr Romance himself. Ooh, but look who he's bringing with him!' she exclaimed, her face lighting up as she stepped past me and embraced Cameron, kissing him on both cheeks. 'I didn't know you were coming, Ron.'

Chapter 37

'I wasn't sure I was going to be allowed in,' said Cameron, his relaxed manner in complete contrast to the head-to-toe tension I was suddenly experiencing. 'Some guy in the hallway is checking postcodes. Hi, Edie,' he added, turning and extending his neck as if about to kiss me, only to then adjust his shirt collar and nod towards the kitchen counter. 'So, do you think you've got enough glasses to last the evening?'

I stared at him, trying to decide how I felt about his arrival, a quick analysis of my feelings identifying a heady mix of irritation, surprise, anxiety and – standing ashamed and trying to go unnoticed at the very back of the queue – pleasure.

'It's touch and go,' I said. 'So let me fill one up for you while I can. What would you like? There are lots of reds here, or whites and beers in the fridge.'

'Some of that would be great,' he said, pointing to the bottle next to me.

I filled a glass and handed it to him.

'Thanks,' he said, saluting me with it. 'And for letting me stay.'

I took a breath and then a sip of my wine, alternately wishing that either he would leave, or that everybody else would.

Andy clapped Cameron on the shoulder. 'It was Patrick who checked Ron's address,' he said amiably, with no hint of the tension he had exhibited at June's party. I wondered if his alcohol intake alone was responsible for his more relaxed mood this evening, or whether his wife's lack of it might be a contributing factor.

I lowered my voice. 'He was telling me earlier that he patrols the avenue and keeps a log of parked cars.'

'He's obsessed with people putting in driveways too,' said Nicky, shaking her head despairingly. 'Gary, from number 12, told me that Patrick hasn't spoken to him since he dropped the kerb in 2015 for his mum's mobility scooter. I mean, personally, the idea of Patrick never speaking to me ever again sounds like a *massive* plus, but poor Gary's actually quite hurt by it.' Nicky sighed and then turned to Cameron. 'But how are you, Ron? Edie says it's mad at work.'

His eyes darted towards me for a moment. 'There's certainly a lot going on.'

'Hiya, Ron,' said Kerry, reaching up to place a hand on his shoulder, as she and Giles joined the group. I watched as Cameron turned and bent low to give her a kiss. Clearly, I was the only woman in the room he couldn't bring himself to have physical contact with.

'Ronal... Ron,' said Giles, extending a hand. 'So pleased you could make it after all.'

Cameron shook his hand – thereby proving that skin-to-skin contact with men was also not an issue for him. 'Me too,' he said, with a glance at Kerry.

She turned to Giles. 'Giles, can you show Nicky and Andy those shelves the carpenter has put in for you?'

He frowned. 'The ones in the understairs cupboard?'

'Yes.'

'Now?' he asked uncertainly.

'Oh yes, please,' said Nicky, putting down her glass. 'Kerry told me about them yesterday, when I was moaning about storage. I think we should get some shelving, Andy.'

'Er...' Andy blinked slowly, swayed slightly, and then shrugged. 'OK.'

'Go and look,' Kerry said, gently nudging Giles and gesturing for Nicky and Andy to follow.

Andy laughed and held up a hand. 'It's OK, Kerry,' he said, as his wife and Giles headed off. 'I trust Nicky with all our major home-improvement decisions. Now Ron,' he said, beaming at Cameron, 'I wanted to tell you about—'

'No, you need to come and see the shelves too, Andy,' said Kerry, linking her arm through his.

'I do?' he asked, with obvious bewilderment. 'But aren't they just long and straight and flat?'

She shook her head. 'Some of them go round corners.'

'Ooooh, corner shelves...' said Andy, allowing himself to be gently guided by Kerry in the direction of the hallway. 'They're my favourite.'

I watched them go and then turned back to Cameron. He raised an eyebrow. 'That escalated quickly.'

I picked up the bottle of red. 'I should go and circulate with this. Would you like me to introduce you to anyone else here? Cormac Walsh over there is a surveyor and an interesting guy — just don't mention the black eye. Or you could join the group in the understairs cupboard, I suppose.'

He glanced around the room. 'I'm here to talk to you,' he said.

Experiencing no surprise, and with unexpected calm, I turned and replaced the bottle carefully on the counter. 'About Alison's offer?' I asked, without looking at him.

'About Alison's offer.'

'Why now?'

'Friends on hand for immediate, emotional support.'

I gazed at Nicky's abandoned wine glass. 'Considerate of you, but I don't think I'll be needing any.'

'I meant for me.'

I looked up to find him smiling.

'Well, I'm glad you're managing to see a funny side to all this,' I said, suddenly feeling distinctly less calm and deliberately keeping the pitch of my voice low to avoid any wobbles. 'But it's my career under discussion and that's never been a laughing matter for me.'

His smile fading, he opened his mouth to say something, but at that moment we were interrupted by a couple politely asking for directions to a fresh bottle of white. Cameron waited until I had pointed them towards the fridge and sourced a corkscrew, and then he touched my arm and gestured towards the darkened garden. 'I know it's cold, but could we step outside? Just for a couple of minutes.'

I closed my eyes and heaved a sigh. 'OK, come on,' I said wearily, walking to the bifold doors and sliding them open just enough for us to slip outside. 'Let's go over there.' I closed the doors behind us and pointed to the edge of the patio. 'I don't fancy being seen or overheard.'

We made our way across the patio, stopping where it ended with a small step up to the lawn. I shivered as we came to a halt. 'Fire away,' I said, clenching my teeth against the cold.

He removed his jacket. 'Here, have this.'

I was about to refuse the offer, before realising that, actually, I was both freezing and miserable, and it was all his fault. 'Thanks,' I said, taking the jacket from him and putting it on, its shoulders sagging and its sleeves extending well beyond my fingertips.

I watched with some satisfaction as he tensed against the cold and then placed his hands into his pockets and studied the ground thoughtfully. 'Right,' he said, after a moment, 'well, with regard to Alison's proposal, I do have a concern.'

'I'd already worked out that much for myself,' I muttered irritably, stamping my feet and looking towards the beckoning light and warmth of the kitchen. 'What I don't understand is why we couldn't have discussed your professional concern in a professional manner, in a professional, *centrally heated* environment.'

'My concern isn't a professional one,' he said, looking at me steadily. 'It's personal.'

'What?'

'It's about our—' he began, before being interrupted by a clattering against the fence behind me. He frowned and pointed over my right shoulder. 'There's a woman climbing...'

'Oh, it's only Stella,' I said, turning towards her, frustrated by the interruption but forcing a smile. 'The doors are unlocked, Stella,' I called. 'Go straight in and help yourself to wine. Giles is in the cupboard under the stairs if you need anything.'

There was a murmured, 'Thank you,' followed by the sound of clogs across the patio and muffled cheers from within, as Stella made her entrance and then closed the doors behind her.

I looked at Cameron. 'Carry on. What do you mean, your concern is *personal*?' I pressed.

He turned his head slowly back towards me, blinking slightly, Stella's arrival clearly having shaken his focus.

'Er, I mean that when considering Alison's offer, our personal relationship is a consideration for me,' he said after a moment.

'Oh, I see.' My shoulders drooped unseen inside the enormous jacket, as irritation was immediately displaced by guilt and regret. I had hoped that Cameron had moved beyond my early injustices towards him, but apparently not. It was a realisation which hurt as much personally as it did professionally – more, in fact. 'I see,' I repeated forlornly.

'It's not an easy matter to raise with you, or with Alison, and definitely not one I'd feel comfortable discussing as a group at our Monday meeting. But at the same time, I don't want to leave you in the dark about my position.'

'Well, thank you,' I said quietly, now addressing my feet. 'And it's fine, I get it. If our situations were reversed, I'm sure I'd have exactly the same doubts and reservations. I should have realised that you might feel this way. From my point of view, I wouldn't feel comfortable working in partnership with you while you're still uncertain or mistrustful of me, but I would absolutely support the idea of you running things on your own, or with someone else, if that's what you and Alison decide. I wouldn't have a problem with that.' I looked up at him and attempted a smile. 'God, maybe I do need a bit of emotional support after all.'

He shook his head. 'I'm not mistrustful of you,' he said. 'I'm attracted to you.'

I was silent for several seconds, before experiencing a need to double check. 'Did you say *attracted*?'

'Yes.'

'To me?'

'Yes.'

I stared up at him, my mouth ajar.

'If circumstances had been different,' he continued, 'I'd have kept that to myself for the moment. But with a partnership under discussion, I'm telling you now because it's something I'd want to know in your position. I'd need to think about whether I was comfortable going into a closer professional relationship with that in the background.'

'You're attracted to me?'

He nodded slowly. 'Yes, Edie, I am.'

'But you were so massively relieved in The Hayes when I said I wasn't expecting you to ask me for a date.'

He looked thoughtful for a moment. 'I was certainly relieved not to have to discuss how I felt there and then. I wasn't prepared for it and it felt too soon. As I said, I wouldn't be raising it now, if it wasn't for Alison's offer. So yes, at the time, I was relieved when you said that you preferred lean men to *earthy types*.'

I put a hand to my mouth. 'Did I say that?'

'You did.'

'God, I can't believe I said that,' I murmured.

'So,' he continued, 'in short: I'm concerned about a personal issue, which might rock the professional boat. If there's no attraction on your side – which I'm guessing there isn't, due to my earthiness – then fine. I'll accept that and don't have a problem with exploring Alison's plan, provided, of course, that you are happy with that. But if you see my current feelings for you as a problem, or if you...' He paused and took a breath. 'If there is anything mutual, or you think there might be, then I'd have doubts about embarking upon a professional partnership, at this time, under those circumstances.' He looked down at me and shrugged. 'That's it.'

Slightly thrown by this rather abrupt end to his statement, I blinked up at him for several seconds, before pulling myself together and nodding rapidly. 'OK. Yes. I get all that. But I need to think,' I said breathlessly, my heart thumping in my chest.

'Of course,' he said patiently, appearing perfectly calm.

I lowered my head, forcing myself to take a moment to consider my feelings and my response. I was, I realised immediately, unequivocally and undeniably delighted on every level imaginable. This kind, intelligent, broad-chested man had forgiven me and wanted to work in partnership with me. In addition, he was attracted to me, and that was, I knew as I looked up at him and met his steady gaze, yet more good news because I was, without a shadow of a doubt, attracted to him too.

I was attracted to his directness, his integrity, his kindness, his talent, his height, his stubble, his width, and even to his anxiety-related Cockney twang, which afforded him a simultaneous air of both strength and vulnerability. I couldn't, in fact, understand what I had ever seen in stringy men. And right now, all I wanted was for us to remain outside on the patio – keeping each other warm somehow – until everyone else had gone home, at which point we would go inside and embark upon a relationship, which may or may not work out, but which would certainly put paid to the single, greatest ever career opportunity of my entire life.

Oh.

My face fell, my heart rate slowed and my excited thought processes rapidly decelerated, before coming to an abrupt halt, as I reached the same miserable conclusion as Cameron. We could have a bash at being a couple, *or* we could form a professional partnership. We could not, with any confidence of success, attempt both.

He was an impressive man, to whom I was at that moment almost irresistibly attracted. But although I was pretty sure I would feel exactly the same way about him tomorrow, next week and next month, what about in *six* months? Or in a year? A split could have disastrous consequences in the workplace, negatively impacting the lives of our clients and colleagues, as well as our own. And even if we didn't split, even if our relationship turned out to be a largely successful one, it could still prove damagingly distracting.

I looked up, resisting an urge to place my arms around his neck and pull him towards me.

'Thank you for being so honest with me, Cameron,' I heard myself say, my voice steady and calm. 'I respect and admire you *very* much, but I'm interested only in a professional relationship. I think we will make a really good team.'

He tensed slightly against the cold and then nodded. 'I have no doubt that we will,' he replied. 'This is a great opportunity for us both.'

Chapter 38

One year later

Roger told us that he wanted no fuss and no mention made of his retirement on his last day in the office. But, of course, we all just rolled our eyes at that and after some negotiation he eventually gave in to an understated single glass of champagne at four p.m. He also agreed to a practice-funded dinner the following evening, to which Alison said partners were invited – a kind offer, even if a largely redundant one, as Luke was the only one of us with anyone to invite along.

'You know, I'm still not sure whether to bring Jem tomorrow night,' he said quietly, as we drank our champagne and Roger chatted with Cameron and Alison on the other side of her conference table.

'Why on earth not?' I asked, pulling a face. 'We all really like Jem and the pair of you are so funny together.' I hesitated for a moment. 'You haven't had a falling out, have you?'

'A *falling out*?' he repeated, with a snort and a shake of his head. 'You sound so like my nan, Edie. Henleaze really rubbed off on you, didn't it? No, we haven't had a *falling out*. It's just that Jem will be the only non-work person there.'

'So?' I shrugged. 'Is that a problem?'

'Not for Jem,' he said. 'But I don't want anyone feeling they can't talk about work, or make in-jokes, because there's someone sitting there who won't get any of it.'

'Don't be so silly. That's not an issue for any of us,' I tutted. 'We just want someone there who'll slap you down when you get a bit much.'

He grinned. 'OK, and—' he began, but was at that point interrupted by Alison, as she stood up and tapped lightly on her glass with a pen.

'Oh no,' groaned Roger. 'I thought we agreed no speeches.'

'We agreed to save the presentation of your gifts until tomorrow evening,' said Alison stiffly. 'That was all we agreed.'

He heaved a sigh and folded his arms. 'Go on then,' he said with a relaxed informality attributable, I assumed, to imminent retirement and a tiny bit of booze.

'Why, thank you, Roger,' she said, coming as close to sarcasm as I'd ever heard.

I glanced at Cameron and frowned, just as he half-turned towards me and did the same. A quick check of Luke showed him to be looking just as entertained by the people he worked with as usual.

Alison downed her remaining half-glass of champagne in one and placed the flute down heavily on the conference table, causing me to look again at Cameron, whilst feeling increasingly uneasy. He was now staring fixedly at Alison, his expression one of determined implacability.

'Roger,' she said, clasping her hands in front of her.

'Yes, that's me,' he grunted.

'What can I say about you?'

'Nothing, preferably.'

Luke grinned and shook his head. 'Just brilliant,' he murmured.

I smiled anxiously and shifted in my chair, wondering if necking my champagne might make me feel any less awkward.

'Roger,' repeated Alison, throwing her head back and addressing the large, white, circular ceiling light directly above her head. 'My co-worker, my friend…' She slowly lowered her eyes to look directly into his, as my palms began to sweat.

'…my soul mate,' she said quietly.

'What?!' I exclaimed, causing all heads to turn towards me. I looked to Cameron, Roger and Luke for some sense of shared amazement, but Luke was quite obviously on the verge of laughter, while Roger looked like he was sitting on a hedgehog and Cameron remained wholly impassive, offering me only a barely perceptible shake of the head.

I looked at Alison. 'What… what a very lovely speech,' I said, somewhat breathlessly, placing my glass on the table and clapping. 'Lovely. Very heartfelt.'

'I'm not sure it's quite over yet,' said Luke.

'Oh, really?' I smiled as broadly as I could. 'I'm so sorry, Alison. Do carry on.' I picked up my glass and drained its contents.

She offered me a nod and returned her attention to Roger. 'You will be missed,' she said and then sat down.

'OK, so *now* you can clap,' murmured Luke. 'Oh no, my mistake,' he added, as Roger stood up and cleared his throat.

'Well, I'm not one for saying fussy stuff,' he said, beginning his speech with an absolutely incontrovertible statement, his focus fixed determinedly on the surface of the conference table, 'but I will say that working here for the past fifteen years has been a pleasure and a privilege. Not only have I worked with a great many talented architects – none more so than the present company – I have also had the good fortune to net a woman who, in my opinion, is almost without fault.' There was a catch in his voice and, as he sat down, Cameron immediately rose to his feet.

'To Roger and his retirement. May it be a long and happy one,' he said.

'To Roger,' we echoed, standing up and raising our glasses, before we all, instinctively and without instruction, returned to our desks.

–

It was a couple of minutes after five when Alison and Roger left the office, bidding goodnight to Luke, Cameron and myself, as if it was any other working day.

I waited until I was sure that they had taken the lift, before standing up and walking to Luke's desk.

'Did you know?' I asked quietly, as he picked up his bags and prepared to leave.

'About Roger and Alison?' he queried, with a surprising lack of drama.

'Yes.'

'She's never said anything,' he shrugged. 'But I'd been pretty sure for a while now that there was someone, and I had a hunch it might be him. He never liked to talk about what he was up to outside work, and then there was the body language between them, and her reliance on his advice, that kind of thing...'

I frowned. 'I didn't have a clue.'

'Surprised face,' he said, looking bored.

I laughed and he joined in. 'Nothing gets past me,' he winked, picking up his bag and sidestepping from behind his desk. 'But to be fair to you, Alison was never one for bringing her personal life to work with her, was she?'

'Best piece of advice she ever – repeatedly – gave me was to keep the personal and the professional completely separate,' I replied, keeping my eyes determinedly fixed on Luke, and refusing to give in to an urge to look at Cameron.

'Not always an easy thing to do though, Edie,' he said, smiling significantly.

'What do you mean?'

'Well,' he said, lowering his voice, 'just ask Vincent.'

'Vincent Lovelock? Ruby's boss?'

He nodded slowly, enjoying the moment.

'Why? What's happened?' I asked, despite already being pretty sure that I had at least some idea.

'Divorcing,' he mouthed.

'Oh no.'

'Oh yes. Jenny, his PA, told me this afternoon, along with the fact that...' He paused and glanced across the office to Cameron, who was currently engrossed in something onscreen. 'Ruby,' Luke mouthed the name soundlessly, 'has left the practice.'

'No...'

'Yes again. She's gone to Ireland.'

'Ireland...' I echoed softly, thinking how relieved Jason would be when I told him. Ruby had recently sent him a birthday card, featuring a Victorian-era painting of a young woman gazing forlornly at a dead bird in her hands. It had unnerved him a little, and had *really* upset his therapist, who had confided to Jason that it had resulted

357

in several disturbing dreams. I did wonder about Jason's therapist at times.

'That's according to Jenny,' said Luke.

'Wow.' I looked at him wide-eyed, relieved to discover that, sympathy and sorrow for Harriet Lovelock and her children aside, I had received the news of Vincent's divorce, and Ruby's suspiciously timed relocation with scandalised interest, rather than any sense of personal distress or connection.

'Indeed,' said Luke gravely. 'And, don't worry, I shall be sure to keep you updated with further details as and when gleaned.'

'Thanks.'

'No bother.' He offered me a salute as he began to walk away. 'Bye, Cam,' he said, as he reached the door. 'See you tomorrow night.'

'Yes, looking forward to it,' said Cameron, looking up, 'and to seeing Jem again.'

Luke paused for a moment and then looked back at me and smiled. 'You two,' he said, tutting and then laughing as he exited.

I watched him go and then wandered over to Cameron's desk, pulling up a chair and sitting down. 'What do you think he meant by that?' I asked, leaning my elbows on the edge of his desk and resting my chin on my hands.

'Who knows?' he murmured, his back to me.

'You working late?'

'No.' He reached out and abruptly switched off his screen. 'In fact, I'm leaving right now. How about you?' he asked, turning his chair towards me.

I sat up and shook my head. 'I've got a few more things to sort out, ready for Gita and Seb starting on Tuesday.' I looked around the office. 'It's going to be a squeeze until we move.'

'Can't whatever it is wait until Monday?'

'I don't want to leave it, in case there's a problem, and I don't want it hanging over me at the weekend, especially not with Anthony coming to stay.'

Cameron smiled. 'Oh, yes, Legoland. I'd forgotten about that. Have they told Harry yet?'

I shook my head. 'I texted Kerry earlier and she says not. Can you imagine the excitement levels when they tell him? I hope they film it.'

He looked at me and smiled in a way which, just for a moment, shook my professionalism to the core. But it was only a moment and then it was back to business.

'Well,' I said, pushing back my chair, 'I'll let you escape.'

He stood up, reaching for his coat and laptop bag. 'Don't work too late,' he said, slinging his coat over his arm and edging past me.

'An hour at most.'

His coat brushed against my arm and I gazed after him as he made his way towards the long glass doors, my mind drifting back, not for the first time, to our conversation of a year ago on Giles's freezing patio. It was, after all, a conversation which had made our relationship what it was today.

'This is a great opportunity for us both,' said Cameron.

I nodded, wanting to say something more but finding myself now unable to speak. Instead, I removed his jacket and returned it to him.

'Thanks.' He smiled, glancing over his shoulder. 'Let's get back inside before you freeze. We can toast our new partnership in the warmth.' He turned and began to walk towards the long glass doors of the kitchen.

I hesitated for just a moment, before rushing to follow and placing a hand on his arm. He stopped and turned, looking first at my hand and then questioningly down at me. 'You don't want to go inside?'

'Not yet,' I said quietly, releasing his arm. 'The thing is, Cameron, I haven't been quite as honest with you as you've been with me.'

'No?'

I sighed and shook my head. 'I mean, obviously I want to take Alison up on her offer, and I do sincerely believe that we would make a very good team professionally. That's all true but,' I hesitated and took a deep breath, 'but I haven't been honest with you about my feelings. My personal feelings,' I added meaningfully.

There followed a pause, during which his frown deepened and I began to shiver and regret handing over his jacket.

'I'm sorry, but I'm going to need more than that,' he said eventually. 'Are you saying that there is still some resentment? Or that you have trust issues?'

'God, no, not at all,' I said hurriedly, shaking my head. 'What I mean is that I'm attracted to you. You know...' I pointed to his face and then swept my hand downwards to his feet, 'physically.'

'Oh, right,' he said, clearly taken aback. 'Right.'

'Yes,' I continued, aware of my hands beginning to numb and now anxious to cover all bases as quickly as possible. 'So, to put my cards on the table: it is mutual. I am attracted to you and I think I might find that hard to set to one side, if we were to start working even more closely together. I mean, even when I was really fed up with you at work today, I couldn't help thinking how good you looked in that shirt. Then, in there, just now,' I said, nodding towards the kitchen, 'when you were touching and kissing everybody except me, I felt really excluded. And when

you were telling me how you felt a moment ago, again I found myself desperately wanting physical contact with you.'

'OK,' he said, blinking a little.

'And you're so right about the need for complete openness and honesty going forward,' I said, still shivering, but grateful to the cold for at least keeping me focused and on-message, 'and, with that in mind, I should be clear that I'm attracted to you on a much deeper level than simply a physical one and wanting to touch you. There's your integrity, your kindness, your intellect – all that kind of stuff,' I continued hurriedly, folding my arms across my chest in a completely futile attempt to generate some warmth. 'But, right now, wanting to touch you is what I'm almost exclusively focused on, so that's why I mentioned it first. I'm sorry. I'm aware that I just agreed to enter into a professional partnership with you and that this probably isn't what you want to hear right now.'

He took a deep breath and then released it slowly. 'If I'm being completely honest – cards on the table – I don't totally hate hearing it.'

'Really? But you just said what a great opportunity—'

'I know, but that was before you kept going on about wanting to touch me.'

'Oh, OK. Sorry.'

He closed his eyes, tilted his head upwards and addressed the night sky. 'I just don't want to screw this up.'

'I know, I know. As you said, Alison is offering us such an amazing opportunity.'

He opened his eyes, lowered his head and looked down at me. 'I didn't just mean my career, Edie,' he said, his voice now a gravelly murmur, as his East London accent broke through. 'Here, take this,' he added, again slipping off his jacket and handing it to me.

I took it from him, smiling gratefully, but far from happy at the prospect of either stifling my feelings, or stalling my career.

'Bye.' Cameron pushed open the office door and strode quickly away down the corridor.

'Sorry, what?' I murmured absently, blinking a little as I returned to the moment, before getting to my feet and hurrying after him.

He was pressing the call-button for the lift by the time I caught up with him, and he turned towards me, raising his eyebrows questioningly. 'Something else?'

I nodded, despite knowing that I had nothing to say which couldn't wait. 'Yes, er, I was just thinking about Roger and Alison,' I said. 'Were you surprised?'

'That they're together?' He glanced up at the digital floor-indicator above the lift doors. The lift was on the top floor and didn't appear to be moving. 'Not really, actually. I can see how that would work. And I'm not surprised that neither of them brought their personal relationship into the workplace. That's Alison's advice to everyone she's ever worked with.'

'True.' I glanced over my shoulder towards the office. When I turned back to Cameron, he was frowning at me.

'Anything else?' he asked, a little wearily. 'Or can I go home now?'

'One more thing.'

'OK, fire away,' he said, looking at the lift with a mild impatience that rather suited him.

'Well, this afternoon – and again just now, actually – I was thinking about our relationship. Do you ever do that? You know, think back to what we agreed that night on Giles's patio and wish for something different?'

He didn't immediately answer and I realised that impatience had now been supplanted by anxiety. 'No, I don't. Are you telling me that you regret this?' he asked quietly.

I shook my head. 'God, no. Absolutely not. Never.'

He looked at me blankly for a moment and then heaved a sigh. 'Well, that's good,' he said, turning away and pressing the lift button repeatedly. 'But thanks so much for asking the question. On a Friday. Just as I'm about to go home and *attempt* to unwind.'

'I think what we agreed was absolutely right *in essence*,' I continued. 'But I do have some issues and concerns and I think I need to be honest with you about them.'

He closed his eyes and his head dropped. 'Go on,' he said resignedly, turning slowly towards me.

'Well… for example… sometimes when I see you here, or rather in there,' I turned and pointed towards the office, 'in the workplace, it doesn't matter what we agreed; I stop thinking about work and I think about…'

'About what?'

I took a deep breath and stepped towards him, taking his face in my hands and guiding it slowly down towards mine. 'About touching you,' I whispered. 'I can't help it and I feel bad that I haven't been completely honest with you about that. You know, about the things that go through my mind when I look at you, when I'm with you, at work.'

'Thank you for your timely honesty,' he mumbled, his ability to articulate significantly impaired by my hands pressed to his cheeks. 'Now can I go home?'

'Are you saying that you never think about touching me? Here, at work?' I asked softly.

I felt him attempt to shake his head. 'Never.'

'Don't believe you,' I said, and then I pressed my mouth hard against his.

Almost simultaneously, his bag and coat hit the floor, and his arms were around me, pulling me towards him, as he kissed me back.

'Wait,' he breathed after a moment, placing his hands on my shoulders and easing me gently away from him. 'We agreed to maintain an entirely professional relationship.'

'Only in the workplace,' I said breathlessly, reaching again for his face. 'So it's fine, because we're not actually in the workplace right now. That's back there.' I flapped a hand in the general direction of the office. 'This corridor is not our workplace, it's a common part of the building. It says so in the lease. I know because I checked it this afternoon.'

He hesitated, frowning for a second, and then said, 'Fair enough, let's go with that,' before pulling me back towards him and kissing me again.

The lift pinged and we hurriedly stepped apart, Cameron desperately combing his fingers through his hair and me tucking in my blouse, as the lift doors slid open to reveal one of the lawyers from the top floor.

'Hello,' she said, looking first at me and then at Cameron, her eyes drifting upwards to his vertical hair and then lowering and coming to rest, with obvious suspicion, on his coat, which still lay in a crumpled heap next to his bag on the floor.

'Hi,' he said, snatching up both bag and coat and stepping inside the lift. He turned to face me, now appearing impressively calm, as he pressed the button to hold the doors. 'Remind me again what time we're expecting Anthony,' he said.

'Eight.'

'OK. I'll pick up dinner on the way home.'

'We need milk and loo roll too.'

He nodded and raised a hand as the doors slid shut with a quiet hiss, and he disappeared from view.

I stood for a moment, smiling at my slightly dishevelled reflection in the grey, steel surface of the lift doors, and then, happy at the thought of going home to Cameron and of the weekend to come, I turned on my heel and headed back to work.

Acknowledgements

First and foremost my thanks go to you, the reader, for being kind enough to give *Working It Out* a whirl – and for then going the extra mile and reading the acknowledgements too. I'm genuinely grateful.

Of course I must also thank those people without whom *Working It Out* would never have made it onto your e-reader or bookshelf in the first place. Top of that list is my agent, Camilla Bolton at Darley Anderson, who believed in me from the word go and who always manages to encourage, cajole, comfort and question just enough to get this anxious author to the point of publication. My thanks also to the talented team at Canelo, in particular to Emily Bedford for her expert editing and, more importantly, for her kindness, good humour and tireless enthusiasm throughout the process.

Finally, a huge thank you to my friends and family in Bristol, Barnstaple, Nottingham, Silsoe, Edinburgh and London for their support and inspiration, and to Martin, Ollie and Betty for keeping things light, making me feel loved and bringing me tea and cake. You're the best.